Praise for David L. Golemon and the Event Group series

"A unique spin on the Book of Exodus and the defeat of Pharaoh's army . . . The mix of legends and history has always been an asset to this series, and Golemon's imagination seems to know no bounds. Fans of the TV series *Warehouse 13* or the action-adventure novels of Cussler and Rollins will lap this up." —*Booklist* on *Carpathian*

"Explosive . . . tense, terrifying—and worth the investment." —Associated Press on *Ripper*

"A tale worthy of the giants of the genre like Clive Cussler, James Rollins, and Matthew Reilly, *Legend* is a definite must-read for action and adventure fans. Don't miss it." —Megalith.com

"The author . . . draws the reader in with an intriguing prologue . . . satisfying adventure." —*Publishers Weekly* on *Legend*

"Golemon can write action sequences with the best of them, and he lands a solid uppercut with this book. The depth of science fiction . . . is surprising and ingenious." —SFSignal.com on *Legend*

"Golemon combines his typical action-adventure fare with more thriller elements this time, and he focuses more on the personal stakes of his characters. . . . Golemon knows how to make readers turn the pages, and *Primeval* will only further enhance his reputation." —*Booklist*

"Fans of *Twenty Thousand Leagues Under the Sea* will enjoy Golemon's recasting of the Jules Verne novel." —*Publishers Weekly* on *Leviathan*

ALSO BY DAVID L. GOLEMON

OVERLORD

An Event Group Thriller

DAVID L. GOLEMON

St. Martin's Paperbacks

OVERLORD

Copyright © 2014 by David L. Golemon.
Excerpt from *The Mountain* copyright © 2015 by David L. Golemon.

All rights reserved.

For information address St. Martin's Press, 175 Fifth Avenue, New York, NY 10010.

ISBN: 978-1-250-01302-6

Printed in the United States of America

St. Martin's Press hardcover edition / July 2014
St. Martin's Paperbacks edition / June 2015

St. Martin's Paperbacks are published by St. Martin's Press, 175 Fifth Avenue, New York, NY 10010.

10 9 8 7 6 5 4 3 2

To my kids, my granddaughter, the kind people who read my books, and to the United States Armed Services—it's time to come home now!

ACKNOWLEDGMENTS

I would like to thank the members of DARPA, as well as the fantastic engineers at NASA. Keep at it, the funding will return and so will we—to the unexplored reaches of space.

To the men and women of the United States Armed Forces: the Army, Navy, Air Force, Coast Guard, and Marines. I told many of you that your reward would soon arrive, and now here is *Overlord,* a small payment for being the best in the world at what you do.

Thanks to MI-6 for answering all the crazy questions this deranged author could think up—at least as many as propriety would allow. And yes, those answers did lead me to suspect that Her Majesty's government may have an Event Group hidden away under the Tower of London! Finally, thanks to the Royal Family of Great Britain for being especially good sports.

PROLOGUE

THE THINGS OF LEGEND

People like us, who believe in physics, know that the distinction between past, present and future is only a stubbornly persistent illusion.

—**Albert Einstein**

700,000,000 BCE

The entire crew with the exception of himself and the maneuvering watch had been evacuated to the new colony on the western side of the giant supercontinent. The captain knew that setting his battle-damaged warship down onto the lush forest and then easing her into the inland sea would be a near impossible task with decks ten through eighteen awash with flames. The last massed assault by the enemy had been catastrophic.

The large eighteen-inch guns had fallen silent when the ship's powerful engines stopped providing the needed energy for the turbo-generators of the massive upper and lower turrets of one through four. Turrets five and six on the underside of the vast ship had been blown free of her superstructure in the warship's last battle above the hostile new world. The crews of those gun-mounts had bravely stayed in place and they had all had died at their stations.

After the loss of the one-hundred-thousand-gallon coolant tanks that supplied the necessary gases to refrigerate the large-bore weapons, his remaining crew had sent the last three enemy vessels to their deaths by ramming them with the wedge-shaped deflector plow at the bow of the battleship. With maneuvering power only the battered ship had limped into low orbit around their new home. The orbital track he had laid into his navigation console was fast deteriorating and the captain knew they either had to obey the orders of a dying race or try desperately to save the last battleship from destruction. He figured the citizens of this new world owed his vessel a better grave than the one he had planned for her—as a floating reminder of a lost civilization that would be seen in the night sky for thousands of years until a decaying orbit sent her crashing into the planet below.

The captain had refused his last order and had decided instead that his battleship would not suffer the same fate as *Ranger, Vortex,* and *Guidon,* the last ships of the grand fleet that had met their fate on the surface of this planet's lone moon. He swore the demise of his ship would not be the same. He gave the order to enter the atmosphere of this hostile planet and face whatever fate would be bestowed upon it by a new, better civilization.

"Liquid fuel maneuvering engines at 100 percent, Captain. We have ejected the main engine core for safety," his executive officer called out as he wiped blood from a gash on his forehead.

"Bring her nose up fifty degrees, set it down easily. Use the trees and terrain as much as possible and slow her down before she breaks her back."

The giant battleship's thrusters were slowly turned and aimed straight down. The articulated jets were never designed for entering an atmosphere nor to carry the bulk of the mammoth warship, but with the loss of the weight of the lower gun turrets and superstructure she just might have enough. She came down fast and hard, trailing a tail of flame that ignited all in its wake. She slammed into the trees hard. Her massive weight crushed the thick, hundred-foot monoliths and her liquid-fueled thrusters started fires that began to rage out of control. The captain saw their approaching target through the electronic view-screen: the giant inland sea.

"Thrusters are overheating, now at 120 percent capacity," the first officer called out. "The lower battle bridge has been sheared away along with the remaining crew compartments!"

The sudden explosion of ion gases burst through their containment bells on the two stern thrusters, taking them and one of the main engines at the stern with it. The enriched gas blew up and the stern vanished in a microsecond, rocking the battleship.

"Stern section has come into contact with the surface, she's dragging and stress forces are at maximum—she's about to break in two!" the maneuvering officer called out.

The captain swallowed as he grabbed the railing lining the center of the bridge, then glanced at the few remaining men on the battle bridge. He was proud of them, as he knew they would die just as assuredly as he in saving their last ship from being just a nighttime display of brilliantly colored debris orbiting a savage world.

They approached the inland sea at fifty kilometers per second. He knew the battleship would sustain massive damage but she would remain intact for the future of their colony if needed again—or some other race for their savagery. His goal was to save the massive eighteen-inch guns in her four remaining turrets. He saw the sea just over the elevated number one gun turret and determined that they would make it to the choppy green waters.

"Gentlemen, fighting alongside of you has been an honor," he said proudly.

The ten men stood at their stations beaten and bloody after their five-day fight to get the colony moved from the moon to the surface of this world.

The inland sea roiled and bubbled as the great bulk of metal eased into the water. Massive steam jets erupted as her engines became inundated with moisture, blowing the mixing chambers of ion particles into oblivion. She rocked as the detonation set off by the heat of the melting main engines mixed with the coldness of the sea. There were several large explosions as it began to sink. Giant pressure-filled bubbles and steam vents were the only grave marker for the most powerful warship ever built.

There the great ship would remain for millions of years until the inland sea on the hostile continent was covered in two miles of snow and ice.

CENTRAL EUROPE
38,000 BCE

The snow fell as the group of quickly vanishing Neanderthals moved across the barren landscape. The wind picked up as the last remaining group of the human subspecies fought their way through the drifting snow. The small clan of twenty-seven men, women, and children were so burdened by the wet skins on their backs that it weighed them down to a point where they could no longer keep from falling and sliding into small crevasses as their footing became perilous.

The large leader of the group stopped as he heard a noise not common in snowstorms. The male shook his head from side to side as the noise seemed to emanate from his own head instead of the sky where the snow was now swirling in patterns never seen before by the group of Neanderthals. As he dropped his long spear and bundled skins and placed his hands to his ears he saw that the same noise was affecting not only the others in the soon-to-be extinct people but the large and voracious timber wolves that were hidden behind the blanket of white and green of tree. The air erupted with the howls and animal screams of other beasts as the ringing struck all in the area. Soon women and then the smaller of the children succumbed to the strange sound and fell to their knees. The wind started to pick up and now the leader of the group was fearful of getting caught in the open plain and buried forever. He had known many who perished because they could not grasp the cruelty of nature.

Suddenly the skies erupted above them. The snow started swirling in an ever-increasing circle. The leader managed to move his aching head to the skies and saw a sight the early man had never seen before. The swirling snow was now highlighted with blue, green, and yellow lights. The miniature tornado trailed down into the plain and struck the ground as if water had been poured from the heavens. The wave of melting snow and ice still moved in an ever-increasing vortex. The strange system started moving toward the small band as lightning and wind knocked the remaining men from their feet. The terror-filled eyes of the first humans watched as the tornado of ice, wind, and snow, highlighted by the colorful streaks, moved toward them.

The alpha male finally managed to gain his feet as his children cowered on the ground, reaching out for him, but he just watched as the strange system moved closer to him and his band. The eye of the storm circled as the tornado came over them. The eye of the storm was clear and the male could see he was staring into a giant tunnel that was violent and terrifying. The blackness at the top of the funnel was filled with stars the size the beast had never seen before. The Neanderthal could never fathom that what he was seeing was not stars, but whole planets—planets that were millions of light-years away.

The funnel cloud passed over them and the long, filthy hair of the small band was lifted as static electricity filled the air around them. The male held out his arm and he could see the soft blue hue of electricity as it coursed around, over, and through his exposed skin. He looked up and could see the interior walls of the swirling mass of ice, snow, and color as the tornado engulfed the small cowering band. The leader watched as first the taller of the men were gone; they vanished right before the alpha male's eyes. Then the children and women followed. It was then he felt the deep penetration of the electrical field as it covered his entire body. Then he was gone.

In seconds the swirling mass of the tornado lifted from the ground and then suddenly turned inside out. It was if someone were shaking out a knotted sock. The tornado shot back into the sky and then vanished. It only took a few moments for the falling snow to start falling in a far more normal pattern. It swirled and eddied as the last of the multi-colored vortex blasted through the high clouds above the earth. Then the strange pattern moved not into the high atmosphere, but back down again into what would eventually become known in many thousand years as the Middle East.

With the disappearance of the last band of Neanderthals in the world, their demise would spark debate amongst the most brilliant paleontologists in the future world as to when and why the Neanderthals had vanished from the face of the earth.

NORTHERN BRITANNIA, THE SCOTTISH HIGHLANDS
117 AD

The four thousand men of the Ninth Legion ceased the chase and laid down moat and stockade for the night's security. The Legio IX Hispana—founded by Pompey Magnus himself and also a legion once commanded by Julius Caesar—was far north of Hadrian's Wall, which dissected Britannia across her middle, dividing the civilized south from the killing grounds in the north. The Ninth was chasing the barbaric tribes of blue-painted Caledonian savages as they tried to put an end to the increased raids into Roman-controlled territory.

The command of all forces north of the wall had fallen to Centurion Flavious Pettellus. With the remainder of the Ninth safely ensconced south of the borderlands, the forces on the hunt felt their vulnerability in this desolate and cold land.

The punitive action against the Caledonians was now entering its seventh month. Pattellus's one hundred cavalry and three hundred and fifty foot soldiers were weary and worn, with many of them having been cleaved to the bone. The soldiers as well as their commander were ready to end this raid and return to Hadrian's Wall.

Pettellus turned his face to the skies as dark rain clouds closed over the last of the sun as the centurion sat by his fire. He removed his helmet and stared into the crackling flames. He didn't notice when his aide removed his red cloak and then placed it over the commander's shoulders for warmth. The sounds of the camp were nothing but muted noises as his eyes remained fixed on the fire even as his body ignored the mist starting to veil the evening under the ominous skies.

"The honor has left this pursuit just as surely as the warmth of the year vanishes around us," he mumbled as his eyes remained locked on the flames.

His aide stopped before entering the tent but decided not to comment on his commander's increasingly sour mood at the lack of success in his campaign to rid the northern regions of the devils that raided south of the Wall. The aide shook his head and was about to step into the tent when he saw the lights to the north. He was about to comment when Centurion Pettellus was approached by the watch commander. Even then the aide's eyes never wavered from the strange sight directly to the north. The green and blue shades of light were unlike the northern lights they had witnessed at these climbs and the aide knew he was seeing something very much different this night.

The watch commander slapped his right fist to his armored chest and then waited for the centurion to acknowledge his presence. The messenger soon realized that Pettellus was not going to respond and hesitantly lowered his hand and arm.

"Sir, we have activity reported by our outer pickets." The man waited but Pettellus remained still and his eyes continued to watch the flickering fire before him. "There seems to be Caledonian movement in force. They may be using the weather for cover for possible attack."

"I would hardly call the placement of fifty men to spy our movements as activity in force, Commander."

"The pickets report—"

"Thus far on this campaign we have yet to see more than a hundred of the savages on open ground, and by the time we react they have vanished as magically as wine and coin in a brothel."

"Sir, these reports are verified. Possibly one thousand to two thousand blue-painted warriors are near our breast-works."

Finally Pettellus blinked and then barely moved his head to look up at the watch commander just as the first real drops of rain hit his face through the gathering mist.

"And with the northern lights having changed their colors the men are not taking to encampment well. They are speaking among themselves about omens and that the lights are a harbinger of disaster."

Centurion Pettellus turned and looked northward and saw the meaning of the commander's words. The northern lights should not be visible at this time in the evening. They were at least seven hours ahead of schedule and the colors were far more radiant. The blues swirled around the green and then those dove into a yellowish mix of reds and orange. The centurion slowly rose to his feet. The red cloak slid from his shoulders as he spied the strange activity of the lights. The rain and wind picked up in strength.

"Bring the men to 100 percent alert. Get my archers to the center of the stockade to await orders. I want my cavalry mounted and ready to move." He turned to his aide as the watch commander moved off to alert the detached men of the Ninth Legion for action. "This is perfect weather for attack. They can hit us and move into the storm and vanish as usual"—he smiled for what seemed like the first time since the pursuit had started many months before—"but not this time."

The aide watched the centurion place his cloak back on and waited for him to tie it off. The helmet was replaced with renewed vigor and the commander adjusted the Gladius in its sheath. The steel of the blade was still shiny and a virgin to enemy blood.

"Sir, this night's lights in the north, this . . . this could be a bad portent of things to come."

Centurion Pettellus turned abruptly to face the aide who

had remained quiet during his exchange with the watch commander. The man was Greek and the Roman knew him to be knowledgeable about the mysticism of the great lights in the north. The man had been a teacher of philosophy many years before his days of servitude began.

"Night arrows!"

Before Pettellus could admonish his aide about his fears, the shout of warning stopped him cold. He immediately took hold of the Greek and threw him to the ground near the fire just as the black arrows started thudding into the ground and tents around them. One of the missiles glanced off of the helmet of the centurion as his aide shouted in terror at the sudden assault from the swirling night sky. Arrows as black as the night struck the fire, tent, and the surrounding equipment of the Ninth Legion. The sound of men shouting and cursing was heard as even more of the black-dyed arrows slammed into the earth around them.

The wind picked up just as the last of the missiles fell. The blow had gone from only a breeze to gale force in less than five minutes. The northern lights were burning through the darkness as they had never done before. At that time every man of the Ninth Legion felt the penetration and assault on their inner ear. It was as if a sharp spike had been driven into their eyes. The feeling soon passed as men fought to get their bearings in the rising storm.

"The attack has stopped!" Pettellus shouted as he stood. He shook his head to clear it and casually pulled an arrow from the lining of his red cloak, then angrily tossed the black stick into the fire. The rain was now falling as if pebbles were being thrown at them from the heights and the wind was threatening the footing of every man inside the stockade.

His commanders were starting to report on casualties and to receive orders when the lights illuminated the entire breadth of the night sky, and that was when the centurion saw what evil had suddenly come upon them. Rock-sized hail started to fall. Some of the ice stones were larger than a man's closed fist, while others were larger than a two- or three-pound stone. The hail destroyed tents and knocked running men from their feet.

"The savages have broken off and are retreating!" one of his men said just as a ball of chain lightning rent the skies above them. Blue and green bolts shot through the swirling raindrops and snaked across the black sky enough to illuminate the circling motion of the storm.

"Tell the men to hold position at the stockade, as I fear this attack may not be over!" Pettellus shouted as his men quickly moved away watching the skies as they did. "This storm may keep them out . . . then again it may not."

As he watched the terror of his men start to show on their faces, Pettellus looked at the sky as lightning again ripped across its blackness. The swirling clouds above the stockade made his blood turn cold. The hurricane-like storm was now directly atop the Roman army. Men were thrown to the wet ground as more of the evil green and blue lightning broke the skies apart with such violence the men of the mighty Ninth Legion cowered in terror. As Pettellus's eyes widened, yellow, green, and orange bolts shot out of the center of the swirling mass above. The air rose underneath the helmet of the centurion. The crack of heat and electricity filled the air and the earth shook beneath their prone bodies.

"The savages are attacking!"

Centurion Pettellus turned as his helmet was ripped away by the wind and rain. The enemy had seen the chance and were now breaching the stockade under the cover of the storm. The moat was now gone, pushed and pulled free of the trench by the storm, and that gave the Caledonians clear access to the wooden barrier.

"Defense!" The order was shouted as men rose to meet the attackers as the barbarians streamed over the stockade in a man-made rush of a waterfall.

The sky exploded.

A green bubble formed within the eye of the storm directly over the battle. The swirling clouds seemed to implode and then expand. At that moment the sky became as bright as the sun and forced every man, both barbarian and legionnaire, to freeze in fear.

The centurion turned to shout orders as the savages broke into the center of his still-forming men. Before he could utter a sound the sky exploded and the buzzing was heard all around them, piercing and deep. The green dome exited the swirling hurricane above and slammed into the ground. Pettellus felt his skin warm and then he felt his stomach heave as though trying to rid itself of the afternoon meal he had eaten earlier. His tongue was like a cotton swab and his vision became nonexistent. Then all was gone. Sensation along with thought vanished as the light washed over him and his men.

The storm stopped as if it had never been. The rain ceased and the clouds circled into nothingness and the mist seemed to climb into the sky and then quickly dissipate. The northern lights were gone and the night was still.

The earth where the stockade had stood was barren. Gone were grass, fire pits, and moat. The wood of the earthworks vanished as though it had never been. Tents, weapons, even the barbarian savages had vanished. Only the strange buzzing continued as the last of the clouds evaporated, and even that eventually faded and then disappeared.

The Ninth Legion and the savages attacking them north of Hadrian's Wall that summer of 117 AD, vanished without a trace, then swelled into one of the great mysteries of the world.

After that night the Ninth Legion was woven into the fabric of legend.

NANKING, CHINA
DECEMBER 1937

Colonel Li Fu Sien of the Nationalist Chinese army anchored the ends of his defensive lines with massed artillery. As he observed the Japanese across the bridge on the far side of the Yangtze River where the enemy waited to cross, the colonel knew his men were ready for what was to come. He removed the binoculars from his eyes and looked down at the commander of his artillery. The hated enemy would not cross the Yangtze River without the loss of many men.

His soldiers were indeed ready. They were near mutinous in their desire to get at the men who had committed the worst atrocity in human history not three days before. The Rape of Nanking would haunt the Japanese people for the rest of human existence. This would be the historical price for the murder of over three hundred thousand civilians inside the city. Men, women, and children had been bayoneted, shot, raped, and beheaded. Yes, his men were ready to exact vengeance on the Japanese soldiers across the river.

The colonel heard the rumble of thunder and as he looked toward the sky he could see the swirling mass of clouds start to collect over the river. The boom of thunder felt as if the guns of the heavens had opened up upon the world. He watched as colors started swirling not only in the winds, but they also illuminated the funnel cloud that was starting to form. He raised his field glasses and aimed them at the Japanese troops across the river. He could see they too were growing concerned over the strange turn in the weather. Suddenly the colonel let the binoculars slip from his grasp as the pain struck first his ears, and then his eyes. He grasped the sides of head in pain, as did the men around him.

Around the two armies the wind started a slow circle as the bright green, yellow, and blue lights intensified, making the Chinese colonel look up. His eyes widened when he saw the swirling, circling funnel cloud moving over the land like a zigzagging snake or a mythical dragon of old. Then he saw the static electricity run over his exposed skin and under his hat. Men were starting to panic as the moving tornado—one that resembled a hurricane more than its landlocked cousin—closed over his men and then the river and finally the Japanese soldiers on the far shore.

The colonel fell to his knees as the gale-force wind struck him and his massed troops. Before he knew what was happening, he, his men, most of the Yangtze River, and finally the Japanese vanished. Each man in both armies felt the penetration of the electrical field as it passed over, around, and then finally through their bodies. Soon each human being just phased out of existence. Equipment, rations, and men vanished in a blink of an eye.

The strange tornado seemed to leap, settle, and then turned itself inside out and then shot back into the skies. In the eye of the tornado the blackness of space could be seen in the far distance. But there was now no soldier, enemy or Chinese, within twenty miles that would ever report it.

The two armies and every piece of equipment weighing less than a thousand pounds had vanished from the face of the earth.

TEHRAN, IRAN
DECEMBER 1978

The streets were now quiet. The rampage of students had settled to an uneasy array of midnight shouts praising God and its oft-mentioned counterpart, "Death to the great Satan."

The slow-moving Mercedes turned and made its way through a small storm of flying paper and other detritus that had accumulated since the revolution against the shah began. As the car's occupants watched through tinted windows a large white van appeared at a street corner and then flashed its headlights. The Mercedes followed suit and gave their return signal. Two large Toyota Land Cruisers sped ahead of the white van as it soon pulled out of the darkened street. The black Mercedes quickly fell in line to the rear of the small column. They were soon joined by five supporting Toyota all-terrain vehicles brimming with armed men.

The two vehicles with their military escort slowly slipped out of town just after 1:45 A.M. and with their escort quickly wound their way out of the still-smoldering city of Tehran. They slid past the darkened United States embassy where student militants were holding fifty-seven American hostages.

The small man riding in the backseat of the Mercedes shook his head. Even though he was younger than most of the occupying students holding the embassy, he knew tweaking the nose of America at this critical juncture of the revolution was dangerous to say the least. Although he had met only three or four Americans in his time at school he knew them to be the most impulsive people on earth—and in his mind that made them dangerous. He watched the students as they lounged around the thick iron gates of the U.S. embassy. The university student took a deep breath and rubbed the skin of his beardless face.

It took thirty minutes to reach their mysterious destination. The van pulled off to the side of a barren road and allowed three of the Toyotas to pull up to the gate surrounding the compound. Three men exited the first vehicle and confronted the uniformed guards at the gate. The small man in the Mercedes watched as the very last of Mohammad Reza Shah Pahlavi's loyal Army members were rounded up at gunpoint. Again the young man shook his head in disbelief as the guards would no doubt be shot at the new regime's earliest convenience.

The young student was beginning to think the revolution was taking on an air of desperation. Many of his fellow intellectuals were as concerned as he. For the moment there was nothing he could do about it. Someday the religious fools would find that the enemy was not within the Iranian state borders, but outside of it.

The man and his roommate had been awoken and taken from their small apartment with no apology and told they were to accompany the armed men on a most secretive trip to the outskirts of the city. The young man had been up most of the night studying and was not pleased with being taken from his bed. He glanced at his friend in the backseat and shook his head once more.

"If they wanted to shoot us would they have taken us all the way out into the middle of nowhere?" his friend asked.

"No, I believe if we threatened them in any way they would just walk into our apartment and shoot us there. No, this is something else. Now relax, worrying about it won't change our fate."

His roommate leaned over and whispered, "They have no compunction about shooting anyone they see as a threat. I've noticed of late quite a few of our forward-thinking friends have suddenly decided to take the short road out of town." The young bearded man looked through the tinted window. "And this is a short road out of town."

The large double-door security gate was finally opened and three of the guards from the first three Toyotas were left behind as the new security for the state-run facility. The Mercedes drew past following the van and the man's eyes locked with the guard that held the gate open. He looked like a brute and a ruthless killer from the old days of the Persian Empire. The black beard framed a face that seemed to be full of hatred.

"All I know is that if they don't get the citizenry under control inside the cities we will have no cities left." The young man faced his friend and fellow student. "They need to stop the destructive ways of the people. The fools just don't realize they have won."

He stopped speaking when he saw the driver of the Mercedes looking at him in the rearview mirror.

As the two vehicles with their escort rounded a bend in the road the two men riding in the backseat saw the building for the first time. It was block shaped and looked nothing like one of the expensive structures that the shah had erected in the past several years. This was functional and any student with a brain could see that this small, ugly facility was military in nature. The Mercedes pulled into the parking area and the motor was shut off. As the tired young man reached for the door handle the driver turned and shook his head.

"You are instructed to wait."

The boy swallowed and released the door's handle. He then watched the white van as a small squad of men exited the rear doors and spread out. Several of those dark eyes were on them. They watched as the right-side sliding door was opened and a small box was placed on the ground. A black-shoed foot exited the van and before they knew what they were witnessing, a tall, thin man stepped quickly up to the door and assisted an elderly man out. The black turban and silver beard with its black streaks were immediately recognizable. The black cleric robe framed the thick, dark, and unforgiving brows as the old man was steadied as he stepped into the night.

"Praise be to God," the young student mumbled as he watched the older man.

The cleric's eyes roamed over the building. Soon other clerics were surrounding the man as he moved toward the glass-fronted building. Suddenly the tall man in the black turban stopped and slowly turned toward the Mercedes. He nodded in that direction and both men in the backseat froze as they knew the most famous man in the known world at that time was referencing them.

"I knew we shouldn't have written that paper on the technological aspect of our relationship with the west. We should have condemned it." The student turned and faced his slightly older partner, but the man was enraptured as he studied the man surrounded by the black-clad clerics.

"This is about something else," the clean-shaven one mumbled.

"You may exit the car, but do not approach the party until you are called on to do so. Any move toward the group will be met with extreme force."

The man didn't even hear the threat as he opened the car's door and stepped out. He stopped and made eye contact with the man centered in the circle. The long gray and black beard was recognizable in any corner of the world as his face had been on television screens across the planet for months. The two students fell in line as the front doors of the blockhouse were opened by men and women in white lab coats.

The large group accompanying Ayatollah Ruhollah Khomeini entered the most secure and top secret facility in all of the Middle East.

*   *   *

The silent group entered a lift that could hold no less than a hundred men. The ayatollah stared straight ahead at the gate in front of him as his advisors spoke in low whispers. The tall man raised his left brow and then turned and faced the two students behind him. The eyes of his advisors followed suit.

"May God grant you favor," he said in Farsi as he faced the young, clean-shaven man.

"God is great," the student said as his throat almost seized as the ayatollah held his gaze upon him.

"You are enrolled at Iran University of Science and Technology?" the ayatollah asked with a barely audible voice.

"Yes, we are in our third year of study."

A man dressed in a white shirt buttoned to the throat and wearing thick glasses faced the two students.

"You are first in your class. I believe your instructors"—he paused and turned to face the ayatollah—"Westerners for the most part"—then he turned back to the two frightened men—"have pegged you as a future leader in the field of high energy."

The young man listened but made no comment. Why should he, he thought. They seemed to know all anyway.

"I am not in the same classes as my friend. I am in the field of agriculture," the younger of the two men braved.

The ayatollah lowered his head, not commenting on the statement from the young man's roommate.

The elevator stopped at its lowest level. The gate was raised and they were met by two men also attired in white coats. The group stepped out onto a bare concrete floor. The man in the white shirt and glasses paused at the entrance and held the younger of the two students back. He nodded with his head that the older of the two should follow the group.

"As it stands, agriculture is not the lesson we seek here tonight, so this is where your journey ends. It was our mistake in assuming you worked with this young man and Professor Azeri." The man pulled the door down and the two students were left looking at each other through the wire-mesh gate. The student inside the lift looked scared.

"Where are you taking him?" the older asked as the elevator started to rise.

"Back to your apartment, of course."

The lift continued to rise. He waited until a hand fell on his shoulder and he turned to face the large man, who gestured that he should follow.

"Where are they taking my friend?" he insisted, not trusting the provided answer of a moment before. This time he asked with a little more force as he was taken by the arm and hurried along a winding corridor made of cinder block.

The man didn't answer a second time. He stepped up to a large door and before the student could ask his question again the steel door slid into the frame and he was unceremoniously nudged forward. The door slid closed behind him.

The room was massive. The small group was situated high up on a catwalk. Newly returned from exile, Ayatollah Khomeini was a few feet away and looking far down into the interior of the room. His arms were folded at his waist with the hands hidden inside the sleeves of his black robes. The student finally realized they were on a viewing platform. When he moved away from the ayatollah he slowly stepped forward and looked down. His eyes widened when he saw the object that was in view of all of the clerics. It was no less than two hundred feet in diameter and at least a story tall in height. It was round and silver in color. There were no identifying marks on its slick skin and the thing looked as if it had been built the day before. Spotlights shined off the skin, giving it an almost heavenly appearance. When he looked back at the ayatollah he noticed the man didn't see the object as heaven-sent at all. The dark eyes were closed in prayer.

Khomeini slowly opened his eyes and then turned and faced the young man without saying a word. The young student finally tore his gaze from his new leader and then faced the object far below once again.

The flying saucer was the most amazing thing he had ever been witness to.

Khomeini watched the amazement as it grew in the young student's face. The new national leader narrowed his eyes and continued to watch the boy's reaction.

The young man was pulled aside abruptly by shaking hands. When he saw who had broken his spell of wonder, he was shocked. It was Professor Azeri. The man was in a state. He was sweating and his beard looked twisted and dirty. His lab coat was askew on his slight frame. He removed his wire-rimmed glasses and looked him in the eye.

"You have a million apologies from me for getting you involved in this. Someday I hope you can forgive me."

"Professor, what is all of this?" The student couldn't help it—he moved his gaze away from the rattled older professor and once more looked down upon the saucer. "Why didn't you tell me?"

The sixty-five-year-old professor stepped up beside his best student and replaced his glasses.

"How could I tell you I was working on a special project for the shah?" He leaned in closer to him and whispered, "Isn't my execution enough? I didn't want you involved." He shook his head, "And now I've involved you anyway." The professor closed his mouth and suddenly froze when he noticed the man in the black suit and half-collared white shirt watching them from the opposite side of the viewing platform, far away from the clerics. The eyes seemed to glow in the darkness.

"Who is that man?" his student asked as he too noticed the medium-sized man with the well-trimmed beard.

"I pray you never find out, my boy." Azeri faced him and sadly looked past his shoulder at the ayatollah as the man in turn was watching him. "At least as well as I will soon come to know him."

His student was about to ask about the strange statement when he saw that Khomeini was slowly walking toward them. His clerics and guards stayed behind. He approached and both student and teacher lowered their heads. The ayatollah placed his hands on top of their heads. Then he used his fingers to gently raise their faces toward his own.

"The demon known as Shah Pahlavi wanted to use this apparatus that was unearthed in the desert?"

The professor swallowed and tried to speak.

"I have heard the tale, but from mouths that are unlearned in this area. Perhaps you can enlighten the unworthy?"

The boy looked at his professor and thought the man was going to have a stroke before he could hear the story that he himself wanted desperately to understand.

"The incident . . ." Azeri paused as he tried to recall the details. "The incident occurred over southern Soviet airspace in 1972. Their border defenses scrambled fighter planes to assist in identifying an object that refused all transmission with ground stations." The professor seemed to relax as he started to remember the event. "Our own air force, that is, the shah's air force, tracked the object that was heading for our northern border. The thought was that the Soviets would get to it first, but then the pursuing Russian aircraft vanished from the radar screens of both countries at the same moment."

The ayatollah closed his eyes as he listened. The young man was hoping the old cleric hadn't dozed off as it seemed the professor was relating chapters from a bad science fiction novel.

"Soon the object passed over our northern and joint border with the Soviet Union. The path brought it into one of the most heavily trafficked air zones in Iran. The air force watched as the object"—he turned and looked at the saucer—"collided with a commercial 727. Everyone onboard the airliner was killed instantly but this object survived. Its crewmen were never found. It was assumed it may have been a drone of some kind. We are still not sure of that."

"A drone?" Khomeini asked as his eyes opened and took in the old professor.

"Yes, unmanned."

"A mindless demon, you mean?"

"Uh, yes, that is a drone. Well, I was contacted as the only man inside Iran who could possibly understand the technology involved . . . that is, without asking our allies at the time, the Americans, for assistance, of which the shah . . . Excuse me." He looked up into the stark features and swallowed as he corrected himself. "The Satan Pahlavi would not do. You see, he wanted the technology to stay inside our borders."

"Yes, I would imagine this object would interest that fool beyond measure."

Both men watched the ayatollah turn away and then he gestured the stranger from across the way to come forward into the weak lighting. He spoke in whispers to the dark man, who stood a full head taller than Khomeini. The stranger nodded several times and then looked over at the two waiting academics. Ayatollah Khomeini tiredly turned back to face Professor Azeri and his prized student. He didn't smile; he didn't even look as if the two men interested him in the least. He looked at them with raised brow that hooded his dark eyes.

"Do you believe in the greatness of God?" he asked as his eyes bore into theirs.

"Yes," both mumbled humbly.

"This . . ." He turned and gestured toward the railing of the platform and the flying saucer beyond. "This apparatus must be destroyed and its mechanics scattered to the sands of our most barren lands. I will not start our world with this . . . this thing of the shah. I wish it burned to nothing."

The professor looked as if he were about to say something in protest, but his student shut him down with a slight touch of his hand and spoke before the Great Leader could see the protest from the older man.

"Of course we agree. This thing cannot be a part of our world revolution. God *is* Great, and this . . . this machine has to be from Satan." He looked directly into the ayatollah's hard eyes. "It must be burned and its ashes hidden from the sight of men."

Ayatollah Khomeini turned and looked at the man he had spoken to, then placed a hand on his shoulder. The old cleric moved off into the group of religious men, who nodded their heads and left the viewing room.

The bearded man then smiled and walked up to the physicist and his student. He placed his hands behind his back and stopped in front of them. He half-turned and looked to make sure they were alone. Then his smile vanished as he turned back to face the two scared men.

"Did you understand the ayatollah's orders?" he asked.

The men didn't say anything but just stood there waiting for him to continue. Instead of continuing he removed a gold case from his suit jacket, opened it, and lit an American cigarette. He blew smoke out and smiled at the two men.

"Secrets amongst friends," he said with a smile as he held the American brand into the air for them to see. "Now, I have been issued the same orders as you—orders that have to be followed to the letter." The man turned his back and walked over and looked down at the saucer. "Conflicts can arise in any given situation. And I have a conflict." He faced the two men once again. "I have been charged with the security of our new country. That is my job and I do it very well."

The young student started to see the flicker of daring in the man's eyes.

"No one will ever know my name. The clerics here tonight do not even know who I am. But you gentlemen will. I have need of you. Are you both familiar with another revolution which occurred not so very long ago—something called the Cultural Revolution?"

"China, Mao, yes we have heard of it," the young man answered, anxious for the man to get to his point.

"And what was the Great Leader's biggest blunder in this so-called revolution?"

The two remained silent.

"It was detrimental to his nation because he set Chinese technology back a hundred years and they are just now fighting to catch up. Gentlemen, Iran cannot make the same mistake no matter what our great man of God says." He watched for a shocked reaction, but was soon pleased to see the two men just waiting for him to finish. "Yes, I am not about to destroy a thing that can guarantee the future of this country." He leaned over into the younger of the two. "When these madmen are finished with it, of course."

"What are you saying to us? You want us to disobey our leader and commit what amounts to treason?" the young man asked, his eyes boring into those of the internal security man.

"Precisely; that is why you were brought here. Your politics are well known in the circles I frequent. You would have been rounded up if it had not been for my protection from afar." He looked at the old, tired man of science. "You and the good professor here." He paused and then seemed to think something over. "To demonstrate how serious and compassionate our new and fearless leader is, your roommate is at this moment being buried in a shallow grave not far from here. The rest of the technicians assigned to this building are meeting the same fate." He saw one of the younger lab-coated science technicians walk past while averting his eyes from the three men. "As soon as it is more convenient, of course."

The anger the young man was feeling was clearly demonstrated on his face after his gaze followed the tech off the scaffolding. He took a menacing step toward the man.

"Take hold of your emotions, boy, it was not I who ordered this. I don't kill children and close my eyes to science. But secrecy must be maintained, so I did not argue the decision that was made."

"But if we do not go along with your treason you will have no such concerns when it comes to killing *us*?"

"Again, you are precise in your assumption and your reasoning."

"What do you want of us?" the professor asked as he twisted his hands together.

"Nothing other than to study and bring this machine back to life, as I believe it may be very beneficial for military use in the future. Oh, we will bury it, but we will be the only three to have a map to its location."

"Yes, we must protect this find," the student said reluctantly, agreeing to this one point as he watched the man standing resolute before him.

"Someday this will make you a great man, my young friend." The bearded enforcer and traitor to his nation's newest cause slapped the student on the back. "The professor is right; you are a very bright student."

With that quick smirk and gesture a deal was struck. The flying saucer was hidden from sight and the minds of those who thought it evil.

The young beardless student looked from the man to the saucer below and its cold silver-colored beauty.

The future president of the Republic of Iran smiled slightly. Mahmoud Ahmadinejad, a boy with very high political aspirations, and now one of three men who had knowledge of a captured UFO in his country's possession, turned and walked confidently into his and his nation's suddenly brighter future.

CENTRAL ANTARCTICA
1987

The four men tried in vain to find shelter from the sudden storm that had erupted around them. They fought the gale-force wind as they crawled through the thick snow and ice. They had been on a British government–sponsored survey of the Bartle Slope, hoping to take core samples of the area they had long suspected of covering an ancient inland sea. Their equipment was now behind them and was no doubt three feet underneath the blowing snow and ice. If it hadn't been for the safety lines attached at their waists they would have been separated to each die alone.

Professor Early Standish of Oxford University finally fell to his knees as a sudden gust of wind that would have clocked in at over a hundred miles per hour struck him. He tried in desperation to hold on as the other three men in his small party hit the snow beside him.

"We have to dig in!" he shouted as loud as he could. "This will bloody well end us if we don't—"

The snow and ice vanished beneath the team as his words fought their way through his frozen mouth. The professor dropped first, followed by the other three as solid earth became thin air in a split second of blurred motion. The four men hit solid ice and then the sensation of speed hit them as they started to slide. Soon the sun and light vanished as they fell away into darkness as the world seemed to open up underneath them. Bump after horrid bump bruised their already frozen bodies as they continued to slide into the open abyss. The safety rope connecting the men together tightened and then snapped as man after man hit his own speed as the hell ride continued.

The professor felt the ice slide give way again to air as he fell from a small cliff and farther into darkness. He hit with a bone-crunching impact. He had his breath knocked from his lungs as he rolled onto his stomach and then felt his eyes burn in pain as he realized his goggles had been shattered. He felt the others strike the ice near him. Several screams of pain and thuds of bodies announced the arrival of his team.

He finally managed to draw a breath.

"Henson, Goodfellow, Wiley, are you all right?" he called out in a coughing fit as air filled his lungs.

He tore at his parka hood and slapped away his broken goggles. Suddenly a bright flare of red-tinted light filled the frozen spaces around him, and he quickly closed his eyes to the harsh light.

"I think Henson may be hurt bad," Professor Wiley said. He was kneeling beside a prone man with the smoking flare alight by his face.

Standish took a cue from his partner and struck alight his own flare. It sputtered and flamed to life as he assisted the others. Wiley stood and shook his head.

"Henson is out like a light—he must have hit his head a good one on the way down. Concussion possibly." The tallest of the group adjusted the light of the flare and looked back at the ice tunnel they had blindly stumbled into in their fight to find shelter from the sudden storm above them.

"Looks like some sort of water runoff maybe, or just one hell of a big crack in the ice strata," Professor Standish said as he examined the area high above them. The blue-tinted ice had not a hint to the daylight that was now possibly a mile above their heads. "Wiley, old man, please tell me your radio is still working and that we have a signal." Standish removed his broken walkie-talkie from his belt and tossed it onto the ice.

Wiley tossed down the flare he was holding and retrieved his radio. He called the basecamp and was happy to get an answer. After telling base to stand by, he nodded at the leader of the survey team.

"Thank God for that, now we better—" Standish stopped when he saw both Wiley and a limping Goodfellow looking past his shoulder. Goodfellow slowly removed his goggles and then allowed them to fall to the ice at his feet.

"Oh, bloody hell," Wiley said as he quickly struck another flare.

Professor Standish slowly turned around as the shock registered on his boys' faces froze his blood far more than the temperature ever could have. His eyes widened as the newly struck flare erupted into a hellish tint of red.

The giant object rose far above them and eventually disappeared into the thick, three-mile ice. The steel was frozen solid and looked as if it was buried in a long-ago green sea. His eyes traveled down its partially hidden length as he felt his bladder threaten to let go of its contents.

"I bloody well think we found our prehistoric inland sea, Professor."

Standish didn't answer as his eyes kept roaming over the giant before him.

The British-sponsored survey team had found far more than an ancient sea. They had stumbled upon the greatest discovery in the history of mankind.

* * *

The small rail line had taken the British government almost six months to complete. The steepness of the ice-water run-off that had created the tunnel had to be shored up and the engineers had finally declared it safe enough to allow the scientific experts access to the site. The five gentlemen of the darkest sections of British Intelligence now stood looking at the object that was estimated to have been buried over a hundred million years before man began scrambling from the trees.

"Well, now the Americans are not the only ones to have something like this to hide," said the young man from MI6. He was portly and stood with his cold-weather clothing masking the heaviness of his body. He smiled and rocked back and forth from heel to toe as he studied the giant object buried inside the ancient sea before them.

"You speak of the Roswell vehicle?" asked his aide. The question only elicited a look of disdain from the science advisor to Her Majesty.

"From this moment on, gentlemen, the need to know on this project is absolutely being apprised through my offices."

"We cannot hide this from the men and women who need to know," said his aide.

The man removed his parka and in the harsh lighting of the portable lamps he glared at the three men before him.

"You will remove the survey team from Antarctica and sequester them until they can be debriefed by me, and me alone. Is that clear?"

"But—"

"Is that clear?" he insisted. He turned his gaze from the men before him back to the object. His eyes traveled the length of the find and he could not help but be amazed at its sheer size.

"Yes, sir," the aide finally said.

"Not even the palace is to know what we have here. This find may make the American discovery from 1947 seem trivial. It seems that strange group headquartered underneath

Nellis Air Force Base in their Nevada desert that we suspect is there is not very forthcoming as far as secrets are concerned." He turned toward the other three men from British intelligence. "It seems we now have a bargaining chip to trade for the future." He smiled. "I love secrets, don't you?"

PART ONE

THE CALM BEFORE THE STORM

Courage is not the absence of fear, but rather the judgment that something else is more important than fear.

—Ambrose Redmoon

1

The man in the rumpled three-piece suit waited in front of Warden Hal Jennings's desk. He stood with his battered briefcase clutched in both hands and was using it as if it were a talisman of some sort as he waited for his ruse to either pass muster, or for his deception to be found out. If he was found out it would be nothing more than an embarrassing episode and predicament he would eventually talk his way out of.

He watched the warden's eyes as he read the letter. Without looking up at the man in the light blue suit, horn-rimmed glasses, and thinning red hair, the warden—who had been running the federal side of Leavenworth—placed his hand on his phone and picked up the receiver.

"Annie, connect me with the FBI field office in Topeka, I need a name run . . . Yes, tell Special Agent-in-charge Klinemann it's for me, right. Thank you."

The visitor in the blue suit smiled as the warden hung up the phone.

"Precautionary. It's not that we don't trust you . . . it's more like—"

"It's that you don't trust me." The man in the rumpled suit smiled.

The warden smiled and then relaxed. "Yeah, something like that. More or less. I was giving you a chance to back out of here without getting arrested if you're lying to me. Trying to see this man you believe is here, if that man existed, could get you placed right next to him in an available cell, or worse."

"Oh, the man exists. That's what we do in our business, Warden Jennings—we make sure we have precise information."

The phone buzzed and the warden picked up the receiver just as the door opened to the office and a large prison guard stepped in. He stood at the door with his eyes on the warden's visitor. The speaker button was pushed and the phone was placed back into the cradle. Jennings wanted this man to hear his report firsthand from the secretary outside.

"Go ahead, Annie."

"His credentials check out. Hiram Vickers, federal employee number 397-12-0989. Departmental information is unavailable but he is a confirmed employee at the Langley, Virginia, headquarters facility."

"Thank you, Annie, that's enough. We just needed to match his identification with his story."

The visitor watched the warden end his call and slide Vickers's CIA identification back to him across the large desk.

"You will speak to Prisoner 275698 on his one-hour exercise period. If he refuses to speak to you that is his prerogative. The only men and women that have direct contact with him are corporate types or weapons theorists in which he has an obligation to speak to according to presidential order, and right now those orders do not include you. I am doing this as a favor to a sister agency. Any deviation from speech or any attempt to touch Prisoner 275698, and you will be shot without warning from the tower. If he refuses to speak with you there will be no comment, no persuasive banter. You will turn away from the exercise yard and exit where a guard will escort you from the facility. Are you clear on the rules?"

"Yes, very clear. I believe the man will wish to speak with me." The visitor reached for his identification and placed it in his suit jacket.

"Then you have one hour. The guard will escort you to the exercise yard."

The visitor smiled and nodded his head and turned away.

"Mr. Vickers," the warden said, bringing the tall man to a stop before he reached the open door being held in place by the large guard.

"Remember, the prisoner you are meeting has no name, has no dossier; in general, he has no life inside or outside these walls. According to special order he does not even exist. If you attempt anything out of the range of description that I have outlined to you, you will be arrested and you will not leave here."

"One of your special rules, I take it?"

"No, Mr. Vickers, not my rule at all but someone else's. It's another name that you may be familiar with—he's called the commander-in-chief."

Vickers smiled. "Yes, so I understand. But he is also a lame duck president who seems to have pissed a lot of people off." Vickers smiled as he started to turn around but stopped and eyed the warden. "And he is also a president you may not want to align yourself so closely with in the near future. Tossing his name around will only make those men and women in power remember *your* name, Warden."

The warden watched the arrogant man turn and leave his office with a smug air about him. The not-so-veiled threat hung in the air as the door closed. The man who had been in the federal prison system for thirty-one years wanted to go after the arrogant little bastard and slap him around, and for the life of him he didn't understand why. His thoughts were interrupted by his door opening after a soft knock. It was his secretary.

"I'm stepping out for lunch, would you care for anything?" the small bespectacled woman asked.

"No, just let me know in an hour when our friend here is done speaking with our guest. I want to make sure he and our prisoner are still in place afterward."

Annie nodded and left. She made her way downstairs and instead of heading for the lounge area staffed for the management end of Leavenworth, she went right and headed for the small area on the grass where men and women usually ate their lunches on fine days such as this. She didn't have to look around as she sat. Lunch for most was after the noon hour, so she found herself sitting alone. She smiled and nodded her head at two passing guards and then easily brought the cell phone to her ear. She punched a preselected number—one she had never had to use before.

"Yes, this is Annie Kline in Kansas. Is this Mr. Jones?"

She waited only a moment until a voice answered at the other end.

"Yes, Mr. Jones, this is Annie at Leavenworth. We've had a visitor for our special guest that was not on the official rolls of authorized visitors. Yes, his name is Hiram Vickers, CIA. Yes, sir . . . yes, sir, one-hour visit. Before you hang up, Mr. Jones, this man won't be in any sort of trouble, will he, because of my actions?"

She waited as a man she had never met explained the realities of life to her from afar.

"Yes, sir, the fifty thousand dollars will come in very handy, but I don't wish to get into trouble. I'm just telling you about a visit to an unnamed prisoner. Yes, I will forward a copy of his ID to you at your office after the warden goes home for the evening. Thank you." She ended the call and then looked up at the imposing structure of USP Leavenworth—and wondered if her small act as informant would go unnoticed in an ever-worrisome world.

The visitor was passed through no less than five security checks on his way to the meeting. Each set of guards eyed him as if he had requested to visit Charlie Manson. The man's prison number drew looks of distaste from each and every man or woman he came across. He soon found himself standing in an enclosed concrete area with high walls and fences. There was no view of the grounds outside those walls and the only evident threat was a guard tower with a uniformed man watching him with a slung Ruger Mini-14 on his back. The eyes of the guard never left the visitor.

Hiram Vickers saw the man in the orange jumpsuit standing and looking at nothing in particular other than the blue sky. Then the prisoner lowered his head and started walking the line around the walls. Vickers watched him for a moment and then approached. He was minus his old briefcase, as it never made it past the first checkpoint.

"Beautiful day for a walk."

The tall, extremely thin man with black hair just kept his gait without looking up at Vickers.

"I don't conduct corporate inquiries out here, so go fuck yourself."

The man kept walking and Vickers moved to pace him.

"Saucy for a Harvard graduate—I think prison has jaded you into being something other than you are." Vickers chuckled as the man kept walking. "I'm corporate, but not the corporate type you believe me to be. My *company* is a bit smaller and based in Virginia."

Vickers could see that the man, although he kept walking, became interested: his breath noticeably caught momentarily with a hitch as if the prisoner was trying to stifle a hiccup.

"I used to have many close friends in Virginia." He stopped and looked at the visitor for the first time. He examined the man as if he were looking at some new and strange breed of bug. "But like most, the rats ran for cover when the exterminator arrived." He gave the man a dirty look and then continued his walk to nowhere.

"And that is the very subject I am here to see you about. It's not the rats I'm interested in, it's the exterminator I want to meet."

The prisoner laughed but kept his stride even and nonstop.

"If you mention the name of that particular exterminator you could find yourself my roommate here"—the tall man gestured about him at the thick walls of Leavenworth prison—"in the Club Med of the plains." The man in the orange jumpsuit laughed and shook his head at the strange and badly dressed man walking beside him.

Vickers matched the laugh with his own chuckle. "Actually, it's the field men I want, not their boss."

Prisoner 275698 stopped walking and stared at the slight man in the rumpled blue suit.

"Don't those people at Langley give you a clothing allowance?"

Vickers, although the insult caught him off guard, ignored the comment because as a matter of fact he didn't get a clothing allowance from the cheap bastards in Virginia.

"To be more precise, Prisoner 275698, I need several of those names—and one in particular."

"Why me? I've been illegally locked up here since 2006. Why should I assist the people who helped put me here—stabbed me in the back, let's say. Why?"

"Because the man who signed your life away is having difficulty hanging onto his power."

"Look, the president who put me away is long out of office, but his replacement still holds the key and he's not going to give it up." The prisoner smiled. "It seems I am not the most popular figure going in the corporate world these days."

Hiram Vickers stopped walking and became deathly serious as he watched the man's back.

"Things change—they can change very quickly, I think. The president doesn't need another problem on his hands with the budget he just turned in. The draft board thing isn't going over too well either. I think you may have some very understanding ears turned your way in the next few months, and that, my friend, is the *why* portion of your question. I can get you out of here and back into the fight that's coming, and along the way maybe we can work together and settle a few old scores."

The prisoner laughed. "You have made an enemy, I think, and whoever it is scares the hell out of you."

Vickers didn't return the laugh as he started walking again. He stopped and looked to the blue Kansas sky.

"My enemies are your enemies. Deal with the devil to get what it is you want most."

"Go ahead," the federal prisoner said. He started to walk around his exercise yard once more.

"The desert, the high desert—need I say more?"

The prisoner looked up at the guard tower where the large officer's eyes never left the two men strolling casually in the yard.

"I don't know what it is you're talking about."

Vickers stopped cold in his tracks and chanced reaching for the prisoner's arm, an action that drew the immediate attention of the armed guard, who shook his head at Vickers.

"The people I seek are in the high desert—or should I say, *under* it?"

"Again, I don't know what it is you speak of."

Exasperated, Vickers nearly reached out and slapped the man but remembered the very lethal looking Mini-14 the guard had on his back.

"Well, I thought I could count on a patriot such as yourself to want to get the hell out of here"—he gestured around him at the exercise yard—"and get into the fight that is surely coming at us."

"What's happened?" the man asked, suddenly becoming interested. .

"Oh, that's right, you're no longer kept in the loop on Operation Magic, are you, Mr. Charles Hendrix II?"

Hendrix wasn't surprised at all that this man mentioned what in this prison was unmentionable: his name.

"They deserve the fate they created for themselves. Nonetheless, Mr. Vickers, you have my attention."

"Good, that's a start. Now, the name of the man who really put you here, who is it?" The two men commenced walking once more.

"He's dead . . . does that surprise you that I know this?

Even I still have sources, my friend; my attorneys are not what they seem sometimes."

"The name, Hendrix," Vickers hissed.

"Lee, Garrison Lee. He's quite an old enemy of my family—an enemy since 1947. But as I said, he's dead and I curse the ground that particular Boy Scout is buried in."

"Garrison Lee, the former U.S. senator?"

"One and the same." Hendrix smiled and looked at his guest. "He was a little bit more than the history books will ever reveal."

"We'll discuss that at length later, after you're a free man. Now, what is the other name I need?"

"Compton, Niles. He's attached to the National Archives and works in that facility you mentioned underneath the desert in Las Vegas."

"Yes, I know, underneath Nellis Air Force Base. Niles Compton, huh?"

"Dr. Niles Compton, yes. And do not, and I mean it, try to match wits with the man. He could outthink you in his sleep."

"A lot of people, much to their regret, thought the same thing about me, Mr. Hendrix."

Hendrix smiled down at the rumpled man. "Is that right? Well, this man has the muscle of the federal government backing him, and he hangs around with some very salty people."

"It's one of those salty people I am seeking. Collins, Jack, colonel, United States Army. Ring a bell?"

"Outside of his famous appearance in front of the senate oversight committee when he threw his commander and several high-ranking politicos underneath the proverbial bus, no. I take it he's running the Group's security for Compton. God knows military men are only good for little else."

Hendrix saw the disappointment in Vickers's face and knew he had the man. "I do have a name that will lead you to this colonel you want so badly."

"Who?"

"Well, at the time of my arrest he was a commander in the Navy." Hendrix's eyes narrowed to slits. "That is one arrogant son of a bitch I wouldn't mind seeing . . ." He looked around. "Gone. His name is Carl Everett, a Navy SEAL."

To Vickers it felt as if he had a chance at getting his life back after reaching a starting point.

"Now, quid pro quo, Hiram. I need a name myself, and it could be a name that interests you and your bosses far more than the ones you asked about. But before I tell you the name *I* want, tell me: Why do you need to find this Colonel Collins, especially with the shit storm getting ready to engulf the entire world?"

"I have to find him and kill him"—he looked over at the taller Hendrix—"before he finds and kills me." Once more Vickers looked away. "I may have inadvertently killed his sister."

This made the man formerly known as Charles Hendrix II purse his lips and shake his head.

"I can understand your consternation, especially since this Group buried in the desert is the favorite of every president of the United States since Woodrow Wilson. And they protect this Group, Mr. CIA man—and I mean *protect* it." He chuckled at Vickers and his little problem that made his own worry seem insignificant. "Yes, I guess you had better find this Collins, because if I remember correctly from my reports on him he seems to be a bit of a stone. Cold. Killer." Hendrix emphasized each of the last three words.

"Thanks for that little bit of info, Hendrix. Now, who is it you want me to find for you?"

"You'll find him in the desert also, just not the same desert as this mysterious Event Group. And believe me, this is a person who would be of much interest to not only your people, but many, many, others with names you cannot even afford to pronounce."

"The name, Hendrix, the name."

"He's got a moniker that is a little off, but you should

have no problem tracking him down with the right leads at your disposal."

"Please," he said sarcastically, "I can find anyone, anywhere." He smiled as the guards were opening the exercise yard. Hendrix's time in the sun was up for the day. "After all, I found you, and you were buried by secret orders of the president."

"Touché, find me you did."

"The name of the man?" Vickers insisted.

Hendrix stopped at the open gate and turned to face Vickers. "He's not a man at all. I will explain to you in no uncertain terms that this name is one of the more valuable in the entire history of this planet."

Hendrix saw the confused look on the CIA man's face.

"I'm giddy with anticipation," Vickers finally voiced.

"The name is Mahjtic, or as his friends underneath Nellis call him—the Matchstick Man."

VANCOUVER, BRITISH COLUMBIA

The blond man in the overly large swivel chair spun around and hung up the phone. He kept his fingers on the receiver and tapped out a gentle beat as he thought. He was well-dressed, wearing a black sport coat with a simple white shirt underneath. His blond hair had grown out over his collar and his face had been unshaven for the past seven months. He pursed his lips, still tapping the phone when the alarm bell pinged on his fax machine. Annie was far faster than he gave the Kansas woman credit for. She had been easy to turn and for this man it came easily and naturally. *"After all,"* he had told her when he gave her an advance of ten thousand dollars, *"it's not like you're giving out the names of good guys here."* The justification was that he was searching for the killer of a dear friend and he thought that anyone visiting U.S. Federal Prisoner 275698 could lead him to that killer. It gave the single mother a chance at excitement in her life, and if she was caught sending him information, well, that was just the way the world worked, in his opinion.

Colonel Henri Farbeaux stood while whistling and made his way to the large credenza by the wall and waited for the fax to finish. When it did he lifted the pages and looked at the face that had been sent to him from a cell phone straight from Leavenworth penitentiary. He looked from the features of the redheaded man to his name. The moniker seemed somewhat familiar to Farbeaux, but for the life of him he couldn't place the face. He examined the name once more and seemed to remember meeting this man somewhere in the past. And then it struck him that he was liaison between the Centauris Corporation and the Central Intelligence Agency—their Games and Theory Department if he remembered correctly, which made sense because when he had met this man he himself had been a contract player for Centauris and their infamous invention, the Black Teams.

"I should have known," Henri said. He took the sheets of paper back to his desk and sat down to study the man and his information.

Henri didn't look up from the fax for a full forty minutes as he thought out his options. He smiled, laid the papers down, and then turned to look out the window. He turned and started typing commands into his computer. The screen was soon showing the tri-color national flag of France and Henri knew the DGSE—General Directorate for External Security—for the French nation had not changed his password. He shook his head, not knowing if he still had friends at the agency or if they were just that slow in their security department.

In thirty minutes Col. Henri Farbeaux had every piece of information on Hiram Vickers the French government had, and as he was beginning to notice it was quite a bit. Finally he printed out a better picture of the CIA agent and stared at it.

"Hello again, Mr. Vickers."

THE HOGGAR MOUNTAINS
CENTRAL SAHARA DESERT, ALGERIA
TROPIC OF CANCER

The four Aérospatiale Gazelle helicopters flew low over the volcanic terrain. They had traveled 1,900 miles from Algiers, being refueled twice on their way to the desolate oasis. The four French-and-British-made helicopters were flying in tight formation after being alerted to a disturbance by, of all entities, the U.S. National Aeronautics and Space Administration. NASA had placed an emergency call through to the Algerian military warning them of a highly unusual weather formation that had sprung up without warning in the region of mountainous terrain where there should be no weather systems at all other than the blazing sun—and a storm forming in or around the mountains was unheard of in the month of June. There was not a history of severe thunder and rainstorms in the entire northern portion of the Sahara such as Talmud. And the storm images taken by NASA declared this to be the mother of storms that came and went in only ten minutes' time.

Talmud Oasis had been a viable source of water for the past five thousand years and was used by men traveling the barren wastes for more than half of that time. The French Foreign Legion made the site famous in many a tale of the Algerian wars. The oasis was home to just under thirty-three men and women who cared for the site and were paid monthly and supplied food by the Algerian government.

The lead helicopter made a slow turn to the north and then the pilot brought the Gazelle to three hundred feet and cleared a small rise. The view that greeted him was shocking at the very least. The spot where the oasis used to be, along with the small grouping of houses, was gone. Not only was the area featureless, there was a thousand-foot-diameter hole in the ground where it had once stood. It looked as if a giant manhole cover had been lifted and tossed aside. The edges of the hole were nearly a perfect circle where the small oasis and village had stood for over two thousand

years. The action could have been done by laser cutting, it
was that precise.

All four pilots and their emergency teams could see
where the storm had washed out most of the sand dunes that
used to line and surround the oasis. Even as they flew lower
they could see small rivers that had accumulated in that very
serious ten minutes of weather. Then they saw what looked
like scorch marks on the sides of the small volcanic hill-
sides, accompanied by glass that shone brightly in the afternoon sun. They estimated that at least one square mile of
sand had been blasted into glass by some form of searing
heat.

The lead pilot in the first Gazelle hovered over the remains of the prehistoric oasis and made the radio call.

How he would explain this was beyond the language
skills of any man he knew of. The world had just pushed the
oasis off the face of the earth, not very scientific but he knew
that was what he would say to his superiors.

Talmud was just gone.

THE WHITE HOUSE
WASHINGTON, D.C.

The president sat with his wife and two daughters and ate a
quiet lunch inside the private residence of the White House.
The two girls, eleven and eight, talked about the plans they
had made for their summer vacation, which just started two
days before. Their mother laughed and spoke as her eyes
drifted to her husband, who seemed to be listening, but she
knew him too well. He was looking, smiling, and even nodding his head at the right times as the girls spoke excitedly,
but his mind was a million miles away. The first lady of the
United States, as well as most Americans, had been watching her husband slowly commit political suicide, and the sad
thing was it was something he had to do.

"Sweetheart?"

The smile slowly left the president's face when his thoughts were interrupted. Evidently he had been asked a question that a nod of his head would not cover.

"Excuse me, I'm sorry, drifted there for a minute," he said, looking first at his wife and then at the two girls, who were just looking at him.

"They asked if you were going to make time to go to Disney World with us?" the first lady asked as her eyes met the president's.

The president finally broke his spell and looked from his wife to the two waiting girls.

"Well, of course I am. The world can just go ahead and miss me for two days."

The two girls laughed and clapped and then stood and ran around the table and hugged and kissed him. He returned the love as the girls broke their hold on him and then exited the private dining room. The first lady noticed his eyes following the girls and the sadness that seemed to be behind those eyes every time he saw his daughters.

"That bad?" she asked as she placed her napkin on her empty plate.

The president took a deep breath as the waitstaff came in and cleared the table. As the last man placed coffee in front of the most powerful couple in the world and left, the president looked at his wife.

"The idiots are not going to pass the bill."

"I know this may sound traitorous to you, but even I would be throwing a fit if I didn't know why you wanted the draft lottery instated."

Again the deep breath. "I've explained to the senate and the house why we need the draft lottery ready to go. Why I need to extend enlistments and why I have placed retirement of any military man or woman on hold for the foreseeable future."

"All of the house and senate?"

The president gave the first lady a bemused look. "Only the few that matter, the leaders of both parties." He shook his head and sipped at his after-lunch coffee. "In other words, every enemy I have on both sides is tearing me apart in the papers."

"Well, maybe it's time you informed the world just what is really happening. I would want to know."

"Like most American wives and mothers, you probably would have had a sense that something wasn't right in the world. But being mere senators and representatives they're a little slower on the uptake."

"How are the branches of service taking the retirement and discharge freeze?"

"The staff at the Pentagon is fielding hate mail from their own soldiers, airmen, and sailors on a scale they have never seen."

"You cannot stick to your timetable. The American people are beginning to think that either you're militarily taking over this country or worse, you've gone completely mad. You have to tell them something. If your soldiers are listening to rumors they're going to react in a negative way. You were a top soldier at one time and you didn't like it."

"I think I fit both scenarios at the moment—mad and a tyrant." The president drank his coffee and then saw his Secret Service guard nod his head. The president stood and tossed the napkin on the table.

The first lady stood and paced to the president's side of the table. She hugged him as he slid his relaxed tie up to its proper place under his chin.

"What is Niles saying?" she whispered in his ear as she kissed his cheek.

"Basically the same thing as you, and he's just as big a nag." He smiled and then regardless of his guards picked his wife up and hugged her.

"I think between your wife and the smartest man on the continent you should have a clear idea on what to say to the American people."

The president finally lowered her and then straightened his coat just as the slight thump of turning rotors was heard coming from the White House lawn.

"Ooh, Daddy, that's a Blackbird!" his younger daughter said as she had sprung from her chair and ran for the window.

"As a matter of fact, that's just who I'm going to speak to right now," the president said. He glanced only slightly toward his daughter, who was staring with wide eyes at the descending helicopter. "It's a Black Hawk baby, not a Blackbird."

The first lady turned his face back toward her own.

"Now don't make him mad. Start off by calling him Niles and not 'baldy,' it puts him on the defensive."

"Yeah, well, you're not even supposed to know about him or what he does."

"Then maybe you should have picked another person to be your best man at our wedding."

"That, my dear, I should have done. That way I would have only one conscience to deal with." He gave the first lady a quick wink.

"Such is life with the president."

He smiled as walked to the door.

"What life?"

The president made his way to the administration wing of the White House. Most of the staff, visitors, and Secret Service men and women saw the same man they had been seeing on a daily basis for almost five years. He was always smiling, always confident. On his way into the Oval Office he nodded his head at his assistant and then nodded toward the door and she affirmed with a knowing look that his guest was inside waiting. His assistant knew almost immediately that the president was off limits for the next hour. However . . .

"Mr. President, House Speaker Camden has been waiting since 11:45. He does not have an appointment nor is he scheduled." Senator and Speaker of the House, Giles Camden of Florida, stood up and got the president's attention by placing his hands on his hips and glaring at him.

The president stopped and with no one seeing his face he

rolled his eyes, but by the time he turned to face the senior Republican from Florida his customary smile was in place. The hawk from Florida was waiting and his hand wasn't out. Even the president's security detail disliked the man immensely.

"Mr. Speaker, this is a surprise, I wasn't aware we had a meeting this afternoon."

"Mr. President, my constituents as well as my colleagues are stupefied as to this draft lottery proposal you have been allowing to leak from your office." The senator looked around to make sure that the ears inside the reception area were all tuned into his voice. "And keeping young men and women ensconced in military service when their obligations have been fulfilled to the utmost standards of the American military, well, sir, that's just a little too much dictatorship and not enough democratic process."

The president lost his smile as he stepped closer to the man from Florida who admiringly stood his ground against the formidable size of the former Army three-star general.

"One thing I don't need from you, Senator Camden, is a lesson on my soldiers, airmen, and seamen, and how well they have fulfilled their duties in the global war on terror. I am well aware of it." The president leaned over as far as he could and took the senator's right hand in his own and shook slowly as he spoke low. "You of all people should know better than to listen to rumors. I have not made any such declarations, at least on an official basis, about either a draft proposal or freezing discharges."

"Then perhaps the president can explain it to an old Southern gentleman the difference between rumor and fact"—he smiled—"as *you* see it, of course."

The president released Camden's hand and was tempted to wipe it on his pants leg, but smiled instead and then looked at his watch.

"If you don't know the difference between the two by now, Mr. Speaker, I would never have the time to explain it to you. If you'll excuse me, I have a meeting."

Speaker of the House Camden watched, stunned, as the

president turned and walked away. The tension inside the reception area was cold and you could cut the atmosphere with a knife. He noticed the Secret Service agent gesturing with his hand toward the nearest exit. Camden grimaced and then angrily looked down to where his own assistant was waiting and gestured for her to follow.

In the corridor he turned fuming to his female assistant. "I want CIA Director Harlan Easterbrook to meet me for dinner. And be sure he brings our good friend Dan Peachtree with him."

"Are you sure that's a good idea? I mean the director is squarely in the president's camp on this issue"—the assistant corrected herself—"the rumored issue."

"What goddamn issue? According to the president there is no issue, just an ugly rumor!" he hissed loudly and started getting looks from men and women lining the outer hallway waiting to see the man in the Oval Office. "Easterbrook knows who it is that controls the budget for his agency and I want Daniel Peachtree there to back us. Even Easterbrook can't argue with his own AD of Operations on how screwed up this thing has become. Aliens, my ass! The president put one over on us four years ago with those damnable images of deep space and the so-called saucers. But where are they? We keep spending billions and what for?" He looked with wide eyes at his assistant. "I want details on what the president is up to and I want to be updated on Chinese and Russian military buildups. Hell, even the damn Brits have upped their naval budget by 100 percent as they are falling for the same crap the president did. And I want a full report on that little bald shit that the president bases all of his decisions on. National Archives, my ass!"

"On the foreign front I'm afraid, according to their governments, they also refuse to comment on rumors on their military. Now about this Niles Compton, Easterbrook and even our man Peachtree have no intel on Compton other than his educational background, which is of course extensive."

"If Easterbrook doesn't explain things to me far more

clearly than they have been, I'm going to leak everything I have to the public and then let the president explain that."

His assistant looked around and nervously leaned into her boss.

"Before you start making that kind of threat maybe we better get a better hold on the situation? After all, he is a lame duck president who doesn't have a successor in any shape, form, or fashion unless you consider the spineless vice president, and Easterbrook will be looking for a job in two years."

"I see. You're saying a far more subtle approach is warranted?"

"It's far better than the other rumors I've been hearing." She again glanced at the faces now turned away from the two visitors.

The Speaker of the House stopped before reaching the outer door and faced the young assistant. "What, there are new rumors?"

"That two like-minded senators and backers of yours have just announced their sudden retirements."

"Yes, Hastings and Schaller, Vermont and Texas respectively. Hastings is citing a pending divorce and Schaller is claiming health issues at age thirty-two."

"Yes, well, some are saying after meeting with the president five weeks ago and them asking rather forcefully about those very rumors that you just mentioned, they suddenly announced their decisions on retiring the very next day."

"Your point?" he asked, getting angry.

"My point is most people on the Hill are saying the president threatened them."

"How do you mean?"

She didn't respond but just looked into the older man's face. He slowly but surely caught her ominous drift.

"Then that makes meeting with CIA Director Easterbrook and our friend Peachtree essential." He turned and made his way to the door. "And remember, we can toss around threats also and Daniel Peachtree has just the man to issue those threats."

The assistant exhaled deeply as she pictured the little creep across the river at CIA. "I can't stomach that little bastard and I wish you would not be associated with him in any way. That Hiram Vickers reminds me of some slinking pedophile the way he looks at people." She shivered at the thought of the little black operations guru over at Langley. "And one more thing, sir, what makes you think it wasn't Director Easterbrook who backed up the president's threat?" she mumbled as she raced to catch up with her boss.

House Speaker Camden only froze for a second at the door as he slightly turned and answered her.

"That will be Dan Peachtree's problem, as he stands to gain the most from . . . complications in the chain of command at Langley."

As the Secret Service agent held the door open for the president, the chief executive paused a moment, took a deep breath, nodded at the agent, and tried to confidently stride into the Oval Office. The president saw his friend immediately. Director Niles Compton was at the window behind the Lincoln desk, looking out onto Pennsylvania Avenue and the five thousand men and women protesting in the street. The placards were offensive to say the least and were saying that the U.S. was on a road to dictatorship. Niles Compton knew his friend was anything but dictatorial. Being a military man from the time he was in college, the president was always terrified of being labeled right wing when actually he thought as many generals do when they got to a certain age: that military power is a dangerous thing in the wrong hands—and even sometimes in the right ones. Niles Compton knew the problem could be in no more capable hands than those of his old friend.

"I'm really surprised you're not out there with them protesting my supposed and *rumored* military moves."

"Maybe they wouldn't be protesting if they knew the whole truth," Niles Compton said as he turned away from the window to face the president.

Niles opened the folder and pulled out his report. "We have chased down every UFO report going back as · as the biblical Ezekiel. Outside of the two Roswell inci- nts we only have rumors of other incidents where a vehi- was recovered with an intact engine."

"So it's just as Matchstick says, then?" The president ught of the small alien who had been in U.S. custody e the Arizona incident in 2006.

'We'll have to place a priority on getting our hands on a er plant when hostilities start . . . if we can knock the n saucers out of the sky, that is."

he president looked a little put out by Niles's comment. lieve your Mr. Ryan brought one down in the Pacific, if ember correctly, with just a Phoenix missile. I think if n do it we can at least get a few of the bastards for hstick to play with."

ouché," Niles said as he slipped the report on the sau- arch away. "We actually may have chance at getting early in any conflict. Then it's just a matter of time aints if we can literally get Overlord off the ground." president raised his brows as he waited for any wel- ews.

tchstick says they cannot come through their travel oles in any large force. Their energy is limited. A few at a time, maybe five or six, and then the Grays have arge before they can continue sending their forces from that extreme distance away. But if they punch enough in the opening rounds their energy problems moot. As Matchstick says, it takes the power of an net to produce the energy needed to produce a time- rmhole."

resident slapped the top of his desk. "And that is hy I want my forces at full potential, Niles. Now, tick sure that this power that creates the wormholes in scope?"

As you know, the home planet of the Grays is dy- forces are growing old and their energy is used in their fleet in space. They have stripped their

The president didn't respond as he stood before his own desk. He gestured for Niles to move.

"Unless you want this screwed up job, do you mind if I sit at my own desk, baldy?"

Niles smiled and then moved. He kept his hands in his pockets as he paced to the front of the room. The president looked momentarily out of the window, then allowed the lace curtain to fall back into place as he turned and sat.

"My so-called good friends in the senate are starting to jump ship. The briefing I gave them four years ago is start- ing to wear off and now they're running for cover. The key people I needed on the hawk side of things have completely flown the coop. My friends on the other end of the spectrum are now feeling the heat because of these rumors and the fact we haven't even had one sighting of anything from space other than our own junk falling from the sky."

Niles finally turned and faced the president as he sat in one of the double-facing couches. He opened his old brief- case and removed a file. "In one brief moment of time many years ago you asked me how I would handle it. I told you."

"You didn't understand the American psyche then as now. So, may I explain it again for you, Mr. Wizard?" The pres- ident saw his friend wasn't going to respond so he quickly continued before he could. "Singly this nation is built of brilliant and smart citizens capable of immense kindness and compassion and a simple vision of the future. My people are smart, Niles. Oh, not like an egghead like you, but smart enough to know the situation and understand it when it's explained to them. But go to the collective mind of those very same citizens and that's where we run into trou- ble, and you know that. Collectively we can be the most frightened nation on this planet if things aren't explained to the extreme point they can be."

"Tell them everything now or call a press conference and deny all the military rumors as a lie, and then stop allowing the military to sway you into this supposed draft lottery. Come clean about everything from Roswell, to the incident with the destroyer in the Arizona desert, and even the moon landings from years ago. Everything." Niles shook his head and then looked at his friend. "And what is this about keeping men and women in the military after their service is complete—is *that* one true?"

The president was silent as he turned his head away from the man he had known since college. Niles Compton was the director of the utmost darkened agency in the federal government. Their existence was known only to a few and answered only to the president of the United States since the time of Lincoln unofficially, and Woodrow Wilson by law. Department 5656, or what was known to a few outsiders as the Event Group, had a mission to uncover the truth about the shared history of the world, as the understanding of the past secured the future. Department 5656 advised the presidency of any correlation between past events and those currently unfolding in the present so he could make a calculated judgment on how to handle any repeat of that history.

"Yes, it's true, Niles. I can't fight a war if my military is stripped down to nothing because of a false sense of security after the war on terror."

"Then explain *why* to the people of the country and of the world. For Christ's sake we're getting ready to watch the Chinese start killing themselves over their military expenditures. The same is happening in France, Russia, Germany, and England. We are the ones scaring the world, not them." Compton pointed toward the high ceiling of the Oval Office and what he knew was the complete future of darkness beyond the high clouds.

"Why haven't they moved on us, Niles? They've been sitting out there ten million light-years from Earth just waiting. I get new images from the Hubble every other day in my security briefing and they haven't moved a light-year in any direction, they just sit there. This is why I have supporters jumping off what they now think of as a rudderless ship."

"Our asset in the Arizona desert reports that the Grays are more than likely here already. They'll strike when they see an opportunity to do so. Thus your military buildup

could be a never-ending nightmare in the ter When they come we have to fight them with t we have already developed and the men and w to fight them. Not with new recruits or angry

The president shook his head and abruptly doing he pushed his large chair back hard er strike the wall.

"Niles, you and Garrison Lee came up w Operation Overlord. For the first aspect of th off I need warships and aircraft. To support Grays strike at them first I need to get my and for that I need control of the oceans. Ar men and equipment left over to secure ou another army as fast as possible for our d this I need experienced soldiers, and in o have to stop them from leaving their resp service. I also need every aircraft we hav desert and every obsolete warship in the adelphia."

"Then tell the people that," Niles sa the first time in the presence of the watched as his friend turned and snat back again to gaze at those very same rumors that were running rampant. " the others are refusing to grasp—an facing it—is that the combined militar planet may not last five days against from the Grays.

"That's why we have Overlord. I fensive strike until Overlord can chance, at least according to our Chato's Crawl."

"And you know damn good an plained that part two of Overlor ting our hands on a power plant fr president released the curtain "Your Group's not confident at t another crashed saucer?"

home world in order to attack us. That is why there is a delay, as they wait for an opening that will be devastating to us."

The president saw the concerned look briefly cross his friend's face. "What is it?"

"In the briefings with Matchstick and Gus, they both get extremely quiet when we talk about the Grays' home world. It seems something has been concerning the little green guy for a few years, but we at the Group cannot explain it, nor will he discuss it."

The president held Niles in his sight and then lowered his head in near despair.

"God, I pray he's not hiding anything from us."

EVENT GROUP COMPLEX
NELLIS AIR FORCE BASE, NEVADA

At 1.7 miles beneath Nellis Air Force Base, the Event Group complex was at its usual brisk pace. Thirteen field teams were crawling through deserts, mountains, and oceans searching for a historical record of downed alien aircraft in ancient times. The push to find an intact alien power plant had stripped the Event Group of most of their divisions and military security personnel, so much so that gate number two inside the Gold City Pawn Shop had been closed due to the lack of viable military personnel to secure the Las Vegas entrance. And with so many scientists and historians in the field the complex was near empty.

The man in charge of complex security on a temporary basis was First Lieutenant Will Mendenhall. Naval Commander Jason Ryan officially outranked the lieutenant but the naval aviator stepped aside due to Will's advanced training in black operations. Both men were standing inside the computer center with Pete Golding, the man responsible for the supercomputer Europa. They stood in front of Pete's personal Europa terminal, and it was Golding who gestured angrily at the six-foot monitor.

"Look, there it is again. What in the hell are he and Gus Tilly working on that's using so much computer time? I have people searching for ancient saucer wreckage and sometimes they can't even log in as Matchstick has usurped the Europa system. Niles and I gave him complete access to the computers but even that wasn't enough. Our green friend is locking out my own teams."

"Have you called out to Arizona to ask Matchstick why he needs so much computer time?" Will looked over at a bored Jason Ryan, who just shrugged his shoulders.

"Gus won't say. He says that Matchstick isn't communicating with him about this suddenly urgent project he's working on outside of the saucer power plant search. Gus also says Matchstick isn't sleeping and barely eating, and Gus is afraid he's going to get sick."

"What does the director have to say about this?" Ryan offered. "I mean, the last I heard Matchstick has total control of Europa whenever he wants it, so why is this upsetting you to the point you're whining like a schoolgirl?"

"The director doesn't know," Pete said as he turned off his monitor and the view of the computer center out in Arizona. They watched the small green alien known as Mahjtic as the monitor faded to nothing. The Group called him the Matchstick Man, as Gus Tilly had been calling him since the old prospector saved the life of the small being after it had crashed in the Arizona desert.

"Well, I would suggest bringing Virginia in on this and get a jump-start on getting some answers while Dr. Compton is in Washington," Will said as he straightened and stretched his back. Pete nodded and started to reach for the phone on his desk, but Will and Jason stopped him by clearing their throats at the same moment.

Pete Golding finally thought he knew what the two military men wanted. He nodded his head and then released the phone. He turned and spoke softly into the extended microphone, and the large monitor above them came to life with a live picture of a giant ice cave. The video was stark as the lights of a surveillance camera glared off the crystalline blue ice.

"Europa managed to break into the British security cameras in the Antarctic. As you can see the ice has been excavated quite extensively in the area of the find. After the initial discovery of the wreckage and the finding of Captain Everett's wristwatch with his and Colonel Collins's DNA upon it, the site has yielded little else."

Three months before they had been informed that a watch had been discovered inside the wreckage of an unknown type of aerial vehicle of Earth origin, no craft like it was now in existence. The plum in that little information was the fact that the British Antarctica expedition that discovered the wreckage found the artifacts under more than a mile of ice. And the kicker to that statement was the fact that the ice it was buried in was more than two hundred thousand years old. Thus they were now in the state they were in three weeks before with Captain Everett in retirement and Colonel Jack Collins suspended from all field operations as per presidential order.

"Are the British going to allow American examination of the craft?" Jason asked before Will could in their never-ending competition to be first in everything.

"Thus far they think the turning over of the watch was enough. Until they have thoroughly examined the ship, or whatever it is, they won't budge. It seems the fight to get the most technology is ongoing. But the strange thing is, Niles, Matchstick, and even Colonel Collins know what the British are up to under the ice but they are keeping it close to the vest."

"Does it have something to do with these strange names floating around security, Overlord and such?" Mendenhall asked.

"Details of that operation will get anyone fired around here for even mentioning it. So, your guess is as good as mine."

"Dr. Golding," Europa announced, "Chato's Crawl has

requested restricted satellite weather data from the NASA mainframe."

"Damn," Pete hissed as he shook his head. "Name of asset requesting data stream?" he asked.

"Identification code: *Magic*."

"Matchstick again?" Jason asked as his smile grew. "The little fella is working overtime, I guess."

"But on what?" Pete asked. "When he requests military data from anywhere he is usually forthcoming about what he's looking for. But now I make requests for verification as to why he wants that data, and he clams up."

Will Mendenhall looked at the clock readout in blue numbers that was projected onto the white plastic wall of the computer center.

"Well, get Dr. Pollock to sign off on Matchstick's request, and I think it's time we pay our friend in the desert a visit. Pete, please keep up on the Antarctic surveillance." Mendenhall hesitated and then faced Pete again. "Without stepping on toes and mentioning this Operation Overlord, whatever it may be."

"Will do. Also, when you get out to Chato's Crawl, ask Matchstick what is so important about Charlie's cryptozo-ology department. He's been spending an inordinate amount of time running through Crypto's files and Charlie Ellenshaw hasn't figured out a pattern to Matchstick's research yet. If he's interested in Crypto, he should ask Charlie directly; he could be more of a help."

"Okay." Mendenhall turned to Jason. "Feel like flying out to Arizona?"

"Sure, beats sitting here listening to Pete," Jason said as he slapped Golding on the back. "But as a field team we need two more security people, buddy, and guess what? We're fresh out of live bodies. Everyone we have in security is either in the field chasing down leads to crashed saucers or on security duty here. As you know, even with gate two shut down we're still shorthanded."

"I've got that covered. Since we need Charlie on this trip he'll be listed in the field report as added security."

Jason smiled as he knew right where Will was heading. "Besides Charlie, who's *they* in that equation?"

Will started to walk up the stairs that led to the theater-style seating above the main floor.

"The last I heard, Antarctica was still way down south. I think Chato's Crawl is safe enough for our intrepid Colonel Collins to join us."

Jason Ryan looked at Pete.

"After finding Captain Everett's watch in two-hundred-thousand-year-old ice I don't find very much safe about anything."

"I hear that."

The knock sounded loudly on his door. His eyes never left the screen full of information that scrolled across his face inside the darkness of his private quarters. The eyes scanned a document he had stared at for hours on end. It was an image of the only scrap of evidence in the murder of a thirty-one-year-old CIA agent. The internal memorandum was of U.S. government origin and was known to be used by three of the top agencies in the country—the FBI, the National Security Agency, and the CIA. The memo directed the young agent to a meeting she never returned from. The key to the document was the small dash-dot system in the left-hand corner. Pete and Europa finally deciphered the code and broke it down to indicate the memo originated at the desk of someone at the CIA.

The subject of the memo was the very man looking at the image supplied by Europa. It was a memo listing his name and day and dates of where he was at. It was a tracking report from a bug that had been planted covertly on his person, and the memo was an order to the contracted satellite company doing the tracking—Cassini Space-Based Systems—by the person or persons responsible for the young agent's and another female's death. The eyes scanned the document one last time and then Jack Collins shut off the monitor and turned his unshaven face toward the steel door of his quarters—or as he had come to think of it, his prison.

"Come," he said as he stood. He paced to the bathroom and splashed water on his face just as the door opened. Will Mendenhall stuck his head inside.

"Feel like getting the hell out of here for a while, Colonel?" Will asked as his eyes studied the usually immaculate quarters. His eyes fell on the empty Jack Daniels bottle and several glasses that lined his desk. The room was a mess and so unlike Collins that Will shook his head.

Jack came out of the bathroom drying his hands on a towel. When he was finished he allowed it to slip through his fingers and onto the carpeted floor.

"What is it, you busting me out?" Jack started to slip into an olive-drab-colored T-shirt over his bare chest.

"Something like that. We're shorthanded on a routine detail and it should afford you to get a little air since it's nowhere near the South Pole."

Collins looked at Will for the longest time.

"Still nothing on the origins of Mr. Everett's watch?"

Mendenhall's silence was enough of an answer. Jack angrily slipped into a wrinkled white dress shirt and started buttoning it. As long as he was restricted to base because of this archeological find in Antarctica he could not get out of the complex to find the killer of the young CIA agent—his sister, Lynn Simpson Collins. He knew the watch had to have been discovered in the efforts to free the largest part of Operation Overlord from the ice, a fact he couldn't share with Will or anyone else who wasn't in on the planned response to a possible Gray invasion.

"Figure we could go out and see our little friend in the desert. It seems he's up to deviltry and it's freaking Doc Golding out."

"What doesn't freak Pete out?" Jack said, feeling better just by talking about normal things again. "Why not," he finally said. "And by the way, you know that anything our green friend wants, he gets, so Pete should just calm down."

Will held the door open for the colonel in silence.

"What's the latest on McIntire?" Jack asked as he gathered his things.

"She's still in Uzbekistan, checking on one of the target areas for the search."

"The supposed Soviet saucer encounter in 1972?" Jack retrieved his sunglasses from the desk and made his way to the door.

"Yeah, looks like another dead end as no one wants to talk to our team or the Russians. Both we and the Ruskies aren't real popular over there. She should be back in a few days. I think Dr. Compton has another search he wants her on."

"Matchstick has no theories on Everett's watch and the Antarctica thing?" Jack knew the link between Operation Overlord and the captain's watch had to be connected, but without telling the top-most secret in the world to Pete and the others they were at a dead end.

"When asked, green boy just looks confused and then says there is no such science as time displacement, no matter what Albert Einstein says, and I guess he would know."

"Why? Most of the scientists around here believe Einstein was one of them anyway," Jack said, referring to Albert's proclivity for being right about everything.

For Will it was good to see the colonel smile, even if it was only a moment of normalcy.

Jack turned to close his door and then hesitated.

"How is Captain Everett?"

"No word. It seems the captain may have found a home in Romania."

Jack nodded and felt better that his friend was at least safe inside Romania.

"Well, shall we go hassle the Matchstick Man?" Collins asked as he gestured for Will to lead the way.

On the way down the corridor Will whistled the old tune the colonel had made him listen to six years before—the 1967 hit by the British rock band Status Quo: "Pictures of Matchstick Men." It was a tune that was hauntingly similar in description to their little green alien friend—Mahjtic.

Niles waited on the president. The way his friend fidgeted about on the facing couch resembled a man trying to find a way to tell his buddy he had a terminal illness. Then the president stood and moved to his desk and used a small key to open one of the many drawers. He removed his own special file and went to the coffee table fronting the two couches, sat on the edge, and then slapped Niles on the knee with it.

"What is this?" Niles asked, refusing to touch it.

"Orders."

Compton saw the president's eyes as they locked on his own. Then his eyes moved to the emblem on the manila file as he saw it was from the Department of the Navy, and a cold chill ran through his body. Finally Niles reached out and accepted the folder.

"Before you open that I have this little problem to deal with and I want to do it in front of you so you can personally pass on what it was you witnessed." The president reached into his suit jacket and brought out a large white envelope and opened it. Without comment the president tore the envelope and whatever was inside of it in two, then tossed the destroyed letter onto the tabletop and faced Compton once more.

"Okay, you have me more than curious. What was that about?"

The president shook his head and turned away, then stood and momentarily squeezed Niles's shoulder. "That was me being a prick, my old friend."

"We've always known that, but why admit to it now?" Compton quipped nervously as his eyes went to the torn-up envelope and whatever secret it held.

"When an officer in the United States military resigns, he resigns, no one says anything, it's deemed personal, and is left alone." The president walked toward his desk and then turned and faced Niles. "That was the resignation letter signed by Captain Everett—not accepted."

Niles started to protest but his old friend held up a warning hand.

"No discussion on this matter will be tolerated or appreciated. It was hard enough interfering with a military man's life, but in this case it had to be done." The president paced toward a silent Compton. "You and General Lee once told me that hard choices were going to have to be made that would send thousands, maybe even millions of boys off to die, and no matter what happens the Overlord plan would have to be adhered to or we would lose to the Grays in no uncertain terms. The debriefing of Matchstick has explained in detail that this planet does not stand a chance of defending itself against an advanced race without Overlord. Lee said it, Matchstick has also said it, and you, my friend, concurred. Nothing interferes with the Overlord plans, especially the second section of that plan. Remember the report you turned in?"

Niles just nodded his head as he slowly opened the folder and saw the thin sheets of military flimsy. The orders were for Captain Carl Everett. He closed his eyes, then the offending file folder.

"Captain Everett has been reassigned to Overlord," the president said. "I need him there and so do you. He's worked closely with several of the engineers and one those engineers in particular. The captain was a part of your original plan four years ago, assigned to the same area of Overlord as this, the Antarctica discovery of his watch and the blood of he and Colonel Collins notwithstanding."

"So no matter what it is we find that explains how Captain Everett's wristwatch was discovered buried in two-hundred-thousand-year-old ice, we still send him out there knowing it could be his part in Overlord that gets him and Jack Collins killed?"

"That's about the gist of it. We cannot alter the Overlord scenario by not having key people where they are supposed to be."

"In other words, the captain is expendable?"

"Very much so—as expendable as the young boys I'm

going to ask to trade their lives for fighting this war. Yes, Niles, we are all expendable."

Niles placed the orders for Everett inside his briefcase. He wanted nothing more than for this meeting to come to a close so he could get outside and breathe where decisions that got people killed were nonexistent.

Before Niles stood the president surprised him and tossed another folder on the coffee table. This one was far thicker than the first. Niles took a deep breath and then looked over at a dejected president.

"Those are orders for Colonel Collins. They are a little more confidential. He is being transferred to Hawaii immediately, along with your young Lieutenant Mendenhall. That smart-ass Lieutenant Ryan will be going with Captain Everett to Houston." The president took a breath and then slowly walked to the couch and sat next to his friend of thirty years. "Jack is now a part of USPACOM."

"The United States Pacific Command—why there? His outline for Overlord never called for that."

"I know, he was to stay with the scientific aspect of Overlord, but things have changed. I want Collins and Everett separated from each other as far apart as possible, and this, old friend, is the only thing I can think of to protect them."

USPACOM was the largest military presence in the world and Niles knew the command would more than likely be at the forefront of any defense the world could establish against the Grays. The Pacific command encompasses about half the earth's surface, stretching from the waters off the west coast of the U.S. to the border of India, and from Antarctica to the North Pole. There are few regions as culturally, socially, economically, and geopolitically diverse as the Pacific. The thirty-six nations that comprise the Asia-Pacific region are home to more than 50 percent of the world's population, three thousand vastly differing languages, several of the world's largest militaries, and five nations allied with the U.S. through mutual defense treaties. Two of the three largest economies are located in the Asia-Pacific along with ten of the fourteen smallest. This area of responsibility includes the most populous nation in the world, the largest democracy, and the largest Muslim-majority nation—India. That was followed quickly by the nation with a military the U.S. intelligence services had shockingly little information on—China.

"Niles, I'm afraid that isn't all." The president pulled a small sheet of paper from his breast pocket and handed it to Compton. "Take this memo back with you and post it for all of my military personnel to read. I will be taking and accepting all military transfer requests to either support roles or any combat command of their choosing. I am reassigning Treasury to assist in securing the Event facility. That and personnel too old for support or combat should be sufficient."

"Why all of a sudden? What aren't you telling me?"

"I'm surprised you don't know already with that criminally controlled computer of yours, but I imagine Pete Golding and his accomplice in crime, Europa, have been busy looking for downed saucers."

Niles was silent, not really wanting to joke about Pete Golding and Europa's diligence at breaking into other computer systems the world over.

The president reached beside him and took yet another folder from the coffee table. It was large and when he pulled the contents free Niles could see it was an image from space. His heart froze momentarily.

"The Hubble?" Niles asked as he took the offered photo.

The president stood and paced away with his hands inside of his pockets. "No, that's a KH-16 satellite image—CIA, actually. That is a shot of the Algerian desert. You notice anything?"

"Yes, it looks like about three miles of earth has been taken out like a plug." Niles examined the picture more closely. He saw roads leading in and then out of the void, but inside there was nothing but subterranean geological formations and dirt. The roads led to nowhere other than the giant hole in the ground.

"That is what's left of a large oasis that has stood for

close to ten thousand years in the Hoggar Mountains of the central Sahara Desert—specifically, Algeria, in the Tropic of Cancer."

"And you suspect the Grays?" Niles asked as he continued to examine the CIA spy satellite image.

"That is the consensus of NASA. There is nothing in the world capable of doing that—to reach down from the sky and snatch a billion tons of earth and rock and make it vanish like a shovelful of dirt tossed over someone's shoulder."

"When did this event happen?" Compton asked, angry that he hadn't been told sooner.

"Six days ago."

Now the president's behavior became crystal clear to Niles Compton.

"Thus the push to build up the military is now escalated to priority one."

"Yes, the Joint Chiefs believe we have already been hit by the Grays, but we have no evidence other than a destroyed watering hole in the middle of the desert. Hardly enough of an incentive to start the largest military buildup in world history, would you agree?"

As Niles examined the space-based image he wasn't sure what it was he was looking at. Something wasn't sitting right with the image. One thing he did know for sure, he was losing two top people and his world of science and fact was slowly starting to go up in flames—just as he knew the entire world soon be burning with that same fire.

The president nodded with satisfaction when he saw Niles hurriedly gathering his case and the orders for Jack and Carl.

The fire had been lit underneath the man that the president of the United States considered to be the smartest man in the world—Dr. Niles Compton.

2

The raven-haired woman stood silently just inside the doorway, leaning against the frame of the dilapidated house with the thatched roof. Her stance was relaxed and motionless with her arms crossed over her chest. She watched the large man in the distance as he sat at the base of the pass, staring out into the valley far below. The summer air had turned warm and the flowers inside the pass brought on a multitude of colors that usually brightened her mood—with the exception of the past week, when the flowers' bright cheerfulness became lost amid an ever-increasing storm front she felt was sliding her way.

Captain Carl Everett seemed content, with the exception of his feelings when night started to descend upon the Patinas Pass. It was at those moments when his past life intruded upon the gentle and loving life he had chosen these past three months. The woman loved Carl and she knew her feelings were returned. But she also knew that very same love would eventually take the life right from the man she fell for. He was not a herder of sheep and he wasn't a farmer and she would be a fool of the highest order to believe he would be content at that over the life he had led just a few months before. His spirit was drowning here in Romania and she knew it.

Anya Korvesky was alone in what was once a bustling village but was now empty, with the exception of a young couple who thought they could leave their pasts behind them and move on into a future that didn't include killing and subterfuge. Anya didn't miss her former life in the Mossad, but she knew Carl was slowly starting to break into pieces. He felt he'd left all of his responsibilities behind; it was eroding what happiness the two of them had found together. She knew the captain loved her dearly, but felt him slipping away in small increments.

"It used to be I could never have crept up behind you without you blowing my head off with a hidden gun."

Anya slowly lost the smile as she heard the voice behind her. As she turned to face the man she cocked back the hammer on a nine-millimeter handgun and patted it on her bare leg. Her smile returned.

"I see you haven't lost your trusting nature or your ability to smell a rat."

The man was dressed in tan clothes and work boots. His bush hat looked ridiculously out of place, as did the large briefcase he carried in his right hand. The men he came with were spread out behind him and were watching the empty village with concern.

"I wouldn't call you a rat necessarily, General, more like an unwanted pest."

"Touché, Major, touché."

Anya closed her eyes at the mention of her Mossad rank.

"As you well know, General Shamni, that is no longer my military rank. My name is now Korvesky, the same as yours." She sniffed as if a bad odor had entered her nostrils. "Or so it used to be."

General Avis Shamni—with his ridiculous safari clothes covering his large and rotund body—stood smiling at the brightest Mossad agent he had ever produced. He held out his hand while his eyes looked at the pistol in her hand. She lowered it and then refused the handshake.

"What do you want, Uncle?" She stepped to the old table that used to belong to her grandmother and set the pistol down. She turned and faced her onetime commander in the Mossad, Israel's elite intelligence service.

"Actually," he said as he lowered his hand, "what I have come about concerns your American friend." He stepped up to the open doorway and saw Carl Everett just below the entrance to the pass mending a small fence. He turned back to face his niece. "And thus, indirectly, you."

"Uncle, I am not returning to the Mossad. I don't belong anymore, my place is here."

"Here?" Shamni glanced around the former home of his elder sister. "My dear, this place is now a part of history. It sits above a fiasco that was once going to be the Las Vegas of Romania, but now sits wrecked, its evil seed returning to the earth." He looked down the mountain through the open wooden shutters of the window and saw the Edge of the World Hotel and Resort Casino lying in ruins far below. Closer were the remains of the tourist attraction, Dracula's Castle, where only its foundation remained after it was destroyed three months before.

"It's something of a home, General. Far more than Israel is."

"Ah, I see." The general opened up his briefcase and pulled out a photo of a man. He held it out to Anya, who tried her best to ignore the offering. "Does this man look familiar to you?"

Anya glanced out the window and saw that Carl had started his descent of the mountain, heading her way. Anya then turned and looked at the black and white photo without reaching for it. The man in the eight-by-ten was thin and looked to have a thinning head of hair. She smirked when she noticed the man was wearing sideburns that almost went to his jaw line.

"Not in the slightest. I've never seen him before."

The general brought out another. "And this gentleman?"

Anya picked up the eight-by-ten and looked it over. This man did seem familiar to her but she couldn't place him. The bright orange jumpsuit was a major clue; the man, whoever he was, was dressed in standard prison fashion. The general could see the face that stared back at her was familiar, so he decided to help out her memory.

"That man once ran the largest arms manufacturing firm in the world. His company was into everything."

Anya tapped the photo with her index finger. "The Centauris Corporation?"

"As the Americans say, bingo! Correct, that is Charles Hendrix II, CEO and chairman. Well, he was, now he's just federal prisoner Hendrix." Shamni smirked with a knowing twitch of his heavy moustache. "Secreted away federal prisoner, I should say. You see, Hendrix doesn't really exist."

"I take it you'll explain this before Carl returns?"

"The man was divested of all corporate holdings, his bank accounts seized and his manufacturing divisions sold off, then he was locked away without trial and hidden away at Leavenworth penitentiary by none other than the president of the United States."

Anya felt the tug of curiosity and then took hold of that old investigative feeling, but hid it away from the general. She handed the photo back to the general.

"Okay, I can see your hobby of photography still has a way to go on quality issues, but other than that, General, what does this have to do with me or Carl?"

Shamni smiled and then cautiously sat in a rickety old chair. The chair creaked and groaned under his immense weight.

"You told me a story when you resigned your position in the Mossad. Maybe you should have kept your secret to yourself, but perhaps it was fortuitous that you did tell me. The story you relayed to me about your American captain and his friend, Colonel Jack Collins, and their search to find the murderer of a CIA asset—an asset that turned out to be the sister of Colonel Collins. It rang a bell, for some reason.

Then I remembered a man buried deep inside Langley who specialized in dirty tricks. He led a group of men that searched out and confiscated new technologies intended for the eventual buildup of military forces the world over. This man restarted one of the more infamous groups in the history of American corporations—the Black Teams, more ominously known as the Men in Black. And the man that ran this desk at the CIA is this man." Shamni once more pulled out the photo of the man in the ugly and outdated suit. "Hiram Vickers is his name. He works directly for, now get this, not the director of the CIA, but the assistant director of Operations, Daniel Peachtree."

"I've read that Peachtree's relationship with the president isn't all that good. As I recall, he was against his appointment but it was pushed through anyway with the help of the Speaker of the House, Giles Camden."

"I see you still know how to read a newspaper and remember briefing reports." Shamni placed the photos of both men into the large envelope.

"As I asked before, what does this have to do with us?" she persisted, not allowing the Israeli general to go into one of his soliloquies about loyalty and how badly the service missed her. She knew how her uncle played the game—he was good at it and very experienced in getting just what was needed for the State of Israel any way he could.

"Okay, Major, we'll get straight to the point, then. It is the opinion of intelligence and a few other departments inside Mossad that the man with the red hair is the entity responsible for the murder of the sister of Colonel Collins, and that this Charles Hendrix gave the CIA, Peachtree in particular, the operational standards and guidelines of his Centauris's defunct Black Teams."

"I suppose you have evidence to back up that rather broad statement?" she asked as she started to see Shamni's game.

"Not one shred other than the fact we have people like you, Anya, that are the best in the world in analyzing enemies and allies alike and can put two and two together." He smiled again. "Besides, it just so happens we have an asset inside

Langley that says this Hiram Vickers is an ass of the first order and no one, and I mean no one, trusts him."

"And you think that you can tell Carl this guesswork of yours and your wunderkind back in Tel Aviv and he'll go running back to the good old USA, and I back to you and the Mossad—is that about the gist of it, Uncle?"

"Something like that, yes."

Anya closed her eyes as she realized that this day was always meant to come. She opened her eyes and watched as Carl stopped at the front gate of the empty village of Patinas. She saw his face as he studied the Range Rover parked along the dirt road. He looked from the car and the driver who sat silently behind the wheel, then to the small house and the men surrounding it. He saw Anya and raised a brow; she must look distressed even from the distance he was standing.

"You know he'll leave for a chance at assisting his friend Jack in finding the lowlife that killed his sister. He may even want to return after he does what needs doing," Anya said with hope ringing her words.

General Shamni stood and paced to the window to let Carl see who was visiting. He placed a hand on his niece's shoulder.

"If it were any other time in the history of the world I would say yes, he will return to you. But these are not times that were meant for joy and happiness. Israel needs all her children to come home for what's heading our way." He held a file in front of Anya and then turned to leave. "Perhaps you'll show him the photos, perhaps you won't." He stopped but didn't turn to face her. "Maybe you can trick him into staying. But the file I just handed to you is top secret and no more than two dozen people in the world know the code names in the contents. That, my dear niece, you can't hide from him. We are just notifying Captain Everett a few weeks ahead of time, is all. Official orders will be delivered to him from the military attaché at the American embassy in Bucharest."

Anya didn't look at the file and she didn't turn as the general approached the door.

"I will have an aircraft standing by to fly you home to Tel Aviv, as we have important work to do." The general left.

Anya Korvesky took a deep breath as she saw Carl being approached by General Shamni. He watched as Carl smiled and took the general's hand in his own. Pleasantries were exchanged but even then Carl was looking past the general's shoulder to view Anya's sad countenance. She quickly turned away and looked inside the folder. She felt the tears well up in her eyes as she saw that it was an absconded copy of a United States Department of the Navy letter. It was an official notice that his resignation was not accepted and that he was to report immediately to Houston, Texas, and the new Naval Warfare Center, permanently attached to something called *Overlord*. She closed the folder and sat heavily in one of the old chairs.

She felt Carl standing in the doorway. Without looking up she slid the large envelope across the wooden table. She placed her hands in her lap as if the envelope had a disgusting feel to it.

Carl ignored the envelope and instead of reaching for it when he approached he went to Anya and placed his large hands on her small shoulders and squeezed lightly. She reached a hand up and took a soft hold on his arm and then just sat that way.

"Carl, you have to sit down and we have to talk."

"The general is recalling you to Tel Aviv, isn't he?" he asked as he kept his hands on her shoulders. He looked at the envelope sitting on the table and that was when he saw the file folder in Anya's free hand. He patted her lightly and then sat and just looked at the large yellow envelope.

"Yes," Anya said as she found her eyes refused to take Carl in. "And I'm returning with him as soon as possible."

Carl sat motionless while his eyes studied Anya's face. Her refusal to look at him told him volumes.

"And you are to be recalled by your Department of the

Navy," she said, still not looking up as she laid the file on the table next to the yellow envelope. Finally her moist eyes rose to meet Carl's. She slowly slid the file toward him and then looked away as he opened it and studied the stolen orders.

"Pretty damn industrious of Uncle General, isn't it? I'm sure the U.S. Navy would like to learn how he got ahold of transit orders before the ink was even dry on them."

Anya smiled at the naiveté that Carl showed sometimes, as he liked to believe everyone in the world was as aboveboard as himself and his friends in America. It was always amazing when she had to explain the hard truths to him.

"The same place your CIA gets their information, Carl, and you know that. Some little analyst with a cheap computer broke into another computer and got the orders before release."

Carl shook his head as he closed the folder. "Yeah, I know about little analysts and their computers and what a pain in the ass they can be. Only the computer they use isn't cheap." He smiled, thinking about his old friend Pete Golding and his "girlfriend," Europa, and then reached out to take Anya's hand. "I guess someone in Washington needs to learn to read a resignation letter. I'm done with all of that." He squeezed her hand. "Just as I hope you're done with the Mossad."

Anya released his hand abruptly and then stood so suddenly she knocked the chair over as she turned for the window. "Carl, I'm leaving for Tel Aviv and you're going home before those orders take effect. You may have enough time before you have to report to Houston to do what needs to be done."

"Time for what, and what needs to be done?" he asked as he finally reached for the yellow envelope. He saw Anya wasn't going to answer so he opened it and pulled the two photos free along with the report that accompanied them. He saw immediately that the written report was butchered by long, black editing lines cutting off information not meant for Carl's eyes. He read as he looked at both pictures. His brows rose when he recognized Charles Hendrix of the defunct Centauris Corporation. He looked at Anya, who was still facing toward the mountain outside. When Carl finished the analyst's conclusions as to the collusion between Hendrix, Assistant Director of Operations Daniel Peachtree, and this Hiram Vickers, he became silent as his fingers closed around the likeness of Vickers. He studied the man's face and didn't notice when Anya turned and went to Everett and sat next to him. She forcefully removed his fingers from the photo and then closed both of her smaller ones over Carl's.

"It's time for you to go home, my handsome captain. Both our countries need us home." She quickly released one of her hands and swiped at the tear that rolled down her right cheek. She hated herself for being a girl as she thought of it, but this was her life, her love that she was going to force away from her. "Your friend Jack needs you, and for the little bit of time you have left before your navy steals you, you can help him end this horrible thing that befell his sister. The general says we are running out of time—about what, he didn't say, but I believe him when he says Israel needs all her children back home." She smiled and leaned across and kissed Carl. "And so does America." She smiled broadly as she pulled back after kissing him. "She needs all of her Captain Americas."

Carl swallowed as he realized his time with Anya was at an end. It was because Carl knew just what the Mossad general was referring to when he mentioned they were all running out of time. It could only mean one thing, and that business had to do with the Event Group's small green secret in the desert. But it was the other that concerned him at the moment. The information he now held could only be delivered by hand to Jack, as he could never trust sending it through any other means. Yes, he knew he had to return to Nevada and he knew he had to help Jack before the real-world problems started burning the world to cinders. Carl lowered his head as he found he was unable to speak. Anya broke down and started to cry, then leaned into Everett and held him.

Deep in the Carpathian Mountains, the sad refrain of a wolf's cry echoed across the windswept peaks.

WARWICK PANGEA BEACH RESORT AND HOTEL JIYEH, LEBANON

On the gleaming coast of Jiyeh sat the refurbished resort hotel that was now the pride of all Lebanon. The hotel had faced destruction many times and was partially burned in the civil war of two decades before. Sitting twenty-seven kilometers south of Beirut, the resort rarely had empty rooms as festive life had slowly returned to the war-torn nation.

On this Saturday tourists filled the spa and pool areas and crowded the many restaurants that served foods from all over the world. The resort was out to make Beirut the place to visit it had been thirty years before.

As the noon hour approached the sun was blotted out by a few clouds that seemed to approach the coast without being noticed by either the guests or the resort staff. As tourists were just starting to lie out on the white sandy beaches while others were heading inside for lunch, the clouds grew heavier and thicker. The guests shielded their eyes against the fading sunlight as they watched the strange clouds swirling right above the resort.

Suddenly thunder roared as more clouds joined the first group. These were darker and strangely enough were tinged with green and blue colored highlights that seemed to emanate from deep within the small storm. As sunbathers stood and started gathering towels and belongings, the wind picked up. It went from a calm five-mile-an-hour offshore breeze to a thunderous peppering of sand and seawater as the guests were pummeled by wind-sped debris.

The hotel staff waved the guests inside as small tendrils

of blackness reached out from the clouds for the earth below. The motion increased and the image of a hurricane filled most with dread. The suddenness of the storm and its power had patrons running in fear.

The circling clouds sped up. The center started down, retracted, and then began to once more creep down from the sky. The few brave guests who braved the stinging sand and sea saw the very center of the storm as it slowly passed the main section of the resort. Eyes widened as they seemed to be looking into the very visage of an angry God. The blackness beyond the dead center of the storm was like the eye of a hurricane, only it was the blackness of space that lay far beyond the top of the clouds.

Suddenly a streak of bright green lightning reached out toward the beach. Running patrons were struck down by the moving electrical fire. More strikes hit the resort. Multicolored yellow, green, and blue streaks slammed the spa area, immediately killing all inside.

Men, women, and children screamed as the clouds suddenly slammed into the earth. Eyewitnesses miles away said it looked as if a dark and viscous liquid had been dumped on the resort. The swirling clouds, wind, and lightning completely engulfed the resort and the land and sea for two miles around. The speeding tornado made the image of the resort a memory.

The storm started to diminish—not slowly, but as suddenly as it had sprung up. As the clouds lifted, the survivors heard the roar and crash of the sea as it rushed in to replace the billions of gallons of seawater that had vanished as surely as the resort itself.

Water seeped into the giant hole that was once the location of the billion-dollar resort. The hotel, all of the outer buildings, and even part of the sea had disappeared—vanished into the tornado-like storm. A few palms fell over as half of their bulk had been stripped away and sent with wood, cement, water, and 4,800 men, women, and children. Water gushed from broken water mains that ended abruptly where the hotel once stood.

The strange phenomenon had sucked up over four square miles of beachfront and had vanished as if it had never been.

SIXTEEN MILES SOUTH OF CHATO'S CRAWL, ARIZONA

The UH-60 Black Hawk hovered one mile away and sent out her coded signal to the security team at the compound. An answering bleep in the pilot's headset told him the code had been read and acknowledged—they were clear to enter the no-fly zone. As the large Black Hawk slowly started forward it was still being tracked by three missile batteries hidden inside the compound and surrounding terrain, ready to shoot down anything that came near to the darkest asset in the United States.

The helicopter rose to two hundred feet and swung slightly west; the compound came into view. The site had changed much in the past eight years since the incursion by the Grays during that horrid summer when so many American servicemen and women had lost their lives.

The large and brand-new two-story Victorian house was the dominating feature with the small tar-paper-roofed shack sitting next to it hidden in its shadows. As Jack Collins, Professor Charles Hindershot Ellenshaw III, and Will Mendenhall watched from inside, they didn't see any of the twenty-man security team they knew to be eyeing the Black Hawk's approach. The pilot aimed for the very small helipad that was camouflaged by a cross of flowers from every angle except straight up. Jason Ryan eased the large Event Group bird down. Charlie started to move toward the open sliding door and was held back by Will.

"Wait, Doc, we don't want to lose you now." The lieutenant eased Ellenshaw back into his seat, then nodded through the doorway at the approaching man in the jeans and blue denim shirt, with a white cowboy hat that had seen far better days. The man waved his hand and then stepped up to the open doorway.

"Colonel, Lieutenant, good afternoon." The man looked beyond the two officers and eyed the professor. "And Doc Ellenshaw." He again nodded, held up a small black box, and extended it to Collins first. "Colonel, if you would squeeze the foam sides of the box, please."

Jack took the Bio-Dynastic cell, squeezed it with his right hand—palm up—and handed it back to the cautious guard. The analyzer beeped twice, then a hidden green LED light glowed softly. Jack's name appeared on the liquid crystal screen with his rank and picture. The DNA analyzer cleared Collins for entrance into the secretive compound. The guard nodded at Jack, peeled away the twin-foam-rubber grips, replaced those with two fresh ones, and handed it to Mendenhall. The process was repeated for him and Ellenshaw. The link to Europa had taken the moisture from their grips and processed it through the DNA autobase she had of every Event Group staff member.

"Thank you, sir." The guard stepped back after checking Charlie's vitals on the screen. He was having a hard time not laughing at the photo of the crazy, white-haired cryptozoologist and the silly look he had on his bespectacled face.

"Sergeant." Jack stepped from the Black Hawk and then stretched. He scratched the itching beard he had yet to shave and then looked at the Marine. "Matchstick and Gus?"

"Well, Colonel, Gus is in the small house as usual. Matchstick is still held up down in the computer room in the big house."

Will and Charlie stepped up beside Jack.

"How long has he been like this?" Will asked, trying to get a firsthand account of what had been happening the past few days.

"Five straight days and nights. We moved a small cot into the basement for the rare times the little guy lies down, and he takes all of his meals in there. The Europa link is running twenty-four hours a day. Not unusual in and of itself, but strange because he doesn't want us looking over his shoulder."

"Yes, we know, that's why we're here." Mendenhall

smiled when he saw the old man open the even older screen door to the small shack. Gus Tilly stepped off the rickety porch and halfheartedly waved at the visitors. He moved toward the group at a slow gait and Jack saw the age Gus had fended off for so long had finally managed to slow him up.

"Colonel, Will." Gus held out his hand and shook the two officers' hands. He stepped up and looked Ellenshaw over. "Professor," he said, taking Charlie by the arm and ignoring his outstretched hand. "Your name is all over that damn research material Matchstick is porin' over, and I need you to slow that boy down before he kills himself," he said, half angry. "What is this about?"

Jack and Will watched the exchange just as confused as Ellenshaw.

"I know he's been in Europa's files from the Crypto department but he's locked the file and we can't get in. He's classified all of his research with a security code."

"A situation that should have been avoided," Mendenhall mentioned as he broke into the conversation. "Pete Golding should not have given Matchstick clearance to secure his own research material or files."

"Look, Niles has given over complete control of certain aspects of computer security directly to Matchstick . . ." Jack hesitated, not able to say too much. "While he does a special project."

Jack stepped up. "Gus, are you all right?" he asked, looking at the thin, frail shape of the old prospector.

Tilly held a hand up and swished it through the air.

"Ah, gettin' old, is all. The Group doc, that Gilliam woman, said it's exhaustion. 'Fraid that little shit in there"—he pointed at the new house—"has me worried beyond reason with his strange behavior. He ain't been to the mine in two weeks."

They were interrupted by one of the civilian-attired guards as he came from the small garden hut that doubled as the main gate for the compound. He was carrying an armload of what looked like newspapers. Jack exchanged looks with Mendenhall as the guard stepped up to the four men.

"Sergeant, Matchstick's daily reading material arrived about an hour ago. I've checked them all for bugs and they're clean. Should I take them to him?" the guard asked the Marine sergeant.

Collins reached for them. "No, we'll take them."

"Tell him now's not the time to hold back secrets from friends, so give the little green bastard a piece of your mind, Colonel," the old man said with a mischievous grin on his whiskered face. "You seem to be the only human that intimidates him anymore. The way he looks at me is like he's in disconnect . . . Sorta sad-like."

A very tired Jack nodded his head and winked at Gus, then started toward the main house. All but the sergeant and guard followed. Charlie thought a moment and turned to Gus.

"Gus, why haven't you two ever moved into the house the people of the United States built for you?"

Gus looked from Ellenshaw toward the large house. "All that place does is remind me about the many American boys and girls that lost their lives in order for us to have that monstrosity. Hell, the only reason Matchstick is in there now is because that damn Europa terminal wouldn't fit into my old shack." Gus's gray eyes lingered for a brief moment longer on the Victorian house, then he abruptly turned and made his way back to the home he and a little green man from space had lived in happily since Gus had found the injured alien in the mountains eight years before.

Charlie frowned, then turned and caught up with Jack and Will.

"Gus is worried more than he's letting on about why Matchstick is behaving the way he is," he said as he adjusted his wire-rimmed glasses.

Collins afforded the naive Ellenshaw a glance. "He's old, Doc. Gus feels Matchstick is ignoring him because of this Gray problem. He's lonely again, is all."

Will Mendenhall stopped before reaching the wide wrap-around porch of the white-painted house. "I take it all of this stuff we're hearing about secret plans for the president is what's keeping Matchstick away from Gus?"

"Maybe, but he always lets us know what he needs. This latest is new behavior."

Two guards greeted the three men and showed them into the basement by hidden elevator. The Europa connection required every inch of four-inch, bulletproof-glassed space. Jack looked inside once the elevator doors opened and saw the mess beyond the glass. Newspapers and books were spread everywhere. The four desks were overflowing with material. Of Matchstick there was no trace.

"Jesus," Charlie said as he examined the interior of the closed off computer area, "what a mess."

Jack saw a pile of newspapers move and then settle. It trembled once more and then stopped again. He quickly adjusted the newspapers in his arms and entered his security code at the station beside the door. The glass panel hissed as it slid open and the three men entered. Collins gave the papers and magazines to Mendenhall and stepped toward the large pile of papers. He brushed some of them away and looked down to see a sleeping Matchstick on the floor, covered in his research material and maps. The little green man was snoring lightly as his small chest heaved up and down. Jack saw the large eyes underneath the opposing lids as they worked back and forth rapidly and he knew Mahjtic was dreaming. Not for the first time Collins wondered what would a small green alien dream about? Home? His slave days amongst the Grays? He leaned down to a knee and lightly tapped Mahjtic on the T-shirt-covered belly. He smiled when he saw he was wearing a *Star Wars* shirt with the wise old Yoda holding up a finger. Jack shook his head and tapped Matchstick once more.

The black eyes sprang open in near panic. The small green alien looked at Collins and then recognition finally reached his very active brain. The alien smiled widely.

"Hi," he said in his raspy voice as Collins helped him to his feet. Matchstick closed the small white terry-cloth bathrobe over the T-shirt and hugged Jack's legs. Then he went to each, Charlie first and then Will, and repeated the process. The three men exchanged bemused looks.

"Here, I guess these are yours." Mendenhall held out the pile of newspapers and magazines.

Matchstick's mouth formed into a small *O* and then he took the offered newspapers and started going through them quickly, tossing first one, and then the next away onto the already paper-covered floor. Then his almond-shaped eyes widened as he found the one he wanted. He held it close to his giant eyes and studied the headlines. Jack, out of curiosity, leaned over and looked at which paper held the small alien's attention. He looked up at Will and Charlie.

"The *National Enquirer*," he said with a curious lilt to his voice. Matchstick dropped that one and then picked up the *News of the World* tabloid from Great Britain. He studied it and then with the gossip rag in his hand turned and went to a small table to sit and read. He completely ignored the three men as they followed.

Matchstick suddenly started pointing and tapping the newspaper violently, then angrily threw the tabloid away from him. He placed his large head in his arms as lowered his face onto the tabletop.

"Okay, Matchstick, what's wrong?" Jack picked up the crumpled newspaper and examined the headline there.

ENTIRE RESORT REPORTED DESTROYED BY STRANGE HURRICANE, it said. Jack held out the front page and showed Will and Charlie.

"What are you working on, little guy?" Collins asked Matchstick as the small alien finally raised his head. "This have something to do with Overlord?"

Will and Charlie exchanged looks as that code name was heard once again. They knew better than to ask Jack what it was, but the name kept popping up from time to time.

Mahjtic didn't answer as he stood and then walked toward the computer terminal. There was no voice synthesizer because Europa had a hard time understanding Matchstick's English vocalizations, so he had to manually input all his requests through the antiquated keyboard, which the Green found immensely and frustratingly slow. He started tapping away with lightning speed with his long fingers.

The three men exchanged concerned looks as Matchstick completely ignored them. Jack's eyes watched Mendenhall as he pulled away some Hot Pockets wrappers and boxes along with forty or fifty empty Jell-O cups, then lifted a file from the debris-strewn tabletop. Will held it up so Collins could see it clearer. It was a Europa printout of a White House security briefing as delivered by the president's national security advisor. Jack took the report.

"Matchstick, you know your limits with Europa, don't you? There was to be no, I repeat, no computer break-ins of any kind where the presidential chain of command is concerned, right? You have to go through channels, and that means Pete Golding." Jack watched as his words seemed to have no effect. "Other than planning for Overlord, you still have limits. We can get anything you want, but we have to know why." Jack turned and made sure his words weren't overheard by Mendenhall or Ellenshaw.

Matchstick suddenly started shaking as if he had become cold; his slim fingers stopped typing on the keyboard. The small being grabbed one hand with the other to control the tremors. Matchstick closed his eyes, sending the side-sliding eyelids to close from the temple area of the head. This happened several times in rapid succession, then Matchstick slowed and opened his eyes wide as he slowly reached for Jack's hand.

"Saucer?" was the only word he muttered in the soft and buzz-filled voice.

"No, we haven't found anything."

Matchstick still held Jack's large hand as his head turned away in thought. Then he looked at the colonel once again, his dark, jet-black eyes intense. Collins hadn't seen the small fella act this strangely since four years back, when he was having psychic nightmares about the events on the moon that led to the discovery of the alien and Martian technology that was recovered. Tech that eventually led to

Garrison Lee and Niles Compton's Operation Overlord plan. Only this episode looked to be worse.

"None . . . of the ancient . . . crash sites . . . yielded a power plant?" Matchstick stumbled with the words.

Only Jack knew any details about the Overlord plan, so Charlie and Will just listened. Part of the plan called for the acquisition of an alien-designed engine from one of the saucers, for what? Jack could only guess as neither Niles, Matchstick, the president, nor Senator Lee ever took him into their confidence on certain aspects of Overlord.

"No, but we're still looking. We have several more leads to follow up on." Collins saw the eyes close and the head shake. Matchstick's hand slowly released Jack's own and he decided to go easy on the green guy for a moment. "Sarah's in Uzbekistan right now and she still has to file a report on the Russian claim of 1972."

He saw Sarah's name made the alien smile for the first time. He nodded his head as if knowing that Sarah was out looking for what they so desperately needed made his burden, whatever it was, far less than it was only a moment before.

"Sarah," Mahjtic said, repeating the name of a woman the alien had always liked. Jack had noticed that she seemed to have that effect on the strangest of people. Henri Farbeaux flashed through his mind and stuck momentarily.

"Now, tell me what's wrong. Will here says you're not sleeping and working far too hard. Let us help with whatever it is. The saucer search isn't what's bothering you. You knew from the start it would be a long and maybe futile effort to find one. It's something else."

Matchstick looked as if he were thinking, then pushed some of the old newspapers aside to find what he was looking for. It was a yellow file folder with 5656 stamped upon the front. Jack looked over at Will and Charlie; they too noticed it was also marked CRYPTO SCIENCES. Charlie stepped forward, took the offered file, and opened it. He quickly scanned a report Charlie had filed himself more than ten years before for a class he instructed at the complex.

"Matchstick," Charlie began, "you were supposed to be assisting us when your other duties allowed you to do so in the Captain Everett situation, and report on any theory of time travel you could possibly know about. Why are you delving into mass disappearances?" Charlie held the file up and Jack and Mendenhall saw the title of the report: WHAT REALLY HAPPENED TO ROME'S NINTH LEGION?

Jack raised his brows and Will stepped up to the small desk, picked up another Crypto file from Charlie's office, and opened it. He shook his head and then also held it up so Jack could read the heading of Ellenshaw's conclusions as reported through Europa. This file was fifteen years old. ENTIRE CHINESE ARMY DIVISION VANISHES IN 1938.

"Do these have something to do with the research you were assigned on the possibilities of time travel and how Captain Everett's watch could be found in ice two hundred thousand years old?" Charlie asked. Collins touched the front page of the newspaper. "Are the Grays responsible for this?"

Matchstick looked up into the face of the colonel and then his eyes narrowed. He shook his head in the negative, which threw Jack a curve.

"Okay, what do you suspect?" Jack asked.

Mahjtic stood and pushed away from his small desk, took Jack by the hand, and led him to the glass wall. Then Matchstick held up his long, thin arms for Collins to pick him up. Jack shook his head but lifted the small being into his arms and sat him on the window sill that looked out on the desert from the ground view of the basement. Jack didn't care for the way Matchstick was acting. He looked out into the afternoon sun with his long fingers framing the sill.

"Someone . . . has . . . a working power . . . plant." His obsidian-colored eyes blinked against the bright sunlight as he turned to face the colonel.

"Sarah and her discovery teams haven't found one trace of any of the crash sites you sent her to. So I doubt anyone, anywhere has a working saucer engine."

Matchstick sat on the protruding sill and then eyed Jack.

"Someone on this . . . planet . . . has a working power plant, and they . . . are . . . creating . . . wormholes." Matchstick hopped down from the window sill and landed at Jack's feet, then pulled the *National Enquirer* from the desk to show him the big hole in the ground where the Lebanese resort site had been. "Wormhole effect when . . . tunnel strikes the . . . surface of . . . the . . . planet."

"I'm not following your logic," Jack said. Charlie and Will came closer as they too became interested in the theory the small alien was putting forth.

Matchstick went back to his desk and with the keyboard humming his long fingers flew across the keys. Soon Europa was online to answer their questions.

"Colonel Collins. It has been determined through debriefing that the technology of wormhole travel is complicated. When travel ends, the wormhole must not be in contact with the destination itself. The exit has to be situated no less than three thousand feet above the surface of target destination. If not, the destructive forces of the transit hole will produce catastrophic effects in the area where contact is made. By contacting the surface of target area the ground is pulled up and back into the wormhole."

"But what about these old disappearances, Matchstick? What do they have to do with this wormhole effect? I mean, they happened so long ago it seems moot." Charlie Ellenshaw raised his glasses to study the diagram of an animated wormhole that looked exactly like an upside-down hurricane formation ending in a faster-than-light-speed funnel cloud.

Collins looked at Ellenshaw and raised his eyebrows.

Europa answered for Matchstick when the alien typed his answer.

"It has been determined by the slave races of their home world that the wormhole effect is also a means of entering and exiting before IP contact is made. Exiting the wormhole before IP contact with the atmosphere of target area will whiplash the traveler inside to another time realm—thus the suspected experimentation with the alien power plant has affected the earth's past in several key points."

"Boy, you have really lost me now," Mendenhall said.

Matchstick quickly typed in more commands.

"The suspected power plant in use must be in an experimental stage as the nation using it powers it up. While miniature wormholes have been initiated by suspected engine, the knowledge to control the wormhole has not been fail-safed or regulated. Experimentation is creating wormholes that are thus far uncontrollable."

Again the three men exchanged looks of incredulity. Matchstick was getting frustrated. He typed in more commands and the Europa screen went to full illumination as an animated effect started. It was a wormhole as produced by Europa and her advanced graphics. The hurricane-like storm was spinning in a counterclockwise swirl. It would slink one way as a tornado would and then straighten. The animation showed the wormhole forming outside of Earth's atmosphere, where it snaked across the screen like an undulating and angry snake. With a bright flash the end of the wormhole opened amid the violence of the storm in space and then a momentary funnel cloud formed. Several saucers flared out of the exit and into the atmosphere.

"This is . . . a wormhole as . . . the Grays . . . use it." He tapped more commands. "This is what . . . is happening . . . now."

On the screen the wormhole suddenly shot downward through the troposphere, then through the high cirrus clouds until the tunnel mouth slammed into the ground. In moments the wormhole started back up and everywhere—land mass, water, or mountain—the hole touched had gone back up with it.

"I see." Charlie lowered his glasses back down to his nose and studied the screen further. "You're saying whoever is experimenting with this power plant isn't using it right?"

Matchstick closed his large eyes and then vigorously nodded his head so hard Jack thought it would fly from his shoulders.

"And the experiments have caused these mass disappearances throughout our history?" Collins asked as he pulled up one of the small chairs and sat next to Matchstick. He looked deeply into his eyes, wanting to understand why the small alien was so terrified. After all, if someone had an engine from a downed saucer it would allow Matchstick and Compton the tools they needed for Operation Overlord— whatever that was. "How are these experiments with a wormhole opening up rips in time?"

Matchstick typed more commands and then Europa tried her best to transcribe them.

"It has been determined that the wormholes are being shut down too soon after contact with the surface of the Earth, thus the victims, or area of the strike, are pulled upward into the exit hole. When power is shut down the affected traveler will exit the wormhole at a point where it wasn't meant to go. As the traveler moves through the wormhole an exit can be found anywhere in time; if the exit appears before it hits space the subject will be tossed out. The time frame runs backward from the initial point of contact."

"So you're saying that the lower in the wormhole you are, the closer to real time. The higher you are the farther back in time you are?" Charlie asked as he went to a knee in front of Matchstick's chair.

The alien nodded again, but he wasn't sure if the humans grasped the science at all—after all, after a million years the Grays still didn't completely understand it.

"Do you need the power plant from a saucer to create your own wormhole for Overlord?" Jack asked, knowing he was entering into very highly classified territory where Overlord was concerned.

Matchstick looked around, knowing that he was told how secure the Overlord plan was. But as he looked into the eyes of Colonel Collins he knew that if this man could not be trusted, there was no hope for this planet anyway. Mahjtic shook his head negatively once more.

"If they don't shoot us for asking, what do you need the engine for?" Mendenhall asked ahead of Jack.

"The . . . power plant . . . gives off a . . . by-product . . .

It . . . is like a . . . breeder reactor. I need not only the engine for power but . . . also . . . the spent fuel . . . from that engine. "

"Why?" Jack knew they were pushing their luck, as Matchstick knew the information was the most highly classified on the planet and he had been told by Niles Compton, General Garrison Lee, and the president of the United States not to mention Overlord to anyone—even the Event Group staff. Matchstick started twisting his fingers and rubbing his hands.

The small alien stood from his chair and then looked at Collins.

"Power, immense power in . . . the . . . spent . . . fuel of power plant. I . . . we . . . the Earth needs . . . this for Overlord."

"Okay, now we're gettin' somewhere," Mendenhall said.

"Yeah, we're getting into the area of treason if the president or Niles knew what we were discussing," Jack said, straightening up and looking at Matchstick. "Now, what happens if we don't recover an old saucer for the power plant?"

"We . . . lose . . . the war in less than six days."

Will looked at Jack. "You mean with all of Earth's firepower we can't win?"

Matchstick shook his head slowly. "We . . . will . . . be totally defeated."

Mendenhall looked away as he heard the word for the first time: defeated.

The room was silent as the statement hung in the air. Collins took a deep breath and decided if he was going to hang for questioning Matchstick, he may as well go for broke in his treason.

"Matchstick." Jack placed a hand on the alien's head and then knelt so he could look into the strangest eyes in the universe. "I know the first part of Operation Overlord because I was in on the planning for troop movements and allied response . . . but the second part of the plan had been kept pretty close to the vest by the president, Garrison, and Niles. What is the real Overlord plan?"

Matchstick shook his head sadly and turned away from Jack.

"I . . . cannot . . . tell . . . you . . . Colonel." He turned and tilted his head at Collins, then gave him a sad smile with the small mouth. "So many will . . . have . . . to be . . . sacrificed to even . . . get . . . to . . . the point of Overlord, that . . . it is best that . . . no one . . . knows." The small alien looked up, sad. "Not even . . . the bestest . . . of friends."

"Colonel, I think the little guy is saying that Overlord includes plans for people we know, and—," Will started to say.

"Those people are expendable and they, or we, are not to know the details." Collins patted Matchstick on the small shoulder and then turned away.

"Mahjtic . . . so sorry . . . Colonel Jack. But many, many, friends will not survive . . . even if . . . Overlord . . . works."

Jack and Charlie heard the low moan escape from Will Mendenhall.

"I knew I should have joined the Coast Guard."

"I think you may want to wait until Matchstick tells us why he's in a near panic to find this outside of the Overlord considerations."

Matchstick realized that Jack was starting to suspect that it was not just Overlord that was weighing so heavily on the small alien's large brain.

"Well, little guy, is there something else you want to let us in on?" Mendenhall asked, far more worried than he had been.

Mahjtic turned away, shut off the Europa monitor, and sat heavily in his chair. He stared at the scattering of papers strewn wide and far. He then slowly looked from one expectant face to the other. The large eyes blinked, sending the double eyelids in from the temple side of his face. They rapidly opened and closed and then settled on the colonel.

"The use of . . . the . . . power . . . plant now operating will force . . . the Gray Masters into . . . attacking earlier than they . . . wanted when they . . . believe . . . the Earth . . . has wormhole . . . technology. We must find the . . . engine . . .

and . . . remove . . . it . . . from . . . the . . . country that . . . is . . . using it."

"What are you saying?" Charlie removed his glasses and wiped at them vigorously with one of the discarded newspapers.

Matchstick looked at the white-haired professor.

"The Grays are coming, Charlieeee."

CIA HEADQUARTERS
LANGLEY, VIRGINIA

Assistant Director of Operations Daniel Peachtree sat before the appointed head of Central Intelligence, Harlan Easterbrook. He had been lambasted by the career law enforcement man for the past hour about a subject that had become a political mess for not only the director, but he himself: Hiram Vickers—special desk for "Dirty Tricks." The euphemism meant Vickers collected technology intelligence from any nation he could gather the information on. The director just discovered Hiram had been doing far more than that.

"First the man runs a tail on a closed operative of the United States Army, and the army is a part of this country, the last that I heard, and like it or not I believe we need them to assist in the securing of this country."

"The tail was just a test and was not meant to—,"

"I don't care, Mr. Peachtree," the director said, cutting his AD off at the knees before he could continue. "You happened to anger the man that appointed me to this very office, a man I owe everything to. The man you tagged is under presidential protection and is assigned to a highly classified position. And this is the man that was incidentally tagged for a test? I have never heard such bullshit in my life. And then this officer's sister, a woman that worked in this very facility, is murdered along with another technician from Imaging and Tracking." The director's glare was murderous.

"Now wait, Harlan, there is nothing to that. Vickers

won't even wipe his nose without permission from me."
Peachtree began feeling very uncomfortable under the intense scrutiny of the director.

"Is that right, Mr. Peachtree? Does that mean you gave him authorization to bug and then tail this Colonel Collins? Did he inform you when he wiped his nose that time?" he asked angrily, tossing his fountain pen on his desk.

"I assure you that everything Vickers and his desk do to fulfill their task is completely aboveboard. Look at the technology he's uncovered. He has been an asset we cannot lose with the trouble coming this way."

"Well, I can damn well get along without that little weasel bastard!" Easterbrook's voice rose to an uncomfortable level.

Peachtree started to say something but the director held up his right hand, staying the response to the insult of a division under the control operations director.

"I was informed that your Mr. Vickers paid a visit to USP Leavenworth to visit a prisoner with no official name or life. A man that it is forbidden to even know exists."

"This I know nothing about," Peachtree said in all honesty. "May I learn the name of this nonexistent prisoner?"

"Not if you want to keep your own freedom. Believe me, you don't want to know. That subject, Mr. Peachtree, is so far above your pay-grade you would think that God himself issued the order that put this man away."

Peachtree hated the silver-haired man sitting before him. He knew him to be, as himself, nothing more than a political appointee by men in the midst of a power struggle. The president of the United States, who appointed the director, and Speaker of the House Giles Camden, who pushed his own appointment through the hard way, were at extreme odds in the world of heavy-duty politics. His main job after the appointment Camden secured for him under Easterbrook was to keep close tabs on the director and his dealings with the president, whom Camden hated with a passion only reserved for the staunchest of political enemies.

"What do you want me to do—shut down Senator Camden's pet project on technology gathering?"

"The Speaker of the House can appoint anyone to any project he wants, but not here. This ends today. I want the Technology Acquisitions desk shut down before too much light is pointed in our direction, as I don't think you really know what your man Vickers has done. I believe he may or may not have informed you about all of his activities. And one more thing, if I hear that stupid phrase 'dirty tricks' around here one more time I'll start firing people in a very public manner. Those days have to be over. We have got to stop making enemies here and overseas if the world is going to get through this crap, and we don't need your Mr. Vickers creating enemies when we need everyone on the planet in the same damn huddle. Am I understood?"

"What do I do with Vickers?"

The CIA director leaned as far forward as his chair and desk would allow.

"I'll tell you what, Mr. Peachtree, you either find a way to get rid of him, or I just may drop a note to an interested party serving with the army about the last official person to see his sister alive only hours before she was murdered. We can go that route if you like."

Peachtree stared silently at the director, as he didn't trust his voice to stay at a calm decibel level. Instead of protesting or giving any credence to the rumors swirling around about Vickers's involvement, which would eventually lead to him knowing the truth about young Lynn Simpson's murder, he would just stall as long as he could to keep Speaker of the House Camden from knowing his man was being fired. He would have to hide Hiram Vickers so deep that no one would ever find him.

"Until I find a way to get Vickers out of here I'll assign him to a post as far away as I can find."

"You can bury your trash as far away as possible, Mr. Peachtree, but the stink may still linger."

Peachtree stood and buttoned his jacket. The director raised his brow, wondering if the assistant director of Operations would try to sway his harsh decision on Vickers. He didn't as he turned and left the director's large office.

Peachtree went to his own office, which was directly connected to the assistant director of Intelligence and her staff. As he walked by the enemy camp—as he came to know it after the Simpson murder—many eyes followed him. He walked past his own assistant and into the seclusion of his inner sanctum. He immediately picked up his secure phone. Peachtree waited while the call was connected.

"Vickers," the voice said.

"Where are you?" Peachtree asked.

"I'm at the Pentagon."

"What are you doing there? I would have thought you would want to stay away from the guys that wear uniforms as much as possible, especially since one of them wants to find and kill you."

"Well, that's what you think. I think I'll find him first. Did you learn anything from the director?"

"Yes, I confirmed he's a colonel and he's in the army. The same thing we always knew."

"Well, I have a lead from a very promising source."

"Yes, and I suspect that is why we need to talk. That source you visited in Kansas doesn't exist and it was reported to the president that you went to see this invisible man. Since he gave us the Kansas asset Black Teams he used to run for his corporate gains, it won't be long before either the president or the FBI put two and two together and realize it was you who hit that secret archives facility in Nevada during that Ripper formula case. The director has ordered me to reassign you to another area of endeavor and then eventually fire you."

"Number one, Daniel," Vickers snidely said, making the name sound dirty, "the use of the Black Teams to secure advanced technology was a plan Senator Camden, yourself, and I agreed upon, so don't even bother to threaten me on that point again. Secondly, as soon as I protect my own ass, Director Easterbrook can have my resignation."

"I can't give you the time it will take to find this man. I

have to reassign you now or our dear director will know because now he's watching things much too closely. With the president's approval ratings plummeting over this military buildup we may be able to hide you in the periphery until he's impeached."

Vickers laughed in that irritating way he had that would set off the normally kind temperament of even the late Mother Teresa.

"And with you knowing what really happened to Lynn Simpson you feel comfortable stabbing me in the back and hiding me away?" He laughed again. "That's the bravest thing I have ever heard, Daniel. I mean, if I'm gone from the CIA this colonel will only have one way to find me, and that's through you."

Peachtree didn't like being threatened by Vickers. But he also realized that the man had the only ace in the deck up *his* sleeve—and that ace was Speaker of the House Camden, the man he owed his allegiance to. He was stuck and knew the only way out was to allow Vickers to track down this colonel and end the threat to their freedom because of the now-defunct Technology Acquisition department. The assistant director knew that this would be the only way he escaped this murderous mess intact.

"You have five days before I have to remove you from your desk. That's all I can give you without the director frying my ass instead of just yours."

"I may not even need that many days. I have a resignation letter in my hand that was filed with the Department of the Navy."

"So, what does that do for you finding out who this army colonel is?"

"Let's just say we may now have a stepping-stone to our army friend."

"Okay, you have your five days, Vickers."

"I need one thing from you to pay off my source that doesn't officially exist."

Peachtree exhaled in frustration and waited silently.

"I need you to get with our Mr. Speaker since he is in the

know on most secret affairs, and ask him what he knows about a project called *Magic*. I need to know the name of that particular asset and where it is I can find her or him. That is the price my prisoner friend demanded. I just need that one thing from our benefactor and this one act will make *his* main enemy in life uncomfortable, to say the least."

"And just what is that one thing, Mr. Vickers?"

"We need to know anything he has on a special project." Vickers hesitated a moment as he thought about the name he was about to say aloud.

"Vickers, you are trying my patience."

"We need to learn what the code word *Matchstick Man* means."

3

Former Iranian president Mahmoud Ahmadinejad was six hundred and ninety feet below the street level of the university. He stared through the two-foot-thick blast-proof glass walls into the chamber where the two hundred men and women who made up the Divine Prophet project crawled in and around the device in anticipation of the next round of tests. The ex-president narrowed his eyes as his aide approached and stood rigid next to his mentor. Ahmadinejad had been at the facility for almost a full year since the edict of the Iranian people that clearly indicated they wanted change and would not support the ex-president's proxy for the position of president. The new president, Hassan Rouhani, would be a change that would bring on better relations with the West—the United States in particular—and that was not sitting well with the man who used to hold the Iranian presidency.

The device he was again looking at would guarantee no backward movement of the revolution with the election of the moderate, and he would need this device he had hidden away so many years before because it was suspected that the next act of the new president would be to start making overtures of recognition to the outlaw state of Israel. This could never, ever happen.

His aide cleared his throat and Ahmadinejad gave the man a look that almost made him freeze. The man's beard had grown longer and his face was starting to show the extreme pressure he was under after the defeat of his man at the voting booths the year before. The lines in his face were growing deeper and far more ragged than they had been just the previous year. He raised his right brow, waiting for the aide to say something.

"Sir, the new president's office has been trying to reach you for hours. The regime wishes to know the status of the project's shutdown."

Mahmoud Ahmadinejad stared at the assistant for the longest minute of the young man's life. The look was as if the ex-president was staring at some form of bug that had strayed onto his arm. The aide was relieved to get those haunted eyes off of him when General Hassan Yazdi stepped up to the glass. The general was silent as he looked inside the chamber. He placed his hands behind his back and looked at the young aide in the black suit. He nodded that he should leave the two men alone. The Iranian general remained silent as he stood next to the man who had made his career advancement possible and eventually placed him in charge of operation Divine Prophet. The very same man who had set the ex-president on this course of action in 1978 was now his subordinate who ran the project.

"Soon we will not be able to hide the continuance of this project from the new president. We short-circuited the entire power grid in the province last time the test was run for a full hour. The grid could not withstand the power of the device and our lines from the nuclear power plant at Cernan have yet to be repaired." The general slightly turned to his left and watched the ex-president as he in turn spied closely the scientists and technicians preparing the Divine Prophet for another test. "They say they need another eighteen hours to find the short in the underground power lines."

"We were very close this last time. The test was nearly flawless."

"Close? Flawless? Is that what you call destroying an entire seaside resort and killing God knows how many people? If you call that close and flawless I have a hand grenade course you may want to instruct, old friend."

Ahmadinejad smiled and then turned fully to face General Yazdi.

"Hand grenades get the job done also, General. I'm sure I need not remind you they kill just as efficiently as any weapon. This hand grenade kills in a wide swath but can also be a little indiscriminate, wouldn't you say?"

He looked hard at the ex-president of Iran. "Too wide. And too indiscriminate."

"That's a matter of opinion. The next test will be closer and we should see the desired effects of the Divine Prophet."

"You don't seem worried that our new president has ordered this project of yours shut down?"

"Yes, I am well aware of that. Now, are you prepared to fulfill your promise to the revolution, General Yazdi—a promise you yourself coerced me into over thirty years ago?"

"Loyalists to the revolution swell our ranks. When we strike at the new president and his backward government he will not be able to withstand the army's wishes, and he will resign to save Iranian lives. Every gaming scenario we have run predicts this fact."

The ex-president placed a hand on the shoulder of the general and patted it twice.

"I have no fear the people will see our new president for what he really is, a new western patsy. But we will need every loyal man to our cause by our side." He paused and looked at the general with his penetrating and cold eyes. "And they may have to make the supreme sacrifice when the world learns of our true intent." He started walking slowly down the curving hallway.

The general grimaced and then turned to follow the man he had created the night he was taken from his student housing the night of the Khomeini revolution.

"Have you prepared for the inevitable military response from the West?" He placed his hands behind his back.

"Our forces are ready with three hundred strike aircraft and five divisions of troops, and that is just for the securing of the capital. I have another full division guarding our salvation here at the university. Project Divine Prophet will remain secure. But if this apparatus fails to do what we want fast enough to stun our enemies in its harshness, we may fail. In the case of an all-out invasion we will not be able to maintain a defense for more than sixteen hours before our enemies knock down anything and everything in this country with the power to generate light from a lightbulb. The securing of the nuclear power generating facilities is paramount."

"Divine Prophet will be operational after our final test. When we strike the Sea of Galilee that will be the precursor to go with our real target."

"If we fail to strike our main target you do realize that Tehran will be vaporized in a microsecond? This act of war will be met with vigorous nuclear retaliation."

"How can our enemy push a button if he no longer exists in this dimension?"

"I pray to God you are right, old friend, or there won't be an Iranian people to lead as we will all be nothing but ashes."

Mahmoud Ahmadinejad turned and looked back through the thick glass at the power plant, the very engine of one enemy that would destroy an even more bitter and ancient foe, and one that would lead his nation into the light of the modern world to take its rightful place. He stopped and saw the round, alien engine with its many vents and steam ports through the thick glass windows as the technicians worked diligently getting the plant back online. As he watched the amazingly varied multicolored lights wrapped around its circumference blink on and off in a series of patterns he would never understand, he saw the glow of the fuel rods inside that made the glass viewing ports on the engine shimmer with magical hues not seen anywhere in the world. Only here in

Iran would the righteous peoples triumph over the Zionist invaders to their south.

"After the strike of the Divine Prophet our enemies will not even have ashes to bury, my friend."

The general saw the confidence in the man's eyes, or was it something else—possibly something that bordered on obsessive insanity toward the one goal that kept the ex–Iranian leader awake at night.

"What of the new president?" the general asked, trying to cover all of his questions before being dismissed by the now very private Mahmoud Ahmadinejad.

"It would take the new regime more than a year to find this hidden facility, and by then"—this time the smile was genuine—"his government will no longer be in existence."

The general watched Ahmadinejad leave at a slow pace toward his room, where only a cot and a desk waited for the most powerful man inside Iran and most of the Middle East. The former head of Iranian intelligence watched the sadness of the scene, then frowned.

"I just pray that the existence you speak of extends to our cause." He started to turn and then stopped. "And also to us."

PRIVATE FLIGHT 3677
ISRAELI AIR FORCE

The military Learjet was cruising at 26,000 feet. The Israeli Air Force pilot relaxed and watched the European countryside far below vanish only to be replaced by the bleaker aspects as they neared their homeland. The small plane carried only two passengers.

General Shamni watched the woman as she stared at the white ceiling. She hadn't uttered a word since their flight had lifted off from Romanian soil. He shook his head as he realized just how much of a son of a bitch he had become. He had used the dirtiest tricks in the book to get back one of his prized agents. He knew just how much Israel needed her children and this child was no exception. Anya Korvesky, again a major in the Mossad, had not said a word since she had watched Captain Carl Everett's plane lift off an hour before their own aircraft. Shamni knew he had succeeded in breaking the young gypsy woman's heart by pulling the mean trick that he had by using something that would drive a wedge between the American naval captain and the major—the attachment the man had with his past in the United States.

"Major, we have a dilemma at home. With this United Nations scare about extraterrestrial incursions running rampant, our friends in the world are starting to arm our old enemies with newer weapons—a lot of them." He glanced at Major Korvesky, but she made no indication that she was listening. "While we suspect that most of these weapons will be utilized against a real and not an imagined enemy like Israel, there are others that may seek to take advantage of the gifts of technology and strike at us."

Anya remained silent and still as the general spoke seemingly to an empty seat.

"We are receiving very disturbing reports from our people inside of Iran. It seems they have redirected several power grids from major cities and provinces for what purposes we can only guess at. We suspect it has nothing to do with the reports of extraterrestrial invasion, as the Americans are also in the dark."

"And this is the reason you have interfered in my life once again?" Anya said as she remained still. "I know Carl would have missed his home terribly, but I was willing to go anywhere to be with him. But you fed him the one piece of information that guaranteed that would never happen. You, Uncle, are a son of a bitch. Why should I risk my future and my happiness for pigs that act no differently than our enemies?" She finally looked at the military man.

He looked at her hard. "Sometimes we have to get into the gutter with those enemies, and you know that better than any agent that I have ever trained. Hell, you were better at this than I ever could be. We need you, Major, and we need to know what in the hell is happening inside the Iranian border. If we don't get answers soon, our prime minister will be forced to act against their power distribution centers."

"You mean their nuclear facilities. That is what you people are fearful of, not the weapons being given to them for an alien invasion that will probably never happen. This is just an excuse to do what you have always wanted to do—destroy the Iranian ability to make nuclear weapons."

The general gave the major a sincere look as he studied her angry features.

"If I cannot convince my smartest pupil, we have no hope of explaining our actions to the world if we do have to strike at the Iranian facilities."

"You have to explain to the young people of our country why we have to be the policeman of the Middle East. If the Iranian nuclear question is so dangerous to us and the world, why aren't our friends and allies backing us in a unilateral attack?"

"Because they may not have the same intelligence we have on the situation." He saw that she was about to throw her same old argument of sharing intel with other nations at him but he cut off the question with his raised hand. "We cannot prove a thing, but militarily speaking something is happening we cannot place our finger on. Military men are not being dispersed as their new president has ordered. Instead of keeping his many divisions on the border with Iraq as per their custom of late, the generals are spreading out divisions in very disturbing and unusual places."

"Such as?" she asked, pretending that she wasn't interested in the least. The general knew he had piqued her curiosity.

"Why place five divisions of their crack infantry in and around the capital without informing their new president of such a move? They have also disbursed many hundreds of their newest fighter jets to the south, and we in Mossad believe those MiG-29s may be pointed directly at Israel's throat."

"The Americans, British, French, and Russians have been quiet on this?" she asked, finally sitting up in her seat.

"We don't even know if they are interested at the moment due to their current political troubles over their military spending. Besides, the Americans are the ones leading the charge in the preparations for this supposed invasion of theirs."

"You're lying to me again, Uncle," she said as she studied the man's worried countenance. "You're not telling me what else you have on the Iranians that is scaring you so badly."

The general reached down, pulled out his small brown satchel, and placed it on his lap.

"What I am about to show you is highly classified. We stole it from the same source that gave us the information for your Captain Everett." General Shamni pulled out a large photo. "This is from a KH-11 satellite flyover of the Lebanese coast sixteen hours ago." He handed the photo to Anya.

"What is it I am looking at—a sea coast with nothing but sand and water?"

"You should know—you had an operational mission there three years ago. As I remember, you eliminated a Lebanese national there for us."

He could see Anya thinking as she studied the black and white recon photo. He saw her eyes widen as they roamed over the small bay area that wasn't supposed to be there.

"Yes, that hole in the beach area there is where the Warwick Pangea Beach Resort used to sit."

She sat up farther in her seat and looked more closely at the print.

"Impossible. There must have been an error in the GEO positioning the KH-11 used for her coordinates."

"That was the initial position of our people in the analysis division, but the prime minister authorized an F-16 recon mission over the site."

"And?" she asked when he paused.

"The resort was ripped from the sea and has vanished.

The place is crawling with a United Nations contingency force and our fighter was lucky to get out before the Americans knew we were there."

"What is the UN saying?"

"They're not entertaining any ideas at the moment other than they believe the attacks from space have started. We have other beliefs."

"And they are?" Anya asked as she again looked at the blank spot in the photo where one of the largest and most luxurious sea resorts in all of the Middle East used to sit. Now it was a torn-out cove of water with geysers of water from broken mains spewing forth their contribution to the mystery.

The Mossad general pulled out another piece of paper from his case after removing the space-based image from her fingers. He handed her a large computer printout.

"As you know we have kept our eyes open for any variance in the Iranian power output because they will need a massive spike to get their breeder reactor up and running. Well, we received a spike in consumption alright"—he paused and then tapped the white printout—"At the exact same moment it is believed the resort vanished into thin air."

Anya looked at the numbers of the output from their three nuclear facilities used for power generation and saw that they had indeed spiked at the same moment it was suspected the attack had occurred.

"No, this is impossible. There is no way the Iranians would have anything near this capability. This would have to be related to the alien question everyone is so worried about."

"Unless the Iranians have found the one thing the United Nations is searching the world for."

"You forget, Uncle, I have been out of the military loop for a few months. You have to enlighten me."

"Oh, yes, maybe I should have had your Captain Everett explain this part to you. The Americans and British are obsessed with finding an operating alien power plant for something they have dubbed Operation Overlord."

"And why would Carl know anything about this?" Anya handed the printout back to Shamni.

He placed the paper back in with the highly classified photo.

"Because, my dear niece, your Mr. Everett was just assigned to the project, whatever it is."

Anya stood so suddenly that it startled the general.

"And that is the real reason you brought me back to Mossad. So I can get the secret information about this Operation Overlord out of Carl once he learns about it!"

"Yes." He looked away in real shame at his actions. "Also for the fact that we need the Americans and their allies to strike the killing blow in Iran and not us."

"You're willing to bet other lives on a strike but not our own?"

"Yes, only because we believe the Iranians have the alien technology. The Iranians are using the mass confusion around them over this alien event so they can strike without anyone getting the wiser on them. But we have."

"You are the biggest son of a bitch I have ever known, Uncle. Tell the Americans, the British, and the Russians what you suspect, let them decide their own fates. We don't have that right."

The general looked out at the growing dark skies that signaled the oncoming night.

"If we don't act soon our right to exist may be at an end."

EVENT GROUP COMPLEX
NELLIS AIR FORCE BASE, NEVADA

Jack Collins had shaved and changed into his blue jumpsuit. It was the first time he had been dressed for duty since Director Compton took him off the field evaluation teams and anything that took him off base. The separation of Captain Everett and himself was due to the finding of the captain's wristwatch with Collins's blood—a timepiece that had been buried over 200,000 years ago. The situation had been especially hard on Jack, who needed to be off base to find the killer of his sister, and that just wasn't happening. He was even having a hard time facing his mother because he could see the question in her sad eyes: had there had been any break in her daughter's case? There hadn't. D.C.'s Metropolitan Police Department and the Virginia state police had yet to come up with any leads. Jack knew they wouldn't find any because Lynn had been killed by one of her coworkers at the CIA.

A light knock sounded at the door and Jack turned to open it. Will Mendenhall stuck his head inside and immediately noticed the colonel's private quarters had been cleaned and the colonel himself was looking like a colonel again.

"Colonel, the director has arrived and Gus and Matchstick are in the conference room."

"Got it." Jack smiled for the first time since the murder of Lynn. He took Will Mendenhall in. "Did the director come down on you for letting me out of my cage?"

Mendenhall looked behind him into the long and curving corridor to make sure there were no ears flapping about.

"Yes, sir, I've only got about half my ass at the moment," he said as he jokingly reached behind himself and hissed.

"Well, that won't be the last ass chewing you get." He smiled even wider. "Especially when you have people like you, Ryan, and Mr. Ever . . ." Jack's words trailed away at the mention of Captain Everett's name. Collins just nodded and Will saw the face of a man who had lost a good friend.

"Nah, when I'm in charge, I'll just recruit better people." Will's smile didn't quite make it as he tried to keep the conversation light.

"The smart move would be not to be in charge at all and refuse all promotions." Collins gestured for his lieutenant to lead the way.

The Event Group supervisory staff had gathered. The sixteen department heads were represented, with the only absentee being the current head of the geology department:

Army 1st Lieutenant Sarah McIntire, who was off in the Middle Eastern desert looking for something they all thought wasn't there. Jack looked at the chair occupied by her second-in-command, Sam Parker, a geologist from the University of Texas. Mendenhall, who was still the acting security chief while Jack was being protected, sat beside Collins. Will knew Jack was used to seeing Everett in this particular chair.

Director Compton cleared his throat as the semiretired Alice Hamilton, whom Niles had called in for the briefing, came through the double doors. She jumped when Matchstick—who had been standing next to Gus Tilly—ran over and wrapped his long, thin arms around her thighs. He hugged her just as he had done with the security team when they had arrived at Chato's Crawl earlier that morning. It was now seven at night and the little guy was still buzzing about the things he suspected were happening.

"Well, hello to you too, Matchstick." Alice tossed her writing tablet and files on the conference table, then picked the alien up to smile at his large eyes.

"Alissssss," Matchstick hissed. His right hand went to the eighty-seven-year-old's cheek and his index finger caressed it.

Alice smiled and then kissed Matchstick on the cheek. Thus far Gus Tilly and Sarah McIntire were the only two people Matchstick allowed to kiss him. The rest, well, he figured a hug was good enough. Alice Hamilton saw that Mahjtic was wearing the smallest military blue jumpsuit she had ever seen. She looked at Will Mendenhall, who was watching them. She nodded her head, suspecting it was the young lieutenant who was responsible for outfitting the alien. She could see that Matchstick loved dressing like the soldiers. She gently placed him in his seat next to Gus, whom she patted on the shoulder lightly; then she leaned in and kissed his grizzled cheek. He swiped at the spot and shook his head. She smiled anyway and then took her accustomed chair next to the director, who sat opposite Virginia Pollock, Niles's number two at the Group.

Matchstick pumped up his chair's riser until his eyes were seen over the tabletop, and then he waited. It had been over six months since he had visited the complex and the small being knew he caused a stir with Event Group personnel every time he showed up. Mahjtic had been adopted by every human he had ever been introduced to.

"Okay, first off, welcome, Gus and Matchstick. It's been too long," Niles said as he stood and nodded at the old man. "I'm glad we could dig you out of that mine shaft for a while."

"Well, I'm a little more comfortable since the first time I visited this place. Never liked the thought of all that unstable sand above your heads." He looked around the large conference room. "But I guess if it hasn't all caved in by now it's not goin' to."

All the department heads nodded their approval of Gus's claustrophobia, especially knowing he had spent most of his life in one cave or mine shaft after the other. He was just mad at being uprooted from his home and flown to Nevada.

Niles nodded in understanding as he moved right into the briefing.

"Before we get to the suspicions of Matchstick and the conclusions he's drawn, let's focus on current events that will lead into our friend's speculation. Virginia, what is the disposition of the field teams assigned to finding Matchstick's power plant?"

Virginia Pollock cleared her throat and then glanced at her notes. Niles could see she wasn't really happy with what it was she had to report.

"Not good. All fourteen teams have come up with nothing." She nodded her head at Matchstick, who was holding the hand of his best friend, Gus, and listening intently to every word. "I'm afraid none of the crash sites mentioned in Matchstick's briefing of four years ago have been uncovered or even documented. The one crash site we had the highest hopes for was the area in which Sarah McIntire's team in Azerbaijan covered fully, but even that led to a big fat zero." She saw Matchstick lower his lightbulb-shaped head.

Niles sat into his chair and quickly made a decision.

"Okay, double the teams and then cover the fourteen sites again. Use a fine-tooth comb, Virginia."

"Niles, we'll have to take some of our science department personnel to cover that order."

"Then do it—we have to find a power plant from a downed saucer. Every attempt at getting the engines of the Roswell saucers operational has met with failure. Matchstick said that the fuel rods inside the engines have been drained fully. That, ladies and gentlemen, is that. The search for the original saucer from 1947 has turned up nothing. We suspect that the Centauris Corporation dismantled it and spread its parts to the winds. Our house guest in Leavenworth, Kansas, is not cooperating with us any longer, for what reason we do not know."

"Maybe he should be reminded of his obligations to the country," Will Mendenhall ventured. "I'll go to Kansas and explain it to him personally if you want," he said with a smirk.

"As much as I would like to see that, we haven't the time."

Mendenhall looked slightly disappointed at not being able to explain things directly to prisoner Charles Hendrix II, the former CEO of Centauris.

Niles nodded his head at the navy communication man sitting at the Europa terminal. On the sixty-five-inch monitor in the middle of even more, smaller monitors, the satellite image of the event in Lebanon came into full view. "Okay, Charlie Ellenshaw has Matchstick's report and his conclusions. Doctor?"

Charlie Ellenshaw cleared his throat and stood. He nodded his head at Gus and Mahjtic and then walked toward the large screen.

"What it all boils down to, Mr. Director, is the fact that Matchstick is a firm believer that this is not an extraterrestrial event, nor a Gray assault. He thinks the disappearance of the resort is due to someone on this planet having an operational alien power plant."

This started everyone talking at once. Niles held up his right hand for silence. He nodded at Ellenshaw to continue, but his eyes studied the small alien who was watching the startled faces around him.

Every monitor around the circular conference room illuminated with photos of events throughout history. On the main viewing screen was the shot of a barren plain in the north of Scotland.

"Mass disappearances throughout human history," Charlie began. "Many here, after the Roswell event, will say that most vanishings, like this one in Scotland of Rome's Ninth Legion, could be blamed on everything from E.T."—he smiled at Matchstick, who looked confused as to the reference—"to earth eruptions that swallowed everything whole, to gravity fluctuation, meaning that gravity just gave way in a lot of these instances."

Matchstick watched the faces of the group and was pleased to see that Charlie had gained their attention.

"Matchstick said many times in his two thousand hours of debriefing that one of the effects of forming a wormhole was a time displacement occurrence that will happen if a vehicle using the time warp exits before it reaches its targeted area. In other words, at a precise moment in the traveler's itinerary the vehicle can jump from the wormhole and hit its target area of the planet but come out in a different time period from the target he was originally seeking. This is what Matchstick claims is happening. Someone on this world has an operational power plant and is experimenting with the wormhole effect, thus the mass disappearances throughout time are occurring. They don't know what they have on their hands."

"I suspect whoever has it may be attempting to use it as a weapon," Jack said, offering a military solution.

"I agree on that point," Charlie said as he moved to the next photo in line. "The United Nations science team investigating the resort area has found some unusual soil samples. The sand had turned to glass. Tremendous heat, and then nothing of the resort was left. I am beginning to think like Matchstick, that this was no accident. Someone targeted the wormhole for that area of the planet."

"But how can Matchstick automatically eliminate the Grays? Can't they be responsible as an opening prelude to an attack?" Virginia asked.

Everyone was taken back as Matchstick jumped upon the tabletop. He vigorously shook his head, then placed his hands over his small ear openings.

"As you can see, Virginia, he adamantly does not think it is the Grays," Ellenshaw said as he tried to explain Matchstick's severe reaction to the question.

"I don't see how he can just reject the Gray theory out of hand; I mean, who would use that as a weapon against our own planet other than an attacking alien force?" Pete Golding asked Charlie.

"Because . . . the Grays . . . know . . . not the theory . . . of . . . time displacement." Matchstick looked around to make sure everyone heard his raspy voice. They had.

"You mean to say that the Grays have had this wormhole technology for a million years and don't know how it works?" Alice ventured.

Matchstick nodded his head yes vigorously as he started to pace the tabletop.

"Remember, everyone," Charlie said, "the Grays are a master race of beings who depend solely on their slaves for technical work and teaching. They don't know how their own technology works because the Greens have kept that little secret from them. And thank God they had the foresight to hide that little trick or we would have Grays bypassing our time frame and going after our far weaker ancestors in the past. Easy conquering of a world, wouldn't you say?"

Matchstick finally relaxed when he saw the looks of the scientists around him. They were starting to understand.

"Charlie, have either you or Matchstick come up with a theory as to how this earthbound entity got their hands on an alien power plant without the rest of the world knowing it?" Niles asked.

"I'm afraid we haven't—at least not yet. Pete and I will be working closely with Gus and Matchstick in the next few days to see if we can come up with something."

Niles opened a folder and slid a paper across the table, where it landed at Mahjtic's bare feet. Charlie picked up the printout and examined it. His eyes scanned the lines of numbers.

"Start there," Niles said.

"What is this, Niles?" Ellenshaw enquired.

"That was forwarded through the president's office. The Mossad repaid some of the favors they owe our government and sent this along as an interesting event in and of itself."

"All I can see is that it's an official energy output for a region inside. Of . . ." He looked at Niles and gave the paper to Matchstick, who also examined it. Charlie was unable to say anything in response to the report.

"That's right, inside the Iranian border—the eastern region. Evidently the Mossad believes they are using massive power outlays for something, and frankly it's making them nervous."

"Nuclear weapons manufacture?" Jack Collins guessed.

"We honestly do not know, Colonel. This may be a coincidence or it may be just what you suggested, Jack, but one thing is clear from Matchstick's briefing reports: it takes more power to start up an alien power plant than we could ever believe. And if they do have one and are using their energy production to get it going they will soon be manufacturing the very by-product that Matchstick needs for Overlord. Both the engine and the expended fuel that is produced by that power plant are essential to the Overlord plan." Niles looked around at his staff. "And as Matchstick has said to the few men and women in the know about it, Overlord is the only hope for the planet, because everything we have weapons-wise will only delay the inevitable."

Pete Golding stood and walked over to a monitor that had the area in question. The map of Iran was multishaded as it depicted the power consumption of each region under Iranian control. The highest output of energy came from the eastern region. The computer genius worked his index finger from the east to the north. He stabbed at the plastic

his hand. "Please. She would be volun-
gerous, stupid assignment the army saw
Please, Niles, pull whatever strings you
arah inside the complex when all of this
d this one thing, Niles."

from Jack to Alice. Jack looked her way
nd then lowered his eyes.

ck, then pursed his lips and slowly nod-

eed her at Group, maybe we can do it
g her from the army. The president may
es, but with everything that's happening,
nything, Jack." Compton stood and with
d from the room.

s stunned. He looked at the folders and
ad changed forever. How would he ever
would be separated for the war that was

d up his orders and those of Captain Ev-
o rise when his cell phone chimed. He
-through from Europa and his eyes nar-
t the brief text message that Europa had

RE PAID OFF JUST AS YOU HOPED. WE

me a long thin line etched with hatred. He
at the bottom and knew the information
r of his sister Lynn had been found. He
ssage and glanced at the signature once

QUBA

nclave of mud brick huts a village was a
ent, even by Azerbaijani standards. The

screen, then went to the conference table and pulled out his
field team briefing report. He shook his head.

"What is it?" Niles asked.

"The suspected saucer crash in 1972 in Russia—or the
old Soviet Union. Look at its suspected track that the Russians have the UFO on before they fired on it." Pete returned
to the map and traced a red line with his fingertip all the way
from Azerbaijan to the Iranian border. The trace line illuminated with Pete's track. "I think we have found one of the
crash sites."

"Whose field team investigated that possibility?" Compton asked as his hopes were raised.

Will Mendenhall opened his security brief, then looked
at Collins first before answering. It seemed the colonel was
already aware of whose responsibility that investigation had
been assigned to.

"Uh, that would be Sarah McIntire's team, sir," Will finally answered.

"What team is that in Israel?" the director asked.

"That is Commander Ryan's team. They also came up
with nothing," Will said as he studied his field team rosters.

"Okay, transfer him and his people to McIntire's team,
get them added security, and then get them into Iran. If I
have to supplement security with Special Forces from the
president I'll do it." Niles exhaled loudly and then looked at
his people. "Matchstick has informed Charlie that if this is
the true case of Iran testing alien equipment they may have
forced the Grays to an earlier attack scenario because they
know what that power plant can do for us technology-wise."

"Mr. Director, that area is not secure enough to send anyone in. The Iranians would capture and execute anyone
they catch. Even with their new moderate president they are
still far from trusting," Mendenhall said. Jack was apprecia-
tive of his pointing out the danger facet to the director.

"Enough said. Contact the lieutenant and get her people
moving. Set up a meet point for Ryan and his team to join
her and then Will, I want you and security to come up with

a plan to get them into the eastern region where someone thinks they have found lightning in a bottle. Okay, Matchstick and Gus will work closely with Pete, Virginia, Charlie, and Europa. We need to get a line on how to get that engine out of there if it's there at all. I'll brief the president."

"Request permission to join the Iranian team."

All eyes went to Jack as he stared directly at the director.

"Denied," Niles said matter-of-factly. "This meeting is adjourned for now. Alice and Colonel Collins, please remain behind."

As the Group members filed out of the conference room, Matchstick held Gus's hand as he approached Jack. To the colonel it looked as if the small green being was empathizing with him over the danger Sarah McIntire was now facing. Jack just winked at the two as they turned and exited.

When the room was cleared Alice placed her writing tablet down, then went to go get coffee for the three of them. Niles slid two folders down to Jack's end of the table. Collins looked them over and saw that one was stamped with the seal of the United States Army, and one of the U.S. Navy.

"What are these?" he asked, feeling his heart sink.

"Yours and Mr. Everett's orders. You have been transferred by the president for work on the Overlord plan. You're being moved to the Pacific area of responsibility. Captain Everett goes to Texas. The president has refused to accept the captain's resignation."

Jack remained silent, knowing that if anything in the Overlord plan called for him and Everett participating in the highly secretive plan, it was placed there by the man who was looking at him right now. Niles Compton and Matchstick, along with the late Garrison Lee and a few others in Britain, had come up with the extensive defensive plan called Overlord. He knew the director found the orders distasteful but was doing it anyway, even though Jack needed time to try and find his sister's killer. He now knew that task might have to wait—a thought that he truly hated.

"You realize that anything we do with Carl could be sending him to his doom in Antarctica two hundred thou-

sand years ago?" Collin
folder to see his new
displacement theory fro
Carl running into one o

"The plan calls for y
sorry. The president ir
Overlord, and that mea
matter what may happ
Houston will keep him

"What else?" Jack
in front of him. She
twitch of her lips. He
as the lie about Carl v
ders and obeying the
send a man he respec
sion was not someth
was the last thing he
danger that Niles, M
sending him to.

"Jack, as much a
gent the president n
ing and protests ov
facing. There is eve
the House. He nee
military personnel
lord concerns and
arise. I'm sorry."

Jack cleared hi
tion of the direct
be assigned?"

"I don't know,

Collins looked
about to do son
interfering with

"Dr. Compt–
"Niles, I want yo
I want her to sta

"Jack, I—"

Collins h
teering for a
fit to send he
have to, but k
comes down.

Compton I
for a brief sec

Niles studi
ded.

"I'll insist
without discha
accede to my
I cannot prom
Alice in tow w

Jack Collin
knew that thin
inform Sarah t
coming?

Collins gath
erett and starte
looked at the p
rowed. He stare
allowed throug

KANSAS VEN
HAVE YOUR MA

Jack's lips be
saw the signatu
was true. The k
glanced at the n
more.

HENRI.

QONAQKEND
AZERBAIJAN

Calling the smal
misleading state

five or six inhabitants tended herds and pastures that had long gone to seed a hundred years before the intrusion of the scientific teams from the United Nations. The few old men who remained watched as the invaders to their small mountain home packed up to leave after an exhausting six-week search for something that just wasn't there. Every piece of modern equipment had been used but no sign of a crash had been detected in the mountainous region of the former Soviet Republic.

Sarah McIntire, barely recognizable as the scarf and hat covered most of her features, handed the last of the soil sample cases to the specialist in the back of the two-and-a-half-ton truck. She heard the Russian army sergeant curse as the weight of the case overbalanced him and he almost fell. Sarah wanted to laugh but was too tired to do so. She pulled the scarf down, shook her head, raised a water bottle to her dry lips, and drank. She looked around the rough terrain. Sometimes she swore she could smell the aroma of the sea in the high pass of the mountain. The Caspian Sea was only fifty-seven miles distant but she knew the smell was more wishful thinking than an actual aroma. She could not wait to get out of Azerbaijan. The saucer crash reported in 1972 just did not happen in this area, if at all. Matchstick had to be wrong about the location.

Most of the sixteen members of her team were made up of an international who's who of geologists and crash specialists from all over the world, but Sarah still found herself far more comfortable around the Russian soldiers than she did the scientists. She smiled as she thought about it. Maybe it was only because as a soldier she could relate to the Russians wanting to be somewhere, anywhere, other than these godforsaken mountains in the middle of nowhere.

She was approached by a Russian lieutenant, who, like herself, was also a geologist. She thought about just how young a man he was and found it hard to believe the boy was a soldier at all.

"Lieutenant McIntire, we have company approaching from the south."

Sarah heard the distinctive thump of rotors. She squinted her eyes against the sun, then placed her sunglasses on. She finally spied the chopper as it came in low over the small clearing between two large mountains.

"Thank you, Uri. Tell the scientists and men that we will be leaving within the hour." She smiled at the young Russian.

The helicopter was a Russian navy bird, a Kamov Ka-27. At one time it was one of the most feared attack helicopters in the world, one that NATO always knew would be a threat in any conflict that would have arisen during the cold war between the two navies. Now it was relegated to scientific duties the Russian Navy conducted in the Caspian Sea. It could hold up to ten passengers and with its twin-boomed silhouette looked amazingly fragile. Sarah hated flying in the thing.

The helicopter slowly settled to the floor of the valley, making the few people still living there come to their door-ways and curse the noise as their few goats and sheep ran off to the wilds of the mountain. The twin, counter-rotating rotors settled and the sliding door opened and out stepped a familiar shape. The man was small and dressed like Lawrence of Arabia, which was exactly the look he perpetuated around the international crew of searchers. Commander Jason Ryan, United States Navy, removed his scarf, shook out his bush hat, and smiled at Sarah.

"I find you in the strangest places." He looked around the ancient village as he slapped away the dust raised by the helicopter. "Qonaqkend isn't much to look at, is it?"

She laughed, as she never expected to see Ryan all the way out here. The last she knew from her briefing was that the naval aviator was searching for another saucer crash site somewhere in Afghanistan.

"Are you kidding? This is the garden spot of Qonaqkend. The Marriott has yet to begin construction on the resort they envision."

Ryan removed his gloves and hugged his friend. He pulled away and then looked around again. "It's still better than Afghanistan."

"Nothing there either?" Sarah saw the weariness in Jason's unshaved face.

"No, and I'm beginning to think that little green bastard has all his facts mixed up about reported crash areas of the past. I'm surely tired of this wild-goose chase."

"Well," Sarah said as she handed Ryan her water bottle, "I guess the goose chase has ended, because we haven't found a damn thing anywhere in the world. Time to go home, I guess."

With a sad look Ryan pulled out a sheet of paper from his flight suit and handed it to Sarah. He shook his head without saying anything.

"You're kidding," she said as she reluctantly accepted the note. She opened it and read. "Damn, where in the hell is this Leschenko?"

Ryan smiled as he watched the activity around him.

"The *Leschenko* is not a place, it's a ship." He turned and shook his head. "You ground-pounder types should at least know your major naval combatants in the world's oceans."

"Okay smart-ass, you can just—"

"It's a Riga-class frigate of the Caspian Flotilla. She's Russian and she's out there." He pointed toward the distant sea. "And she awaits your lovely face, Lieutenant."

"What's happening?" she asked as she folded the orders from Niles Compton and handed them back.

"I haven't the vaguest notion, my dear. But your new friends here aren't invited. They are to pack up and go home. It's only us and your Lieutenant Uri . . . Uri . . ." Ryan patted his pockets looking for another note he had written.

"Lieutenant Uri Petrovich."

"Yeah, that's it. Well, we're to report to the *Leschenko* to meet with a Lieutenant Colonel Pavel Krechenko, a Russian Army type."

"Who in the hell is that?"

"The director wouldn't say. We are to report to the frigate, where all will be explained."

Sarah frowned at Ryan, knowing the navy man never

settled for surprises. She could tell by that evil smirk of his that he had other information.

"Okay, Commander Dipshit, what did Europa tell you when you queried her on this colonel fella?"

Ryan's features twisted in mock surprise. "Would I do that? I mean, that's a criminal offense, getting Europa to search for something without Pete Golding knowing about it."

"Okay, so you placed a call to Pete and since the good Dr. Golding always kisses your ass, you found something out."

"Well, yes. But it doesn't explain anything—in fact, it makes it far more mysterious than before."

"Jason, come on!" she said, grabbing his coat collar.

"Our Russian lieutenant colonel is the commander of an assault unit operated by the Russian Army, the 106th Guards Division." Ryan saw the blank look on Sarah's face. "It's the Russians' most elite airborne division. It seems that two thousand of them have been transferred to the Caspian Flotilla. As a matter of coincidence most were transferred to the very same Riga-class frigate where we're now headed."

"Oh, shit," Sarah said.

Ryan winked. "My sentiments exactly, Lieutenant McIntire."

THE WHITE HOUSE
WASHINGTON, D.C.

The president entered the Oval office with the thick file that had been sent over from the Event Group that morning. The briefing with the small green asset in Arizona had given them one hell of a pill to swallow and the president knew that pill could choke them all to death.

As he made his way to his large chair behind the Lincoln desk—nodding to acknowledge the five men who had been waiting for him—he paused momentarily by the window, tempted to glance out at the protesters who had grown in number even since that morning. There had been another leak to the press about information pertaining to the expenditures being mounted by the military. The president was close to crying "uncle" and telling the world what it desperately needed to know. He eyed the five men and motioned for them to sit. The faintest of protest calls entered the room from the outside.

"Gentlemen, we have a growing mess on our hands that can no longer be contained." He opened the folder and scanned the front briefing page. Niles Compton had been direct and to the point with his old college buddy in explaining how important tracking down this possible lead was to the coming fight. He understood what the Overlord plan called for, but to go to war over finding the engine they needed was the straw that would break this particular camel's back.

The men facing him remained silent. Only the two military men in uniform actually knew about the orders the president had issued six hours before. Now they and the Russian president were in the know.

"If the power plant is found to be operational, as my sources say it is, we have to move decisively. After that I have to come clean to the American people." The U.S. president again eyed his guests. "Especially if the mission we have planned fails and the Iranians take nuclear offense. Admiral, do we have any asset we can use in the Caspian area to support the Russians in the assault if it comes to that?"

Rear Admiral James Fuqua cleared his throat. "Mr. President, we have never had a dependable asset in the Caspian Sea. The Cold War has long been over and that was an area of responsibility we always hoped the Russians would take seriously when it came to a nuclear-armed Iran lurking at their belly."

"Director Easterbrook?"

"Nothing, sir," the silver-haired CIA director answered. "We will have two KH-11s in orbit over Iran, but not knowing when or even if the Russian assault happens we cannot guarantee eyes-on target. Viewing would be purely by chance. As for the human asset on the ground, we have nothing."

The president took a deep breath and then looked at U.S. Marine Corps general Maxwell Caulfield, the chairman of the Joint Chiefs of Staff.

"Max, please tell me you had luck with your counterpart in Moscow. Has he relented to allow at least one American Special Forces team in on the assault?"

"No luck, Mr. President," Caulfield answered. "It seems some old Cold War jitters still persist on both sides."

"So the only American assets we have are a navy lieutenant commander and an army first lieutenant?"

"Well," the Marine general said with a small smile on his lips, "that's more than we knew. Do you mind if I ask just who these officers are?" Caulfield suspected that although he might not know the men, he did have a suspicion where these two sprang from—that quirky little think tank situated under Nellis Air Force Base.

The president looked up from the file. "The naval officer was in Afghanistan and the lieutenant was in Azerbaijan. They were part of the power plant search. Hell, I guess we're lucky the damn Russians allowed them in."

"I suspect because whoever these two officers are they have an idea just what an alien spaceship engine looks like," Harlan Easterbrook said with his silver right brow raised.

"If this alien power plant is found and the Iranians will not give it up peacefully, will they go to war to protect it?" The president ignored the remark about Event Group expertise, but stared at his CIA director.

"No," Easterbrook said confidently. "The newly elected president, Rouhani, would never risk his government over something he may not even have control over." Easterbrook opened his briefcase, then passed around a singular report. "We have made several enquiries since you informed us of this new information. As of fifteen days ago the city of Birjand, a pretty large city in eastern Iran, received a new citizen who's taken up residence only two blocks from the

University of Applied Science and Technology: the former president of Iran, our old friend, Mahmoud Ahmadinejad."

A chill went through the president's body. The ex-president of Iran had been a thorn in the side of every U.S. president since Bill Clinton with his anti-western rhetoric and his outright hatred for the State of Israel. If he was in charge of this project, the president suspected that maybe far worse was happening in fundamentalist Iran than what they knew about.

"Jesus," the president said. "Harlan, I need to know if the new Iranian president is backing this project if it is in existence."

"Hassan Rouhani is a moderate cleric who is attempting to end the hostility between Iran and the West. Our intelligence analysis of his demeanor does not support him as the hardcase here. He's trying desperately to heal old wounds and keep the peace with the more hardline clerics. No, sir, I am adamant in my belief this new president would not be a part of this—if this is really happening and they actually have a saucer engine."

"Just look at the satellite photos of that damn resort that magically vanished, Harlan," the president said angrily. "That should give you an idea about the validity of this event."

"Yes, sir, I stand corrected," Easterbrook said.

"Sidney, I need to speak with President Rouhani, ASAP. Can you arrange it please?"

Secretary of State Sidney Washburn nodded his head vigorously as he removed the cold pipe from his mouth. "Most definitely, Mr. President, and I concur one hundred percent that this is the way to go. He may even come in handy if the situation . . . well . . . worsens to the point that Ahmadinejad, if he is the culprit here, utilizes what we know the Iranians have been hiding in that nuclear closet of theirs."

"Thanks, Sidney, give me an hour and then arrange the call. I'll need you in the room with me as he may take some convincing. The last I knew Rouhani hadn't been briefed on Magic and assuredly not on Overlord. The Russian president has to be conferenced in and I want to speak with him fifteen minutes before the Rouhani call. He has to kowtow to the Iranians if he doesn't want a bunch of dead Russian boys out there."

"Yes, sir."

"Mr. President?"

The commander-in-chief looked up from writing his order to the secretary of state and into the eyes of the man he had very little respect for in the few meetings he had been involved in. No, you could say Assistant Director of Operations Daniel Peachtree was not a presidential favorite over at CIA. He knew whose man Peachtree was—Speaker of the House Giles Camden.

"The ever silent Mr. Peachtree, what can help you with?" The president leaned forward to complete his order.

Harlan Easterbrook cringed, knowing he had made a mistake in bringing the man to the White House. He also knew any operational questions would have had to have been directed at his operations man, but that didn't mean he had to like it. He waited to see what Peachtree had to ask.

"Sir, it would be most helpful if I could get briefed on this asset you keep referring to. If I'm to make a strategic evaluation, that would go a long way to—"

"That is none of your concern, Mr. Peachtree," Easterbrook said before the president could do so himself.

"He's right, Mr. Peachtree," the president finally said with a withering look at the AD. "The Chato's Crawl information is on a need-to-know basis, and you, sir, don't need to know." He smiled broadly for the first time in what seemed weeks. "Neither does the Speaker of the House."

The room went silent as the other men wanted to shout that it was about time the president called a spade a spade—or, more accurately, a spook a spook.

"Okay gentlemen, let me have my talk with the Russians and Rouhani and see if we have a larger mess on our hands than we previously thought."

As the five men stood it was Harlan Easterbrook who saw

the two words that Daniel Peachtree had written in his notepad, but he didn't think anything more of it at that moment.

Chato's Crawl.

Peachtree closed his notebook and followed the others
out of the Oval Office, a light but confident smile on his lips.
The president had obviously not intended to say the name
of the location aloud. A location that the assistant director
of Operations at the CIA knew well.

Chato's Crawl, Arizona, was where Harlan Vickers's
search for the mysterious asset would start.

4

Speaker of the House Giles Camden listened to the man he had pushed into his position at the CIA, Daniel Peachtree. His eyes kept flitting toward the man who sat in the high-backed chair next to him, Hiram Vickers, with apprehension as Vickers kept looking at his watch and his cell phone. Peachtree thought they had a golden opportunity to kill two birds with one stone.

"I don't see how the president can get out of this one," Camden said. "I mean, starting a war over this silly space engine? The American people would crucify him, and they will after he has to go public with the fact that we and the Russians are taking on the Iranians over a possible fairy tale."

"I'm beginning to think that it may not be as big a fairy tale as you may think," Vickers said. "Back in 2006 during another administration, the CIA filed some very strange reports on an incident in the Arizona desert. I've sent the reports to your e-mail and would like your opinion on them."

Camden eyed the man and then cleared his throat.

"Mr. Peachtree has informed me of the president's little slip about Chato's Crawl and I did some snooping on my own. Yes, the CIA did make an attempt in 2006 to acquire that very same asset the president is leaning on so heavily, but was informed by the field commander at the site that the alien involved was killed during the event. Our predecessor never pursued it."

"So this action in the desert actually did take place?"

"As far as I can tell, yes. And that in and of itself backs everything the president has deemed necessary for us to hear in order to get his military toys in order. Everything else regarding Operation Overlord is being guarded from the public and certain aspects of our government in a far more secure manner than even the Manhattan Project was in the forties. Yes, gentlemen, I believe there is something imminently bad happening and it's scaring the hell out of not only our president, but the Russians, Chinese, French, and British. And when all of those military machines start getting scared other bad things are bound to happen."

Vickers cleared his throat, knowing he was still in very deep and hot water where Peachtree and Camden were concerned, so he chose to speak only when it benefitted him. "Did the field reports from the company name the man that was in field command of the event in the desert in 2006?"

"You know it did, Mr. Vickers. The commander was a Colonel Sam Fielding, 101st Airborne Division, killed in action, same mission." Camden watched Vickers for a moment and saw the disappointment on his face. He shook his head. "But I'm here to tell you Vickers that this, while maybe not your lucky day, may be a godsend for you . . . and us."

Peachtree looked from Camden to his associate, who looked up expectantly.

"Yes, his name is all over the reports; even received a presidential citation—a citation that lists no unit or even his real military rank."

Vickers began to smile. "Jack Collins." It was more of a statement than a question.

"Yes, it seems we may have lucked out on this one. Now here is something you're both not going to like." Camden picked up a thin sheet of paper and handed it to Peachtree.

"The man you used to formulate and reinstate the Black Teams for Mr. Vickers. Your Leavenworth asset?"

"You know what the code name means?" Vickers pushed in rudely with the question.

"It's not a code name, young man. With a little arm twisting I finally got to the truth. The name you referenced, the Matchstick Man, is what the surviving alien is being called by this mysterious think tank the president uses. Real name is Mahjtic."

"I'll be goddamned," Vickers said aloud. "Mahjtic, Magic, they can't be that simple?"

"So simple the CIA and your good offices couldn't connect the dots, and if you ever use the Lord's name in vain again in my presence I'll make sure you wind up counting Russian penguins in some far off, very bad locale. Am I clear?"

Vickers wanted to look at the Speaker of the House and flip him the bird but at that moment he thought that would not be a positive career move on his part. So he just nodded that he understood the threat.

"Now that you know just about what you need, Colonel Collins will not be touched or harmed in anyway."

Both Peachtree and Vickers leaned forward in their chairs. Camden frowned and then held up a hand to stop the protests that were going to spring forth from the two CIA men.

"You two gentlemen have to stop and think. The blunder that Vickers here did by killing Collins's sister is getting ready to come home to roost right here in this office—if I know your competence like I think I do." Again he held up his hand when Peachtree wanted to exclude himself from the blunder that caused this whole mess. "Mr. Vickers, get one of your Black Teams together and gather as much intelligence on this Chato's Crawl facility as you can. The president has been lying to the American people for nearly eight years about a battle in the American desert that may lead to this world being invaded by a hostile force."

Peachtree relaxed when he saw where the Speaker of the

House was going with his thoughts. Vickers, on the other hand, did not.

"As for your other man, this Captain Everett, he just landed right here in Washington, D.C.—possibly to reverse the presidential decision to revoke his naval resignation." He looked at Vickers and smirked. "Or he's coming here to see you, Mr. Vickers. If that is the case I would start my Arizona assignment as quickly as possible, because you know who else's name is in those Arizona reports?"

"Captain Carl Everett," Vickers stated flatly.

"That's right, and I suspect he works in that same desert think tank that this Colonel Collins is assigned to along with that strange little bald man with glasses the president seems to lean on so much. Get to the desert, Mr. Vickers, with all haste and find out what you can to assist me in stopping this military spending insanity by the president, or guess what? You could have some very disturbing company coming your way. So don't fail me, Mr. Vickers."

Hiram Vickers had all of his power stripped from him and had been reduced to a field agent with the responsibility of a house cat. He decided that for the moment he would have to play their game. He stood, nodded at the two men, and left the office inside the gorgeous brownstone.

Camden watched him leave and then looked at Peachtree.

"That man is not to go to Arizona. I suspect that those two crazy bastards are coming after him, and if they get Vickers I'm afraid we will become exposed and brought into his foolish attempts at playing master spy. I want him elimin—" Camden stopped short of saying it. "Well, I guess I don't have to voice that order to you of all people, do I, Daniel?"

"Vickers will be dealt with by one of his own Black Teams"—Peachtree looked at his wristwatch—"in just about thirty minutes. I've already warned all three Black Team leaders of the situation."

"I don't want particulars. The president seems to have ears everywhere."

"You are not involved in this. Vickers has served his purpose. The technology he and his Black Teams came up with has made us quite a sum of money, thanks to the president buying up any and all war material for this fictitious fight."

"Good, now let's later discuss this so-called Russian invasion that's brewing in Iran. If it succeeds, or even if it fails, I am going to crucify that sanctimonious son of a bitch in the White House, if it's the last thing I do."

Peachtree stood and buttoned his coat. "You don't think Vickers would do anything on his own with that little green asset in Arizona, do you, if he makes it out of Washington?"

"Vickers doesn't have the brains to screw me over, Daniel."

As Vickers drove away through the quiet streets of Georgetown, he smiled. He had all three names and now he even had a location on where to start. He turned on his radio and started whistling a tune.

"Jack Collins, Carl Everett, and the Matchstick Man," he mumbled to himself in the form of the song that was currently playing on his car's radio. "All in all, not a bad meeting."

EVENT GROUP COMPLEX
NELLIS AIR FORCE BASE, NEVADA

Niles, Virginia Pollock, and Matchstick had been sequestered inside the conference room for the past twelve hours. The remains of their dinner were spread across the large conference table, as were the many field reports from their field teams across the globe and others from archeological digs in France, England, Germany, and Russia. These countries knew the importance of finding a downed saucer with a mostly working power plant. If the president could not talk the Iranian leader into surrendering the prize, its recovery would cost many Russian soldiers their lives, not to mention the lives of Jason Ryan and Sarah McIntire. Thus far he hadn't been able to convince their foreign ministry to even allow the president to speak to Rouhani. Niles laid down the report from China and removed his glasses in frustration. He looked up at Virginia.

"What did General Electric have to say about their attempt to restart the Chato's Crawl engines?"

"No luck whatsoever. They lost two of their technicians just providing a nuclear jump-start to the pieced-together power plant. The explosion nearly took out their New Jersey facility."

Compton laid his glasses on the table and rubbed his eyes. He looked back up, into the dark eyes of Matchstick. The small being sat silently on an elevated chair and chewed on a pizza roll that the chefs in the cafeteria had made especially for their guest. The remains of Gus Tilly's sandwich sat untouched beside Matchstick. Six and a half hours ago the old prospector had excused himself and, with the assistance of Dr. Denise Gilliam, had gone to the clinic to be checked out for exhaustion.

Matchstick chewed on another pizza roll but remained silent, occasionally looking at the empty seat beside him left by his friend Gus.

Niles placed his glasses back on his nose and then looked up as the double doors to the conference room opened. Alice Hamilton, wearing a new, fresh dress, entered. Compton looked at his watch and noticed the time was three in the morning.

"What are you doing up and out at this ungodly hour?" he asked.

Alice walked over and kissed Matchstick on his green and very bald head and then looked at Compton. Matchstick smiled up at the woman and offered her one of the cold pizza rolls, which she accepted and popped into her mouth. She smiled and then made a face of disgust but managed to swallow despite the cold taste of the pastry. She held up a file and then slid it down the table to Niles. She returned to the head of the table to sit at her customary spot to Niles's left.

"Your pitch to the Joint Chiefs of Staff paid off," she said as she nodded a greeting to Virginia. "Three of them already had his name at the top of their own lists."

Compton opened the file folder and perused the list of

names, concentrating on the one name at the top and the number of staff members who concurred with the name submitted by Niles and the president of the United States. He nodded and closed the file. He knew that only a very few select personnel in six governments knew who led the list. Alice reached into the pocket of her print dress and placed two small black boxes on the tabletop just out of reach of Compton. He raised his eyes and took in the eighty-seven-year-old woman.

"They just came in this afternoon. I took them to the jewelers in Las Vegas and had the backs engraved."

Niles smiled for the first time in what seemed months and then looked at Virginia.

"In 1941, what did congress and the higher-ups in the army think about President Roosevelt's and General George Marshall's decision?"

Virginia Pollock smiled. "Not well at all. As a matter of fact there was a significant push to have Chief of Staff Marshall removed from his post. Most said he had become incompetent, and that his choice of field generals was a clear indication that the old man could not begin to handle a world war. They wanted him removed, Niles"—she smiled even wider—"just like the politicians will want your head when that name is presented to them."

"Well, personally the sons of bitches can have my head if this plan fails."

"That's only because if you and the president fail with Operation Overlord, there won't be anyone around to demand your heads," Alice said in her businesslike manner.

Niles laughed. "That's what he and I planned—the perfect crime."

Matchstick was listening and was very curious about the small boxes at Niles's fingertips. He stood on the chair and, like a small child, stepped onto the table with his mouth full of pizza rolls and retrieved one of the small boxes, turning it over with his long fingers. He looked at Niles and the director nodded that it was all right for Matchstick to open it. He did, and his obsidian-colored eyes widened and his mouth

formed the shape of that familiar *O* he had a habit of doing
when amazed. The two stars gleamed in the recessed lighting inside of the conference room. Matchstick reached down
and snapped up the other satin-lined box and opened it.
There, a pair of stars were shining and the *O* was there again
on the mouth of the alien.

"You know this hasn't been done officially since the beginning of World War Two," Alice said as she watched the
reaction of Matchstick to the boxed ranks inside of their
gilded cases. "I think the last man who wore colonel's eagles and was selected to be a brevet general was Dwight Ei-
senhower. Congress is going to shit wide and hard when
they get wind of this."

"This war may be well over before they even become
aware of it," Niles countered with a sad smile. "Especially
if that power plant is not recovered."

Matchstick looked up from the two boxes as he snapped
the lids closed. He looked at Niles long and hard.

"We will recover the engine." He locked eyes with the
small alien. "I promise."

Matchstick seemed placated by Compton's reassurance
and returned to his chair, started to pop another pizza roll
into his small mouth, and then quickly thought better of it.
The information about the failure to find one of the many
alien crash sites had taken a toll on his appetite. Mahjtic
knew that without that alien power plant there would be no
war, only a slaughter.

"Well, let's get Jack in here as soon as we can and get a
message and recall order out to Mr. Everett in Romania,"
Compton said.

Alice didn't respond. She exchanged a look with Virginia, who sat directly across from her. The assistant director of the Event Group saw that Alice was concerned about
something as she slowly pulled a note from the same pocket.
She looked it over and then looked up at Niles.

"Carl is no longer in Romania and Jack left the complex
twelve hours ago."

Niles was speechless.

"Jack left a message for me, with instructions to open it at eight tomorrow morning. Then I received a report from the State Department, telling me that Carl had used his passport to fly home on a commercial flight."

"Where is he going?" Niles asked and not politely.

Alice remained silent for thirty seconds. "Washington. Carl flew into D.C. early this morning. If anything is going to happen it will be there. I took the liberty of opening up Jack's e-mail early; it seems he had recent communication from Colonel Farbeaux. The subject matter in all of this is this man." Alice opened her folder and pulled out the same photo Henri had sent Jack.

"Why does this guy look familiar?" Niles asked.

"That's because you've sat in more than just one security briefing with the man. CIA—I think Jack and Carl, along with our French friend, have found the bastard that murdered Jack's sister."

"Did Jack and Carl have communication at any time in the last two days?" he asked as his anger grew.

"Not as far as Europa knows. Jack hasn't seen or spoken to Captain Everett since the Group left Romania. I even went as far as checking out Anya Korvesky's location."

"And?" Niles fumed.

"She's back in Israel, on active duty."

"Which is a clear indication that something unforeseen has happened to make these three people move as quickly as they did. Carl would never have left that woman, he loved her," Virginia said, trying to assuage Niles's anger as much as she could. "And Jack knew that we had major problems mounting here. Besides, would he have left the complex knowing that Sarah was heading into harm's way in Iran?"

Niles again angrily shook his head. "I didn't tell him. Jack knows nothing about what we have ordered her and Ryan to do."

"Niles, Jack should have been informed." Alice knew that she was pushing the wrong buttons at that very moment, adding fuel to the fiery anger of Niles Compton.

"Jack is a soldier, he does not have to have everything

explained to him. He cannot protect people all of the time. Sarah has a job to do." He reached out, took the box that held the two shiny stars, and threw it against the wall. "And so did he, goddamn it!" Compton hit the second box and it also flew to the far wall and landed on the carpet. Niles placed his head in his hands and cursed again.

"Do you think Jack would do it?" Virginia asked.

Niles looked up with his swollen and reddened eyes. "You know he will, and Captain Everett, like a damn lap-dog, will be right beside him. And then the two men we rely on the heaviest outside of Matchstick will be in jail for murder instead of where Matchstick and Garrison wanted them during the war. Damn it, Jack!"

Alice knew what had happened as soon as she received the note from Jack. He and Carl had somehow found out the identity of the person who killed Jack's sister, Lynn Simpson. She shook her head, knowing that there was one thing in the world you could make a sure bet on: the fact that Jack Collins would kill the person responsible, and there was nothing anyone could do about it.

"What do we do, Niles?" Virginia asked.

Compton stood as he watched Matchstick slowly slide out of his overly large chair. He quickly came to a decision.

"Alice, call Kyle Stimson at the FBI and tell him to pick up Jack and Carl and place them into protective custody. Get them off the fucking streets before Overlord loses two valuable chess pieces that cannot be replaced. Inform Houston about the delay in getting Everett out there, and then inform General Wheeler in Japan that Jack is also on assignment but will arrive ASAP."

Alice wrote all of this down.

"Are you going to inform the president?" Virginia inquired.

"What, that two of the main cogs in the wheel just went off to commit what amounts to premeditated murder? Oh, that would go over real well with a man that has more on his plate than Wilson, Churchill, or Roosevelt ever had." He shook his head. "No, I will deal with this myself."

Niles slowly walked to his desk and sat heavily.

None of them noticed that Matchstick had retrieved the two boxes and was staring at the stars inside. He looked up, walked over to the large desk, and placed them on the top even though he wasn't tall enough to see it. The long fingers pushed them toward the director, then he turned and left the conference room.

Niles lowered his head, knowing that he needed to take the attitude that Matchstick was taking. He smiled lightly and reached for the brevet promotional ranks, then tapped his fingers on them.

"Jack, what am I going to do with you now?" he mumbled, then looked at Alice, who always had words to smooth things over.

She smiled in her coquettish way and batted those green eyes of hers at the director. She then became serious.

"What will you do with Jack?" She looked from Niles to Virginia and then back to the director.

Niles looked lost.

"This is what you do, just like you and I used to with Garrison: you sit here and hope that our agent in the FBI can stop them. If not, we hope he and Mr. Everett catch up to whoever this murdering son of a bitch is and kill him. Society can overlook this one minor infraction, I'm sure." Alice gathered her things, then went to Niles and kissed him on the cheek and patted his shoulder. "That's what you do, Niles—trust in Jack, either way."

CIA HEADQUARTERS
LANGLEY, VIRGINIA

The field glasses were tinted with an electrified liquid crystal, the newest creation of the Bushnell Corporation's advancement in binocular technology; it assisted in the elimination of glare bouncing off the tri-lenses of the viewing system. The man saw the target emerge from the main building after nodding his head to several of the CIA guards who roamed the outside, looking as if they were men and women taking after-lunch walks. The watcher adjusted his lenses so he could make out the feminine features of the subject he was tasked to follow.

Henri Farbeaux tilted his head at what he would call the audacity of the man as he just strolled out the front doors of the CIA headquarters as if he hadn't a care in the world. The colonel lowered his glasses and shook his head. He raised his small radio and hit the transmit button two times, then waited until he heard the responding three clicks in return. Once he had received the response he raised the glasses and studied Hiram Vickers. *"Yes,"* he mumbled. He knew automatically that this was the same man whose picture had been forwarded to him from Leavenworth. Farbeaux lowered his glasses and walked out from behind the stand of trees that fronted the open gates of the Langley facility. He walked to the small side street that was only a hundred and fifty yards away and waited. Soon a black rental car pulled up and he stepped inside. He took a deep breath and then looked at Colonel Jack Collins.

"That's him." He pulled out his cell phone and looked at the one message he had waiting for him. He frowned, then placed the cell phone in his pocket. "We can pick him up when he gets to Colonial Farm Road. That will be his way home."

Jack didn't say a word as he placed his foot down hard upon the gas pedal. The black Chevrolet sped into the morning sun.

"I suppose you still refuse to be persuaded to wait, Colonel?" Henri asked.

"This needs to end, and end now." Jack looked at Henri, his enemy for many years; the man he knew beyond any doubt was in love with Sarah McIntire. "The world is not going to wait on me. I'm out of time, Colonel."

Farbeaux took a deep breath and then looked out of the side window. This favor he owed, he knew that, but to willingly walk into a murder was something Farbeaux liked to do of his own volition, not on the whim of a man he hated for allowing his wife to die in the jungle eight years before. He looked at Jack as he drove and knew that the man he faced was not the person he always thought he had been. This American colonel was unlike any individual he had ever known, and if a man like this could love a woman such as Sarah McIntire there had to be more to him than his enemies ever saw. He had started to reassess his opinion on his wife's demise in the Amazon at this man's hands. Farbeaux had his doubts that Jack was capable of cold-blooded murder.

"Listen, I'm a little more experienced at being a bad guy. I think you should allow a professional to do this. From what I've learned, this man that you want to kill can be retired without any fuss."

Jack said nothing. The light-gray suit Collins wore and the white shirt underneath were starting to darken with sweat as the man neared his prey. Henri had the same physical reaction as Jack when it came time to finish business that was long in coming. He knew then that the colonel was going to carry this thing through to its obvious and, to him, logical conclusion.

"Turn left and we can beat him to his town house." Henri realized that trying to talk this man out of what he was about to do was no use. He knew because he had been there himself.

GEORGETOWN
WASHINGTON, D.C.

Hiram Vickers stepped from his car and glanced around. The early evening was warm. A slight breeze brushed his sweaty features and he tossed his keys in the air. Before they reached his hand he felt the gun at his back. The keys fell to the pavement of the parking area. Vickers froze.

"Man, there are security cameras all over the place. Maybe you should have picked a better robbery target, or at least another location."

"Tell me where the cameras are so we can wave and

smile," came the slight French-accented reply. "Now, shall we go inside and talk? Ah, ah, pick up your keys. And please lower your hands and quit being so melodramatic. After all, this is Washington, not your Dodge City. We don't want to attract the attention of your influential neighbors, now do we?"

Vickers reached down and retrieved the keys, then straightened. He managed to see the face of the man who held the silenced weapon at his kidneys. While his face seemed familiar, he couldn't place where he had seen it before.

"Who in the hell are you?" Vickers asked as he was not too gently pushed forward toward his first-floor apartment door. He reached out to place his key in the first door he came to and was stopped by Farbeaux.

"Now why would you attempt to go into your neighbor's house? Try the next one."

Vickers knew then that he was in some serious trouble. He cursed his poor attempt at trying to fool the man with the gun. He went to the next apartment and shoved the key in and opened the door. Henri pushed the man inside and quickly reached behind him to lock the door, all the while keeping the gun leveled at Vickers's kidneys.

Vickers almost lost his balance and bladder control when he saw the man in the gray suit sitting in his living room chair. The intense blue eyes bore into his frightened ones. But the one object he noticed even more than the man's blue eyes was the silenced Beretta in his right hand. His guest was sitting casually as the barrel of the weapon gently tapped his knee.

"Look, you guys really don't know who you're fucking with here," he said as he gestured that he wanted to reach into his coat. Jack Collins nodded his head that it was all right. The blue eyes went to Henri, wanting him to shoot the man if anything untoward came free of his coat. Vickers pulled out his CIA identification and tossed it to Jack, who caught it but didn't examine it. Instead he just placed it on the small coffee table to his left and stared at the cowering man before him.

"You don't know me?" Collins slowly stood from the chair and faced the man he had wanted to meet since his sister's murder six months before.

"Why should I?" Vickers said as Henri strode away and into the man's kitchen. Jack heard the refrigerator open and the Frenchman rummage through it.

"I thought since you knew my sister that you just might know me."

Vickers felt his heart slip a notch in his chest as he realized just who was inside his home. All thoughts of the Matchstick Man were all but gone—along with his future.

"Look, I really don't have any idea what it is you're talking about. Who is your sister?"

Henri Farbeaux stepped from the kitchen with an opened can of Coke and watched the activity he found immensely amusing. He did notice a momentary flare in Jack's eyes. It wasn't one of anger, but one of doubt when Vickers said he didn't know what the colonel was referring to. Henri sipped the cold drink.

Jack walked toward Vickers with a purposeful stride. He stopped only inches from Vickers's nose.

"Lynn Simpson . . . Collins."

Vickers's eyes flitted to the Frenchman, who raised his soda and nodded. Vickers didn't know if he was praising the cold drink or saying *we gotcha*.

Jack knew the man they sought was right in front of him. "Why was she killed?"

"You can't shoot me right here in the middle of Georgetown for something I am not involved in. I don't know what—"

The gun's barrel struck the CIA man on the side of the head, making him yelp in pain. He looked at his hand when he pulled it away from his ear and it was covered in blood.

"Who said anything about shooting?" Henri said as he sipped from the can. "There are quite a number of ways to use a gun, my friend, and I think the colonel knows them all."

"But I—"

Another gun-barrel blow to the other ear and Vickers this time went down.

"Why?" Jack persisted.

Vickers looked up at Collins and saw no mercy in the eyes of the man.

"Okay, okay," the CIA man screamed as he tried to stand. The gun came down again, sending him to the braided carpeting. *"What was that for?"*

"I believe he was telling you to be forthright and straight with him before you speak again," Henri said as he raised the can to his lips. He froze when he felt the weapon digging into his backside. The can stopped at the lips and he didn't move.

Jack saw the other three men but it was too late. They were drawn on before he could react. They had been in the apartment the whole time and Jack hadn't checked when he entered the building. He cursed himself for his unprofessional act.

"This man has done quite enough damage," a tall, thin man in a black Windbreaker said as he stepped around Vickers to remove Jack's weapon. Henri was simultaneously pushed out of the kitchen's doorway. He was as angry as Collins for being taken by surprise. He quickly surmised that although they were both extremely adept at battlefield prowess, they were sorely lacking in the fine art of cold-blooded murder tactics.

"Maybe we should have planned this a little better, Colonel," Farbeaux said as he joined Collins in the living room.

Collins counted four men in total. There was one more outside the front door as he had seen a shadow pass the window a moment before. They were all wearing black Windbreakers and at that moment Collins knew just who it was they were dealing with. The infamous Men in Black that had been reborn, and now he knew who it was that had reinstated the teams—the CIA. Everything became crystal clear to Jack.

Vickers finally stood and wiped the blood from both ears, then bravely punched Jack in the stomach. The colonel barely winced. One of the Black Team snickered when Collins didn't even flinch at the assault. Instead he looked at Henri.

"Not only did this asshole kill Lynn, Henri, these are the wondrously patriotic gentlemen that hit our complex six months back, looking for the Ripper formula." Collins turned back to face the man standing next to Vickers.

"Not us, but our commander, Mr. Smith. Don't tell me you're the men that dispatched him and his team?" the thin man asked.

"You bet. Killed every one of the bastards," Jack said as he looked into the steady eyes of the man in black.

"Enough of this crap—kill the son of a bitch!" Vickers said.

The man turned the weapon away from Collins and shot Vickers in the meatiest section of his right calf. Hiram screamed and went down, sliding to the carpet against the wall.

"You must remain quiet as we attempt to sort through this, Mr. Vickers."

Jack was surprised but held the expression in check as Vickers rolled on the bloodstained carpeting in agony. He looked up at the team leader.

"What are you doing?" he wailed as he tried to hold his wounded calf.

"You are no longer head of your desk, sir. They told me to tell you one fuck-up is all that is tolerated." The man took deliberate aim at the face of Hiram Vickers, who covered his eyes as blood from his hands dripped onto his face.

Jack hit the floor as the front window exploded into the room as a silenced weapon opened up. The first bullet struck the man with the gun in his exposed hand, dropping him to the floor. Jack fell upon him. Henri ducked just as three of the bullets flew past him. One struck the man at his back in the nose, dropping him as if he were a mere sack of potatoes. The two men standing behind the first hit the floor as the front door was kicked in. Several more rounds found their mark, hitting the men in their exposed backs.

Jack wrestled with the first gunman, then wrenched the weapon up as the trigger was pulled. Collins felt their rescuer run into the apartment and down the hallway, where several more shots were fired just as his own efforts caught the struggling man in the lower chin. A bullet exploded into the assassin's brain. He went limp. Henri ran by and took one of the weapons from the two fallen men and ran to the front door. As Collins pushed the dead man in black away with disgust he looked around but didn't see Hiram Vickers. He saw the blood trail leading out of the front door. Henri stepped back inside with the silenced weapon still smoking after discharge. He shook his head.

"Your target just ran for the hills, Colonel." Henri looked at the hallway and was surprised when a familiar face emerged from the bedroom, dragging one more of the men in black by the collar. He was also dead.

"Always have a navy man plan your ops, Jack, you know that." Carl Everett let go of the dead man's collar and looked over the others.

Collins finally managed to get to his feet and shook some of the blood from his exposed hand. He looked at Carl and shook his head.

"I thought you had a woman to look after in Romania?" He went to the door and looked out past Farbeaux. Vickers's car was gone. Jack looked at the gun in his hand, then tossed it on the couch next to the door.

"Ah, she left me for another man, a general in the Mossad, as a matter of fact." Carl slid his nine millimeter into the belt at the back of his waistband. He looked at Henri and tilted his head. "And a good thing too, it looks like you're starting to hang out with characters that can get you into a lot of trouble."

"You can't be here, Carl," Collins said. "I'll explain later but you cannot be around me."

"Well, if that's not a thank-you, I'll—"

"Jesus Christ!" a voice from behind Jack said.

"We are really losing our touch," Henri said, realizing they had been taken by surprise once again as he spied the man with the drawn weapon standing in the doorway.

Collins turned and immediately recognized the Group's man inside the FBI.

"Agent Stimson, how are things?" Jack wiped his hand on the white curtains at the window.

The agent placed his weapon in its holster and looked at the scene inside the apartment.

"I don't know how in the hell I'm going to explain this one to my boss." The FBI special agent stepped inside and eyed the three men. "Jack, you have put me in a hell of a spot here."

"How did you know where to find us?" The colonel looked from Everett to the man he had recruited himself five years before.

Stimson looked at Collins and shook his head. "How in the hell do I know how your people find these things out? I'm just an errand boy here." Stimson shook his head as he examined the scene again, trying to make sense of what he was seeing. "Well, I guess it doesn't matter now, the Bureau's had orders for a couple of months to keep tabs on our Mr. Vickers. It seems the Oval Office doesn't like certain factions over in Langley and wanted to start a file on more than just a few of their operatives."

"Bullshit. Dr. Compton authorized you to use the computer chip tags Mr. Everett and I have in our arms."

"Okay, that too." The agent again shook his head as he looked at the three men before him. "By the way, you three . . . well, you're under arrest."

"Now you know better than that," Carl said as he raised a brow at the agent.

"Look, you guys can take me down but I have to tell you that I have eight more agents outside. We have enough of a mess around here. By the orders of the president of the United States you are hereby placed into protective custody."

"President, my ass. I smell Niles, correct?" Jack asked.

"I don't know about these gentlemen," Farbeaux said,

"but I'm a foreign national who has nothing to do with secret groups or even the president of the United States. So, if you would excuse me, I'll say—"

"You'll say thank-you and be grateful you're not in handcuffs, Colonel Farbeaux," Stimson said with an angry glare.

"Yes, Colonel Collins, I would say your little bald employer is indeed behind this." Henri walked up to Jack and smiled as he slightly raised both hands. "I guess if you can't get one bad guy, your boss thinks another will be just as good. At least enough to appease your president over this mess." He gestured at the dead men around him.

"No, I'm afraid your own government wants to speak with you, Colonel," Stimson said.

Henri deflated before their eyes when he realized his time on the run from his own government was now at an end. He took the gun from his pants and handed it to the agent. The look he gave Jack was not a pleasant one, and Collins knew trying to explain to Henri that he had nothing to do with his arrest would go by the wayside. Henri Farbeaux never forgot a slight and Collins knew he was back to square one with the Frenchman.

"Come, gentlemen, we have little time. We have to get you clear of this and cleared fast. Things are starting to go to hell in a handbasket across the globe. The president just placed the rapid deployment force in Kuwait on alert for action inside the borders of Iran."

Jack was taken aback. "I didn't know FBI field agents were briefed on presidential orders?"

"He didn't brief me, Director Compton did. And he told me to tell you that the Azerbaijan field team is involved. I guess you're supposed to know what that means."

Jack's face went slack, a reaction that both Carl and Henri noticed.

"What, Jack?" Carl asked.

"Sarah is on the field team in Azerbaijan."

"Then we must obey your orders," Henri said, becoming dead serious.

The men were led from Vickers's apartment. It was Jack who remembered what they had come here for.

"Vickers could not have been working alone, you know that?" he asked no one in particular.

"I'm afraid the men he does work for are untouchable at the moment," Stimson said. He led the men past his special agents as they rushed into the slaughterhouse that was once a beautiful condo inside Georgetown. "Call the forensics team and issue an all-points for Mr. Hiram Vickers. This is his place and his mess," he said to the team inside.

"And why are the men in black untouchable?" Everett asked.

"Because priorities have shifted, gentlemen, from passive preparedness to a war footing. Dr. Compton said you would understand. He said to tell you, Operations Magic and Overlord are on. And that you picked one hell of a time to go rogue on him."

Farbeaux didn't know what either meant, but became concerned when he saw the countenance of Jack Collins go from worry to fear in a split second. "If you don't mind telling me, what do those terms mean?"

Jack stopped before reaching the FBI sedan.

"It means, Henri, that the war we've been fearing is starting."

COMMERCIAL LANDING FIELD
MASALLY, AZERBAIJAN

The three Russian-built troop transports, the Ilyushin IL-76 D "Desantnyis," sat at the far edge of the northern-most runway. The security aspect of what was now known as Operation Zeus dictated the large force stay as far from the prying eyes of the Azerbaijani military forces as possible. From a distance the newest sets of eyes on the airstrip watched the activity of the Russian paratroopers as they made ready for their flight into Iran. It had taken close to three hours to get the Azerbaijani government's permission to use Masally as a staging area. As it was, several large western newspapers and networks had gotten wind of the operation but were kept at bay at the main civil terminal far away.

The lone helicopter sat between the large troop transports. The pilot made ready for the flight into the Caspian Sea staging site. His passengers had just arrived and were being outfitted inside the three large tents they had set up.

Two miles away inside the run-down terminal, two Russian soldiers made their way through security and past the many prying eyes of the civilians waiting for their flights. The two officers, a man and a woman with very dark hair, turned sharply into the airline pilots' ready room. The woman removed her cap and held a hand up, stilling the man as he stepped in behind her. She heard a shower running and a man somewhere inside the locker room whistling. She gestured for the man to take the whistler and she would address the shower situation. The man nodded, reached into his uniform jacket pocket, and removed a small syringe. He looked at the raven-haired woman one last time and she gave him a warning with her raised brows. He smiled and walked off.

The woman pulled a duplicate syringe from her own pocket and with one last glance at her male counterpart moved to the shower stalls that lined the back of the pilots' ready room. She heard the shower turn off and the soft humming of a woman as she opened the stall door. The woman in the absconded Russian uniform moved quickly to jab the female shower taker in the arm, then held the woman's head as she easily collapsed into her arms. She laid her gently on the tiled floor, then looked over at the man who had accompanied her as he dragged the whistler into the shower area.

"Place them in the janitor's closet and seal the door. Someone should free them tomorrow morning when their cleaning shift arrives."

"I don't think that's wise. This fellow"—the man lightly tapped the drugged man with his right foot—"got a good look at me before I stuck him." The dark-haired woman removed the combat fatigues from the wall hook, held them up for sizing, and tilted her head, thinking the large fit would have to do. She finally spared the man a hard look.

"The last I heard, Israel wasn't at war with Russia. We're here to observe and report, that is all. If this weapon the Iranians have is meant for Israel, we have to know."

"You're the boss, Major, I just work here."

Anya Korvesky looked at the man, then nodded at the captive at his feet. "Then by all means do your work and hide these two." She looked at the wall clock. "And hurry, we're on the clock."

Anya was bone weary. The two Mossad agents had been airlifted twenty miles out from Masally and had to walk in from there. Now they had but five minutes to make the flight line to be in on the raid into Iran. She was there to confirm the suspicion that the weapon the Iranians were using was being directed at the State of Israel. If it was, the Russians would have one chance to destroy it, and if that failed it would be left in the hands of the Israeli Air Force, which was on standby just outside Tel Aviv.

Anya dressed quickly and looked around the locker room until she saw the briefcase. She opened it and made sure the two people they had replaced had all of their documentation and necessary credentials; they did. The man and woman the two agents replaced would have been the scientific advisors on nuclear energy and would be allowed on the raid to assist the American team flown in from a cruiser out in the Caspian Sea. Only it would be she and her partner who would be in on the combat jump into Iran instead of these two.

Dressed in their combat gear, they walked out of the pilots' ready room and into the night.

The Mossad was jumping tonight with the elite of the Russian military.

Sarah nervously watched as the twin-rotor helicopter started up before them. She and Ryan were sitting on that cold tarmac next to a set of giant landing gear of one of the Ilyushin transports when the pilot of the helicopter waved them over for their flight to the Riga-class frigate *Leschenko* awaiting them in the Caspian Sea. They stood and both knew they were heading into a situation neither had expected.

"Right about now would be a good time for the colonel and Mr. Everett to make an appearance." Ryan threw his bag over his shoulder and looked at Sarah.

"Yeah, it would be nice to have them along," Sarah agreed as Ryan helped her to her feet.

"No, not to come along, but to replace us. I don't know about you, but those Russian boys don't look like they're heading for a picnic."

Sarah watched as the paratroopers of the elite Russian 106th Guards Division started loading onto the three transports that would take them into harm's way.

"Strange how soldiers look the same all over the world, isn't it?"

"It's the look in their eyes," Jason replied.

"Look?"

"Yeah." He took Sarah by the elbow and started steering her toward the idling helicopter. "The look that says they would sure as hell rather be somewhere else."

Sarah had to agree. She started forward when she accidentally bumped into a soldier making her way to the second Ilyushin in line. The two women locked eyes for the briefest of moments but it was enough to make Sarah stop in her tracks. Jason Ryan saw exactly what she had seen. Sarah managed to get her feet moving as Jason pushed her forward.

Anya Korvesky felt her heart sink when she saw who had bumped into her. She knew Sarah was going to say something and then that, as they say, would be that, and their little ruse would be over before they entered Iranian airspace. Both parties managed to separate without a word.

Sarah slowly turned her head just as Anya did. The two sets of eyes met again and then they both turned away.

"What in the hell is she doing here?" Sarah asked as Jason managed to get her moving again. "Where's Carl?"

"I don't know, McIntire, but if we draw attention to her

we could damn well be responsible for getting the major shot, so move on and let's forget we even saw her—at least until we can inform Group."

Anya turned one last time. She had met the two Americans in Romania and knew them to be Carl's best friends outside of Colonel Collins. She was grateful that Ryan and Sarah seemed to realize what would happen if Sarah had exposed her identity. With a sigh of relief Anya Korvesky adjusted her chute and equipment, then stepped onto the rear loading ramp of the Ilyushin just as it started to rise, closing out the sight of the small helicopter lifting off with Sarah and Jason.

As the ramps of the three transports closed, a large red flare shot into the sky, and then the first of the giant transports started to roll.

Operation Zeus was on the move.

5

Hiram Vickers winced as the bullet was slowly pulled from his upper right calf. He hissed as the old doctor removed the insulting object from his body. He was lying on a gurney in a shabby office of a man he had only sent people to for injuries—never, ever his own.

"Aw, come on now," the old doctor said in German-accented English. "It barely qualifies as a flesh wound. I've done worse to myself with a—"

"Shut the fuck up and keep your witticisms to yourself. Can I travel without too much discomfort?"

The doctor allowed the misshapen bullet to fall free of the clamp and Vickers heard the *ting* of the bullet as it hit the stainless steel bowl. He then placed a gauze bandage over the wound and started to tape it.

"As I said, it was nothing more than a flesh wound. It barely hit the muscle. If you can withstand a little discomfort I'm sure aspirin will cover it."

Vickers eyed the man and was about to comment on the doctor's opinion of his pain threshold when his cell phone chimed. He cursed when he saw the secure number displayed. He pushed the old doctor away and answered it.

"You son of a bitch, do you think this is going to stand?" he said angrily into the phone.

"You brought this down on yourself. You gave us no choice in deciding your fate, and you knew going in that if your dirty tricks and acquisitions department became public knowledge you would do what needed to be done. You didn't do what was expected, so your retirement was determined to be essential. As I said, you brought it on yourself, and unless you have a plan that will make the president of the United States forgive and forget, some sort of leverage, you will be the most hunted man in the country. The FBI has already tagged you for the murder of four men at your apartment. Believe me, if I were you I would handle my retirement myself and not allow Jack Collins to do it for you. And you know that you can't go and turn yourself in—we can get to you anywhere."

"Listen to me, Mr. Peachtree, if you don't help me get the hell out of here I will do something that will not only ensure that I hang, but you and several others will also."

"You have nothing on either me or Speaker of the House Camden. You started the department and you are the one that went rogue on us and killed two American citizens, and agency people at that. No, I think the best way out for you and your family name is to do the retirement ceremonies yourself. Or your very own Black Teams will hunt you down and do the retirement in a most brutal manner—their way."

"Listen to me, I will—"

Vickers cursed when he realized he was speaking into a severed connection. He closed the cell phone, then looked at the doctor, who was wiping his hands on a towel and looking his way.

"Find something funny in that?" he asked as he slowly slid from the table.

"Yes, as a matter of fact, it's not often that I treat a dead man. May I suggest you run for your life?" He smiled as he started to turn for the door.

Vickers angrily reached into his coat, pulled out the .32

automatic, and fired six times into the old doctor's back. He limped over to the fallen man as he rolled over.

"Still find it funny?" he asked, and fired two more times into the upturned face.

Vickers turned and rummaged in the medicine cabinet until he found some pain medication, then quickly swallowed three pills. He reached out with his good leg and kicked the doctor's head to remove the staring and blank eyes from him. He shook his head as he realized that the entire law enforcement community of the planet would be looking for him. He knew he needed leverage, the likes of which would sway the president into not proceeding with his retirement. He stepped around the murdered doctor and faced the far wall.

"I'll bring you all down before this is over," he said as he leaned his head against a large wall map of the United States. He knew he was a lost man as he took a deep breath and straightened. His eyes fell on the map and then they strayed to the western part of the United States. They centered on the southern portion of the multicolored map and he slowly started to smile, feeling better almost immediately with the sudden burst of inspiration. He stepped back and looked at the map and his smile grew. He knew he had found his get-out-of-jail-free card. His hand reached out and slapped the area he was staring at. He smiled at the streak of blood he left on the spot. He then turned away and left the dilapidated office building, exiting Washington for the last time.

On the wall map there was a blotch of red blood smearing the small town in Arizona that would see Vickers free of his dilemma: Chato's Crawl—the home of the Matchstick Man.

USNS *ALAN SHEPARD*
UNITED STATES NAVAL SUPPLY VESSEL

The *Alan Shepard* rose on the twelve-foot swell and then rolled slightly to the starboard beam as her blunt but powerful nose fought free of the foam and sea that had so suddenly sprung to life around her. She went from a five-knot wind and light seas to having to take on ballast to keep her firmly placed in the water. Her captain leaned forward and peered through the wipers that tried in vain to keep her bridge windows clear. The swirling skies above were taking on a shape that the young captain didn't like at all. He turned and looked toward his executive officer.

"I want damage control to stand by near the ammunition lockers. This would be the time we find out that someone went slack on their loading procedures because no one was expecting this an hour ago."

"Already done." The exec reached for a control panel just as the *Alan Shepard* rolled again, this time to port. Lightning illuminated the interior of the bridge and many worried looks from her young crew were exchanged at the sudden appearance of the swirling storm.

"Captain, we're starting to get a severe current slamming us from the starboard side. We're having a hard time keeping course."

"Maintain course, bring speed up to fifteen knots. I want to get out of this corkscrew. This is beginning to look like a typhoon."

"I heard the North Sea was rough, but this is ridiculous," the exec said as he finally gained control and steadied.

"Captain, you better look at this," called out one of civilian load handlers. He was looking through binoculars and gesturing in the growing darkness of the raging storm. The captain grabbed a pair of glasses and turned to his second-in-command.

"Get a message off to Southampton and warn them about this. They have to get word out to those deep-sea oil platforms—this thing could tear them apart. Message the Royal Navy that they may have a situation brewing out here."

"Aye," the exec replied and moved off to get the word out.

The captain quickly raised the glasses to his eyes as the *Alan Shepard* went deep into a trough of water that plunged her no less than a hundred feet down a steep waterfall of terror. She corrected and then her bow shot almost straight up. Lightning flashed and eyes flinched as they broke free to the surface once again.

"My God," the captain said beneath his breath as he eyed the most amazing sight he had ever seen in the natural world—one he knew few had ever seen before. The clouds swirled in a clockwise motion high above them and thirty miles to the south. It looked as if it was a hurricane forming but the captain knew it was swirling far too perfectly. What he was seeing looked almost animated. The colors of blue, purple, green, and reds turned at an amazing speed. The sea directly beneath was churned up into a whirlpool that covered no less than ten miles of the North Sea. A giant wall of water was reaching up to touch the bottom of the tornado of light. The captain flinched and turned away when the windows were blotted out by a thousand streaks of lightning as they broke free of the swirling mass and struck out into the sky in all directions.

"Captain, sea temperature has risen by ten degrees, current winds approaching one hundred miles per hour!" The shout came as the captain regained his sight and once more looked out into the raging hurricane.

"Bring us hard to port—get us the hell out of here! All ahead flank!"

The large supply ship turned hard as the captain saw a sight that froze his blood. Far above and twenty miles away the great tornado of clouds, water, and Lord knew what else, slammed into the sea. The two met with a powerful explosion that sent the sea three miles into the sky, and that still was not enough to hide the terror of the mass of swirling light as it met the ocean. The captain turned away just as the bridge windows exploded in. He looked up and then his heart sank just as five objects of tremendous size exited the twirling tornado. The sound they made even broke through the passion of the raging winds—a deep base tuba that hurt the ears of men twenty miles away. Five times the excruciating noise broke through as the sound of the objects exiting the storm finally diminished and then was gone. The giant round structures then vanished into the eruption on the surface of the North Sea. They disappeared as fast as they had arrived and even then the captain truly wondered if he had seen them at all. .

"God!" came a scream of terror as the *Alan Shepard* rolled hard to starboard as the rogue wave slammed into her. Men lost their grips and fell. Cargo meant for the USS *Nimitz* carrier battle group broke free and crushed many below decks, and still the giant supply ship rolled. A tremendous scream rent the air as the ship began her death roll.

Three minutes later the bottom keel broke the surface of the North Sea and the USNS *Alan Shepard* rolled lazily on the now-gentle surface. The sun gleamed off her red-painted underside as men started to bob to the surface of the cold sea one and two at a time. The storm had completely vanished as if it had never been there at all. There was only the debris of a once-proud supply ship that marked the graves of many a sailor.

UNIVERSITY OF APPLIED SCIENCE AND
TECHNOLOGY
BIRJAND, IRAN

Mahmoud Ahmadinejad looked on angrily from behind the protective three-foot glass wall as technicians raced to put out the fire that blazed at the base of the alien power plant. General Hassan Yazdi was standing beside him and too saw the debacle that the final test had turned out to be. He felt the anger rolling off of Ahmadinejad in waves. The ex-president reached out and struck the intercom button with a closed fist.

"Turn off that cursed alarm," he said over the intermittent beeping of the fire warning system. He waited as the alarm was finally silenced. He turned to the general. "As if these incompetents couldn't realize on their own that they had a fire, they had to be warned?" He shook his head as he watched the fire being brought under control. "How does the placement of your men progress?"

"The First Guards Division is entrenched outside of Tehran, and the Third Guards are at this very moment approaching the holy city of Qom. We will have no trouble from the clerics—nor, dare I say, the ayatollahs. The bulk of the men believe they will be preventing a coup, not initiating one. Once the president falls, the religious right will fall in line with the plan, especially since it will be too late to stop it." He looked into the dark eyes of the smaller man. "That is if this infernal device works correctly and the target actually is struck."

Ahmadinejad remained stoic as he held the general's eyes. "That is something we shall see about right now."

As the two men watched a large glass doorway parted and the lead physicist stepped out. The giant, round, mostly glass and strange steel power plant was still and dark behind him as other technicians scrambled on and over it. The man used a white towel to wipe his hands. He angrily removed the white lab coat he was wearing and tossed it aside. He rummaged in his shirt pocket and pulled out a pack of American cigarettes. He caught himself just before he lit up and looked at the dark eyes staring at him. He cleared his throat and apologized, then placed both cigarette and lighter back into his pocket.

"Well, what happened to the test?" Ahmadinejad asked, still eyeing the bald man.

"We had a power spike from the blasted power plant itself."

The two men just stared at the physicist.

"The power we were supplying it was too much; the damn thing seems to be correcting its output on its own. The technical advancement of this engine is so far beyond our understanding. It's like it is healing itself after being inactive for so long. It's actually correcting the adjustments we had made to it."

"Talk straight, man," Ahmadinejad said angrily.

"It has made an adjustment entirely on its own that actually made it more efficient. It went out of control momentarily and didn't target anything on this planet. There was no ground strike, it just dissipated into space . . . we assume."

"Will the machine work in the manner we need it to?" Yazdi asked. "I have half a million men with their lives hanging in the balance if it doesn't work, you fool."

"Oh, yes, yes, very much so," the man said, wishing for a cigarette in the worst way. "We now know what to look for and will prevent the power plant from spiking. We'll adjust our input of power to compensate for what the engine provides."

"Will it work?" Ahmadinejad asked as he leaned forward into the scientist's face.

"Yes, the targeting will be accurate to the foot."

Mahmoud Ahmadinejad finally dipped his head. He turned and faced the general. "Make final preparations to eliminate the key government personnel we have selected—seal the capital off, General."

The taller man came to attention as the once and now future president of Iran turned to the shaking physicist.

"Correct your machine and make it operational within the hour. No more delays."

"Yes, sir," the man shakily answered.

"A complete strike package will be delivered to you in one hour. Target: Tel Aviv."

SSN *SUFFREN*
NORTH SEA

The boat was new. She was on her third shakedown cruise deep in the North Sea as the French navy unveiled its latest attack submarine: the Barracuda-class *Suffren*. Her design and construction had been done in secret and the French people had been shocked when news leaked of the Barracuda class of boats. Protests from Paris to Toulon took up every available minute of news time on television. The anger stemmed from the program's prohibitive cost, for the six new boats of the Barracuda class would cost the people of France eight billion Euros—roughly twelve billion dollars. The citizens could not grasp the need for such an expensive weapons platform when the world—so it was thought—was drawing down from the war on terror. It seemed to the French nation that military spending was on the rise just as it was in other countries. Every western nation along with China was trying to quietly bring on new and expensive weapons platforms for no apparent reason or perceived threat. Riots in every western nation soon followed the discovery of new weapons programs that no nation on earth could possibly afford after the costly war on terror. The anger stemmed from not having a justification for the buildup.

Captain Jean Arnaud, a veteran of every class of submarine the French navy had produced since the end of the Cold War, sat at his elevated station just above the navigation console. Arnaud was close to his retirement from the sea and was preparing to drive a desk after the *Suffren* had been thoroughly put through the ringer on this, the last of her shakedown cruises.

As he looked around the silent control room he wondered if the protests back home would eventually shut the most expensive naval program in the history of France down before the second boat, the *Duguay-Trouin,* could be launched early next year. He shook his head in wonder at the way civilians thought. He knew the program was needed, but he had to admit that in this day and age it was hard to justify the expense of such a massive weapons system when the terrorists of the world were on the run and the old Soviet Union didn't exist. As far as the Chinese went, they had been silent for the past four years on anything concerning their military. Rumors of a massive Chinese buildup could be the force factor in the West's rearming.

At the moment the *Suffren* was running a standard station-keeping drill in the thermal cline a thousand feet below the surface of the roiling North Sea. If the new boat could keep still at the thermal cline—which was a layer of current that separated deep water from shallow and had varying degrees of current and temperature—her shakedown would be complete. Thus far the *Suffren* had not moved three feet in either direction. Her thrusters kept her nearly motionless in the dark waters as the rough current tried to push her first one way, and then the other.

"Very nice. Enter the specs into the computer along with the time and note it. Gentlemen, let's bring her up to five hundred feet at a bearing of 237 . . . let's take her home."

He saw the relief on the faces of the young French sailors as the order was given and the shakedown was officially closed. The *Suffren* had passed all of her tests. Even his officers were relieved to learn they were headed back to L'Ile Longue submarine base.

"Sonar, do you have anything in the vicinity?"

"Conn, sonar, no close-aboard surface contacts and nothing below."

The captain nodded his head and then started to relax.

"Five hundred feet and zero bubble, Captain."

Arnaud heard the chief and smiled. "Gentlemen, push the fish out of the way and let's get back home with our newest fleet boat. Watch commander, all head two-thirds."

"All ahead, two-thirds, aye, Captain."

The *Suffren* and her new power plant pushed her silently and efficiently through the frigid waters of the North Sea.

HMS *AMBUSH*
TWENTY-SEVEN NAUTICAL MILES EAST OF
SUFFREN

The French navy was not the only nation in Europe with the latest in attack submarines. The Royal Navy was in the middle of producing its own—the Astute-class submarines would lead the empire into a future of subsurface warfare that was on a par with the United States and her Virginia-class line of superboats. The *Ambush* was the second keel to have been laid down at the shipyard and her crew was well aware that theirs was the leading class of attack boat in the entirety of the Royal Navy.

"It looks as if our French friends may be satisfied. It seems they are headed home, Captain."

Captain Miles Von Muller took the report from the sonar officer, examined it, and handed it back.

"I see old Arnaud worked out the station-keeping problem they had with their thrusters."

"Yes, sir," Von Muller's first officer, or number one, said as he folded the report. "It looks as though the Marine Nationale have a keeper on their hands."

Von Muller nodded his head. "For now we'll await them to egress from the North Sea. Then we'll come shallow and report to the admiralty that the *Suffren* is now a viable asset for our friends across the channel."

"Aye, Captain," the first officer answered.

Von Muller started to rise from his chair. "Until then, match speed and course and let's follow *Suffren* a while, and collect what we can from her power plant noises. Keep her at fifteen knots and three hundred in depth. Let's stay above the thermal cline for the moment." He smiled, "No sense in letting our friends know we're near and interested."

"Very good, Captain."

"I think I'll take some tea and settle in for a while. You have the conn, Number One."

"Number One has the conn."

Von Muller started to move aft, patting men on their shoulder and nodding his head in thanks at their performance.

"Conn, sonar, we have a light contact bearing two-three-seven. Contact is intermittent at this time."

The captain immediately stopped and looked back at his first officer. He watched the man take the 1MC mic from its stanchion.

"What do you mean intermittent?" The first officer thought a moment and then clicked the mic to life once more. "Either the *Suffren* is there or it's not."

"Sir, this is not the *Suffren*. The Frenchies are slowing to five knots. I think they see and hear the same thing we are."

The captain strode quickly back into the control room and nodded his head, indicating that he would take it from there—his tea would wait.

"Captain has the conn," his first officer said as he turned and sped for the sonar shack.

"All stop, quick quiet," came Von Muller's order.

"Captain, sonar," his first officer called from the aft compartment, where the Thales Underwater Systems Sonar 2076 was located. The Thales system was the newest and latest in British technology and the men were well aware of its sensibilities. If she said there was something out there you could bet your mother's pension check that there was indeed something in the tree line. They all felt the massive submarine decelerate as she came to a full stop. "I believe we have a contact two kilometers to the south. It comes shallow and then goes deep. We have a hard time tracking her below the layer. Captain, there *is* something out there."

"Americans?" the chief of the boat asked the captain in a low tone.

"No, the Americans know the way the game is played. They bloody well invented shakedown tracking. They have other things to concern themselves with in the South China Sea, with the Koreans. This is something else. What is the *Suffren* doing?"

SSN *SUFFREN*

Arnaud had ordered all stop as his sonar was below the thermal cline and thus had much better information than their British counterpart. They could see the object at one half mile away holding perfect zero-bubble station—as if it were waiting. Arnaud noticed that the target was sitting right in the middle of the swiftest current in the North Sea and she refused to budge one inch in any direction, up, down, sideways, or backward—the object was anchored like a rock at six hundred feet.

"What are the dimensions?" Arnaud asked as he leaned

over the operator's shoulder to see the multicolored water-fall display on the screen.

"We may be having an issue here, sir. We think it may be as much as six hundred feet . . ." The young operator paused. "In diameter, Captain."

"Diameter? You mean this thing is—"

"It's round Captain. That is not a submarine. I don't know what it is, but it's not a normal submersible."

Captain Arnaud turned to face his second-in-command and leaned toward him, as he looked like a man wanting to say something. "What are you thinking?"

"The alert we received from Fleet before leaving on our first shakedown last month. Any abnormal contacts beneath the surface are to be reported immediately when contact has been confirmed not to be a submarine."

"We don't even know that yet. We cannot report a partial contact no matter what mysterious orders we have from Fleet. We need—"

"Captain, contact is now active and it's moving straight toward us at high speed," the operator said.

"What is their speed?"

"No speed estimate at this time; the computer is having a hard time keeping up."

"Bring the crew to battle stations, submerged." Arnaud hurried back to the control room. "Weapons," he called back to his first officer. "Load tubes one through four with war shots."

"Aye, Captain, tubes one, two, three, and four with Sharks."

The Black Shark, as the Italian-made torpedo was known, was a heavyweight in the world of submerged warfare. The fiber-optic-controlled weapon could speed out of the tubes at over fifty-five knots. She could punch a hole in most anything even without her powerful warhead detonating.

Arnaud entered the control room to face the uneasy faces around him.

"Range to target?" he asked as he studied the sea and its surroundings.

"Target aspect change, it's now slowing, slowing . . . It's stopped dead in the water again, Captain."

"Stopped where, sonar?"

"One moment, conn . . . Conn, contact is at one hundred meters to our bow. Target is holding station."

Arnaud looked to his first officer. "The goddamn thing is nose to nose with us. What in the hell are we dealing with here?"

"Captain, we are close enough to use the camera in the sail. Bring the exterior tower floodlights up and see if we can get a look at this thing."

Arnaud nodded his head. "Weapons, stand by, we may have to shoot from the hip." He smiled in false levity for the benefit of his young crew. "As our American gunslinging friends might say."

The lightness the captain displayed brought some uneasy smiles to the men manning their stations, but no real relief.

"Lights are up 100 percent, camera coming online."

Most submarines of modern navies are equipped with cameras hidden behind high-pressured glass located in the tall sail structure. It was used for driving boats under the ice and close-in situations where radar and sonar could only give you numbers, while high definition and ambient light cameras gave you real-life viewing.

Captain Arnaud took a few steps toward the twenty-seven-inch monitor as the picture started to clear. The bright floodlights illuminated the bow of the new submarine, and through the bubbles rising from her steel, sound-absorbing skin Arnaud saw the object. His eyes widened and he looked at his first officer.

"Jesus Christ, what in the hell have we here?" Arnaud asked as curious eyes tried to get a glimpse of the thing blocking their way home. "Maneuvering, back us off to five hundred feet—dead slow."

"Dead slow astern, aye." And a few seconds later: "She's answering two knots astern, Captain."

They all felt the slight movement as the *Suffren* slowly

eased back from the saucer-shaped object. Arnaud watched as the distance grew between the two very different vessels.

"Conn, sonar, target shows no aspect changes at this time. It's not following."

"Orders, Captain?"

"We already have our orders, Number One." His eyes met those of his younger first officer. "Directly from Fleet at L'Ile Longue. I'm beginning to believe someone knows something very peculiar that they're not telling us. Well, I guess that's beside the point now, our orders are to report immediately so that's just what we'll do."

"I assume those orders don't include not defending ourselves if we have to?"

"Orders sometimes can be very ambiguous." He smiled at his first officer. "Weapons officer, if that thing so much as blinks put four Sharks down its throat—I don't care how close it is. Set your safeties on the fish accordingly."

"Aye, Captain, fish are warmed and ready, safeties set to three hundred feet," came the call over the overhead speaker.

Every sailor who heard the command knew that the distance was not far enough to avoid blasting open the hull of their own boat if the warheads detonated that close.

"Give me ten degrees up bubble—bring her up slow like she was made of glass, Number One. Periscope depth, please," he said.

The hull pops and creaks meant the boat was slowly coming shallow.

"Standby radio room for flash traffic to fleet."

"We can—"

The cannon fire from the saucer flashed three times and the bolts of blue-green light smashed into the sonar dome of the *Suffren*'s rounded bow. The heavy submarine rocked as its nose was blown free of the boat. Water cascaded into the forward spaces faster than anyone could react to close all hatches. The nose of *Suffren* went down and the French navy's newest sub started heading for the bottom of the sea two miles below.

"All back full, blow ballast, blow everything! Weapons,

match bearings and fire!" Arnaud called out as loudly as he could. Even with the noise of the fast-sinking warship the captain could feel the four successive jolts as the high-pressure air sent the four Shark torpedoes flying from their tubes. One of the fish caught on the wreckage of the bow and snagged but the other three raced to the target. The flying saucer moved down and the resulting wash of the sea broke the fiber-optic cables guiding the Shark torpedoes. The weapons spun off into three differing directions as the guidance to the *Suffren* was severed.

"Put the reactor into the red, we're going down stern first. Full power!" Arnaud shouted. "We need—"

Another salvo of green-blue light struck the *Suffren* amidships as she spun counterclockwise in her race to the bottom. The cutting beams smashed into the sound-reducing hull and penetrated into the pressure vessel itself. Before anyone could scream, the *Suffren* came apart.

The fall of the French navy's newest boat would take a full two hours to reach the bottom of the sea two point seven miles beneath the surface.

HMS *AMBUSH*

Captain Von Muller's eyes widened as he listened to the recording of the attack. At least he was assuming it was an attack.

"Target is moving off at high speed, Captain." The sonar operator looked up with an uneasiness he wasn't accustomed to. "One hundred and twelve knots' speed. Target is now off the scope." They saw the sonar rating's face go white.

The first officer looked from the operator and then leaned over to a switch on his console just as the sonar technician removed his headphones and lowered his head as the sounds of men dying came across the speakers. On the acoustic display and on the sound system inside the sonar room they heard the most horrible noises any submariner could ever hear while submerged. It was the bursting sound of twisting steel and clanging metal.

"*Suffren*'s bulkheads are collapsing. She's breaking up." The operator slowly shook his head as the sound of the French navy's pride and joy died only a mile and a half away.

"My God, Number One," Von Muller said as he hurriedly reached out and shut off the echoes from the audio separation mode. "What is the complement of their new boats?" he asked, fearful of the answer. Every man inside the control room could see it in his eyes.

"Forty-seven enlisted personnel and twelve officers."

Von Muller felt his stomach lurch. He shook his head.

"Do we have a course bearing on the target?" He lowered his head and then nodded at his first officer to get to the radio room.

"Last aspect change had target heading north toward the ice pack."

"Maneuvering, all ahead flank, take us shallow to fifty feet. Make ready to raise radio mast."

The HMS *Ambush* was about to pass along a message the military forces of the world had been waiting to hear—the first shots in a new kind of war had been offered up. A war some had been planning for since 1947—people who knew exactly who the fight was against.

The Grays had arrived.

TOKYO AIR TRAFFIC CONTROL CENTER
EIGHT MILES NORTH OF TOKYO, JAPAN

The semi-darkened room seemed far quieter on the midnight-to-eight shift than third-year controller Oshi Yamamura was used to. The number of flights into Japan was virtually cut by a third in the early morning hours. He noticed some of the more experienced controllers actually had time enough on their hands to share conversations about their experiences, unlike the overtaxed men and women on the day and evening shifts. The atmosphere was light and easygoing and that was just what the young controller wanted.

Oshi's shift supervisor stopped by his station and momentarily looked over the young man's shoulder to examine the flights on his scope and their numbers.

"Ito is going to go on his break. Think you can handle a Continental heavy out of Honolulu?"

Yamamura smiled and nodded his head. The supervisor slid the flight and its info card into the slot just above his board. He patted the young man on the back and then made his way to the next controller to further divide the breaking man's flight responsibilities.

"Korean Air 2786 to Tokyo Center, over," the voice in his headphones said.

"Korean Air 2786, this is Tokyo Center, good evening." The young dark-haired man answered confidently, making sure to speak loud enough that his supervisor could hear.

"Tokyo Center, we have traffic off our starboard wing, about two miles out and below our six. What do you have in that area? Over."

Yamamura examined his scope and saw Korean Air at twenty-nine thousand feet on an easterly heading. The only other flights in the immediate area were a Nippon Air thirty-five miles south of the Korean flight and the Continental 747 he was just handed at twenty-six miles north of Korean Air.

"Korean Air, I have no traffic in your vicinity at this time, over." He again examined his scope for something he might have missed. The sweep was clear except for his three immediate aircraft responsibilities. "We have the storm cell to your rear and clear skies with a twelve-knot tailwind; other than that we are clear on the scope. All other traffic is local and feet dry, nothing over water, over."

"Tokyo Center, we are being paced by an aircraft with very bright anticollision lights and it's less than two miles distant. The lights are brilliant. We have been observing aircraft since breaking into clear weather, over."

Yamamura watched his scope but the sweep remained clear. He was almost at a loss for what to say. His supervisor came over and also examined his radar sweep and was satisfied the kid had missed nothing. He placed his clipboard down and then connected his headset with Yamamura's console.

"Korean Air 2786 heavy," the supervisor said as his eyes remained on the screen, studying the lone IFF designation of the Airbus A350 as it made its way toward Tokyo. "Come right to heading 314 and climb to 31,000, see if traffic remains on current course."

"Roger Tokyo Center, come right to—"

The silence was sudden. Yamamura looked at the supervisor, who just clicked his mic twice. There was no problem on their end.

"Tokyo Center, this is Continental 006 heavy, we have a bright flash of light approximately twenty to thirty miles to our north, very high altitude, over."

"Continental 006, wait one, please. Korean Air 2786, repeat last message. Korean Air, please report, we have—"

"Oh, God," Yamamura said as he nudged his supervisor on the side and pointed at the scope just as the blinking symbol for Korean Air 2786 heavy went dark.

"Korean Air, do you copy? Over."

"Tokyo Center, this is Continental 006, we have traffic to our immediate front and just above our position. Tell whoever that is to mind the rules of the road, we are—"

The Continental icon blinked three times and then it too went dark. The Boeing 747 just vanished.

"Continental 006, come in, over. Continental 006, say again." The supervisor slapped Yamamura on the shoulder to get him out of the trance he was in. "Get Kadena Air Force Base in Okinawa on the line and ask them if they have any traffic in the air that can report on what's out there. They're closer than we are."

As they moved to get to the business of reporting downed aircraft, another of the controllers started talking loudly,

trying to raise a commercial heavy, a Qantas 777 out of
Anchorage, Alaska, as it too vanished thirty miles from
the scene of the first two. All of this at 2:30 A.M. on a cloud-
less and moonlit night.

KADENA AIR FORCE BASE
OKINAWA, JAPAN

The two Japanese Air Self-Defense Force F-16 fighters
lifted off on full afterburner just minutes after the call came
in from Tokyo Center requesting assistance. The Fighting
Falcons jumped into the air and instead of heading for their
normal hot spot in the Sea of Japan and the hostile Korean
Peninsula, they headed east toward the Pacific.

Lieutenant Colonel Naishi Tomai brought the venerable fighter's nose up and climbed. As he did he had to think
back to the very brief weather report from the base. Cloud-
less, it had said, but just as the thought came to him the F-16
along with his wingman rose into a heavier, darker mass of
weather that seemed to be stationed over the sea at sixty
miles. He knew he would never be able to see anything from
that altitude so he nosed the fighter down, trying to ease the
light aircraft into the sudden storm. He hoped his wingman
was hugging him pretty close as they slowly came through
the low clouds. It seemed the dark clouds held nothing but
potholes as his small fighter was tossed up and down and side
to side as he eased the Falcon through the rain and swirling
winds of the storm.

The two F-16s broke free of the squall at eight thousand feet and that was when the lieutenant colonel could
not believe the sight he was seeing far below on the surface of the sea. He unsnapped his oxygen mask and shook
his head at the impossible view. Spread out on the ocean for
hundreds of miles around was the wreckage of the three
commercial aircraft. Three distinct spots on the sea eight
thousand feet below. For the colonel it looked as if the
waves had caught fire.

The attack that killed over seven hundred and twenty civilians had lasted less than thirty-two seconds from beginning to end.

CAMP DAVID
FREDERICK, MARYLAND

Jack, Carl, and Henri sat in a closed and windowless van that either had the air conditioner on the fritz or the four FBI agents watching over them wanted them to suffer for some reason or the other. The mess they left back in Georgetown was more than likely the reason. Farbeaux had listened to the two Americans speaking and tried his best to follow the complicated conversation they were having. Henri adjusted the handcuffs on his wrists.

"And the British, who were out in the middle of the Antarctic for who knows what reason," Everett said, "found my watch buried in two-hundred-thousand-year-old ice? And this was the reasoning behind you leaving me out of the hunt for your sister's killer? Just to keep us separated? *Your* blood on *my* watch, found at a level in the Antarctic ice that is over a hundred and eighty thousand years old."

"That's about it." Jack glanced at the Frenchman, who acted as if he weren't listening. "Now, as for the British, I know some parts of the Overlord plan, but not the main cog in the wheel. I'm beginning to think they found that watch during the excavation of something else under the ice."

"That's a little thin, Jack." Everett also looked at Farbeaux, who only winked at the captain. "Niles has got to have more on this."

Jack adjusted his hands so he could get some relief from the handcuffs on his wrists.

"I believe he does, but he, Matchstick, and Garrison Lee have been so tight-lipped about Overlord that they won't let anyone in. I handled some troop reports and dispositions of war material for the plan, but after that, it's like the Manhattan Project was reactivated."

Carl just raised his brows when Matchstick and Lee were mentioned.

"As far as I can tell without butting my nose into secret stuff is that only a few people, mostly heads of state and their immediate military commanders, even know the word Overlord."

"And?" Carl persisted.

"Well, I guess Matchstick says that no matter what we do to prevent you from being lost two hundred thousand years ago, it will more than likely cause you to be lost. He said you were too vital to Overlord."

"So the little guy will just chuck my ass right under the proverbial bus to prevent us from changing the outcome?"

"I guess that's the way it is. He says you may be the reason we win or lose the war."

"It's called a paradox, gentlemen. One cannot change the past, nor dare I say the future. Time and physics will make the changes so it comes out the way it was meant to be."

Both Everett and Collins stared at the Frenchman as if he had just fallen from the Darwinian tree.

"So now we know the truth—you used to write for *Star Trek* or something, right?" Carl joked as the van's sliding door flew open.

"The powers that be, Captain Everett, have deemed you expendable and no attempt is to be made to change the fact that your watch ends up two hundred thousand years in the past. I guess for whatever war that is approaching they need you doing what it was you were meant to do."

"Henri, why don't you take your theories and shove them right up your—"

"Gentlemen," said one of the agents in a navy blue FBI Windbreaker, "please follow me. You will now be separated."

Henri only smiled at the uncomfortable frame of mind he had put the navy man in. He winked at Everett as he was led to a black sedan only feet away.

"I hate that guy, Jack," Carl said as he was led to a second car.

"Really? I couldn't tell."

* * *

Three separate vehicles moved slowly down the winding roadway. Jack Collins was in the backseat of the lead vehicle, driven by a healthy looking young Marine corporal. The guard next to him kept his eyes straight ahead and did not once look back at the career army officer. As they neared the front gate Jack saw the security team of five Marines awaiting their arrival. They all wore gray combat fatigues and all watched the three sedans intently as they approached.

As the rear door was opened for Collins he looked back and saw Carl and Henri step from their cars and look around. Carl knew exactly where they were. As for the French Army colonel, he looked at the secure surroundings and figured this was one of the nicer prison properties he had ever seen. He started to step toward the two other men but a burly Marine stepped in front of him. Another three Marines escorted Henri toward the back of the large wooden residence.

A Marine captain soon stepped from the house and walked down the pathway toward Jack and Carl. He was examining two photographs and then held up a small black box the two Event security men knew immediately. Collins and then Everett both held out their cuffed hands and their right thumbprints were taken and compared to Department of Defense records. The captain nodded his head and then gestured for his security team to disperse. He eyed first Collins and then the much larger Everett. His eyes settled on the blond man as he removed first Everett's and then Jack's handcuffs.

"You may not remember, Captain, but we served together once at Camp Pendleton." He gestured for the captain and colonel to follow him toward the front of the less than ostentatious home.

"I'm sorry, Captain, it's been a long day," Everett said as he looked back at Jack.

The Marine captain paused at the double front doors. "It's about to get a lot longer for you," he said without a smile just as a two-and-a-half-ton truck pulled up to the front yard. Twenty Marines hopped down from its tarp-covered back. Jack looked at Carl as they both noticed the heavy ordance the squad of Marines carried. Collins raised his eyebrows when he saw the three men carrying the very heavy hellfire missile tubes.

"I take it you're having trouble with the animal life around Frederick?" Carl asked, not really feeling comfortable with the small joke.

The captain looked back at the dispersing Marines as they vanished into the thickly lined tree-covered property. He ran an electronic keycard through the security lock and the door opened.

"I cannot comment on that aspect of security at the camp, gentlemen, not even as a professional courtesy." He pushed the door opened and gestured for the two officers to enter. Jack held his place and looked at the young captain.

"What about our fri—" He paused in his description. "Our colleague. Where is he being taken?"

"That will be explained to you later, Colonel." Jack and Carl looked up in time to see a very weary Niles Compton step into the foyer. "Until then, let's just say the Marine security unit at Camp David becomes a little nervous when a known criminal enters the compound." He nodded at the Marine captain until the man turned and with a dip of his head left the house. "And frankly our friend the colonel is not well liked by the president, especially after his miraculous escape from custody six months ago." He looked sideways at Jack and Carl as he spoke. "So, after we talk maybe you can see Henri again, but not until a few things get out in the open." Niles turned and walked down the hallway he had just exited. "Until then we have a meeting with a very angry and put-out president."

Everett looked at Jack and raised his brows. "I probably chose a bad time to come home."

Collins looked from Carl's eyes to the watch he wore on his right wrist. He looked back and then just nodded his head. It probably was not the most opportune time to help Jack out with his personal problems.

They followed the director of Department 5656 into the bowels of the Camp David White House, eyed by even more menacing men, only these were the standard Secret Service team that always stayed close to the president. The men were serious looking. Jack and Carl immediately noticed that the agents all wore a sidearm fully exposed on their hips and every other agent carried a small briefcase that obviously held something far more lethal than a standard nine millimeter. They watched the two visitors very closely and that got the two Event Group men thinking that something in the equation had changed. They passed through a small living room where an agent stood beside the doorway and as they did they could hear the laughter of two small girls; when they walked by, the two officers, both observant men, spied the first lady sitting on the carpeted floor playing with her two daughters. She looked up and met Jack's eyes, and what he saw there made him worry even more. The first lady looked frightened.

Niles Compton opened a large door and stepped inside. When Carl and Jack followed they saw a sight that was reminiscent of the old photos from the war that depicted President Roosevelt sitting at a conference with Churchill and Stalin. Three men sat around a large table, looking at the newcomers very closely, as did two men standing off from the round table. Both Jack and Carl knew the five men from photos and briefing reports and they immediately came to the position of attention even though they weren't in uniform. The president of the United States angrily nodded his head toward the desk that sat in the corner of the room. He stood and said something to the other four men. Niles escorted Carl and Jack toward the desk, where the angry man from the Oval Office met them.

"Have a good time in Georgetown, did you?" The president placed his hands on his hips. He wore no tie and his shirt was slowly turning a darker shade of white from sweat. Jack and Carl remained quiet.

A knock sounded at the door and a Secret Service agent escorted another two men into the room; the president gestured for them to join him. With a nervous glance at the four men sitting around the table, the two men advanced.

"Gentlemen, this is my director of the CIA, Harlan Easterbrook, and the assistant director of Operations, Daniel Peachtree."

Easterbrook nodded his head and quickly looked down at his shoes. Only Peachtree offered his hand for shaking. Collins looked from the outstretched hand and then up to the man's dark eyes. Jack turned away and looked at the president as if he had been set up.

"Colonel Collins, I believe Mr. Peachtree has something to say to you." The president's hands remained planted on his hips, a stance every American knew meant he was angry and wanted something concluded. The four men at the table quietly spoke amongst themselves as the American problem played out on the other side of the room.

"Colonel, believe me when I say how much this ugly episode has upset the agency."

Collins stared at the man as if his words went right past his ears without entering. His blue eyes bore into the man's darker ones and before the assistant director of Operations knew it he had taken a step back.

"Upset the agency?" Director Easterbrook said as he heard the words come from Peachtree's mouth. "Colonel, we are even now tracking down the murdering bastard who killed your sister and her colleague. We will not rest until he is hanging from the highest tree the agency can find, and the man to tie the knot in the rope is Mr. Peachtree here, especially since it was in his operational area that Vickers committed his crimes."

"Enough. For right now the colonel will be satisfied with your response—won't you, Colonel Collins?"

Jack didn't give the president the courtesy of looking at him. "No, sir. As soon as I'm cut loose from here I'm going to hunt Vickers down myself. These gentlemen have lost credibility when it comes to policing their own agency."

"And he'll have company dong it," Carl said as his eyes did find the president.

"Thank you, gentlemen," the commander-in-chief said, ignoring both Jack and Carl for the moment. "Our regular security briefings are cancelled for today, as you see I have other guests." He gestured toward the four men sitting at the table. Peachtree and Easterbrook nodded their heads and Peachtree took a wide path around the two military officers, who only glared at the two CIA men.

The president faced Carl and Jack and shook his head.

"You had your shot, Colonel, now allow the FBI to do their work. They have several men they need to speak to, not just Hiram Vickers."

Jack's face took on an angry countenance as he listened, but soon softened when he saw Niles and Carl and was held in check by a look from the two men. The president nodded at Collins as he saw that the colonel immediately regretted his action while in the presence of the boss.

"I would want to punch me too, Colonel, but this job sometimes requires a bit of bad taste to get people to listen. Your participation in this matter of your sister is now concluded."

Jack started to say something, but the president held up a hand to stay him.

"Vickers took orders from someone. He gathered war material and several men used it to profit while saying they were patriots. Bullshit. I suspect I know who was behind it and I need the FBI to prove it or nothing will ever be done about it. As I said, your and Captain Everett's participation in this is at an end. We will track the son of a bitch down and then I'll let you throw the switch that sends ten thousand volts through Vickers's black heart."

"Now, let's get down to business because, as you see, we have men waiting." Niles Compton tried to get the meeting back on track and to get Jack's head away from the immediate situation. He looked at his watch, knowing what he had to say next would place Jack's mind back at the business at hand. "We have about an hour before the Russians strike at Iran."

The president raised his brows as he gestured for Everett and Collins to join the men at the table.

"And you don't know this, Jack, but we have two of our own heading into harm's way."

"Who?" Everett asked.

"Sir, your call went through," a Secret Service agent said from the doorway. Another handed Niles a phone.

Compton looked at the president, who grimaced and then turned away to join his guests. Niles handed the phone to Jack, who gave him a questioning look.

"It's Lieutenant McIntire."

Still, the questions filled the cautious look from Jack, and even Everett stopped in curiosity.

"Colonel, this is a presidential favor." Niles held his gaze on Collins. "Sarah and Lieutenant Commander Ryan are going in as consultants to the Russian strike team."

It was Everett who said what Jack was thinking. "Oh, shit."

Carl stepped away to give Jack some privacy.

Jack turned away to take the call. He didn't care how this looked to the powerful men in the room, as all thought of the events happening in the world fell away from his thoughts the very moment he heard Sarah was heading into danger.

"Small Stuff." He almost choked on the nickname by which he had always called her.

"Hey, baby," she said, her voice sounding distant and scratchy. "Jack, are you all right? Niles said you were away for a while?"

Collins caught the inference about his mission to kill the man who ended his sister's life.

"That's not important. You need to pay attention out there and get your small ass home in one piece. Ryan too."

"Jack, we have so many Russian commandos here that you better worry about how many times I have to fend them off. I don't know if those guys ever get time to see any women, the way they train."

Collins was silent for the longest moment as he swallowed, and thought about the misery he would feel if Sarah was lost to him. "Look, baby—"

"Jack, I have to go; something's happening here. It looks

like we have a massive power surge coming out of Iran. They may be testing again. If they are they could lead the Grays right to us."

Jack's heart froze. He looked over toward Niles and the president as several signals officers urgently passed messages to the men around the conference table.

"Listen, I love you."

Silence. Sarah had been disconnected as the Russian ship she was on went black, meaning the Caspian Sea task force had gone into communications blackout. Jack knew they were getting ready to strike. He turned away and locked eyes with Everett, then tossed him the now silent cell phone. Carl could see the pain in his friend's eyes as he strode to the conference table just as the president stood with message in hand.

"Gentlemen, we just lost three commercial jetliners in Japanese airspace, and the navy is reporting that we also lost a United States naval supply ship in the North Sea."

The president of France cleared his throat, then sadly shook his head. He had been conferring with the prime minister of Great Britain, Hamilton Lloyd.

"I must also sadly report that we have also lost contact with one of our submarines in the North Sea. It has been confirmed by a subsequent British report from a submerged source in the same area." He placed the message he had received back on the table and lowered his head.

"Gentlemen, the time has come. We must assume we are under attack and the strike on Iran is now paramount to recover the alien engine." The president turned to the leader of Russia. "Sergei, are your follow-up forces ready in case the first strike at recovery fails?"

"Yes, we have the Nineteenth Guards Division ready to move in from Azerbaijan, if needed."

The president sadly shook his head, and sat down while looking at his old friend Niles Compton, who was seated along the wall. The eye contact was brief but they both knew that the plan they had drawn up along with Matchstick and the late Garrison Lee was now fully on the table. The fate of the world was now predicated on a small green alien and a man who died a year ago, along with two college friends who just five years before had never thought anything like this could ever happen.

"Gentlemen, Operation Overlord is now in effect. We have a lot of work to cover. Colonel Collins, we better start the brief. When the Grays strike in force, you will be immediately transferred to another location."

Collins was shocked he had been mentioned at all. Every set of eyes was on the forty-two-year-old career army officer as his gaze went from Niles to Everett.

"You, Colonel, will be instrumental for the time we need to make Overlord work, and that may be quite some time. You will lead a fast-reaction unit of Special Forces to secure the Overlord location."

Again all eyes went toward the head of the table and focused on the president's words.

"Gentlemen, alert your home forces and let's prepare to defend ourselves."

The world was going to war—and they would fight as one.

PART TWO

THE FAILINGS OF MAN

Never in the field of human conflict was so much owed by so many to so few.

—**Winston Churchill, 1940**

6

The three Ilyushin IL-76 Ds started to disgorge over two hundred and fifty of the most highly trained soldiers in the world. Colonel Vladimir Tiushkin was in constant verbal communication with the Russian government as he watched his elite but truncated 106th Guards Airborne Division start their HALO (High Altitude, Low Opening) jump into harm's way. The colonel was the last soldier to leave the safety of the aircraft. His unit was tasked to secure the university science buildings and then allow the Russian and American propulsion specialists to deactivate the alien power plant and secure it for transfer back into Azerbaijan, and then from there to whatever secret destination was called for. The colonel knew that if his unit failed a full-scale invasion was being prepared by not only Russian forces from the sea, but also from NATO forces based out of Afghanistan.

In the final twenty minutes of their flight the colonel had been told that they were being tracked by a possible hostile flight of aircraft that may or may not have originated in Tel Aviv. The operations intelligence people had told him that

they had picked up transmissions from Israeli fuel tankers
leaving their immediate area and they could only figure it
was a flight of Israeli fighters that were going to finish what
the Russians might have started. Now the colonel had Israeli forces to contend with as well as an undetermined
number of Iranians. He only prayed that more levelheaded
minds prevailed inside the halls of the Iranian government.

FIFTY MILES EAST OF BIRJAND, IRAN

The commander of the 50th Mechanized Division of the
Iranian army had placed his tanks well away from the city
and university and was hidden well behind a series of small
hills surrounding the valley. His instructions were simple:
move fast after the attack on Tel Aviv and secure the university. Other forces would move on the government in
Tehran and secure the capital. The rumor that the new Iranian president had been having high-level talks with the
American president weighed heavily on his mind as this act
of high treason meant that they were going to hang if the
attack and coup failed.

The general only prayed that the new president ignored
the Americans.

UNIVERSITY OF APPLIED SCIENCE AND
TECHNOLOGY
BIRJAND, IRAN

The first Russian troops landed hard just inside the university compound. It had only taken seconds for the first warning shots by security forces loyal to Mahmoud Ahmadinejad
to respond. Several of the highly trained commandos were
killed as they touched down, forcing others to start firing
before they hit the ground. This was a scenario they had
expected and the excellent marksmen of the 106th Guards-
men soon settled the initial security situation of the attack.

Thirteen of the ex-president's men hit the ground dead before the first Russian soldiers had removed their jump equipment.

The commandos knew exactly what to do and immediately assembled inside the large university grounds. The initial assault on the applied sciences building began at exactly fifty-five seconds after the campus was secured.

Inside the large facility, at the bottom-most level, noise from the outside world could not be heard as the large alien power plant started its initial sequence in initiating the elements of the wormhole to open. The weather over Tel Aviv was light wind and no cloud cover. The Iranian technicians knew that if they had targeted the large city correctly the skies over Israel would soon cloud over as the machine gathered bits of moisture from the surrounding air and sea into the swirling mass that was the alien wormhole. The only three recon satellites of the Iranian nation had been re-tasked six hours earlier so they could witness the destruction of the Israeli problem firsthand.

"Power is at 80 percent and rising," came the lead coordinator's voice over the intercom as Ahmadinejad listened and watched through the thick glass. He was anticipating many things this night—not only the destruction of Israel, but also his anointed return to the head of Iranian government.

His smile wanted to break free from his stern countenance. The general seated at his side was on the opposite end of the spectrum as he watched the activity of the alien engine startup. He was overly concerned about his forces and their ability to secure the capital and reinforce the university. Thus far the only word that had come in was from the university element that awaited his word in the hills surrounding the city; that they were in position and prepared to defeat any opposition from the outside world. There had been no word from his division commanders outside of the capital or the holy city of Qoam. He knew that if Rouhani was not taken into custody and the ayatollahs kept under lock and key until after their power base had been secured,

the entire coup would be over before the plan had been fulfilled.

Ahmadinejad turned in his seat and examined General
Yazdi's face. "Are your units prepared to enter Tehran?"

The general wiped the small bead of sweat from the
space between his upper lip and pencil-thin moustache and
nodded.

"Yes, my president, the forces loyal to you are moving as
we speak," he lied.

"Good. I want my cabinet inside the capital in one hour.
They are to secure all government office facilities and dis-
arm the Revolutionary Guard."

"My men have their instructions and will report soon."

Ahmadinejad's eyes remained on Yazdi for the longest five seconds of the career officer's life, then finally
turned away as the lead technician joined them from the
laboratory.

"We are prepared to initiate the wormhole. Do I have the
president's permission to start the attack on Tel Aviv?"

"Yes, let's end this. Commence the operation."

The technician stood rigid and then moved to the communications panel on the glass wall.

"Form the wormhole."

The plan was simple. The wormhole would form around
the capital of Israel, engulf the entire region, and then shut
down. Like the resort a few days before, the entire Israeli
government and the city of Tel Aviv would be whisked away
to a place only God would determine. Five thousand years
of Hebrew domination of the Middle East would end as suddenly as it had begun in 1947. The Israeli dogs would simply
cease to exist, at least in this dimension.

Ahmadinejad felt the hair on his arms and neck start to
rise as the alien power plant built up to maximum power.
Blue and green swirls of light started to escape the containment vessel of the engine. The interior of the glass-enclosed
space started to shake and vibrate as the alien technology
started to explode free of the building. The large tunnel

opening to the laboratory opened to the sky six stories above, to allow the wormhole effect to escape.

Suddenly an explosion rocked everyone in the sublevel of the university. Ahmadinejad thought the power plant had exploded as the men inside hit the ground for protection. Just as suddenly, the lights were gone and the alien power plant started to power down with an ear-shattering screech. Shots rang out from every direction as stun grenades started to explode.

Ahmadinejad hit the floor and turned to the general. "Signal the reinforcements to move in. We are being attacked by Israeli or American forces. Hurry!"

Yazdi stood and raised his phone. "Move in!" he shouted—and then the general's face exploded onto the ex-president as a bullet entered the back of his head. Ahmadinejad watched in stunned silence as men moved in, dressed in black commando uniforms. One of these placed three more rounds into the general's head, then pulled Ahmadinejad to his feet. The ex-president was immediately swarmed by several men and made secure by a nylon strap that was brutally applied to his wrists. He could hear the men speaking into their headsets and the language they spoke was a shock. They were speaking Russian, not American! Flash-bang grenades exploded all around him as technicians inside the chamber went down one and two at a time as the commandos killed them. In the flash of the grenades and the hum of flying bullets he watched men from another nation spoil the plan of thirty-five years right before his eyes.

The man leading the assault yelled into his mouth microphone. "All secure, power plant is disabled."

The general in command of the forces arrayed to resist the Russian assault was getting ready to order his mechanized forces forward when his second-in-command jumped onto his armored personnel carrier.

"Our new president sends his regards." The colonel raised his automatic and fired two shots into his general's head.

The American president had finally gotten through to the government in Tehran and convinced them of the plight Iran was facing. In a matter of mere hours men had been moved into place to thwart the coup attempt, which none of the junior officers of the treasonous divisions had been aware they were doing. Across the board every commanding general and their adjutants of every frontline Iranian division had been so disposed of. The coup had become a complete failure.

CAMP DAVID
FREDERICK, MARYLAND

For the first time in recorded American history foreign nationals were allowed into the most secure location inside the United States—with the exception of one facility in Nevada. Russia, Great Britain, Germany, France, and China were represented by their countries' highest political figure. All eyes were on the live video feed supplied by the joint resources of the United States' NSA and Russian Intelligence platforms that amazed the other leaders in clarity and real-time exposure to the assault in Iran. The men in the situation room watched as a live video feed from Tehran took up a large portion of the main viewing screen. Iranian president Rouhani watched the satellite feed of the assault on his complex with trepidation. The view inside the university was confused and erratic. The men watched as cameras were tussled and images obscured. They heard the real-time shouts of men doing a devastatingly effective assault. The screams of Iranian technicians and the calm voices of men killing them thrilled and sickened the powerful men sitting around the large table.

Rouhani lowered his head as he watched helplessly as the men of his nation were cut down in the most ruthless manner. He now understood the dynamic of what the Ahmadinejad had planned. The scope of the coup and the planned attack on Israel had been explained to him by the many leaders gathered today. He now understood what had been at stake and had decided that his national goals would now coincide with the plans of the western and eastern worlds. Still, the sight of his countrymen being killed so ruthlessly was a vision that froze his blood.

Jack Collins and Carl Everett watched from seats situated along the wall with military assistants from the other nations. Every man knew the efficiency of the Russian assault and feared for the men involved. They had watched the entire assault without comment.

As Everett watched, his breath hitched in his chest when the all-clear was announced. The assault had been an overwhelming success. Carl saw Jack tense when he recognized the faces of Ryan and Sarah as they entered with the rest of the United Nations technical team who were there to secure the alien technology. It was Carl who wanted to stand when a face he recognized came into a soldier's camera view: Anya's. He looked at Jack with an almost panicked look. It was the president who eyed the two officers that offered an explanation.

Another monitor along the wall sprang to life and the prime minister of Israel appeared. The Intel chiefs of the varying nations knew the man next to him was the head of Israel's intelligence agency, the Mossad. General Shamni was being viewed publicly for the first time as a good-faith measure for the peace of mind of the gathered nations.

"Mr. Prime Minister, is your government satisfied the rogue element inside Iran has been curtailed, to the point that you can stand down your military forces and recall your strike elements?"

The small and elderly prime minister closed his eyes momentarily, then looked into the monitor and just nodded his head.

"Yes. As of one minute ago, General Shamni has recalled all Israeli forces and lowered our alert status. Do we have reassurance that former president Ahmadinejad's forces have been neutralized, and that there will be no reoccurrence of hostilities from the new Iranian government?"

It was Rouhani who answered from his monitor.

"I can assure the State of Israel that not only will there be no occurrence of hostile intent, but also that Mr. Ahmadinejad and his cohorts in crime will not see the light of the dawning day. Furthermore, with the agreement of the clerics of our nation, Iran is prepared to offer this sign of peace and friendship. We are prepared to publicly announce that we as a people recognize the State of Israel's right to exist, and I am prepared to offer full cooperation in our new and hopefully continuing relationship between our two nations."

The many varying national personalities of the world's most powerful nations rose as one around the large conference table and applauded the most decisive decision in the history of the Middle East. At long last the coup not only failed, but ushered in a new age of cooperation between the two nations of Israel and Iran.

"We are most pleased to accept your very kind and genuine intent of friendship across the board," the Israeli prime minister said with a nod of his head. "I am sorry for your losses in this sordid affair. May I offer assistance to not only the Iranian nation, but also the gathered nations planning for what is to come?"

"Thank you, Mr. President, and you also, Mr. Prime Minister. I will be in contact very soon so your governments can liaise with our military forces for training and instruction," the president of the United States said with a grim smile and nod of his head.

Rouhani nodded and his monitor went dark. He had a new government to form and a very long explanation for the people of his country on how close they had come to war with the rest of the world. He should have no trouble with the changing of power from his people. The Israeli leader removed his glasses as his monitor also went dark.

The president nodded toward the opposite end of the table and the president of Russia.

"Our assault division will remain on station until the technology is crated and moved to Overlord's transit location. This will be confirmed by members of the assault team under United States control." The Russian turned and faced the leader of America and shook his head. "I fear with the reports from Great Britain and France that we may have run out of time."

"First we have to confirm that the Iranian scientists have actually managed to power up the alien power plant and have succeeded in creating their wormhole." The president looked at Niles Compton, who stood and went to the large monitor. He held the phone in his hand as he connected with his element in Iran.

"Lieutenant McIntire, have you procured the test sequences from the Iranian experiments?"

There were several beeps and static sounded over the speaker system in the situation room. All eyes watched the strange balding man as he waited. Soon the image of Sarah came into view. Jason Ryan was standing near her.

"Yes, sir, what we have thus far is their experiments were charted into five differing areas of Earth's past." She held up a printout and pointed to several lines of code. The view changed on the Russian-supplied camera to show one of the leading Iranian technicians as he confirmed the time differential. "The first wormhole created a tunnel that accidentally targeted an area of northern Europe right around 38,000 BCE. This is verified by charting the skies and various planet locations. The second was 117 AD, location was the Scottish highlands. This corresponds with the disappearance of the famous Ninth Legion." Sarah looked at the camera. "It seems the Iranians were responsible for this and several other incidents of mass disappearances over the course of history. The next was 1558 near Roanoke, Virginia. It is estimated—"

"Very good, Lieutenant. Then we can confirm that the alien technology has been successfully powered up, and that an immediate transfer of the unit can be accomplished as soon as it's dismantled and crated for transport?"

"Uh, yes, sir," Sarah said as she knew the president had cut her short on the report.

"Lieutenant, you and Commander Ryan will stay with the power plant until it arrives at its final destination—is that clear?" Niles Compton said.

"Yes, sir."

The picture went dark and Niles returned to his seat.

"Mr. President, the People's Republic understands the need for the alien technology, but I believe the time has come for the United States to"—the Chinese president looked around the table—"as you Americans say, 'come clean.' We need to know the source of your planning. We, the many nations represented here, have invested our entire treasuries to something that may or may not work, as this has turned into the most expensive project in the history of the world. And now the peoples of our nation are starting to become very anxious over the unbridled spending. We are going to lose the confidence of the people, and then all will be lost."

"Gentlemen, many of you have wondered about my friend and colleague sitting with our group today. May I introduce Dr. Niles Compton." He nodded at Niles, who made his way to the podium at the front of the room. "Dr. Compton is the head of a think tank, or advisory group, located within the borders of the United States. Operation Overlord was conceived in part by him and two other men. Doctor, you may start at the beginning."

Niles nodded his head, removed his coat, then took a sip of water. He glanced at his oldest friend, the president, who nodded and smiled as the truth the United Sates had held in secret for sixty-five years was about to spill forth. Niles pushed a button and a view of vault number 28967, buried deep inside the Event Group complex, appeared. A giant black tarp was laid over an object of tremendous size. It was pulled away by several men. The round, broken, and incomplete skeletal remains of the two Arizona saucers appeared and the leaders of the world sat forward in their chairs as the sight amazed them. Only the British prime minister did not seem shocked.

"1947, Roswell, New Mexico," Compton began. "A flying saucer was indeed captured, just as many of you have speculated. The incident was covered up by then President Harry S. Truman. We had been attacked. In the summer of 2006, it happened again . . ."

Jack and Carl listened as Niles spilled the secrets of the Event Group and the United States, baring the soul of secrecy that had been hidden since the end of World War II. The leaders of the world's most powerful nations had been told about the attacks and shown proof earlier after the moon missions to uncover alien technology, but never the source. The two officers listened for an hour as the story was related. When he was done, Niles looked at the faces staring back at him.

"We inside France knew the United States, and to some extent Great Britain, had some valuable information they hadn't shared with the world, but we also have belief inside our intelligence community that perhaps you are still not being truthful to the full measure. Since the British find in Antarctica, you have yet to explain the way in which you devised a way to power up the device discovered. Who has been assisting your government, Dr. Compton?"

Carl Everett looked at Jack and mouthed the question *"What device?"*

Jack raised his eyebrows and shook his head, indicating he had no idea what the president of France was referring to.

The American president nodded toward Niles, then looked at his colleagues and laughed. They looked at him, confused.

"Dr. Compton has been in control of an asset we have been hiding since 2006. Yes, it is the very same incident that he described concerning the attack in the Arizona desert. Thus far the need to know the whole truth of the matter has only extended to Her Majesty's government, due to their extraordinary find in Antarctica." The president again smiled his strange little smirk. "Niles, please make the introductions."

Jack and Carl saw the familiar face of Virginia Pollock come onscreen. She sat next to a chair that was turned away from the camera. She smiled at the gathered men in the situation room, and as she did, she turned the swivel chair. The faces around the table drained of color.

"Good God," the president of France proclaimed as he rose in his chair. The president only smiled wider.

"Gentlemen, may I introduce our friend. This is Mahjtic. Along with the late senator Garrison Lee and Dr. Compton here, this being is responsible for the planning of Operation Overlord."

Jack had to join the president and smile as he watched Matchstick blink his large, black eyes at the camera—and then wave to the gathered men with a quick, childlike gesture.

It was the French president who summed it up for the world leaders.

"Incroyable!"

Jack had to admit as he looked at his small green friend, that yes, it was incredible.

The president of the United States stood, placed his hands inside his pants pockets, and walked to the front. He nodded at Niles, who replaced his coat and seated himself between Jack and Carl. He looked at them and winked, knowing that he had just introduced to the world the most important being on the planet since the arrival of Jesus of Nazareth. Jack pursed his lips in a silent whistle, showing that he had been impressed with the information about Matchstick being finally out in the open.

Before the president could speak, the German chancellor rose to his feet. "I may assume we can have access to this . . . this . . . being for questioning?"

"No. Mahjtic is in a secure location that is inaccessible to the rest of the world, even myself." The small lie came easily to the president. "If the enemy knew we had a Green being in our hands they would search until they found him and eliminated our only asset. Mahjtic is the only advantage we have in the coming days. If we lose him, we lose the war."

"And this being is trustworthy?" asked the president of the People's Republic.

"Mahjtic has proven himself over and over again in the past. It was he who led us to the discoveries on the moon and the technology found there. But for argument's sake, the man your military leaders chose to lead the combined Special Forces Fast-Reaction Force, Colonel Jack Collins"—the president gestured toward Jack, who just looked on as he still didn't know what he was there for, and was hearing certain things for the first time—"has worked with the asset many times and will vouch for his commitment to our fight. Gentlemen, Mahjtic was a slave to the beings threatening us; there is no love between the two races. He is reliable."

A member of the Secret Service knocked and entered the room.

"We have a communication directive from China for the president . . . err, Mr. President."

The president nodded his head as the agent delivered the flimsy communication teletype to the small and portly leader of China. The man read and then frowned as he turned to the agent.

"Please have your communications people verify this and inform us right away, please."

"Is there a problem?" the president enquired.

The man cleared his throat, then slowly placed the communication on the tabletop.

"We are starting to get confirmed reports from Japanese sources that we may have indeed had several instances of downed civilian airliners off their coast." The Chinese president motioned for an assistant to distribute copies of his Intel report. "It seems that if we couple this report with the incident in the North Sea concerning our friends the French and British, we must assume we are facing the initial stages of war."

The American president lowered his head and then looked up at the gathered men.

"Thank you Mr. President." He knew the man he had helped gain power inside China was right. "Gentlemen, I think we can all concur: it has started. And may I suggest we waste no more time."

"Yes, I believe we should initiate Operation Cut and Run immediately," the British prime minister announced.

"Very well. Then we are all in agreement?"

One by one each member of the world council raised their hands and lowered their eyes. France, Great Britain, Germany, China, Russia, and the United States all voted together for the first time in military history. The president moved to the door and opened it to allow the chairman of the Joint Chiefs of Staff to enter. General Maxwell Caulfield stood rigid as he came face-to-face with former enemies and allies alike.

"General, please alert your counterparts across the board, Operation Cut and Run has been initiated as of this date and time. Start hiding them."

With one last look at the men at the table the general nodded and then left.

In the next fifteen minutes every army, naval, and air force asset in the world would go to Red Alert. Every warship assigned to a fleet would take to sea and every warplane the world over would be dispersed to undisclosed airfields in every country that was part of the alliance.

Jack looked at Niles, still not understanding what his and Everett's parts in this plan would be.

"Gentlemen, let us prepare to defend ourselves," the president said.

Jack wanted to ask Niles about their role but kept quiet as the world spiraled toward a war of the worlds—the like of which had never been thought of before, in life or in their worst nightmares.

The world was about to change forever.

CATOCTIN MOUNTAIN PARK
THURMONT, MARYLAND

Hunting Creek Lake was located inside the confines of Cunningham Falls State Park and was situated only fifteen miles from the fortified residence of the president at Camp David.

The sun was just beginning to set behind the trees as Jim

Macdonald and his two sons, Bobby and Brandon, twelve and ten years old respectively, were just starting to pack up from their end-of-the-month hike through the lake country of the park. Ever since Jim had been coming here, he and his boys had occasionally run into either Secret Service or State Park employees making routine sweeps over the area even when the president wasn't in residence at the Camp David Retreat. This day had been different as they had come across not only the Park Service and the Secret Service, but also full combat-dressed Marines. Needless to say the heavy presence had put a major damper on the day for him and his two sons, even though they had shown nothing but excitement at seeing the Marines in the woods.

Jim admonished the boys to hurry packing the remains of their lunch and hiking gear, as their mother expected them home for dinner before the sun fully set. The father was also in a hurry because the security people they had run into had advised being out of the area due to the heavy police and federal presence surrounding the parks.

They had just finished packing when a small rain squall washed over the area. The man and his boys looked around and up as the sudden wind and rain caught them off guard. The small storm lasted only a minute and the skies quickly cleared.

"Well, that was different," Jim said as he tousled the now wet hair of his youngest son.

"Now I'm all wet. Mom's going to have a hissy fit," Brandon said as he shook off his father's hand.

Suddenly a shrill whistling was heard from the twilight sky above them. Jim looked up and saw at least a thousand large balls of silver falling toward the small lake and shoreline. At first he thought it was an optical illusion and he was watching a bizarre meteor shower that just looked as if it were heading straight toward them, but then the whistling became loud enough that his two boys placed their small hands over their ears.

Jim realized they were indeed falling objects and they were definitely heading straight for them. He grabbed his sons in both arms and sprinted straight into the trees lining the lake. He was nearly out of breath as he pulled up and turned in time to see the first of the objects strike the water and the shoreline. He tried to count them as the hissing orbs struck, the splashes rising high into the air. The objects that struck the small shoreline also hissed in the wet sand and threw up a plume of steam. Jim had to stop counting after he hit over a hundred of the silverish objects, and still more pierced the sky and landed anywhere from the lake to the forest surrounding it.

Brandon grabbed his father's legs in a hard hug as Bobby hid closely behind the tree. The objects came to rest; some sank in the cold water while others struck trees and careened off into the woods. They heard a loud crack as one of the strange balls came down near them and crashed against a tree. The eight-foot-in-diameter spherical object left a scorch mark on the bark of the tree, and when it rolled twenty feet and came to rest it started the loose pine needles on fire.

Jim took hold of both of his frightened boys and drew them close. Brandon whimpered as the silver ball started to slowly open along its center-line mass. Jim gagged as a horrid smell struck his nostrils as the ball split open. The three started to slowly back away from the grounded object just as a pole-like device came up from the center. Steam slowly rose and the hissing sound; the small ball was hot enough that Jim felt the heat from ten feet away.

"Daddy, what is it?" Brandon asked, wanting to pull his father away from the frightening scene.

Before Jim had a chance to answer, something uncurled and stood from the inside of the strange craft. It had a large, thin body and as it rose to its full height, Jim thought that he had had enough hiking for the day. He turned with his boys in tow and he came face-to-face with another of the things. The helmet it wore was a dark purple but that didn't stop Jim from seeing the horror that was behind the visor. The eyes were black and ringed in yellow, a brightness of color that frightened Jim beyond measure. The tall being was holding a large pole half as long as its entire body in its gloved right hand. The other hand reached down nearly to the being's knees, which were turned backward.

Jim pushed at the boys and they quickly ran past the strange creature. Brandon was crying and Bobby was admonishing him and his father to hurry. As they cleared the woods they came to a screeching stop only fifty yards from the small lake. Over three hundred of the creatures were lining the shoreline or emerging from the water. It seemed every one of them was looking right at the three humans.

A low moan escaped the lips of Jim Macdonald as the Grays approached. He almost fell to his knees as the closest one removed the helmet that had been covering the worst feature of all—the head.

As the sun set over the small lake in the even smaller park, the humans' screams echoed through the area. Then the Grays moved off toward the north—toward Camp David.

CAMP DAVID
FREDERICK, MARYLAND

The leaders of the world broke into several small groups as they sent out their alert orders; the military establishments, not understanding the entire plan, moved to protect their nations. Coffee and tea were brought in but many, including the president, chose to have something a little stronger— after all, it wasn't every day that the entire world acted as one in a matter of life and death. The president secured his drink as he approached Niles, Jack, and Carl. He was soon joined by the Chinese president with his cup of tea in hand. He spoke before the president could.

"Colonel Collins, it is a pleasure to finally meet you." He sipped his tea and then smiled. "As I understand it, you were quite instrumental in securing the technology in South America. I must say the report that your president gave all of us read like an American adventure novel."

"Thank you, sir, but I'm sure it was nothing that thrilling," Collins said.

"Still, it was enough for my military people to concur with these men that you are the right person for the mission at hand." He smiled again, then nodded at Niles and Everett and moved away to sit and talk with his counterparts.

"I suppose you are at least curious as to what that mission may entail, Colonel?"

"All I can hope is that it's something that will assist you in this massive undertaking," Jack answered.

The president took a sip of the watered-down whiskey and nodded at Niles Compton.

"I'll leave it to your director to explain as much as he is able. I'm sorry the whole picture cannot be painted for you, Colonel, and Captain," he said, looking at Carl. "But as you know, we still like our secrets around here. Hell, we would all die if we didn't keep something in the dark—after all, we're politicians." He moved away with a smirk at Niles.

"Captain, you are hereby transferred to a location in Houston for training at the request of one of our leading engineers at NASA. Your transport is waiting outside." Niles held out his hand to Everett, his eyes going from his face to the wristwatch he was wearing on his right hand. Carl shook. "Godspeed, Admiral," he said as he handed Everett a small box. Carl opened it and saw two stars. He was shocked. "I'm afraid it's only a temporary-grade promotion, but it was needed for you to command who it is you'll be commanding." Everett looked at Collins.

"Congratulations . . . sir," he said with a smile as he too shook his friend's hand.

Carl was speechless.

"And these are for you, General Collins. Same brevet rank, I'm afraid," Niles continued without a hitch.

Jack opened the box and saw the two stars of a major general. He too was shocked.

"Believe me, when I heard you went to Washington, I

thought we had lost the opportunity to see the faces you are wearing right now."

"I don't understand, why—"

"It's not your place to understand, General. And don't think that you no longer work for me, because when this is over you both are going to be returned to Group at your former pay-grades."

Niles smiled and then removed his glasses. "Jack, you will be working with the finest men in your field. It will be a fast-reaction force designed to protect the asset known as Overlord. I cannot give you details, but it will be up to you and your unit to give us the time we need. To give Carl the time he needs to fight back."

The two officers were as confused as ever.

"Jack, we assembled men from Special Forces around the world; some of them you have worked with before and have been assigned to you. Carl"—he faced Everett—"learn fast, get through your training, and save the fucking world."

"Niles, we—"

He held up his hand with his glasses still clenched in his fingers, stopping Jack's question.

"Will Mendenhall, or should I say, Captain Mendenhall, will join you as your aide. He's waiting outside. You will also take Colonel Farbeaux with you as your adjutant." Again he held up his hand when Collins started to protest. "Jack, he's the best the French have and they saw fit to give him to us, thus saving his life. They wanted to hang him, after all."

Niles relaxed and then shook his head.

"I wish I were going with you, but know this: at Group we are going to help you in every way that we can. You know our people, we will find a way. Good luck . . . my friends."

Niles Compton turned away quickly as he choked up.

Both men looked down at their new brevet ranks and then both looked up. It was Everett who broke the uneasy silence.

"I would give a year's pay to see old Henri's face when you tell him, Jack."

"Admiral, you know what?" he asked.

"What, General Collins?" he said with his smile growing.

"You can kiss this old ground-pounder's two-star ass."

EVENT GROUP COMPLEX
NELLIS AIR FORCE BASE, NEVADA

Matchstick was sitting beside Gus's bed. The old prospector was exhausted as his age was really starting to show. He was dozing as the small alien watched from his chair. The small feet dangled three feet off the ground as Matchstick reached out and took the old man's hand and lightly squeezed. Gus's eyes fluttered open and then closed, but in that brief moment he felt the presence of his small green friend. He relaxed, then slept more soundly.

Earlier, long before Matchstick had been introduced to the men at Camp David, Dr. Denise Gilliam and Virginia Pollock had sat the small being down and explained for the first time how tired Gus truly was. Matchstick had blinked several times in his fight to understand what it was they were telling him.

"You fix Gus, like you fix Mahjtic?"

Denise and the best medical men and women in the country had saved Matchstick from the growing fate of his race. His body had been overwhelmed by pollutants from his home planet, but with the perseverance of the medical staff they were able to control all of the infectious materials inside the green alien's body. They suspected they had saved his life from one of pain and death. They had no such hope of saving the old prospector. Gus was old beyond his years and was slowly letting go of this life in his own ornery way.

Virginia had kneeled beside Mahjtic and looked into the large, obsidian eyes.

"Gus is old and tired. This is the way of our race. The reward for being us is the chance to rest and sleep. We here at Group do not yet understand your belief system on your home world, but we sense . . ." She stopped and thought a moment, then corrected herself. "No, we believe that once you die, you are allowed to see and be with the ones that you loved in life. I believe that you and Gus will be together again. Right now he's just tired and old."

"Gus, die?" Mahjtic said as his eyes rapidly opened and closed, the eyelids sliding inward from the side of his head. "You cannot fix?"

"Gus has lived a long life," Denise offered as she started to choke up.

Matchstick had simply lowered his head, then wrapped one arm around Virginia's neck and one around the leg of Denise. That was when the two highly trained doctors broke down and cried. Matchstick and the two women had stayed that way for the longest time before they left the two friends alone. Matchstick was content to sit and watch Gus breathe contentedly in his sleep.

A light knock sounded on the door and Mahjtic eased the old man's hand from his own and hopped from the large chair. The Group had placed them inside the quarters they usually reserved for the president of the United States on his frequent visits to the Group. The small apartment was well appointed and Gus had complained to no end about the accommodation, but had finally relented. The small alien made his way to the door and pulled it open. He blinked several times as the light in the curving, circular, plastic-lined hallway struck his eyes. He saw Pete Golding and Charlie Ellenshaw standing there smiling. Charlie leaned into the darkened room and saw that Gus was fast asleep.

"Uh, we thought since you were introduced to the Overlord security council gathered at Camp David this afternoon, you may want to come down into the computer center to watch the president address the nation and the world," Pete whispered.

Charlie and Pete saw a concerned look cross the alien's features and then he tilted his head.

"From where?" Matchstick asked.

The two brilliant men were confused as Matchstick quickly stepped from the guest quarters and into the hallway. With one last look back at Gus he eased the door closed.

"We will watch in the—" Pete started to answer.

"Where . . . president speak?" he asked hurriedly.

"They haven't left Camp David; I imagine the speech will take place there," Pete finally answered.

If it were possible, Pete and Charlie would have sworn Matchstick's face drained of color.

"Any . . . broadcast . . . to . . . the . . . public . . . will . . . be . . . in . . . the . . . clear . . . not . . . like . . . the closed . . . communication . . . with . . . us. The Grays will . . . triangulate . . . and know . . . they have . . . been . . . discovered . . . they will . . . know . . . where . . . the president is!"

Suddenly Matchstick turned and ran for the two pneumatic elevator banks and waved Charlie and Pete forward while crying out.

"No, no, no, must stop, must stop, must stop!"

The two men watched as Mahjtic vanished into the elevator and then they both hurriedly followed.

GEORGETOWN, MARYLAND

Speaker of the House Giles Camden watched the president as he was being broadcast live from an undisclosed location. The senator's eyes studied the other men seated to the president's right and left, with the flags of their various nations behind them; centered in the middle was the blue flag of the United Nations. Camden had listened to the president's explanation concerning the Russian assault on Iran. He thought the man actually looked pleased that he had set up the Russians for an eventual takeover of that region. Another reason for the need to get this maniac out of office—he was losing control of everything from his military to the influence of the U.S. when it came to gathering new allies in the hectic Middle East.

Camden had excused his aides before the speech had started to allow him and Daniel Peachtree to sit alone. He was free to speak his mind now that his young aides were visibly absent. Peachtree, with his recent failure in the Hiram Vickers fiasco still vivid in not only his but Camden's minds, sat silent when the Speaker of the House again started his ranting about the president.

"And let me tell you one thing, if he thinks his entire military is backing him he is sorely mistaken. I didn't spend all those years in the senate not making friends myself! I have plenty of generals and admirals, people that are not happy with the unplanned, unfettered spending that's happening!"

"You still are not onboard with the president's plan for defending the planet, even though all these world leaders are? I mean hell, Mr. Speaker, most of them are as big a hawk as yourself. The new Chinese president is a known right-wing fanatic and he believes what his scientists and the president have outlined."

"Yeah?" Camden snapped his head around to look at the assistant director of Operations of the CIA. "And what about the report that emerged from your own boss at Langley that said the president had been instrumental in bringing that nut in China into power, after being a cohort in the previous chairman's assassination after the moon landings?"

"That is speculative at best. We have no proof of that. It may have been a military coup because the former chairman was not pleased with the money spent on going to the moon last year. That was why he was . . . well . . . removed."

On the screen the president was in the middle of explaining the events that had taken place in the desert sands of Arizona back in 2006. He had finally admitted to the world that the famous Roswell incident had really happened, and thanks to that episode they had the ability now to fight back.

And he was warning the world that a fight was indeed coming—and now he had the leadership of the most powerful nations on Earth backing him. Camden saw no way to stop the massive spending that was going on and the president knew that—that was why this very press conference was taking place.

Assistant Director Peachtree rolled his eyes at the Speaker's ranting. As he looked at the television screen he saw that the president had life-sized cutouts of a small Green, and a rather aggressive and very much taller Gray. He swallowed as he looked on. As for Camden, he scoffed at the likenesses of the aliens as the president explained the difference between the two races. Peachtree wanted desperately to get out of there and get out west to track down that bastard Hiram Vickers before he was caught and spilled his guts on what he and Camden knew. That was what was worrying him, not the president and his no-longer hidden and secret agenda.

"As of right now, we and the rest of the world are destined to go broke because these fools believe in fairy tales!" Camden bellowed.

As for Daniel Peachtree, he didn't think the man on television was bluffing. He was beginning to get a little frightened.

EVENT GROUP COMPLEX
NELLIS AIR FORCE BASE, NEVADA

Charlie Ellenshaw and Pete Golding were right behind Matchstick when he burst into the computer center. Europa had the president's address to the world on most of the large monitors that ringed the large room. They watched him run down the flight of stairs in the amphitheater-style arrangement and streak toward the weather-recon section. Mahjtic looked up at the computer-generated vision of the world and watched it intently. Most of the planet seemed calm to Pete's eyes as he and Charlie finally managed to catch up to the small alien.

"Hey, hey, what's the matter?" Pete asked as he finally managed to get some of his breath back after the long sprint down to the center. Many of the one hundred computer techs moved their eyes from the president on television to the commotion on the main floor.

"No, no, no, no," was all Matchstick said as his large eyes centered on the eastern portion of the United States.

It was Charlie Ellenshaw who understood first. He leaned over and spoke to Pete, who finally registered the relief he wanted after Matchstick had frightened him so.

"Matchstick, the president and the council are safe. No weather patterns that would indicate a wormhole are anywhere near the Washington area. Besides, their people and Niles have the information needed to detect a strike. They know what to look for."

Mahjtic ignored Pete as his eyes continued to scan the area of the East Coast. Finally the alien sat at Pete's desk and brought the Cray Supercomputer to life.

"Europa?" he said with his strange but now stronger voice.

"Good evening, Mahjtic, how can I help you today?" The computer's voice program still sounded like Marilyn Monroe after eight years.

Matchstick started to talk but in his excitement he couldn't get the words out fast enough. He turned and started hitting keys on Pete's computer at a blinding rate with his long, articulated fingers.

IS THERE AN ION READING WITHIN THREE HUNDRED MILES OF MARYLAND? he asked quickly by keyboard. The words started springing up on the monitor.

Pete and Charlie, along with many of the other techs, watched with curiosity.

"There has not been any sign or reading that would indicate electrical activity in the vicinity of Maryland since nine A.M. eastern standard time," Europa said.

Matchstick closed his eyes. Then he sprang to life again and started banging on the keyboard.

PLEASE, CAN YOU BACKTRACK AND SHOW ELECTRICAL ACTIVITY AT THAT TIME?

On the main viewing screen the scene switched from the president and his Overlord Council to that of a swirling weather pattern that had only lasted a short time and then had cleared up. The swirling pattern was light and vanished almost as quickly as it had formed.

"Now there, you see?" Charlie said. "That was no wormhole, Matchstick, it was a small pattern of rain clouds that wasn't enough to compete with the regular morning dew."

Matchstick turned and faced Charlie. "It formed . . . from almost . . . nothing," Mahjtic protested. "It is . . . possibly . . . a raid!"

"But Matchstick," Pete said as more technicians started to surround them because they had detected the fear in the alien's voice, "that brief weather cycle was not big enough for a wormhole. The ship transiting it would have had to have been far smaller than anything we have ever encountered, or any you have warned us about in your briefings."

Matchstick became angry and turned on Pete.

"The Grays . . . can come . . . through the wormhole in . . . capsules! You must . . . get the president and the . . . council out of . . . Camp David . . . now!"

"I don't understand what you're telling us," Pete said as Virginia Pollock entered the comp center after being alerted by security. She heard what the alien being was saying and waited for Charlie and Pete to explain.

"They are here. They may have . . . connected to the . . . communications coming . . . from Camp David during the . . . raid in . . . Iran. They . . . know about the . . . engine . . . and now . . . the president's . . . address . . . to the world . . . is being broadcast in the . . . clear. They know where the president . . . is and the power plant. They will move . . . on them and eliminate . . . the threat they pose." Matchstick's voice and speech pattern were clear and precise, but in his excitement certain words seemed to catch in his throat. He turned and stood up, looking again at the weather patterns the world over. His eyes widened as he pointed at the screen directing everyone's attention to the borders of Iran. "Look!"

They all turned and saw a huge storm starting to form over eastern Iran. As they all watched stunned, the space-based image showed the giant swirling pattern of a large wormhole starting to gather moisture and electron particles from the air.

"Pete, warn Niles at Camp David, get those men out of there. Tell them we suspect, as does Magic, that ground penetration by the enemy may have been achieved earlier in the day. And get a message out to the Chairman of the Joint Chiefs. Warn the Russians in Iran they are about to have company—a lot of it!" Virginia started by slapping Pete on the shoulder, "Go, go!"

On the large computer screen the wormhole over eastern Iran grew to tremendous proportions as red alarm lights started sounding throughout the complex.

CAMP DAVID
FREDERICK, MARYLAND

There was a line of vehicles waiting to leave and even more waiting to enter at the now camouflaged and sandbag-buttressed security entrance to Camp David. Jack and the newly promoted Captain Will Mendenhall stepped from the green government sedan and walked toward the car behind theirs. Carl Everett stepped from the backseat while his driver stayed behind the wheel.

"Damn, it's harder to get out of this place than it is to get in," Everett joked as he took in the new silver bars on Will's uniform. "It must be the shock of seeing Will weighed down by all that hardware."

Jack smiled and Mendenhall frowned.

"I don't think the Secret Service and these Marines care much that I was promoted to be a secretary for a new

two-star general," he quipped, then caught himself as he
was now addressing not only a two-star admiral, but also a
newly promoted two-star general. He relaxed when he realized that these temporary ranks would never change the way
these two men looked at life.

"I'm afraid we've been held up because the Secret Service and FBI have yet to deliver my new adjutant." Jack
looked at his watch. "Which should have been five minutes ago."

"With our luck old Henri probably stole their keys and
has already escaped," Everett said in all seriousness.

"My luck isn't that good," Jack said with a frown as he
looked around, wondering what was taking security so long
to deliver the Frenchman.

Jack was about to tease Will even more when every alarm
bell inside the Camp David compound started blaring with
intermittent and very loud warnings.

The Secret Service broke into the live broadcast of the president's address and ran to the podium, pushing and pulling
him and every member of the council out of the small room.
Marines formed a perimeter as the group was hustled out.

"What's going on?" the president demanded as they were
ruthlessly shoved into a tight formation as they neared the
back of the main building. The other leaders of the world
were just as shocked as their own security elements joined
the rush to get out as warning bells sounded everywhere.
The few members of the world press who had been invited
up to the press conference now were left standing with
mouths agape at the sudden action.

"We just received a coded warning from 'Magic' that an
attack is imminent on this compound!" Niles Compton said
as he joined the group of world leaders. They were now surrounded by fifty Marines in full battle BDUs. "The same
warning is going out to the technical team in Iran. It looks
like a giant wormhole is forming over the eastern section—
they're going to be hit. It must have been the last test and
our own communications that led the Grays to the univer-

sity. Your broadcast was like leaving a bread-crumb trail for the enemy to find *us* and *them*."

"The power plant, that's more important than us. Can we get it out of Iran in time, Niles?" the president asked as they were being hustled toward a reinforced bunker a hundred yards from the main house. They heard the scream of F-15s as they streaked low over the densely forested area. Soon the thumping of rotors broke through the noise of the warning alarms and the jet noise as more Marines were brought into the compound.

"We've got the warning out to the Russian and Iranian forces. Luckily the Revolutionary Guard detachment was still in the area and is moving on the university to assist," Niles answered as they reached the steel door of the shelter. "The power plant had already been crated and our people have begun to move it out of the city, but we don't know if it's in time."

A loud explosion rocked the area and then they all heard screams as the early night was now alight with flares. Large shadows ran through the trees, and then bright streaks of laser light pulsated out toward the Marine detachment. Several men were caught before they could react and were sliced in two. The others started to return fire at the unseen Grays, but they were well hidden inside the tree line. The president and the Overlord Council were hustled into the bunker, followed by a full squad of heavily armed Marines and Secret Service personnel. Niles Compton looked back as the door was closed. He prayed that Jack, Carl, and Will Mendenhall had cleared the Camp David compound in time.

Jack hit the ground and Everett and Mendenhall fell on top of him. The world came alive with flashes of light as an unseen enemy opened up from thick surrounding trees that obscured the Marines' return fire. He heard an explosion overhead and they all managed to look up in time to see a Marine Corp Black Hawk start spinning into the tree line, where it hit and burst open, killing all inside. Three Marines in battle fatigues ran by them and were immediately struck down by bright flashes of light. Jack winced as a headless torso struck the ground next to him.

"Come on, we're going to get cut to pieces if we stay here!" He reached for a fallen M-4, the shortened version of the venerable M-16. He also reached for the nine-millimeter Beretta that was still holstered in the Marine's web belt and tossed it to Everett.

The three men ran to a defensive position being set up by the remaining Marine detachment at the front gate.

As soon as Will Mendenhall slid to a stop beside Jack and Carl he found another M-4 lying on the ground, just out of reach of a dead lance corporal a foot away. Will reached for it, then shielded his eyes as flares burst in every direction.

"I think the war may have started," he said as he tried in vain to find a target. He ducked behind Collins as three streaks of laser light reached out toward them. They struck a tree and burned through the thick trunk. It started to fall over as several Marines broke their cover and ran to a new position.

As Collins raised his head he saw the outline of one of the Grays highlighted by a floating overhead flare. He took quick aim at the distant target and fired off three rounds. He watched the tall, angular Gray stumble and fall to the ground.

"Good shot, Jack," Carl said as he too fired off his own M-4. Marines from every direction started firing as they acquired targets.

The men from the Event Group knew from their experience in Arizona, from autopsies, and from Gus Tilley's debriefing that same year, that the Grays would be notoriously hard to kill because of their having two hearts. Everett remembered the same thing.

"Aim for the heads!" he shouted out to the Marines around them.

The volume of fire escalated to a loud din as the Marine detachment started to get their bearings.

Will saw something rushing at them; he kneeled and fired a long burst into the dark. He saw as well as heard the

tracer rounds as they struck the Gray. Its forward momentum brought the alien over the fallen tree they were behind
and struck Will and they both hit the dirt. In an instant the
Gray was on him, jabbering and screaming as bluish blood
pulsed into Mendenhall's face. Everett jumped onto its
back and fired four rounds from the Beretta into the creature's head. It rolled off and Carl assisted Mendenhall to
his feet.

"Just like old times out at Tilley's place, huh, Captain?"
Everett said over the noise of bursting grenades and gunfire.

Before Will could comment an Apache AH-64 Longbow
attack chopper streaked low over the trees and the men
heard the screech of missiles being launched into the woods
surrounding the compound.

"This is a major strike element—if Apaches are firing
directly next to the compound this has to be an assault on
the men inside. They're serious." Jack rose up from the
ground and chanced a look around. He saw Grays coming
in from the surrounding woods. He counted at least twenty
before a hail of laser shot forced him to duck. "Fellas, we're
about to get major company."

"Damn it, Jack, I've got about five rounds left in this
thing," Everett cried out but immediately rose and fired at
the line of tall Grays coming at them. "Make that none."
Carl hit the dirt beside Will and Jack. "Well, I got two of
those ugly bastards!" he said as he ejected the magazine.

Collins managed to rise and watch as the Grays advanced. Suddenly a loud explosion rocked the ground beneath them and they were tossed against the underside of the
green sedan. As his vision cleared he looked back and saw
a tall column of smoke rising from the direction of the living quarters of Camp David. Jack grimaced as he started
fearing the worst.

"What we've got here sure as hell looks like a murder
raid, General," Everett said as he too examined the Grays as
they came out of the tree line. They held what looked like
long shafts. He turned and looked at their rear and his heart
froze. Ten of the Grays had managed to work their way

behind them and what was left of the Marine detail. He saw young men being mowed down by weaponry he had only seen in movies.

Jack yelled in pain as one brief shaft of light grazed his shoulder with the full wattage of the laser round striking the dirt next to him, sending up chunks of bright red clay.

"Gentlemen, I think it's time to get the hell out of Dodge."

Jack stood with Everett and Mendenhall right behind. Just as fast they were frozen in solid bright light coming from the opposite direction.

"Collins, hit the dirt!" came a voice amplified over a bullhorn.

The three men didn't need prompting and did as ordered without much thought. Before their ragged breathing could stir up dust, a horrid sound started. It was a shrill whining and then all hell broke loose. Jack raised his head slightly and looked from under the rear of the car. He saw Grays being torn to bits. The brutes were being mowed down by something Jack now recognized as a five-barreled Gatling gun. He looked behind and saw over a hundred Marines making their way toward them. Before he knew it the noise had stopped and the ringing in his ears began. Soon arms and hands were lifting him to his feet.

Jack, Carl, and Mendenhall were stunned to see one particular man among the Marines. He had a smoking M-4 assault rifle in his hands and a set of handcuffs dangling from his right wrist. Henri Farbeaux looked around him as if he were in shock. He watched as Marines continued to shoot some of the Grays as they struggled to get to dropped weapons, but soon even that noise fell silent. Farbeaux shook his head as he approached.

"Makes you appreciate a human enemy, does it not?" Henri said as he handed off the empty M-4 to a passing Marine. "I don't suppose you have a key for this, do you?" Henri held up the dangling handcuff. "I think my days of hiding and running are over."

Will Mendenhall was grateful to see the Frenchman, but Jack and Carl only looked at him in amazement. Then at once both men came to the realization of what really just happened.

"Come on," Jack said. "Niles and the president are back there!"

Farbeaux watched the men start running back up the road without a second glance at him. He looked at the dangling cuff, then cursed and followed his new allies.

Around them, the remaining Marines started checking the dead Grays, with several of the toughened veterans getting ill when examining the alien species up close. There had been several shots ringing out in the growing night as Grays were dispatched by very angry soldiers and state police. Soon officers with cooler heads stopped the executions and they began the grim task of gathering dead and wounded from both sides.

Over 2.78 billion sets of eyes had watched live on television as the leaders of the most powerful nations on earth had been hustled off the podium at Camp David. The camera was left on and the billions of citizens of the world were left looking at an empty stage with shouts, screams, and gunfire erupting through their speakers. Men, women, and children were left astounded, and all were in the dark as to what was happening at the small American villa in the Maryland woods.

Jack, Carl, Will, and Henri all ran toward the rear of the devastated compound. Secret Service, state police, FBI, and Marines were running everywhere with weapons at the ready. No less than a platoon-sized element of Marines had surrounded the rear of the house and grounds. Many Marines and agents from every branch of service lay dead or dying from the assault of the Grays, over a hundred of which had been cut down and were lying dead on the ground; some even in the trees.

"Oh, God," Will Mendenhall said when he saw fifty or so men trying desperately to clear the entranceway to an underground bunker.

Men were tossing chunks of concrete left, right, and over their shoulders. Finally reinforcements started to arrive by helicopter and by road. All concern for security had gone out the window as even the servants stationed at Camp David were joining in the efforts to free whoever was trapped below in the bunker. Sirens blared and large Marine Corps helicopters circled above as they cast bright lights on the surreal scene below. Off to the left Jack and the others saw the president's helicopter, Marine One, on its side and burning. Apache Longbow helicopters were now orbiting in force. A lone Gray rose from the ground and charged at the rescue workers. Before Jack could relax two FBI agents spun and fired at the alien, but its momentum carried it forward until it struck the workers. Three Marines immediately dispatched the enemy, then several others struck at it with anything they could get their hands on.

Jack grabbed a Marine sergeant as he trotted by, making the kid almost fall to the ground.

"Where's the goddamn president?" he shouted over the din.

All the boy could do was turn his head toward the bunker. Jack released the kid and looked on at the continuing efforts to free all inside. Even Farbeaux was stunned at what he was seeing. Relief flooded their features as they saw the prime minister of Great Britain and then the Chinese president as they were assisted from what now looked like a grave. The Chinese leader looked as if his arm was broken and the prime minister was cut but unharmed. He was desperately pointing back toward the collapsed bunker and insisting that he be allowed to help the rest of the council.

Jack felt his body deflate as a man was brought out, his head and left leg missing. Jack looked around, fearing what was coming next. He glanced at Will Mendenhall and his heart ached for the young captain. Will was so angry that a single tear coursed down his face.

Collins was soon tapped on the shoulder and he turned to see the chairman of the Joint Chiefs. He was ragged looking, with his uniform jacket ripped and his face bloodied. He tossed away an old M-16 and as it clattered to the ground he looked at the four men around him. He flinched when the roof of the main house collapsed and a shower of burning embers lit the night around them. The rescue workers were removing many of the house staff covered in sheets or curtains, anything they could find.

"How in the hell did they get so close without us knowing about it?" Jack asked angrily.

"As I'm not supposed to know about you people out in the desert, all I can say is that we were warned at the last second by that asset out there, *Magic*. If we hadn't been warned none of us would have made it out alive." General Caulfield wiped blood from his broken nose.

"But how did they get so close, goddamn it?" Jack insisted, as his eyes probed the site for Niles Compton.

"We think they may have arrived early this morning. It was purely a ground assault, which was why that damn wormhole wasn't large like the others."

Finally it was Everett who called out. "Niles!" All to a man they ran forward. Niles was covered in blood as he was helped from the rubble. His right hand was held over a large gash in his head that completely covered his eye. Will tore off part of his shirt and applied pressure to the wound. Jack and Carl and even Henri assisted the director over several of the fallen Grays. Will even managed to kick one of the dead beings in the head with brutal force. Suddenly Niles, acting delirious, turned and wanted to return to the smoking hole in the ground.

"The president—we have to get to him!" he cried as he struggled against the restraining arms.

"There he is," General Caulfield said as he rushed forward.

Niles stilled his protests when he saw his best friend being carried out by five filthy Marines. His arms were hanging loose and as the men watched, doctors ran toward him. Jack's heart froze as he watched the president of the United States laid on the ground. Caulfield turned and faced the men.

"He's out cold, has a massive gash on his head, and he may lose an arm—it's crushed bad. God, what are we . . ." The general looked up and grabbed the first Secret Service agent he could find. "Get the word out: the vice president needs to return ASAP to the capital."

Niles collapsed into the arms of his men. The president was hurriedly rushed to a waiting Marine Black Hawk and was immediately lifted out, along with the Chinese president.

Caulfield again grabbed for a man. This one was a Marine medic who had been working on the president.

"Is he going to make it?" he shouted.

The young medic shook his head. "He's bad, real bad." The boy ran off to assist in the treatment of other wounded people.

Jack assisted the director to the ground and saw that Niles's right side had taken a devastating beating. He knew the man was going to at least lose his right eye, and his left arm had to be shattered.

"General, you had better get to the vice president soon. This may not be over."

"Look, we passed the information along, but—oh, hell, I would want to know if I were you," Caulfield started to tell Jack, "because I know you have people in theater, Magic also relayed that there may be a massive wormhole forming over Iran."

Jack stopped briefly as his thoughts went out to Sarah and Ryan. Then he just nodded his head once at the chairman and then pushed Everett, Mendenhall, and Henri forward.

The men started to assist the Marines, Secret Service agents, and firemen helping the survivors. Henri started to follow but a long-fingered hand wrapped around his ankle, stopping him. The others stopped and turned and saw that a surviving Gray had stopped the Frenchman. The being was uttering something Henri couldn't understand. With a quick look at Jack and the others the former special operations man for the French army leaned down and pulled the long, spotted, and sickly fingers from around his ankle. He squatted over and stared at the Gray for a few seconds.

Eyes much smaller than Matchstick's obsidian ones gazed up at Henri with their yellow tint, the mouth working enough that he could see the creature's small, clear teeth. The Gray had three bullet wounds to the chest and abdomen. The clothing it wore was jet black in color, highlighted with purplish hues.

"Let me be the first to welcome your kind to Earth," Henri said as the others watched with interest. Even General Caulfield was interested in what the Frenchman was up to.

Henri Farbeaux slowly stood up and, with the eyes of an enraged mercenary, raised his right foot and brought it down on the Gray's neck, easily snapping the strong spine.

They all realized at that moment just what kind of war was being brought to Earth's doorstep.

7

Before Vice President Sol Stevens knew what was happening, ten Secret Service agents and as many of San Francisco's finest had whisked him out the back doors of the new terminal building he was dedicating. He was roughly shoved into the back of an SFPD SWAT van and moved to the east end of the airport. He was held in place by SWAT team members who hadn't issued one word to explain the situation.

The van soon stopped and the rear doors opened and three men climbed in beside him. One of these men was his chief of staff, who was visibly shaken to a point that he looked like he was going to be sick.

"What in God's name is going on, Stanley?" Stevens asked as the door was closed. The van once more sped off, followed by ten police cars and as many motorcycles with sirens wailing and lights flashing.

Stanley Whalen had been with the VP since he was twenty-two and was thrilled when the president had chosen his man after the former vice president was ousted before the last election. Now he wasn't so sure it had been a good thing. He choked out something that was incomprehensible. It was the second man who answered for him when the assistant broke down.

"Sir, the president is close to death at this moment. Camp David was hit with a strike team as yet unidentified."

"Who in the hell are you?" Stevens asked, straining to hear over the wailing sirens.

"I'm Frank Deveroux, special agent in charge of the San Francisco FBI field office."

"Who hit Camp David?"

"That has not yet been confirmed, but the president is in surgery at this very moment. The German president is dead, the Russian president won't make it, and the other members of the summit are bad off. Most of the president's staff is dead. We have to get you to Oakland and a secure location ASAP. The president is unable to perform the duties of his office. Do you understand what I am saying, sir?"

Vice President Stevens sat heavily against the side of the large, black van as the eyes of every man inside looked toward him.

The VP looked into the agent's face. "Was it . . ." He looked at the SWAT members guarding him, but thought he didn't care about security, especially since the president was supposed to have explained to the world what was really happening. "The Grays?"

The agent nodded his head just once. "Right now we have an Air Force Pave Low waiting to take you to the Presidio. We have word out and the airport is going to close down immediately."

The vice president, along with most citizens of the planet, had not fully understood the nightmare scenario the president had tried to explain to them. Now it hit home that this was not some fictional story or new game that just came on the market—this was going to be a war, one that he prayed they had prepared for.

Ten minutes later, with ten F-15 Eagle fighters flying overhead for protection, the Air Force MH-53J Pave Low III

helicopter slowly lifted free of the tarmac as aircraft of
every kind was being cleared from the skies. The giant five-
bladed rotors crushed the air around it as it rose into the sky,
flanked by two Apache Longbow attack helicopters. The
helicopter dipped its nose and fought its way into the sky just
out over the bay.

Flight leader Sam Ellington, better known as "Viper," led
his flight of ten F-15s as they supplied combat air cover for
the Pave Low. He was flying low in, dangerously close to
the commercial flights inbound to San Francisco, frightening more than one pilot until they screamed bloody murder to San Francisco control at the dangerous conditions.

"Hercules flight, we have an intermittent contact bearing
three-five-seven degrees heading your way. Flight speed
estimated at four-seven hundred kilometers per hour. Suspected contact is confirmed hostile. You are free to engage.
Say again, you are weapons free," came the call from the
Naval Air Station in Oakland. "We have support coming
in from USS *George Washington,* six Hornets on your
six, over."

The only answer from the Air Force flight leader was two
clicks on his radio. He was thinking that the Air Force
would not need support from the Navy on this one.

"Air Force Pave Low, hit the deck and scatter to dry feet,
over."

The giant helicopter dropped low and when only ten feet
from the choppy bay waters leveled out and made a run
for land.

The small saucer was almost invisible as it came in from
the sea. It flew beneath the Golden Gate Bridge and swooped
low over the waters of the bay. It capsized over twenty sail-
ing vessels out for the beautiful evening as its V-shaped vortex shattered the waters around them. The flight of fighters
turned to meet the incoming threat as it slowed to under
Mach speed for its attack run. Flight knew immediately
that the small craft was coming for the man they were protecting.

"Hercules flight, engage!" he ordered. The F-15s broke and peeled off in twos to meet the incoming threat. As the giant Pave Low made for the docks near Fisherman's Wharf, the fighters started launching long range AIM-120 AMRAAM radar-guided missiles at the small attacker. The saucer jigged and then went low, confusing the seeker heads of the advanced missiles with its speed and maneuvering. The missiles struck water and several large container ships by accident. The evening sky was illuminated as an oil tanker exploded with a blinding flash. The saucer rose before a second volley of missiles could leave the rails.

The Pave Low never stood a chance as the saucer easily sidestepped the protection of the fighters as it made its attack run. The initial laser flash missed the helicopter and slammed into the sea with a loud hissing noise, but then the beam was adjusted until it contacted the aluminum housing of the giant Air Force bird. It sliced through the tail boom and the Pave Low spiraled into the sea, to break apart in the water.

As the small saucer, measuring no more than fifty feet at its widest point, turned nose up, five AIM-9 Sidewinder missiles struck its rear section, pushing it down into the sea. The saucer, now smoking, rose once again. Five more missiles struck and it wobbled, then briefly made for higher altitude. But its momentum ceased and the saucer crashed into a very crowded Fisherman's Wharf and exploded, killing well over a thousand people.

The second assassination inside the American chain of command had taken place, and the might of the U.S. Air Force had been powerless to stop it.

UNIVERSITY OF APPLIED SCIENCE AND TECHNOLOGY BIRJAND, IRAN

Sarah watched as the massive alien power plant was lifted free of the science building, through the giant skylight that had been built when it first arrived five years before. The circular engine was taxing the crane used to lift it. The cables strained and the Russian engineers cringed every time the wind gusted to fifty plus miles per hour. Sarah glanced at the sky and then toward the plastic shrink-wrapped engine as it finally settled on the bed of the Iranian army's largest transport. As she allowed her nerves to settle she felt the first drops of cold rain strike her face.

Jason Ryan and Mossad agent Anya Korvesky approached. Anya had now been officially cleared by the president and the Russian authorities to be officially on location. The Israeli prime minister, as well as Rouhani of Iran, had been thoroughly briefed on the new alliance of nations and were fully onboard. Egypt, Syria, Afghanistan, and India were not.

"I don't care for the looks of this. The Russian military meteorologists said this formation of clouds has sprung up from nowhere." Sarah felt the electricity in the air. She used her hand to brush the hair on her head back into place.

"I've never seen anything like this in this region. There are storms over the Caspian Sea quite often, but never anything that resembles a hurricane," Anya volunteered.

They turned toward the sky and braved the unusually cold rain drops to see the clouds as they formed and then were snatched away, where they joined others in a massive swirling pattern that reminded Ryan of a vortex of draining water. They could see very clear sky at the exact center of the cloud formation. Small particles of hail started to fall.

"Jason, remember the Magic briefing about the formation of wormholes?" Sarah asked.

"You don't think this—"

"Yes, that's what I think. It's a wormhole."

At that exact moment sirens sounded and Russian and Iranian military personnel started to scramble around the university. Sarah was shocked to see over a hundred Iranian Zulfiqar tanks, the new armor built by Iran to combat the forces of the West, coming through the main gate of the university. What was even stranger was the fact the 106th Guards Division of the Russian army was riding on the tops of the tanks alongside the Iranian crewmen. They screamed left, right, and were in moments totally surrounding the many science buildings. Iranian infantry from the very units that had been assigned to attack them earlier that day were now on guard and ready to defend the power plant at all costs.

"Oh, shit, this isn't good," Ryan shouted into the increasing strength of the storm.

"You're not saying the Iranians have another operating engine, are you?" Anya asked. Ryan pushed her toward the large transport, where riggers were making fast the power plant to the bed of the giant tractor trailer.

"No," he shouted at Anya as they ran, "not exactly the Iranians. As you can see, they're on our side."

They stopped at a grouping of soldiers who would be transporting the power plant to the docks for sea transport across the Caspian. The commander of the 106th Guards Division was shouting orders to not only his subordinates but to the new Iranian allies as well. He saw the two Americans and then grabbed Sarah by the collar, making Ryan become defensive until he saw he was giving orders.

"Get to the transports and get the hell out of here. We have something coming through this storm. Space-based imagery is showing a massive power surge connected with this activity. I'm afraid your president's scenario is not just prophecy."

Sarah, Ryan, and Anya all looked at the strengthening storm that had come out of nowhere. The swirling clouds had intensified and now there were bright streaks of blue, purple, and yellow lights shooting out like lightning. Several of these actually burst free and struck some of the surrounding buildings.

"Go get this thing to safety. We will do what we can!" the general shouted, pushing Sarah away. He and his staff ran to take control of his ground forces.

The three ran for the line of trucks that were waiting. The semi-tractor trailer with its heavy burden wasn't even waiting for the Russian riggers and engineers to clear the flatbed as the driver, with seventeen Russian commandos riding on the back, shot the large vehicle forward. Ryan took the driver's seat of an old university-owned car that happened to be a 1978 Ford LTD, a leftover from the days of the shah. He threw the heavy touring vehicle into gear as soon as Anya and Sarah were safely inside. They all heard the hail, which had grown in size, start pummeling the vehicle just as they fell in line inside the large convoy of trucks, cars, and armored personnel carriers assigned to the transport of the engine the hundred miles to the sea.

Sarah leaned her head into the windshield as the hail cracked the glass, and heard a sound that could only emanate from a nightmare. The bass throng of noise shook the car and as she placed her hands over her ears she saw that the Russian and Iranian ground forces were hitting the wet ground around them as the noise literally threw them to the earth. The ungodly sound seemed to intensify as they moved toward the main gate.

The first two saucers through were one hundred feet in diameter and they separated as soon as they cleared the swirling vortex of moisture. They went in opposite directions trailing moisture, lightning, and hail in their wakes. Then another two of the same-size saucers entered Iranian airspace and they also spread out high and low over the university.

The world stopped working momentarily as a bright and blinding flash illuminated the air around the university as the largest saucer came through the eye of the storm, taking the cloud formation down with it. Its speed actually burst the eardrums of over fifty of the closest men as it slammed into the largest science building. The structure pancaked as the violence of the collision broke the earth three hundred feet around the building's foundation. Earth, water, and men were thrown two hundred feet into the rain-swept sky as the giant saucer came to rest. All inside the five-story building had to have been crushed to death. Electrostatic lightning shot from the the five-hundred-foot-diameter saucer. Its roundness was almost beautiful to behold as it settled in the rubble of the science building. Steam jets burst through the air as its skin was cooled by the falling rain and hail.

Anya ventured a look out of the now cracked and broken rear window of the LTD. "My God!"

Sarah turned in her seat as the Ford sedan shot through the front gates of the university. She saw the Iranian tanks open fire on the downed saucer, and then to her amazement Russian commandos rushed forward to engage the enemy. Her eyes widened in fear when she saw one of the smaller saucers streak low over the remaining buildings and start to shoot the very same laser systems she knew they had recovered in South America. Blue light reached out and cut the new tanks into pieces. Explosions rocked the grounds. Russian handheld missiles left their launch tubes and small arms tried desperately to fire on the smaller saucer. Sarah couldn't take it all in as she saw the large saucer open a fifty-foot hatchway, and she choked up when she saw the dark images of hundreds of Grays as they ran down a ramp and started their assault on the facility. Russian soldiers were very brave as they ran to engage the enemy.

"It's going to be a massacre," Anya shouted as ten more of the Iranian tanks exploded. She saw streaks of armor-piercing rounds strike the larger saucer and she was seeing damage as large chunks of metal were thrown forth into the dwindling storm. Explosion after explosion rocked the car as they watched helplessly as the Gray attackers over-whelmed the small force of Iranian and Russian troops, but they were taking a healthy host of attackers with them. Anya and Sarah saw Grays falling by the tens and twenties as Russian marksmen and missiles found their marks.

Ryan was mentally willing the transports to move faster as a new sound entered the din of the attack. Russian MiG-31s screeched across the sky and then climbed toward the fast-disappearing storm clouds. Missiles and ground-penetrating bombs struck the large saucer but Sarah saw they were doing nothing but denting the large machine. Somehow the saucer was starting to generate a force field that adhered to its bright metal skin. Still, it took damage.

She realized this was a suicide attack and quickly surmised this craft was never meant to lift off again.

Sarah turned in the front seat and looked at Ryan.

"You don't have to say it, I'm scared as hell myself. I don't care what weaponry we've come up with in the past five years, I don't think we can stop something like this." Ryan blared his horn for the armored transport ahead of him to close the gap between him and the transport ahead.

All Sarah could do was look at the tarp-covered alien power plant on the flatbed ahead of them in the column, and pray that the little man they knew as Matchstick knew what he was doing with the plan designated Overlord.

GEORGETOWN, MARYLAND

Speaker of the House Giles Camden watched the news footage being split between Camp David and Iran. The scroll at the bottom of the large screen was mentioning disjointed attacks in San Francisco, Beijing, and Cologne, Germany. Specifics thus far were only speculative on the reasoning for these strikes.

Camden accepted the drink from Daniel Peachtree, who was anxious to leave the Speaker's house and get back to Langley, as he knew the director was probably reeling after news of the Camp David strike had become more specific. His cell phone was now turned off as he waited for his new lord and master to set him free. As it was, Camden didn't seem to be in a hurry as the smallish, portly man sipped his drink while shaking his head.

The ornate study was starting to fill with assistants and interns from the Speaker's offices, and many were in shock at what was happening here and around the world.

"Okay, we need a little damage control here, ladies and gentlemen; after all, it was me who has been decrying this military spending of the president's and now it seems because of well-kept secrets from our nation's past it very well seems justified. You need to come up with a quick course change to minimize the damage."

"Don't you think the president should have brought you in on this, to make spending these billions upon billions of dollars more acceptable to the nation, and yourself?" Peachtree offered, not really caring to air his opinion inside a room full of Camden's people.

Camden sniffed loudly and then held his empty glass out to be refilled, which an aide promptly did.

"Not when one considers how much that man hates my guts. Hates my state, hates my budget crunching—when it's not my party in power, of course. But hate nonetheless."

On the television screen the view of the Iranian situation went from split screen to full as it showed the downed saucer that had completely obliterated the large building on which it rested. It was smoking and had finally been smashed by the remaining tanks of the Iranian army. Camden watched as Russian soldiers rushed from spot to spot, trying to dispatch areas of resistance. Gray bodies lay everywhere and Camden grimaced when a news camera came close to one and he saw in detail what they were fighting. The dead yellow-ringed eyes stared off into nothingness, and the sickly gray skin that was exposed underneath the strange-looking suit they wore gave the Speaker a small, cold chill.

"It seems the Russians and the Iranians dispatched the attackers soundly." Lyle Morgan, the Speaker's chief of staff, accepted a drink as he watched the screen. "They seemed to have destroyed the large saucer quite quickly and efficiently, if you ask me."

"They're saying it wouldn't have been so easy if those four smaller saucers had stayed on station, but they left in a hurry for some reason. Now we hear that the large saucer was nothing more than a transport of some sort not designed for sustained attack. It had thick armor, but no electronic shielding. It just housed attacking troops. So, we may not know as much as our new Russian allies think," Camden said.

The sliding doors opened and the Speaker's housekeeper came in and whispered to Daniel Peachtree. The CIA assistant director handed her his glass of whiskey and then nodded his thanks.

"I have to leave, something big is coming down and—"

Peachtree was cut off as five Maryland state troopers burst into the study, at least ten Secret Service agents along with them. The staff was pushed aside and one of the dark-clothed agents went straight to Camden. With the assistance of two of the troopers he lifted the Speaker of the House from his large chair.

"What are you doing? What is the meaning of this?" Camden insisted.

Lyle Morgan tried to stop the men from handling his boss in such a rough manner. He was pushed to the carpeted floor and two agents placed their nine millimeters close to his head. Morgan froze.

"Do not interfere, sir," one of the agents said.

Peachtree was in shock as he first thought that the authorities had caught up to Hiram Vickers and the little weasel had spilled his guts.

"Gentlemen, I'm Assistant Director Peachtree, CIA. May ask what is happening?" he ventured, terrified he would be placed into handcuffs soon.

One of the agents holstered his weapon and then nodded to the state troopers that they could ease up on the Speaker's staff of frightened men and women. His chief of staff was lifted from the carpet as the security detail calmed a bit.

"Apologies, Mr. Speaker, POTUS is down and the vice president was just killed in San Francisco. For the time being we are here to transport you to Fort Meyer, where we can properly secure you. Your staff will be sent for."

"The president is dead?" Camden asked as he was moved to the doors. "The vice president also?"

"We don't know the details, sir, but we do know that under the Constitution we are obliged to get you to safety."

Camden was in shock at the change in luck. He realized

after a moment's hesitation that he was in a direct line of succession to the most powerful position in the world—the presidency of the United States.

CAMP DAVID
FREDERICK, MARYLAND

It had been three hours since the president had been flown out to Walter Reed hospital. Jack, Carl, Will, and Henri Farbeaux were covered in dirt, sweat, and gore as they watched the last of the world Security Council being airlifted out. Jack took a deep breath and walked toward the last remaining ambulance. He saw paramedics still working on slowing the bleeding of his friend and mentor, Dr. Niles Compton. Will Mendenhall placed a hand on Collins's shoulder. Will finally turned away as Carl and General Caulfield approached. They watched as Niles tried to sit up on the gurney. Two medics yelled at him that he could not move. Niles struggled for a few more moments and then settled. Jack's eyes never left the director.

"General," Caulfield said, trying to get Jack to look away from the scene. "We have some updates."

Collins swallowed as he feared the worst from Caulfield's tone. He hated the title of his new rank because it made him feel that much more powerless in light of what was happening. He turned to face the chairman of the Joint Chiefs. The man had his nose bandaged and his cuts tended to. He looked tired and haggard in his ripped uniform. Collins nodded his head that he should start with the bad news he knew was coming.

"To start, from what we know in Iran, your people are safe. The power plant made it out just as the attack began. Russian forces took heavy losses and the Iranian armor division has just about ceased to exist. We have more people on the ground now, but they were hit hard."

"One thing I've learned as well as you, General, is the fact that you always deliver the good news first." Jack waited for the other shoe to fall.

"The military way, huh?" Caulfield looked from Collins to Carl, then the Frenchman as he joined them.

Will Mendenhall had eased closer to the ambulance to try and let the director of the Event Group know that he was near. He swiped at his face, angry at himself for being so emotional.

"The vice president is dead. His helicopter was shot out of the sky over San Francisco Bay this evening, moments after the attack here."

"Any word on the president's condition?" Everett asked as he used a towel to wipe his face.

"It doesn't look good at this point. As of right now they placed him in a medically induced coma, whatever the hell that means. His injuries are extensive, I'm afraid. The Chinese president died in the air. A heart attack, of all things."

"What a fucking mess," Everett said as he angrily tossed away the filthy towel.

"That, my friend, is the understatement of the year," Caulfield said. Jack knew immediately that the other shoe would now come down as assuredly as Henri's foot on the alien's neck had.

"What is it?" Collins ventured.

"The line of ascension for the presidency goes to the Speaker of the House."

Collins felt his stomach roll as he angrily turned away. Henri tried to follow what was being said beneath the actual words. He stepped closer to the men.

"Besides the insanity that comes with all politicos, may I ask the significance of this action?"

"Henri, you study history, and I assume you're well versed in the classics. What does the name Cardinal Richelieu mean to you as a Frenchman?" Carl walked past and joined Jack.

Henri looked taken back. The cardinal was a scoundrel of the first order in Dumas's *The Three Musketeers*. "This man, this speaker of the house is a—"

"He's no friend to the president, or to us," Everett finished.

"What he's saying, Colonel, is that this man Camden will most assuredly cause problems for Operation Overlord—our only chance at winning this thing," Caulfield said.

Jack shook his head, angry that his role in Overlord was being kept from him because of the dangers he and the others faced in being captured by an enemy that, as of that moment, looked unstoppable.

Will Mendenhall ran toward them.

"Colonel—I mean, General, Doc Compton wants to see us." He looked at Henri. "All of us."

Collins and the four others rushed to the ambulance, where the two medics were angrily holding the rear doors open.

"Look, make it fast, this man has serious blood loss and he's lost his right eye. His left arm is going to follow and then his life, if we don't get him—"

The EMT was pushed aside so the four men could gather around the back of the ambulance. Jack had to push Niles back down when he tried to sit up.

"Easy there, we can hear you, Niles."

Compton seemed to relax and then patted Jack's restraining hand as he settled.

Will momentarily turned away when he saw the white blood-soaked gauze covering Compton's face. The damaged arm was placed inside a clear plastic cast and the director's white shirt had been ripped open to expose several large gashes to his chest.

"Get to . . . your . . . new stations . . . imperative . . . imperative." He was running low on steam. "Overlord . . . must . . ." Niles coughed up blood.

"Goddamn it, we have to get this man to the front gate, we have air transport standing by there," the medic insisted. Jack gave the man a withering look until he lowered his eyes, and then turned back to his director.

"Jack . . . Jack?"

"I'm here, Niles."

"Get word . . . to Virginia . . . get out . . . here . . . and . . . take my . . . place . . . on the . . . council."

"I will before I leave for Hawaii, I promise." Jack watched Niles trying to find his glasses on his head. Jack knew the man's glasses were long gone and felt so bad that he choked back his anger and sorrow.

"Jack . . . you . . . don't understand . . . this isn't right . . ." Niles's voice became a whisper. "General Caulfield?"

Maxwell Caulfield stepped closer so he could hear. "I'm here, Doctor."

"You two . . . tell Virginia . . . something is wrong."

"What do you mean, Niles?" Collins glanced at Caulfield, who shrugged his shoulders. He didn't understand the comment either.

"Matchstick . . . Matchstick . . . is not telling us something. It may not . . . matter in the end . . . but he knows something that . . . he's kept from us."

Jack felt the blood rush from his face. But . . . "I'm not following."

"He . . . knows . . . he . . . knows . . . why.   He . . . lied to us . . . The Grays aren't here . . . for the planet, or resources . . . they . . ."

Niles passed out. Jack and the others were roughly pushed aside by the attendants and the doors closed.

"Sorry, he's got to go," the man said as he rushed to the front of the ambulance. It screamed off toward the distant front gates of Camp David.

"What in the hell did that mean?" Everett asked.

Collins waited until a Black Hawk went by overhead as he turned to Caulfield. "I have a call to make, General. Can I get to a secure phone somewhere?"

"Use my car, there's a secure phone there with a scrambler." Caulfield removed his coat and took another from his aide. "Someday you people have to tell me just what in the hell you do for the government. The president told me never to ask, but I would really like to know."

Everett watched Jack run toward the parking area with

the general's aide close at his heels, then turned to Caulfield.

"No you don't, sir, you really don't."

Will Mendenhall sat on a small outcropping of stone and watched as the FBI and Marines rounded up three of the Gray aliens and bound them hand and foot to each other. The beasts hissed and spat until several of the soldiers placed black hoods over their heads. Even then the Grays fought to free themselves by kicking out with their nylon-bound legs. Will wondered just what was behind this attack, as it hadn't matched up with anything the Event Group had come to expect from the briefings that Matchstick had given over the past eight years. He shook his head and thought about not only the president but about his boss, Niles Compton. He never knew how close he had become with the surly little man who protected his secret department like a mother bear defending her cubs. He was distant at times and hard to like, but the one thing you could never take away from the director of Department 5656 was the fact that he was serious about the charter of the Group—he knew the answers to everything lay in the shared past.

Carl Everett sat next to Will and saw what he was looking at. Carl picked up a small stone and lightly tossed it over toward the three Grays. The rock struck the middle one and again it began to hiss and spit under the black hood. The three Marines guarding them turned and looked at Everett. Carl just held up his hands in a *What?* kind of gesture. The Marines turned back to their charges.

"The closest I can come to figuring this out is I believe this was a suicide attack. Over a hundred sacrificed themselves to get at our chain of command."

Both Carl and Will looked up and saw Henri Farbeaux standing over them. The Frenchman had managed to find water and a rag and cleaned himself up. Everett and Mendenhall looked as if they had come out of a cave-in in some distant coal mine.

"I have to agree with you, Colonel," Carl said, standing and keeping his eyes on the three prisoners for a moment. He turned to the Frenchman. "This doesn't make one hell of a lot of sense. If they just want the planet, why attack the chain of command of any country? Just come down and start cleansing the world would be the order of the day. It makes no difference who goes first."

"Confusion, I guess," Will said as he stood, his eyes still planted on the three prisoners. He finally looked away. "The old take-the-head-of-the-snake-and-the-body-will-die thing."

Everett smiled for the first time that day. "Is that the way they put it at Officers Candidate School, Captain?"

"Yeah—I mean, yes sir, something like that."

"Well, maybe he has some answers for us, or at least new orders that make sense."

Everett and Mendenhall looked in the direction that Henri had come and saw Jack returning from his call. He was joined by General Caulfield, who gestured that his staff and aides should stay back from the small group of men. The general had just been updated by the Pentagon on what was happening elsewhere in the world. They all noticed that Jack and Caulfield had the same look on their faces—they weren't happy.

"Well?" Everett was anxious to hear what both men had to say.

Collins looked at Caulfield. "General, you may not know what we really do in that desert facility you know about, so I'll just say this: we are run specifically by the president of the United States, as I know you're aware. You and just a very few others suspect we are even there, and that's the way it's been since President Woodrow Wilson. Only the director of the National Archives and the head of the General Accounting Office know we're officially there."

"Okay, do you have to shoot me or something for knowing?" the general joked.

Jack finally smiled. "No, but whatever happens, Virginia Pollock, our assistant director, has a special file just in case this exact scenario ever happened." He looked at Will and

Carl. "It seems our esteemed director was smart enough to cover all his bases, and he covered this one particularly well. Under no circumstances is the new president to know about the Group. By law he is to be informed of our existence no later than ten days after taking office and is to be briefed by the director of the National Archives and the General Accounting Office. Now, no sitting president can ever dissolve our department; we are law. We are there to stay. But the president can also hamstring us. I and Ms. Pollock believe, and Niles concurred, that Camden would indeed hamstring us, thus damaging the Overlord plan. This cannot happen. You will be the only one in his cabinet that knows anything about us and it must stay that way until . . ." He swallowed. "Until we know the fate of the president and Dr. Compton."

"Well, I don't understand, but if that is what the president wants, who the hell am I to disagree?"

"Wait, what are you saying, Jack?" Carl asked.

Collins looked from face to face, then closed his eyes for the briefest of moments. He opened them and then kicked at a small piece of rubble that used to be a part of the family residence at Camp David.

"Giles Camden was just sworn into office five minutes ago at Fort Meyer."

"Wait a minute, the goddamn president isn't even dead yet!" Everett protested.

General Caulfield turned away, then looked up at the dazzling night sky full of stars.

"The president is now unable to fulfill his duties as commander-in-chief. Until such a time as he is mentally and physically able to perform his duties, it falls to the vice president."

"Who's dead," Will Mendenhall said with a sigh.

"In that case it falls directly to the Speaker of the House."

"Senator Giles Camden." Caulfield turned again to face Jack and the others. "I don't know how long I'll be able to protect you or your group, General Collins, but one thing I do know for sure is the fact that this Camden will fire me the first chance he gets. Had too many run-ins with the bastard, and he is no friend of the president's."

Jack placed a hand on Caulfield's shoulder. "Do what you can, while you can. The biggest priority according to Virginia is to keep Operation Overlord alive. They all say without it we cannot win this war."

"I'll do what I can." Caulfield held out his hand. They shook and the general nodded at the others. He took a particularly longer look at the man he had seen in handcuffs not five hours earlier, Henri Farbeaux. "Damn strange outfit," he said as the strange group of men watched him leave. The general was quickly joined by his aides and they walked out of Camp David.

"What's up, Jack?" Everett asked as the four men gathered around.

"Virginia is using a Nellis fighter to fly to Washington; she is officially taking over Group. She'll fight for the plan as it stands, but she can only do so much. Matchstick has requested a prisoner be taken back to the facility. I arranged that already with the FBI through General Caulfield's people. He goes back with Will, Henri, and me. Carl, you're to get to Houston on the first military flight you can get. Arrangements have been made at Andrews Air Force Base. As for us, we have a few pointed questions for Matchstick that he has to answer before we head to Hawaii."

The four men stood facing each other with the whine of helicopter turbines ripping the air around them. Carl Everett looked his companions. He turned to Will Mendenhall and held out his hand.

"You take care of this guy, Captain."

"I'll do what I can," Will said tightly. He always hated good-byes. "And if you run into that navy flier anywhere, tell him I said he better get his ass home safe," Will shouted over the mounting noise of the Black Hawk.

"I think you may see Ryan before I do, but if I do, I surely will pass it on."

The two men shook hands and Everett turned away from Mendenhall quickly and faced his friend.

"Jack," Carl said, not knowing just how to say good-bye.

Collins looked at the watch on Carl's wrist and then nodded his head.

"Swabby, I don't know just what Niles, Director Lee, and Matchstick had up their sleeves, but I swear to God, it better be worth it. You are the best man I have ever known."

The two men shook hands. Then to the astonishment of all Jack bear-hugged his friend. They stayed that way for a moment.

"You better knock it off. I mean, we're a long way from don't ask, don't tell," Carl said as they parted.

"Kiss my ass, Navy," Jack said as he backed away.

"Ditto, you Army puke," Everett said with a smile. "We'll meet again, Jack, you better believe it. Maybe not here, but some place where we can raise hell."

Collins nodded and then started walking toward the waiting Humvee. Carl turned to Henri.

"I don't like you, Froggy, I think you know that."

"I do indeed, Admiral."

"But that man sees something in you the rest of us don't. Don't let him down." Carl, against his better judgment, held out his right hand. "Get everyone you can home safe. I don't think I'll be there to see it."

"Understood."

The two antagonists shook hands and then Henri Farbeaux left Everett with a small salute to the man who had been chasing him since 2001.

Carl watched the Humvee leave with a last wave of Jack's hand. He smiled as he knew he would more than likely never again see the two men he admired. With a thought toward Sarah McIntire, Jason Ryan, Niles Compton, Alice Hamilton, and the rest, Admiral Carl Everett turned and made his way toward the waiting Black Hawk and his ride to Houston.

Collins smiled, as did Will. They both realized they might never see the man they had come to admire more than most.

It was Henri Farbeaux who put the whole scene into context.

"Gentlemen, I doubt that is the last good-bye we'll be making. I suspect that we will have many more." He smiled sadly. "And very possibly not many hellos and welcome homes afterwards."

The three soldiers turned and looked at the three hissing prisoners bundled in the back of the Humvee.

8

Sarah, Anya, and Jason Ryan were sitting inside the small hut, watching the Russian language news reports coming out of the United States. Many more Russian officers, scientific technicians, and civilian engineers were stunned at what was happening. Sarah knew Jack and Everett were at Camp David during the attack, but a quick, secure phone call to Nevada had informed them that the two men were safe. Sarah had a chance to speak with Pete Golding, who was now in charge of the Event Group facility since Virginia Pollock had been called to Washington. Sarah knew something was wrong when she had asked why Virginia and Niles Compton were both in the same place at one time outside of the complex and Pete Golding had become quiet for ten excruciating seconds on the international phone line. Then he said it looked as though, along with the president of the United States, the Chinese president, and the chancellor of Germany, Niles might not make it.

Since she had heard the bad news from Camp David it seemed as if the world had turned into her ultimate nightmare. Ryan watched the television as Anya Korvesky explained what was being said; she understood the Russian language fluently. Earlier Anya had been informed by General Shamni in Tel Aviv that she was now a military liaison with the project that had been formed to combat this terror from space. She was just as stunned as the rest of the world at learning they had basically been at war since July 1947—the very same year her nation, Israel, had been born. She glanced at Ryan when the news report showed the Walter Reed military hospital in Bethesda, Maryland. She saw his jaw working and then he kicked out with his foot, sending a small trash can flying through the air.

A small Russian nuclear technician nodded his head and then sat the trash can upright. Everyone in the room was as angry as the American and wanted to do the very same thing—kick out and strike anything.

"Look," Ryan said as he turned to face Sarah, "Did Pete say anything about when my real orders would come through? I mean, we've babysat this fucking power plant long enough." He looked around at the Russians and the fifteen naval police guarding them. "The damn thing seems to be in good hands, they don't need us anymore."

Sarah walked over and faced Jason, then smiled. "We all want new orders, but we're supposed to take this thing wherever the Russians are taking it and inform Niles and Virginia when it's on station—wherever that is. Until then we have to bite the bullet just like everyone here."

"Goddamn it, Niles is probably dead along with the president, and do you think for one minute the Chinese are going to look kindly on how well we protected their president? This whole alliance could come crashing down around our ears and here we sit. I'm a United States naval aviator and I want out of here. I want orders cut by Virginia, Pete, or whoever else may be in charge releasing me from Group. I want to fight, not babysit something that may be nothing more than a small alien's pipe dream!"

"And you shall get your wish," an officer in a snow-white naval uniform said as he stood just inside the doorway. He quickly gestured for the naval police of the Russian navy to escort the nuclear technicians and engineers from the small office. He stepped aside for the thirty-plus people to pass. He removed his saucer cap and then closed the door. "Maybe not one of your super carriers, but it is a warship. You three are to accompany me to your transport."

He started handing out identification badges with their pictures on them. Even Anya received one. She looked at it and saw it was a picture from her Israeli Army days. She was surprised at how the Russians got ahold of it. Then she saw the workings of Mossad. She immediately knew that General Shamni had her placed here in the guise of an army major, not a Mossad agent—it probably would make for a harder working relationship with the Russians if they knew who she really worked for.

Ryan looked closely at the man's white uniform and the two shoulder boards he wore. The man was a captain, second rank.

"My name is Captain Vasily Lienanov. I am the first officer of the ship that will transport you and this power plant that cost many Russian lives to its destination."

Ryan stepped up to the man and saluted. He accepted the shipboard identification and placed it around his neck.

"May I inquire, Captain, if this engine is so important and speed is of the essence, why the alliance isn't transporting the power plant by military cargo plane?"

Sarah placed her ID over her head and then watched the two naval men discuss the situation.

"I guess you have not been updated on the military situation," the dark-haired and handsome Lienanov began in very passable English. "All aircraft outside of military fighter cover has been grounded. The alliance issued the orders after the civilian airliner attacks in the Pacific and the downing of your aircraft in San Francisco. Our transport may be somewhat safer, but almost just as vulnerable. We will depart with one of the most powerful Russian fleets ever assembled." The Russian captain lowered his head in near shame. "And then we will slip away from that fleet in the middle of the night and make our run for our destination."

"Alone?" Ryan asked incredulously.

"Yes, we will run at flank speed for forty-eight straight hours."

"Can you tell us what our destination will be?" Sarah asked as she and Anya exchanged curious looks.

"No, I cannot, as I have yet to be informed by my captain. Now, if you will follow me, we are to be underway in less than fifteen minutes—the fleet awaits."

As they joined the rest of the technicians and engineers in the back of a two-and-half-ton Bulgarian-made truck, Ryan was still angry at his assumption he was being allowed to wither away babysitting and not fighting. Sarah felt as angry as he but unlike Ryan she suspected they were a part of something that was extraordinary. She just smiled and patted his leg as the truck sped off. They were followed by the captain in a second transport with the remainder of the techs.

Ten minutes later the truck stopped and the tailgate was lowered. Two men in black Nomex, carrying the short version of the venerable AK-47 assault rifle, allowed them to hop down. They were soon joined by Captain second-rank Lienanov, who gestured them to follow him. They walked around the transport and faced a sloping hill that ran downhill toward the naval base proper. Ryan's eyes widened when he saw the ship they were to make the passage on. He turned and faced the Russian, who was smiling.

"May I present to you, our latest naval achievement: the nuclear-powered missile cruiser, *Pyotr Veliky*."

The warship was the newest, largest cruiser in the world. Ryan had heard the rumors of her launch and even seen mockup drawings of her design. But that could never compare to the gleaming gray hull of her massive shape. It was one of the most beautiful sights any naval man in the world could ever behold. This was the Russian navy's equivalent to the Nimitz-class carriers of the American navy.

The Russian started to explain, but Major Korvesky beat him to it. She had known about this warship even before the Russian engineers laid down her keel for her initial construction.

"The flagship of your Northern Fleet, Kirov class, although that is more of a lazy designation because she is a class of ship all her own. She displaces 26,000 tons, about the same size as a World War II aircraft carrier. She has a suspected top speed of thirty-seven knots and has a crew of nearly eight hundred sailors. It is also suspected that her weapons arsenal includes, but is not limited to, twenty SS-N-19 Shipwreck missiles, designed to engage large surface targets. Air defense is provided by twelve SA-NX-20 Gargoyle launchers with ninety-six missiles and two SA-N-4 Gecko with forty-four missiles." Anya looked down on the ship and was truly as impressed as Ryan. All Sarah knew was that this was one of the more beautiful ships she had ever seen, with her sharply angled and raked bow and gorgeous lines. She also noticed the roped down and secured, shrink-wrapped cargo on her aft decking where a helicopter would normally be—the alien power plant.

"Impressive." Lienanov eyed the Israeli woman closely. He and Ryan exchanged glances. Ryan only grimaced as he suspected Anya might have blurted out a little too much knowledge.

"Just a hobby of mine." Anya had been so impressed that she forgot just who she was in company with. She smiled at the captain, who didn't bother returning it.

"As I said, your ship awaits."

One hour later the *Pyotr Veliky* put to sea. She was joined by the most powerful assemblage of Russian naval power ever documented, her course heading south.

FORT MEYER, MARYLAND

There were no less than three hundred agents from the FBI, the Secret Service, and the Capital Police on duty at the nondescript building, surrounded by even more armed U.S. Army personnel. Radio traffic was limited and the only outside communication came in from old-fashioned landlines buried deep underground.

Speaker of the House Giles Camden was sitting in an

ornate room that was once used by former General of the Army George C. Marshall when he was at Fort Meyer for his weekly riding at the local stables. The senator saw the many portraits of the general and felt somewhat intimidated for the first time in his many years in Washington. The room was ripe with military history, a subject Camden was short of memory on, with the exception of military contracts and the rewards they could provide.

A light knock sounded at the door and his chief of staff entered. Lyle Morgan cleared his throat and then stepped up to the senator.

"The president was wheeled out of surgery ten minutes ago. Our friends at the White House are keeping the news of his condition secret for the few moments it will take to brief you on the situation."

Camden looked up and grimaced.

"This should have been over with by now. The entire political system knows those people are just playing for time. What is the president's real condition?"

"Right now it's fifty-fifty that he recovers. He's still in a medically induced coma."

"I want his cabinet signed off on this, I want everything aboveboard. He obviously cannot fulfill the duties of his office at this time, so let's get this show on the road, shall we?"

"We do have one slight problem in the works."

Camden just stared at the young chief of staff and waited. He removed his glasses and then wiped them clean on a handkerchief.

"It seems the military has been placed on alert by the president's National Security advisor and the Joint Chiefs."

"Well, even I can see the need for that; after all we *were* attacked. I have no reason to call off the alert. I already have to bite the bullet for not believing any of this outer space crap to begin with. I will have to mend some very high fences."

"That's not the problem. Our own military forces have been placed on alert for actions in other parts of the world; it seems promises have been made to other countries in this so-called coalition formed by the president's office and our allies, including the Russians and the Chinese."

"And where did you come by this information?" Camden asked as his temper started to flare.

"I have my military sources. Some high-ranking officers are not pleased that we would designate forces to defend other territories outside of our own borders before we know just where any attack would happen. It's all preplanned."

"As soon as this official swearing-in ceremony is finished I want to speak with Caulfield, the chairman of the Joint Chiefs. That man has been a pain in my side for nearly five years. This country comes first; I want to hear his reasons why that shouldn't be the case. And don't wait until I'm sworn in, I want you to get word out to the directors of the CIA and FBI that I would like their resignations on my desk an hour after I'm sitting in the Oval Office. Is that clear?"

"Is that wise? I mean, so soon in a time of emergency? My advice is to wait, and then if you have to, you sack the whole cabinet at once and bring in our own people. But after things calm a bit."

Camden's face soured at the thought of having to work with the president's men. He hated them, but even more, they despised him as much as their boss.

He was about to speak when the door opened and most of the president's cabinet entered the room. Camden almost smiled but caught himself when he saw that the last man to enter was the chief justice of the Supreme Court of the United States, attired in his long, black robes.

The Speaker of the House rose to be sworn in as the next president of the United States of America.

THE PENTAGON
WASHINGTON, D.C.

The chairman of the Joint Chiefs of Staff was haggard as he waited inside his large office. Several doctors had checked him out from head to toe as he made his phone calls. As he hung up his call from COMSURPAC, the commander of Surface Forces—Pacific, the door opened and the president's national security advisor walked in and started pacing. General Caulfield nodded that everyone should leave the office. He sat at his desk and waited.

"I guess you feel the same as I do? Pressing duties keeping you away from the swearing in of the new president?"

"Please tell me that Operation Cut and Run has been initiated to its fullest?"

"It has—all with the exception of Centurion. General Collins is enroute to Nevada to finalize plans with Magic. He will depart for Hawaii within the hour. His team is waiting for him there. The new president will soon have knowledge of the Overlord plan, with the exception of our fast-reaction force."

"Good. You know how he'll react—he'll recall all naval forces as soon as he can. The president knew all along that Camden would never go along with the placement of U.S. troops in any land other than this one. We predict he will run scared and then cancel Overlord. If we are hit he will insist this country comes first."

"I have ordered Admiral Fuqua to see to it that his forces remain on course for action in any part of the world. We may be able to initiate world defense before our new man in office can stop it."

The national security advisor stopped pacing and then faced Caulfield. "It's treason on a massive scale, but I'm willing to hang if Overlord can continue. I hope you're of that same opinion?"

Caulfield just smiled and then sat back in his chair. "If our new president finds out, that's the least he will do to us and a thousand others. In case we are caught, it's imperative that at least Centurion is operational. That could assist our allies and not affect the readiness of our armed forces."

"In case they are called upon, is this Collins up to the task of holding the flood waters at bay?"

"I believe so. At least he has the respect of most military organizations in the world—yes, I think he can."

"Who in the hell is this guy that the president places so

much faith in him?" the national security advisor asked. "I mean, between him and that little bald guy lying in the hospital, most of our fates lie in their hands."

"That little bald guy Compton and General Collins have been there before, many times. If they can't pull this off, then we won't have long to suffer the new president. Our asses will be kicked as thoroughly as Custer's was at Little Big Horn."

EVENT GROUP COMPLEX
NELLIS AIR FORCE BASE, NEVADA

Jack and Will sat inside the conference room. Both men had hurriedly packed and sat waiting for Matchstick to be brought in. While they waited Collins had requested that Pete and Europa try and contact Sarah McIntire. Pete reported just a few minutes later that Sarah and Ryan, and, to the surprise of both Will and Jack, Anya Korvesky, had put to sea six hours before and could not under any circumstances be contacted. The entire Russian battle fleet was off the air and would remain so. This all came from the orders pertaining to Overlord.

The conference room doors opened and Gus Tilly, dressed in a long robe, walked in holding the hand of Matchstick, who at the very least looked worried about Gus. The old man looked worn to the bone, which made Jack apprehensive about broaching the subject of trust with the small alien, as he knew upsetting Gus would do no good. Matchstick made sure Gus was sitting comfortably and then walked to a chair, where he climbed up and sat looking straight at Collins. Pete Golding, acting as temporary director of Department 5656, sat in on the meeting. It was he who spoke first.

"Jack, General Caulfield contacted us through the Oval Office. He is furious that you, Will, and Farbeaux haven't departed for your duty stations yet."

Collins only nodded his head. "Anything else?"

"Yes, Colonel Farbeaux is waiting in the hallway. His uniform's arrived and he looks as if he's miserable."

"Good, he needs to be miserable. Thanks, Pete. Have a seat, you need to hear this too in case the new president throws Virginia in jail and Niles . . . remains incapacitated."

Pete nodded and then slowly sat down. He didn't bother to sit in Niles Compton's chair. Everyone could see the computer genius was devastated that his friend was lying in critical condition in a Washington hospital. Jack hit the intercom to the outer office.

"Okay Alice, you can come in."

Alice Hamilton opened the double doors and came in with several large photographs. She handed them to Jack and then sat down next to Gus Tilly, who had been adamant about being with Matchstick. Collins accepted the photos and then looked at the large and very long conference table. There were so many missing faces that he had to clear his throat.

"You haven't been totally honest in your debriefs about the Grays, have you, Matchstick? We brought back a Gray prisoner from Camp David. You have had several hours with it. Now we need to know what you know because Alice and Pete say you have stopped talking."

"What's this about?" Gus asked as Matchstick remained quiet.

"Niles suspects that Matchstick is keeping something from us." Jack had his eyes on the alien and not Gus.

"Matchstick, it's too late in the game for you to hold back. In order for us to fight what's ahead, we need the truth," Alice said with a comforting smile.

"I think over three hundred and seventy hours was enough of a strain on this little fella to explain his actions," Gus said as his temper started to rise. Matchstick reached up and easily patted the old man's hand in an attempt to calm him.

Jack pushed a photo toward Gus and Matchstick. "Niles began to have doubts about his honesty when these showed up on the Hubble telescope."

Gus looked at the photo, but Matchstick did not. It was the now famous photograph of the armada of saucers thousands of light-years away from Earth that had spurred the nations of the world to action. Jack tapped the photo.

"Why are they there?"

"I think he explained all of that stuff to you and every other egghead on the planet more than just once," Gus said as he eyed Collins.

"Yes, we know Matchstick's planet is a dying world; we assumed that was the reason for the mass exodus of saucers. Over seven hundred and fifty thousand of them, at last count. We understand that they plan to colonize this world and take it down for their own. The Grays do have a plan, which Niles is sure of. It's just not what Matchstick told us their plan was in reality."

"Look, you better explain," Gus said tiredly, feeling betrayed by men he had come to trust. "Why is he being asked these questions? Does it really matter in the long run?"

"Matchstick," Mendenhall said, trying to take some of the pressure off of Jack, "there are no less than five thousand habitable worlds just inside the Milky Way galaxy alone. Any one of them is suitable for habitation by yours and the Gray species. I think you better tell us, why Earth?"

Matchstick remained silent as his eyes traveled to Alice Hamilton, the kindest person outside of his best friend Gus Tilly he had ever known. She nodded her head that he should tell the truth. Still he remained silent as he dipped his head and squeezed Gus's hand that much tighter.

Jack looked at his watch and then shook his head as he knew his secured flight to Hawaii was close at hand. He had to leave and he didn't know if Alice and Pete were strong enough to force the truth out of the small green alien. He hated treating Matchstick like this but they had to know everything because it impacted the way Earth would fight this war.

"Every science fiction story ever written has the main reason for extraterrestrial invasion as a fight for our resources. Water, timber, minerals—but that isn't it, is it? We have since discovered that fresh water is readily abundant throughout the galaxy. Minerals, there are whole worlds of precious metals just waiting to be discovered. Now, what do the Grays want?"

Matchstick released the hand of Gus and then wiped at his large eyes. Jack felt horrible as he realized he had never seen Matchstick cry before. Alice walked around the table and placed her arm around the small being, then looked at Collins and shook her head, indicating that he should stop the questioning. Jack returned the look and shook his head.

"Why would the Grays try to take out the chain of command? They have the power to come here and destroy whatever they wanted to destroy with practical immunity. They wouldn't care who was in charge and they certainly wouldn't risk a ground incursion. They would come in blasting and you know it. Now why did they do that?"

"That's enough. Isn't it ample that they have come, just like he told you in the past? Does it matter what they came for?" Gus stood from his chair as Mahjtic tried to stay him.

"Yes, Gus, they could come here and just start killing all. I mean, that is their main goal, is it not, the complete subjugation of the planet? Why would they kill the leaders of the world? There is no need."

Gus sat back down and then took Mahjtic's hand once again. The alien nodded his head at Tilly and the old man turned white as he couldn't form the words. Matchstick looked from him toward Jack. A single tear fell from his large, obsidian-colored eye. He wiped it away and then with a final look at Alice he started to say something. Gus stopped him, and then nodded his head also.

"There is one thing . . . that . . . is not . . . abundant . . . in this . . . or any . . . other universe, Colonel Jack."

Collins and Mendenhall leaned forward and Pete Golding stopped writing on his notepad. Jack nodded his head that Matchstick should continue. It was like the Green alien was hiding something that pained him to the extreme and he wanted to excise the thing so bad that its poison ripped him apart as he tried to say it.

"We're your friends, Matchstick—always have been. And nothing you can say will ever change that."

"My race is . . . all . . . dead. That Gray Master you brought . . . here . . . said so. They are all gone.

"What happened to them—did they die out?" Pete Golding asked, starting to feel sick for Mahjtic and his kind. Slaves to the death.

"Their . . . fate will be . . . our fate," he said, looking from face to face.

"They were killed off?" Will asked, getting angry for the small friend before them.

"Yesss," Mahjtic said, drawing out the answer as he lowered his eyes.

"What do they really want?" Jack said with a growing feeling of dread.

"There is . . . one . . . natural resource . . . not readily . . . available . . . in the universe, Colonel Jack. Not water, not minerals . . . but people." Matchstick looked from Collins to his friend Gus and the old man nodded that he should continue. "They sent the Talkan to your world six years . . . ago, not to kill off your species . . . but . . . to study . . . your . . . close in . . . defenses. Your ground . . . attack . . . methods."

Jack exchanged looks with everyone at the table and they all remembered the battle in the desert sands of Arizona where many a soldier had fought and died, killing a species of animal they had all assumed, and were told by Matchstick, was a war of extinction.

"I . . . I . . . was mistaken . . . that was not the truth." He stumbled on his words. He looked at Gus for help as he choked up.

"Damn it, Colonel, the goddamned ugly bastards are here for one thing and one thing only."

Jack stood from his chair and then paced with his back to Matchstick.

"What?" Pete asked, feeling ill himself.

"Food to feed their home fleet. They cannot take the planet while their own kind is starving."

"Us?" Pete almost shrieked.

Jack turned around in stunned silence.

"The Greens, Matchstick's kind, the slaves have all been

consumed for the Grays' benefit, Colonel. Their kind is starving on those saucers you see in that picture. Horrible but true. Now they are coming for the one resource only found here. Food. That's why they are not attacking in force, they cannot afford to kill off the one thing that can sustain them—their food source."

Gus took hold of Matchstick and they went silent as the small alien cried into Gus's robe. He sniffed and wiped his eyes. He looked at Jack with guilt written on his face.

"When . . . their . . . starvation . . . is . . . relieved . . . they . . . will . . . come . . . in . . . force . . . but . . . first . . . they must . . . secure enough . . . food for . . . the major attack . . . Right now . . . they . . . are too weak."

Jack turned and faced Alice. "Keep this quiet for right now. It won't do anyone any good to hear this."

Alice nodded her head, agreeing with his decision.

"Thank you, Matchstick. We won't let it get that far."

It was Mendenhall who stood and placed his hands on both Gus and Mahjtic. He patted them on the back and then left the room.

The horrible information was sickening, but to Collins it didn't really matter what the motivation was for the attack. It just didn't matter—one reason was as bad as the other.

"Pete, there is no need to pass this on to Virginia. She has enough on her plate for now."

Pete stood and nodded his head and then held out his hand to shake. "Good luck, General, we'll be working here for you." He looked at Matchstick and Gus. "All of us."

"I know that." He shook Pete's hand and then reached over and hugged Alice. As he did, Mendenhall walked back into the room and up to Matchstick and Gus.

"I've wanted to give this to you for a while now. I guess this is as good as time as any." Will held out his hand to Matchstick. "Put these on your little collar. You've earned them, Captain."

Matchstick's eyes widened even larger than normal as he accepted the gift of the single silver bar of an Army first lieutenant. Gus smiled and patted his small friend on the back.

The new captain and Jack's aide knelt down next to Mahjtic and looked at him closely.

"Do you trust General Collins and me?"

Matchstick wiped his almost nonexistent nose and nodded his large and bulbous head.

"I promise we'll get those bastards for what they did to your kind. Isn't that right, General?"

"Damned right." Jack and Will started to leave for the Nellis airfield. He stopped short of the door and turned. "Alice, when and if you get a chance, get word to Short Stuff for me; tell her I love her and we'll see each other again. Either here, or somewhere else where soldiers always meet after the shit of the world has been cleaned up."

"I will, Jack, I promise."

"Pete, find a way to help, if you can."

Pete just nodded as Jack and Will left the conference room.

"What did he mean where soldiers meet?" he asked Alice.

It was Gus who answered for Alice as she choked up and wiped at her eyes with a Kleenex.

"It was his way of saying good-bye, Dr. Golding. The man doesn't think he'll see any of us again."

THE ARK, EVENT GROUP COMPLEX
NELLIS AIR FORCE BASE, NEVADA

Pete sat with a beer and a shot of Jack Daniels and stared at the shiny bar top. He was twisting a napkin into knots.

"Buy you one?"

Pete Golding looked up and saw Charles Hindershot Ellenshaw III standing by the stool he was sitting in.

"I've already got one . . . or two," he corrected himself as he noticed the untouched drinks in front of him.

Charlie got the bartender's attention and waved him over to order more drinks. He sat next to Pete and then looked at the bottles arrayed behind the bar. Pete sniffed and noticed Charlie, the old Cal-Berkeley hippie, had indulged in a practice that Niles Compton ignored most times.

"That shit will warp your brain, Charlie," Pete said as he downed the shot of Jack Daniels.

Ellenshaw accepted the drinks and then nodded at the bartender, a retired Air Force sergeant.

"Your point?" Charlie asked as he too downed his fresh shot.

Pete looked at the cryptozoologist and then shrugged his shoulders. "I guess I don't have one."

Ellenshaw didn't say anything.

"We're going to lose a lot of friends, Charlie."

"Yes, I think you're right, my friend." He slid a fresh shot of whiskey toward Pete.

Golding looked at Ellenshaw, then nodded his head and downed the drink.

"Charlie, you didn't think much of the military before knowing Carl, Jack, and the others, did you?"

"Well," he said as he sipped at his glass of beer, "I was always a pacifist, you know that. I mean, Cal-Berkeley was not a haven for military leanings during the sixties." Ellenshaw took another deep swallow of beer. "But the men I've known here at Group have shown me something that I never knew." He placed the glass on the bar and turned to face the computer genius. "The people we serve with are the best men and women I have ever had the privilege to know. Now I'm just afraid I could never live up to what they stand for."

"What do you mean?" Pete asked as he too joined Charlie in drinking his two beers.

"They stand and fight for people who can't fight for themselves. They fight the bullies in the world that we"—he nodded his head toward Pete—"could never stand up to. I for one am going to move heaven and hell to get my friends home. That's all we can do, Pete—fight for our friends and those other soldiers who are going into harm's way. We have

a chance here to help, what assitance that is I don't know
yet, but I for one will do anything to get these people home.
That's what hanging out with Jack, Carl, Will, Jason, and
Sarah has taught me: try your best." He looked at his friend.
"And that's what you'll do too. You were meant to be one of
them, you and Europa, and you will prove it once this thing
really starts, because like Niles is smart, Jack is brave, you're
a genius, and you'll do what needs doing." Charlie finished
off his beer and then looked at Golding.

Pete looked at Charlie and smiled. "You have any more
of that crap you smoke? I think it's time to embrace the radical left."

"You bet. Let's retreat to my inner sanctum and figure
out how to help those boys and save the world."

The two men toasted and then left the Ark.

LAS VEGAS, NEVADA

Hiram Vickers stood outside the MGM Grand and waited.
He had just watched the news broadcast and had been so
shocked at the reports of the Speaker's swearing in as the
president of the United States that he felt like laughing. His
luck had gone from bad to worse in less than twenty-four
hours.

His cell phone rang. Looking at a few of the passing
guests, he cautiously answered.

"It's about time. I was wondering if you and the new
president were going to call my bluff."

On the other end of the line, calling from his private and
secure cell phone, was Daniel Peachtree. "Do you think you
can try and blackmail the new administration in the middle
of a war—an interstellar war, at that?"

"You don't think the press would love to hear that the
man they billed as the most despicable man in the House
was in an arms purchase, possibly even the murder and
cover-up of a U.S. field agent? I would think again, Mr. Future Director. With the information I have on both of you

making money buying up that new technology for a war the Speaker never thought was true in the first place, and then covering up the fact that your man, me, killed two American citizens? I don't think you would be in your new office for very long, do you?"

Vickers was starting to think that the assistant director had hung up on him before he heard the man laugh.

"As it so happens, Mr. Vickers, there is now a need for a man such as you."

Vickers eyed two men walking into the MGM and then turned away from them, careful to hide his face.

"And what special need is that—a target for one of your field agents?"

"Mr. Vickers, you landed at McCarran International at 7:45 this very evening. You are now standing in front of the MGM Grand looking rather nervous. If I had wanted you dead any one of three very despicable people would have sliced your throat a minute into this call."

Vickers looked around nervously. He saw about a hundred people standing around the entrance of the hotel. Any of them could be the assassins Peachtree spoke of.

"Okay, you have eyes on the target. What do you want?"

"It's what you want we're going to discuss, Hiram."

"And what's that?" He avoided a small woman with a handbag the size of Detroit as she approached.

"You wish to have this nightmare end and receive the forgiveness of the new president—and of course myself."

"What game are you trying to run on me? Ten hours ago you had half the agency tracking me down to kill me, now you want me to come back?"

"That was then, this is now. You know how quickly things can change in Washington. Before you left Langley, you contacted several members of your now-defunct Black Teams for assisting you in a delicate matter in the Arizona desert. Well, those men reported directly to me, and explained how you were going to gain leverage on us by taking a very secret military asset and holding him hostage until we saw things your way."

Hiram Vickers had sorely underestimated the assistant director of Operations. The man had been five steps ahead of him at all times.

"What is it you . . . I mean Camden wants?"

"Why, nothing more than you and your Black Teams as originally intended. You see, there is a plan in effect that our former friend in the White House had devised with certain allies. This plan was thought up by the people who guide whoever you were tracking in Arizona. This asset, as you remember from your talks in Kansas with Mr. Hendrix—the man in prison with no official name—is code-named Magic. You see, Mr. Vickers, the new administration wants to speak directly to this Magic."

"Why, if you follow Operation Overlord, you would undoubtedly get access to him, whoever he is, eventually."

"Please stop thinking, Mr. Vickers, and listen. We want that asset in our pocket and not hidden away by any think tank the former president has hidden away. We want *our* military people to evaluate this war, and whoever this Magic is has the information they will need. Get him. If it takes three months or three years, get Magic for us. Your Black Team is standing by. May I suggest you stake out that house in Arizona; Magic will show up there eventually. And if this strange group is in charge of security there, I would be extremely careful."

"And then I will be allowed back? The Black Team won't have orders to kill me after we take him?"

"As I said, Vickers, we could have gotten you at any time, but now you are too valuable. Get that asset so we can get the information we need for *this* country, not everybody who has a gun and a few tanks. Now, accept the package the man behind you is holding and get to work. This is one mission you don't want to screw up, because if you do a certain army major will discover right where you are waiting. And he will assuredly kill you in a most brutal manner."

Vickers's eyes widened when a rather large hand came over his shoulder. A plastic bag was there and he turned to see the leader of the last Black Team on the CIA's books.

The man shoved the bag at him and he finally took it. Vickers felt the weight of the weapon and took a quick look inside. It was a Glock nine millimeter and a cell phone.

"Be useful to us, Hiram, and all is forgiven. Use the secure cell phone and not the one you used to call me—we don't want certain people tracking you down the way we did, and stopping you before you secure this Magic. Good luck and don't fail."

The phone went dead as he turned and faced the man in the black T-shirt and blue jeans.

"What are your orders?" he asked as he tossed his old cell phone in a trash can.

"To follow your orders. Other than that, we have orders that if we can't secure the asset in Arizona, we kill him, or her, whoever the case may be."

"And then kill me." Vickers frowned.

"It won't come to that. You know how good we are. I guess you can say we never fail to get our man."

Vickers frowned as the large man gestured for him to follow. He knew his men to be stone-cold killers if they had to be.

Now he actually felt sorry for the asset known as Magic.

SOUTHERN ATLANTIC OCEAN

The *Pyotr Veliky* signaled the Russian flagship of the Red Banner Northern Fleet by signal light. The night was warm and moonless and the giant silhouette of the missile cruiser was hard to discern. Aboard the *Pyotr Veliky* Sarah, Ryan, and Anya had been allowed out on deck to observe the highly dangerous maneuver that was about to take place. Sarah watched the skies and wondered if their movements were being tracked by someone other than the American NSA or the Russian Security Service with their highly technical tracking satellites. In all honesty she wished it were the Event Group's KH-11 Black Bird ASAT, code-named Boris and Natasha. It would make her feel more at home if she knew family eyes were on them. But she did know one thing that was certain: the *Pyotr Veliky* was on her own from this point forward.

The sixteen warships of the Red Banner Northern Fleet made a sharp turn to the east and made for the coast of France while the giant missile cruiser heeled sharply to port, cutting dangerously close to a small Russian destroyer, so much so that the large cruiser sent the smaller vessel rolling high in her wake. The great missile cruiser was now traveling in the opposite direction as the flotilla.

The three guests standing along the stern railing had to hang on tight as the ship rolled hard at full maneuvering speed. Seawater cascaded onto the deck as the powerful warship heeled hard over in what was known as a slink-and-dive turn. This meant that she hadn't slowed by one single knot as she made the maneuver.

"Whoa!" Ryan said as he made to grab both Sarah and Anya as they came near to sliding over the side of the railing.

The enormous missile cruiser finally straightened and then settled back deeply into the sea as her speed increased even more than western intelligence agencies ever thought possible.

They watched the darkened forms of the sixteen ships as they made for the French coast, hopefully taking any curious, watchful eyes from space with them. The ruse had started and they all hoped it worked because now they were truly on their own.

Sarah was the first to see the after-watch take their battle stations and she was curious to know why.

"We will run the rest of the way to our destination at action stations," came the voice from the darkened area between the fantail and the aft missile mount. They looked up and saw the first officer as he stepped onto the fantail. Captain Vasily Lienanov nodded a greeting as he joined his guests. "I would have thought you would be down with the rest of the engineers and technicians."

"We can only listen to so many sad songs of home," Ryan said as he shook his head. "I mean, talk about gloomy."

"This is a ship full of frightened men." The first officer stepped to the railing and breathed deeply of the sea air. "They fear they will never see home again."

"Strange, I have the same feelings myself, but I'm sure as hell not going to sing about it. Bob Dylan, I ain't." Ryan hoped to squeeze some information from a fellow seaman. "Speaking of said event, if we do die, just how far from home will we be?"

The captain smiled and then turned to face Ryan. He looked the small American naval aviator up and down and then turned away. "You should go below; they are fitting our passengers with gear from the ship's stores."

"Gear?" Sarah asked as she and Anya joined the men.

"Yes, you will have need of special equipment when you arrive at our destination."

Ryan exchanged looks with the two women and frowned as he suspected the captain wasn't going to volunteer anything.

"Can you feel them?" Lienanov asked, looking at the dark waters of the Atlantic.

"Feel what?" Anya asked after no one else inquired.

The captain turned around and faced them. "We have company out there. I don't know what good they would do us if our Gray friends strike, but it's comforting to know they'll be along for the ride."

"Who?" Ryan asked.

"Out there we have assembled no less than four Akula attack submarines, joined by a screen of two Los Angeles–class attack boats. They are riding shotgun for this little suicide run."

"Submarines?" Anya asked.

"Yes, so you see, we shan't die alone."

The smile of Lienanov made them all nervous.

"Perhaps you should get below and receive your allotted equipment, and get some rest. You will need your strength in about four days' time."

Anya, Sarah, and Ryan started to turn. It was Ryan who stopped and confronted Lienanov.

"I know secrecy orders, Captain; we are in the same trade. But as you can see, none of us are ugly, and definitely not Gray in color. Where in the hell is this ship taking us?"

The captain lit a cigarette and then exhaled. "I gave these up when I graduated the academy," he said, looking at the foul cigarette, and then he tossed it over the side. "Bad habit, smoking and . . ." He looked directly at Ryan. "Talking."

Sarah watched the man closely, as did Anya.

"If you must know, Commander Ryan, you will be issued cold-weather gear and, when the time comes, also weaponry." He turned away and made for the hatchway.

Ryan was stunned as he faced the women.

"You're the navy man," Sarah said. "What do you think?"

Ryan shivered in the warm night air.

"Antarctica."

INTERNATIONAL SPACE STATION
HIGH EARTH ORBIT

Greg Worth, a visiting atmospheric scientist from the University of Colorado, watched from the porthole on the hugely expensive international boondoggle known as the space station. He could never get enough of the view. He floated freely while his companions ate their dinnertime meal and laughed at the way the newcomer managed to look out of the window every two minutes.

Dominique Vasturi, an Italian photojournalist, approached Dr. Worth from her position forward. She held a freeze-dried bag of casserole in her hand as she grabbed for the support ring close to the window. She gazed through the glass and saw Earth far below. The sun was just rising over the Asian continent as she joined the curious American.

"I take it home is still there?" She offered Greg some of the terrible tasting casserole. He grimaced and shook his head.

"God, you really don't appreciate the planet until you can

see it from this vantage point," he said, turning away from the offered meal and the gorgeous Italian photojournalist.

The woman agreed as she zipped the Mylar bag of dry casserole closed. "Well, let's hope the news footage we saw tonight was not the beginning of something." She looked out of the porthole. "Because it looks like a long way to fall."

Greg finally pulled back from the window and then glanced over at the Russian and American astronauts as they went about their business. They were soon joined by Nemi Takiyama, another guest who had arrived only three days before on the same flight as Greg.

"Are you scared—I mean, being out here?"

"I think if they attack, I would just as soon be here as there." The Japanese scientist glanced out of the window as he floated up to the two observers.

"Okay, everyone, it's time to power down. We have a lot of work to do tomorrow." Peter Blasinov, a Russian Air Force colonel, started throwing switches that would send the expensive space station into sleep mode.

Greg frowned. The one thing he hated about being here was to be strapped into a sleeping bag–type device and hang from a wall just to get forty winks.

As the three young people moved from the window they heard a sharp alarm sound in module C-11, the next compartment down. They heard the call from one of the U.S. Air Force communications men.

"We have a hatch warning in the physical training module."

"That can't be, there's no one in there." The Russian maneuvered past the three startled people. The warning buzzer kept up its shrill call. "Shut down that alarm!"

The buzzer stopped and then they felt the entire station shudder.

"What in the hell was that?" Greg asked as he felt the shudder again. "Is it an open hatch venting gas to the outside?"

"No, we haven't lost atmosphere." Blasinov quickly took

handholds and shot into the physical training module through the connecting tunnel. He saw immediately the hatch ring was turning. He hurriedly floated toward the hatch and tried to force the handle back into the locked position. It started to move back and then a tremendous force outside the door started moving the locking ring back to the open position. "Damn, help me, Lieutenant!" he shouted at the young American communications man. He was floating nearby and his eyes were as wide as spotlights.

"Come on, that's impossible!"

"That seems to be a moot point at the moment. Something is forcing this seal open—now help me!"

The three young people watched from the module's opening. Greg sprang forward, quickly traversing the exercise equipment, and then was able to take hold of the door's locking ring located in the middle of the hatchway.

"Who's out there?" Dominique asked.

The Japanese weather specialist floated over to assist. As he did he hit the window covering, sending it up and into the composite hull. His eyes widened as he saw just who it was that was turning the handle. He used his feet to spring backward with a small yelp of fear.

"What in the hell is that?" he yelled.

Blasinov looked up. Staring right at him was the most horrible thing he had ever seen. The Gray was helmeted but they could clearly see the yellow-ringed black eyes as they looked inside the station. The thing opened its mouth and he could swear the creature had smiled at him.

"Environmental suits and helmets, quickly!" Blasinov shouted. He fought to hold the handle closed. He was losing the battle. As he chanced another look he saw several more of the strangely dressed Grays as they floated up to the doorway. Too late, the handle turned and opened.

The atmosphere of the station vented outward with an explosive crash of passing air. Men and women were tossed and blown toward the open door. Blasinov was forced out through the three-inch gap between the hatch and the rubber seal. He was crushed as his large body was forced out into space, where it was immediately grabbed by one of the assaulting Grays.

Men and women quickly placed their helmets on in the midst of the flying paper and other debris forced into a whirlwind by the venting oxygen. The Grays opened the hatchway completely, and five of them entered the International Space Station.

Outside the large station, two of the silver-colored saucers held station. They were soon joined by a much larger alien vehicle as the station was raided.

The Gray assault on the blue planet below had begun in earnest.

UNITED STATES SPACE COMMAND
THE PENTAGON, WASHINGTON, D.C.

Major General Walter Shotz watched the monitor and his face turned white as he and two hundred radar and imaging technicians witnessed the International Space Station explode. The devastation was silent as large pieces of composite material, aluminum, and plastic arched into the black void of space.

"Get me General Caulfield on the horn and sound the incursion alarm. We have a serious attack starting on our front door," he said as calmly as he could, as the horror of what just happened etched deeply into his brain.

9

The blue and white Bell helicopter set down easily on the pad. Admiral Carl Everett, attired in his summer whites, watched as a small crowd gathered around the NASA helipad. They looked as if they were wearing Event Group blue jumpers and for the briefest of moments he thought about home. The illusion was quickly dashed when he saw the horde of Air Police surrounding the group of men and women. He allowed the two-bladed rotors to whine down before the crew chief slid the large door open. As he reached for his seabag the crew chief took it first.

"All this will be brought to your quarters, Admiral; you are scheduled for meetings throughout the night."

Everett nodded, then reached through the compartment and tapped the pilot on his shoulder and nodded his thanks. He stepped from the helicopter and placed his saucer cap over his blond hair and then came forward. He was quickly approached by a young woman wearing the blue coveralls bearing the NASA emblem on her left breast.

"Admiral, we expected you two days ago," she said, saluting.

Everett returned the salute and then saw the Air Force lieutenant insignia on her collar.

"Had problems arise, as I'm sure you've heard, Lieutenant." Carl moved forward as the lieutenant caught up.

"Yes, sir, it's just that one of the propulsion engineers has been screaming bloody murder since your original arrival date came and went. He's been a real bear, sir."

Everett turned on the young officer. "Look, Lieutenant . . . ?"

"Branch, sir, Evelyn Branch."

"Branch, I couldn't give a damn about any civilian engineer who is upset that a small alien incursion has happened and I was delayed in transit. So inform this asshole, whoever he is, he can—"

"Toad, you son of a bitch, I knew I'd get you out here sooner or later!"

Everett froze. The recent past came flooding back on him as the young lieutenant smiled and then stepped out of the way to join the rest of her team watching the anticipated reunion. Everett turned to find one of his worst nightmares staring him in the face.

United States Navy Master Chief Archibald Jenks stood leaning on a cane. He removed the stub of a cigar and made a kissing motion by pursing his lips. He finally smiled.

The last time Everett had seen the master chief he was being carried off on a stretcher to a local Los Angeles hospital after the Event Group incursion into Brazil and the search for the not-so-mystical El Dorado mine. Jenks was now attired in a lab coat that did his rotund appearance no good at all. His eyes went from Carl to the young lieutenant who stood in line. His eyes wandered over her tight-fitting jumpsuit and then he again made eye contact with Carl and raised his brows twice in succession.

"Master Chief," he said as he finally found strength in his legs to step forward. He eyed the man up and down and smiled. "Or is it *Mr.* Jenks?"

"Just Jenks will do, Toad, or if you insist, Professor Jenks, asshole." He held out his hand.

Carl shook and then looked around at the young people he was surrounded by. "What are you running here, Jenksy, a day-care center?"

Jenks looked at the NASA men and women and replaced the cigar stub in his mouth. "Yeah, it's like the Amazon all over again, huh? I mean, these kids are young enough to be in high school." He grinned. "But we did get those kids in the Amazon home again, didn't we?"

"Yes we did, Chief."

The chief's demeanor instantly changed. "After you and that crackhead army major trashed my boat, my baby!"

"Look, Master Chief, *Teacher* saved all our lives, and with my last look at my pay voucher I was still paying for that damn boat, one dollar a month for the rest of my life."

"Hah! Got you there, didn't I? It's got to be hell at tax time trying to explain that one."

Everett remembered the beautiful boat, USS *Teacher,* an experimental river craft of the chief's design and construction. The genius little engineer had built the most magnificent and advanced boat he had ever seen, only to have Everett and Jack Collins ram it into an ancient gold mine and sink her in a bottomless lagoon. He coughed and cleared his throat.

"And that's now *General* Crackhead, Chief," Carl said, referring to Jack's new brevet rank.

"Jesus, the military is really hard up, ain't they?"

"Hard up enough to give *me* a brevet rank also, you old goat."

Jenks eyed Everett up and down, his eyes finally settling on the admiral's shoulder boards for the briefest of moments. Then he removed the stub of cigar and tossed it into the wind.

"Yeah, the navy always gives you the candy before the medicine, if I remember right." He eyed Carl and then shook his head. "Well, this time I'm afraid you'll earn it, Toad, my boy."

The master chief gestured for the young NASA officers to scatter as he and Carl moved toward the elevator on top of the roof. The men and women all looked on in shock, as they had never seen the man that had driven them crazy for the past year so cowed by a mere man before. They immediately had respect for anyone that could do that with the old chief designer.

"Just what in the hell is going on, Master Chief?" Carl asked as Jenks growled at two lieutenants when they tried to get into the elevator with them, sending them scurrying for cover.

"These young folks are going to make you an astronaut, Toad. And the plan is we're going to try and save this fucked-up planet." He hit the floor button he wanted. "What for, I'll never know, as I never found much use for it, or at least the species that occupies it much."

Carl was ashen faced as the elevator doors slid closed. "Astronaut?"

"That's right, my boy, a fucking astronaut. That's what I call military preparedness." He hesitated and then smiled wider than before. "Admiral." He laughed all the way to the fifth floor of the astronaut training center.

The space arm of Operation Overlord had its commander.

WALTER REED NATIONAL MILITARY MEDICAL CENTER BETHESDA, MARYLAND

Virginia Pollock sat next to the bed and reached over to take Niles Compton's left hand, careful not to touch the cast of his right arm. The doctors had barely managed to save the limb after sixteen hours of complicated surgery. The entire right side of his face was covered in white-gauze bandages and that was the injury that made Virginia tear up. Niles had lost the eye and he would have a scar running down the side of his face for the rest of his life. He had not awakened since her arrival.

She looked up at the silent television as President Camden was seen visiting his comatose predecessor as he lay in bed in severe critical condition, as the multitude of specialists proclaimed he may or may not pull through. Many people saw the disgust in the face of the nation's first lady as the new man in the Oval Office shook her hand in condolences. It was no secret that the first lady shared her husband's contempt of the former Speaker of the House; the distaste was hard to miss.

Virginia turned at the sound of a light knock on the door. She crossed the room and opened it.

"Acting Director Pollock?" A small man with glasses stood massaging a briefcase that had seen far better days. Another taller and very much thinner man was standing behind him. He looked more nervous than the smaller gentleman.

"Dr. Pollock," she corrected apprehensively, as she didn't know these two in the slightest.

The tall man nudged the smaller man in front of him.

"Of course, my apologies." The man eyed the taller, dark-haired Virginia nervously.

"What can I do for you gentlemen?" she asked abruptly, not wanting to disturb Niles.

"Dr. Pollock, my name is Sanford, Max Sanford. I am the director of the National Archives, and this is Mr. Halliburton West, of the General Accounting Office."

A light came on inside Virginia's brilliant head and she stepped aside to allow the men in. They stood before the bed and looked down on Niles. The smaller man looked as if he were about to cry. The taller one moved to inspect Niles's face. He also shook his head.

"God, look what they have done to him," Sanford said. He straightened and then placed the briefcase he was carrying on a nearby chair.

"I take it you gentlemen are here because of the succession regulations?" she asked in a whisper.

"Yes, Doctor." Sanford looked from Virginia toward a departing shot of Camden on television as he waved his hands at the reporters gathered at the scene. "As you know—or may not know," he corrected as he looked down on Niles's still form, "we have to brief the new president on Department 5656 no later than ten days after he takes office. That's the law as set down by President Roosevelt in the forties."

Virginia turned away and cringed. The thought of an enemy of not only the president but of Niles Compton taking command of the Group made her almost ill.

"Doctor, we have no desire to do that, but according to law we have no choice. My job is to budget Department 5656 and hide just where that budget has come from. There is no choice but to brief the new commander-in-chief on your department's charter and budgetary limitation, or its extremes," said West.

"No."

They all three turned. Niles was awake.

"Niles," Virginia said as she hurriedly approached the bed.

"I will . . . order . . . Virginia to . . . blow up . . . my facility before . . ." Niles drifted away as Virginia took his good left hand in her own.

"What do you want us to do, Niles?"

The two men exchanged brief looks and then a conspiracy-laced mask crossed their features as they too stepped up to the bed.

"That man is not to know about us . . . until . . . Overlord is . . . off . . . the ground. He . . . is . . . never to . . . know . . . about Magic."

"What's Magic?" Sanford asked in a whisper.

"An Event Group asset that occupies the house you gentlemen paid for in Arizona," Virginia said, just wanting the red tape boys to be silent as she got her orders.

Both men knew of the expenditures in time and material for something just south of Chato's Crawl, Arizona, but had never thought anything about it. They nodded their heads, still not understanding.

"We . . . need . . . your . . . help . . . gentlemen," Niles whispered. "Get lost until . . . until . . ." Niles coughed lightly and then opened his good eye against the pain he was feeling. "You'll know when . . . the departmental briefing on . . . my . . . Group . . . can . . . take . . . place . . . Just watch the news."

The two men exchanged looks. They had battled with Niles Compton for over fifteen years, and Senator Garrison Lee before him, on budgets and allocations for the top-secret agency. They grimaced at the thought of lying to the president, but nodded their agreement anyway.

"We'll do what we can, Dr. Compton," West said.

"Good . . . good," he said as his good eye closed. "Virginia?"

"Yes," she said as she leaned in closer.

"You have to . . . help . . . Overlord . . . make sure . . . our . . . people . . . do . . . their jobs. Carl and Jack will need . . . their help. The unexpected . . . will . . . arise . . . and I only . . . trust our Group, understand?"

Virginia backed away when Niles gestured for the two men to come forward.

"Thank you . . . I'm afraid all . . . I can . . . guarantee . . . you . . . is a . . . possible . . . hangman's noose."

West straightened, smiled, and then allowed the director of the National Archives to answer for them both. "A noose doesn't sound that scary, Doctor. Have you ever been a bureaucrat?"

"It's quite boring, I assure you," Sanford finished.

ONE HUNDRED NAUTICAL MILES EAST OF
PEARL HARBOR, HAWAII

The C-130 Hercules made a sharp turn to the starboard as the Air Force transport awaited clearance to enter Hawaiian airspace. The trip across the Pacific had been fraught with choppy weather and high winds. The main reason for that was the combat altitude they flew since leaving Edwards Air Force Base in the high desert of Southern California. The Hercules never once rose above two thousand feet of altitude, necessitating the extended flight time. They had four extra flight crews on board for relief because of the strain caused by flying so low an altitude.

The skies had been cleared of all civilian aircraft and the

world travelers were not at all happy about that as people were all stuck in differing ports of call with no way to get home. The Air Force knew if they had any idea just what could be waiting for them they wouldn't complain that much. Thus far the only thing the Hercules radar had picked up was the many combat air patrols the navy was running to protect the Seventh Fleet that had hightailed it out of Pearl two days before.

Strapped in his seat and dozing, Henri Farbeaux had relieved himself of his French Army uniform and replaced it with the desert BDUs—battle dress uniforms—of the United States Army. The only difference was the small French flag on the left breast. The colonel had slept through some of the roughest air of the flight.

Jack Collins, now dressed the same as Henri, and replete with two black stars on his collar, read from a thick file that had been delivered to him, left by a Pentagon courier at Edwards before they departed. Jack took a deep breath, then unsnapped the seat belt holding him into the barbaric canvas seat. He maneuvered around a few of the resting crew that had been relieved an hour before. The men were worn out and slept soundly. He sat next to Farbeaux and slapped him lightly on the knee. Will Mendenhall stirred across the aisle and moved his cap from his eyes to look at Collins. Jack nodded his head and slapped Henri once more.

The Frenchman woke and yawned. He saw Collins and sat up. Will noticed the Frenchman didn't look thrilled to awaken to his old enemy staring at him.

"I would prefer to wake up to a beautiful woman, General." He straightened up and yawned again.

"Yes, I suspect you would."

"Are we there yet?" he asked.

"Almost." Jack opened the folder and then waved Will over. "I need you to witness this, Captain."

"Yes, sir." Mendenhall crossed over and sat on the opposite side of Farbeaux.

"Colonel," Jack held out an official looking document, "before the attack at Camp David, the president signed an order." He gave the paper to Farbeaux. "This order was also countersigned by the French president."

"Two men that are at this very moment very possibly dead?" Henri said with a smirk.

"Possibly," Jack answered. "But that doesn't make this piece of paper any less enforceable. It is a binding and legal document."

Henri Farbeaux looked it over and his brows rose.

"Basically it absolves you of all crimes on U.S. and French soil. The price of this is your complete and utter cooperation in the aforementioned Operation Overlord."

"Why such an honor, General Collins?" He saw Mendenhall roll his eyes.

"It was actually my idea. The alternative was seeing you taken away in handcuffs for immediate prosecution for crimes against both nations, and then for whatever nation was willing to wait in line to get at you."

"I see. Am I supposed to say thank you?" he asked with not so much as a small smile.

"No, Colonel, you are not." Jack closed the large file and sat back. "It was either you die in prison, or—"

"Die somewhere else?" he said, cutting Jack off.

"Exactly. But I'll profess that your fate will be no different from mine or Will's. I need you, Colonel, for what . . . I don't know yet. But I suspect it will be dirty and in your field of expertise. You are going to be my dirty-deeds man, along with your duties as my chief of staff."

"Oh, joy." Henri folded the paper and placed in the large breast pocket. "Have you any idea what it is we're assigned to?" Even Mendenhall leaned forward, hoping for an answer.

"Not a thing, other than we are a part of a fast-reaction force of very special soldiers."

"Special? You mean expendable?"

Jack smiled and then relaxed. "All soldiers are expendable, Colonel, you know that."

"That's why I got out of the business and went to freelancing."

"And look how good that turned out," Will said with an even bigger smile. Then he looked at the silver eagles on the man's collar and decided that maybe chiding him wasn't the best idea at the moment. For all he knew, the Frenchman had stolen a gun from one of his guards earlier.

As they relaxed, an airman came forward with his mic cable dangling from his flight helmet.

"General, the pilot thought you may want to see this. Right over there on the port side." The airman moved off back to the flight deck.

The three men moved to one of the few windows on the large transport and looked down. Three miles away was a sight none of them had ever been witness to before.

"Wow, I always wondered what Mr. Everett and Ryan played with when they were with the navy," Will said.

In battle formation was the entire Seventh Fleet of the United States Navy Pacific Command, with the exception of the far eastern battle squadrons. In the direct center was the USS *George Washington,* flanked by her entire support group.

"They are scattering to keep the Grays guessing. The president and the other leaders were smart enough to get every warship in the world worth anything at sea at the first sign of trouble. This group is out of Pearl and every other Asian port of call and is now awaiting orders." Jack returned to his seat as the Hercules started its climb to altitude for landing at Hickam Air Force Base.

As the *George Washington* battle group steamed beneath them far below, Jack Collins knew that the task force was more than likely headed to the same area of the world where they were destined to fight the war—and the new general had no sound idea where that was.

THE WHITE HOUSE
WASHINGTON, D.C.

Giles Camden was wide awake at three o'clock in the morning. He walked around the Oval Office and paused to look at the ornate rug in front of the Lincoln desk that depicted the seal for the president of the United States. He smiled as he remembered the fight of the past six years to occupy this office. Once called the most hated politician in the nation by the left-wing and middle-of-the-road newspapers and news outlets, until finally his friends of the more right-wing-leaning news organizations started distancing themselves from him, he now stood on the precipice of complete power. It was now time to consolidate that power.

He walked to the window and looked out at the extensive White House lawn and the many batteries of National Advanced Surface-to-Air Missile Systems (NASAMS) that crowded the green grass. Air Force personnel manned each battery and three companies of Marines had joined the force of capital police and Secret Service agents that stood a watchful eye over all. To cap off the entire defense were fifty Delta Force operatives spread throughout the grounds. The acting president placed his hands inside his pockets and cursed his luck that the very same action of the Grays that placed him inside the Oval Office was also the action that was going to keep him, although temporarily, out of it. The Secret Service director had informed him personally that he was to be moved to a more secure location within the hour. He had only come to express his condolences to the first lady in a more private manner.

Camden sniffed at the rebuke he received when the first lady refused to meet with him for the second time.

He left the window and paced to the boxed and sealed articles of the man he was replacing that were stacked in the far corner of the room. He sneered at the personal effects of the comatose man who had hated him beyond measure. He wanted to kick out at the sealed containers but refrained when a knock sounded at the door and it immediately opened.

A young Secret Service agent stepped aside to allow the new president's press and public relations team inside. Two men entered and the Secret Service agent left without so much as a word or a glance back. Camden had noticed the tightness of the White House staff and security people toward him since he had arrived that afternoon. He knew he had caused considerable controversy when he abstained from staying at the temporary quarters they had waiting for him at Blair House, and had ordered the immediate transfer to his real offices. The first lady had moved with her children into the suite of rooms next to her husband's at the hospital.

"Mr. President, we're getting flak from CNN and NBC Overnight about your hurried entrance into the White House while the nation is still in shock over the attacks. We're going to take some gut punches on this."

Camden eyed the two men and then walked to the window, looked out, and then quickly sat down for the first time behind the Lincoln desk.

"I cannot project the power we need with other nations by hiding over at Blair House. For the good of the nation we need to be seen on the job. Besides, the damn Secret Service is moving me to a more secure facility very soon, so CNN and NBC can report that one if they want. In the meantime you people get some fodder of me at the White House and on the job to calm the people."

"Yes, sir." The younger of the two journalistic wunderkinds wrote in his notepad. He stopped and then looked up. "We had a call from General Caulfield's office. He was concerned that your earlier statement undermined the seriousness of the attacks in Japan, Iran, and the International Space Station, by saying that the issues are not as clear cut as they may seem. You stated, without running it by us or your national security advisor, that the attack in Iran was unclear at this point as to who was involved or responsible. That the situation was still unclear because of a possible coup attempt by Ahmadinejad."

The second man walked to one of the two couches and pulled a *Washington Post* from his briefcase. "Also, that an 'accident' had occurred on the space platform. Mr. President, it has leaked out everywhere that the so-called incident was actually recorded by Space Command. There is direct evidence undermining your statements."

"Gentlemen, we need to slow this thing down until we get a grasp of what is really happening."

The two young press gurus exchanged looks.

"Sir, wouldn't it be wise to continue the military policy of the former staff and cabinet at this time? If anything goes wrong no one would hold you responsible. But if it goes right, you can take the lion's share of the accolades."

Camden stood and faced the men with his best Harry Truman pose as he leaned over with fists planted firmly on the desktop.

"From what I understand of this so-called plan of the former administration, we were to strip our defenses here at home and support operations overseas if the main attack occurs there. This I will not do. This country will not be attacked while our forces are out protecting former antagonists."

"But sir—"

"That's all, gentlemen. Please have a press release in my hands by no later than airtime for the morning shows to broadcast. I want to make it clear that we are responding accordingly and that the American people will be protected— so much so that I am going to partially lift the no-fly ban in the continental U.S. no later than noon today." He smiled. "After all, America needs to go to work, don't they? Now, you two find out from the Secret Service just where it is they are going to hide me, and get that statement prepared."

The two young men stood and with one last look back at Camden, nodded their heads and left the office.

The younger of the two ran a hand through his hair and then looked at Camden's secretary, who looked as fresh as the morning as she glared at them. Then he eyed the Air Force colonel sitting in a chair against the wall. He was holding a large aluminum briefcase. The young press secretary knew that the briefcase was called "the football"; inside it were the codes the president needed to launch the nuclear weapons under his direct command. He took his partner by the arm and steered him away when he too was caught looking at the officer. The Secret Service detail looked them over and immediately dismissed them, then stepped to the Oval Office door and opened it.

"Ten minutes, Mr. President." The man closed the door and eyed the two press men closely as they moved away from the door and into the hallway.

"Do you know what that little meeting reminded me of?" the press secretary asked as he looked around him to make sure no one was in earshot.

"I can think of a few things," the taller of the two said as he tossed the edition of the *Washington Post* in the trash receptacle.

"The last few days inside the bunker in Berlin. Why, I would—"

"That's enough; we both know that our new acting president has ears everywhere."

"That's what I mean, my friend. This is a little frightening and this is no game that's going on out there. An accident on the space station? Unclear what really happened in Iran? If he keeps that up he won't have a military friend left in the country, because even those he's influenced over the years will run for cover."

"Well, come on, we have to go play Joseph Goebbels and get this press release ready."

The younger of the two got a pained look on his face.

"Oh, that was a low blow."

MUMBAI, INDIA

In the late afternoon the populace of India's largest city went about their routine in the crowded confines of that nation's most advanced and cultured metropolis. Home to its entertainment industry, and with its natural deep-water port, it was also the commercial center for the entire country. With a population of over thirteen million people it easily outsized the nation's capital, New Delhi, by many millions.

Lieutenant Colonel Rahim Rajiv was on leave from the Indian Air Force and was in the city to visit his ailing mother.

He had just left her small apartment and was waiting on a cab inside the crowded market district of the city. He saw a taxi a block down and started waving his hand. He was in uniform but that didn't mean much inside India, as the military was not very popular and never had been among the vast population of the country. The men and women of India would never understand the expenditures of the government in the pursuit of new ways to kill their fellow man—even with the threat of Pakistan on their doorstep. The cab approached and then slowed and then immediately sped up and passed the uniformed colonel. He frowned and started searching for another when the loud rumble sounded far above the skyscrapers of the city.

Thousands of pedestrians and street vendors bent low as thunder boomed in a clear evening sky. Rajiv flinched as the rumble subsided and managed a look upward. Streaks of lightning suddenly lit up the sky, forcing the colonel to duck his head again, this time behind a cart of fresh fruit. He again looked skyward and saw that dark clouds were beginning to form out of the clear evening air. He frowned as he watched, thinking this weather pattern was anything but normal. The clouds went from white and fluffy to dark and menacing in a matter of mere seconds. He stood and walked out into the street, causing traffic to stop. People were honking horns and screaming obscenities at him as he watched the clouds start to rotate in a counterclockwise motion.

"What the hell?" He shaded his eyes as electrical discharges started in earnest. Yellow and white bolts streaked across the sky as the cloud cover intensified. The wind began and he lost his saucer cap, but didn't notice as many more people started to leave their vehicles to witness the strange weather.

The clouds turned dark and then the first hailstone struck his exposed head. He ducked under a theater marquee as the hail pummeled cars and people as they broke for cover. The wind had increased to fifty plus miles per hour and the clouds continued to form what looked like a hurricane above the city. Only this formation was defined and clear and looked like a special effect from some multimillion-dollar science fiction film.

The colonel started to get a cold feeling in his stomach as the lightning increased in intensity. Blue, red, and yellow streaks that resembled no electrical storm he had ever seen before struck the tall spires of the city's skyscrapers. He estimated the rotating clouds that were swirling above Mumbai were at approximately twenty thousand feet. He pulled his cell phone from his uniform jacket and punched in the number for his air force base just outside the city. The phone didn't ring and as he looked down the lighted screen went dark, just as the power to the multitude of buildings blinked once and then went out.

A tremendous rumbling sounded and he heard a woman scream. She was soon joined by others as the lightning started striking the street and buildings around them. Colonel Rajiv kneeled low as the most horrid sound he had ever heard pierced the dark skies above his head. It was like a deep, bass tuba had gone wild. The sound reverberated and shook the large buildings around him. He felt the sound through the soles of his shoes and then it broke windows in those same structures. He placed his hands over his ears as the tuba sound increased. It was joined by an ear-splitting crack, and as he looked up his eyes widened in terror as the first of six saucers broke through the bottom of the hurricane-like formation. Each time one was seen flying out of the extreme hole that had formed in the swirling mass above, the tuba sound and reverberation echoed, ear-splitting decibels tearing through the city. Six of the metallic saucers broke free and immediately spread over the city with Mach 1 speed.

Men and women started to panic and break their cover as the hail and noise increased. Men fell in their scramble to move someplace, anyplace other than where they were. Then the sound went dead. As Rahim looked up he was pushed to the ground by an air pressure wave that flattened everyone in the city who had been standing. Glass shattered and even the headlights on cars burst as the pressure changed so rapidly that the atoms that made up the glass broke free of one another.

Then the colonel saw it. A massive saucer, larger than three city blocks, broke free of the wormhole and as it did it took most of the clouds down with it. The ship was so large that the storm accompanied it through the atmosphere. Rajiv braced himself as best he could against an iron fire hydrant as the giant saucer fell through the sky and slammed into the tallest buildings in the direct center of the city. The buildings were crushed under the weight of the great saucer as it pancaked the Reliance Communications skyscraper at the heart of Mumbai. Two hundred buildings next to it disintegrated as the extreme weight of the saucer exploded into the city. It came to rest, crushing the lives of two hundred thousand people in the rubble of the skyscrapers.

The six smaller saucers split apart. While three of them hovered over the city-sized ship, the other three made for the Port of Mumbai and splashed into the deep water. The wave they created capsized three container ships tied to the largest dock in the world. They were smashed by the sea and sent to the bottom.

Colonel Rajiv stood, his head bleeding from ten large cuts and his eardrums burst. He looked at the devastation around him and knew the world had changed forever.

The lightning decreased and the cloud cover started to dissipate. As the city started to rise from the dust and the flying and falling rubble, the screams of people could be heard and then the panic started.

One of the largest cities on planet earth was now under Gray attack.

THE PENTAGON
WASHINGTON, D.C.

The extreme size of the Pentagon situation room was alight with massive projected high-definition screens that showed the world as it was on that first day. Army, navy and air force personnel manned every console in the theater-style complex inside the fourth ring of the building. The center was located sixteen floors beneath the hustle and bustle far overhead.

Marine Corps four-star general Stanley Roquefort stood on the upper balcony at a large glass podium and watched the main console in the center of the room. He saw the swirling weather pattern over western India start to dissipate. He pursed his lips and almost reached for the red phone beside the podium, but held his hand in check as he tried to see far beyond the national weather service satellite. He cursed under his breath as his vision was limited to nothing more than a cloud of smoke rising above the city of Mumbai. The scene was eerily reminiscent of the images of 9/11 when the twin towers had collapsed. The general's frustration was evident in his tone. His words were straight but a little louder than he was known for.

"I need Space Command to get me eyes on Mumbai now, not later!" He adjusted his view to the naval assets the United States had in the immediate area and saw that the *Nimitz* battle group was too far south in the Arabian Sea to get eyes on target. "Do we have an Air Force asset in the area so we can get some drones in the sky?"

His adjutant walked up and handed him a slip of flimsy and he scanned it.

"The only thing we have are Predators and they're in Afghanistan, too far off at the moment. We're trying to get Pakistan to get one up in the air but it's business as usual there. They won't lift a finger at the moment to assist India until they know what's going on," the Air Force colonel said and then moved off.

"I want a full squadron of F-15s from Bagram Airfield in Afghanistan to get into the air with tanker support. I don't care what territory they invade, I need real-time intel on this ASAP! Tell the goddamn Paks to get the hell out of our way. If they refuse over-flight shoot their aircraft down! Contact Space Command and get me a recon bird retasked for western India, now!"

The men sat at their consoles and started making calls. The projection screens started showing the displacement of the Indian Air Force as they started to scramble their fighters.

"I need Indian naval assets in the Arabian Sea projected. Come on, let's move!" The general reached for the red phone on his podium. The direct line to the chairman of the Joint Chiefs of Staff connected immediately.

"Caulfield," came the tired voice.

The general was a personal friend and fellow Marine of the chairman; they had served together in both Iraq and Afghanistan and knew each other and how they would react. Both Marine Corps men were not used to having to wait to make decisions.

"Max? Stan. We have an event happening real time in Mumbai. As far as we can see with only weather sats is a smoking hole in the center of the city. Whatever happened, it took out a good portion of downtown. We had a massive weather front that coincides with what we were briefed on to look for. Max, I think this is it." The general went on to explain what he had ordered done and Caulfield agreed with the decisions thus far. "I recommend we go to DEFCON One and set our overseas status accordingly."

Caulfield hesitated, which was unlike the general. "No, not at this time. Go to yellow and bring the alert level up, that's all at this time."

"India may be calling for assistance at any time. I would like to start to move at least the *Nimitz* battle group to a northerly station in the Arabian Sea."

"You have permission to turn the group around, but no action is to be taken at this time. Listen, Stan, we don't know if this is the only incursion that's going to happen. So wait, I have to inform the president of what's taking place. We have had major terror attacks in Afghanistan and the rebels inside Iraq are starting to smell the blood in the water. They think we're too busy to fight, so they are taking advantage. I have to tell the new commander-in-chief, and God knows which direction he'll come out swinging. This may have a direct effect on our Overlord efforts."

"Shit, good luck on that one," he said with a frown. "I wish—"

"There is another severe weather pattern forming over mainland China!" came the loud voice of the weather and atmospheric officer for Asia and Asia Minor. "It looks like we have another event."

"Hold on, Max." Roquefort scanned the data streaming across the far-left screen. He again turned to the phone. "We may have another incursion, Max. This one is forming . . . Oh, shit, it . . . it's forming right over Beijing."

The alarms started sounding and even more military personnel started running to other stations.

"Got to go, Max. Get some clear definition of our orders, especially our ROE when it comes to defending other nations' territories." He was asking for direct Rule of Engagement parameters for his overseas commands.

The line went dead but Roquefort was unaware as he lowered the phone. He watched the hurricane-like formation begin in earnest over China.

"God help us."

BEIJING, CHINA

It was still evening when the multitude of citizens rallied in the streets and squares of the capital. The nation was still in mourning and shock over the sudden death of the president. Signs and posters bearing the man's likeness were held high in recognition of the forward-thinking man who had replaced a tyrant four years before.

As the million-plus men, women, and children milled the streets, few noticed the surface-to-air batteries as they motored into the city. They did become somewhat apprehensive when the Chinese National Army started to take up positions on every street corner and darkened alley, and hundreds of citizens of China's capital city thought it was beginning to look as if the acting president was getting ready to start a crackdown on the rights and privileges they had started to receive under their dead leader's sponsorship.

The attack on Camp David had aired live in China, and most were aware of the devastating news that it was an attack initiated by an extraterrestrial source. Thanks to the advances of the World Wide Web and the country's new right to use it freely, the idea that the attack had been conducted by an alien enemy was not as farfetched as it had once been. Most citizens had watched in quiet fascination as the president of the United States had explained the timeline of events leading to the historic meeting of the great powers at Camp David.

Xiang Lei, a newspaper reporter for the Xinhua News Agency, the equivalent of the Associated Press, watched the soldiers dispersing into the crowded streets with trepidation. He took out his cell phone to call his editor about the developing deployment of troops inside the capital. As he connected with his office he heard a click and then nothing. He looked at the phone and tried several buttons again. The battery was fully charged but the face of the instrument had gone dark.

"Damn, now's not the time for this," he mumbled. He looked around for a phone kiosk. As he did he saw several other men and women trying their phones and he could tell from their reactions and cursing that they were also having trouble. Suddenly the street lights went out and as he looked up he saw that dark clouds had rolled in. There had been rain earlier in the day, but the skies had cleared just before the sun started to set. Now it looked as if the storm was returning. He cursed his luck again and began to walk.

"Look at that," he heard several people say as he crossed the wide avenue in front of the National Ballet of China. He saw that the many citizens who had been watching the evening performance, along with some of the dance company, had moved out of the large theater and were pointing to the sky. He again looked up and saw that the clouds had doubled in size and were now moving in a slow, counterclockwise pattern against the increasing winds. His hair was tousled by static electricity, and then he felt the first raindrops.

The crash of thunder sounded and he heard the nervous laughter of the few dance troupe members still braving the rain. The clouds increased in size and speed of motion and then the first lightning strikes burst from the formation. Soon a blaring warning sounded that momentarily drowned out the blast and crash of lightning and thunder from above. The air raid sirens that stood dormant since the Vietnam War began to sound. Lightning again flashed as the newspaper man ran for cover.

He turned as the first frightened screams joined with the cacophony of noise as fist-sized hailstones struck men and women as they also started to run for cover. Two million people had been caught in the open and even the soldiers broke and tried desperately to find shelter.

Blue, yellow, and white lightning lit the early evening as if a million large artillery pieces had gone off at one time. Buildings were struck and several hundred mourners died in an instant as the tentacles of electricity reached for the ground. Like fingers of a terrible octopus they reached out and fried anyone near the strikes.

Xiang Lei had to brave the danger to be an eyewitness to the event happening in the capital. As the air raid sirens sounded he stepped out of the protection of a store awning and looked skyward. His eyes widened when he saw the impossible pattern in the sky. The clouds were moving at an incredible rate of speed in that horrifying circular path. Tendrils of dark cumulus broke free of the high winds, dissipated, and then more, darker and thicker clouds formed to take their place. The center was directly overhead and he accidentally let out a moan of despair when he saw stars inside the clear center of swirling moisture.

The deep sound of bass drums and horns seemed to come from everywhere, enough so that he had to cover his ears at the assault. It reverberated through the capital, drowning out the frightened screams of the populace. Windows shattered and dead streetlights burst and fell into the throng of people. Xiang Lei watched in awe at the amazing spectacle. He was bumped and pushed aside as soldiers broke in earnest from their posts. Missile batteries and gun emplacement crews, along with the crews of armored personnel carriers, ran in abject terror.

With a loud explosion of a million bass drums and a vibration the likes of which the newspaper man had never felt, the first saucer broke into the skies over Beijing. It was soon followed by five more. Then the world was turned upside down as the saucers started firing infused-light weapons at specific targets throughout the city. People panicked as they fled into any building they could. Soldiers tried to fight the rising tide of humanity and return to their batteries after being harangued by their officers, but it was too late.

The skies erupted and the swirling clouds burst apart as the largest object Xiang Lei had ever seen fell from the sky. It looked like it wasn't under any form of power. It fell like a rock. The giant saucer hit the speed of sound just as it struck the China Central Television building and the International Finance Center. The bulk of the massive ship slammed into and crushed the Natural History museum in the center of the city, pounding it to dust along with the accumulated knowledge of five thousand years of Chinese history. The middle and southern seas, lakes that had stood the turbulent test of time at the heart of the city, burst into mist as the saucer came to rest. Steam exploded from the moisture of the large lakes and the waters evaporated in an instant. Fifty square blocks were crushed. A million and half Chinese citizens were crushed or burned to death in the resulting fires.

Xiang Lei never saw the impact of the saucer as the pressure wave preceding the strike had crushed anyone exposed to the sudden downrush of air. His body had turned into a fine mist, blown away on the winds.

Three of the hundred-foot-diameter saucers broke from the city and made for the deep-water port of Tianjin. The three vehicles were fired upon by coastal batteries, twenty-millimeter rounds bursting against the hulls of the speeding ships. The rounds glanced off the smooth surfaces of the metallic saucers. One by one they smashed into the sea. As ships were capsized and dock workers were swept away and killed by the small tsunami created by the impact of the three invaders, the UFOs sank deep into Bohai Bay.

The three remaining saucers came low to the ground, hovering just above the larger object as it continued to settle into the crushed city center beneath.

A loud crack was felt and heard as the top of the giant saucer exploded outward. Cables the thickness of telephone poles burst from the vehicle. On the tip of each was a pointed arrowhead of an anchor as they pierced the evening with a scream. They rose to an altitude of seven thousand feet. The apparatus resembled a basket as it covered the skies. After reaching their highest arc, and then starting down into the outskirts of Beijing, they slammed into the ground, buildings, and homes, and then buried themselves deeply with an explosion of earth, concrete, steel, and humanity.

A half hour after the fall of the giant saucer into the center of Beijing, twenty of China's latest generation of fighter jets, the Chengdu J-20, overflew the strike area. What the pilots saw was a glowing mass of lines that covered the entire city. The bluish glow emanated from the tendrils of cable that had been launched from the saucer. The entire city looked as if it had been covered in a large woven basket that glowed blue in the darkening skies of China.

The second assault on the planet had taken place. The nations of the world trembled as the true power of the enemy was demonstrated with extreme violence.

SCHOFIELD BARRACKS
HONOLULU, HAWAII

Jack Collins, Will Mendenhall, and Henri Farbeaux had been met at Hickam Air Force Base and escorted by Humvee to Schofield Barracks. As they passed through the main gate they saw elements of the 25th Infantry Division loading gear onto two-and-a-half-ton trucks. It was Farbeaux who noticed that the busiest area they had seen on their drive through the post was the activity at the main armory. Jack also saw but didn't comment on the fact that the division was loading up live ordance. He also noticed that they were being escorted by four Humvees with the 2nd Stryker Brigade Combat Team designation on the bumpers of the vehicles. He exchanged looks with Will, who just raised his brows from the front seat.

Before they had offloaded from the C-130 Hercules they had been briefed on the events in India and China. Since they had left the west coast of the United States the world had become a battleground.

The five Humvees drove to the oldest section of Schofield and pulled onto a gravel drive that had seen better days. Jack recognized the area as the oldest barracks still standing in the state of Hawaii. The last men to occupy this area left their souls and their lives in the most horrible places on Earth: Bataan; Corregidor; Luzon. The area had not seen live activity since the end of World War II.

Jack stepped out of the back space of the Humvee and started to reach for his bag and briefcase, but was halted by the staff sergeant who had accompanied them from Hickam.

"Sir, we'll take responsibility for your gear. You're needed inside ASAP."

Jack took his briefcase with a nod of his head and without comment as the occupants of the other four Humvees exited with M-4 automatic weapons. They took up station at the front door of the old wooden structure.

"I think the last time I saw one of these old barracks was at a museum at the site of old Fort Ord in Monterey, California," Will said as he saw the peeling light green and brown paint that once covered the building.

"Hey, my father graduated basic training from there, Captain, watch it," Jack chided as they were escorted up the old wooden stairs.

"I think you people love old things so much they obviously

felt at home bringing you here." Henri touched the old wooden railing of the stairs and snatched his hand away when he picked up a splinter. "But then again, rank has its privileges," he grumbled as he followed the two Americans inside the dimly lit and dusty barracks.

Jack stood for a moment and then removed his sunglasses against the dimness of the old building. His sense of history was alive and well as he saw a worn picture of the World War II pinup girl, Betty Grable, back to the camera, looking over her shoulder, in her famous pose that had excited men since 1944. Her legs—the bottom half of the print— were missing.

The sergeant gestured to three chairs in the center of the once green linoleum. As the three men looked around, the sergeant from the 2nd Stryker Combat Team went from window to window and pulled down the hastily installed blinds. He nodded his head and then left the barracks through the back door. The lighting was yellowish and reminded Will of an old classroom, one that he was not particularly comfortable in. A man in a black suit entered and placed a tray of coffee on a small table. Jack quickly noticed he had the credentials of the FBI hanging from his neck. Without a word the man left and the three were left alone.

Henri walked over and poured himself a cup of black coffee, and then returned to his seat. Will also sat but Jack remained standing. Soon two more FBI agents entered, wheeling in a large stand, and set up a fifty-two-inch monitor they plugged into a long extension cord.

As they left they saw a figure enter the main barracks from the old room in the back that used to be the quarters of the platoon drill instructor. The gentleman was short and stocky with a head of distinguished gray hair. He was wearing a brown suit of good style and an old-fashioned bow tie. His glasses were thick and his beard as gray as his hair.

He walked up and studied Jack for a moment, then nodded his head at Mendenhall and Farbeaux.

"As imposing as I was led to believe," he said in a thick British accent, placing his hands behind his back and rock-

ing on his heels. He smiled and turned his attention to Jack.
"I once knew a man, a rather big gentleman, he had the kind
of stature that you have. Oh, he was a bear of a man, blind
in one eye and mean as a snake. You remind me of him."

Jack looked down on the man and didn't say a word, not
knowing if he were friend or foe.

"He had the odd name of Garrison, and the poor sot
chose a life of military adventure over the thrills of politics
many years ago. I believe he ended up running some sort of
boring think tank underneath some desert or other in the
States. Does this sound familiar to you, General Collins?"

Jack saw the stern look that replaced the smile for the
briefest of moments before the friendly grin returned.

"Sir, I have never heard of such a man, and am not aware
of any think tank under any desert, in America or any other
country." Jack remained still, watching the man who had
just tested him, for what reason he didn't know. He
chanced a glance back at Will and Henri and saw that they
were both stone-faced.

"Yes, I believe you are just like this man, this Garrison
Lee, General Collins."

"I'm afraid you have me at a disadvantage, sir."

"Yes, that's a position I prefer, but alas I don't have the
luxury of time to play my little games." He held out a soft
hand for Jack to shake. "In my country I am known as Lord
Harrison Durnsford, of Her Majesty's MI6."

Jack shook his hand and then released the manicured fingers. He gestured to the two men seated behind him as
Mendenhall and Farbeaux stood. Henri continued to sip his
coffee with his cold blue eyes on the English lord, one of the
queen's spies.

"May I introduce Captain—"

"Newly promoted Captain William Mendenhall." He
shook Will's hand. "A soldier who has risen through
the regular army ranks, which I admire very much." Lord
Durnsford slowly turned to face the Frenchman. "And this is
Colonel Henri Farbeaux, a man I am most familiar with, as
he has recently been absolved of many, many crimes inside

the borders of the Empire. I learned to become a grand ad-
mirer of your exploits, Colonel, even though my organization once had a kill order out on you."

Henri sat his coffee on the vacated chair and stepped forward and to shake the Englishman's hand. Jack noticed he
remained quiet, as a man under scrutiny should.

Lord Durnsford turned his attention back to Jack. "General, we have little time before your rather dangerous flight
to the south. I pulled my strings and then even stamped my
feet to get this meeting with you before your departure."

"Well, then, I guess you won out," Jack said as he sat down
in his chair.

The man from MI6 again rocked on his heels and waited
for Jack to get comfortable.

"Gentlemen, it is most fitting that our first meeting takes
place here. After all, it was at this very post and at the naval
base in the harbor that World War II started for the American race, and most fitting that your war begins here also."

Henri felt the setup even before Jack did. Mendenhall
knew something was up but wasn't sure what it was.

"Gentlemen, since the assault on your Camp David, we
have lost the services of not only the driving force behind
Operation Overlord, the president, but also a man we now
know will be desperate for support from the world—the
president of China. The German chancellor was officially
pronounced dead at three A.M. These men were three very
important cogs in the alliance."

Lord Durnsford paced away from the three attentive men
and then lowered his head with his hands still behind his
back, like a college instructor lecturing a group of students,
which was exactly what Jack felt like. Henri was taking it
like he did when he was in War College in France—bored.
He took a drink of his coffee.

"Gentlemen, the alliance will not stand in the face of
these attacks." Durnsford turned and gave the three a ten-
tative smile. "My department says so, and so does your
CIA, or at least the director of said agency. The biggest threat
outside of the Gray incursion is the acting president of the

United States. We surmise that this . . . gentleman will not fulfill his obligation as laid down by the men before him. He will call it 'national priorities,' of course, and most likely he will ask for and receive the backing of the American people in this time of crisis. He is very persuasive that way."

"Lord Durnsford, we know and understand what the temporary man in the White House is capable of. He's a hawk and lover of the military, but only when it suits his needs. He will make friends very quickly in the halls of the Pentagon with men of equal ambitions."

"As I said, General, you are Senator Lee's double, or at the very minimum, related to him in some way. Well, we have an answer for him." He pulled a gold pocket watch from his vest and snapped it open. "We are short of time, so I will not beat around the proverbial bush as you Americans like to say. The director of your . . . think tank, Dr. Niles Compton, is a very dear friend of mine, one I have had many run-ins with, but a man immensely respected in my offices. You, General Collins, are the answer to the alliance falling apart—a little more so since the Camp David incident."

Jack was stunned that this English lord knew about Niles Compton just as he claimed to know Garrison Lee, but he remained silent, not revealing his surprise.

"He foresaw this happening in the event something took place—not that he predicted the attack and the succession of power in your country. He was my friend and if we lose him we have lost one of the best hopes for our world. You gentlemen will be tasked to end the threat against us with a volunteer force of the best-trained and well-equipped soldiers in the world. You will have men selected from most nations on Earth that will be dedicated to the destruction of our enemy, and not even their own governments can pull them back. They are even now awaiting you at your final destination."

"Your brief is as confusing as the past four days, Lord Durnsford." Jack again looked at his watch, wanting to get to the secure computer center located at the headquarters building. He was hoping Pete Golding had fulfilled a small request he had asked of him and his supercomputer, Europa.

"Calm, General, I have arranged your phone call with your young Lieutenant McIntire." Durnsford gave Collins a look over the top of his glasses. "I suspected you would wish to know your people are safe. They are—at least for the moment, as they are transiting some quiet waters. Their ordeal will soon start as our little ruse to get them free of the North Atlantic has worked, but I'm afraid the Grays will catch on eventually and the very power plant they are escorting will lead the Grays straight to your friends. I suspect a rather large engagement at sea before too long."

Will looked at Jack. The concern for Sarah and Ryan was evident.

"I suspect you will keep that to yourself when you speak. Remember, I am granting you this privilege, General."

With one nod of his head Jack knew he was cornered and could not warn Sarah and Ryan what might be coming.

Durnsford reached into a coat pocket and used a small remote to activate the large monitor that had been set up. Two split-screen views of the attack zones in Mumbai and Beijing illuminated and they saw that they were live views.

"Your Lieutenant McIntire and the others are transiting the sea in one of the most powerful warships afloat, and they will meet other, even more impressive assets the closer they get to their destination." Durnsford again looked at his watch and then snapped it closed. "I am sure I have confused you enough. I just need a man like you to know, General, because you are known to follow your orders to the letter." He smiled at the three men before him. "At least to a point, and that is the point I wish to expand on." He leaned over and looked Collins in the face and became deadly serious. "No matter what orders you receive to the contrary, General, you and your men will do the job that is assigned to you. You will possibly be pressured by higher influences, even be threatened with courts-martial and death; be called a traitor to your nation, as will the men under you. But stay the course, General, stay the course. If you do, the odds of our world climbing out of this bloody mess will increase a thousandfold. Far worse than the view you see here." The small British spy gestured at the two smoldering cities.

Jack knew he was talking about the changes at the highest levels of government in his and other nations. That deals had been struck in order to make Matchstick's grand plan of Overlord become reality. He also knew that he would come down on the side of Niles, Lee, and—as he looked at the small man before him—Lord Durnsford.

"Stay the course, no matter what, General." He finally smiled as he toyed with his pocket watch. "If I'm still breathing, and if needed, I promise I'll have your court-martial littered with sympathetic ears. You still may be shot, but you'll receive a much better last meal."

Mendenhall looked at Henri and then Collins and shook his head. "I knew this Hawaii thing wasn't going to last."

"Precisely, young captain." Durnsford opened his watch and looked at the time. "Gentlemen, good luck and God's speed. You have a rather large Galaxy transport aircraft to catch and again you have to fly rather low to the ground. You may make your phone call enroute, General."

With that Lord Durnsford nodded his head toward the back of the room and a door was opened. With one last sad smile and nod of his head the man from MI6 turned and left.

The three men stood as a man gestured for them to follow him outside. And again it was Will who put things into proper perspective, as young soldiers usually do.

"I am so very glad we now know what's happening and are totally clear on our mission," he said in mock understanding as he placed his cap on his head. "I think they are out to kill us in the most dramatic way possible." He looked at Farbeaux with a sour look. "And why do I think hanging out with you, Henri, has something to do with it?"

"For the first time since I've known you, Captain, I find myself in total agreement. I understand nothing." Henri turned toward Jack. "I imagine it's far too late to accept that invitation for that long stay at your Leavenworth prison?"

Jack shook his head. "I think it's too late for a lot of things, Colonel."

MUMBAI, INDIA
2200 HOURS

One hundred Russian-manufactured Su-27SK "Flanker" fighter aircraft flew at Mach 1 toward their designated target, which was entrenched at the center of Mumbai. The entirety of the strike force was going to lay waste to the four targets painted on their radar screens. The flight leader of the strike orbited at twenty-seven thousand feet in an Airbus A20 radar and defense aircraft, a cheaper variant of the American AWAC. It was on the Airbus where the air assault would be coordinated.

The large saucer had deployed the same apparatus as the vehicle in China. It was glowing a soft blue hue in the dark nighttime skies. And thus far all attempts at breaching the defense shield had been fruitless. Probes by the thirteen infantry divisions deployed around Mumbai had found that any form of contact with the alien cable network had been met with no resistance or event.

The airstrike was in support of elements of the 50th Parachute Regiment (Special Forces) and the full force of the 411th (Independent) Parachute Field Company (Bombay Sappers) who had been on station since the incident began six hours before. The infantry divisions would be the follow-up strike after the Sappers had gained the interior of the alien shielding.

The 411th Bombay Sappers had started testing the thick cables that had been buried deeply into the ground since ten that evening. The barricade was crisscrossed in three-foot squares and the Sappers thought they could get the entire regiment through under the cover of the Air Force fighters when they arrived. The fence had been tested and thus far appeared dormant. It looked as if it was just a steel cable fence. They had managed to get over four thousand of the city's residents out through the less than formidable shield. One of the regiment's helicopters had even managed to land on the structure and thus far had repeated the maneuver sixteen times in differing areas, giving them hope that when the airstrikes began they could blast holes through the steel "basket" and bring in the many attack choppers of the 125th Aviation Battalion that had been quickly recalled from the Pakistani border.

General Jai Bajaj, commander of the combined 1st and 3rd Armored Divisions, stood atop the tallest building outside of the city. The American-owned Century Records Building was thirty-five stories tall and afforded him an excellent view of the city and the giant saucer sitting in its crushed and still-smoking city center. The utility companies had arranged emergency lighting and over five thousand high-powered spotlights were illuminating the giant craft.

The general moved his glasses to the streets below and saw over two hundred of India's newest main battle tanks, the Arjun Mark II. They were joined by four hundred Tarmour AFV armored personnel carriers with over three thousand men awaiting orders to advance into the city. They would be his spearhead.

"Inform the strike coordinator to start the air attack, please," the general said as he moved the glasses to the caged-in city. "This ought to provoke a response," he said under his breath.

The glow of the giant "basket" remained constant and the Sappers lining its outside started using cutting torches to break their way in while army tunnel teams began digging underneath the shielding. Men stood at the ready as the sparks of hundreds of torches shone around the entire circumference of the three-square-mile shield as Sappers started to penetrate the pretty but ineffective cage.

The shriek of jet engines pierced the clear sky above as the Indian Su-27 fighters made their initial runs on the center of the city. Their target was the very center of the large saucer on the two-city-block-wide upper dome. One by one the incredibly fast fighters dove on the target ten thousand feet below. The general had chills as he watched the Air Force start its music from above.

The initial weapons to be released by the first ten aircraft were the latest in Indian technology: the Sudarshan laser-guided bomb. The commander watched the sky but all he could see was the ten fighters as they swooped low and then climbed after releasing their loads. Immediately cheers erupted around him as two of the bombs struck the thick steel mesh and detonated high above their target with a bright flash of explosive force. The rest of the eight laser munitions penetrated the cable shield and struck the enormous saucer directly on its top-most section where the giant cables had deployed from earlier. More cheers sounded as men saw what looked like large chunks of the vehicle fly skyward.

"That's it!" the general yelled as loud as the men around him. "If you want to just sit there and take it, we will accommodate you!" he yelled enthusiastically.

Three more of the weapons made it through the mesh while others detonated far above the saucer. More cheers. The general switched his view to the men using cutting torches far below. It looked as if they were making good progress.

"Armored lines three and four, open fire!" he called out. "Artillery, commence fire!"

His radioman immediately made the call and an instant later the main battle tanks of the Indian Army started their barrage as the first line of tanks started firing point-blank into the shield where they detonated, ripping huge holes in the pattern. More aerial bombs fell; these were the old-fashioned dumb iron bombs that hit everything—saucer, buildings, and even the smaller alien vehicles that were there to protect the larger. The one thousand artillery pieces of the Indian army opened fire from the small rises of hills around the city and from the docks of the city.

Explosions rang out loudly throughout Mumbai to the cheers of the infantry soldiers waiting to breach the iron shield.

General Jai Bajaj watched as the top dome of the larger saucer seemed to be withering under the onslaught of pinpoint bombing. He saw pieces flying high into the sky and was hoping it was the material the craft was made of and not just the shrapnel from the old-fashioned iron bombs.

"Our Sapper units report that they have opened sixteen gaps in the shield and ask permission to enter in force," his adjutant said, holding the phone close to his ear.

"Permission granted. Order the cease-fire of all aerial bombardment and get me my paratroops on top of that shield for entry from above, now!"

The adjutant passed on the order and the general moved his field glasses toward the base of the enemy shield. He couldn't believe an advanced race of beings would ever think that a wire fence would keep his forces from entering the city. He hissed approval as he watched elements of the 1st and 3rd armored regiments start to pour through the gaps in the line.

"Inform the prime minister that we have breached the enemy defenses and are advancing into the city. No enemy resistance thus far detected."

The information was passed on to Delhi as the troops entered the holes the Sappers had cut.

"Okay, gentlemen, get the first element of tanks through as soon as the holes are widened."

Overhead, four of the Indian Air Force's mighty transport planes, the Russian-built IL-76 aircraft, started to disgorge the airborne units of the proud military. Some units were designated to land on the shield cables and place explosives, then rappel down to the top of the saucer's dome and the surviving buildings of the city. The remaining units would penetrate the shield directly from the air and land atop the vehicle and place charges at the anchor points of the cables, the direct apex of the center-most dome. The Indian army and air forces were about to take the fight directly to this barbaric enemy. The airborne units would be supported by the armor of two full divisions. The general estimated full incursion in less than thirty minutes.

"There they are," his adjutant said as he pointed to the first chutes of falling airborne. The white of their canopies shone brightly in the light-blue haze of the enemy shield and the reflection off the saucer of the thousand high-powered spotlights.

"Excellent," the general said as he turned his glasses skyward. The powerful main battle tanks that remained outside of the steel-like fence kept up their fire. Rounds were now striking the three hovering saucers and it looked as if they were being rocked by the detonations against their hulls. The general watched as the leading saucer in front of the larger platform wobbled, and then straightened as two armor piercing dart-like Sabot rounds caught it along the centerline mass. He was amazed it recovered so quickly, straightening and then rising back into formation.

"They won't last long after our infantry and airborne troops start hitting them with Dragon Missiles."

More cheers sounded from below as men started pouring through the widened gaps in the shield.

Before anyone realized what was happening, the shield went brilliant blue. Men caught entering the gaps in the line immediately ceased to exist, vanishing micro-seconds before they could even feel the searing heat that caused their deaths. The holes that had been cut in the cables started to regenerate and connect once again with the squares of cable directly above, beneath, and at the sides. The system of defense was actually healing itself, looking like growing snakes as they regenerated and connected once more. It was as if the cables were living things that had sprung to life.

General Bajaj's heart skipped a beat as he turned his attention to the falling chutes of his airborne. His fingers tightened on the field glasses as men started to land on the upper portion of the shield. In magnificent flashes of blue and white light his brave men started bursting into flame. As he zoomed in the general could see that it wasn't the men flaring and burning, but their clothing and equipment. The flesh of his soldiers had immediately turned to ash as they hit the shield. They were being exterminated just as bugs in an electrically charged zapper would be when they ventured too close. All around the city above and below the shield was healing itself and his infantry started disintegrating by the thousands before his eyes.

As he shook in rage at the enemy ruse, he heard as well as saw the three smaller saucers start to move over the city. He watched as the round vehicles started to fire on his infantry inside and outside the shield. Large bursts of an energy weapon, the likes of which he had never seen before, started blowing men apart from their insides. They exploded as if they had swallowed a grenade. The few tanks that had entered the city were cut in half and the men inside died in the resulting explosions of their ordnance. The large saucer also flared to killing life as thick, purplish light fired from the upper dome. The sky illuminated with exploding and falling aircraft, both fighters and the transports that were still dropping men from their doors. The defense by the saucers was like watching a western light show as bolt after bolt of energy was cut loose.

"Oh, no, no, no," his adjutant said as he gestured wildly toward the bottom half of the large saucer.

Large doors that were at least a thousand feet wide slowly opened and large rounded shapes of chromed steel rolled out like balls from a pinball machine. Thousands of the objects rolled through and over the rubble of the buildings, surprising the three hundred men who had gotten close to the seemingly dormant craft. The soldiers started hitting the rolling machines with small-arms fire and then fifty-caliber weaponry from the few armored personnel carriers nearby. That seemed to stop them. The general had his hopes raised only momentarily as the sixteen-foot-diameter balls stopped suddenly as if they were stuck in the asphalt of the street and the crumbling concrete of the destroyed buildings; then they sprang open like an animal trap. His eyes widened further when he saw that the balls had expanded to manlike shapes. The automatons were chromed steel monsters. Their bulk was tremendous as their heavy weapons started to open up on his exposed troops. The machines were firing high impact, exploding kinetic rounds directly into flesh. Men were exploding into bright red bursts of mist as they were struck.

"Look!" men started shouting from their vantage point of safety outside the shield.

The general looked through his glasses as the Grays showed themselves for the first time. They charged through the open portals in a mass concentration, but didn't start attacking the remaining ground forces inside the shield. They charged directly into the standing office buildings and apartments that were abundant in Mumbai. They streamed into homes, the subway, and other places of sanctuary where the population had taken shelter.

"What are they doing?" his adjutant asked in a stupefied and frightened voice.

The tall, thin Grays, dressed in their purplish clothing and carrying long weapons of a sort that was unknown to the soldiers, entered the buildings by the thousands and to everyone's horror they started dragging people from the safety of their homes and places of work where they thought they had survived the opening assault. They were pushed and rounded up like herds of sheep and made to walk, crawl, or die. The Grays were taking them into the large ship thousands at a time.

The general lowered his field glasses and felt his blood run cold. The enemy had lain in wait just to demonstrate their power. Now he didn't know what the enemy plan was. The metal machines walked on two legs and started to track down his men who had escaped the initial confrontation; they too were taken by the hundreds. They were dug out of small pockets where they fired their weapons to no effect. He saw several of the walking machines go down after being struck by the old Dragon Missiles given to India by the Unites States, but he saw that the remaining men would not have a chance of taking down thousands of the evil, mechanized brutes. They were slaughtering men at every street corner and every hastily prepared position, even as the citizens of Mumbai were being dragged into the large saucer.

The carnage continued above as well. Airborne troops,

who had managed to start their assault by rappeling down lines, were shot by laser fire and burst into small fireflies of flame by the gunnery located at the top dome of the large saucer. They fell like embers from a bonfire until their remains littered the top of the dome.

The shield glowed brighter than ever as the power of the grid increased, causing his tanks that had come too close to melt under the intense heat of the mesh-like cage. Men jumped from their burning and melting armor and were cut down by the mechanized monstrosities that were now at the shield wall, firing into soldiers and equipment that were still outside the trapped city.

The main strike force, the most powerful assault element ever assembled by an Indian army in the field, and its proud air force had been defeated in less than fifteen minutes after the enemy had shown itself for the first time.

The largest city in India was delivered to the Grays with the loss of over eighteen thousand men and forty thousand tons of equipment, and the Indian air force had virtually ceased to exist.

Mumbai was now lost to the world and its millions of citizens taken for reasons that would shake the planet to its eternal core.

10

The *Pyotr Veliky* had set a new world record for a southern
Atlantic Ocean transit for a ship of war. She had surpassed
her top speed of thirty-seven knots no less than six different
times as she made the southern crossing. Her nuclear reactor had gone into the red twice when the giant missile cruiser
had hit bad weather, this just to keep her speed over thirty
knots. The crew was exhausted after their 50 percent alert
status had gone into effect after she had departed the fleet.
Thus far the ruse had worked as they had received flash
radio traffic that the 123-ship Northern Fleet had been
overflown five times by a craft they never laid eyes on. The
rumor that they were being hunted had quickly spread
throughout the ship. Jason Ryan had reminded both Sarah
and Anya that the Russian Navy was no different from any
navy on earth—believe only 10 percent of all rumors and
you should come out ahead on any bet made.

As he stood looking at the tarp and plastic covered alien
power plant, Jason was fearful that he had been overzealous
as far as his rumor estimate. As he looked skyward into the
crisp late afternoon sky he had the distinct feeling that the

Pyotr Veliky was now entering a kill zone. That naval officer feeling that comes on career sailors who have seen death up close. He felt that was what was stalking them—death.

Jason watched as five of the Russian and Polish nuclear technicians checked the tarp covering the power plant, making sure none of the sea spray had compromised the sealing plastic underneath. The technicians looked short and bulky in their heavy arctic parkas as they moved about. Jason got a chill and placed the fur-lined hood over his head. He had been on deck for twenty minutes to avoid Sarah's sad eyes as she spoke to Jack from the radio center of the large missile cruiser. Anya had also excused herself, wishing she had an opportunity to speak with Carl, but she figured that the new admiral had plenty on his plate at the moment.

Soon he realized he wasn't alone. He turned and saw Anya standing beside him as she stared out over the railing. Jason walked three paces over and joined her.

"Homesick already?" he asked.

"Already?" She smiled and then lost it as suddenly as it had arrived. "I've been homesick ever since I said good-bye to Carl. He's my home, not some barren patch of land." She turned back to look at the sea and shivered. "So in that sense, yes, I am extremely homesick."

"I miss my friends. I think I may go on missing them too." It was Ryan's turn to look down and away from Anya's eyes. "When we got that report that Niles was seriously injured in the Camp David attack it was like a portent of things to come, and I realized then just how close I had become to all of my people at Group." He looked at her. "I mean friends."

"Mumbai has just fallen," came a small voice from behind them. "The Indian Army was defeated in just a little over twenty minutes after they had thought they had the upper hand."

They turned and saw Sarah as she came from the upper decks, careful to avoid the six sailors coming off of watch. The men were in a hurry to get out of the cold air that was increased in misery by the ship's torrid speed.

Jason and Anya saw the worry on the young lieutenant's features as she pulled the drawstrings of her hood tighter to fit her small head.

"How is the colonel . . . I mean the general?" Jason asked.

"Alive at the moment. He, Will, and Henri are in transit, wave hopping south." She smiled finally. "They are wave hopping on a southern course trying to evade prying eyes. And you know how he hates flying anyway."

"Yeah, so does Mendenhall. I imagine he may even be frightened enough to be sitting on Farbeaux's lap right about now, which would thrill that thief to no end."

The moment of tension was broken and the three laughed.

"You know, if they are heading south, it's possible they have the same destination as ourselves, which means you might just see Jack real soon."

"I know," Sarah said. "But is that a good thing or not? I mean, where we are going might not be the safest place to be."

"Any word on Beijing?" Anya asked, changing the bleak subject to an even blacker one, but also one that wasn't as personal as the current question.

"No, satellite images are showing the city is ringed with the largest Chinese army ever to take the field. But after the Mumbai disaster they are holding. The enemy hasn't made any move like they have in India, and the Chinese right now like it that way."

"Unlike India, they have a massive troop presence inside the city already. Someone over there was forward thinking enough to get about a hundred thousand men and some heavy armor into Beijing before the Grays' arrival. Captain Lienanov said that their intelligence shows about a thousand tanks and half that in artillery pieces. But right now the commander of Chinese ground forces is satisfied that the Grays haven't budged."

"How about the new president—how is he taking the news?" Ryan asked.

Sarah turned and looked at both Anya and Ryan. "He's

talking about pulling back all American forces to protect the homeland first. Virginia is going to sit in on a meeting with the British, French, Russian, and Chinese delegates and present Matchstick's analysis of the attacks thus far."

"No, they can't expose Matchstick to that man in office, at least right now." Ryan saw a confused look cross Anya's face. He ignored her ignorance and stared at Sarah.

"Camden and the others won't know exactly who they are talking to; a few of them, like the British and Chinese, know about our asset, but all most of them will learn is that he is an asset with vast knowledge of the enemy. Most have guessed, I think, but don't know for sure we have him in our corner. He'll be speaking through Europa. Virginia has seen to that. As long as the president is alive she will keep Matchstick away from the Speaker of the House."

Ryan finally smiled. "That ought to give everyone a thrill, to have Marilyn Monroe explaining things to them. I would like to see their faces on that one."

"Who is this Matchstick Man?" Anya asked as she couldn't hold the question any longer.

"You mean that the great Mossad is actually in the dark about something the United States is doing?" Ryan laughed. "God, the world is in a tailspin."

"Maybe not the Mossad, but I am," she answered.

"Let's just say he's a friend that would give his life for his new home," Sarah said, warning Ryan with a look about security. "Anyway, I would like to hear what he has to say myself. We may be able to—"

Sarah was cut short by a blaring announcement over the ship's speakers. Anya turned to the railing once more and leaned over just as the alarms sounded abovedecks. Before they knew it sailors were rushing to stations. The speed of *Pyotr Veliky* increased just as she started to heel to starboard. She turned so sharply that Ryan had to reach out to keep Anya from being flung headfirst into the sea. He pulled her back and they both slammed into the steel decking. Sarah immediately saw why the giant warship made such a severe turn.

"Oh, my God," she said as the saucer surfaced in front of the *Pyotr Veliky*. Water was running off the one-hundred-foot-wide metallic vehicle and she seemed to be stationary in the calm seas. Before Sarah could say more the three were practically lifted off their feet by four burly Russian seamen and hustled to the stairs that led to the second deck. Sarah was in the rear as they rushed up the slippery steel steps but she could not take her eyes off the saucer as it remained in the path of the missile cruiser.

"Get inside and to the evacuation stations immediately!"

Ryan was pulled inside along with Anya by Captain Lienanov.

As Sarah finally entered the hatch the door was sealed and dogged tight.

"Hurry, we have just gone to general quarters. I must get to the bridge!" The captain left the three.

As the captain made his way forward they heard the rumble of four Granit SS-N-19 "Shipwreck" antiship missiles leave their tubes. The entire cruiser shuddered under the launch of the heavy weapons. Then the deep rumble of the ship's twin AK-130 130-millimeter/L70 gun opened fire. The ship was still leaning heavily to starboard.

On the bridge second captain Lienanov joined the commander of the vessel, Captain Andre Vileski, a no-nonsense and by-the-book man. He was watching the saucer take hits from the heavy-caliber 130-millimeter weapons and just as Vileski ordered the helm hard to port, they saw the four missiles strike the alien vehicle. Two of the Shipwrecks hit the uppermost, raised dome of the saucer and the next two hit the curving edge where the rounded metallic edge met the sea. They were all direct hits.

As the *Pyotr Veliky* completed her turn five more of the Shipwrecks struck the saucer, and still the craft made no defensive move to save itself from the hard-punching offense of the Russian missile cruiser.

Captain Vileski watched through the large bridge glass windows and nodded his head as the saucer was momentarily blocked from view as several missiles and 130-millimeter rounds detonated at the same moment against the enemy's hull. The vehicle vanished under a bursting cloud of smoke and debris.

"These bastards will soon learn the difference between battling the Indian Air Force and the Russian Navy!" he shouted. His men on the bridge started to take heart that the brand-new *Pyotr Veliky* would possibly survive the encounter.

As the warship completed her turn to port and straightened her bow into the light wind, Lienanov tried to remind his commander of the tactic they had been warned about directing them to keep up concentrated fire on the enemy and to not let up. The saucer had obviously taken damage because Lienanov had seen large chunks of flying metal being torn from its upper half before the whole scene became obscured with smoke.

"Captain, we must maintain fire and try and move off as fast as we can. We have orders to avoid a confrontation!" Lienanov knew the missile tubes had gone silent as the fire control teams in the command and control section far below on deck six awaited the order to continue. Only the 130- and twenty-millimeter weapons kept up a constant fire. Lienanov had a distinct feeling they were witnessing the exact same thing that the Indian commanders had in Mumbai—the enemy was waiting for the right time to make their move. "Captain, put up a defensive screen of torpedoes in the water as a shield and allow us to digress, give the trap a chance to work. This action is not in our orders!"

"I think you need to learn your place, *Second* Captain Lienanov. We are to take advantage of the situation. We will—"

"Look!" his lookouts on the bridge wing called out as they caught sight of the ship, the last of the smoke whisked away by the winds its bulk and engines were creating.

The hearts of the men on the bridge froze momentarily. Instead of seeing the saucer in pieces, it was slowly starting to rise completely from the sea. The water beneath the enemy ship was being pushed aside as her engines whipped the freezing ocean into frenzied white caps. But the one thing they all saw at once was the last of the holes created by the Shipwreck missiles fast closing, healing over like a wound forming a scab. The metal that replaced the damaged areas was lighter in color, but it was metal just the same. The saucer was now undamaged from the massive strike of the missile cruiser.

"Lock on missiles and continue fire!" the captain yelled, and ordered another hard maneuver to starboard.

Too late the mighty ship heeled over, exposing her waterline completely toward the enemy. A straight line of light shot from the upper dome as the saucer made a course correction to match the turn of the *Pyotr Veliky*. The intense beam struck the bridge section and then sliced through with blinding quickness downward toward the water line and then hissed as it struck the sea. The great warship shuddered and large plates of hull simply fell off as if it had been sliced by a large knife. Water cascaded into decks five, six, and seven. The bridge burst into flame as the laser sliced cleanly through Vileski and his helmsman. The bridge wing with the lookouts came apart and the men fell into the freezing sea, yet still the missile cruiser continued her heel to starboard.

After hitting the deck Lienanov felt the heat as the thick laser beam passed over his prone body. His uniform jacket began to burn and he rolled over in an attempt to smother the flames. All around him men were being fried as the enemy weapon continued to pummel the *Pyotr Veliky*.

On deck five Ryan rolled on top of the two women and they angrily pushed him off. They felt the electricity produced by the laser as it came into contact with steel and aluminum. Sarah was screaming that she didn't want to die in the belly of the ship if she started to go down.

"Come on, if we get hit again we'll lose the ship and the power plant!"

"You want to go out there?" Ryan struggled to regain his feet under the shuddering deck.

"We have to cut the retaining ropes on the power plant or she'll go down with the ship. She'll float, Jason. We have to give it a chance to be picked up by another ship!"

"Okay, but it's going to be a mess outside."

"I agree, I don't want to die in here," Anya chimed in as they heard one of the missile tubes abovedeck cook off as another laser strike hit the launcher. The cruiser shuddered again as she was starting to feel every hard blow of the enemy. The great ship rocked and actually left the water as her aft missile mount and loader exploded in a blinding flash of light and power.

The three started to fight their way against the tide of sailors running to and from their posts as the lights flickered. If the ship lost power from her nuclear power plant the vessel didn't have a chance in hell of making it out alive.

Jason ran into a roadblock of dead and dying men as they made it to the outer hatch that would take them to the ship's fantail. He struggled trying to move the sliced and burning bodies of men that blocked the hatch. It was too much. Every time he tried to move one of the poor boys the body would simply separate into pieces.

"Back, go back!" he shouted just as a large explosion rocked the fire and control stations on the deck one. The *Pyotr Veliky* shook as if it had been grabbed by a rabid dog. As the three tried to run back the way they had come they all felt the temperature rising around them. The steel bulkheads started to heat up from being struck with the laser weaponry of the saucer.

Jason knew the *Pyotr Veliky* was done for.

The saucer completed its maneuver, successfully blocking the path of the ship that was three times the size and weight of itself. The waters were being churned in a froth of green sea as her engines provided the power to keep it in the air and produce the energy needed to attack. The missile batteries had gone silent but the brave Russian sailors kept up the 130- and twenty-millimeter assault. Even the torpedo tubes lining the lower deck came to life as the weapons officers for each harangued their men to fight. Whatever happened to their ship, they would fight until they had nothing to fight with.

Eight VA-111 Shkval supercavitating torpedos were the fastest in the world and carried a punch like no other western or NATO weapon. It was designed to be fast and unstoppable. Its design was made for antisubmarine warfare, but could be detonated electronically by sight if need be. Each of the torpedo tube weapons officers now had direct control of the weapons they launched from tubes that had been angled out from the lower deck of the missile cruiser. As the eight torpedoes traveled under the now hovering saucer they entered the choppy sea directly underneath. The weapons control officer and their tube captains detonated each of the eight. They exploded with the power of a ton of high explosive force, bringing the sea up to meet the saucer's underbelly. Again the enemy disappeared from view, only this time by seawater.

Sarah, Anya, and Ryan finally cleared the last obstacle to the fresh air outside. Just as they opened the hatchway at the stern they felt the sea rise up around them as the ocean erupted. They were thrown to the wet deck as the water was so churned up by the detonations of the eight torpedoes they thought the final death blow to the missile cruiser had been dealt.

Jason gained his feet and assisted the women to theirs. They saw a horrible sight as the wave of water washed many of the Russian and Ukrainian nuclear scientists over and under the stern railings as the fantail became a hell of green seas. The explosive wash of water had cleaned the deck as efficiently as a fire hose cleaning a parking lot.

"They had the same idea," Ryan shouted as he ran toward the strapped-down power plant. Several of the ropes had already been cut away and the large engine was held in place by only six of the thick straps that held her to the deck and railings.

"We have to cut the rest!" Sarah yelled as seawater cascaded from every direction.

* * *

Captain Lienanov finally staggered to his feet inside of the smashed bridge. Bodies and parts of bodies of the bridge crew lay on and over their consoles and equipment. He struggled to get an assistant helmsman to his feet.

"Get this ship moving!" he ordered the young and very frightened seaman.

The man struggled to his feet and swiped at the scorched area of his forehead and then struggled to the damaged helm station.

"Course?" He screamed to be heard over the din of dying men asking, praying for help.

"Ram that son of a bitch!" the captain shouted. He never realized that the first and only command he had ever given inside the bridge in the midst of battle would be to destroy his ship and everyone onboard. He would ignite the thirty remaining Shipwreck missiles in their launch tubes directly under the saucer, creating the force of a nuclear weapon. Lienanov could not allow his ship to go down with their precious cargo without taking the enemy with him.

The new captain of the *Pyotr Veliky* fought his way to the 1MC microphone and hit the switch as he unceremoniously kicked out at a young man who had grabbed his legs begging for help.

"Weapons, set your safeties to zero, set your warhead to automatic. I will detonate from here," he screamed into the mic. "Helm, all ahead, flank speed, direct line of sight, ram her." His eyes blazed with angry fire at the imminent death of the proud missile cruiser. "We'll see if this fucker can play the Russian way!"

The *Pyotr Veliky,* with her engines pushed to their limit, started forward, her bow digging deeply into the sea as her large bronze propellers bit the water. She was heading directly for the saucer sitting in her path at two miles.

The saucer waited and readied for the final death blow her weapons would bestow on the *Pyotr Veliky.*

The world exploded around the saucer. A naval warhead, the likes of which had never been used before in an act of war, penetrated the saucer's hull at over Mach 7.5, almost 7,000 miles per hour. The warhead burst open like a morning flower meeting the sun. Its petals spread wide as it pushed through the saucer, ripping a massive hole in her side. It tore through and continued to rip the insides of the enemy warship. It passed completely through the unknown metal and exploded out of the opposite side. The saucer wobbled, then straightened, and the hull began healing itself once again. But this time it didn't have a chance as four more of the strange warheads erupted inside her. Again she shook and struck the sea with a loud hissing noise. More of the rose petals opened and began forcing themselves into the interior and began breaking the saucer apart. Naval rounds struck the silverish skin and began ripping the guts out of the enemy.

Unable to heal itself fast enough, the power systems of the saucer started to melt down and her ability to reatomize the hull ceased. Internal explosions ripped her apart and in one blinding flash it vanished in a large mist of expanding metal. The remains of the enemy saucer rained down upon the hard-charging *Pyotr Veliky*.

Lienanov could not believe what had just happened. He scanned the area in front of his speeding ship and saw one quarter of the saucer bob in the churning sea; then it sank into the Southern Atlantic and exploded below the surface.

He quickly grabbed his binoculars and scanned the seas to his stern. His eyes widened in amazement as he saw the strangest sight he had ever seen in his twenty years in service. He lowered his glasses and said a silent prayer as he started to shake in near shock at seeing their savior for the first time.

At the stern of the *Pyotr Veliky*, Ryan was actually smiling as he too spied the strange vessel emerging from the mist of battle. He dropped the restraining rope he was attempting to cut and grabbed Sarah and Anya and pointed. He shook his head as the rumors he had been hearing out of the Department of the Navy had been confirmed for the first time. The people that had been stationed here in the South Atlantic had finally came to their aid.

"Thank God," was all he could say.

The USS *Zumwalt* was unlike any destroyer that had ever plied the oceans of the world. It was the first of her class and the only warship that was completely stealth in nature. At $3.5 billion, it was also one of the most expensive weapons platforms ever invented and was one reason why the injured president of the United States had become embroiled in arguments over military spending. With its strange angled shape she was a sight to behold.

The most amazing part of her design was the equally strange turret mounted on her angled decking. It was two-barreled and resembled two clear plastic ballpoint pens. The barrels were actually the twin alternating weapons that generated opposing electrical fields that launched an Argon-based projectile, or solid shot. In this case it had been what the U.S. Navy had dubbed "the Blossoming Rose," a kinetic warhead that had been seen ripping the insides of the saucer apart.

The weapon was called a rail gun, the latest in naval weaponry, and it had just saved the lives of over six hundred sailors onboard the *Pyotr Veliky*.

The United States Navy had arrived on station.

THE PENTAGON
WASHINGTON, D.C.

The situation room was unlike anything in the western world. Designed originally as a war room to administer American military conduct of a global world war, it was equipped with every piece of modern electronics tracking and communications available. It was staffed by over two hundred of the brightest military technicians in the American armed forces. Army, Navy, Air Force, and Marine personnel ran the communications boards that were connected directly to the heads of every foreign government in the world. It also provided real-time communications with the commanders of NATO and the Pacific, Indian Ocean, Mediterranean, and Atlantic areas of responsibility. The same mix of men and women operated the many situation boards spread along the walls that had every continent, every capital, and every city on the planet scanned into its computers and operated on holographic images to give the commanders, or in this case the remaining leaders of the allied coalition of Operation Overlord, the advantage of real-time data.

The leaders of France, England, and Russia were joined by the representatives from China and Germany—men sent to take the place of the late chancellor and president. They sat with Acting President Camden as they watched the satellite imagery of the action in the southern Atlantic Ocean. The images from last night's battle of Mumbai were weighing heavily on everyone's minds. The bulk of the allied coalition was very concerned because of Camden's stunned look. Utter shock had been etched on the face of the man ever since he had witnessed the massacre in India. The sight of seeing so many innocents being captured and led into the large saucer was hard enough that even the supporters of the Operation Overlord plan had cringed at the despicable turn of events.

The men at the main conference table had watched in awed silence at the dramatic rescue of the *Pyotr Veliky* by the USS *Zumwalt*. The small man with the bow tie sitting next to the prime minister of Great Britain, Lord Durnsford, tired after his long flight from Honolulu, leaned over the PM's shoulder.

"Finally something went according to plan. Stationing the *Zumwalt* in the area has paid dividends. I'm glad something has worked in this bloody mess of a day."

The prime minister looked at his intelligence chief of MI6, raised his brows, and nodded toward Camden, who sat with a stern look on his face as he shot General Caulfield a cold and withering look.

"I don't think our newest member liked the fact that one

of his warships was doing something he had no knowledge of, even if it was his predecessor's idea and plan," the PM whispered. "I think I'll throw a line in the water and see how our new member reacts."

The prime minister cleared his throat and stood. A satellite image showed the USS *Zumwalt* holding station guard against another saucer attack as two American Perry-class frigates came alongside of the *Pyotr Veliky* to tie up and tow her to her destination. Her nuclear propulsion plant had scrammed and she was sitting there like a dead duck in the Atlantic, with only enough battery power to keep her out of the dark.

"Mr. President, congratulations on a most satisfying conclusion to this dastardly attack by the enemy. Your newest weapons platform performed most admirably," the PM said with a nod toward the man sitting at the head of the conference table.

The men from Germany, France, and Russia rapped their knuckles on the tabletop in support of the comment. The new representative of China remained still as he eyed the group with something akin to suspicion.

Camden looked at the men around the table. "I'm glad we could assist our friends at sea," was all he said as he nodded toward his British ally.

The prime minister remained standing as he returned the stiff reaction to his comment.

"Now, gentlemen, we are close to the time that you will have a chance to speak directly with the asset that has provided this group with so much valuable intelligence. Who was also instrumental in formulating Operation Overlord, along with our good friends, the late Senator Garrison Lee, and Dr. Niles Compton. And by the way, we all pray for a speedy recovery of both Dr. Compton and the president. This esteemed gathering will miss their valuable guidance."

Again, all but Camden and the representative of China rapped their knuckles on the shiny tabletop. With a glance at the thick glass that separated the conference room from the frenzied activity below, the prime minister continued.

"Gentlemen, the asset that is so very valuable to our efforts against the Grays has requested that his identity remain anonymous because of the very real chance that he would be tracked by the enemy to his secret location." The PM looked at the faces around the room. He knew that the only people here who knew of Matchstick's real heritage were he, the Russian president, and the leader of France. The gentleman from Germany and the new man from China were kept in the dark. No one was to know the Mahjtic secret but a very select few. "The ability of the enemy to track down our valuable assets has been demonstrated by the attack on the Iranian University, where the alien power plant was being tested. We will not challenge the enemy's willingness to destroy anything that will help us survive this fight. As a group we have given this asset full cooperation in keeping his identity secret. Even his voice will be disguised, as will his person. He will be speaking through a computer-generated voice, but will answer any and all questions or concerns you may have."

"Let me understand this. You want full cooperation for this audacious plan that you have kept from certain members of this panel, and you are unwilling to supply us with his real identity?" Camden looked harshly again at his military advisor, General Caulfield, who held up admirably against the hate-filled glare of his new commander-in-chief.

"Mr. President, I don't even know, nor does Mr. Devinov, nor Mr. Arneu, the exact identity of the man that the president before you and the one before him, trusted implicitly," the PM lied. "We trusted the president in his judgment, as I'm sure you, Mr. Klinghoffer, and Mr. Xiao do also."

Camden was maneuvered perfectly by the prime minister. What was he to say, that he despised the president who sat in this very chair and that he was the last man in the world he would trust? No, he was caught and had to nod his head at the man from Number Ten Downing Street, whom he knew to be extremely close to the former president.

"We have a moment before our asset's representative arrives to take part in the discussion, so why don't we take a small break. I know I can use one after that dramatic rescue by your magnificent new warship."

Camden was cornered again by the praise and could do nothing but lean over and tell his aide to get in contact with the one of the only allies he had in Washington.

"Get Assistant Director Peachtree in here immediately. I need him to sit in on this, and then I want the identity of this so-called asset on my desk after this meeting of the new order dismisses," he hissed under his breath.

The acting director of the Event Group, Virginia Pollock, was standing outside the *E* ring of the Pentagon. She paced as she smoked a cigarette, a bad habit she had given up just after college twenty years before, but now found she needed the distraction—after all, it wasn't every day that you came to see the president of the United States and knew beforehand that you would lie directly to his face. Virginia was a rabid constitutionalist and despised the idea of not allowing the chain of command to operate as it was designed. But she knew that this man Camden was an enemy of everything the Event Group stood for—their forward-thinking philosophy.

She angrily mashed out the cigarette in the receptacle and then saw the man approaching that she had been waiting for.

The gentleman was of medium height, black, and wore a tailored suit from Harrods of London. Virginia recognized him immediately as the former congressman from the state of Pennsylvania, Lee Stansfield Preston. She had heard he was in private law practice with a very select clientele. His briefcase was made of alligator skin, which depicted his extremely good taste in the finer things in life and immediately placed Virginia on edge. She didn't admire anyone who used animals for decoration.

Virginia had been ordered by phone from Pete Golding at Group Center to wait on this man to arrive, as he would be joining her before taking her place with the leaders of the coalition for their clandestine meeting with Matchstick.

"Dr. Pollock?" he asked with his million-dollar Hollywood smile. His beard was expertly trimmed and he wore just enough jewelry to show his success.

"Yes," she said, becoming concerned.

"Lee Preston."

"I know who you are, Congressman. I have seen you on television quite often since you left office."

"Yes, the camera does seem to seek me out on occasion."

"Mr. Preston, can you tell me why was I instructed to await your arrival before entering the situation room? It's bad enough that I missed most of the meeting, but our new president is a bear and also a man that particularly despises my boss."

"So I understand. I have been retained by Mrs. Alice Hamilton, and she, Madam, is a particular friend of mine." He mocked her slightly as he smiled. "So, President Camden has been 'checked' in that regard. He has his peculiar group of friends and so does Mrs. Hamilton. I am one of them."

"Just what are you doing here?" She removed a cigarette from her pocket and started to light it.

"I am here to protect you and certain other people we both know from implicating yourselves in treason, Doctor." He removed the cigarette from Virginia's lips and tossed it away into the receptacle. "You will say nothing in that meeting unless I say to do so. You work clandestinely for the president; I, however, most assuredly do not. You are bound by your oath; I, again, am not. Stay silent and follow my lead, and Mrs. Hamilton can have her friends back in one piece after this mess is sorted out."

Virginia swallowed as she listened. If Alice Hamilton had sent this arrogant man to assist in getting Matchstick through this, then she had no choice but to allow Preston to do his work.

"Now, shall we go see the great men of the world conducting the momentous work of our times?"

Virginia stood rooted to the spot next to the former congressman.

"I know, it's mind-boggling to be so close to great men in perilous times." He gestured toward the door and the Marine guard standing there.

"Some of them inside are great. Others? Well . . ."

"Who's talking about them? I meant me." Preston walked to the door and held it open for the shocked and staring Virginia.

Virginia and Preston were issued Pentagon identity cards and allowed past the posted Marine guards. They both noticed that the Marines were attired in battle dress and wore menacing sidearms in holsters strapped to their chests.

"Makes one feel rather warm and cozy doesn't it?" Preston said.

He and Virginia were directed to two seats facing the table, but far enough away that they felt like eavesdroppers. "I haven't had seats this bad since the Lakers-Celtics game in '89."

They both sat and it was time for Virginia to ask herself if Alice Hamilton had made the right choice in selecting Lee Preston as her consul in this rather serious game of hiding the real truth from the new president.

The members of the allied council had reconvened as still shots of the sieges at Beijing and Mumbai flashed across the one-hundred-foot screen in the center of the situation room. As the members settled into their seats an Air Force officer and two men came into the room and set up a high-definition screen so all could see. Virginia wanted to smile as she saw the likeness of Pete Golding appear. He was in a suit and tie, clothing she had never once seen the computer genius wearing, and it looked as if he were about to crap his pants. The committee would never know that Europa, Pete's supercomputer, was streaming the live feed from over one and a half miles below the desert sands of Nellis Air Force Base.

It was the British prime minister who took the lead as he and the French and Russian presidents were the only members left inside the Pentagon besides Virginia who knew the full details of everything concerning Magic and Operation Overlord.

"Gentlemen," the prime minister started, and then in deference to Virginia's presence, nodded her way. "And lady. I believe we are ready to begin our question-and-answer session with our main asset in this war against our Gray enemy. May I introduce Dr. Peter Golding of the Garrison Lee Institute of Strategic Science, a broad-based and voluntary group sanctioned by the office of the president of the United States for the gathering of intelligence on the hostile force we are now facing."

President Camden scribbled something on his notepad and slid it over to Daniel Peachtree, who had joined the meeting. The move had not gone unnoticed by Peachtree's boss, Director Harlan Easterbrook, who knew Camden was starting to consolidate his power base and place people that only he trusted in certain key positions—replacing the director at the CIA was going to be one of his first moves in that regard.

Peachtree quickly scanned the note.

"It's that damn clandestine group out west again. Find out who this Golding is."

Peachtree nodded and then sat back as the PM continued.

"Dr. Golding will be acting as liaison with the subject, code-named Magic."

On the large monitor there was a picture of a blacked-out shape of a man as Pete's image vanished.

"Dr. Golding, is the subject ready?"

"Yes, he is, Mr. Prime Minister. You may ask your questions."

Camden became uneasy as he was not used to having others run the show, especially a foreign national inside his country. This was proof the former president had gone too far in relinquishing the role of the United States as the leader of the world.

"Magic, thank you for taking the time to answer some questions for our newest members of this esteemed council.

Just be straightforward in your brief and we'll try and let you return to your work as soon as possible."

"Thank you." Europa spoke for Matchstick as he typed the answers on a keyboard with lightning-fast speed. The members of the allied coalition exchanged glances around the table as the synthesized voice of Marilyn Monroe came through the speakers.

Virginia couldn't help it, she had to smile as even Lee Preston's brows rose at the sound of the synthesized voice program.

"I think I would like to meet this Magic face-to-face."

"I think you two would make a good match," she said as she finally got a brief moment of levity in on the arrogant but brilliant counselor. "You're both very clinical in the things you do. Yes, I believe you and she would get along just fine."

Camden gave the two people sitting against the wall a look and then returned his eyes to the screen.

"Magic, I would like to start out by asking what many here are desperately curious about." The PM sat back down in his chair as he tried to guide the meeting in the direction he and the former president, along with Niles Compton, wanted. "We expected a full-scale invasion by the enemy. Why have they initiated full attacks in only two parts of the world?"

Camden watched with interest along with Peachtree, who was guessing the video stream was coming in from that rumored base in Nevada. He didn't mention this to Camden as of yet, as he wanted to know what game was being played by Niles Compton and the former president.

"The extensive civilian population of those two cities and the density of that populace are the driving forces for their initial attacks. After the attacks have succeeded they will move on to another major population center for exploitation."

"Magic, why is the civilian population so important in a matter of world domination?" The PM watched the faces around the table, paying particular attention to Camden.

There was a long pause as Matchstick needed urging from an off-camera Pete Golding to continue and tell the council the truth. Virginia could picture Matchstick at his small keyboard banging away and Europa synthetically reading his answers. She couldn't help but smile at the simple subterfuge.

"The Grays are starving. The attacks initiated on the Earth since 1947 have been geared to dominate until such a time as they can consolidate a foothold for processing the populace and wildlife, domestic plant and animal life of the planet, for transport back to their home fleet to feed the remainder of their kind."

As the sensitive voice of Marilyn Monroe answered, the room erupted in outrage. The PM rapped his knuckles on the table to get everyone to calm down. Only Giles Camden remained silent as he looked at the screen.

"Why doesn't the enemy attack in force against many cities at once, why piecemeal?" asked the French president as the PM nodded his thanks in assisting with the questioning. "And what I see is a major flaw in the Gray tactic is the fact that they have left our entire inventory of communications satellites in orbit. Why?"

"They are limited by power restraints. Generating the power to open up a transit wormhole takes a vast amount of energy. They can only send through a limited number of warships and processing plants at one time before their power base can regenerate. This will eventually be solved by the Grays when they take certain areas of conquered territory by utilizing the nuclear facilities of these fallen countries. As to your query on why they have left the Earth's communications satellites alone, that is simple—it is their way of gathering intelligence. They have found that the Earth is quite talkative when it comes to secrets. This is why Overlord utilizes—" Again the men around the table heard Pete Golding admonish Matchstick about saying too much.

The leaders and representatives around the conference table were shocked by the brutal truth being told to them.

"Gentlemen, I would like to pause the questioning only

momentarily and show intel on something that may interest you. It seems we may have caught a break with the satellite footage you are about to see." The prime minister nodded his head at Lord Durnsford, who in turn gave an Air Force lieutenant the okay.

On the large screen the view of the blacked out Matchstick and Pete Golding vanished, to be replaced by a green-tinted night view of Mumbai. It was the man from MI6 who explained what they were about to see.

"The footage we will see here is from one of Great Britain's satellite systems that was retasked over India last evening." The view was on the city and the saucer sitting in its center. "This was one hour after the attack. As you watch, the three smaller vehicles are dormant as they keep station watch over the larger; now you see another saucer enter the shield area from the south. It was discovered through independent observers that this saucer entered the city from the bay only a few miles away. Electrical readings of the shield had shown a 70 percent power loss after the attack by the Indian Air Force and Army. Now as you see, the shield has dimmed somewhat since that attack. Now watch the approaching saucer as it lands on the very top dome of the larger craft. You see it has landed." The view showed a mating of the smaller and larger vehicles.

The next scene came on and the PM explained further. "This was an hour later; you see the smaller craft lift off and then exit the alien-controlled area. See the brighter, stronger glow of the shield once this mating was complete? British Intelligence had the readings verified. The shield was back up to almost 100 percent efficiency after this mating."

"Are you saying that this smaller craft transferred power directly into the large one?" the German representative asked.

"Yes, that is our belief," Durnsford said. "The battle of Mumbai, although a failure, has given us some rather valuable insight into our enemy's limitations. The fighting and defense of the three ships inside the shield were drained in fending off the attack."

"So what if we use special weapons? Would that not drain their power source completely?" the German representative continued.

"That is a question for another time and men such as yourself who are policy makers, not a simple man such as myself. But I would believe the question that stands before us is how do we save lives, not destroy them. A nuclear strike may disable the attackers, but would also completely destroy the city under attack. Rather wasteful, I should think."

"Thank you for that insight, Lord Durnsford," the PM said, trying to get the subject of the matter out in the open. "Magic, are you there, sir?"

"Yes, and I agree with the gentleman. The use of nuclear weapons unless out in the open will cause irrefutable harm to the planet and only hasten the downfall of mankind. You will die long before the Grays run out of invasion ships."

"So, let's move on, shall we? What you are saying is that the Grays do not want this planet for her natural resources as we suspected, but are treating our world as a food processing plant for their fleet of warships. Why not just come and take the entire planet after our military has been subdued?" The PM's eyes stayed on Camden.

"Their populace is in need of nourishment; they are a dying race. Once they have a healthy diet they will come in force and take all animal life on Earth."

"Magic, based on your calculations and those of the Garrison Lee Group, and after studying the Hubble telescope images, what do you estimate the Gray population onboard their home fleet to be?"

There was a long pause as Pete was heard admonishing Matchstick that he had to answer the question. Finally Europa interpreted the query for him.

"Over seventy billion."

The group sitting at the table erupted as they realized what it was they were facing. The PM allowed the men to state their fears in the open, as he knew this could only scare them into action and possibly sway President Camden into the Overlord camp.

"Once a power base has been established they will land in force and overwhelm not just the military, but the entire world population. Then the Grays will move on. They have already killed many, many species, including—"

Pete was heard stopping Matchstick from elaborating.

"This is kind of disconcerting," Lee Preston whispered to Virginia.

"You don't know the half of it."

"Magic, does the plan code-named Overlord have a chance of succeeding?"

A very long silence came through the television monitor and the PM hoped Magic would fudge the answer like it had been discussed weeks ago by Compton, himself, and Mahjtic. The small alien's answer threw that right out the window.

"Ten percent chance of success."

"Only 10 percent?" the PM asked, disappointed that Matchstick had not been reminded to exaggerate their chances of success to a point where there was hope.

"Yes, the variables and design of the weapon have not been established or tested. The alien power plant recovered in Iran has to be adapted to the working model and is far from guaranteed to supply the—"

Again Pete Golding stopped Matchstick cold before he said too much.

"That's about enough of this dog and pony show, sir." Giles Camden stood and then paced to the monitor and snapped it off. "I must admit, I was never a believer in this alien attack, and have been made the fool in its obvious reality, but I will not sit here and allow the people of my nation to be the subject of an experiment in defense when we don't even know who"—he looked directly from the prime minister to the two people sitting away from the table, Virginia Pollock and Lee Preston—"this asset—this so-called Magic is. I have taken an oath to protect the citizens of my nation, gentlemen, and I will not strip her defenses for something this man"—he slapped the top of the monitor for emphasis—"claims has only a 10 percent chance of working. Whatever this weapon of yours is. No, I will recall all forces of the United States back into home territory and fight them our way." He turned to General Caulfield. "General, we need to talk after this meeting is adjourned."

Caulfield nodded his head as he chanced a look at the PM.

"Gentlemen, I recommend that you also prepare to defend yourselves." Camden walked back to his chair and took a seat.

Now it was the time for the Chinese representative to stand. He was solemn and had not uttered a word since sitting.

"The People's Republic is under direct assault by this race of barbarians, and now you propose to leave us at the mercy of their onslaught, to allow our population to be taken away, all to benefit you so you can consolidate power back home. This act, gentlemen, is unacceptable. You have lured the People's Republic and our dead leader into this undisclosed Overlord plan to give your nations time to fight your own battles at home. China's obligation to this council and this alliance is at an end. We will most assuredly test this power theory advanced by your intelligence services, we thank you for that. Good day, gentlemen."

The representative started walking from the room, quickly followed by his aides.

"Mr. Xiao, please—"

The doors closed as the German representative stood, bowed, and then also left without a word.

Camden was not finished.

"Who are these two people?" he asked, as he gestured toward Virginia and Preston.

"Mr. President, if you would direct your questions to me, I will be happy to answer all you wish to know . . . to a point." Lee Preston stood and faced the president.

Camden grew furious as he took in Lee Preston. There was no need to make the introduction as he was well aware of the former congressman's name and his reputation as a bulldog. Most of the time his attitude had been directed at people like himself.

"What do you mean 'to a point'? I am the president of the United Sates and you will answer any and all questions I choose to ask."

Daniel Peachtree cringed at the way Camden was speaking to a very deliberate and smart man. Preston was no one to have a pissing contest with. The counselor looked at Camden but didn't respond as he waited for a question to be asked.

"What are you doing here, Mr. Preston? This is a closed military evaluation committee and you are not welcome."

"From what I've heard here today, I believe this concerns everyone on the planet, not just the military."

"I again state my question, Mr. Preston: why are you here?"

Preston pulled out a document from his briefcase, stepped to the table, and slid it down unceremoniously to Camden, who didn't bother to reach for it.

"I am here to represent the asset you now know as Magic. To preserve his rights as a free citizen of this country, and his right to remain anonymous in the face of the situation he is involved in. He is a private citizen. I represent Mr. Mahjtic Tilly, and his legal guardian, Augustus Tilly, both residents of the State of Arizona." He took his seat once more.

Daniel Peachtree was shocked but kept the emotion in check, as he had just confirmed the fact that this Magic *was* the asset that was being hunted by Hiram Vickers and his Black Team. He placed a hand on the president's arm and patted it lightly, indicating that he should hear Lee Preston out.

"As to Dr. Virginia Pollock, she is here because she has been tasked, through presidential order, to look after and secure the subject known as Magic. And at this moment she is under the protection of that same presidential order."

Camden didn't like the smug look on Preston's face as he held eye contact with the counselor. He quickly decided to allow the matter to rest as he knew that Peachtree wanted to pass something along to him later.

Before Preston could continue the men inside the glassed-in conference room saw the activity in the strategic center below pick up as several screens came alive with a satellite view of Texas. At that moment a Marine courier entered the room and passed a note to the president.

"This is why we are pulling out of any agreement my predecessor has made to this council." He held up the note just as the red alarm lights started flashing below in the information center.

"What is it, Mr. President?" the prime minister asked, fearing the worst.

"First, the Pakistani Air Force has gone to full nuclear alert for preparations to defend themselves against the attack in India. They say they will not allow the saucer to move on them after they have finished in Mumbai. They said they will destroy the landing craft before they can move against Pakistan. They claim the Indian government has not done everything in their power to stop the enemy. Thus, the Indian government has reciprocated and brought their border forces to red alert for action against their neighbors if they move to strike at the alien assets at Mumbai."

The prime minister lowered his head as he saw Overlord vanishing before his eyes.

"What else, sir?" Peachtree asked. His assessment of the situation as explained to the president earlier had come to fruition.

"Houston, the Johnson Space Center in particular, is now under full-scale enemy attack."

With that short and blunt announcement that history may never record, the coalition of allied nations disintegrated.

11

JOHNSON SPACE CENTER
HOUSTON, TEXAS

Admiral Carl Everett watched the drill being conducted by
SEAL Team 5 out of San Diego. The action was taking
place underwater in the large Space Center pool. Everett
was there also, wearing the bulky spacesuit that had been
trimmed down from its nominal requirements for space ex-
cursions. He hated the feeling of restriction the suit added
to an already difficult training exercise. This was coupled
with the simple fact that he was still in the dark as far as his
mission parameters were concerned. He was working closely
with a mix of navy personnel and Delta Force of the U.S.
Army.

The specialized commando force was working as a team.
The SEALs were the access assault team and the Delta personnel the action team that would enter the target and set an
explosive device that the military had yet to explain. Carl's
job was to make whatever their mission truly was go off
without a hitch. Thus far they had been training in a near-
weightless environment against a mockup of a metallic access point that the SEALs would breach and then secure the
interior compartments of an as of yet undisclosed alien

location. Before breaking ties with the coalition, the Chinese had forwarded the specs for the entranceway through photo recon of the Beijing craft. Still, Everett came to the conclusion that because of security, or the fear his units would be captured because of the events at sea and in Iran, his mission would undoubtedly fail because of a lack of free-flowing intel.

He had spent very little time with Master Chief (retired) Jenks as the mad engineer was off in the simulator area working on one of his strange vehicles. Everett thus far was not pleased at what he had been seeing as far as cooperation between the Army and the Navy. The Delta men complained bitterly that it was taking the SEALs far too long to gain access to the mock-up of the two large metallic doors, and that they, the interior team, were being left exposed outside whatever craft it was they were assaulting. Instructors inside their small cubicle kept blowing horns when the team, in their estimation, had been wiped out before entering. Where these fail-pass parameters came from Carl didn't know, but he was determined to find out. He could not train men like this.

The Delta team was limited as far as the weapons they carried and complained bitterly that the SEALs had all of the serious firepower. Delta carried strange-looking sidearms that were mocked up in plastic and they resembled no handgun they had ever seen. The SEALs had a much stranger shoulder-fired assault weapon and had no idea how it worked. Again, training blind was the way Carl looked at it. He was becoming furious at the strange compartmental way the secret project was being run.

The design bureau at the DARPA—Defense Advanced Research Projects Agency—complex next door said they would have working weapons within the week. Everett wasn't so sure about the estimate when he saw Master Chief Jenks raise his brows in doubt at the claim while attending a design meeting. When they asked the master chief about the progress of the assault platforms he shook his head and smiled.

"Well, if you consider the fact that we have blown up in simulation no less than fifty-seven times, and the two ships have collided only twelve times with the simulated loss of all onboard, if that's progress, then yes, the *Asimov* and *Heinlein* are almost certainly ready to go." That comment was the forbearer of the explosion of temper from the master chief claiming that he couldn't run his shop like this.

Carl was as lost as ever as Jenks had refused to divulge the nature of the project he was in charge of. He had hints when Jenks had claimed on more than one occasion that the NASA, Boeing, Lockheed, and DARPA engineers he was working with were a bunch of candy-asses that were good for nothing other than protecting their own skins. He knew it was a vehicle of some kind and that his men, his uncooperative assault element, would use the two vehicles to enter some sort of alien craft. He was lost after that as the "need to know" was driving him crazy.

Everett slapped the side of the clear visor–encased helmet when his communications shorted out. He shook his head inside the environmental suit as this was the fifth time he had lost communications with his assault teams.

As he slapped his helmet again, he saw one of the SEALs turn and shove away the Delta commando who was looking over his shoulder and giving his unwanted advice as he was trying to assist laying the explosive against the mock-up of the entrance point. Several other SEALs joined the first and then they were soon at odds with five more Delta team members as they all came together in a shouting match. Everett shook his head and then pushed off from the bottom of the giant water-filled tank. Two navy divers hooked his breathing pack to a hard point and then hoisted him up and out of the pool. As the divers released him to the deck team, Everett pointed harshly to the helmet as it was removed.

"The goddamn radio shorted out again. Tell whoever designed this fucking thing that it's for shit. It may work well in space, but a water environment? It leaves a lot to be desired. Now someone get on a radio that works and get those idiots to the surface!"

The assistant handlers had never seen the admiral lose his temper before and they were humbled as they moved off to get his commando teams out of the pool.

As Everett was stripped out of the tight-fitting environment suit he was approached by the man running this insanity, General Perry Cummings, commander of the Space Center special training unit.

"Look, Perry, I need to know what in the hell this fucked-up team is supposed to assault. I haven't a clue and don't hand me this 'need to know' bullshit. In case these boys or I are captured before the mission sets off, we'll blow our own damn brains out. Now get me some answers."

"Carl, I really don't know. This shit is so compartmentalized we'll be lucky to have men that speak the same damn language." The general, a Marine Corps two-star, the same rank as Everett, helped him slip on a white robe with the NASA emblem embroidered on the breast. "All I know is that the men we were given is all the Army and Navy can spare. The Air Force commando teams have been secured for whatever project is happening with the alien power plant. The rest of the Navy and Army units are off gallivanting around with a general named Collins somewhere in the world."

"Collins? You mean Jack Collins?" Carl's astonishment was written on his face.

"That's the scuttlebutt I hear. Do you know him?"

"Yes, I do know him, and now I wonder what new and inventive way the Army has designed for killing him."

"Probably not as inventive as what NASA has planned for you, would be my guess."

Everett nodded and smiled briefly at the general as he tossed the man his towel. He heard the argument reconvene on the surface of the pool between the SEALs and Delta teams. He regained his land legs and slowly and deliberately walked to the far end of the giant pool as the men were hoisted from the water.

As the admiral approached the men still arguing over the finer points of ingress into a sealed target, they noticed the admiral had a very serious scowl on his face. The large, former SEAL took in the men as they were mostly in a state of undress. They turned and halfheartedly stood at attention. Everett saw the sloppiness their basic training was displaying.

"Is that how the Army teaches you to stand in the presence of your commanding officer?" he asked the young Delta captain in the center of the group. "You assholes have been off in the wilds of Afghanistan far too long. Back in the world you are soldiers again."

The man stood ramrod straight, as did his bearded Delta team. Everett turned next to the lieutenant commander leading the SEAL detachment.

"And the last time I commanded a team, we didn't start fights with other team members."

"I . . . I . . ."

"What, Commander, are you having trouble speaking?" Everett admonished. "This crap has to stop and stop now. Delta, you stay clear of those hatchways until you are called in. SEALs, get that damn hatch open faster, these men are sitting ducks to enemy fire while you play with that explosive. If you don't work together you'll all get your asses flamed in the first minute of the assault!" He saw a young SEAL with a blond beard that had yet to see any thickness to it. He was too damn young. "What is it?" Carl asked, making the boy flinch back.

"I . . . well, we heard, sir, that this was a one-way mission."

"So, aren't SEALs and Delta used to that? Every time you put on assault gear someone is trying to kill you, both on the enemy side and ours. Now get over it. We have millions of people dying out there and they expect you to do something about it. You want out?"

The young SEAL looked insulted. "No, sir, of course not."

"Do any of you want out?" Everett demanded as he looked from bearded face to bearded face. No one moved or answered. They all looked at their bare feet. "Now get that fucking gear back on and the next man that doesn't cooperate with his brother—and you are all brothers regardless of

pretty uniforms,"—he thought of Jack, Will, and Ryan—"I
will personally make sure his life is a living hell, because
I will ship all your asses off to military reservation land
reclamation. That means you'll be draining swamps for the
rest of your worthless careers. And believe me, gentlemen,
it will take approximately a decade to process your resignation requests. Am I getting through to you prima donnas?"

The two officers leading the assault teams stood rigid
and that told Everett they did indeed understand. The two
captains were stunned to be dressed down in front of
their men.

"Now, get back in the water. And remember this, you assholes: you're not going up against a bunch of backward-assed
terrorists on this one. These things will have new and inventive ways of killing every one of you. Then after that
they will come down here and use the same methods on little
Sally and Billy and Mom and Pop, got it?"

Before the men could answer alarms started sounding
throughout the complex. Air Police and NASA security personnel started running and warning men to get to their designated shelters.

Everett grabbed ahold of the first passing airman he
could reach. "What is it?" he yelled over the din caused by
the alarms.

"Houston and the Space Center are under air attack. All
of your men must get to the hardened shelters immediately!"

Carl didn't know how, but the enemy had discovered the
fact that a plan was being worked out, no matter how bad
that plan was, and decided to put up a fight.

The Grays were striking at the heart of the American
space program.

Everett, instead of running for the designated deep
shelter for his command, made sure his men were secured
and then sprinted for the roof of the large training facility.
He had to be witness to the defense of the Center. He had to
know the capabilities of what his team was up against firsthand.

The first explosions rocked him as he struggled to climb

the steel stairs. Carl lost his balance and started to fall backward as the loose-fitting robe tangled his legs. He thought
he would tumble down the two flights of steps when two
large hands grabbed him and pushed him forward.

"Come on, twinkle toes, don't want to lose you now,"
Jenks said, and ruthlessly pushed him up the stairs.

The master chief too was climbing to the roof to see what
they were up against.

The twisted form of the wormhole had started over the Galveston area. It had snaked and crawled the distance between
the island and the outskirts of Houston. This time as soon
as the formation of clouds was recognized for what it
was the combined strength of the 149th Fighter Wing lifted
off the ground. The Air National Guard unit had been brought
together in one spot for a combined strength of over forty
fighters, eighteen F-15 Eagles, and twenty-two F-16 Fighting Falcons. They would support the ground element made
up of the Army's 3rd Cavalry Regiment.

Someone had actually planned for the defense of the
Space Center, and placed the regiment inside the Center to
protect the men being trained there and the experimental
craft Jenks and his team were working furiously on. The
nickname of the cavalry unit was the "Brave Rifles"; today
that name would be put to the test. At last count, ten of the
smaller attack saucers had entered the atmosphere and by-
passed the civilian population centers of Galveston and
Houston and shot straight for the Space Center. The two
sides would collide to bring about the largest land engagement on the American continent since the Civil War.

The first of four saucers spread out and concentrated
their laser fire on the mission control center. Blast after blast
of the bluish-green light punctured the thickened walls of
the building. The high-intensity beams smashed through the
cinder block and cascaded through the billions of dollars'
worth of equipment.

M1 Abrams tanks wound their way through the streets
fronting the many buildings of the Center and took up station,

hiding themselves the best they could with only their 120-millimeter smoothbore cannons exposed. The saucers were moving too fast for the tanks to traverse their turrets to aim properly, so the Cavalry Regiment opened fire with small-arms and heavy-caliber weaponry.

Four more of the saucers started attacking the personnel quarters of the Space Center to devastating effect. As Everett and Jenks broke through the roof doors of the training center they saw over a hundred men of the 3rd Cavalry Regiment holding station. They flinched as five man-portable Stinger-B antiaircraft missiles left their launch tubes. The five missiles struck the second saucer as it tried in vain to maneuver away from the infrared seeker of the small warheads. All five of the missiles struck the aft quarter of the vehicle and sent it wobbling, momentarily out of control. That gave two M1s their chance to lock on the target. As the saucer started to straighten and climb, two sabot rounds struck the craft and sent it spinning into the Interstellar Sciences Building. The depleted uranium rounds penetrated the thin skin of the attacker, ripping out her guts until the dartlike projectile struck its power source. The resulting explosion tore out her entire bow section and the ship cascaded in pieces into the building.

As Jenks pointed skyward Carl saw three of the saucers strafing the personnel center and family housing located just outside of the training facility. Everett felt helpless as he saw at least eight Stingers track and then lose lock on the fast-flying ships. Before he realized what was happening the logistics center blew skyward as the laser fire hit the main gas lines connecting the underground lines leading to the next. A series of explosions rocked the next building and then the next, until the entire personnel housing area was in flames.

"Goddamn things are kicking our asses," Jenks cried as he watched more men on the roof open up with more Stingers and small-arms fire. He heard the Abrams tanks far below open up with their turret-mounted fifty-caliber machine guns. Soon Stingers and tracer rounds stitched the sky in a vain attempt to bring down the remaining alien craft.

"Get down!" Carl yelled, and pushed the master chief away from the edge of the roof. A line of laser fire burned through the concrete and threw up large chunks that peppered both men. As the saucer rose after the strafing run, they were stunned as two AMRAAM missiles struck the stern section of the vehicle. Two large explosions shook the building as the saucer very quickly lost altitude as it struggled to stay in the air. Before they could mentally wish the saucer to crash, six more of the long-range deadly missiles struck it and sent it spinning crazily into the NASA museum pieces lining the lawn of the flight control building. The remains slid into the welcome center and then came to an abrupt halt.

Carl leaned over the side of the building and saw at least three surviving Grays as they tried to exit the burning saucer. They were met immediately by heavy cannon fire from six M1s. The HE—high explosive—rounds were different from the dartlike sabot shots as these large, armor-piercing rounds blew the craft to pieces. The Grays were caught as they struggled free of the wreckage. Heavy weaponry from fifty-caliber rounds to grenades dispatched them with a vengeance only shocked and angry soldiers could provide.

Two Abrams and three Bradley Fighting Vehicles broke cover as their gunfire and cannon discharges brought them unwanted attention from two low-flying saucers. Before the five vehicles could find more cover, laser fire started to take them out. A Bradley Fighting Vehicle took a direct hit in its personnel compartment and the tracked machine careened into the side of a building as the men tried to scramble free over the now-exposed rear ramp. One of the Abrams tried to turn sharply to give the men cover fire, but it too was struck in its hindquarters and immediately exploded, with a force that tore her turret free from the armored chassis.

"Damn it!" Everett cursed. He felt helpless as he watched with nothing more than a bathrobe on. Jenks stood and with his cigar clenched in his teeth shook an angry fist at the climbing saucers that had killed at least thirty men with the two strikes.

He didn't have long to curse as the cannon fire from an F-16 Falcon connected solidly with the domed upper section of the lead saucer, damaging it just enough that it slammed into the grassy front lawn of the Sciences Building. Everett flinched as at least five Sidewinder missiles slammed into the metal body of the saucer. The resulting explosion once more knocked the men down. They ducked again when an F-15 Eagle slammed nose-first into the guard post at the front gate. Everett looked up and saw the pilot's chute as it billowed three hundred feet above their heads.

Jenks once more screamed in anger as one of the remaining enemy craft slammed into the pilot as he tried desperately to get to the ground. A red mist marked the spot of the Air Force pilot as his chute fell free and gently floated to the ground, twisting inside out and then coming to rest on the museum grounds.

Everett cursed as loud as the master chief and pulled him away from the wall. As he did he was amazed to see the saucer that had slammed into the building slowly start to rise, even as an AMRAAM missile struck it again. It wobbled, fell back to the earth, and then with its entire aft quarter still aflame it started to rise again.

Three hidden M1s added their firepower to the assault on the damaged vehicle. Carl grimaced as the saucer returned fire, striking the first charging Abrams. The cannon was cleanly sliced away as the beam adjusted and then bit into the frontal armor of the heavy tank. The beam punctured and passed by the driver and impacted the ammunition storage area in the back. Carl pushed Jenks down hard as the Abrams blew up, heavily damaging the second and third M1s close by. Three tanks had been knocked out of commission by a single laser of the enemy.

Everett gained his feet and again started pushing Jenks back toward the roof door as men continued to fire at the downed saucer. Again it rose and to everyone's amazement it was starting to scab over with new material. Finally at full power once again the fires were extinguished and the vehicle shot back into the air. As Carl pushed Jenks through the door he turned and counted a total of five saucers still in the air, striking every building more than once. Every ship they thought they had destroyed had regenerated and risen to fight again.

A second squadron of navy fighters joined the fray from the naval air station at Galveston. The FA-18 Super Hornets came in low and were carrying heavy ordnance. Several of the armored cavalry units started lasing the saucers from the grassy area just below Carl and Jenks. Everett had to watch the men below as they braved the low-flying craft as they used the large laser designators to paint the saucers that flew low to the ground, and then Hornets let loose their laser-guided weapons. As the lone alien vehicle hovered near the smoking ruin of the flight control building, eight 500-pound bombs struck it directly on the top. The bombs traveled from the just-regenerated stern area to the center dome and then the undamaged front section. The saucer evaporated, taking one of the Hornets with it. The jet had come in too low after load release, and the blast slammed it into the earth, creating a massive fireball.

Two more saucers launched a withering barrage of light at the main training center, the first of which struck next to Everett and Jenks. The concrete and gravel roof burst open like an eggshell and peppered both men. Carl saw the ground personnel of the 3rd Cavalry Regiment take heavy losses as the laser cannons blew them apart.

SAM batteries finally found their targets and at least five of them started streaking after the remaining five saucers as they tried to climb and evade the fast missiles. Two of them didn't make it—the large warheads struck and blew them apart, turning them into falling debris. The power of the ships must have been decreasing rapidly after the attack because the powerful warheads of the SAMs hit hard enough that two of the alien craft couldn't regenerate and fell in pieces to the ground. The mission control building was completely destroyed, taking over a hundred of the Armored Cavalry infantry units with it. The resulting explosions once more knocked Everett from his feet, skinning his bare legs against the steel doorway. The master chief was once again lying across him.

Still the saucers attacked.

Carl sat up and realized he wasn't hurt, then assisted Jenks to his feet. Immediately they were knocked down again as a tremendous explosion ripped through the training center. The roof gave way and Carl found himself flying in midair. He struck the steel stairwell and his head hit the steps with a bone-jarring impact. All went dark as the carnage raged around him. The last thing his conscious mind picked up was the sound of streaking jet fighters and the boom of cannon fire from the remaining Abrams tanks.

The Johnson Space Center had been totally knocked out of commission and the men who would assist in the combined efforts of Operation Overlord were either dead, scattered, or buried alive in the rubble of America's only advanced center for space exploration. The training center with all of the alien mock-ups was destroyed, and the only hope of salvaging the precious training records was seriously dashed.

The one thing that went right for the entire planet was the fact that it was Houston and the Johnson Space Center that were hit, and not the main Overlord base in the south, in Antarctica. Garrison Lee's plan to use the world's communications satellites to keep the aliens guessing had worked. They had tracked the heavy radio and satellite traffic to the wrong base by listening in on radio calls from the military. There was almost no electronic communication engaged at Overlord; it was all done by old-fashioned dialing.

The obsolete landlines of the old AT&T phone system had saved the world for the time being.

PART THREE

UNYIELDING FORCE

I believe in one thing only, the power of the human will.

—Joseph Stalin

12

Will Mendenhall nudged Jack awake as the LC-130 Hercules made a wide turn to lose altitude. Collins awoke suddenly, feeling as if his entire body was still back at Christchurch, New Zealand, where they had hurriedly exchanged aircraft from the relative comfort of the C-5A Galaxy to the cramped confines of the ski-equipped Hercules. Jack looked at Will as if he didn't know who he was, then slowly he came awake. He looked from the captain to a slumbering Henri Farbeaux, who was stretched out across two of the foldable airliner seats just aft of the cockpit.

"I hate to tell you this, but the base they've sent us to isn't much of a going concern." Will stepped back so Collins could sit up and look out of the small window.

To Jack it seemed as if the Air Force pilot was rubbing it in a little as the Hercules concluded its hard bank to the right so they could get a good look at the small hellhole they had been sent to. The research base was that in name only, as it appeared to be nothing more than eight plastic construction-style buildings that were raised on thin stilts. A large British flag flew and was rapidly waving in the brisk winds of the area.

"Oh, shit," Jack mumbled as he took in the atmospheric research complex.

"My exact description, General," Will said as he shook Farbeaux awake.

The Hercules was now at a thousand feet of altitude as the pilot came on over the intercom. "Gentlemen, please fasten your seat belts for landing. They haven't had time to scrape the runway since the last storm so it may be rather rough. Temperature outside is a balmy minus-forty-seven degrees Celsius—that's below zero. Welcome to Halley Station." The colonel flying the aircraft hesitated just a second before clicking off his mic. The three officers in the belly of the Hercules heard laughter just before it became silent.

"I think that pilot is what you Americans would call an asshole," Farbeaux said as he strapped in and then looked out of the window.

The Hercules came down hard with her front skis banging against the ice and snow. The Herky-Bird on skis reversed the pitch of her four powerful propellers and then her flaps flew high in the air as the pilot gave it everything the old bird had to slow her down without having to hit the brakes. The nose skidded right and then left and the pilot adjusted through the rear stabilizer to stop the swaying motion of the Hercules.

Jack, Will, and Henri felt their stomachs as they ejected somewhere near the front of the landing strip. The Hercules bumped, rose into the air momentarily, and then came down again as she caught the nose-on winds. Then she finally settled to the ice and slid to a stop.

"Crazy bastards," Jack mumbled. The whine of the LC-130's turbofans slowed in pitch as the aircraft taxied toward the nearest buildings. Collins saw several men in white snow gear awaiting their arrival. He also saw three Black Hawks with their rotors already turning. They were flanked by two British Gazelle Attack choppers that also were warmed and ready to fly.

"I guess we're not done flying yet," Henri said as he stood and stretched his arms.

They started gathering their gear, and heard more laughter from the cockpit as the snow-crazed pilots had their fun at their passengers' expense.

A man wearing white arctic gear with his face covered in a ski mask approached the men as they exited the Hercules into the breath-freezing environment of Antarctica. The man's goggles covered his eyes and Jack, through his sunglasses, saw the British Union Jack on the stark white parka.

"General Collins?" the man asked as the three freezing visitors hit the bottom of the loading ramp. Farbeaux cursed as the wind struck him and nearly froze his feet to the cold aluminum.

"I'm Collins," Jack said. The man before him held out a white-gloved hand.

"I am Colonel Francis Jackson Keating, of Her Majesty's Special Air Service. Welcome to Halley Research Station, sir."

"Wonderful spot you've chosen in which to vacation, Colonel." Jack quickly looked away from the offered salute of the well-trained soldier from the SAS. "If you don't mind, Colonel, it's too damn cold out here to stand on ceremony; shall we get to where we're going before my ass freezes off?" He ignored the military gesture of respect from the Englishman, as Jack was in no mood.

The colonel lowered his hand, then gestured to the first Black Hawk.

"Yes, sir." The colonel reached into his parka and pulled out several flimsies and handed them to Jack. "These flash messages were sent over about an hour ago from the Alamo, sir." Collins took the message traffic and saw that they were from Lord Durnsford and countersigned by General Caulfield. "Now, if you would, General." Keating gestured to the waiting Black Hawk. "Right this way." He sprinted toward the warming helicopter along with his four men.

Jack and the others were relieved of their gear as they climbed into the relative warmth of the rear compartment of the first Black Hawk.

Once airborne, Collins placed a headset on underneath his cold-weather parka as the Black Hawk, piloted by men from the British Expeditionary Force, started a trek on a southerly heading, with the other Black Hawk and Gazelle attack helicopters flanking it. Jack gestured for Will and Henri to also don their headphones, then quickly studied the messages from the strange little man from MI6.

"News from the real world?" Will asked as he settled into the cold, hard seat.

Jack was silent as he read the communiqués from Durnsford. He looked at both men with worry etched on his hard features.

"They hit the Johnson Space Center hard. Downtown Houston was spared for the most part, with most of the damage coming from our own downed aircraft and friendly fire from the Center. Thirty-two fighters, both Navy and Air Force, were lost, plus the bulk of the Third Cavalry Regiment. It's basically ceased to exist."

Mendenhall looked out of the side window at the featureless expanse of Antarctica as it sped by below. He turned and faced the general.

"Any word on . . . any word on Mr. Everett?" he finally asked.

Jack didn't answer as he moved to the next message. "The Chinese are preparing to attack the enemy that occupies Beijing with everything they have short of nuclear weapons. The Paks are mounting an offensive force along the Indian border in preparation of attacking the landings there. They claim the Indian government is wasting time by not using every weapon at their disposal for eliminating the threat to the entire region."

Jack shook his head and then saw Henri with his "I told

you so" look as he turned away. Like Mendenhall, he watched the passing white of the land beneath them.

Collins read the last signal from Durnsford, then closed his eyes as he passed the message to Will. Jack leaned back as he realized that things were not going according to the plans of Lee, Matchstick, Compton, or their newest spook, Lord Durnsford. He didn't say anything when Mendenhall read the operational order aloud.

" 'From General Caulfield, Chairman of the Joint Chiefs of Staff, to all foreign commands. Cease offensive operations directed at the enemy. Return to your home bases of operations immediately. Defensive strikes against the enemy are only to be conducted for the defense of your commands. 7th Fleet operations are to cease and return to Hawaiian home waters. This order has been deemed necessary at this time. NATO command is hereby ordered to exit European theater of operation and return the 4th Infantry Division to Fort Carson, Colorado, immediately. All Persian Gulf commands will hold station and current defensive posture until further evaluation on enemy strategy has been investigated.—signed, Caulfield.' "

Henri finally sat up, slowly removed the message from Will's hand, and read it himself. He handed it back, shaking his head.

"I think you are beginning to see why I have made the choices that I have in regard to government service, Captain."

Will finally nodded his head, agreeing that Henri more than likely was right.

"What about this operation we are on, General? I mean, do you think an official recall will be ordered?"

"It doesn't matter, Will, you heard what Durnsford said back at Schofield: stay the course. And until Doc Compton or General Caulfield tells us differently, that's just exactly what we'll do."

Farbeaux smiled and shook his head in wonder.

"Tell me something, General Collins. What will happen when you discover this Overlord plan is nothing but what you Americans call a pipe dream, as much as these new orders for separation of defensive moves against the aliens? And with the destruction of your space facilities, that scenario seems to be the way this is headed."

"I don't have an answer for you, Colonel, as I'm sure the men that planned this don't either. We just have to trust Matchstick and his judgment."

"Well, either way one thing is for sure," Henri said as he leaned back in his seat. "Just as soon as the Pakistanis and the Indians start launching nuclear weapons at everything in sight, we won't have to worry too long about the shortcomings of your Operation Overlord."

Jack didn't respond as he knew the Frenchman was dead on in his judgment.

"General," came the English-accented voice of the pilot, "we're approaching Camp Alamo, sir. You can view it out of the left-side window."

Will moved over to Collins's side of the Black Hawk; so did Henri. Below was the site where the salvation of the entire world was being planned.

"Correct me if my American history is lacking, gentlemen, but was not the Alamo a defeat, a rather nasty one?" Farbeaux began to laugh, then turned and flopped back into his seat. The despair was showing the only way the Frenchman knew how to vent it—in black humor.

"Oh, I feel sick," Will said as he too sat back down with a long sigh.

Jack just closed his eyes against the sight that greeted them. The hopes he had felt, the trust in the powers that be, and the dreams of life someday returning to normal were fast evaporating as he closed his eyes against the sight from below. He heard the mocking laughter of Farbeaux over the sound of the twin turbines of the Black Hawk as the doubts about the abilities of his director, Niles Compton, and of a small green man, and a once brilliant one in Garrison Lee, entered his thoughts for the first time.

Camp Alamo was the last hope of the human race. It was five small huts and a helicopter landing pad. One guard stood outside one of the plastic-coated environmental enclosures and waited for the commanding general of all defensive forces in Antarctica to arrive and take charge.

Collins opened his eyes and examined the spot for Earth's last defense, if it came to that. First the destruction of the Johnson Space Center and the possible loss of his friend, Carl Everett, and now this.

Camp Alamo existed to house the staff and military personnel of Operation Overlord, but looked deserted with the exception of the lone man waiting outside who shooed away two penguins that were playing at his feet.

Hope was fast fading from the mind of the ever-trusting Jack Collins.

CHATO'S CRAWL, ARIZONA

The Cactus Bar and Grill had slowly slid downhill since the establishment had been sold by its former owner, Julie Dawes, after she and her son Bill had moved to California, where Billy was attending college at San Diego State. Gus Tilly and Matchstick had made sure the young single mother and her son would never want for anything again. She had left the small town of Chato's Crawl after the incident with the saucers and the firefight in the desert in 2006. When Gus died Billy would inherit not only Gus's entire fortune reaped from the Lost Dutchman Mine, discovered accidentally during the same incident, but also the mine itself and the guardianship of one Mahjtic Tilly.

Hiram Vickers entered the now dingy bar, removed his sunglasses, and squinted into the dust-infused lighting. He saw the man behind the bar as he was cleaning glasses. The only other patron was a slim man standing at the old-fashioned jukebox in the corner. Actually, the music machine seemed to be keeping the old-timer from falling over, more than providing music. He walked up to the bar.

"So this is the famous Cactus Grill," he said as he looked around. The front glass was cracked and the bar had seen far better days. He smelled at least fifty years of burnt hamburgers and stale beer clinging to every inch of the rotted wood and stained linoleum. "Not much of a going concern, is it?"

The heavyset man looked up, then just as fast ignored the remark and returned to rinsing his glasses.

"I mean, this place being so famous and all. The stories I've heard said this was a joint that saw a lot of action in the dust-up of 2006."

"I wouldn't know about that, mister, I bought the place from an ad in the paper. What happened before me ain't my concern and none of my business. Now, you want a beer, or is this just a question and answer session?" He placed his last glass on a towel to drain and then looked at the thin man with the red hair. The bartender was figuring the fella for a pansy type out of Phoenix.

"Well, partly a question and answer session, I guess, but I will have a whiskey sour in the prelude to our conversation." ·

The bartender looked at him, reached for a glass, poured him a flat beer from the tap, and pushed it toward him.

"There you go, one whiskey sour. Anything else?"

Vickers looked at the glass of beer that resembled urine, then smiled but didn't reach for the offering. But he did reach into his pocket and pulled out a hundred-dollar bill and place it by the dirty glass.

"An old man, Tilly. Gus Tilly lives hereabouts?"

The man eyed the bill before him from the man he suspected was mocking his country accent, but didn't reach for it. Instead he grabbed a bottle hidden under the bar and then opened a refrigerator and brought out a plastic container. His hands disappeared below the counter and Vickers heard the tingling of ice being placed in a glass. Then his hand reappeared with a fresh glass of whiskey sour that he pushed toward the stranger. He took the hundred-dollar offering as he dragged his hand away. Vickers reached for the drink and took a sip. He set it down, then pointed at it and winked, and nodded his head one time.

"Haven't seen Gus in a while—he usually stops in around the end of the month to pick up the things he orders and then leaves. But he's been a no-show so far this month, and that makes him about ten days late." The bartender placed the bill in his filthy shirt.

Vickers drank again and then stared at the man while he crunched ice in his mouth. The sound made the heavy man wince.

"Things. What kind of things would he order from you?" He continued to chew the ice without looking away or duplicating his earlier kind smile.

"About the only things you can get from a distributer out of Phoenix for a small bar. Couple'a jars of beef jerky, some pickled eggs—a lot of pickled eggs—and a case of frozen pizza rolls. The rest of his goods, I guess, are brought in from the Piggly Wiggly over in Apache Junction by the folks that watch over his place."

"Folks?"

The man didn't answer as he removed the stale beer and then drank it himself.

Vickers nodded his head in understanding at the bartender's hesitation. He took another drink of the whiskey sour and then bit down on more ice. The burly man smiled as the redheaded visitor reached inside his pocket again. He brought up the silenced Glock and aimed it at the bartender's chest. He crunched the ice again and then raised his thin red brows. The big man in the dirty shirt took a step back.

"He's got several men staying with him out at his place. I think they just look after the old goat. That's all I know. Since Gus has been gone, they come in a little more regular and knock a few back. Not the same guys, though, these fellas look like . . . well . . . they look older, not quite as tough as the regulars."

With his left hand Hiram Vickers reached for the drink and then drained it, leaving the ice for last. He was satisfied that whatever body guards this asset had were no longer there, but had been replaced by other less formidable men.

"So, let's sum it up. Gus Tilly is gone, the fellas that

watch over his place aren't the regular ones who have been there previously, and you supply them with—well, let's face it, crap to eat. Is this all correct?"

"Yeah, but I don't think the pickled eggs and pizza rolls are for him, because Gus once said the stuff makes him want to puke. So I'm guessin' they're for those men out there, or someone I never see."

"Now, that adds up. Thank you for the drink and the answerin',", he said, mocking the drawl of the bartender. He didn't turn when the small bell sounded over the door and two men in black shirts and Windbreakers walked inside. The first through the door nodded his head once to the reflection of Hiram in the dirty glass behind the bar. Vickers placed the gun back into the waistband of his Dockers and then finished crunching the ice he had in his mouth, never looking away from the frightened man.

The second man through the door walked over to the phone line that ran in from outside, and ripped it out of the wall. He lifted the phone that was next to the damaged line, listened, and then hung up, satisfied that the old system wouldn't work.

"There's no cell phone service here, and now no phone either," he said to Vickers, who was intent on watching the bartender's eyes.

"Okay, I think we're done here. By the way," he said as he smiled, "these two men will be staying here with you." He looked around the bar and grill. "To help out. It looks like you could use some assistance. We need to know when these new men from Tilly's place show up, and we need you to point them out." He smiled wider and then placed another hundred-dollar bill on the counter. "Sound good?"

The man just nodded once but didn't reach for the bill.

Vickers winked at the man and then left the bar. The two men in black sat down and then without the same smile as Vickers displayed reached for a dirty and creased menu.

Hiram Vickers wasn't pleased at the result of his interview. The two members of his Black Team had passed on the

information that the rest of the town was deserted. The Texaco station was boarded up, and the hardware store had
burned and, from the looks of it, had also fallen into the
ground somehow. The ice cream parlor was likewise boarded
and so were the rest of the small hovels that passed for
houses in this godforsaken part of Arizona. Chato's Crawl
was a ghost town in the strictest sense of the word. He shook
his head and walked toward the large Chevy Suburban, then
climbed into the front seat.

"What's the plan, Hiram?" the leader of the Black Team
asked from the backseat, making Vickers's first name sound
like it was shit, only pronounced differently.

"The plan is we wait." He turned his head and looked
back at the brown-haired man behind him. "That's what
you're good at, isn't it, waiting?"

The man didn't react to the question until he returned
Vickers's arrogant smile.

"Yes, that's what we do, we're patient, Hiram. Very patient." The smile widened. "Until it's time to stop being
patient."

Vickers turned back around and told the driver to park
inside the garage at the Texaco station. He never realized it
was the same location where Colonel Henri Farbeaux once
waited with his men a long time before as they planned to
enter the underground hell of the animal known as the Talkan—or as Matchstick had called it, the Destroyer.

"Well," he said, "they'll eventually show and Chato's
Crawl will be the place it all ends for this Matchstick Man."

The dark blue Chevy drove straight to the station and
vanished around the back, where the men in black would
start their vigil and patiently wait for Hiram Vickers's bargaining chip to come home.

BEIJING, CHINA

General Xiao Jung was a man who was most responsible for
bringing their former leader to power. Since the incident at

Camp David he had his plans for China's commitment to Operation Overlord overruled by the new president, Dao Xatzin—a man who had been waiting to take power in the wake of the military's bold move four years before when they ousted, rather forcibly, the man that stood in the way of China's cooperation with the rest of the world. The power had not passed to Xatzin, but to the Western-leaning man who had died at Camp David. Now General Jung was at the mercy of the man who ordered China's withdrawal from the agreements with the West.

As he watched from National People's Park two miles from the city of Beijing, he knew that this improvised plan had a chance of failing spectacularly. Even with the secret communiqués from the chairman of the Joint Chiefs of Staff, Maxwell Caulfield, advising the general on the intelligence that the new representative of President Xatzin had failed to pass on to the military. It was risky, but Jung thought if the attack could be coordinated correctly, they had maybe a 10 percent chance of saving Beijing.

In just the sixteen hours Jung had been observing, he had been fed intelligence from his forward units that over two and half million of China's citizenry had been taken into the processing ship. As far as the air force could tell him the power-replenishing saucers had risen only once from Bohai Bay to regenerate the large saucer's power shield. The plan would succeed or fail in that area alone. He must stop the processing craft from getting the needed power that prevented his military from regaining the capital. Thus far the new leader had been silent on the plan of attack, offering no guidance—as if he would not take the blame if the plan failed, but would gain the favor of the people if the general succeeded. Frankly thinking, Jung would rather have the politicos screaming at him for action rather than the silence coming from their hidden bunkers along the Yangtze River.

The roundup of Beijing's citizens had deeply affected his army as they awaited the ground attack to commence. They had watched as screaming and pleading women and children were taken from their homes, streets, and other hiding places and dragged into the processing ship. The general's mind screamed at him for action against this barbaric enemy that had shown no mercy for his people. The fate that awaited them once inside was one that any human being could not think about for very long before their spirits flagged in this desperate hour.

Jung placed his hands behind his back and looked out toward the sea. His navy was out there, waiting to spring their surprise on the ships hiding in the bay. The navy's twenty attack submarines would be joined by the *Liaoning*, the first aircraft carrier in the People's Liberation Army Navy. Its keel was originally laid down as the Admiral Kuznetsov–class multirole carrier *Riga*, for the Soviet navy. She had been purchased and refurbished and made China's own by the People's Republic shipyards.

The *Liaoning* waited twenty miles out to sea for any sign of the power-generation saucers that could escape the speedy and dangerous Type 093 Shang-class attack subs. Ten of these fast-attack boats, which looked amazingly like the older Los Angeles–class submarines of the U.S. Navy, would be assisted by five of the old Russian Akula-class boats and five of the Han-class subs as they would attempt to track down the three saucers before they could assist the larger processing craft in the heart of the city. The plan, code-named Operation Wrath, depended upon the navy to do their job and do it well. They were all expendable toward that goal, even General Jung himself.

As he turned and looked at the dark city before him, only the soft glow of the enemy shield cast any light on the dying capital. The surreal illumination was also a fear-inducing factor among the largest attacking force the People's Republic had ever mounted. Over twenty thousand artillery pieces would be joined by an attack force of over five thousand Type 99A2 main battle tanks. These units would use their full complement of shells and special sabot rounds to weaken the shield and draw the energy-producing saucers from their hiding places. They would be assisted by a thousand long-range missiles fired from the five Shagshu-class missile cruisers a mile offshore. Add five thousand surface-to-surface missiles launched from hidden batteries in the outskirts of the city itself.

Jung looked at the forces poised inside the park and the surrounding suburbs of the capital. Over three million men would rush the shield if and when it went down. They would have orders not only to rescue as many of the citizenry as possible, but to avenge the millions that had already been butchered like cattle inside the cursed processing vehicle.

The general looked at his watch in the soft glow of the distant enemy shield. Two minutes until the air force started their attack runs. Bombers of the 10th People's Air Wing would strike first with small battlefield nuclear bombs. One-megaton warheads code-named "The People's Vengeance" would pummel the top of the shield in the hopes of draining the power of the enemy protection and craft and, with luck, maybe even destroy it. This plan was not the general's but the commanders of the military advisory committee that sat safely beside the new leadership in their deep bunkers along the Yangtze.

"General, it is now 0230 hours. Shall I give the order to the orbiting bombers?" His aide also watched the quiet city two miles distant. He noticed the general had refused to wear the protective clothing provided to higher command officials. Jung would suffer the same fallout fate as his men. The aide silently and almost motionlessly laid his mask and plastic-lined protective gear aside, and waited on the man he and all the soldiers of his command respected beyond measure.

Jung just nodded his head as he faced away from Beijing.

The men could hear the engines of China's latest miracle of aviation, the H-8 stealth bomber. The bat-winged craft was identical to the American B-2 and was just as deadly. The silence of the night was broken by two million men of the People's Army taking cover as the loud warning sirens sounded from around the perimeter of the enemy shield.

A second warning sounded in a series of alternating blasts from the mobile communications vans that ringed the city. The general had to be pulled by his staff into the makeshift bunker near his command-and-control hut.

The dark-skinned bombers streaked overhead from twenty thousand feet in altitude. Suddenly thick laser beams were projected onto the saucer from hidden places inside the smoldering debris outside Beijing. These laser-targeting guides were being cast by ten volunteers who had family inside the capital. Jung closed his eyes as he thought of the brave men who were sacrificing their lives.

The night became like day as the first one-megaton warhead detonated against the force field. Then three more struck the upper section of shielding. The scene became like an X-ray to those that braved the sight before them. The punishing winds tore through the city and the surrounding forces of the People's Republic. The men inside the general's sandbag-reinforced bunker felt the earth shake as three further detonations rocked the capital. Men all around Beijing fell when the impacts happened in rapid succession. The general heard screams of frightened men around him as he prayed to the unjust gods above that the enemy couldn't withstand such an evil power as man's nuclear arsenal.

The last of the nuclear smart bombs struck the direct center of the dome even before the heat had begun in earnest from the first three weapons. The cable of the shield cooked and melted but immediately started to regenerate before the heat started to dissipate. The two guarding saucers were immediately knocked down by the pressure wave that forced itself through the powerful shielding around the capital. The first hit the larger processing craft and then slammed into the surrounding buildings, while the second saucer was simultaneously smashed two miles distant from where it had been hovering. Then it impacted the shield, sliding down it like a bird caught in a net. It lay there smoking and melting. From the outside the men who braved a look saw the massive cables of the shield shake and vibrate and they momentarily thought that they would give fully. Instead, the blue glow increased, adding its own light to that of the nuclear detonations.

The night sky around Beijing looked as if the sun had exploded directly overhead. The noise was deafening as the explosive wave struck the surrounding troops. Armored vehicles rocked on their hardened springs and tanks bounced as if they were toys. Several thousand men were incinerated as they tried in vain to see the devastation and they vanished in a blinding wave of heat. The Grays were no better off. Spotters estimated that at least five or six thousand of the creatures had been caught in the open, along with several hundred of their walking automatons. At the same time it was reported that many hundreds of thousands of citizens were also killed from the 10,000° heat caused by the attack.

The general could not wait any longer. He rose from the plywood flooring of the bunker and raced outside, followed quickly by his entire staff. Jung threw up his arm as the heat wave continued to burst into the outskirts of Beijing. He turned his head and felt the hair on his head and arms crisp and fly away into the storm of wind and dirt.

Before the order was given, the three hundred JH-7 Flying Leopard fighter-bombers tore through the maelstrom of fire coming from the electronic shielding of the saucer. Without even the slightest estimation of the damage caused by the nuclear attack, the fighters released their loads of unguided bombs against the burning shield and city beneath. Strike after strike erupted on the smoldering upper dome. Ten thousand bombs fell from the night sky that was no longer dark. The attacking fighter-bombers were outlined by the glowing sky around them as the largest air assault in history continued.

The general raised his field glasses when he thought it was safe enough not to burn his pupils out from the amazing site before him. The city of Beijing was awash in a tremendous light that could never have been imagined and still the bombs fell from the sky.

"Get me intelligence from our forward spotters immediately. Is the shield holding?" he shouted as he tried in vain to penetrate the thick billowing smoke caused by the bomb impacts.

As a hard wind came in from the north, the answer was clear. The blue glow of the enemy protection was still alight with energy. The general saw the saucer that had slammed into the larger vehicle slowly rise from the rubble at its base and then start toward his waiting forces outside the capital. The large saucer was burning in several sections but was still there and still viable as it rocked and then settled once again. The streets had been sweeped clean of Grays, but also sadly many thousands of men, women, and children.

General Jung stilled himself against the failure of the attack and then lowered the glasses. The plan had to move forward through the disappointing failure.

"All commands, open fire!" he said angrily as he looked toward the target of Beijing.

In the next three seconds, twenty thousand artillery shells and five thousand sabot and high explosive tank rounds arched and streaked into the shield wall. It was as if a million fireflies struck the electronic dome at once and then kept alighting to the surface in an unyielding cacophony of sound and never-ending explosions. It was now a battle between the ancient gods of old as they struggled for supremacy.

The Chinese army was unleashing Earth's version of hell against the invaders of their world.

BOHAI BAY, BEIJING

The three smaller saucers began the rescue of their processing ship by burrowing out of the sand and mud where they had lain undetected for three full days. They spun the bottom of the bay into a spiraling vortex of ocean life and water as they rose toward the surface. The Chinese navy finally had found the saucers' hiding place and went on the attack.

Captain Zen Lee of the People's Republic Submarine S-78, the *Great Leader*, was the first to confront the lead saucer as her sonar detected the movement through the deepwater port.

"Lock on and engage," he calmly ordered. "Tubes one through six, full spread."

The large submarine was based on the stolen design of the old Los Angeles–class boats built by the American General Dynamics Corporation. She shuddered as six YU-6 torpedoes, based on the design of the U.S.-built Mark-48s, sped from their tubes just aft of the sonar dome. The heavy-kill weapons sped to their maximum speed of fifty-two knots, catching the first saucer as it shed the mud of the bottom of the bay from its metallic skin. All six struck the craft at the midsection and then they detonated simultaneously, sending debris from the bottom through the thick environment to the surface where the impact explosion rocked the waves high above. The column of seawater shot to a height of three hundred feet and that was a marker for the fighter aircraft from the aircraft carrier *Liaoning,* as sixty of them had been orbiting the bay high overhead. The fighter-bombers of the 3rd offensive wing struck with the very deadly Mongol missiles. The tremendous rush of air caused by the streaking jets shattered the column of water and struck the saucer as it tried to reach the sky.

The *Great Leader* and four of her large sisters let loose a spread of YU-6 torpedoes that were targeted just beneath the falling vessel. The wire-guided weapons were electronically detonated sixty feet below the dying saucer.

Suddenly the second and third saucers charged through the dense waters of the bay, loosing cannon fire against the fast-attack boats of the Chinese navy. As the first saucer sank deeper into the water the warheads of no less than thirty-one YU-6s exploded just beneath her. The resulting cataclysm warped the saucer until it broke into three separate sections and then the remains swirled to the bottom, too damaged to heal itself.

The *Great Leader* heard the breaking up of the first saucer and her crew cheered. The captain ordered silence as he heard through her sound-dampening hull the terrible whine of the streaking saucers as they came on at the grouping of attack boats at over 200 knots. The captain never had the chance to order maneuvering to take evasive action as the first long line of laser fire cleanly sliced the *Great Leader* and her four sister boats into an exploding mass of steel and composite material. The crews of five of the largest submarines in the world perished as the remaining two saucers rose through the sea to confront the air attackers with a vengeance.

THE PENTAGON
WASHINGTON. D.C.

The situation room far beneath the *E* ring of the colossal building was silent as the real-time satellite images streamed in from three KH-11s and -12s as the battle for Beijing took a turn for the worse. Not only was the largest military bombardment and shelling against a single target the world had ever been witness to a complete failure, the entire attacking force of the Chinese navy's surface flotilla and her underwater assets, twenty of the finest submarines in the world, had been destroyed.

Many angry eyes turned toward the upper balcony, where the military technicians knew the acting president sat with his young advisory staff. The men knew they had failed the Chinese, but the president wasn't seeing it that way.

Camden watched the giant processing saucer as it slowly rose into the sky. Fighter jets of the People's Republic continued to pummel the shield that had withstood no less than ten small nuclear weapons and millions of artillery, tank, missile, and air strikes and had still survived.

The gray image from high above showed the watching Americans the powerful might of the enemy as the large, thick cables of the shield wall burst like a balloon; then the cables cascaded to the ground as the saucer began to climb into the sky. The shield was shed like the skin of a rejuvenated snake. They watched as the remains of buildings were also shed like a dog shaking off water. Still the great saucer rose into the dawning light of day. The two smaller saucers climbed with it as the two remaining craft that had refueled the power source shot off to the south. Tanks and artillery pieces adjusted aim and continued to pummel the unyielding saucer as it rose. Fighter aircraft dove in and several even made suicide runs and crashed into the upper sections, all to no avail. The craft simply rose at a leisurely pace as it burst through the thick columns of smoke that covered the remains of Beijing.

"General, the CIA sent this analysis over from Langley." Caulfield's aide handed the shocked Marine the bad news.

The general read the report and then passed it over to the remaining members of the Joint Chiefs. They too read the damage estimates to the People's army, navy, and air force. All the chiefs were stunned with the exception of Admiral James Fuqua, who had resigned just after the destruction of the aircraft carrier *Liaoning*. She had gone down with all hands battling to the end. With her aircraft all shot from the sky the giant ship had died a violent death as she was ripped apart like a tin can by the remaining two saucers that had arisen from the bay and exacted a terrible revenge for the death of the third craft. Admiral Fuqua had begged for permission to send the three Virginia-class subs in the area to the rescue of the surviving crewmen of the carrier who were fighting for their lives in the sea off of China's coast. He turned and pleaded with the new commander-in-chief to allow him to turn the 7th Fleet around and assist the Chinese in their effort as agreed upon by his predecessor, but it was all to no avail. The president merely shook his head in complete deference to the horrible disaster happening halfway around the world.

Caulfield lowered his eyes as he studied the angry military personnel far below in the situation center. He had watched an infuriated Admiral Fuqua as he stormed from the conference room; the president had accepted his immediate resignation. Caulfield watched as his friend's replacement had been waiting in the hallway leading to the situation room.

Virginia Pollock, still there as an observer, patted the

general on the arm and then she too left. She wanted to go to the ladies' room and be sick, as she had never imagined that such carnage could be absorbed by one nation. She left with her head hung low.

General Maxwell Caulfield slowly turned away from the horrid aerial views of the burning capital city of China. He placed a hand over his eyes and then sat at the main conference table, never so ashamed in his life.

On another set of monitors flames rose high over the completely destroyed city of Mumbai. The Indian air force had attempted the same attack method as the Chinese, only they had used almost their full arsenal of nuclear missiles. The large saucer had survived the strikes of no less than the combined megatonnage of fifty warheads. With the aid of the two replenishment craft that had completely destroyed that nation's surface fleet near the Strait of Mumbai, she had shed her defensive shield and now the giant processing vehicle was rising from the ashes of the once proud city as she too started to head for space and the raging wormhole the American imaging section said was forming. The craft entered the swirling mass of light and then departed for her home fleet with no less than three million souls in her cargo holds. Despair covered the entire world.

"This is why I will not sacrifice the military forces of this nation in a plan that would result in this." Camden stood and gestured at the two completely destroyed cities on the screens below. "The American people will back me on this."

Caulfield raised his head and took in the man standing at the thick glass. "You don't know them, do you?"

Camden turned at the sound of the general's voice. "Excuse me?"

Caulfield stood, shaking off the restraining hands of his Air Force counterpart as he foresaw the confrontation developing.

"I said you don't know them very well, do you?" Caulfield stepped around the large table and strode to face the president.

"Know who?" Camden was joined by several members of his young staff, who feared they were about to witness something unprecedented.

"The American people!" Caulfield turned and gestured at the screen below that showed the two lost cities. "Do you for one minute think that they will be proud of what happened last night? We had a chance at a united defense with weapons developed just for this scenario, but we failed them, Mr. President. If word ever leaked out, and it will, that we basically stabbed our allies in the back, they will crucify you and I'll be there to help. Americans don't run, never have. Despite what most think, we do like the rest of the world, and would never, ever wish to see this tragedy befall anyone. And we refused to even assist in the rescue of drowning seamen?" He shook his head and started for the door, joined by two of the chiefs and, to Camden's surprise, many of the politically neutral civilian staff.

"My resignation is in your security advisor's hands," Caulfield said.

Camden wanted to smile as he nodded his head at the security advisor, who held up the resignation letter that had been delivered to him by the general's aide not long after Admiral Fuqua had left the room. He then opened the door to allow General Sydney Lefferts, the new head of the Joint Chiefs, into the room. The plan for getting rid of all the former president's remaining cabinet had been initiated.

"General, are you prepared to defend the nation?" Camden asked as he placed his hands behind his back.

The U.S. Army four-star general nodded his head as the remainder of the chiefs shook theirs.

"Sir, we have recalled the 82nd and 101st from their former stations that were a part of this Operation Overlord. Thus far there has been no response, but we should be able to track them down now that the head has been removed from the traitorous—"

The rumble of men in the room voiced what most were feeling at the moment by the use of the word *traitorous*. Many, while not backing General Caulfield's and Admiral

Fuqua's actions in this highly secretive plan, would not stand by and allow this man to say such a thing about an American officer who had dedicated his life to the nation.

Camden felt the first rift among his people and didn't like it.

"Being traitorous is for history to decide. We don't wish to stir harsh emotions in this room."

"Yes, Mr. President," Lefferts, said bowing to the man's wishes. "We have thus far initiated military law in all cities above a million-person population, and the smaller cities will be under military control over civil law enforcement."

Camden was shocked when the CIA and FBI directors also got up and left without a word.

"Thank you, General. I want your new staff to get me a battle plan immediately that I can fully explain to the general population. No need to keep them in the dark. We must let them know their leaders are going to protect them far better than those in other nations."

"Yes, sir, our National Guard units are rolling into New York, Chicago, Houston, Dallas, Los Angeles, San Francisco, and other cities as we speak. I believe the populace will be willing to listen to anything you have to say very soon."

Camden nodded his gratitude and then left with his staff following close behind—all except the two men who shared the president's public relations duties. They exchanged looks of horror as they stood, stunned, as the calligraphers gathered their materials.

"This is beginning to smell bad. Control the civil population?"

"Those cracks yesterday about the Berlin thing, that's not sounding that ridiculous any longer." The taller of the two was betting his Harvard law degree that once Camden seized control there would be no wresting the power from his tight grip that he now seemed to be consolidating.

The two men didn't know what they would do, but knew they hadn't gotten into the political side of things to be a part of a coup, no matter how ingeniously it was disguised.

"Feel like taking a side trip to Walter Reed?"

"Yeah, why not? I would rather get shot trying to warn someone than be ordered to fall on my sword when we don't agree with something this man says."

The two men left the situation room more scared of their commander-in-chief than by the enemy that had just destroyed two of the world's most populated cities.

13

Carl was sitting against the deep subbasement wall and was struck in the face by a pair of tan naval dress pants. He looked up at the cigar-chomping master chief as he stood before him.

"Where did you dig these up?" Everett asked. He tried to clear his head after being knocked into a semiconscious state after falling through the training center roof.

Jenks became sullen as he removed the stub of cigar from his mouth and then fixed his old student with the look that said it was time to buck up and listen.

"Plenty of uniforms and everything else lying around; hope they fit."

Everett stood and removed the bathrobe that was covered in blood and then accepted a torn T-shirt from the master chief.

"Well?" Carl asked. "You're not one for dramatics, Jenks, what's the score?"

"As far as I can see, we just got our asses royally kicked. Can't see much from under here until they dig us out, but you can bet there's not much left up top." Jenks looked away

at the memory of hundreds of F-15, F-16, and Hornets falling from the sky like hailstones before he had slipped down
the torn and twisted stairwell to get to the admiral moments
before the building started to collapse around their ears.
"Got a few boys down here in the subbasement, some of
them are hurt real bad, but it's better than what it is out
there." He gestured at the collapsed concrete and steel
above their heads. "We lost a lot of good people, Toad."
Jenks looked sad, unlike him according to Everett's memory. "My whole goddamn engineering department is gone."
He looked down at his feet and then angrily threw the cigar
away. "I think I was a little hard on those kids."

"You didn't kill them, Jenksy," Carl said as he slipped the
filthy T-shirt over his head.

"Yeah, I guess." He reached into his scorched lab coat
and brought out five plastic disks. "But all their work didn't
die with them." He held up the computer discs. "I have all
of our simulations right here. All we have to do is get them
to where my babies are waiting. I think these hold the keys
to the bugs we sorted out."

"Your babies?" Everett looked around the dimly lighted
area beneath the training center.

"Yeah, the goddamn vessels that will get your boys to the
target. They're not here. Thank God some moron was bright
enough not to have the ships and the men that would fly
them in one place. No, my two girls are down with the rest of
Overlord."

Admiral Everett was looking at the angry men in the
basement until he saw a familiar face. It was the young navy
SEAL he had confronted during the training exercise that
very morning. He was leaning over and tending to the wounds
of a Delta sergeant sitting against the cinder-block wall. He
saw Everett and then stood.

"How many made it to the shelters?" Carl asked as he too
leaned over and examined the Delta commando's wounds.

"I'm not sure, sir. The whole damn building came down
around our ears as we tried to get below." He looked around
at the remaining men of the admiral's command. "I think

all of the officers from both Delta and the SEALs were killed, I'm not sure. At least half of the . . . the . . ."

Jenks walked up to the young SEAL and whispered something to him as Carl watched. The kid straightened and then faced the admiral. "Sorry, sir, it looks like we'll be down to half strength."

Everett nodded his thanks and then allowed the SEAL to continue tending the soldier, who looked as if he were going to join those already killed by the enemy's surprise attack.

"How in the hell did they allow this to happen?" he asked Jenks as he turned angrily to face him.

The master chief managed to find another fresh cigar in the rumpled lab coat and stuck it in his mouth.

"We always knew it was a possibility, that's why the separation of the engineering boys down south and the training of personnel here in Houston. We couldn't take the chance of having both elements together. It just so happened that those Gray bastards singled us out." He removed the cigar and fixed Everett with the look that made the master chief the terror of the United States Navy during his long tenure. "So don't go thinkin' your bosses left you and your men hangin' out to dry, they didn't. What we have to do now is get our shit together and head south as soon as we can pick up the pieces. As far as your command is concerned, you'll have to pick up some warm bodies from the command already down south."

"Why not here?"

"Because, as of six hours ago, this entire unit is ignoring the orders directly from the president of the United States. That means we're not only deserters, Toad, but now a bunch of pirates that's soon to be on our own."

"All right, Master Chief, I've had about enough of this secrecy crap. What do you know?"

Jenks finally laughed out loud, drawing questioning looks from the men left in the basement.

"You orderin' me to answer, Toad?" he asked as his smile remained.

Carl took a deep breath and then shook his head. "No, I'm asking not just for me, but them." He gestured at the dead and wounded men around them.

"Goddamn, that's below the belt, Toad."

"Yes, it is."

"This Overlord plan is so departmentalized for security reasons I only know my part . . . and yours. The rest is as big a mystery to me as it is to you. Whatever the large part of Overlord is, it's bigger than anything I can imagine. If they are using my designs for what they are intended for, I really do want to see the delivery method."

"Explain," Everett said, not letting up.

Jenks lit his cigar in the darkness of the basement. "Okay, Toad, we have one of the original simulators for one of my babies right down here." The master chief turned at another set of steel stairs and then stopped. "Well, you wanna see or not?"

Everett followed Jenks into the bowels of the subbasement.

When they got down the two flights of stairs Carl saw a large object covered in plastic sheeting in the center of a large room. Jenks went to a desk that was covered in dust and then found a flashlight in one of its drawers. He flicked it on and gestured for the admiral to follow.

"This was the original prototype of my initial design. We worked out the engineering with some of those boys from DARPA and NASA. But it's my baby, make no mistake about it. They helped some, I guess, but mostly on the subsequent versions." Jenks pulled the plastic away from the large vehicle.

"What in the hell is this?" Carl asked. He had to step back and look at the amazing sight before him.

"This is the landing craft *Spruance*." Jenks's eyes traveled over the graceful lines of the spacecraft. "The first of her kind and the lead vessel for a new class of transport—smaller than the space shuttle, but sturdier and a whole lot faster."

Everett examined the lines of the ship. It did look like a smaller version of the shuttle, with the exception of the wing assembly. These were short and stubby, almost nonexistent.

The tail boom was that only in name, as it ended abruptly just aft of what Carl assumed was the cargo hold.

"Seats a command crew of six, plus the load master. She's capable of transporting a strike element of fully equipped, fully suited commandos to their final destination. She is armed with two five-thousand-watt laser cannon designed by the boys at DARPA and the Raytheon Corporation." He turned to face Everett. "I understand that you may have had a hand in securing the technology somewhere in South America." He smiled. "If the rumors are true."

Carl didn't answer as he examined the snow-white skin of the landing craft. He saw the collar on the front nose of the ship below the pilot's compartment and the ring that would secure it to whatever target it was sent against. It was designed to mate with another craft, but Carl didn't know what that craft was, but knew his men had been training for its eventual use on the destroyed mock-up that came crashing down with the training center.

"There, now you know as much as myself, Toad, my boy." Jenks turned and admired the obsolete version of the ship that he had designed. He puffed on the cigar vigorously as he turned back to Carl. "Now, you gonna go with it, or do you want to sit down and cry your little pussy eyes out over the fact that not everybody hands out secret shit like Halloween candy—you little shit-ass."

Everett turned and faced his old SEAL instructor and shook his head as he returned his gaze to the amazing seventeen-ton craft sitting on its pedestal.

"I think I'll come along for the ride, you old, crusty son of a bitch."

"That's more fucking like it, you candy-ass officer."

CAMP ALAMO
ANTARCTICA

The winds had picked up just after their arrival at Camp Alamo. Jack stood warming his hands at the space heater as

Henri fumbled with the bulky arctic gear, trying to remove the warm parka. Will Mendenhall made no bones about staring at the young British SAS officer who sat at the small desk, writing out the departure time of the helicopters that had delivered the three to the most desolate spot in the world.

Will leaned over and showed him the black captain's bars on his collar. The SAS lieutenant looked up and gave Mendenhall a brief smile and nodded his head in approval, then returned to his logbook.

"In America," Will said, drawing his words out like he was explaining something to an immigrant that spoke very little English, "a captain outranks a lieutenant. How about in your country?" he asked as Jack looked over with a small smile. Henri stopped struggling with the bulky parka and watched the exchange. The lieutenant had remained silent since their arrival and that was also getting on the Frenchman's nerves as much as Will's.

The lieutenant stopped writing and then fixed Will with that irritating grin.

"Yes, sir, the chain of command is very much like your own. However, the man who will answer your inquiry will arrive shortly." He smiled and nodded his head. "Sir."

Mendenhall gave the SAS lieutenant a dirty look and then turned to Collins. "These guys keep a secret better than the director." He too went to the space heater and warmed his cold hands.

The lieutenant finally stood up as the buzzer on the plastic wall went off. It was like an old-fashioned telephone ring that shut off after only a second. The lieutenant walked to the far wall and faced the still struggling Farbeaux, who had finally removed the difficult parka.

"Colonel, please step aside. Professor Bennett has arrived." The lieutenant gestured for Henri to step closer to Jack and Will.

The three men heard the soft whine of an electric motor and then the plywood flooring gently parted near the far wall. As it did the two halves slid back, revealing an opening that was dark and foreboding. As they watched in amazement a man in a furry winter coat rose from the darkened abyss. The disguised elevator stopped and the man stepped off.

"Does the same guy that invented half the stuff at Group design stuff for everyone?" Will asked as they watched the man with the thick, horn-rimmed glasses approach them.

"Evidently," Collins answered as he took in the average-sized man.

"General Collins?" He held his hand out to Jack.

"Yes," was the quick answer as he shook the man's offered hand.

"Bloody good." He shook first Will's and then Henri's hands. "You made the perilous trek in one piece, good show. No unexpected in-flight horrors, I take it?"

"If you call potholes in the sky a horror, we had plenty of those," Collins said as he examined closely the strange man before him.

"Potholes," the man repeated, and then got what Jack was saying. "Ah, yes, potholes. Good show, old man. Yes, I can only guess at the rough air you must have traveled through all the way from the States."

Collins exchanged looks with Mendenhall and Farbeaux. Henri just closed his eyes and shook his head as he listened to the Englishman. The man just continued to smile without saying a word. Collins shook his head.

"I'm afraid you're the second gentleman from your country that's had the advantage over us when it comes to knowing names in the past two days."

"Oh, my, yes, that would be appropriate, wouldn't it?" He smiled but still said nothing until Jack raised both brows, urging him to connect the dots. "Damn, I'm just excited that you're here, General. My name is Bennett, Charles Darcy Bennett, professor of Astrophysics and a member of Her Majesty's Design Bureau, and former Dean of Sciences at Cambridge University."

"Sir Darcy Bennett," Henri said as he looked from the

crumpled man to the general. "He's got so many letters after his title that you may as well throw in the alphabet; his credentials would be shorter and more to the point that way." He surprised both Mendenhall and Collins with his sudden burst of knowledge.

"You've actually heard of me? Good show, old man." Bennett was impressed by the Frenchman's knowledge.

"Yes, well, I ran into you a few years back, I believe. You had just misplaced a rather expensive particle accelerator from the University of Sheffield laboratory."

The man allowed his mouth fall open in surprise. "Yes, but how would you know about—"

"Professor," Jack interrupted as he shot the French thief a cold look. "You really don't want to know. Let's just say Henri here was aware that your government misplaced that particular piece of priceless equipment and leave it at that."

Mendenhall smiled and shook his head knowing that it was Farbeaux who had relieved the British government of their little science experiment. Henri just smiled at the professor and said nothing more.

"Well, I'm sure you're exhausted and would like to get below. We have a rather long day ahead tomorrow." Bennett leaned in closer to the three men like a conspirator. "Our package is due to arrive."

Collins nodded his head as if he knew what the package was. He looked over at Will and sadly shook his head.

"Now, shall we descend into madness, gentlemen?" Bennett gestured toward the lift and the dark hole beyond. "Lieutenant Davidson, you may tell your man outside to place his detonator on hold for the moment." He smiled and looked at the three men. "Our guests' DNA analysis came back and they are whom we believed they were."

The SAS lieutenant nodded his head and smiled at Will Mendenhall. "Yes, Professor," he said as his eyes finally left Will's, and then he raised a small radio and did as he was instructed.

Bennett saw the questioning look as the three men hesitated at the lift.

"Oh, sorry, the lieutenant and his man, who is hidden quite well outside, had orders to blow you all to hell with twenty pounds of plastique—rather nasty stuff—if your DNA sequences weren't confirmed when you walked inside and breathed the air of this room. Sorry, we're cautious buggers around here." He walked to the lift and then waved the men on. "MI6 is running the security for our little band of mad scientists."

Jack, Will, and Henri cautiously stepped onto the lift with the smiling Bennett. The professor stepped on a hidden switch buried in the steel grate and the elevator started down into the solid ice.

"Rather much I know, but the James Bond attitude is seriously warranted after the attack on your Camp David, and especially after the disasters of last evening in Mumbai and Beijing."

Jack looked at the man and raised a questioning brow.

"Oh, of course you couldn't have known. Both cities have been totally destroyed after the Gray sots absconded with the bulk of their populations. Yes, I'm afraid the fun and games around here are over."

"I would think so," Will said, becoming angry at the professor's flippant remark.

The man became serious as he saw the upset way in which the young captain responded.

"I didn't mean to make light of the horrors of what happened, young man, but you must realize that we are in no better position here at Camp Alamo—thus the name the soldiers have given it."

"Why is that?" Mendenhall asked as the lift continued down into the blue ice.

"Because, old boy, the men and women here at Camp Alamo fully expect to die in this rather bizarre endeavor, and have volunteered for Overlord regardless."

"Well," Henri said as he felt his stomach lurch as the lift sped up and safety bars rose on all sides of the platform, "I haven't volunteered for anything."

The professor laughed heartily. "Again, good show, old

man, always keep that sense of humor, it will help you in the coming days. You French, always the kidders in the face of danger, very admirable."

Henri Farbeaux cursed his luck. "Who said I was kidding?"

The lift traveled down seven hundred feet through thick, blue ice, and that ice caused the professor's laugh to echo endlessly off the carved walls of the shaft.

As the four men stepped off the lift they were confronted by no less than twenty armed United States Marines. The professor waved his hand and then nodded at the gunnery sergeant leading the squad. Jack was the first to notice the strange weapons in the hands of the Marines. They were lightweight and made of composite plastic. They were also crystal-tipped-barreled rifles, the sort Charles Hindershot Ellenshaw III almost blew both of his hands off with in a deep South American tunnel four years before as he fired off an alien designed weapon.

"It seems at least some of the alien tech is paying off," Collins said as three of the Marines stepped forward and relieved the men of their bags. The gunnery sergeant stood at rigid attention in front of Jack.

The Marines were dressed in white colored BDUs as half of the twenty men stepped onto the lift and began the long climb to the surface. The rest of the Marine detail left the group of men as Professor Bennett waved the men forward from the elevator gallery. As they entered a carved-out section of ice the men had to stop as they gazed upon what looked like a large crystal tunnel system that stretched for miles. Five arms of tunneled-out ice went off in varying directions as small tram cars loaded with soldiers, sailors, and technicians in white lab coats transited to places unknown. The ice should have been melting in the comfortable atmosphere of the tunnels, but the general noticed the coolant lines that ran just beneath the surface kept the ice sound.

"Yes, a marvel of engineering by one of your universities—Montana, I think. Yes, Montana State. I'm afraid without the coolant lines we would all be bloody swimming." Bennett approached a tram that was waiting for the three new members of Overlord. "We are surrounded by a very ancient inland sea, thus a lot of frozen water."

The tram was plastic and traveled along an embedded rail that coursed through the floor of the tunnel system. As Jack and the others climbed onboard the professor punched in his desired destination. The sixteen-person vehicle silently moved off without the aid of a driver.

"Camp Alamo has one thousand different laboratories, five hundred shops for engineering purposes, along with research and development. We have personnel space for ten thousand military personnel and technicians. Completely separate, of course, is the center of the lake system where . . . well, where Overlord really resides."

The tram moved forward without a question being asked because each of the three knew that any questions would bring on only more confusion as just another compartmentalized secret.

"We have to make arrangements for about a thousand additional personnel as we bring in survivors of not only the trainees from the Johnson Space Center, but we'll soon also have guests from the Russian Navy. I understand a rather large vessel of theirs will never see the ocean again after it docks. She took quite a beating a few days ago not far from here." Professor Bennett looked momentarily saddened. "Bloody shame, actually, as we owe that ship and her crew everything."

Collins looked over at Mendenhall as they both thought the same thing at once. Sarah and Jason, if they were still alive, would be here shortly.

The tram arrived at a location that was filled with activity. The structures surrounding a large square were made of thick plastic and glass. The roadway here wasn't ice but asphalt. The tram moved off as the men exited. They were in front of a large structure that flew the blue flag of the United Nations, with the corresponding flags of the once cooperative nations flanking the taller pole in the middle.

"Before we enter the briefing, gentlemen, two young men have requested an audience with you, General. Something about being old acquaintances or something like that. When you finish, feel free to join me inside." The professor moved off and immediately started to greet others entering the structure with the many steel steps leading to double doors that were guarded by SAS men. These were identified by their red berets.

As Jack, Will, and Henri examined the surroundings of ice walls and the perfectly carved tunnel system, two men in battle whites approached. When Jack saw them he was amazed, to say the least. He had been told his command would involve specialists from all over the world, but never in his wildest imagination did he expect to see these two. He smiled and approached them as they stopped and saluted. Jack ignored the military protocol and held out his hand to the first man.

"Lieutenant Tram, you're a long way from home." Jack shook the small Vietnamese officer's hand. He had served with Van Tram in the same South American action of four years before. The Vietnamese national was possibly the best man with a rifle he had ever seen, and had demonstrated that ability time and time again in the deep mines of Peru.

Tram smiled as he lowered his hand after Collins forsook the salute, then took Jack's offered gesture and shook stiffly at first, but then with more enthusiasm.

"It is . . . good . . . to see . . . you . . . again, General," Tram uttered in his attempt at English.

"And speaking the barbarian's tongue too," Jack joked, easing the small man's demeanor.

Collins turned to the larger of the two. This officer was dressed the same as Tram but had a blue beret over his blond hair. The colonel held out his hand and Major Sebastian Krell of the German Army nodded his head and shook the general's hand. The major had been one of the best assets he had in the same operation in which Tram had assisted. He had led the defense of the mines in Peru against an army of mercenaries; without him the technology stash would have never been recovered. Krell was also an officer who had been personally trained in black operation by Jack himself.

"Jack," Major Krell said, forgoing all signs of military protocol as he shook his hand. "Glad to see you finally made it. I guess we volunteered again."

"So you did, Sebastian, so you did. Don't tell me you two are assigned to me?"

"Well, I don't know about our little communist friend here, but when the chancellor said you would be leading the defense of some out of the way and likely dangerous place, I came."

"Yeah, sorry about the death of the chancellor. I understand he was instrumental in getting this thing"—he gestured at the strange base that surrounded them—"off the ground."

"Whatever this thing is," Mendenhall said as he shook first Tram's hand and then Krell's.

"*Captain* Mendenhall? Now that's rising fast through the ranks," Sebastian said as he released Will's hand. "It must be nice to have friends in high places . . . like generals, huh?"

"I was railroaded, just like the general." The four men laughed. Will stepped back and gestured toward Henri. "Gentlemen, Colonel Henri Farbeaux of the French Army," he said with the slightest trace of humor edging his voice.

Sebastian Krell hesitated before taking the Frenchman's hand. "Colonel Farbeaux. I believe I've heard that name before." He shook despite the fast-returning memory.

"Only if you've been in the post office and seen his picture," Will not quite jokingly quipped about seeing a wanted poster of the infamous colonel.

Farbeaux shook both men's hands and then looked around.

"Perhaps you can shed some light on what this is all about?" Henri asked as he was noticing soldiers of every nation on the planet as they went from place to place. The one thing he noticed the most was the strange uniforms of some of them. They were completely different from most as they were coveralls and had the emblems of NASA and the

European Space Agency emblazoned on their breast pockets.

"Well, we were hoping you would share that with *us*. All we've done is train with our foreign buddies here"—he touched Tram on the shoulder—"and start to take courses in direct-line combat with the boys from your 82nd and 101st Airborne. And then more classes on armored tactics with the 23rd Armored Division of the German Army, which I understood even less than the American classes."

Jack had no answers for the two officers, but he knew that he wanted to keep these two men close to him, Will, and Farbeaux. He owed these two men that much at the very least.

"Look, I guess I'm the man in charge," he said, looking from Krell to Tram, "So I guess I can do whatever I want around here. So, you two consider yourselves a part of my staff."

"Deal," Sebastian said as he smiled over at Tram, who looked on in a fog of confusion.

Jack, Will, and Farbeaux were led directly into the large building constructed of aluminum and plastic. The barren walls attested to the fast fabrication of the council chamber and only the electronics suite and the monitors lining the walls were anything like normal to the men from the Event Group. Inside Collins and his men were introduced to General Dave Rhodes, commander of the 101st Airborne Division, whom Jack knew almost as well as his friends at Group. The last time Collins had seen Rhodes he had been a captain leading a company of Rangers during the Iraqi invasion. The men shook hands and then Jack was led to Colonel Wesley Bunting, acting commander of the 82nd Airborne. Then finally to one-star general Heinrich Bader, a stern-looking Wehrmacht officer commanding the controversial new German Armor Corps, the 23rd Panzer Division.

Jack shook the general's hand as the man stood rigid. He knew the officer was the leader of the most controversial division on the planet simply because of the designation of the unit. The 23rd Panzer Division was famous for one thing in history: it was once known as the most brutal component of the once famous Afrika Corps. The 23rd had been disbanded after World War II and the new German chancellor, before his death, had reinstated the famed division, despite the protests of its own citizens. The memories of those hard days had yet to wane in the minds and hearts of many Germans. The strain of commanding such a division was clearly showing on the general's face.

"General, I've heard good things about your new division. Top notch, I understand."

"General Collins, my men will do their duty. As you know, the savior of our division died for us—not directly, of course, but he was responsible for us being reborn."

Collins looked the tall German in the eyes and then smiled. "Well, from what I understand, you'll get a shot at the animals that killed him."

The general clicked his heels, then moved off to join the two other commanders of the defensive units.

Jack turned and faced Will and Henri. "I wonder how long until all three of those men are on the traitors' block when and if they refuse a direct order to come home?"

Farbeaux watched as they were approached by Sir Darcy Bennett. He leaned in so only Mendenhall and Collins could hear. "The better question, General, is, does it matter if we are all hung at home, or die amongst the ice and snow of this barren land? All in all, I think it doesn't matter anymore, because whatever they have in store for us in this most bizarre place, it will end up accomplishing either outcome."

"Colonel, you have to quit being so damn optimistic."

Jack smiled at Will's retort as Bennett walked up and gestured for the three men to take their seats. Then he walked to the front of the room and removed his heavy jacket and remained standing. Besides the military officers, Jack saw ten other men in varying states of dress. Most had lab coats on, with about a hundred pens and pencils in each pocket.

"Ladies and gentlemen, this is the first full staff meeting of the defense group for Camp Alamo. Since the arrival of General Collins this afternoon, this is the first full defensive meeting since Operation Overlord came into being four years ago."

Jack sat at the opposite end of the table and noticed many of the faces were looking at him. Many shied away but most had the look of hope that he was capable of performing whatever his duties might entail. In other words, there was worry on most of those faces.

"General Collins will be addressing you later in the evening, once the old boy gathers his wits about him after his long and perilous journey. As for now we need all commands and civilian defensive groups to have full equipment and capability studies delivered to the offices of the commanding general no later than"—Bennett looked at the wall clock—"eighteen hundred hours." He looked at Jack for confirmation, but the general remained silent and didn't react. How in the hell was he supposed to know when the reports should be delivered? He was sure the cooks in whatever mess hall they were going to eat at knew more about his duties than he did at the moment.

"General, we have developed some amazing defensive equipment for your units to operate with that should provide an edge, if and when they are needed. But after Beijing and Mumbai, we truly hope those measures won't be needed, and we can get Overlord up before the Grays know what is happening right under their noses."

General Bader stood and in a nod of deference toward Bennett, apologizing beforehand for interrupting, he partially turned to face Jack.

"Herr Bennett, General Collins, I must know the timetable for my men to take to the field for operational training on the new cannon for our tanks and armor. We have no OJT for maneuvering in this kind of environment. We attend classes, but as the general knows that is no substitute for field training—especially with equipment never before used in combat. That amounts to a disaster in the works."

The general sat down to the nods of the men from the 101st and 82nd Airborne.

Collins saw the academia shaking their heads in disagreement. It was a woman who stood as the buzz of conversation went around the compact room

"Professor Kenilworth, you have something to say?" Bennett asked as he looked at the woman and then shook his head in Jack's direction, privately indicating to him that this was an ongoing argument between the engineers and the military, something Jack knew was always prevalent between the two. He realized how closely this team resembled the makeup of the Event Group. The dark-haired woman faced the men around the table as the room became silent.

"We have told our friends time and time again, we completely sympathize with the restraints that we have put on you in regards to training. But if we expose a large force of men outside of this complex for training and maneuvering exercises it can do nothing but attract the very element we are hiding from," the woman said in her British accent. "As far as your vehicles and their new tracks, we can guarantee they will work in this environment."

It was Dave Rhodes who stood next. He nodded at the professor as she sat down.

"The question is, are we prepared to do what is asked of us in the defense of this camp and the subsurface areas beneath us? By our understanding, Overlord must be protected until such a time as whatever she is, is ready for action." He turned to face Jack. "General, we have not even been provided working plans of the sub areas of the ancient lake. We have no way of setting up any form of defensive line." He turned to face the academics to the front of the table. "I must tell you, for all the brain power sitting around this table you are rather short on the knowledge of the difference between the ice Overlord is buried in, and the snow that sits above our heads. Vehicles react differently between ice and snow, new track or not. We need to know what it is we're protecting and how to do it. This we cannot do without the plans of the frozen lake beneath our feet."

Jack finally stood and faced the men and women of the defensive group of Operation Overlord.

"I haven't had time to even brush my teeth since my arrival," he said to some nervous laughter. He faced the three military officers who sat hoping for some form of good news from their new commander. "But I think I can safely say this: Whatever the defensive posture of this area is, I will study it, learn it, and I will get your men acquainted with their equipment some way, somehow, without upsetting your"—he faced the engineers—"*our* security concerns. And if we have orders to protect an area of Camp Alamo that I am not aware of, and we have no detailed plans being offered us, then I guarantee that will change, and change immediately." This time Jack's eyes met those of Bennett's and didn't waver. The three military commanders seemed satisfied for the moment.

"I'm afraid that will have to be taken up with Lord Durnsford when he arrives, and of course with Admiral Kinkaid and Admiral Huffington—all men who won't take too kindly to your request, General."

One name Jack knew. Admiral James Kinkaid was a legend in the United States Navy. Carl Everett had spoken about the man many times. He was considered the Hyman Rickover of the twenty-first century; a man who had pushed the antiquated postwar naval forces into the future with the advent of nuclear propulsion. Kinkaid was the same with his rumored involvement with trying to get the navy to be more advanced in the area of space. Jack had heard the rumor he had been shunted aside after particularly bad run-ins with more than one secretary of defense through the years.

As for Admiral Huffington, it was known he was a tenacious Brit who hated any and all things in the nature of surface forces, a man the Royal Navy hid from sight for his addresses to parliament on the endless manufacture of ocean-going vessels that would be sunk in the outset of any major engagement against the Russians or the Chinese. Evidently the powers that be had found usefulness out of these two pariahs, and now the general would have to work with the men the rest of the world leadership and military hated and despised.

"That I will, Sir Bennett. If they want whatever this base is hiding protected, I need to know how to do that, or their plans won't see the light of day. I have seen the way the Grays fight and they will eventually lay all of this"—he waved a hand around the room—"to waste until there is nothing here but melted ice."

That seemed to get the attention of all, as the room fell silent. Eyes looked away from Jack's angry demeanor and looked at nothing. Collins sat down.

"Very well, I think we can adjourn for now to allow General Collins and his staff time to study his rules of engagement and start to evaluate men and equipment. General, we are all at your disposal, as we are desperately seeking the same goal: We must protect what is hidden below us at all costs, even if even we all have to face the two admirals on a daily basis."

Laughter erupted almost immediately from the academics as the tension was broken. The men and women stood and started making their way to the door, with many of them stopping and shaking the hands of Will, Henri, and Jack on their way by. When the military commanders nodded their thanks, it was Farbeaux who once more summed it up.

"Tell me this isn't a government operation. Situation normal—"

"All fucked up," Jack and Will said simultaneously, finishing the old military axiom for the acronym SNAFU.

EVENT GROUP COMPLEX
NELLIS AIR FORCE BASE, NEVADA

Matchstick always drew a crowd of the curious whenever he ventured into the cafeteria. Many stopped by just to say a few words to the small green alien as he sat propped up in a child's seat at the round table. Matchstick was unusually quiet as the men and women of Department 5656 moved off, wondering what had affected the small being so, as he was just staring at the large slice of cheese pizza on his tray. Denise Gilliam sat next to him, watching, sipping her coffee, and worrying about the state of mind of their guest. As her eyes moved around the almost deserted eatery, she was saddened by the fact that it was abundantly clear that most of the military personnel were absent from the complex. The cafeteria was normally a place where the Group's academic and military arms came together and formed what the Group was known for—closeness. She shook her head and felt what Matchstick must have been feeling—a sense of loss.

Matchstick reached out and placed one of his long fingers next to the slice of cheese pizza, touched it, and then pulled his hand away. Dr. Gilliam knew that when Matchstick wasn't either eating or talking about eating, there was something definitely on his mind. Finally the small alien looked up at Denise, who smiled, trying to ease the being's troubled mind. Mahjtic didn't say anything and then returned his large eyes to the cold pizza.

Charlie Ellenshaw cleared his throat. Both occupants of the table looked up and saw him and Pete Golding standing by the table. With a look from Pete, Denise got the hint and then reached for her coffee.

"If you'll excuse me, I think I'll go and bother Gus in the clinic. He's particularly tired and grumpy today."

Matchstick looked up at the departing Denise Gilliam and then started to get down from his elevated chair. It was Charlie who sat next to him and smiled.

"Matchstick, you have a minute?" he asked as he pushed back some of his white hair from the frames of his wire-rimmed glasses. Alice Hamilton entered and also approached the table. She held a file in her hand.

Matchstick looked from face to face, fearing they were about to deliver bad news about Gus, but then Alice opened the folder and removed several photos. She held them while Pete explained why they were there.

"Mahjtic," Pete began, letting the alien know it was serious by his use of his real name. "We just received the latest deep space images from the Hubble."

Matchstick's demeanor changed as he had been waiting for the deep-space imagery to come in for the past sixteen hours.

"It seems the final phase that you warned us about has commenced." Pete nodded that Alice should show him the black and white imagery. She slid the first picture toward the extended, elongated fingers. "We haven't forwarded these to Dr. Pollock as of yet because we wanted confirmation before alarming the rest of the world." Pete shook his head sadly as he realized with the evidence they were holding, Operation Overlord, whatever that truly was, was now out of time. Matchstick looked at Pete and Charlie, then the obsidian orbs settled on Alice, who smiled and gestured that he should examine the first photo. Pete gestured that Alice should continue.

"At 2200 hours, local time, three nuclear power plants inside Russia were raided by many support ships of the Grays." She pointed to the picture of the blank spot near the Vistula River Nuclear facility. She placed another photo of another site. "This is a military reconnaissance view of the Hanford Nuclear Labs inside Washington State taken six hours later. A raid was conducted there; every one of two thousand personnel were killed in the attack. Very experimental energy storage units were taken and then the facility was destroyed, just as the three power-generating plants at other locations, sixteen plants in all. The support saucers entered a transit wormhole and vanished."

Matchstick studied the prints and then blinked several times as he took in the images. The eyes were wide and attentive as he examined them. Alice pulled two more photos from the packet.

"As I said, these were taken by the Hubble. It shows the alien fleet at Point Hermes, still the same location and still many thousands of light-years away." She gave Matchstick the photo. He looked at it and then at Alice. "This one is a shot, blurry though it is, of the large processing ships rejoining that fleet after they lifted off from our world and exited the atmosphere through a return wormhole." She pointed at the fuzzy image of the larger craft as they took up station inside the formation of ships.

Charlie noticed the grip of Mahjtic tightened on the photo.

"Now, the largest ship of the fleet, the one that we now know, thanks to you, is what you have called their main energy-production vessel. You can see it here." She pointed once more at the same photo. "Now, the saucers that conducted the raids at the nuclear plants inside Russia and at the Hanford facility are seen here after their arrival through another wormhole." She gave Matchstick another photo, leaving only one inside the folder. "They have linked with this other, the largest vessel in the alien fleet. Perhaps transferring power, we don't know. Now the disturbing thing is that you always told Garrison Lee and Niles Compton that we would know when the full-scale attack would occur— when this energy ship came up missing from the fleet. Well," she gave Matchstick the last shot the Hubble had taken, "it has. It and what we estimate as close to five thousand of their processing and attack saucers have vanished from Point Hermes."

Matchstick didn't even look at the last as he knew what it would show. Europa was always deadly accurate with her calculations. If she said these attack saucers were missing, they were indeed missing from the remainder of the alien fleet. That, coupled with the absence of the island-sized power ship, meant the Grays were on their way to Earth in force.

"Your opinion, my friend?" Charlie asked as gently as he could. Matchstick looked up and fixed them all with his black, obsidian eyes.

"There . . . is . . . only one . . . event . . . that could . . . cause . . . our enemy . . . to accelerate . . . their attack . . . schedule. The . . . Gray . . . Masters . . . have . . . found . . . something . . . that . . . must . . . be . . . destroyed . . . immediately," he struggled to say aloud. He closed his eyes and sat silently. "You must pass this . . . on . . . to . . . Camp Alamo."

"What could be so important that they have to attack before they are fully capable of doing so?" Alice urged and then her own eyes widened as she realized what Matchstick knew.

"Operation Overlord," Charlie said.

"Somehow they have learned the location of Overlord and are coming to destroy it with an overwhelming force," Pete said as he watched Mahjtic shake in his small seat.

"Alice, get these off to Virginia and then copy the colonel—I mean, General Collins. Virginia will know how to reach him. Tell them the jig is up and they have limited time."

Alice stood and then paused. "How much time do you estimate, Matchstick?"

"Soon, very soon the Grays will strike . . . and then all . . . is . . . lost . . . for Overlord."

Charlie Ellenshaw reached out and took the long fingers of Matchstick's shaking hand and squeezed. The old cryptozoologist tried to smile but found he couldn't generate the appropriate muscle movement for that simple task, because if the truth be known he was far more scared than their small green friend.

"Go ahead, Alice, send the message," the acting complex director said with a faraway look.

"I believe I should say what we suspect the Gray target is in the open, so there can be no misunderstanding," she said.

Pete forlornly nodded his approval.

"Target is Overlord."

WALTER REED NATIONAL MILITARY
MEDICAL CENTER
BETHESDA, MARYLAND

Virginia Pollock accepted the coffee from Lee Preston with a nod of her head. The constitutional attorney had been impressed by this tall, skinny, and very tenacious woman since he had met her. She seemed to be able to stay awake for days at a time and not lose any of her powers of conclusion or reasoning. He was curious as to what she did, exactly who this highly educated woman was, and how she came to associate herself with his friend, Alice Hamilton.

Lee Preston was silent as he sat down next to Virginia and looked at her. She felt the man's eyes on her and then raised one of her pointed brows in his direction. She didn't want to talk, but she knew a question was forthcoming. She looked from the lawyer to the sleeping form of Niles Compton.

"You and Dr. Compton have worked together for a while, I take it?" he asked in a low voice.

Virginia sipped the coffee and grimaced, then reached out and placed it on the small table next to the window. Preston smiled and then did the same thing with his cup.

"I know it's bad. But with all of the security running around here with the president right down the hallway, it's very difficult getting to the cafeteria."

"It's okay; I think my kidneys are floating anyway. Thanks, though. And yes, we've worked together for the better part of fifteen years." She looked from the bed to Preston. "I don't know what I would do without him there to guide me through the things we have to do sometimes."

"Well, Mrs. Hamilton speaks very highly of him . . . and you. She told me that if you cannot be protected by my constitutional prowess, she would geld me like a worthless horse."

Virginia laughed for the first time in what she thought was a month. She nodded her head.

"How would you ever come to know a woman like Alice?" she asked.

"Well, I'll make this short, because I only have to say one name that I am sure you are familiar with. Garrison Lee. I was a young buck on the constitutional congressional hearings on budget restraint, and it was rumored I was close to finding out some rather disconcerting information on a

rather large department that was hidden deep in the power
base of government." He looked sideways at Virginia and she
only winked. "Well, the rumor got out, I'm afraid, and I got
a call from President Clinton at the time. He asked if I would
meet with a gentleman who might have some information
for me concerning said investigation. Well, being stupid and
naïve and thinking the president must mean business—you
see, he was going through a rough patch as far as his personal and professional conduct were concerned—so I said
yes, as a favor to his office I would meet said gentleman."

Virginia smiled as she knew just where this story was
headed.

"We were to meet at my office, but instead as I was leaving home one morning a rather scary gentleman with a limp,
a cane, and an eye patch was sitting in my car that was
parked in my garage. Without looking at me he introduced
himself. The name, of course, was familiar, as most heroes
of the old war years are around this city. Well, he calmly
asked if I preferred to go on with my professional life or go
for a ride with him."

"I see. A long ride with Garrison Lee. Not one I would
like to take."

"I thought at the time that he couldn't threaten a member
of Congress like that. Well, my phone rang in the car and he
nodded that I should answer it. I did. It was the president;
he asked if I had met Mr. Lee and I said yes I had, as I
watched him out of the corner of my eye. The president
asked if I was going to work or go out riding with the man
in the car. I couldn't believe the offhanded way the president
of the United States had just threatened me. Well, I told him
I'll just go to work. The president said good, that was what
he would do in my place. Then he said that he suspected
that all inquiries regarding the rather large budget of the
National Archives would"—he smiled—"just slip by the
wayside. I said yes, they would." Then Lee reached over
and pushed my automatic garage door opener. It opened
and a lovely older lady walked in the garage as if she owned
the place, opened the rear door, and stepped in with a brown

paper bag. She handed Lee a coffee, me a coffee, and then smiled at me from the rearview mirror. We sat and had coffee, and Garrison and Alice explained to me a little of what they did for a living. And that's how I met Mrs. Hamilton."

Virginia laughed out loud at the story, as it was so much Alice and Lee that she would have had nightmares for a year if it had been her. "I doubt very much if Alice would have harmed you. You see, she, like me, is a rabid constitutionalist."

Lee Preston turned away and looked at the ceiling of the hospital room.

"I noticed you didn't mention Garrison Lee in that sentence." He turned and smiled.

"Yes, I am aware of that." The smile remained.

"Well, if Mrs. Hamilton is a friend of Dr. Compton's, he's a friend of mine." He turned and looked at Virginia. "And after learning a little bit about what it is you people do, even I can live to be a little light on the constitution."

Before Virginia could respond, the door opened and a man the acting director of Department 5656 recognized immediately, stepped into the room. He paused at the bed and looked down on Niles Compton and shook his head. He had his hands on his hips and made a *tsk, tsk* sound as he looked. The man turned and walked to the far side of the hospital room and pulled up a chair to face Lee Preston and Virginia. He placed his hands in his lap and smiled.

"Assistant Director Peachtree, what brings you here?" Virginia asked.

The middle-aged man with the perfectly coifed hair looked from the two and then at the darkened screen of the television.

"Oh, well, I guess you've missed the news waiting here like you are. It's *Director* Peachtree now. It seems my old boss, Mr. Easterbrook, has opted for the private life of a country gentleman." The smile was wide and genuine.

Lee Preston crossed one leg over the other and remained silent, as did Virginia.

The attention went to Lee Preston. "I think you should

know, Mr. Preston, I have initiated an investigation through my good friends at Homeland Security for your part in the illegal immigrant litigation currently happening in Arizona. It seems you may have received monies from sources on many, many enemies lists of that particular federal agency."

"I was wondering when you people were going to pull the old 'security risk' file out and dust it off. I guess I was bound to become a nuisance when I filed court documents trying to stop the good people of Arizona from putting up an electrified fence around their common border with Mexico, and killing Lord knows how many people in the process. Well, take your best shot, Mr. Director, I'll be waiting in my office with *my* copy of the Constitution."

The man nodded and turned his attention to Virginia, then he glanced at Niles across the room.

"Now you, young lady, I need to know where your asset is being held. We would like a chance at debrief."

Virginia smiled as best she could, but the action never reached her lovely eyes. Preston saw this and leaned back, not wanting to get any venom on his expensive suit.

"I guess you must have missed the part where I told you to go fuck yourself." She glanced at the dark television screen. "But I guess you were too busy stabbing your boss in the back to have heard."

"The asset, Ms. Pollock," he said without his condescending smirk. "The asset known as Mahjtic Tilly—we want him and are going to get him."

"*Dr.* Pollock," she said, batting her eyes the way Alice Hamilton had taught her over the years.

"The president of the United States has issued me orders to debrief your asset at the earliest possible time as the security of the United States is at risk—and that, *Doctor,* gives him special powers."

"Debrief," Preston said aloud. "An old CIA euphemism for torture in the rough, tough, Cold War days." He looked at Peachtree. "If I recall correctly."

"If it comes to that. After all, the asset isn't really human, is he? He's one of them," he said, his eyes rolling toward the ceiling.

"Maybe not," Virginia said, leaning forward in her chair, "But Lynn Simpson Collins was very much human, wasn't she?"

The look on Peachtree's face was priceless as Lee Preston suddenly became very interested in the name just mentioned by Virginia.

"We know more than you ever could fathom, Mr. Director, and someone, someday is going to answer for her murder. I suspect that may end at the White House in the long run, and the man that will explain it to you and the president can get to you anywhere, anytime."

"I believe you just threatened the president of the United States," he said as he stood suddenly.

"No, I believe she just made a statement about a murderer being caught, nothing about that murderer being the president. Is that what *you're* saying?" Preston said as he too stood and buttoned his coat.

Peachtree smiled and then relaxed as he realized he didn't have the upper hand any longer.

"Very well, Dr. Pollock, a warrant will be issued and delivered to Nellis Air Force Base in Nevada at the earliest opportunity. I suggest you heed the warrant when issued, even if your complex is buried beneath the desert. We want the asset, and we will get him." Peachtree started for the door, stopped and looked at the unconscious Niles Compton, and then turned back to face them. "One way or the other." He left.

"I hate to say it, but right at this moment that man is holding all the aces in the deck, and even the deck belongs to the White House."

Virginia knew she had to get Matchstick out of the complex. She shook her head as the door opened once again. It was one of the president's loyal Secret Service agents; she recognized him from his constant vigil over the comatose president. He walked straight to Virginia and handed her a note.

"This was just passed to us from the president's private phone system. The first lady asked me to pass it on to you." He left the room.

Virginia knew that the message had come to her through the official channels that included the president's laptop and through his close ties with the NSA. She read the note.

"Damn," she said aloud as she looked at Lee Preston. "Mr. Preston, I thank you for being here and helping me with Peachtree, but I have to ask you to leave me alone with Director Compton for a moment."

"I understand," he said and started to leave.

"Mister . . . ," She stopped and then thought better of her lead in. "Lee, please corner that Secret Service agent in the hallway. Ask him to find General Caulfield and get him here as soon as possible. He should know how to get ahold of him."

Preston nodded his head and then left. Virginia went to the bedside of Niles Compton. She saw him sleeping but leaned over and spoke.

"Niles, wake up, it's happening. Operation Overlord is going to be attacked. Niles, please wake up."

Virginia looked around the room in despair as Compton remained out.

With the president's men going after Matchstick, and the Gray situation going critical, she was faced with having to go directly through the official chain of command. That meant dealing with Giles Camden's new staff, where she knew a sympathetic ear was going to be impossible to find. She looked at Niles and frowned as he seemed to be dreaming in his sleep. She turned away as the door opened once again. She was disappointed that it wasn't General Caulfield or another friendly face, but two men she had seen on television standing behind the new man in office.

"Look, assholes, I've had enough threats for today, so you can kiss my—"

"Dr. Pollock, we're not here to threaten you," said the smaller of the two with his briefcase held tightly in his grip. "I think we've come to help. We want to know if there is anything we can possibly do to assist you and whoever it is that you work for."

Virginia was stunned as she remembered the two young faces from the news reports.

It was the two young public relations experts for the new president of the United States, and they looked very frightened.

14

A thousand Argentinean and British soldiers watched as the *Pyotr Veliky* was towed into port by the two frigates of the U.S. Navy. The men gathered at the large dock were amazed at the damage incurred on the giant missile cruiser that looked as if she was about to succumb to the calm waters off Orkney. The sight even curbed the historic hard feelings between the two nations that had battled two decades before over the Falkland Islands. No man wanted to be witness to the scene of the proud warship as she was assisted into port.

Two of the men who had joined the crowd of onlookers were Admiral Carl Everett and former Master Chief Jenks who, with their men and materials, had just arrived by C-130 Hercules transports and now awaited their transfer to Camp Alamo. Carl had sent his remaining fifty-two men onto the large airstrip to load what gear they had remaining after the Gray strike on the Space Center.

Everett had explained to Jenks that Sarah McIntire and Jason Ryan, along with a woman he knew, was supposedly onboard the *Pyotr Veliky*—although he still didn't know if the trio were alive or dead. The report had filtered through the soldiers waiting at the dock that the cruiser had suffered catastrophic losses in her brief engagement with the Grays. Everett saw the men who had saved the missile cruiser from going under start to line the decks as she was finally tied off and technicians ran aboard her like ants swarming a wounded elephant. They all saw the men of the battle-hardened ship wave as the vessel that had saved them moved quickly back to sea after escorting her in. The strange shape of the USS *Zumwalt* moved slowly past her damaged charge and blew her horn in salute to the proud Russian vessel. The men on the cruiser's deck waved and hollered their thanks at the American seamen lining her stealth-designed angled decks.

"Glad to know the goddamn navy can get something right from time to time," Jenks hissed as he puffed his cigar.

"Damn thing looks too small to fight a battle," Everett said as he watched the stealthy frigate leave the small bay.

"Yeah," Jenks said as he looked at the taller Everett, "well, everything tough doesn't have to be big, does it, Toad?"

Carl laughed as he knew the master chief was referring to himself. "No, but it sure helps sometimes."

Jenks cleared his throat and spit and then glared at Everett.

The men on the dock watched as a large Royal Navy shipboard crane started to lift a large object off the fantail of the listing cruiser. Technicians were screaming at the operators to lift it slowly. It was eventually placed down on a large transport awaiting its delivery. It was being taken to the hold of the large C-5a Galaxy waiting for it on the airstrip.

"I guess they're in a hurry before all of this activity attracts prying eyes from up there," Jenks said as he looked skyward into the crisp, cold air.

Carl joined Jenks in looking apprehensively into the sky. The combat air patrols by a squadron of Sea Harriers of the

Royal Navy had ceased two hours before the damaged *Pyotr Veliky* had entered the bay. Too much attention to the area was the reason, he figured.

Jenks stepped back as a dark-haired woman grabbed Everett by the fur-lined jacket he was wearing and turned him to face her. She kissed him deeply as Jenks raised his thick brows in wonder. Carl picked Anya Korvesky up and swung her around. He hugged her and then set her down with a serious look on his face.

"Sarah and Jason?"

Anya pointed to the ship's gangway she had just run down to the consternation of the safety officials on the dock. Sarah and Ryan were walking down the thick planking with their bags. Sarah saw Everett and she waved, surprised to see him. Ryan was stunned as well as they reached the bottom and then hurried toward the waiting trio.

"Well, I see you're done cruising with the Russian Navy," Carl said as he hugged Sarah. He shook hands with Ryan, who immediately saw the new shoulder boards on the admiral's fur-hooded parka. His eyes widened.

"Whose ass have you been kissing . . . sir?" Ryan asked as he turned to Sarah in mock horror.

"He better start by kissing mine since I have the fate of his men in my ample hands," Jenks said as he eyed Anya up and down appreciatively.

"Master Chief?" Sarah said for her second shock in as many seconds.

"Hello, little lieutenant, glad to see you and Mr. Ryan made it off the communist pig boat alive." He accepted the strong hug from McIntire. Jason shook the man's hand and then shook his head. He turned to Anya and explained.

"Once upon a time, the admiral here sank the master chief's boat . . . on purpose, if I remember."

Anya smiled as she saw the memory was an especially fond one for Carl and Ryan, but not so much to the scowling little man they faced.

"Goddamn right it was on purpose." Jenks started to turn away from the group. "And it's *Professor* Jenks to you from now on, Commander Short Shit," he said to Ryan as he started to walk off. "Now if you ladies would like to escort an old sea dog to his aircraft, we have a flight we have to catch."

"I too have a flight to catch," a voice said from behind them. Carl looked up and saw a Russian officer as he approached.

"Captain Lienanov," Sarah said as she saw the man in full black dress uniform. "What's going on?"

"It seems the powers that be have declared me shipless. The *Pyotr Veliky* has been declared unfit for sea duty and is to be scuttled immediately in a very much witnessed fire at sea, so as to make others believe she succumbed to her battle damage with her cargo still strapped on her deck." He looked back sadly at the ship he had commanded for only five days. The very same crane that had lifted off the alien power plant was now lowering a duplicate mock-up onto the fantail where men of the missile cruiser were waiting to tie it down.

"I'm sorry, Captain, for the loss of your command," Ryan said in total sympathy. The Russian officer raised his seabag and then stared at his company.

"Thank you, but she wasn't really mine."

"What now?" Sarah asked as Carl realized exactly what was planned for the captain.

"I would guess that the orders in your pocket are directing you to a place called Camp Alamo?"

"Yes, they do, and a transfer to another ship, but my orders are confusing at best," he said in very good English as he looked closely at the twin stars on Everett's shoulder boards. "Excuse me, Admiral, but they are rather ambiguous orders. It seems I'm being transferred to a vessel that is situated in the middle of Antarctica."

"Well, Captain Lienanov, welcome to the world of ambiguity, and I suspect you are hitching a ride with us." He pointed to the large transport truck leaving the dock area with the power plant strapped to its giant trailer. "And that too, to the aforementioned Camp Alamo, another rather ambiguous name that has connotations in American history that my colleagues here will gladly explain to you later." Everett gestured for the small group to follow the master chief.

With one sorrowful look back at the now doomed *Pyotr Veliky,* Captain Lienanov turned and walked away from his first command.

The two enormous C-5M Super Galaxies were fully loaded to their capacity. Two hundred and seventy thousand pounds of men and cargo crowded the largest aircraft in the United States inventory. Sitting next to the Super Galaxies was the most obscure aircraft to take to the skies in many years. This strange aircraft would be carrying only one item in its bulbous belly: the alien power plant.

The colossal storage area of the French-owned Airbus A300-600ST "Beluga" had absorbed the heavy power plant like a hungry animal as the strangely shaped Airbus began lowering her top-mounted loading bay. Two other French-built Airbus A300-600ST Belugas had taken off earlier as a decoy and these too were flanked by two C-5Ms from Airlift Command in an attempt to fool any prying eyes that may be watching, as it was the designers of this part of Operation Overlord who knew they were pushing not only the program's luck, but were also betting the lives of over six hundred men, women, and soldiers that transporting them in the bright sunlight of day would catch the Grays off guard.

The eight combined and extremely powerful General Electric TF39 Turbofans of the two Galaxies were brought up to full power, drowning out the full three squadrons of Royal Air Force Sea Harriers as they flew up and over the long runway at Orkney. The fighters would escort all three aircraft most of the way to McMurdo Station's Pegasus runway, where the American weather station operated the only landing site on the Antarctic continent that could support the heavy transport aircraft that was arriving there.

As the Beluga lifted off with her heavy load, no less than sixteen Sea Harriers took up station, above, beside, and under the French Airbus. The Beluga made a radical change of course and then climbed to the north before they would make a course correction and hopefully one that would confuse any unwanted onlookers.

Admiral Everett was invited up to the Galaxy's large fly-by-wire cockpit as a courtesy to the navy by the air force and allowed to sit at one of the engineer consoles as the colossal transports took off. Once in the air the pilot nodded his head at his copilot and the Air Force colonel removed a message flimsy from his clipboard and tapped his headset so Everett could put his on so he could hear over the roar of the powerful turbofans. Carl slipped the headphones on and accepted the message.

"Just to let you know, these four aircraft are hot. I think the Defense Department has them on their stolen vehicles list." The colonel looked to the pilot and then back at Everett. "The acting president and his new chairman of the Joint Chiefs ordered us home two days ago, but we all developed engine trouble in the extreme cold down here," the copilot said as he smiled with tongue firmly planted in cheek. "The Air Force Chief of Staff and the head of Air Force Intelligence send their regards and hope this operation is worth it."

"So do I, Colonel, so do I."

Carl raised the message and read.

Gray attack on Camp Alamo and Operation Overlord imminent . . .

Operation Gray Strike is fully activated with truncated training schedule . . .

Defensive command at Alamo has been warned as per this message . . .

Operation Overlord will commence within two days . . .

Good luck and Godspeed . . .

                              Caulfield, General (USA Ret.)

Carl folded the message, then thought better of it and handed it to the engineer, who noticed the worried look on the admiral's face. He accepted the message, tempted to see what it said.

"Destroy that as soon as you can, but pass it around to your men first, they deserve to know." Carl removed the headset, then stood and first patted the pilot and then shook the colonel's hand in the right seat. "Thank you, gentlemen . . . for everything. As soon as you make your drop-off, get the hell out of Dodge as soon as you can. I have a feeling the skies in this part of the world's going to turn hot real fast. Get home safe."

Everett moved off and down the stairs and saw his friends as they explained what they could to Captain Lienanov. Jenks was at one of the fold-down desks that were arranged for the relief crews to file reports during flight. He had headphones on, listening to his engineering notes. He nodded his head at Sarah, Ryan, Anya, and Lienanov, then moved aft and down another short flight of steps and saw the men he was looking for.

He saw the two teams of commandos as they rested against the vibrating skin of the giant aircraft. He shook his head as he noticed that the SEAL and Delta teams were still separated by their disrespect for each other's abilities. He became angry but held it in check as he grabbed hold of a safety strap and leaned in to the two operational leaders of the two teams. Both officers were new as the first two had never made it out alive after the attack on the Space Center.

"I want these men broken up into mixed teams."

The naval lieutenant and the army captain looked up. Both had questioning looks on their faces as Everett leaned in.

"Sir?" The SEAL turned and offered the same questioning look to the Army Ranger picked to replace the Delta team leader. The Ranger just sat there with his training schedule locked in his hands.

"Look, I know the engine noise in here is loud enough to drown out a locomotive, but if I have to say things to you gentlemen twice I'll throw your asses right off this aircraft. Do you understand what I'm saying now?"

The Army Ranger braved getting thrown off the Galaxy. "I hear you, sir, but don't follow."

"Yeah, you're Army, all right," he said. The Navy SEAL tried to hold back the small snicker that escaped his mouth. Everett just leaned closer to the SEAL and glared. "I know the SEALs have changed since my days in Team Five, and the navy has had to make hard choices about who they accept these days for the duty, but don't advertise the fact that you're a dumb fuck that doesn't know shit, all right, Lieutenant Shit-for-brains?"

Not even the Army Ranger was tempted to laugh at the dressing down of his counterpart.

"Now, take your rosters and mix these men up evenly between ingress and assault. I want the new team rosters before we land at McMurdo. Is that clear, or do you want me to stand here and explain why an admiral always gets his way?"

Both young officers remained silent for the longest three seconds of their lives.

"Yes, sir," both said simultaneously.

"I'll meet the men in fifteen minutes to explain why their part of this mission will be either their moment of triumph or the biggest cluster-fuck since Operation Eagle Claw in Iran. It all depends on how they work together. Am I clear?" The famous 1980 foul-up in the Iranian desert had occurred when differing and mixed commands brought the rescue operation to free the embassy hostages to an abrupt and disastrous conclusion.

"Yes—"

"I said, am I clear?" he shouted, getting the attention of the two teams lining the bulkheads of the Galaxy.

"Yes, sir!" the two officers said as they jumped to their feet, colliding with each other as they did.

Carl let go of the strap and then started to say something else, but was interrupted by a familiar voice from behind.

"Admiral, can I have a minute?"

Carl turned, ready to continue his tirade against whoever had the balls to interrupt him. His eyes took in Jason Ryan as he removed his cold-weather parka and then held the cold, blue, angry eyes of his friend.

Carl turned and gave the two men a look. They were still standing at attention even with the heavy rocking motion of the transport.

"Gentlemen, rosters before we land, and tell the men I'll speak to them in fifteen." Everett turned and followed Ryan back toward the front of the Galaxy.

Ryan stopped near a pile of strapped-down gear and turned to face Carl. "Admiral—"

"Look, don't do that." Everett too removed his cold-weather jacket and then tossed it on the cargo netting holding some of the assault gear in place on their pallet.

"Do what?" Ryan asked, knowing full well the meaning of Carl's statement because he had felt the exact same way after being promoted to full commander a month earlier.

"Address me by that rank."

"Okay, then I won't call you that, but they will," he said, pointing toward the two frightened officers he had just left.

Everett lowered his head and then turned and looked at the two men as they looked lost and at a loss on where to start with the extraordinary orders they had just received. He turned back and took in the small, dark-haired naval aviator.

"They don't know you as Carl, or Captain, or as a friend from a closed Group. Those men know you as Admiral Everett and will never know anything else. They have come to terms with the fact that someone far over their heads thinks of you as someone who can pull off whatever way they have designed to get you"—he again nodded back at the men—"and them killed. But maybe, just maybe those people who saw fit to promote you actually knew what they were doing, Admiral, just like they knew what they were doing when they placed Jack into the same situation. They have seen you two work together and know that they have a fighting chance to succeed with you two in the positions you now hold. Those men deserve Admiral Everett, and not the SEAL you still think you are. Because to tell you the truth, they *are* that good and will die proving it."

Everett eyed his friend for the longest time and then shook his head. "Just when in the hell did you become so deep thinking?"

"I guess being separated from Will has made me look smarter. I'm still the same ruggedly handsome naval aviator I was a few days ago."

"Well, thanks anyway." He started to turn away and return to the men he was to train, but stopped and held onto some loading straps to face Ryan. "And I guess those same powers that be saw something in you also, Commander Ryan."

"Nah, they were just mesmerized by my rugged good looks too."

BLAIR HOUSE
WASHINGTON, D.C.

Giles Camden listened to his new designee for the directorship of Central Intelligence, Daniel Peachtree, as he explained his run-in with Virginia Pollock at Walter Reed.

"And she still refuses to give us that damn asset of theirs?" the president asked, fuming over this woman's refusal to fear his office.

"Not only that, she practically dared us to come after him," he lied.

"Well, we have the men in the area and I have warned the director of the FBI that he had better come up with an exact location of this complex and raid the damn thing and get me that alien son of a bitch. How these people could be so gullible as to believe the same kind of beings that eat people is beyond me."

Camden's chief of staff cleared her throat to get the two men's attention. With a wary eye toward Daniel Peachtree she stood and handed the president a report in order that the subject be changed from that mysterious base hidden in the desert of Nevada, to a more real threat to his power.

"Sir, General Caulfield sent this message through the auspices of the National Security Agency and routed through the communications hub at Fort Huachuca."

The president read the message and then angrily tossed it into the trash next to his desk.

"What this treasonous action amounts to is a general military coup. I have to bring the military's refusal to follow a presidential directive straight to the American people. This is unprecedented." He fumed and then stood and paced his office. "I want Caulfield brought up on charges, along with the people responsible at NSA for forwarding this message. I also want the Air Force Chief of Staff's resignation on my desk immediately!"

The female chief of staff looked petrified at the orders. "Sir, if we bring all of this out into the open more than it already is, the faith in this office is going to tumble even further than it has to this point. The press is asking a lot of questions as far as the resignations of the former president's staff and the firing of so many military advisors."

"What in the hell do you mean, even *further* than it already has?" he demanded.

"Mr. President," she started, facing the man directly. "Our friends in the news outlets have seen a trend and they don't particularly like it. Even though the American people had disagreed with the spending on military preparedness, they now know the reasons why, and are starting to wonder why so many of the cabinet and military personnel are quitting over your new Home Shores First policy."

"That is exactly why I have to tell the people about the refusal of the men around me to do as they are instructed to do to protect *them*." He waved his arms maniacally. "When they find out that we have designed a defensive plan developed by one of those alien bastards, they will see why that plan cannot, should not be trusted."

"Sir, announcing a possible coup by your military, a scenario that has not once been uttered in the history of the presidency, will not bode well with the current emergency happening. It will only further confuse the issues you are trying to make clear to the American people," Peachtree said. He finally got the first warning signs that Camden had lost control of the situation.

"This also came in," the chief of staff said as she handed the president another message from the Pentagon. Peachtree shot the woman a look as if she had just thrown a can full of gasoline onto an already out of control fire. "It seems the 7th Fleet has turned around to conduct rescue operations in and around the South China Sea. The situation is confused at the moment, but the communiqué looks as if it was forwarded through the offices of the NSA. I have looked into the matter and haven't found any smoking guns thus far, but I am still checking."

Camden sat there stunned at the information.

"Also the Air Force is still slow in implementing your order to cease all cooperation with this Operation Overlord. They claim bad communications due to alien activity coupled with bad weather. I've checked through the Pentagon and the area of concern is clear skies and no communication interruption."

"It *is* a coup," Camden mumbled as he looked at Peachtree.

"Mr. President, allow whatever it is to happen. We'll fight this in our own time with the Constitution in our corner. But for right now you need to explain to the citizens why you are wholeheartedly against this plan of action."

"To do that I need that asset that's hidden away from my CIA and the rest of my people. I need that Matchstick, or whatever its name really is!"

"With the threat I made at Walter Reed to that Pollock woman, we may see some progress in that area very soon. In the meanwhile, there is a bit of good news."

"Oh, please tell me," Camden said with sarcasm lacing his voice.

"It seems the message sent to the Overlord command structure has warned of an imminent Gray attack on their hidden facilities. We may have little to worry about in that regard very soon. Then you can claim that you were right in not backing the former holder of this office in his plan for defensive cooperation. Also, not all of your military is refusing your orders. The task force consisting of the *George Washington* and *John C. Stennis* Battle Groups have turned away from their ordered route toward the Antarctic. They will not be there if called upon for support. It seems the admiral in command was not a friend of Admiral Fuqua, nor, dare I say, General Caulfield."

"So you recommend that we do nothing for now, just play the 'little boy being picked on' by the military bullies in power?"

"Exactly."

Camden thought about this as he returned to his chair and sat. He paused as he looked at his Chief of Staff, who nodded her agreement.

"All right, I'll wait to cry wolf at the door, but I need that alien and I want to know what it knows. I am a firm believer that the former president has been lied to; even he couldn't be that big of a fool."

Peachtree turned to the president's chief of staff. "Would you excuse us for a moment, please," he said with a smile.

She looked frustrated as she never trusted the man standing before her boss, but moved to the door and left regardless.

"I didn't mention this before, but that Dr. Pollock knows a little too much about the murder of Lynn Simpson Collins, and has threatened us with that knowledge."

Camden couldn't believe what it was he was hearing. The same nightmare he had faced before taking office was still rearing its ugly head—the one thing that would not only get him thrown from office, but also would send him to prison. He remained quiet.

"I have informed the Black Team in Arizona that they are free to get their hands on this alien asset any way that they can."

"And?" Camden asked expectantly.

"And to immediately eliminate the only bread crumb in the trail leading back to us."

The president knew he shouldn't have listened to Peachtree

in the first place when it was suggested they use Hiram Vickers to find the asset. But he had, and there was no sense barking about it now.

"It's about time. Kill that stupid bastard. It seems everything has gone wrong for us since he mindlessly murdered that girl and brought her brother closer to finding out who Vickers really worked for."

"That is already in the works, and we have the men that will not only do that, but get the asset as well. You'll get the truth of what's happening from the mouth of that little alien very soon."

Camden nodded and could only mumble the words of possibly the only thing that could save his presidency: "The Matchstick Man."

CAMP ALAMO
ANTARCTICA

Jack and his new staff gathered inside of the office that he was assigned. The new men, Major Sebastian Krell and Lieutenant Van Tram, had been assigned to coordinate getting men and equipment outside for training purposes, a topic that had been both men's main gripe since meeting up with Collins. Meanwhile, Will Mendenhall was standing over the desk, feeding the general sheet after sheet of paper with the assigned troops under his command, while Henri was assigned to liaise with the troops of the 101st and 82nd Airborne Divisions and the German 23rd Panzer Division. Henri's fluency in all languages guaranteed confusion but Jack had no choice. Farbeaux knew battle tactics as well as himself. He had handed Collins the status of his command. The general had over seven thousand combat troops and their equipment, sixty-five Leopard II main battle tanks, and two hundred armored personnel carriers of both Bradley Fighting Vehicles and the German-made Fuchs 2 wheeled personnel carrier.

Henri had reported that he was concerned about the

wheeled vehicle of the German Panzer division and the way
it would handle in the ice and snow when called upon to run
interference for the Leopard IIs.

"Colonel, I suggest you bypass the nomenclature of the
book specs and go directly to the soldiers that operate the
system. They'll tell you straight if they believe the Fuchs
can do the job or not. If they can't, get them off the line. But
I suspect they will."

"I will do that," Henri said as he passed another report
and design specs toward Collins, who picked it up and
looked at it. "These are the design specs for the new tracks
for the Panzers and the Bradleys. You see why the planners
are so nervous about the maneuvers you have requested. The
deep-seated spikes can really tear up the ice and could be a
possible trail for anything with eyes to follow straight back
to the facility."

Jack examined the new design and saw that instead of the
normal padded tread of the American-made Bradleys and
the M1 Abrams, these were heavily spiked. Those steel an-
chors designed for traction purposes would find purchase in
this environment by digging in deeply.

"Damn, I hate to say it, but Sir Bennett and his people
have a point. Damn, is there any chance of getting the Panzers' and Bradleys' old padded tracks on?"

"Again, military planning," Farbeaux said with a smirk.
"They weren't sent along with the replacement parts or
equipment."

Collins rubbed his eyes and then looked at Mendenhall.
The captain shook his head.

"Do you think we'll even have the time to get a training
and maneuvering field test in after the warning from General Caulfield?"

"It would have been nice just to find out if the damn
Panzers could even move out there."

Van Tram and Sebastian Krell joined them at the desk.
"The SAS colonel has requested extra security for something they call Poseidon's Nest," Major Krell said as he
handed Jack the communication. "He says at least four

hundred men from either the 82nd or 101st would be adequate."

"Oh, is that right? And what am I supposed to do when those commanders scream bloody murder because I'm taking away from their already short-staffed divisions?" Jack looked at Krell, not expecting him to answer.

"The men he would take are very important to both divisions, sir. He wants the fast-reaction force that is to plug any gap in the lines if and when the Grays get close to this Poseidon's Nest, whatever that is."

"Thank you, Major." Jack stood and walked to the wall map of Camp Alamo and the design of its interior. As he looked he saw a large blank spot that wasn't filled in with detail. He jabbed at the section that lay ten miles distant and was connected by only one ice tunnel. "Major, I suspect your Poseidon's Nest is right there, as everything else is in use and explained."

Krell stepped forward and examined the spot Jack was pointing at. "Yes, sir, I agree."

"That's about enough of the compartmentalized and need-to-know bullshit. Will, get me Sir Bennett on the line. I need a meeting with him and our mysterious Admirals Kinkaid and Huffington within the hour. Say I insist for security reasons."

"Yes, sir."

"Henri, you feel like getting out of here for a while?" Collins asked while staring at the blank spot on the map.

Farbeaux laid the multitude of paperwork down and then looked at the general.

"Why do I get the honor of getting out of all of this wonderful paperwork?" the Frenchman asked.

Collins turned and faced him. "Because if they don't show us what in the hell they're protecting, I need you to get us inside there. And if the SAS is protecting that site, I need all the sneaky-bastard stuff I can get to bypass the most dangerous security in the world. After all, it was the Special Air Service that trained us both, as I recall. And besides, all they can do is shoot us."

Will paused with the phone in his hand. Tram and Krell smiled.

"Well, I didn't get all dressed up to do paperwork. After you, General Collins."

Fifteen minutes later both Farbeaux and Collins were sitting in the main conference building facing Professor Bennett and Admirals Kinkaid and Huffington. The men didn't look too pleased at being ordered by this man to a meeting that was not planned.

"General, I appreciate the difficulty you face not knowing certain aspects of Overlord, but I must say what you ask just isn't possible at the moment, at the proper time we—"

"Now, sir," Jack said as he eyed the man in charge of Alamo.

"General, Sir Bennett is only responsible for the defense of Alamo, not the area in question. That is ours and ours alone," Kinkaid said. "The SAS is under the strictest of orders from not only Lord Durnsford, but your own president and your Dr. Compton, to keep this played as close to the vest as possible, and to keep that area secured. So no, your request is denied until such a time as we see fit to explain."

Jack had been thinking about this area and had decided to play a hunch as he remembered everything ever explained to him by Niles Compton. He was about to bluff his way into Poseidon's Nest.

"Look, I know the British government discovered the site. I know that artifacts were uncovered there that may or may not affect me, and a colleague of mine, directly. Your dig may have started out as an archeological function four years ago, but you found more than just a watch there. You found Overlord. Now, how close did I come?" He eyed both naval men, who sat with their mouths agape.

Professor Bennett laughed lightly.

"Well, you were warned when the general was assigned that he wasn't your typical soldier and was capable of deduction beyond the officers you are used to working with."

"I . . . I . . . ," Kinkaid started but didn't know how to be-gin his denials.

"Gentlemen, it's time we show the general what he is here to protect. I believe the time for spy versus spy has passed, as we are dangerously short of time. You gentlemen have yet to install the power plant that is still in transit from McMurdo Station, and have even yet to see if the bloody thing will work with technology it was never meant for—after all, we only have the assurance from our small alien friend that the two systems are even compatible. Let us share with the general what it is Her Majesty's government un-covered over thirty years ago and has spent the fortunes of six countries to develop and repair, shall we?"

Admiral Huffington slammed his palm down on the tabletop. The Royal Navy man was furious, but he was in a tight corner because everything the professor had said was true—they were out of time. He nodded his head in agreement.

"Well, General Collins, gather your staff and tell them to meet us in section 2287. It is a very long ride. And tell them to dress warm."

Jack stood as well as Farbeaux and was soon joined by Sir Bennett.

"Shall we go and introduce you to Overlord?"

Sir Darcy Bennett, Collins, and Farbeaux met Sebastian, Tram, and Will at the large junction that had tunnels carved in the ice that ran off in differing directions like the spokes of a wagon wheel, with the exception of one. This one was closed off to the men and women of Camp Alamo and sealed with a large steel door. Standing guard at the door were five SAS soldiers in white camouflaged battle dress, with two fifty-caliber machine guns stationed on either side of the dual sliding doors.

As they waited a tram pulled up with Admirals Kinkaid and Huffington, who looked none too pleased at the fillet-ing of their security precautions. General Collins's outright refusal to add additional security, as per their request, probably did not help matters. Collins steadfastly refrained from answering, only saying that he was fearful that by breaking up individual teams from the 101st and 82nd, especially with their lack of Antarctic training, would muddy what little teamwork the two divisions had established during their original mountain training of six months before. To break up men who had at least that much training together, sending 10 percent of them to Overlord, would disrupt Jack's command. As the defense leader he had that right to refuse—that's why he had the two stars on his collar. Thanks to Sebastian, Tram, and Henri, the admirals never thought that Jack's staff could find enough excuses to refuse them, and they were, to say the least, put out by this.

The two men waited inside the automatically driven tram as the men loaded in. The SAS watch commander checked the identification badges that hung around their necks; even the two admirals were questioned and then finally passed through.

The men were placed inside the tram in groups of threes and the final two rows of seats were reserved for four heavily armed SAS soldiers. Admiral Huffington nodded at the gate security and from a glass-enclosed booth the guard opened the automatic blast doors. Collins watched from the second row of seats as first one set of doors opened left to right and slid into the ice wall on either side; then just as rapidly a second set of heavier, thicker doors slid up and into the ceiling and floor. As the men looked beyond they saw that the track was concrete and that it vanished after only a few feet inside the large-mouthed tunnel. The tram started forward without any noise other than the wind rushing down the tunnel. The temperature dropped dramatically as the car moved in.

As they watched the crystalline ice slide by, the speed of the tram increased, creating an additional freezing wind that reddened their faces. Then the car angled down sharply. Jack heard Will Mendenhall yelp—Will was afraid of anything that moved without him being in control. That was thanks to Jason Ryan. Ryan scared the young captain any chance he got with his flying and the driving of any wheeled vehicle. Jack had always meant to talk to the navy man about freaking everyone out with his prowess with machines, but never had gotten around to it.

Professor Bennett, sitting next to Jack, started to explain that which he had already partially guessed, but never in his wildest imagination did he expect to hear the real story of the origins of Operation Overlord. Before Bennett started, a glass bubble came up from both sides of the tram and then a clear glass shield did the same at the front and the rear. The tram slowed while still on a downward angle and then came to a stop. Before anyone could even think about what was happening, the tram started straight down on an elevator the men never saw. It started traveling at a high rate of speed and then suddenly stopped, and then before that shock wore off the tram started forward once more, this time at a slower rate of travel. As the lighting came up at a higher illumination, Collins and the others could see that the strata of ice had changed dramatically. It was now mostly solid and transparent. It was literally a block of ice they were traveling through.

Sir Bennett placed a small headset on as the two admirals frowned, and started telling the tale they all had waited to hear.

"Gentlemen, what you see all around you is a prehistoric inland body of water, named the Shackleton Sea. It was discovered approximately thirty-five years ago by a British survey team sinking test holes for volcanic activity. In the estimation of our science boys, and through the efforts of the University of California and the National Weather Data Center in the United States, we have come to the conclusion that the Shackleton Sea is well over 700 million years in age."

Collins looked back and saw that his four staff members were duly impressed as the frozen sea whizzed past them at thirty miles per hour and was still traveling deeper as Bennett continued.

"Species of microbial life from the time before the continents separated have been recovered during excavation—animal life never before seen or documented. As the geology teams continued to drill for core samples, some very amazing things started to be brought up from this very, very deep sea. Things, gentlemen, that had no right to be anywhere on this planet at any time in its history—shards of metal, pieces of dense unknown carbon fibers, and, dare I say, even human remains."

Farbeaux had his sense of wonder piqued as he looked from the green-tinted ice toward Mendenhall, who didn't look like he was enjoying the tour one bit as the tram traveled even deeper. Bennett seemed to sense Will's unease and added another little trivia fact.

"I dare say that we have one point eight miles of inland sea above our heads at this very moment."

Mendenhall lowered his head and it was the small, very intrigued man from Southeast Asia that gave Will a sympathetic pat on the shoulder as the captain just realized that after his trip into outer space and his ride to the moon, he had developed an extreme case of claustrophobia.

"Through an accidental break in the ice in the eighties, a weather team of scientists discovered something rather bizarre that sent our world into chaos. After we achieved access we sent large teams down into the sea and started analyzing the find. Finally, after we analyzed the samples of composite fiber, plastic, and steel from an ancient discovery, we were shocked to see the artifact, to say the least, was viable to the point that it looked brand-new, despite the scorch marks and damage it had sustained during some confrontation or the other. Four years ago, after the moon missions and the discovery of alien technology in South America, we started to share our amazing find with our counterparts in America, and thus we learned about your little house guest in Arizona. We learned the tale of the tape, so to speak, of the ancient war between Mars and our common enemy, the Grays. Then it all started to make sense with the information of the finds on the moon and the magnificent technology uncovered in Peru."

Jack knew the story, and hoped Will could come up for air long enough to explain to the others, as they only knew their little contributions to the entirety of the tale.

"Through the cooperation of entities inside of America"— Jack knew Bennett was referring to that little secret facility in the desert—"a deal was struck to give our government and others a certain amount of access to Mr. Mahjtic. His explanation of the disastrous war 700 million years ago sent us off in a new direction as far as excavating this site was concerned. But the current defense plan was not engineered until an old plan was taken from the files of Garrison Lee, a man I greatly admired and one who was familiar with the head of our MI6, Lord Durnsford. That gave Senator Lee's conclusions instant credibility, at least in our eyes. It seems Lee, being responsible for the conclusions reached at Roswell those many years ago, came to the conclusion, rather quickly, that we hadn't a chance of fighting such a war with the Grays. We would lose and lose badly. The obviousness of his findings was what led to the creation of Operation Overlord, with one vital piece missing."

"The use of alien technology to fight," Jack mumbled as he watched the passing ice sea.

"Correct, General, very good." Bennett smiled over at the two stone-faced admirals. "Senator Lee's conclusions were reached after he studied what remained of the evidence at Roswell. But, gentlemen, he never realized that an earlier war had been fought millions of years before the event at New Mexico. But when the mine system in Peru was discovered he became aware in the final moments of his life what the finds really meant, and passed this on to to your president while he laying dying inside Air Force One on the runway in Peru."

Collins now remembered that Alice and the president were the last to speak to Garrison Lee in the moments before his death and now he knew what was told to them by Lee: recover any and all Martian war material for use in the upcoming fight. He knew that man's true ancestors, the very beings that made Earth their final refuge, had left the means to do battle.

The tram started to slow as they approached another, even larger gate system.

Bennett removed the headset and mic from his head, then leaned over to speak with Jack privately.

"As we expanded the archeological site surrounding the Shackleton Sea, we found something that confused everyone in the know on the events on the moon, in Peru, and here, General."

"You brought up Carl Everett's wristwatch containing samples of my blood," Jack said, not looking at Sir Darcy Bennett.

"And that, coupled with what you are about to see, made us keenly aware that you and Mr. Everett had to be onboard the team no matter what, because the finding of the watch in such an ancient sea dictated your involvement in the project. Frankly, General, we couldn't afford the chance that removing you would change our destiny."

"Thus the secrecy and the need to know."

"Precisely."

The project leader stepped from the tram and turned to the other members of Jack's staff.

"Our alien friend in Arizona struck on the Overlord plan after we found what you are about to see. He knew the ancient power source of a Martian engine would not be viable after seven hundred million years and knew we had to replace that source. The only thing that could do that, I'm afraid, died with the Martians before the continents separated."

"The Grays had the answer," Collins said as he watched the SAS security team advance on the tram and its occupants. "We needed the power plant from the downed saucer at Roswell. When we didn't have that we had to turn to the two downed ships in Arizona six years ago." Jack turned and faced the two admirals as they listened, trying to get under their skin as much as possible with the realization that their little secret was never as secret as they were led to believe.

"When the damage to them was proven too great to repair and the fact you were having a difficult time reverse-engineering the two power plants, the search for other downed saucers throughout our history commenced. Then one was finally found, in Iran, and thus the small battle of a week ago."

Sir Darcy smiled and looked at the two admirals, who were shocked that so much information could be delivered by Collins.

"Oops," Bennett said in mock astonishment. "It looks like the secret is out, and only several thousand people besides the general have more than likely figured it out for themselves."

"Okay, we were bloody wrong about security. You have made your point, General Collins," Admiral Huffington said, defeated.

With his staff gathered around him, Jack continued to finish his conclusions.

"Now that the power plant is obviously enroute, you intend to fulfill Senator Lee's and Mahjtic's plan. All we need to know is what it is you found that gave our alien ally the slightest hope that we can be saved before the full-scale assault begins."

Bennett nodded his head at the SAS guards, who turned away from the group and activated the large blast doors to their front.

Jack and the others stepped up as Sir Darcy placed his hands behind his back, and like his boss, Lord Durnsford, did at Schofield Barracks, rocked back and forth on his heels as the doors opened.

"Gentlemen, I give you the answer you have been waiting to hear and the means of defeating the invaders of our world. This is the heart and soul of Operation Overlord."

The blast doors parted in their double-axis sliding fashion. The men stepped up to the brightly illuminated and enormous excavated cave, and the truth of their combined history was theirs for the viewing.

"My lord!"

Major Sebastian Krell summed it up for the staff of General Jack Collins as the doors opened wide. And even the normally silent Tram started talking in Vietnamese when the sight was finally revealed.

Jack took in the most unbelievable sight ever created by the hand of man—a Martian hand for sure, but a human too, nonetheless. At that moment the real truth of Operation Overlord overwhelmed his thoughts.

The object was so large that it had to have been built by the hands of the ancient gods.

"Gentlemen, I give you Her Majesty's Ship *Garrison Lee*."

15

As the four-man staff of General Collins stepped forward and looked down upon the ship lying in a fog of thick condensation, they saw the immense cavern that encompassed no less than four square miles of excavated Inland Sea, which explained the large blank spot on the map of Camp Alamo.

As Jack Collins stepped forward he noticed that they were perched high on a ledge that looked down upon the vessel—a viewing gallery. The first thing he noticed was the enormous bow that was equipped with what looked like a giant sharpened plow. That tapered off into a long girder-style superstructure that he could see housed pressure- and outer-space-resistant compartments that had small portholes lining them. As he took in the whole of the colossal ship he saw that it resembled two World War II battleships sitting bottom hull to bottom hull. The superstructure rose to a height of five hundred feet above the hull and contained radar, sonar, and other turning dishes whose use Collins could not begin to fathom. The structure was duplicated, or exactly a mirror image on the underside of the ship, and was hanging low in an engineered basement of sorts to accommodate its enormous size.

"I think someone finally made something you couldn't steal, Colonel," Will said, wide-eyed, as he looked at the size of the vessel below.

All Henri Farbeaux could do was whisper his agreement, as even he was shocked at what the planners had come up with.

Tram was pointing at the upper deck that really did resemble an old battleship. Lying on two differing elevated decks was the forward armament of the ship. Two turrets that were the size of at least four of the USS *Missouri* gun turrets stood out in majestic power as the three guns in each lay dormant. Jack saw the large crystal bulbs on the very tips of each of the six weapons. The turrets themselves looked as if they could house a gun crew of over a hundred. The muzzles of each, capped off for now, were ten feet wide at their base as they disappeared into the turrets, and the muzzles were at least sixteen inches wide before they hit the larger crystal knob at their tips. Collins realized they were looking at laser cannon. They were the type that Sarah had explained they found on the surface of the moon in the crashed ships they had uncovered there.

Inside the immense cavern, thousands of torches were flashing and sparking as the repair to the ancient vessel was continuing even as her proposed launch date was soon arriving. Large patches of damaged hull, the girder system, looked new as other parts were old and rusted. These were in the process of being ground down and painted by the large work crews manning her decks, both upper and lower. The bottom half of the ship was almost an exact duplicate of the upper only the large towers were far shorter. But the resemblance was complete when they all noticed two of the same turrets on the bottom half. That made for six of the large weapons systems in total and that didn't include at least fifty smaller, twin-barreled turrets lining her superstructure. The staff realized that the ship, if viewed from the side, would have looked like a vessel sitting in calm waters with her reflection displayed perfectly in duplicate, top and bottom. They also realized that the crew of the lower half superstructure would be upside down; utilizing the zero gravity of space they would be operating just the same as the upper crews.

"The vessel—we could never decipher her name in the Martian language—was heavily damaged. So much so it took the combined treasuries of six nations to repair her," Admiral Kinkaid said as he stepped up to Collins. Jack could see the pride in the faces of both of the brilliant naval engineers as Huffington joined them. "Perhaps it's better explained by looking at the silhouette on the wall." He pointed to a large, illuminated design etched on glass sunk into the ice wall.

Jack and the others turned and watched as Admiral Huffington took over the explanation.

"Whatever battles this ship was in, it took an inordinate amount of damage. We have had to replace, or reverse-engineer if you prefer, over 40 percent of her bulk. We have had to replace her six engine bells and mixing chambers at the stern and every one of her sixteen maneuvering jets lining her midsection." He pointed to certain areas of explanation on the lighted depiction of the *Lee*. "The crystal laser enhancers on every one of the eighteen guns had to be replaced, as they were cracked and broken whenever the ship came into contact with the sea due to the enormous overheating. Cold water and extremely hot glass of any sort do not mix well."

"What are . . . these tanks . . . inside the hull? They . . . look new?" Tram asked in his limited English, as this was the first time the small man had said anything in English.

"Very observant, Lieutenant," Huffington said, surprised by the knowledge of the average soldier. "Those are five-thousand-gallon coolant tanks, fifteen in all, upper and lower decks. They are used to flush each of the large barrels at the time of discharge to cool them from the heat of the Argon laser system. Without the coolant, the barrels would melt after the second or third firing of the weapons."

"Have the guns been tested?" Jack asked.

"Yes, they have, General. Raytheon Corporation built two turrets with three weapons apiece at the Aberdeen Proving Ground two years ago. At first the crystals blew apart, but with the assistance of the Hillman Corporation of Liverpool, England, and their vast history of lens grinding capability, they fashioned new crystals that were able to withstand over a thousand discharges of the system before eventually cracking. We have calculated that we'll eventually need far less than that from each barrel."

Collins knew the connotation of the admiral's words because he knew that the ship wasn't meant to last that long in battle with the saucers. He didn't expand on the subject of duration.

Kinkaid tapped the body of the nearly holographic view and it changed, rotating 150 degrees. "As you can see, the vessel is enormous in size and weight. Her thrusters were never meant to lift her off an atmospheric world, thus our dilemma." He stepped away from the diagram and pointed to the spot on the *Lee* where engineers were busy attaching what Collins and his staff realized were hundreds of powerful solid fuel booster rockets along her midsection.

"They look like space shuttle booster rockets," Mendenhall ventured.

"Exactly, Captain, only far more powerful. Morton-Thiokol Corporation took three years designing and developing the new system and that should be capable with the one hundred and twelve boosters to get the *Lee* into the air with the assistance of her many maneuvering jets, all one hundred and fifty thousand tons of her."

"I hate to be the realist here, but where is this ship supposed to fight?" Farbeaux watched the five thousand workmen busily going here and there in all locations of her superstructure.

"Hopefully not too far from here," Sir Darcy said, glancing upward toward the ice ceiling five thousand feet above their heads. "It really depends upon the Grays and where they place their energy-producing vessel when it arrives for the main invasion." He looked at his watch for the dramatic effect. "Which should come at almost any time, according to our small alien friend."

"The main armament of the *Lee* cannot destroy this rather larger saucer on her own, gentlemen," Huffington said almost sadly. "She can only defend and protect, for as long as she can, the two ships of the boarding party that will assault the enemy vessel and destroy her from within. This is the job of the HMS *Lee,* to fight as long as she can against overwhelming odds to hold station while our people enter the energy ship. Because without that, the Grays cannot bring the rest of their fleet to us. They will wither and die in deep space."

"Oh, I thought for a minute there we didn't stand a chance. But now that you've explained it, I see not one obstacle to your plan." Farbeaux shook his head at the arrogant audacity of these men.

"Now you can imagine, Colonel Farbeaux, the hardship that we endured getting other nations to join in the allied coalition," Sir Darcy stated flatly.

"And what does Mahjtic say about the chances of success?" Jack wanted to know the truth, not just for him but the many thousands of men and women that were going to die in the attempt. He realized now the distant and tired look of Niles Compton the past five years; this knowledge had weighed him down like a drowning man holding cinder blocks while trying to stay afloat.

Sir Darcy Bennett looked from Collins to the two admirals, who looked away from the group. Then the professor turned back and faced the expectant men before him.

"Ten to 20 percent."

Jack's staff was silent as they realized that the great hope of the entire world boiled down to a mere fraction of what they had hoped.

"Now you know why your Dr. Compton and Lord Durnsford kept the information making up the Overlord plan so compartmentalized. If the percentage of possible success leaked out before we were ready, the world would just give up."

Before anyone could bravely say anything in response to deter the fear they all felt, a loudspeaker came to life and over the noise of machinery and cutting and welding torches came the announcement.

"All propulsion engineering personnel please report to your stations. All heavy load handling crews, man your cranes. All riggers to their stations. Arrival of power plant is estimated in fifteen minutes. Repeat, all propulsion engineering divisions prepare for power plant arrival."

Jack saw the activity below increase as a loud cheer went up from the many thousands of workers who had slaved for the past four years on the most expensive project ever initiated by mankind.

Collins turned to his men and nodded for them to return to the tram. He then turned to the three men who were responsible for the reverse-engineering of the former Martian battleship, the HMS *Garrison Lee*.

"Thank you, gentlemen. Thank you for the truth."

WALTER REED NATIONAL MILITARY
MEDICAL CENTER
BETHESDA, MARYLAND

Niles Compton was sitting up as far as he could in the bed. His right eye and forehead, along with the right side of his face, was still covered in heavy gauze. He had awakened from a state of near-coma to see Virginia Pollock sleeping with her head on her arms at the foot of his bed. He had been awake for the past forty minutes, trying to get the fog of his memory back before he attempted to speak. He watched Virginia and realized that she must have planted herself here in the hospital, which wasn't a good sign. He would have thought she would have been with the president's cabinet working on the Event Group part of Overlord.

Niles moved his left foot and Virginia came awake with a start. It was if she was falling from a cliff, which is exactly what she had been doing in her waking hours. She blinked several times and then noticed that Niles was staring at her. His one brown eye took her in and the director of Department 5656 actually managed a small smile.

"How many days?" he asked in a whisper.

Virginia stood and walked to the head of the bed, then leaned over and kissed her friend of fifteen years lightly on the top of his balding head. She wiped at a tear and then smiled at him as she took in his battered features.

"I must say, you look the mess, boss."

"I feel a mess. Now, how many days was I out?" he persisted.

"Six."

Niles closed his good left eye and then leaned back against his pillow.

"The president is still in a coma," she said as she watched Compton's face for a reaction. There was none. "Vice President Stevens was killed in San Francisco by a Gray attack similar to the Camp David strike."

Niles acted as if the news didn't affect him, but Virginia knew the news about his best friend had shaken him to his core.

"Giles Camden is now the acting commander-in-chief."

"Overlord?"

"At the risk of every one of the president's cabinet, and most of the military basically under threat of treason, it's still going forward. The engine arrived in Antarctica this morning. Jack, Carl, and the rest have arrived safely and are on station."

"The Grays?" he asked as he finally managed to open his one good eye.

"Mumbai and Beijing have been destroyed."

This time a moan did escape the director's mouth. He turned away for a moment to gather his thoughts. He faced Virginia once more with a questioning look.

"The Grays have come to take people, Niles. To . . . consume us. Matchstick held that back from us. They emptied Mumbai and Beijing and then the saucers left. We have them on the Hubble back at their fleet."

The horrible truth as to the Gray intent was clearly written on Compton's face. He shook his head, understanding why Matchstick had been so secretive.

"Niles, the largest energy-production ship has left the rest of their fleet, along with over a thousand attack craft—the invasion is about to begin. India and China were nothing but test platforms for the real thing. And nothing the Chinese or the Indian militaries threw at them worked. They shook off even nuclear weapons and completed their raids and then left."

A light knock sounded at the door and General Caulfield looked in. He was dressed like Niles or Virginia had never seen him before. His civilian clothing made them feel the loss of control more than anything thus far.

"I should have known you were awake, Doctor. It seems you and the president are mentally linked or something." Caulfield entered the room.

"Jim is awake?" Niles asked hopefully.

"No, but the doctors said his brain activity is rising very quickly. He should be able to open his eyes soon."

"Thank God," Virginia said as she shook the general's hand.

"Overlord?" Niles asked, trying to swallow. Virginia took the glass of water and placed the straw in his mouth and Compton drank deeply.

"Being rushed, I'm afraid. We're fast running out of time."

"Everything is in place?" he asked as Virginia pulled the glass away.

"All, with the exception of the two battle groups assigned for the defense of Camp Alamo. I'm afraid our President Camden has a friend in the task force commander." He saw the sad look cross Niles's uninjured side of his face. "But with General Collins there, I feel somewhat better about giving Overlord a chance at getting off the ground. Everything else is getting back to the normal plan, thanks to two young men who saw what was happening with their new boss the president, and scattered the airwaves with false orders directed from the White House through the NSA, which immediately forwarded them to all commands." He smiled. "Even though the NSA director across the river knew them to be forged orders. We owe those two men in the president's press corps a lot. Especially now that they have been arrested at the direct orders of Camden and director of the CIA designate, Peachtree. Those kids are now in jail, charged with falsifying federal documents and the rumor is a charge of treason is forthcoming, all at a time of war, which means they'll hang if convicted."

"We have to see to it they don't," Compton said.

"Niles, there is one more thing I need to tell you," Virginia said, not wanting to add to the director's already burdened mind. "Peachtree and Camden want Matchstick and they will raid the complex in order to get at him. We now suspect that it was Peachtree along with the killer of Jack's sister that arranged for the first raid on the Group six months ago, trying to procure that aggression formula uncovered in Mexico."

Niles shook his head adamantly even though it caused him pain to do so.

"Get Matchstick out of there. He's given Overlord all he can; it's time for him to go home, where our men can protect him and Gus."

"I'll see to it," Virginia said. "General, I know it's asking a lot, but can the FBI give us the men we need to cover the house and property in Arizona?"

"With the resignation of the president's man at the FBI and Camden's new choice in that position, no, I'm sorry. If I ask it will only tell Camden and Peachtree exactly where your asset will be."

"I want Pete Golding to stay with Matchstick and Gus. Keep them safe. I also want any other civilian volunteers at

Group to go with Pete. With our military arm spread all over the globe, it's our only security besides the retirees we have watching the place," Niles said as he felt his strength waning fast.

"Get some sleep, Dr. Compton, we'll do what we can from here," Caulfield said as he and Virginia watched him fall asleep.

"I'll get these orders out to my Group to get Matchstick and Gus out of there; you stay with the president and let us know as soon as he awakens. Camden has to be stopped before he interferes with Overlord any more than he has."

Caulfield nodded, took Virginia's shoulder and squeezed, then left the room.

Virginia stayed a moment looking at Niles. She shook her head as she realized just how much Niles had personally altered the world they knew. She again wiped a tear away as she moved for the door.

The world would never know the names of Niles Compton or that of the Matchstick Man, and Dr. Virginia Pollock knew that to be wrong and unacceptable.

CAMP ALAMO
ANTARCTICA

Jack was sitting at his desk in his assigned quarters six hours after the incredible tour of Poseidon's Nest. He was short on sleep as he had been for the past six months since the death of his sister, Lynn. Collins had two pictures on his cluttered desk that he kept looking at: one of his sister and mother, posed together in the last photo ever taken of the two women a year before Lynn was murdered; the second of Sarah. She sat on a rock somewhere in the middle of a desert, smiling into the camera, and Jack imagined from time to time it was he who had taken the snapshot and that they might have even been on a vacation together. He closed his eyes momentarily and then went back to his battle plans.

A loud knock sounded on his door and he stood and

stretched. He rubbed his sore eyes and then walked to the plastic door and opened it. Before he knew it someone was on him and he stumbled back into the small room, then hit the bed and fell backward. The next thing he realized was that Sarah was kissing him all over his face. He laughed and then while on his back lifted her into the air. He then brought her down and kissed her deeply. After a full minute—a minute that he would never forget as long as he lived—he pushed her off and then while on one elbow looked into her sea-reddened face. Her smile was enormous.

"I see your pleasure cruise has finally docked," he said with a smile he no longer thought he had been capable of.

"Yeah, it sure had, General," she said in amazement. "Boy, I can't wait to spend all of that extra money at the end of the month," she said with an even larger smile as she leaned over and kissed him again.

Jack finally pulled away again. "Sorry to disappoint you, but the president didn't see fit to give me the pay-grade advancement with the brevet rank; I guess he spent all of his extra money down here."

"Damn, Jack, how in the hell are we to live off a colonel's pay?"

He smiled again and then stood from the small cot, then pulled her to her feet and held her at arm's length to look her over.

"I see the Russian Navy must have behaved themselves while you were onboard."

Sarah got a serious look on her face as she reached out and placed her arms around Jack.

"I'll never tell," she said with a sadness Jack detected immediately.

"Lost a lot of good men, I hear," he said as he hugged her back.

Sarah didn't answer as she buried her face in Jack's chest, and that to him was good enough.

"Where's Carl and Jason?" he asked.

Sarah finally pulled back and her smile returned. "They

were absconded by a funny little man with a lab coat, Sir . . . or Lord something or other. They're taking some sort of magical mystery tour. I was supposed to go but I escaped to see some jerk with two new stars on his collar."

"Well, they're in for one hell of an eye opener. You should have gone."

"I wanted to see only one thing," she said as she smiled wider.

"And that is?"

"Will." She laughed before she could get it fully out.

"Ass," he said.

"One more surprise, Jack, you'll love this one."

"What?" he said expecting a gift as she turned away and then looked at him with wide eyes.

"Master Chief Jenks is here."

Collins turned a nice shade of white as the image of the short, meanest son of a bitch he had ever had the displeasure of meeting came into his mind. He felt like he needed to sit down as he remembered crashing the master chief's boat, USS *Teacher,* inside the El Dorado mine.

"You look a little put out, General; don't tell me that man makes you slightly uncomfortable?"

Jack's eyes narrowed. "The first time he calls me Captain Crunch, or even General Crackhead, I'll have that seagoing bastard shot!"

"Aw, he likes you too."

After the brief about HMS *Garrison Lee,* which had left Admiral Everett, Jason Ryan, Anya Korvesky, and Captain Lienanov stunned, Everett turned to Jenks, who sat smiling inside the tram with his booted feet up on the console.

"Compartmentalized, my ass. You knew about this all along." Everett zipped his cold-weather parka back up and then climbed inside and sat hard onto the plastic seat.

Lienanov, Ryan, and a silent Anya followed suit and the tram started moving again in the opposite direction. Jenks ignored Everett for the moment and turned in his seat to look at the white-faced Russian.

"You wanna tell me again about how *big* that Russian pig boat was you served on, my Red friend?"

The Russian captain squinted his eyes at the gruff master chief and then shook his head in wonder at the size of the grounded battleship he had just seen up close.

"Always buy American, my friend, more bang for the buck." Jenks puffed on the cigar as he laughed at his own joke. "Now, to your question, Toad. Yes, I knew about the *Lee,* had to because I designed her escape pods *and* the assault craft that will ride inside her superstructure until we're ready for you hero boys to do your thing. I had to know what in the hell ship I was attaching my work to. And I can tell you one thing, I had those two admirals, Kinkaid and that limey Huffington, so angry they shit gold bricks. But I withheld my designs until they showed me what I needed to see." Jenks got a bad taste in his mouth and tossed his cigar onto the long dead ice of the inland sea. "Now that I know the whole truth, I wish I would have built a better beer can."

Everett studied his old friend and then looked back at Anya, who also realized that Master Chief Jenks knew what was at stake.

Jenks faced his old friend and looked at him closely.

"Just make sure you're not on that battlewagon when she shoves off, Toad, because she's never coming home again." He plopped a fresh cigar in his mouth with a far different demeanor as he looked back at the Russian naval officer. "You either, my Red friend. I think losing one ship at a time is quite enough."

Lienanov listened to Jenks's words and thought about them.

"As an officer, I will go where I'm needed. And I am not a Red, as you say. I am Second Captain Lienanov of the Northern Fleet."

"Well, Second Captain Lenny Popoff, I admire your spunk. But just to let you know, the *Garrison Lee* is a death ship in waiting, and she will be crewed by men also not meant to return. So put that in your babushka and smoke it, and then find another way to glorify Mother Russia."

Everett looked at Jenks, really not liking him that much at the moment, but then he saw that the former navy man was sad enough that he couldn't look back at his old trainee and friend. Carl knew then that the master chief was on the crew list for the HMS *Garrison Lee*.

16

Matchstick was again at Gus Tilly's bedside as the old prospector slept a rough sleep. Every so often Mahjtic would
reach up and take Gus's hand when the old prospector
started to awaken. Once the long, green fingers wrapped
around the man's hand, he would go silent and let out a
long breath and then he would breathe normally. Matchstick
really couldn't fathom his friend growing old, he had been
so vital in his introduction to Earth and her ways. The man
had not rested since he had arrived so many years before.

Matchstick would watch Gus's closed eyes with own obsidian, oval-shaped ones, and then he would see the eyes
under his lids start to move rapidly as Gus started to dream.
Mahjtic didn't know what he was dreaming about, but he
sensed whatever it was made the old man happy, and that
was good enough for him. He released the wrinkled, liver-
spotted hand and then started to read the briefing from
NASA on the destroyed space station.

Matchstick reached over and popped another pizza roll
into his small mouth and crunched down upon it. He found
eating allowed him to concentrate far better as a writer

would consider smoking in the same regard. As he chewed the frozen snack he tapped the photo of the debris field as captured by earth-bound telescope with the tip of his long finger. While he did this and chewed the ice-covered pizza roll, he hummed the old song that Charlie had introduced him to that he was now hooked on and hummed constantly without knowing it: "The Purple People Eater" by Sheb Wooley. The fifties' novelty hit was a favorite of Charlie Ellenshaw when he smoked that strange tobacco Matchstick always wrinkled his small nose over.

Suddenly Matchstick tapped the debris field as he noticed the full moon in the background of the starfield. It was the moon that had caught his attention and the small alien sat up in his chair. He looked closer and then it dawned on him why the Grays had gone out of their way to destroy the International Space Station when they had left all of the other earth-orbiting objects like satellites alone. The space station provided real-time visuals of the moon and it would have an unobstructed view of it from their position. That was why it was destroyed.

Matchstick spit out the frozen dough and cheese and made a beeline for the door.

The target area for the IP point of the Gray invasion had been discovered, and now Matchstick knew where the Power Vessel and the saucer armada would gather for the attack on Earth: the far side of the moon.

It had taken Europa only minutes to break into as many as two thousand telescopic devices the world over. Pete had been confronted by a very excited and incomprehensible Matchstick in his office just as he received the warning from Virginia in regard to getting Matchstick and Gus back to Chato's Crawl. But all that was forgotten for the moment as Pete was now in the computer center scanning the area around the moon, selecting the satellites and telescopes that would give him the best view of any dimensional wormhole that would form in space to announce the arrival of the vanguard of Grays and their irreplaceable power-producing saucer. He realized that the Grays weren't that stupid—why risk entering the atmosphere of Earth and open themselves up to attack, when all they had to do was come in covertly and strike at will from anywhere and never announce their presence with the forming vortex of the wormhole?

Alice Hamilton, who was staying on at Group, came in and traversed the steps to the center's main floor. She raised her glasses and studied the still shots of the moon provided by Europa and her stolen signals.

"Do you think Matchstick has something?" she asked, looking over at the alien as he popped another frozen pizza roll into his mouth.

Pete looked at their small friend. "Yeah, I think he's hit on something. His evidence is flimsy, but the attack on the space platform didn't make any sense at the time. Now it does."

Alice smiled at the chewing Matchstick and winked as she lowered the glasses on their chain.

"Looks like you may have a starting point for Operation Overlord," she said to Mahjtic. He smiled and nodded his bulbous head. Alice patted Pete on the back. "Let's get this out to Camp Alamo, tell them they will have a target very soon."

"I just checked the status. Since you briefed me, Charlie and I kept an eye on the landline communications down there. It's a damn good thing I never ordered Europa to dump her memory discs of the analog phone system. As I understand it now, they've had some kind of accident down there."

"What accident?" she asked.

"After Matchstick verified that the power plant would work, some tech down there hooked something up wrong and they nearly lost the entire ship when a coolant line ruptured."

"God, what next?" she asked herself.

"What's next is that Virginia says that Matchstick and Gus are in danger because the president and the new head of the CIA want our little friend here in the worst way and will breach our security if they have to. We have orders to get the little guy back home, where we believe he'll be safe, because no one knows about Chato's Crawl."

Matchstick continued to eat and then began humming "Purple People Eater."

Both Alice and Pete looked over at Matchstick.

"I don't know about you, Alice," Pete said, "but I can really live without that."

CAMP ALAMO
ANTARCTICA

On the fifteenth try the mixed units of Delta and SEALs finally broke through the composite hatch of the power distribution vehicle mock-up. Everett was pleased when he realized that combining the teams and mixing specialists had paid off. Doubly pleased thanks to the Chinese government, which had been so pleased by the return of the 7th Fleet to assist in rescue operations of their seamen that they had sent several large fragments of the downed saucer from the wreckage of Beijing. That made the ingress into the power supply ship realistic in that regard. They had found out that their protective shield was only good when the cables were deployed and a grid was activated because, as the DARPA and General Electric technicians had explained, the shield grid was only viable when the interconnecting cables were in contact with the next, and the next, and so on. So if they hadn't planned on setting their shield up in space, Carl's men actually stood a chance of breaking in with the explosive teams.

Carl was drying his hair with a towel after exiting the freezing pool and was approached by Anya Korvesky. She was smiling as she pecked the admiral on the cheek. He looked up and saw to his relief that his men were still in the process of being lifted from the pool and hadn't seen.

"Okay, I give up, Major. What's got you so happy?" He tossed the towel at her, wrapping it around her face.

She laughed and removed the damp towel. "Because the whole time I've been on this mission I couldn't understand why I was chosen to be here by the general. Now I do. I thought I was going to be condemned to sit here like a frog on a log while everyone else was doing something worthwhile."

"That's *bump* on a log, darlin',' not a frog."

"What? I always thought it was a frog," she said in all seriousness.

"Again, why so happy? And no witty Americanisms, please," Carl said, finally breaking out in a smile.

"I have a gift of the Israeli government for Operation Overlord," she said as five SAS soldiers rolled in a large wheeled cart with four bright yellow aluminum containers strapped down to it. Carl saw the nuclear warning device emblem stamped on them and stood up with his eyes locked on the containers.

"Okay, you have my attention." He glanced at the major out of the corner of his eye. "And if you want a frog on the log, that's okay too, because any woman that carries around that kind of firepower can say whatever the hell she wants."

Anya Korvesky smiled. "Good."

"Now, explain your gift," he said as his men started to gather around in various states of dress. They saw what was on the four-wheeled cart and one of the SEALs whistled.

"General Shamni realized, once he read what charge would be used on the power production saucer, that your battlefield 'backpack' nukes were a little small and rather bulky; the megatonnage was lacking, in his opinion. So after conferring with your General Caulfield he decided to give you one of Israel's most guarded secrets: the Horn of Gabriel. Or rather, *Horns* of Gabriel, plural. Ten times the size of your American backpack nukes for each of the twelve units and packing one hell of a lot bigger punch."

Everett and the team leaders of both the SEALs and Delta approached the cart and looked the boxes over. Each man had been briefed and had trained on setting off the

American versions of the weapon, but were now doubly anxious to see this rather bizarre Israeli surprise.

"How big of a punch?" Carl asked with due respect.

"Twenty megatons each. Each unit can be carried by one man. I believe that will be double the amount needed to blow anything up."

Both SEALs and Delta teams smiled as they exchanged looks, knowing they had just found a new best friend in Major Anya Korvesky.

The arrival of Lord Durnsford caused quite a stir among the hierarchy of the Overlord staff. Sir Darcy, Admiral Kinkaid, and Admiral Huffington watched along with the gentleman from MI6 as he studied the training exercise in the large mock-up of the number one gun turret. The sides were cut away to give the Royal Navy evaluation teams clear access to view the loading and firing procedures of the gun crew, all fifty-six of them.

They had already lost one of the real mounts on HMS *Garrison Lee*'s number five turret on the underside superstructure that placed it out of action early this morning, when one of the shipyard workers inadvertently struck one of the thick coolant lines with a cutting torch, touching off a large chain reaction when the explosive gases mixed together in the oxygen-rich environment. The resulting explosion killed sixty-one yard workers, most of whom were working on the outside of the turret while performing their jobs on the elevated scaffolding that was needed to get to the upside-down superstructure. These were yard personnel that could not be replaced due to the time restraints and the strict requirements of the security background checks involved.

Lord Durnsford, the leader of the world's effort on Overlord, watched the gun crew inside the mock-up insert the particle canister into the large-bored breach and then slam the tube closed. They stepped back and covered their ears as the power surge from the generators began to pump over a thousand cubic feet of Argon gas into the mixing chamber just forward of the gun's breach. As the power built to 100 percent the first blast of nitrogen gas was injected into the tungsten-lined barrel, effectively freezing the hybrid steel before the shock of the blazing hot laser fired. The simulation went off without a hitch as the blank round of canister shot pellets, small steel ball-bearing-sized shrapnel injected into the barrel to be carried by the electrical impact of the light weapon and then pushed through the thirty-five foot gun. Once it neared the tip of the crystal the pellets were redirected around the light enhancement crystal so as not to blow it apart, and then once outside of the barrel the light wave would carry the particle beam shot at the speed of light to its intended target. The bolt of steel-infused light, a particle beam in essence, would slam into an enemy vessel, ripping its target area like a shotgun blast. Then a blast of nitrogen coolant would be flushed through the barrel to cool it before the next loading process began anew.

"I'm glad to see we worked out the damaged crystal mishaps," Durnsford said. "That was fast becoming an expensive proposition."

The gunnery officers had made adjustments to the redirection of the canister shot after numerous mishaps had not directed the steel pellets far enough around the expensive light enhancement crystals, causing them to be smashed by their own gunfire.

"Yes, it took our American colleagues at Raytheon far longer than we would have thought to reverse-engineer the barrel openings. The rifling that sent the pellets around the crystals were installed backwards from the original Martian design." Sir Darcy hoped the explanation didn't bring on the famous temper from the gentleman from MI6.

"What is the status of the number five turret?" he asked as he watched the two hundred welding machines at work trying to repair the platform.

"Not as fast as we would like. After all, the men have to work precariously upside down and it gets rather tiresome,

I am told. We are having to switch crews far too often. The turret may not be available when the time arrives."

"In other words, due to tired crews and careless workmen we may have lost one-third of her firepower?"

Lord Durnsford took a deep breath and then looked away from his battleship. He needed Niles Compton here to assist him in holding his famed temper at the lack of progress. He faced his number two man in Sir Darcy Bennett.

"Tell me the fame that preceded our infamous Professor Jenks has paid dividends?"

"I'm pleased to say that the former naval master chief was everything he was advertised to be. The escape pods for not just half, but the full complement of crewmen have been installed ahead of schedule. The two assault craft are complete and ready to go."

Lord Durnsford raised his bushy brows in surprise.

"It's just that Jenks is the most disagreeable bastard I have ever had the displeasure to know."

"Yes, Dr. Compton warned us about that."

"Yes, that may be, but I wish we had ten more engineers like him, regardless of his feelings toward the established way of doing things." Admiral Kinkaid defended his Navy man as best he could, no matter how hard it was.

Durnsford stepped back from his elevated view of the dockyard and faced all three men. "When will the power plant test take place?"

It was Admiral Huffington's turn to speak. "We have already powered her up and it didn't blow up the bloody ship, but now I'm afraid to push our luck."

"I am not in the mood for humor, Admiral. I'm quite tired and still have to meet with General Collins and Admiral Everett and field their vast concerns."

"It wasn't an attempt at humor, my lord, but the God's honest truth. All we have in hand is the plans supplied by Dr. Compton. If that alien bloke is off by the smallest parameter in his engineering, we could very well blow up half of the bloody continent of Antarctica."

"Admiral, Mr. Mahjtic has been right on with all of his calculations thus far, has he not?"

"But something with this much power . . ." Huffington stopped when Durnsford held up a restraining hand.

"He was an engineer in his slave capacity, was he not? He was also a crewman on a saucer, was he not?"

"Yes, so the Americans claim."

Durnsford shot Huffington an angry look and then narrowed his eyes underneath his glasses.

"Niles Compton believes everything Mr. Mahjtic has said in his many thousand hours of debriefing. I have had a chance to personally do so. I will not hear another excuse about your having doubts on his ability. As I recall you two forward-thinking geniuses were adamantly opposed to having a mere Navy master chief on your design team." He paused for the briefest of moments and then exploded. "And he's the only engineer that delivered what he promised!"

The men lowered their heads as they realized how wrong they had been to doubt the small alien engineer.

Durnsford calmed himself with a look to his friend, Sir Darcy.

"Gentlemen, I expect the test no later than 2200 hours this night. Due to unforeseen developments our timetable for launch of the *Lee* has been pushed up. The enemy has made a mistake caught by the very being you have doubted all along. We know where they are going to place their power disbursement vessel, and the HMS *Garrison Lee* is going to be there to meet it."

All three men were stunned at the announcement.

"Now, no more delays, gentlemen. I appreciate the hard work and sacrifice, but now is the time for action and not doubt." He turned and looked down at the men working and those training. "We owe them that, don't you think?"

With that Lord Durnsford turned and left with Sir Darcy in tow.

"My old friend Dr. Compton is awake in Washington. We have hopes that the president will soon follow, but he may not be awake in time to stem the crazed orders of that madman occupying that particularly powerful office. General Collins will have his hands full if he has only the air cover of our very limited Sea Harriers. Now I have to go and tell Collins that good news." Durnsford paused and then eyed his friend closely. "Tell me the crew of that bloody ship is ready and that Commodore Freemantle can do the job."

"He'll be meeting with us, General Collins, and Admiral Everett. I think that question has to be put forth by you, my friend. Freemantle will know the true gravity of the situation then."

"Why will he meet with the Americans?"

"Because the commodore needs to look in the eyes of the men that will be responsible for allowing him the time to get the *Lee* in the air, and once it is there to make sure his one-way trip is not for nothing. Also because he needs to see two Americans that don't give a good goddamn who he is or what his reputation for being a hard-ass is."

Jack had toured the storage areas for the equipment and logistics needed by the two airborne divisions and inspected armor in place at the dispersed location where the Army Corps of Engineers had dug out emplacements for the Panzer division. Without maneuvers, his men were as ready as they would ever be. He and Everett, who said his assault teams would never be prepared enough for their mission, sat and waited for an important meet and greet with the commander of the HMS *Garrison Lee*. Jack turned to his friend.

"You're going with your men, aren't you?"

Everett smiled and then looked at Jack from across the table. He knew before the meeting what was going to brought up between his friend and himself.

"I can't let them go out there without me, Jack, just like you're going to place your ass on the line up there when the time comes. I'm taking Ryan with me, if that makes you feel better. The little bastard gave me those hurt puppy-dog eyes when he learned I'm going. Besides, the commander can keep me company on that flying death trap they named after our friend. Can you see Lee right now if he knew what the name was on the fantail of that crate?"

Jack snorted laughter at the thought. Garrison Lee would have screamed bloody murder over the honor and then limped up a scaffold and personally scratched his name from the fantail.

"I clandestinely took a picture of the name and secretly used Europa to send it to Alice." He looked away for a brief moment. "I think she'll get a kick out of seeing it."

Carl removed his wristwatch and looked at it. He then offered it to Jack.

"Look, if it makes you feel better, go ahead and keep it for me until I get back."

Again Jack laughed lightly. "No, as Henri said, time paradox and all of that Isaac Asimov crap. Just bring it back in one piece, swabby."

Everett looked at the watch and then slid it back over his thick wrist. "I'll do what I can to do just that, General."

At that moment a lone figure strolled through the door and Jack recognized him immediately. He had first met the man at Aberdeen Proving Ground, where he had been a guest instructor on the theory of astrophysics, and then a second time at a NATO conference on the interaction between naval forces and army special operations. The sudden recognition explained why Carl Everett was doing the mission he had been assigned. This man's pet theory was that Special Forces combined with naval tactics could achieve more by stealth and audacity than a large-scale invasion. Jack Collins despised the arrogant British naval man like no other allied officer he had ever met.

"Oh, crap," Jack said under his breath as Lord Commodore Percy Freemantle, the Third Lord of Sussex, entered the room. Jack and Carl stood up.

The tall, thin figure took in the two American officers, then stepped to a chair and placed his bag on the top of the table. Without looking at either officer standing at attention, he sat.

"At ease, gentlemen, at ease." The commodore opened his briefcase and pulled out some papers.

With a worrisome sideways glance at each other Jack and Carl sat.

They studied the blond-haired graduate of Her Majesty's Royal Naval Academy, a man who had graduated number one in his class; who would look down upon Jack for finishing third in his West Point class, and definitely down upon Carl for finishing tenth in his at Annapolis. He was dressed in the new blue computer-designed print camouflage BDU, which looked quite out of place on the prim and proper naval genius, but still enough of a difference that Jack and Carl simultaneously noticed their own wet and filthy white camouflage that had already seen better days.

"I want you gentlemen to know, in the interest of being honest, and *my* nature of full disclosure, I was against your appointments to your current duties." The commodore didn't show the professional courtesy of even looking up from the paperwork he was perusing. "General Collins, I know that you are a capable officer, but your duties away from the army of your country has . . . well . . . let us just say you may be a little rusty. And that fact, coupled with your limited knowledge of large-scale defensive tactics, *I* believe is a hindrance to giving me the time to get my ship off the ground." He finally looked up at Jack to see his reaction. There was none. The commodore smiled at something only he was privy to.

Carl looked at Collins, who sat stoically and silent. Everett raised his brows and waited for the insults to his appointment to commence. The commodore returned to his papers, making Carl think he wasn't important enough to address. He was wrong.

"Admiral Everett," Freemantle said, and to Everett the word *admiral* sounded as if the commodore had just taken a large bite out of a shit sandwich. "I am so disappointed that Lord Durnsford chose a political appointee over my suggestion for an SAS regimental combat team to achieve the goal of gaining access to the power replenishment vessel." He looked up at Carl. "The impact of this decision, in my humble opinion, could lead to disaster."

The two men exchanged glances and then smirks as the commodore continued his reading. *Or acting job,* Jack thought, *if you would prefer that description.*

The double doors opened and an SAS commando stepped inside. He looked at the occupants of the room.

Jack and Carl stood as a line of Gray captives entered with only pants covering their disjointedly backward-working legs. All five had black bags over their heads and were shackled together. The line of Grays was flanked by heavily armed SAS men who had their short and compact Heckler & Koch HK-417 automatic assault weapons at the ready. The Grays were ruthlessly shoved into the meeting room. Everett and Collins relaxed while Commodore Freemantle never even turned. The captives were followed by Lord Durnsford and Sir Darcy Bennett, who strolled in as casually as you please. The Grays were made to sit on the cold floor along the wall. Several of them hissed and snapped underneath their hoods.

"I see you gentlemen are getting acquainted?" Lord Durnsford sat at the head of the table while Sir Darcy remained standing, looking at the captive Grays with distaste.

"Yes, I was just telling the general and admiral what a pleasure it is to be to working with them. I am truly excited about our chances."

"Please, Percy, cut the crap, I know you a little too well." Lord Durnsford shook his head. "General Collins, Admiral Everett, Commodore Freemantle is the right choice for the command of the HMS *Garrison Lee*, but his manners and professionalism are at most times called into question." He looked at the commodore, who only smiled up at him. "Even Her Royal Majesty thinks he is a bloody pain in the bum."

"Thank you, Harrison, a better introduction could not have been written more profoundly by myself."

"Time is short and I wanted to meet with you gentlemen and wish you luck. Your timetables have been advanced, hopefully before the Grays make their initial move. We now know, thanks to your little friend in the desert"—he looked and Jack and Carl—"that the Grays are going to seek the protection of the far side of the moon, thinking we cannot get at them from here. That is the reason for the attack on the International Space Station. We plan on surprising them."

The Grays in the corner started hissing and kicking out with their legs, as if they understood what Lord Durnsford was saying. Sir Darcy stepped back next to one of the SAS guards.

"We have brought these creatures in for your benefit, Percy"—Durnsford eyed the naval man closely—"to show you what will be inside every city, every village, and every home if you fail. I hope your arrogance doesn't cloud over the fact that you have one hell of a lot of people on this planet depending on you."

"There is no more capable man in the service of Her Majesty, I assure you of—"

A member of the SAS suddenly burst through the doors and handed Sir Darcy a slip of paper. The small man grimaced and then handed Lord Durnsford the message.

"Gentlemen, the time for demonstration is at an end. You must now go to your commands. It seems our enemy is moving far faster than we thought. A dimensional wormhole has been seen developing in space, two thousand miles above the surface, on the dark side of the moon. Good luck, my friends."

Jack and Carl stood, but Collins hesitated a moment as he eyed Lord Freemantle as he quickly gathered his papers. He then looked at the SAS men gathering their captives.

"Lord Durnsford?" Jack said.

"Yes, General?"

"Were these prisoners meant for anything other than demonstration purposes for the sake of the commodore?"

"No, as a matter of fact."

Without saying another word Jack paced the twenty steps to the now standing and struggling Grays. He quickly pulled out his holstered nine millimeter and before the SAS guards could react, shot each Gray in the head, dropping them to the floor, and then fired three more times into the hearts of the hard-to-kill prisoners. An SAS soldier started to reach for Collins's weapon, but Durnsford stopped him.

Jack Collins holstered the Beretta and then faced Commodore Freemantle.

"That's what you can expect, Commodore—ruthlessness." He took a step toward the shocked naval genius who had never fired a shot in anger in his entire career. "Now, are you up to the task?" Jack joined Everett and they both walked out to the smiles of Lord Durnsford and Darcy.

"Damn, Jack," Carl said as they both bounded down the steps.

PART FOUR

INVASION

War is Hell.

—**William T. Sherman**

17

The dimensional wormhole formed out of the thin upper atmosphere. The powerful event was tracked by weather satellites the world over and immediately reported to their corresponding stations.

Europa was the first system to know what the wavering displacement of atmosphere meant, and the first system to announce the dimensional rift to the command and control element at Camp Alamo.

The first line of defense put into action was the vanguard of missiles hidden away inside five different communication satellites that had been decommissioned five years before and then refurbished by the European Space Agency, under the guise of saving the platforms from a decaying and thus dangerous orbit.

Twenty 100-megaton warheads were targeted at the mouth of the dimensional rift that started the initial forming of the wormhole. As the first saucer exploded out of the tunnel-like tornado in the upper atmosphere, ten of the warheads, in anticipation of the appearance, detonated after launch from two hundred and fifty nautical miles above the Earth.

The resulting heat wave in space knocked the first small attack ship backward, where it collided with the next two, which in turn exploded, taking out six more of the attackers. The next ten warheads caught the second formation as they made the initial entrance into Earth's atmosphere. The first missile was a direct hit, disintegrating the saucer, and then the rest of the missiles detonated in quick succession, destroying no less than sixteen of the attackers. The violence was recorded from a KH-11 operated by the Pentagon. This information flashed across the screens inside the situation room far beneath the E-Ring of the Pentagon where several officials watched, including the acting president of the United States.

THE PENTAGON
WASHINGTON, D.C.

Acting President Giles Camden was far more comfortable with the replacement staff of military men that he trusted. He had worked closely with these men in his time on the Senate Armed Services Committee and they had been extremely loyal to the House Speaker beyond those days. After all, the new president had made most of them a hefty sum of money geared toward their retirement.

The president watched from the upper tier through the thick glass as the men and women below went about their duties tracking the forming dimensional rift. He felt the eyes on him from below as the soldiers, sailors, and airmen waited for him to give the orders that they expected for him to issue. On the big board, a three-dimensional map of the world, the 7th Fleet-Asiatic Squadron was still conducting rescue operations with the Chinese navy. Camden had come to terms with the admiral commanding that particular task force and through the offices of his new chairman of the Joint Chiefs had even managed to make him look good, as it was reported that the president had sent the large force in to assist their friends in their time of need. Some of the press had accepted and reported that it was a brilliant and gracious move on his part, but others, more than he cared to admit, felt the president was only trying to save face after a major policy blowup with his military chiefs.

He stood with his hands behind his back as the White House official photographer snapped picture after picture, depicting the commander-in-chief in complete charge of the situation. When the photographer was finished instructions were given that the images should immediately be sent out to the AP and Reuters news agencies as soon as possible in an attempt to get his latest and dismal approval ratings up.

Daniel Peachtree entered the situation room and went to the president's side.

"The president is awake," was all he said. Camden tensed.

"I need the attorney general and the chief justice brought here immediately. I want the truth about the laws regarding that man retaking power and I want it now."

"I've already done that. They're enroute."

"What progress on the asset in Nevada?"

"The FBI has basically refused to enter the grounds of a federal installation unless a legal warrant signed by a federal judge is issued. Until then we are helpless. But I did find out that they may be in the process of moving our boy to another location."

"I need . . ." Camden caught himself as he saw Peachtree flinch at his loud voice. He mentally forced himself to be calm. "I need that thing now. Is there any hope the asset will return to where our people are waiting?"

"I am a firm believer they will take him to what they think is a bigger secret than their own complex, Chato's Crawl."

"This is not just about me hanging onto this damn office any longer; it's about going to jail. Now get it done," he hissed.

Peachtree went to his chair that was situated around the long, oval conference table.

Camden relaxed and looked at the situation in Antarctica. The two battle groups were still moving away from the continent and would soon be too far away to assist in the defense of Camp Alamo and whatever project had been hidden from him.

"Sir, the first saucers have exited the rift and are approaching the south pole at a high rate of speed," an airman said as he read the sit-rep coming from Space Command three floors up. "McMurdo Station, Antarctica, is requesting assistance." The young Air Force officer looked at the president's back.

If the president had been facing his new subordinates inside the military arm, he would have seen them shift in their chairs uncomfortably when he remained silent. Finally he turned and faced the communications officer.

"Inform McMurdo that the situation is currently being evaluated, and assistance will be forthcoming."

"Sir?" the airman said with his pen poised above his pad.

"Send it, son."

"Yes, sir."

The new chief of the Joint Chiefs looked at his Air Force commander and frowned. They might owe Camden for their sudden rise to power, but it was tearing their guts out not going to the aid of American forces calling for assistance. Lefferts nodded for the Air Force commander to meet him out in the hallway and they were soon joined by the Marine Corps commandant.

President Giles Camden never noticed that a few of his rats were considering jumping ship.

WALTER REED NATIONAL MILITARY
MEDICAL CENTER
BETHESDA, MARYLAND

The door to Niles's hospital room burst open and without ceremony a civilian-attired Maxwell Caulfield entered pushing a wheelchair. Virginia—who had been speaking with her boss and relaying the bad news about the early attack by the Grays that was currently in progress—almost peed herself as the general threw back the sheet and blanket covering Compton's battered body. He tossed the director a pair of glasses he had absconded with from his personal belongings that had been recovered from his quarters at the ruins of Camp David.

"Mr. Director, we've been ordered to attend an emergency meeting, now!" The general assisted Niles up, careful not to hurt his broken left leg and his shattered right arm. Virginia, meanwhile, placed the director's replacement glasses onto his heavily bandaged face. "The chief justice and the attorney general are already there, along with the directors of the FBI, the CIA, and the rest of my staff."

"A meeting with whom, may I ask?" Niles weakly asked as he was carefully lifted by the large Marine into the waiting wheelchair.

"We are going right down the hallway. When the president calls, we act. Now hang on!"

Caulfield turned Niles and out the door they went with the president's Secret Service detail clearing the way. The entire hospital was abuzz with relief as the news quickly spread that the commander-in-chief was awake and talking his head off with the assistance of his first lady. Secret Service and capital police were busy wheeling large television monitors and communications equipment into the president's hospital suite. They even saw the president's two young daughters carry armloads of bottled water inside.

The political war was also just beginning.

CAMP ALAMO
ANTARCTICA

Jack almost slammed into Sarah and Anya just as the action station alarms started blaring their warning. She was on her way to his quarters as he and Everett had sprinted to get to their stations. They both stopped and, out of breath, couldn't say anything at first. Collins looked at Carl as he quickly kissed Anya and then pushed her at arm's length.

"Gotta go, baby," he said and then kissed her again. Then he quickly turned to Jack and Sarah.

"Take care, McIntire." He then faced his friend and held out his hand. Sarah quickly pecked him on the cheek and then backed off. "Jack, tell Will—hell, just tell him something." Carl took the general's hand and briskly shook. "See ya, ground pounder!" With that Everett jumped upon a speeding tram. Before Jack could say anything his friend was gone.

Anya quickly slapped Collins on the chest, giving him a quick and soldierly good-bye, and then turned and watched the tram with Carl inside disappear downward into the tunnels.

"Short Stuff, get to your bunker and keep your ass down." He quickly kissed Sarah and then held her a moment.

"I love you, Jack," she said, loud enough to be heard over the blaring horns.

He smiled and then before Sarah realized it, he was gone.

Anya turned back and took Sarah's hand, then started pulling her away in the opposite direction they had been told to go when the shit hit the fan.

"The bunkers are in that direction!" Sarah said.

"I don't know about you, but I'm a soldier and I intend to die out there, not in this frozen icebox."

Sarah started sprinting. "I knew I liked you, and thought Carl couldn't do any better."

The two women sprinted for the SAS arms locker that Anya had accidentally stolen the key to.

Admiral Everett met up with his team at the main elevator leading down into Poseidon's Nest. As they traveled downward he saw the young face of the SEAL he had chewed out at the Johnson Space Center. His face was now clean-shaven and he looked even younger than he did four days ago. Carl winked at the boy of twenty.

"Ready, son?"

"Not at all, sir!" he said loudly as the others laughed—SEALs and Delta together.

"Now you're a SEAL!" Everett said as he slapped the boy on the back.

The view from above was one of organized confusion as yard workers started cutting the fifty-six enormous ten-ton braces that held the battleship upright when the British engineers had freed her from 700 million years' worth of ice. Scaffolding was being cut with acetylene torches and was falling free to crash onto the frozen seabed. Fuel specialists scrambled to load the full complement of liquid nitrogen into her vast tanks and live ordance was being loaded by giant cranes to feed the large 70- and 105-millimeter rail guns. Yardmen were quickly tearing away the tent structure they had erected for the installation of the alien power plant that had been seated inside a ten-foot-thick wall of titanium alloy to protect it from enemy cannon fire. The workers knew that the alien-designed engine had yet to be tested but didn't really care, as their yard supervisors urged them on with their destruction of the support systems.

Commodore Freemantle stopped and turned as the doors for the elevator opened. He faced Lord Durnsford and Sir Darcy Bennett.

"Good luck, Percy, old man," Sir Darcy said.

Lord Durnsford held out his beefy hand to a man he had very little love for but respected immensely. "Look, I know we've had our differences, old boy," Freemantle said, "but I wonder if you'll do me a favor. I was caught off guard and forgot to say good-bye to my wife. She frets ever so much."

Lord Durnsford realized the man before him was saying good-bye in the only way he could. He nodded his head and then shook his hand. Freemantle smiled and then saluted the two men. Then he turned and hurried to the upper gangway.

The two men stepped out on the elevated platform

and watched the 4,000-man crew scramble aboard. Lord Durnsford glanced up toward the area where the engineers had tunneled out four square miles of tundra and frozen seawater and then filled it in again with a pattern of much thinner and well-disguised ice.

"I hope Niles Compton was right about our General Collins."

"All we need is an hour, one bloody hour." Sir Darcy Bennett stepped by Lord Durnsford and entered the elevator.

With one last look at the enormous battleship, Durnsford joined his friend inside the lift. The last view they had was of the American SEAL and Delta teams hurriedly loading their special gift from the government of Israel.

MCMURDO STATION
ANTARCTICA

The twenty-five saucers streaked low over the frozen earth as they hit the speed of sound after their dive from a hundred and fifty miles up. They flew in a *V* formation as the powerful attack ships blew snow and ice in their wide path toward Camp Alamo, a location they had discovered while tracking the Super Galaxies two days before.

As the first attack craft breached the coast, the lead saucer broke formation and sped toward the one base in the direct line of communication to the Alamo: McMurdo weather station. As men, women, and weather observers ran for hollowed-out bunkers, the saucer struck. Its rapid-fire cannon burst from the lower dome at the center of the ship and stitched a pattern that tore the 100-year-old base to shreds. The insulated metal buildings rocked and then burst into flames as the powerful laser cannon did its deadly job.

When it was finished the saucer didn't even slow down. It jumped back to altitude and reformed at the rear of the assault flight.

The twenty-five saucers were now on a direct line of attack to Camp Alamo.

Admiral Jim Sampson sat on the admiral's flag bridge, drinking a cup of coffee when the captain of "Big George" handed him a message. The commander of the carrier watched the admiral's reaction as he read the note. He looked at the captain and set his cup of coffee in its holder on the arm of the large chair.

"Now?" he asked.

"Yes, sir, he's on the command phone." The captain was pleased to see the blood drain from the man's face. "The message relaying the time has been decoded and authenticated as coming from National Command Authority. It is the president." He removed the heavy phone from its cradle and held it out to the admiral, who then took a deep breath and reached for the instrument.

"Admiral Sampson," he said into the phone. The captain, standing by the admiral's chair, could hear everything because he had turned the volume to full before handing the phone over.

"Admiral, do you recognize my voice?"

"Yes, sir, Mr. President."

"Glad to hear it," came the tired but firm words. "Admiral, it seems you backed the wrong goddamned horse in this particular race."

"I was following orders from the commander-in-chief, sir, I would never have—"

"I don't buy that just-following-orders crap, Admiral, and you know that. Now turn those two groups around immediately and steam at flank speed for the coast of Antarctica. Assist the ground element on station in the defense of American and allied lives. Is that clear, sir?"

"Yes—"

He was speaking into a dead instrument.

A short time later, the *George Washington* Battle Group, with the USS *John C. Stennis* Group in tow, made a dramatic full-speed course change to the south.

CAMP ALAMO
ANTARCTICA

The first three advance scouts crossed the outer markers without any defense being thrown at them. The scouts slowed to subsonic speed as they came low. One stopped to take heat emanation readings while the other two sped ahead.

The entrenched men of the 82nd Airborne observed but did not report, as per their orders from General Collins. They were to report only when the main element arrived. It was tempting to send the battery of TOW missiles toward the slow-moving targets, but the men realized they would have plenty of saucers in their laps soon enough.

The advance element of Airborne waited.

The three saucers rose in height and hovered, waiting. The hidden 23rd Panzer Division was targeting these ships but had no orders to fire. The same went for the fifty emplaced and well-disguised M-109-A12 Paladin Self-Propelled Artillery. The specially modified Paladins had recently been redesigned and had their 155 Howitzers replaced with M-9780-A2 Standard Rail Guns, the exact same weaponry that had completely gutted the saucer that had attacked the Russian missile cruiser in the South Atlantic. The trick would be for the saucers to slow down enough for the geopositioning targeting systems to function correctly.

Collins was watching with his staff in a specially prepared bunker two miles from Overlord. He watched the close-looped monitoring system and saw the three saucers just silently hovering near the exact center where Poseidon's

Nest lay. It was excruciating waiting for the real assault to begin. It was the silence before the storm that precedes every major battle, and Jack Collins knew the game well—it was knowing when to make the other guy flinch.

Colonel Henri Farbeaux was monitoring the technician that watched the advance BQPP-7 special radar system built to pick up the barest minimum trace of a stealthy aircraft by reading trace elements of the environment—in this case, snow and ice as it was disturbed by a speeding aircraft from almost any altitude. The Frenchman watched the scope intently as he was unprepared to die in this frozen hell.

The Air Force technician, a volunteer from Edwards Air Force Base and now a part of the general's staff, pointed to his scope silently. He looked up at Henri and nodded his head.

"We have contact, General," Farbeaux said confidently as he patted the airman on the back.

"Positive contact?" Will Mendenhall asked.

"Unless a flight of giant pterodactyls just flew over the warning line," he said as Henri placed his web gear on and then charged a round into his nine millimeter handgun, "I think the enemy has arrived."

Tram and Major Krell did likewise and made ready to evacuate the general when and if it were called for. Will Mendenhall stayed close to the phones and radios to relay the orders as the situation dictated. Collins leaned forward and studied the twelve battlefield monitors at his disposal.

"Inform Alamo and Poseidon's Nest, we have incoming."

Will relayed the information and then swallowed, wondering how in the hell everyone could be so cool. But as he looked at the many faces inside the command bunker he saw the same fear in their eyes as his own.

The radio monitored by 101st Airborne personnel sprang to life. "Incoming, seventeen ships behind the first scouts, crossing into zone 1187," came the excited voice.

Jack calmly looked into the appropriate monitor and saw the snow being churned up before he saw the saucers. The three scouts remained in their hover. Collins nodded and Will responded as calmly as he could with the radio.

"Fire Team Bravo Five, take out the scouts. Fire at will!"

Six TOW missiles streaked into the air from two different hidden locations as fire teams from the 101st opened fire.

The wire-guided weapons made a beeline for the saucer at the forefront of the hovering vehicles. The first three struck its metal body and knocked it sideways, but it quickly recovered—just not before the second set of three hit it. This time the saucer dipped and dug its nose into the snow and ice. It came to rest just as thirty more TOW missiles broke free from camouflaged positions. Missiles struck the two still in place as at least five missed altogether. The alien craft now reacted and streaked toward the line of fire, firing their laser cannon as they went. Carefully prepared positions started to explode in a hail of ice and snow as men and equipment were blown apart.

"Eighteen saucers on the scope." Henri turned to face Jack.

"All positions, open fire, fire at will!" Collins said, a little louder than he had intended.

All hell broke loose as the Paladins opened fire. The rail guns were the only thing visible as the mobile weapons system moved far enough forward to uncover their twin-barreled batteries.

"Order the 23rd to scatter and confuse!" Collins calmly commanded as he watched his orders being carried out.

Mendenhall shouted into the radio and Jack looked at him and mouthed the word *calmly.* Will immediately lowered his voice. Tram, after loading his old M-14 American-made rifle, smiled as his adrenaline started pumping as fast as the young captain's.

"We have ground movement from the first downed saucer," Major Krell said as he watched on the perimeter monitor.

Jack watched as the 23rd Panzers broke cover with their armored bodies breaking free of the camouflage netting and snow. It was a magnificent sight as the large main German battle tanks opened fire even before they were free of the earth they had been buried in. They immediately scattered to try and make the saucers spread out their fire to protect the troops on the ground. Collins switched views and then saw at least fifty Grays breaking free of the downed saucer.

"What are you waiting for, Major?" Jack said to a stunned Krell as the German officer saw the Grays for the first time. He quickly snapped out of his trance and then grabbed the radio and the map.

"Victor Seven, Victor Seven, we need you at . . ." He looked at the premarked map for his grid designated points. "Coordinates 27-89. Fire for effect!"

The line of buried 155 Howitzers of the 82nd Airborne fired all twenty of their large guns at once. The heavy shells arced into the sky and came down directly on top of the slow-moving Grays as they attempted to get away from the small-arms fire from the entrenched infantry to their sides and rear. The ground around the twenty survivors erupted in a hell storm of shrapnel as the Grays were engulfed with fire and death. When the wind blew the smoke away there was nothing left but a large hole in the ground.

The Paladins were taking their toll. The remaining two scout ships had succumbed to the twin rail guns' rapid rate of fire. The two vehicles lay in pieces as the radios were crackling to life with the sound of targeting requests coming in.

Several of the attacking enemy broke free as they started becoming more coordinated in finding their own targets. Laser cannon erupted and several of the expensive Paladins exploded deep in their revetments.

Calls from calm but determined groups of Airborne began to get more frequent as the enemy started stitching the frozen world with far more accurate fire. Men started to break cover, running from one protected position to the other.

Jack looked at the Frenchman and nodded that it was time. In the din caused by the loud discharge of the rail guns and artillery, Farbeaux made the call to the orbiting British Sea Harriers.

"Eagle flight, Sentinel. I repeat, Sentinel," he said matter-of-factly into his headset.

The American Airborne troops wanted to cheer out loud as the British air arm made its dramatic appearance in the skies over Camp Alamo. Missile after missile struck the saucers from above as they attacked the maneuvering tanks and Paladins, not realizing they were being hunted from the air they thought they had under control.

The enemy recovered quickly as even the first of the downed craft began healing faster than the defense was led to believe they could. The damaged craft slowly spun up into the air. It was like a shooting gallery where the little ducks kept getting up. Collins didn't know how long his forces could hold out against such technology.

Mayday calls began streaming in as the Sea Harriers were starting to succumb to the rapid-fire lasers of the enemy. Smoking ruins marked the grave sites of the Royal Navy aviators as they rode their antiquated birds into the ground. Vapor trails and missiles along with cannon fire filled the blue sky as dogfights broke out and then quickly ended for the Harriers as their Sidewinders and AMRAAM missiles had little effect against the advanced technology of the Grays.

The enemy had quickly regained control of the skies around Camp Alamo and was now free to stalk and kill the fast-maneuvering Panzers and the men they were there to protect.

General Collins ordered both the 82nd and the 101st to use their TOW missiles and then break for the fall back positions code-named DiMaggio.

Henri Farbeaux called into his radio as Will helped Lieutenant Tram and a young airman start to gather their gear.

"All units, DiMaggio. I repeat, DiMaggio!"

The defense had now retreated to only a mile from Poseidon's Nest.

* * *

Everett secured the weapons next to the arms locker in the assault team's ready room, where his men hurriedly started dressing in the layered plastic suits that would protect them in the hard environment of space. Carl followed suit. He started with the blue long johns and that was covered by an ultrathin layer of chest armor made from Kevlar and other dense carbon fibers. Then the suit itself: the nylon-based clothing was not much different from the atmospheric suits the shuttle astronauts wore, but were far more lightweight in nature. He placed the oversized boots on and then zipped them up, but left the combat gloves dangling by hooks from his wrists. He checked his thirty-man team and saw that they had completed their dressing in far less time. He checked them one at a time.

Carl then ran to the forward bulkhead to check the status screen of his area of responsibility and saw that all of his personnel were accounted for. Along with the assault element, his weapons specialists would wait until the giant battleship gained the unrestricted confines of space before arming the fifteen nuclear devices supplied by the Israeli government.

The warning alarms were silenced from the outside but the red blinking call to stations was still active throughout the ship. Everett turned and ordered his men to strap in to the Velcro-secured stations where the team would ride the initial flight into space, braced by nylon and canvas straps. He made sure all were secured, starting with the ingress team who would be the first to enter the assault craft. He examined his men as they were lined up against the forward bulkhead like tin soldiers. He made sure each was holding their helmets and they would stay that way until ordered by the ship's crew to don the expensive acrylic 360° vision visors for takeoff.

When he was finished he turned and ran for the automatic bulkhead doors that remained open until the ship's captain called for all doors and hatches to be closed a minute before launch. His feet were sticking to the deck as his boots were designed with microfiber Velcro that adhered to the same hook-style fabric that clung to the soles of his boots like a cocklebur to a sock. The admiral ran through the companionway until he reached the large launch tubes that were the home to the two assault craft that would be used to take his men to their assignments. The six-man crew of each was going through their final checklists and the Air Force pilots were doing it rapidly. The great warship started to shudder as the alien power plant was brought online for the first time.

Every man in visual range stopped as their hair came up as static electricity coursed through them from the decks and bullheads. A swirling sense of dizziness struck every one of the four thousand crewmen and all to a man or woman wondered if that was a normal thing—and no one really knew the answer.

The shuttle bay was wedged into the girder system of the main decking superstructure and looked out of place. It was nothing more than two separate pressure chambers that were not part of the original Martian design. As Carl crossed the connecting ramp he saw that if he missed a handhold he would tumble more than a thousand feet down to the cave's bottom that was fast being evacuated far below. He ran across the connecting bridge and saw Jenks struggling with the main engine bell of one of the shuttles. A large chuck of ice from above was wedged into the housing as he started kicking at it. Carl wondered if the crazed bastard knew that he was actually dangling a quarter mile above an abyss. As he started to say something the chunk of ice fell free and Jenks turned and ran for the safety of the girders that held his two shuttles secured. Everett reached out and grabbed the master chief by the arm and pulled him through to safety.

"What in the hell are you doing?" Carl screamed over the powerful noises coming from three hundred feet aft as the six main engines came to life. The ion-based technology was the reason for the electrical discharge that had coursed through the vessel.

"That goddamn vibration from the battle above is

knocking ice from the tunnel down onto everything. I warned the damned limeys about it. I told them they have to erect shielding, but the pansy-asses think they know everything!"

"Well, don't you think once this thing starts rising with all of those thrusters out there it will melt anything that isn't steel and composite material, you old goat?"

Jenks stopped and the looked as if he were considering the monumental thought that Carl just passed on. He unzipped his shoulder pocket on his coverall and popped the stub of a cigar into his mouth, then shook his head.

"No, I didn't think of that," he said as an angered admiral pulled him back into the companionway. He resisted and then told Carl to be on his way, that he was going to ride the rocket from his place in the number one shuttle. He said he felt safer there.

"Okay, you stupid bastard." Everett held out his hand. "I'll see you up there!"

The two men quickly shook hands and then Jenks smiled and tossed his cigar out through the extensive steel girders that made up the ship's superstructure.

"Watch your ass, Toad, my boy." He vanished into the raised doorway of shuttle number one. As the door closed Everett saw that someone had painted a name across the shuttle's heat-reduction tiles: *Virginia*. Carl shook his head, realizing that the master chief was still carrying a torch for the assistant director of Department 5656 from their time together in Brazil.

"Hey, I know I'm only excess baggage on this little cruise, but don't you think you better get back to your station?"

Carl looked at the next shuttle station where Jason Ryan was hanging out of the doorway like a small monkey.

"I ordered you to the command bridge with Captain Lienanov where you might be useful, you little pain in the ass!"

"Borrrring," Ryan said as he acted the insulted commander.

"You better hope this ship blows up and we're all killed, because . . . because—"

"Go get 'em, Admiral." Ryan quickly ducked back into assault shuttle number two.

Everett cursed and then had to laugh as he ran back across the connecting bridge to the relative safety of the pressure hull. The second officer called over the loudspeaker from the sixteen-story bridge high above.

"Defensive force has fallen back to the DiMaggio line, enemy penetration is imminent. All personnel secure for launch sequence. Security detail standby on the main deck to repel borders until final countdown begins. All hands, man your launch stations."

"Repel borders?" Carl said to himself over the noise surrounding the ship as her ion engines were at station keeping.

"All hands standby, commence charging boosters."

Everett knew that was the last resort as the electrical connection was made to all one hundred and twenty dry chemical booster rockets attached to the *Lee*'s outer hull, along the massive girders that made up her main deck.

"Oh, shit," he cursed. The rumble and clanging of steel restraint started in earnest as the full weight of the battleship came down on the remaining support structures keeping the *Lee* upright. Everett realized that gravity was starting to take effect on the 125,000-ton structure.

"All hands, final warning: secure all decks for launch in ten minutes. Defensive command reports Gray penetration of safety zone is under way. Defensive line DiMaggio has been compromised."

"Damn it, Jack, get the hell out of there!" Carl spat out the words just as he reached his launch station on the uppermost deck, which was the most exposed area of the *Lee*. As Everett strapped himself in next to his men, he could see clearly outside as men hustled from her decks. He and his men would have the best view as the colossal battleship rocketed into the sky.

* * *

On the upper command bridge, Commodore Freemantle looked over at his new aide, a man who had virtually no training on bridge operations but might come in handy if he lost immediate communication with his command technicians monitoring and operating all the shipboard functions thirty feet below. Freemantle strapped himself in the upright position and braced with a steel station so he could remain standing at all times during launch and battle.

He examined the Royal Navy seamen below and was pleased with the calm approach they had during the most stressful event of their young lives. They called out shipboard status of all thirty-two decks. Freemantle knew that the HMS *Garrison Lee* was launching light, meaning to say the ship was carrying a minimum of food, water, and other necessities needed for an extended stay in space. Freemantle and the planners had figured the great battleship could only last less than an hour from launch to assault. Their job was to give the Americans time to reach the power refurbishment saucer.

"Rather exciting, isn't it, Captain Lienanov?"

Lienanov stood next to the Englishman, in awe of what he was seeing through the large plates of thick, triple-paned glass that made up the bridge windows. Black Hawk and Gazelle helicopters buzzed like small bugs in and out of view above the *Lee*'s wide decks.

"Strap yourself in, Captain." Freemantle saw that the Russian was frozen in wonder at the events he was now a part of.

"'Exciting' wasn't the word my limited English would have chosen, Commodore." Lienanov sat in his plastic chair and pulled the triple harness over his head and snapped it into place.

Next to him Freemantle laughed heartily as the pressure of the past four years bled away as the moment approached. His number one, feet sticking to the material-covered decking, stood rigid next to Freemantle and held out a flimsy.

"Flash message from the States, sir." The first officer held firm to the railing lining the upper battle bridge.

"Read it please, Number One." The commodore watched the activity outside the large windows. He reached over and made sure his helmet was nearby and then faced his first officer.

" 'The hope of the world rides with you, good luck,' signed, the prime minister."

"Rather nice of the old boy. Now enter the message into the ship's log, Mr. Jennings, and take your station."

"There is one more, sir, a warning from NASA. The United States Space Command and the European Space Agency have long-range telemetry showing the invasion fleet is now moving away from the dark side of the moon. Course is plotted and confirmed; they're on their way here. Estimated time of arrival is twenty-five minutes."

"Bloody cheeky bastards, aren't they? Not waiting and hiding. Well, let's give them what for, shall we?"

"Yes, sir!" the first officer answered. He momentarily stood at attention, then quickly moved away to his launch station.

"All hands, prepare for launch, five minutes until power-up. The DiMaggio line is in full retreat."

The commodore heard the announcement sent from his communications center and then grimaced and was mumbling to himself, but Captain Lienanov overheard nonetheless.

"I must apologize personally to General Collins, he gave me ten minutes longer than I needed or expected." Commodore Fremantle lowered his head. "Good show, old man."

Jack had watched his command being mowed down one unit at a time and knew that over a quarter of his men lay dying in the snow and ice. The German Panzers had finally been decimated as they fought to give the 101st and 82nd Airborne time to break from their defensive positions on the DiMaggio line and head for the deep shelters that had been designated for complete withdrawal. It had been hard for Collins to have the order issued.

"General, it's time for you to go." Will Mendenhall thrust

Jack's web gear into his arms. "We'll get the rest out, now go, your Black Hawk won't last long out there. We just received a message; we have over a hundred Super Hornets heading in from the *Washington* and *Stennis* Battle Groups. Go, General."

Collins nodded for Farbeaux and the others to get to the Black Hawk. Sebastian and Tram gathered their gear but refused to move until the general came with them; he was now their responsibility. Jack locked eyes with the Frenchman as he eyed the young captain.

"General, a ground attack force of Grays, over a thousand strong, is heading straight here and are only three minutes out."

"Okay, get out," he said to the young 101st Airborne communications man.

The soldier looked at Mendenhall and the Frenchman. "I'll stay, sir."

Henri removed the nine millimeter and chambered a round, then holstered the weapon. He looked from Collins to the young black man he had never cared for. Now he knew the reason why: he never liked the perception of lacking in dedication to his craft, as he saw from the young officer studying him. He nodded at Will and then turned back to Jack as laser blasts started shaking loose ice from the last control bunker still operating.

"I'll be staying as well, General," the Frenchman said, to the amazement of Mendenhall and a stunned General Collins.

"It's not your style, Henri," Jack said as he was starting to be pulled away by the remainder of his staff to get him to leave. He angrily pulled away.

"It once was, Jack, now kiss little Sarah for me." He picked up the radio to prepare to make the call that would call down death from above.

Jack turned to Will and stuck out his hand. "The best damn soldier I've ever known. So long, Will." He dropped the offered hand and hugged the young captain.

"Sir," Mendenhall said, knowing that anything else

would be pointless. He had to give the general time to leave. "Kick Ryan in the ass for me."

"Damn you, Captain, I should have left you at home." Jack Collins released Will and took a step back.

Mendenhall smiled and looked back at Henri, who had turned away and was leaning heavily on the desk where the radio sat.

"You know I wouldn't have accepted that. Now go, and when you get home, tell Doc Ellenshaw to keep swinging away, the rest of the world will catch up to him eventually." Will smiled and then looked at Farbeaux. "You know, Jack, he's not Ryan, or the rest of my friends, but I could go out with a far worse soldier."

Jack nodded, unable to say the words he so wanted to say to a friend, so he turned and left. He ran hard toward the waiting Black Hawk as if the running would stop the feeling of utter despair.

Will zipped up his parka and then faced Farbeaux and the 101st Airborne lieutenant. He then removed his own automatic and chambered a round, then nodded to Henri, who raised the microphone to his lips as the sound of the Black Hawk started moving away. Jack was safe for the moment to fight again. The Frenchman waited until Collins and his team were clear and the Grays thought the line was still holding the defense. He made the call.

"St. Bernard, St. Bernard, this is Raven's Wing, this is Raven's Wing. Broken Arrow, I repeat, Broken Arrow," Henri called and then gently placed the radio down. "I don't know about you gentlemen, but I would prefer to be outside in the fresh air."

Will nodded in total agreement with the man he had hated for many years, who was now going to be with him for a very long time.

"After you, Colonel—sir."

Jack looked out of the Black Hawk's large door window as Tram and Sebastian lowered their heads in shame for leaving the three men behind. They knew it was a necessity to delay the Grays as long as possible to bring them into the killing zone, but that didn't make the two professional soldiers hurt any less.

As Jack Collins watched, over a thousand Grays surrounded the last remaining bunker on the DiMaggio fallback position just as the roar of the attacking air wings of the United States Navy was heard four miles distant. Then the world exploded right over the top of his friends.

18

As the last Black Hawk fought for altitude, a hundred streaks of blue and green laser light lit the skies around it. The army warrant officer pulled hard right on the stick and brought the large helicopter almost to a stall position to avoid a line of tracer-like cannon fire. They were being bracketed by not only five of the remaining twenty saucers but also the surviving Grays of the ground assault.

U.S. Navy Hornets buzzed the battlefield in an effort to engage the enemy, but the saucers were much too fast to get missile-lock. The naval aviators finally started using their twenty-millimeter cannon to engage at close range. Their goal was to protect the remains of the German infantry element left stranded by the destruction of their own shield of burning Panzers. The two airborne units had climbed aboard anything that was still operational when the orders had been given from the command-and-control bunker to break for the designated deep shelters prepared months in advance of the attack. For the first time since Operation Market-Garden during the air assault and invasion of Holland in World War II, did the two American airborne divisions actually leave a battlefield in the hands of an enemy. The soldiers of the 101st and 82nd did not like what was happening.

The retreating soldiers set up pockets of rearguard action and fired TOW missiles from the backs of Humvees and Bradley Fighting Vehicles; they struck mostly air as the wire-guided weapons flew past the speeding saucers. The Gray reinforcements on the ground were paying a heavy toll for every foot of ground they took as missile after missile struck among their ranks. Heavy-caliber weaponry fired by the rearguard sent thousands upon thousands of tracer rounds into the saucers and the Grays on the ground. The effect was chilling to behold as the airborne units and the German infantry fought for all they were worth. Bradleys opened up with their Bushmaster weapons and started mowing down the Grays as they advanced, with each armored transport succumbing eventually to enemy hand-held laser fire. The mechanized monsters Jack remembered from the Peruvian mines made their appearance as they rolled free of the saucers and then broke into their original forms and started deliberately walking toward Poseidon's Nest. Their arms were extended and heavy-caliber kinetic weaponry opened up in all directions as the enemy advance continued.

The command Black Hawk swooped low over the retreating units as the men inside wanted desperately to join them.

Jack slammed his hand into the glass of the window as he saw three Bradleys explode simultaneously below.

Four more of the saucers had landed at the spot where the command bunker used to sit and thousands of Grays and their automatons ran down the metal ramps. It was like watching ants emptying a hill.

The American and German forces had been completely overrun and were now just trying to survive.

The Black Hawk pilot slammed the stick to the left as a line of cannon fire hit her four-bladed rotor. The helicopter shook but remained in the air and the pilot cursed as he brought the army bird directly over Poseidon's Nest.

* * *

The three tons of charges had been placed when the false
ceiling of the three hundred tons of camouflaging ice had
been frozen over by the U.S. Army and Royal Corps of Engineers years before in anticipation of the *Lee*'s breakout of
Poseidon's Nest. The loud warning blasts of horns could be
heard throughout Camp Alamo and Poseidon's Nest and every man and woman braced for one of the largest explosions ever detonated by man over an occupied zone.

"All camp personnel brace for shock wave," came the
automated announcement that echoed off the ice walls of
the now-deserted hangar.

Carl and his men looked at one another and most felt as
if they would never reach the IP position for their assault to
take place. The men in the two squads had set their odds
of the *Lee* making it into the air as 75–1. Everett had not
wanted to place his money on the outcome because the odds
he had figured were far worse.

Inside the hangar the sound of the powerful ion engines
pulsed with the power of the alien power plant. Blue-colored
venting started to flare from her six thirty-five-foot-in-
diameter bell housings at the stern of the battleship. The
paint marking the name *Garrison Lee,* stenciled on the fifty-
foot fantail, started to peel and fly away from the tremendous
heat being generated from the giant engines. Plastic wire-ties
left by the workers flared and melted away, and even a scaffolding left by the yard started to melt like ice cream in the
summer sun until it fell like melting wax to the frozen
ground beneath the last of the support struts, and even these
enormous pieces of steel started glowing red hot as the engine exhaust became too much, even with the six engines at
idle.

The HMS *Garrison Lee* was as ready as she ever would
be as she shook in her red-hot mountings with the power of
the Martian technology flowing through her structural lines.

"Ceiling detonation in ten, nine, eight, seven . . . ,"

Carl braced himself for the impact that would be caused
by one hundred tons of hardened ice striking the ship as the

man-made roof opened to the sky. He hoped the Martians
knew what they were doing in their design of the large battlewagon.

The Black Hawk took another direct hit on the tail boom
and the rear rotor barely hung on after ten feet of aluminum
housing tore free.

Suddenly the world seemed to go silent. The illusion
could be attested to by men caught in the opening moments
of an artillery barrage as the mind played a protecting trick
on the body. It was if the world slowed down so the human
reaction could spark movement in the speedy detonation
around them.

The Black Hawk vanished in a hail of shattered ice as the
false roof of Poseidon's Nest exploded upward. Four square
miles of ice and snow disappeared in a millisecond as
the explosives were electronically detonated by computer.

The passengers and crew were thrown against the sound-
reducing roof of the helicopter as the impact first lifted
and then flipped her onto her side, and then the Black Hawk
rolled over upside down. Her tail boom was ripped completely free of her main body and the five-bladed rotors
were sheared away by one-ton blocks of ice that were
thrown into the sky like Styrofoam. The helicopter spun in
a dizzying circle as she fell from the sky in flames and falling ice.

Everett closed his eyes as the impact started beating a horrible sound against the *Lee*'s superstructure as the millions
of tons of ice fell free and onto the decks of the warship. The
giant battleship shook and was nearly pushed from her remaining support beams as she righted herself and then
shook even more as five delayed charges exploded against
her superstructure. When the shaking and battering stopped
and the *Lee* ceased her frightening roll, Carl chanced a look
onto the upper deck of the battleship to see falling blocks of
ice striking the ship with terrifying loudness. The view that
he had was amazing and horrifying at the same time, even

as several of his assault team members shouted their approval at the adrenaline-producing scene.

Everett's eyes widened when he saw amongst the falling ice, the dark shape of something his brain didn't recognize at first. Then he realized it was the damaged main section of a Black Hawk. It struck the deck and then bounced, stopping only when it was inundated with falling ice from above. Carl immediately released his harness and sprinted for the emergency hatch only feet away. The opening would lead him toward the deck and superstructure beyond. The two Special Forces lieutenants had seen the same thing as the admiral and also unsnapped their harnesses and ran after Carl, finding it hard to lift their feet against the grip of the Velcro flooring. They admonished the rest of the men to stay put as several of them attempted to follow.

Everett ignored the hatch-open warning and even the yelling from the engineering section on the bridge to secure the hatch. He finally managed to break the hard seal and he was nearly crushed as ice continued to fall. He covered his head, cursing himself for not bringing his helmet as he was joined by the two team leaders. They dodged and ran along the laced girder superstructure that made up the forward decking just aft of the giant deflector plow. The Black Hawk was starting to burn as it was wedged into the sharpened rear of the immense plow.

"Check the other side!" he yelled as he ran for the shattered door of the upside-down helicopter. Ice fell and warning alarms once more sounded inside the immense cave.

"Booster ignition in two minutes," came the announcement that eerily echoed and bounced off the ice walls three hundred feet away.

The three men struggled getting both sets of sliding doors open. Finally Everett smashed the Plexiglas and slid inside, careful not to puncture or slice his environmental suit. He bounced down inside the upside-down compartment. He landed on at least two men. The two team leaders could not get the wedged-in door open and couldn't reach the glass window because of the immensity of the deflector plow. They ran to Carl's side and helped him lift the first live passenger out. It was a small man, to the relief of the Delta and SEAL as they roughly pulled the man free.

Lieutenant Tram was seriously hurt from a bleeding head wound as the Delta lieutenant threw him over his shoulder and ran for the open hatch thirty feet away, still dodging the falling ice.

Everett checked the next man after discovering the two pilots dead in the seats. He rolled the large body over and saw that it was Major Krell. His blank and staring eyes told the admiral the major was dead. This gave him a start as he realized both men were a part of Jack's command staff.

"Jack!" Everett yelled as the countdown outside started at exactly at one minute.

Finally Everett found Collins lying underneath their field gear and rolled him over. His head was bleeding from several large gashes and he looked as if he were having difficulty breathing.

"Oh no, you don't—not here, not now!" he shouted into Collins's face as the big SEAL lifted him free from the debris. He practically tossed Jack through the broken window and didn't wait to see if anyone caught him as he too scrambled free of the Black Hawk.

"Booster ignition in thirty seconds," the computerized voice stated.

Carl quickly ran for the fast-retreating Delta lieutenant, who had the heavy general in a fireman's carry as he made for the hatchway. Carl wasn't far behind.

Helping hands took Jack and placed him on the deck. Then the men quickly strapped themselves in. Everett and the Delta lieutenant threw themselves on top of the two unconscious men and braced them as best they could. Several of the assault team reached out with their legs and slammed their booted feet down across the two men and the rescued passengers to assist in holding them down.

"Three, two, one, ignition."

Outside the pressure hull a tremendous explosion rocked the *Garrison Lee* as one hundred and fifty solid fuel boosters flared to life at once. The *Lee* shook and then rocked in her cradle as the giant battleship dangerously rolled to starboard as the synchronization of the igniting rocket port boosters was off by 2.3 milliseconds. The men hung on as the *Lee* bounced several times, crushing the remaining support beams holding her in place.

Flames erupted all along the central line of midsection of the battleship as she strained against gravity to rise. On the command bridge the officers and men were being shaken as if a 12.0 earthquake had erupted under the ship.

"Gimbal main drive engines one to six to maximum down angle," Commodore Freemantle said calmly into his headset and mic. "Maneuvering thrusters 150 degrees down angle, full power, gentlemen. Let's see if the Martians knew how to fly!" That command was the only excitement they had ever heard from their stoic commander.

The added thrust of *Lee*'s six main engines coupled with her maneuvering jets pushed the *Garrison Lee* into a slow climb.

The power of the booster and the main engines melted ten million gallons of ice lining Poseidon's Nest, instantaneously inundating the superstructure with a wall of water.

The *Lee* rose like a slow-moving airship as her boosters lifted her clear of her remaining support beams. As it did the thrust melted even these.

Still the enormous battleship rose majestically skyward as embedded cameras broadcast the images to the world as major networks were ordered from every capital on the planet to break in.

The HMS *Garrison Lee* broke through the remaining ice that clung tenaciously to the sides of the tunnel walls. Melting ice fell like Niagara as her engines burned and scorched steel support beams holding the walls intact, and still she rose.

The battleship shook and rocked as her bulk finally cleared the opening. Two of the hovering saucers were hit hard and bounced away as the *Lee* blasted into the open with brilliant sparkles of sunlight illuminating the thirty tons of ice crystals whose luminescence was excited by the combination of heat and color as the engines exploded her into the clear.

The world watched in awe as Operation Overlord became active and the *Garrison Lee* rose faster and faster into the brilliant blue sky, incinerating thousands of attacking Grays on the snow-covered ground.

The Earth trembled at the hybrid mix of Martian and Earth technology, and the idea advanced by a small alien in Arizona became reality.

Operation Overlord was going on the attack.

WALTER REED NATIONAL MILITARY MEDICAL
CENTER
BETHESDA, MARYLAND

The president was propped up in bed. His eyes were both blackened and his head was still bandaged. Both arms had been broken and the casts were being held up by nylon lines that kept a tight traction on the arms and shoulders. The first lady was standing next to her husband and as they watched the *Garrison Lee* rise into the air, the water glass she was holding slowly tilted forward and water inundated the commander-in-chief. He didn't notice as his lips were moving but nothing was coming out of his mouth.

Niles Compton was at the foot of his friend's bed and Max Caulfield and Virginia Pollock were at each of the handles of the wheelchair, watching in awed silence as the scene from Antarctica was played out before them and six billion other citizens of the world. In an instant the military expenditures incurred by the major contributors to Overlord immediately explained the enormous bill for the project as every advanced technology made by every nation on Earth was utilized in the discovery, excavation, reverse engineering, and repair of the Martian technology that was 700 million years old.

It was two of the six Secret Service agents who voiced the hopes of the world as they simultaneously screamed encouragement as the stirring sight unfolded before them.

"Go, go, go!" they shouted, ignoring the flinching people around them.

Finally the man who had just awakened from a coma less than three hours before joined the men in their enthusiasm. He tried to swing his arms but only succeeded in knocking the rest of the water glass being held by his wife onto his head and he still didn't notice; neither did the first lady.

As the *Lee* rose higher and higher, a chase plane from the USS *John C. Stennis,* an old Grumman A-6 Intruder, had to turn sharply out of the path of the largest object to ever move on land, sea, or air, but her cameras kept rolling. It was Niles Compton who saw the carnage on the ground as the Intruder's cameras caught the scene as she straightened and accidentally showed a panoramic view of the battlefield beneath the *Garrison Lee.* He looked at the view of devastation as hundreds of burning and smashed armored vehicles were clearly seen below. Men of the 101st and 82nd Airborne and the German 23rd Panzer divisions were lying dead across the scorched field of ice. Aircraft from the Royal Navy and the remains of Hornets from the *Washington* and *Stennis* aircraft carriers were crushed and in flames where their sliced and smashed aluminum frames had impacted the ice.

Niles lowered his bandaged head as he realized it was his plan that had sent so many men and women to their deaths. Max Caulfield, ever the general who cared for his men, had seen the same devastation as Compton, and Virginia allowed her tears to flow for the first time without wiping them away. Niles was only seeing, within his deepest soul, the smiling faces of the friends he had sent into harm's way—friends who could never be replaced. Caulfield squeezed Compton's undamaged shoulder in sympathy because he knew exactly how the director felt. Virginia Pollock could no longer stay in the room and turned and left.

On the television screen the *Lee* burst through the thick-ened cumulus clouds and vanished.

THE PENTAGON
WASHINGTON, D.C.

Acting President Giles Camden realized that many of the soldiers who owed their allegiance to him were the loudest of all the officers in the situation room. He turned as the British-christened warship reached the sky and the cheers inside the room erupted in earnest. For show the president waved his official photographer over by whipping his head around. The man raised the camera and started taking shots as he stood on his high perch and placed his hands over his head and clasped them together and shook them like a prize fighter after a KO.

Daniel Peachtree watched the show put on by the presi-dent and knew that somehow he was to be blamed because the grand experiment had succeeded when he said it would fail and Camden had gone with his advice.

The military men who had been in the acting president's camp earlier in the day were now stunned at the exhibition being put on by a man they knew had wished Overlord to fail; who had insisted it wasn't real in the first place. As for Peachtree, he wanted to throttle the man because he wasn't watching the rats leaving a sinking ship, he was ac-tually pushing them off himself. It didn't take long for many of the enlisted personnel to see the man above them behind the glass and they slowly lost their enthusiasm for cheering. Finally Peachtree stood and moved to the front and acted as if he were studying the situation boards. Since the awakening of the real commander-in-chief, not only had the two battle groups changed course and assisted in the battle in Antarctica, the *Nimitz* Battle Group in the Arabian Sea was steaming at flank speed toward the Indian coast. The man having his picture taken had yet to realize that he was no longer in charge. As he stepped to the glass he spoke out of the side of his mouth to get the fool to acknowledge the reality of what was happening.

"The president is giving orders from Walter Reed, if you hadn't noticed."

Camden nodded at the photographer and then turned around. "I am well aware of that, and that is why I have had you summon the chief justice and the attorney general."

"Well, they're meeting with *a* president, but it's not you. My men tell me they're currently inside the president's suite of rooms, more than likely telling him the procedures for getting you out of his office."

Camden lost a lot of the bravado he had been feeling just a moment before.

"Either that or he's asking for arrest warrants for a few men that seem to have been at odds with their oaths of office."

"What are you saying?"

Peachtree wanted to turn and shake the fool out of his dreamlike slowness. Finally he turned and faced him directly as many eyes turned their way.

"This is not about hanging onto power any longer, it's about what prison they send us to after that power is yanked right out of your hands. We have to stop everything right now and put an end to . . ." he stopped for a moment and lowered his voice to a hard whisper, "Recall the Black Team and immediately eliminate Vickers—he's the only one that has more than just innuendo and rumor on us. He has knowledge that can hang both of us, and not just about technology buying and selling. Other things."

"Well, we had already decided that, so what?" Camden said, still not fully grasping the situation. "When he goes, the problem goes."

Peachtree gave up and walked out of the situation room.

The moment he was outside in the grassy area between the E ring and the glass doors of the D, he pulled his cell phone out and hit one number.

"Yes?" came the cold voice.

"Mission cancelled. Eliminate the problem that you have currently in your possession."

"It looked like the asset wasn't going to utilize this out-of-the-way facility anyway, and the other problem is right in front of me at the moment."

"Also, after you finish, lay low for a while, a long while. Your payment has been deposited in your regular account."

Peachtree didn't wait for a response. He closed the cell phone and then looked over at the two Marines standing guard by the glass doors. For some strange reason it seemed as if the two men knew what sort of man he had become, like they could see his very thoughts. He decided that he would return to his office and await the fate that had been destined for him since he first threw in with the likes of the former Speaker of the House.

This particular rat was on the gunnels of the ship and he was seriously thinking about jumping.

CAMP ALAMO
ANTARCTICA

Poseidon's Nest was now completely destroyed. The HMS *Garrison Lee* and her powerful booster rockets, coupled with her ion drive engines, had completely melted the entirety of the ancient inland sea. As the command group, Sir Darcy Bennett, admirals Kinkaid and Huffington, and Lord Durnsford watched from monitors inside the defense zone created by the SAS, the tremendous heat had caused the largest cave-in in world history. Water heated by the ion drive had created waterfalls that cascaded back into the light green, blue, and white void that once was the birthplace of the *Lee*.

All eyes went to the surface cameras and they knew immediately that the Grays had not taken too kindly to their destruction of their landing force and were even now landing two of their saucers to eliminate any further threat from the site. Camp Alamo, however, was buried so deep not even their powerful lasing systems could strike at them.

"Well, gentlemen, it seems our little secret is out and the landlord has come to evict us." Lord Durnsford stood from his chair and walked closer to the nearest monitor. "How far out is the remaining Royal and U.S. Marine force from the *George Washington* and the *Stennis*?"

Admiral Kinkaid looked at his watch and then frowned. It was Huffington who answered.

"It seems we will be getting our hands dirty before they arrive."

"Oh, Lord," Sir Darcy said as he too stood and watched the embedded monitors that showed the battlefield high above their heads. "There are men still alive out there."

As all eyes went to the many screens around the command center they saw boys being rounded up by the advancing Grays. Men no older than these gentlemen's grandsons were being pushed and prodded toward the waiting saucers as thousands of Grays were rounding up the survivors of General Collins's defensive forces, and from what they could see there were far more survivors than the men ever thought possible.

"Can we help those men?" Darcy asked as he sadly looked on.

"With a thousand SAS personnel, old boy, we can't even defend ourselves," Lord Durnsford said as he watched the horrible spectacle before him. "We will have to arm every technician, doctor, yard worker, cook, and kitchen personnel that we can find to delay the enemy long enough until help arrives. Which, I'm afraid, could be long on promise and short on delivery."

"What the bloody hell," Admiral Huffington said as he pointed to the screen. "What force is that?"

All eyes again turned to the screen. It was impossible but a force of at least two hundred men were actually advancing on the Grays, who were too intent on rounding up the survivors that they hadn't noticed the spider traps that the SAS had installed weeks and months before. The trapdoors were open and men were streaming from the interiors and firing on the surprised force of Grays. With the two enemy vehicles on the ground the human element advanced quickly as they laid down a withering fire. They were soon joined by the surviving armored personnel carriers once thought destroyed but obviously had made it out before the crushing "Broken Arrow" attack by the U.S. Navy. Also at least three to four hundred of the battered 82nd and 101st Airborne troops and also men dressed in tank gear and German support troops were also among the hastily formed and very mixed composite regiment trying to save their brethren from being taken like broken cattle back to the waiting saucers. At least twenty of the German- and American-made vehicles were on a rapid advance to cover the fire team that had been hastily organized by someone inside Camp Alamo.

"Look, General Collins has saved his attack helicopters!"

Long streaks of Hellfire missiles arched into the ranks of the Gray rear guard. Explosions wrecked their loading ramps as once more the Gray ground element had been caught off guard by the combined strength of over thirty attacking AH-69 Apache Longbow gunships and more than fifteen Gazelles of the British Army. Hellfire antitank missiles were joined by twenty-millimeter chain guns of the Apaches and the thirty-caliber weapons of the fast Gazelles as they joined together against the attacking Grays, to devastating effect.

"Good show, Jack, old man," Lord Durnsford said under his breath as he leaned in to better view the attack. Suddenly an inspiring thought entered the old master spy's head. He turned to the two admirals. "Gentlemen, as they say we must not look a gift horse in the mouth. This is the time that courses and outcomes of battle are made. Admiral Huffington, order every man, woman, and whoever else you can, get them with our SAS boys and get them out there. We either defend from the ground or die like rats inside here, and unlike our German foe Herr Hitler, I don't intend to go out that way! We owe it to General Collins at the very least."

Huffington sprang to action as did Kinkaid, and for the first time the two men didn't argue an order as they came to the same conclusions as Durnsford.

"Shall we get our best winter clothing on and join those men, Darcy?"

"By all means. I would very much like to meet the person responsible for getting a force together so quickly while we sat here and predicted our demise."

"Then, after you, old man."

Sarah McIntire had sat and watched Jack's entire force be decimated on the surface during the defense of Camp Alamo. She had felt sorry for herself for all of ten minutes and then her eyes settled on the men, women, technicians, shipyard workers, and extra military personnel who had no orders for what to do after the *Lee* had been launched. She saw the frightened eyes and knew they couldn't just set here and wait to die. She knew she had at least three thousand able-bodied personnel that would rather be outside fighting than in here waiting on the Grays to dig them out. She stood and so did Anya Korvesky after coming to the same conclusion.

"We have fifty arms lockers right out there. Now you can either sit in here and wait on those ugly fuckers to come and get you, or we can get out there and help those boys that gave us the time to do our jobs."

The eyes looked at her from benches; mouths that had been whispering in hushed tones were now closed. It was a burly welder from the shipyard who stood and looked at the gathered personnel in the largest of the bunkers, looked at the diminutive female soldier, and decided she was right. The Englishman looked around at the men and women who had worked for years to get the prize put back together and get her launched.

"I don't relish the thought of waiting here for those ugly bastards with a bleedin' welding torch. Let's take it to them before they know what's happening!" The men and women, cooks and bakers, military computer personnel, and even the cleaning crews slowly rose and looked toward Sarah and Anya.

"The least we can do is help the survivors get back inside," Sarah said as she yelled, "This way to the armory!"

Word had spread that an attack was going to be mounted, and everyone who foresaw their deaths at the hands of the Grays decided in an instant that they would rather go out with a weapon in their hand instead of waiting for mercy from a merciless race.

Bunker after bunker had emptied out as SAS guards knew they couldn't contain the rush of humanity who charged the four armories they were to guard. Before they knew what was happening they too started issuing weapons and ammunition to the workers. The fever had spread like a virus and the carriers of this new disease were two women who now fought for men who possibly would never return.

19

Colonel Henri Farbeaux fought to get the ice and the remains of the command bunker off his body. It felt as though the very life was being squeezed from his lungs as the weight of sandbags and snow covered him from head to foot.

He had lain there for what seemed hours and it wasn't until the heat from the engines of the rising *Lee* had struck him that he realized he was still alive. He felt the earth shake and the weight of the debris press down even harder as the remains of the bunker pressed harder into his hurt body. He remembered he and the young captain had just broken free of the entrance when the lights, the air, and the world vanished around them as the attacking carrier aircraft laid waste to the command post.

Henri felt strong hands reach into the rubble and pull him ruthlessly out of the situation he was in. He wanted to curse at his rescuers for the indelicate way they were going about it when he heard the familiar hissing and cursed language of the Grays. He knew then that it wasn't friendly hands freeing him.

He was finally pulled out and thrown onto the ground, and just as he opened his eyes a long sharpened staff came down and stabbed him in the right shoulder. Farbeaux screamed as he felt the alien weapon drive deep, and then among his own scream of pain he heard a satisfying hiss of a Gray as he stood over him. Henri cursed in his native tongue and then tried to roll over and away from the assault, but the Gray grabbed him by the white, blood-soaked parka and threw him again onto his back. Before he could curse again he saw three more Grays in their purplish-colored and strangely styled clothing. The Grays were showing their faces to him as they picked him off the ground and made him stand before them. The Frenchman kept his eyes on the taller Gray that had ruthlessly tested him for life with the sharpened edge of his laser staff. Henri angrily spit out at his tormentor, wanting the animal to finish the job and quit stabbing at him like a trapped and injured fly by a mean-spirited child.

He heard a loud grunt as another captive was thrown down at his feet. It was Will Mendenhall; the boy was out cold. Henri watched as the Gray that had captured his prize also sent the spearlike tip of his strange weapon deeply into Will's leg. It produced not so much as a cry of pain.

"Bastard!" Farbeaux took a step forward and was mercilessly kicked and beaten to the ground. The assault continued for what seemed like minutes and he thought he was going to get the final coup de grâce, but the killing blow never came. Instead Henri heard a single gunshot and when he managed to look up he saw the three remaining Grays kicking and punching at the young captain, who had curled up in a tight ball to protect himself for the brutal blows. The smoking nine millimeter was lying a few feet away and Farbeaux had to admire the kid for getting at least one of the brutal bastards before they fell on him. Will's victim was on its knees, still breathing and looking dumbfounded with a nice clean bullet hole in the center of his chest. Mendenhall must have hit at least one of the Gray's two hearts because as the Frenchman watched the alien just simply rolled over and then fell face-first dead into the snow. Its sickly greenish-purple blood stained the burnt and crusty snow around it. The beating of Will came to a stop as the three Grays hissed and spat. One raised the laser staff and took aim at the now unconscious kid. Henri rolled over and placed his body over Will's. He was also pummeled but not shot. When the beating was done he was again lifted to his feet.

Henri realized that his right leg was broken and at least four ribs felt as if they had been snapped in two. He had never felt such pain in his life and thought the same as the captain that it was better to go his way than being slowly beaten to death. But as he looked around he saw other survivors of the battle, boys no older than Will being revived and pushed toward two saucers that hovered only feet off the snow and ice. Like Mumbai and Beijing they were being herded together and marched to a waiting butchering at the leisure of their ruthless and barbaric foe. He had decided that wasn't the way his story would end, it would end the way Mendenhall's had—on his own terms, not these bastards'.

Farbeaux closed his eyes and thought for the briefest of moments of his long-dead wife, Danielle, the woman whose death had been blamed on Jack Collins for years, and he smiled, knowing that soon enough he would join her in a far better place. He also thought quickly of Sarah McIntire, the complete opposite of his wife but just as loved for no better reason than he saw a kindness to the woman he had never seen in anyone else. With those faces in front of him he charged and the first Gray raised his weapon.

The field of battle once more erupted in gunfire and explosions. Henri felt bullets whiz by his exposed head and the Gray who had just had the intention of ending his life went down in a spray of sickening blood. Once again Farbeaux hit the cold earth and rolled as more fire caught the next two captors and sent them reeling backward. Still the rounds came in a ruthless but satisfying abundance that hit everything near and far. He realized that whoever was firing had very little discipline as to who they were shooting at. He covered his head and waited for the bullets to end what the Grays had started.

He heard Will's name called in the din of battle and he managed to look up and see many hands pulling at the unconscious captain, then other hands were on him and he knew that the Grays had probably beaten whatever attackers had momentarily saved him and were back in control. He heard the missile strikes and the sound of helicopters buzz past, shouts and screams of men and women as they surrounded him. The hands that picked him up were strong and not very delicate, but he realized that the blessed hands were at least human.

"There, a little worse for wear, but still breathing," said a Cockney-laced accent as he came face-to-face with a large brutish man with a thick dark beard.

"Who in the hell are you?" Henri managed to ask of the same yard worker who had earlier echoed the commands of Sarah and Anya. The brute of a welder stared in wonder at the injured soldier before him.

"A bleedin' Frog, will wonders never cease!" the man said and then ran off.

Henri wobbled on his feet and then slowly looked around and saw the attackers were a motley mix of men and women in varying states of dress. The one thing they had in common was the arms they held and the way they used them. His eyes widened when a lab technician—a woman no older than a twenty-something punk rocker with pink and blue hair streaming from her parka's hood—kneeled only feet away and cut loose with a Heckler & Koch German assault rifle on full automatic. The weapon was spitting bullets as she lost control and sent the rounds into the snow-covered ground and then stitched a pattern that ended up going straight into the air. The woman was nonplused at her inaccuracy as she immediately sent the spent magazine flying and quickly inserted another and then recklessly charged forward.

An American Apache Longbow attack helicopter streaked low overhead and sent a pair of wire-guided Hellfire missiles straight into the open hatchway of the far left, hovering saucer.

The interior of the alien vehicle exploded outward in a hail of strange material and flying bodies, then it fell to the ground, where a loud Bushmaster twenty-millimeter cannon mounted on a surviving Bradley Fighting Vehicle slammed its large exploding rounds into the remains of the saucer.

Henri was shoved in the back and as he turned he saw none other than Sarah McIntire, wearing the white camouflage BDUs of a soldier. She was screaming at him to get down as she fired at something rushing their way. Her bullets riddled one of the shocked Grays as it charged them maniacally. The Gray hit the ground and its large body dug a path as it finally slid to a stop.

"Come on, Colonel, help us gather these men together and get them the hell back to Alamo!"

Henri was still in shock at not having his life ended, and further stunned to find out just who his rescuers were.

For a five-mile radius around the crater left by the departing *Lee,* three and half thousand civilian and military personnel were fighting for their lives as they attempted the rescue of the remains of General Collins's defensive force.

As they fought and died to save their own, a roar filled the sky high above. But before the force of civilians and military could spy the new threat their attention was forced back to the ground. Amid the explosions of Hellfire missiles and mortars they saw the attacking Grays streaming from another saucer that had landed. The rescuers were now slowly being surrounded.

And still the roar overhead continued of what could only be assumed were even more saucers coming to assist the Grays' landing force.

TWO HUNDRED AND SEVENTY NAUTICAL MILES ABOVE ANTARCTICA

The mistakes in their reverse engineering and even the technical instruction given to the engineering teams by Matchstick in the mating of the Gray power plant with the Martian-designed ion drive were readily apparent as the *Lee* gained high orbit. Fires broke out in the engine spaces as the reverse-flow generators cooling the power plant went into the red and coolant leaks sparked a blazing inferno as engineers, both civilian and naval, fought to extinguish the hell that had erupted in the tight spaces. The only way they could see to put the fires out was the use of emergency venting into open space; the vacuum would suck the inferno out of the large hatches designed just for the scenario.

The bridge was loud as technical men and women were taking emergency calls from almost every deck on the battleship. Commodore Freemantle felt the powerful ion-drive engines shut down as the *Garrison Lee* became the largest object in the history of the planet to be an out of control, floating, and spinning object in space.

Captain Lienanov unfastened his safety harness when he saw the red blinking lights coming from the engine room, six decks high and as many deep at the stern of the ship. He saw the temperature in those spaces rising rapidly as the fire alarms were tripped. He heard the frantic calls coming from those spaces and he roughly shook the commodore by the shoulder to get his attention.

Freemantle immediately placed his headphones back on, and then said into the mic, "Permission granted. Open all vents and hatches to space. Get the fires out and shut off the coolant flow to the mixing chambers, for God's sake, before they explode and take the bloody engines with it!"

"Commodore, we are also venting oxygen into space from numbers three, six, and fourteen tanks," the atmospheric officer two tiers below the main deck of the bridge called into his communications mic.

"We can't do anything about that right now—we can't spare the damage control parties to fix them. Shut down and transfer as much O_2 to the remaining tanks as you can."

"Aye, sir," the man said and then relayed the order.

Suddenly sparks flew from the maneuvering panel and the four men and two women monitoring the now shutdown maneuvering jets fell back onto the steel deck and rear consoles, their feet losing grip on the Velcro-accented station. They floated free.

"Keep your harnesses on, people, how many times did we drill for that?" Freemantle said as calmly as he could. The *Lee* shook and rumbled and was pushed thirty kilometers from her position as more alarms announced a fracture somewhere in the superstructure.

"We have hull breach!" came the voice of the damage control officer below them. As more technical support personnel floated free of their stations, Commodore Freemantle held his temper in check.

"Calmly, people, calmly, now. Shut down the hull breach alarms, Lieutenant Stevens, that is not a hull breach, it's the bloody venting ports open to space. Now please shut off that damnable noise."

The young man felt foolish as he did what he had been ordered.

The *Lee,* to the casual observer from the vantage of the Earth, was upside down, but the crew never realized it. The alarms were slowly being shut down as fires and other small emergencies were brought under control after the men and women in all departments slowly became used to zero-gravity maneuvering in the spaces throughout the ship.

"Gentlemen, I need engine status or we're going to have Grays sitting in our lap with no engines or weaponry. Radar, enemy fleet status, please?" Freemantle tried his best to be a calming influence to his crew as no men or women in the history of the world had ever faced something as traumatic as this—technology that had gone out of control with no prior testing in the ship's natural element of outer space.

"Thus far they have not rounded the moon." The radar officer and his seventeen operators adjusted set and bandwidths. "We are receiving telemetry from Sydney Station; they're bouncing a signal off of the Mars relay station. The enemy is still being screened by the moon. We are not, I repeat, not being tracked by enemy sensors at this time."

"That will change as soon as they get in direct line of sight with us." Freemantle looked over at Lienanov and winked. The captain could not believe he was on this mission in the first place, and was nervously watching men and women who really didn't know what they were doing. He released his handhold and then went to a standing chair and strapped himself in. "People," the commodore said, "I need the status on my engines. Without them we have no generators, and without the generators we have no gunnery at all. We will only have the kinetic weapons and the rail guns, and I'm afraid that will fall far short of what we need."

"Power plant is still offline, Commodore. Engineering is getting assistance from shuttle management, and he is—"

The commodore and everybody else heard the cursing over the intercom as someone below was haranguing the engineering crew to shut the magnetometers down, that they were electrically interfering with the power plant's flow of energy to the main mixing chambers. Freemantle recognized Professor Jenks immediately—who else would call his engineering officers a bunch of pussies that couldn't turn a monkey wrench?

"Commodore, we have extraneous personnel interfering with operations down here. We need to—"

Freemantle hit his transmit switch and cut off the engineering commander down below. "What you need to do at the moment is listen to the master chief. He seems to be the only one that has an idea of what to do."

"Yeah, did you hear that, you limey, snot-nosed little shit? Quit being a tattletale and get your ass over to the mainframe coupling and turn it on. I don't relish the thought of floating here and being used as fucking target practice. Now move."

In the background everyone heard the master chief as he took control. They also heard a voice remind Jenks that they were still transmitting to the bridge.

"I don't give a good goddamn who—"

The command bridge intercom was shut down when Freemantle gave a slice-across-the-throat gesture.

"I particularly do not like that man, but I must say he is one colorful . . . whatever he is," the commodore said.

"Permission to join the master chief below?" Lienanov asked.

Freemantle just nodded his head as he studied the motion control board before him. He saw that they had at least 60 percent of their monitors out as the *Lee* spun crazily out of control.

"Now gentlemen and ladies, I need my eyes back online. Can we do something about that, please?"

Carl Everett checked Jack's status as the Delta medic looked him over.

"As far as I can see, Admiral, he's got one bad concussion and maybe some glass in his side, but other than that, I think he's just out." The medic turned to Tram, who was finally sitting up and being held in place by three men as his body wanted to float away. A sergeant walked toward Tram and offered him a pair of Velcro booties to slip over his white combat boots. Everett turned his attention to the small Vietnamese sniper. Another SEAL passed him an environ suit that should fit the small officer. The suit floated in front of Tram, which caused him to get dizzy and almost vomit.

"Pretty bad down there?" He kneeled as best he could next to Tram inside the zero-gravity environment.

Tram held the Velcro boots close to his chest, pulled the clothing down into his lap, and lowered his head.

"Captain Mendenhall? The Frenchman?" Carl hesitated but asked anyway.

Tram shook his head as he finally looked into Everett's face. The admiral just patted the famed Vietnamese sniper on the shoulder and then gestured for the medic to get that head wound tended to and for others to get him and the knocked-out Collins into spacesuits.

Everett stood with his feet secured by the antigravity boots and looked out into space from the large porthole. The remains of the Black Hawk were now gone as he spied the roll of the battleship.

"Well, things don't look like they went according to plan in phase one of this operation." He looked down at Jack as he lay on the plastic deck. "We're sitting ducks out here."

Commodore Freemantle floated to the elongated damage control station and watched his people working the boards. Thus far the fires had all been extinguished without the use of mass venting, thus saving precious O_2 that they couldn't spare or replace. They had lost three of the nitrogen coolant tanks used for the enormous turret guns, and thus far they were lucky as far as deaths and injuries. Twenty-two dead and one hundred and fifty injured. For a launch that had gone off without a hitch the *Garrison Lee* soon reminded the crew how dangerous this mission was from start to finish. He realized the training they had the past four and a half years told all personnel in no uncertain terms that this was nothing more than a one-way trip to begin with. They all wanted to get at least a chance to prove to the world, and to themselves, that the *Lee* could make a difference.

"How are the repairs to the power plant? We need at least maneuvering as soon as possible. Right now we wouldn't even give the bloody Grays a fright, not spinning like this."

"Professor Jenks said it was nothing more than the arrogant bastards—sorry, sir, his words. The engineers at the Royal Institute of Technology and the techs at General Electric misinterpreting the American asset's design drawings and installing the twin plasma pumps backward. They said they didn't look right and changed the specs. It tested well, but when full power to the ion engines was engaged they backed up and shot pure plasma into the cooling system, causing the overload. They are in the process of changing out the lines now. The two plasma pumps have been taken out and reversed."

Freemantle shook his head. "Awful brave of those engineers who aren't on this little ride to change the specifications of a being with the intelligence quotient of four hundred of those bloody sots."

"Yes, sir," the female American navy motorman said. The twenty-two-year-old had been one of the first volunteers when the assignment was offered to members of the American navy.

Freemantle took hold of the handrail and pulled himself to the radar officer. "Any sign of the bastards?"

"No sign of the large power ship yet, sir. One of the small attack ships nosed over for a look-see and then vanished from the scope in a flash three minutes ago. Gave me a start, I can tell you."

"Any indication the scout saw us?"

"I don't see how he could have missed us with the spectacle we're putting on."

Freemantle had to smile at his radar officer's observation. Down the line radar personnel from the Russian, American, and British navies watched their scopes closely. Some of the sets were calibrated at differing wave bands to cover the full spectrum in order to defeat the stealthy design and materials of the alien vessels.

"Well, we have to assume they know we're here and just don't know what to make of us as of yet. That time could cost them if we get the damned power plant online," he said angrily.

"Or maybe they're just laughing too hard to come at us," the officer interjected. "I mean, they haven't had to deal with this class of ship for seven hundred million years."

Freemantle had to laugh and that broke his momentary spell of anger. He had been too long absent from the real navy and real seamen and knew they joked at the harshest of times. He nodded his head, feeling better about his crew.

His damage control officer joined him as he floated up and took a hold on the same railing, letting his feet secure themselves to the Velcro adherent on the deck.

"Mr. Jenks reports two minutes more will be needed to flush the coolant and plasma lines. He cursed me for not having the foresight to add lengths of ceramic lining to our ship's stores before takeoff." The officer looked behind him. "I think he ate all of my behind on that one, sir."

"Well, he has a point, but it wasn't your fault, lad. I'm afraid I cut what I thought were all nonessentials from the stores list. Just don't let on to the master chief, eh? So what did Jenks use for the ceramic lines?"

The officer grimaced. "He bloody well tore out the officer's zero-gravity toilets. He used the small sections of ceramic tubing, nonconductive duct tape, and aluminum foil."

Freemantle was stunned.

"He said the officers can shit themselves for getting them into this mess."

"Very well, I'll give up my toilet privileges if the damn thing will just work."

Freemantle let go of the handrail, peeled his boots from the deck, and launched himself up and over the two tiers of battle bridge technicians to grab a firm hold on the captain's station, where he came to a twirling stop. He would never admit this to his men, or even his wife—if he ever returned home that is—but he had become totally infatuated with the zero-gravity travel from one spot to the other. He settled to the deck and then strapped in. He placed his mic cord into its station and then cleared his throat.

"All hands, this is Commodore Freemantle. I have been informed that we will be testing the power plant repairs in just a few moments. Please take your stations and secure all material."

The *Garrison Lee* was still spinning crazily in a wide circle.

"What do you mean, they're just gone?" Admiral Everett said to the attack craft commander of the first shuttle.

Five men were floating free in the bay next to the two ships. The locking gear firmly held them to station but they also did not escape damage from the engine meltdown. Everett counted at least ten serious-sized holes that had to be patched on the outer docked attack ship. When three of the large booster rockets attached only a hundred feet from the shuttle bay were jettisoned, the explosive bolts holding them in place blew them off. But there had been an inordinate amount of dry chemical still left in the booster from the countdown misfire that delayed its activation, thus when the bolts exploded the rest of the fuel was redirected from the containment housing into the girder system of the superstructure. That, in turn, was vented directly to the exposed fuel lines attached to the outboard shuttle. The explosion not only knocked holes in the DuPont-designed heat tiles, but also killed the pilot and copilot of shuttle number two who were strapped into their stations nearby—another safety flaw of the hurried design.

"Commander Roberts and Lieutenant Rodriguez were blown out through the deck and into space," said the Marine pilot of the number one shuttle, Commander Emily Coghagen. The two men had been her friends and she had trained with them on Master Chief Jenks's design for the past two years.

Everett angrily kicked out at nothing, forgetting he was floating and momentarily throwing himself into a slight spin. Jason Ryan reached out and steadied his friend.

"Can you make two trips?" he asked Coghagen with little hope of a positive answer.

"Not in the time frame we'll need to get two teams inside. The first will already have found their way deep into the energy ship before we returned with the second assault element."

"So, you're short one pilot and copilot and have a damaged ship?" Ryan asked with a brightening smile.

"Forget it, Commander, you're not qualified," Everett said angrily, knowing the young aviator would pull something like that.

"Yeah, well, I wasn't qualified to land the LEM on the moon either, but guess what?"

"What in the hell is he talking about? What is a LEM, and what fucking moon?" the Marine pilot asked astounded at the claim by the cocky naval aviator. "Sir."

"Landing Excursion Module. Mr. Ryan accidentally

landed one on the moon four years ago." Everett shook his head at the astonished men floating next to the grinning Ryan.

"You see, Commander, the navy doesn't tell the corps everything it's up to—we keep some secrets to ourselves," Ryan said as he returned his attention to Carl. "Now, either you think you can blow that thing up with one assault element, or you allow me to at least try to get your second team over to the opposite side. I'll even take that asshole friend of yours along to show me the way of things. I'm sure those engine room boys would love for Jenks to get the hell off their ship anyway."

Everett looked at his watch for no other reason than to see the time, because in reality he didn't even know if they could get the *Lee* back into action long enough to find the power ship.

Ryan was watching, no longer concerned with his request as he noticed the thick blood clinging to the admiral's watch. Without even asking he knew it was the blood of Jack Collins and everything he had learned about the British find came flooding back. He swallowed but refused to point that out to Everett.

"Okay." Carl turned to the Marine commander and her copilot. "You have until launch time to get this asshole up to speed on the fly-by-wire control system of that bird, and you make him understand it and understand it good." He turned to face Ryan. "Pay attention and no smart-ass comments or observations, is that clear, mister?"

Ryan nodded, smiling at last, letting the vision of the blood-covered watch go for the moment.

"Great." Coghagen looked from the admiral to a cocky Ryan. "No matter if he understands something or not, he'll say he does. I know these carrier jocks."

"She's got you pegged already, flyboy."

"I love you too, Admiral." Jason blew the retreating form of Everett good-bye. Ryan soon lost his smile as he turned to face the commander. "Let's get to it."

The Marine Corps pilot saw the sudden change in Ryan's

demeanor as soon as the admiral was out of sight. Gone was the man she had seen moments before; now Jason Ryan was all business.

She had no way of knowing that Ryan had just sworn to himself to try and change the destiny the Event Group, Matchstick, and the planners for Overlord had in store for him. Even if it cost him his life, Admiral Everett, his friend, would not die in the Earth's ancient past if he could help it.

Ryan entered the damaged shuttle without another word.

"I want the drone launched immediately; I have to know the disposition of the enemy ships. How many are they, what does their fleet consist of, where are the processing vessels? And most importantly, the number of attack ships protecting the power distribution craft. As soon as the computers are up and propulsion systems restored I want that probe on the way. We're not getting telemetry from the Earth stations since their jamming started."

"Probe is ready and in the launch tube, Commodore."

The lieutenant in charge of torpedo tubes 1–18 answered the commodore from his computer station. Jenks walked behind the kid and slapped him hard on the back. "Son, you take that system off-line while we try to crank this ion pump up; if she blows again it'll take your torpedo tubes up with it. So safe all your weapons, is that clear?"

"Clear, Master Chief," the young Royal Navy officer said, just grateful the master chief didn't yell at him the way he had the commodore earlier when asked for the status of the ion drive.

"Good boy, now all hands strap in." Jenks paused. "Ah, hell, hide behind something and take those damn Velcro boots off or you'll break your ankles if we start venting again. Just hang onto your ass or the guy's next to you. Everyone, helmets on." The master chief and once proud professor looked at the Royal Navy female ensign standing next to him and raised his brows. "You stay by me, doll face. Okay, let's start the music, sound the warning alarm, and tell the bridge we're tryin' her now."

The alarm echoed through all eighteen decks of the *Garrison Lee*. Silent prayers were said and men and women closed their eyes as they waited for the loud sound of rushing coolant, and prayed that the new lines didn't leak into the plasma containment tanks.

"Tell the computer to start, son, she ain't going to do it without you."

The propulsion officer swallowed and turned the switch, thus allowing the computer system to take over.

A loud whoosh sounded in the engine spaces as the coolant flow shot into the lines. Everyone cringed and then waited for the lines to back up into the plasma generator again, but this time the lights all turned green. One by one the plasma containment indicators switched on in the slowest manner possible. All twenty indicator lights were now in the green, or safe mode. Coolant was heard pumping through the lines at a rapid rate.

Master Chief Jenks closed his eyes and pursed his lips, surprised his jerry-rigging was successful. The propulsion officer sitting at his console watched as the power plant was now receiving the required amount of coolant and she slowly came online one system at a time.

"You did it, Master Chief, she's up!"

Captain Lienanov, who had been hastily assigned to watch the plasma tanks for escalating pressure buildup, turned and echoed the officer's words.

Jenks opened his eyes after his silent prayer and then looked at the computer showing full power had been restored. He raised the glass visor in his helmet and then stuck the stub of a dead cigar in his mouth, much to the horror of the safety officer, then turned to the men he thought of now as his people.

"Of course it is, what do you think it was gonna do, you bunch of—" The master chief looked at the young female ensign and then thought better of what he was going to call the men in the engine room. "Well, of course it works!" he said instead.

Jenks floated over to the intercom and slammed a beefy

fisted glove into the switch. He removed the stub out from his mouth.

"Bridge, engine room. Full power restored. Now you have maneuvering capability, but don't go slammin' her into the moon or anything!"

Commodore Freemantle stood at his station and shook his head at the very unprofessional man he had in charge in the engine spaces. But he was thankful the gruff old engineer was there.

"Starboard maneuvering watch, fire jets one, five, and eight. Stern, reverse thrust of jets twelve and eighteen."

The commands went without comment as the silent roll of the *Garrison Lee* started to slow.

"Port jets twenty, twenty-four, and fifty-one, fire now!" he said, overly excited to get the command out.

"She's stabilizing, sir," the helmsman called out. "Roll has slowed, slowing . . . stopped."

"All jets cease burn. Helm, please give control back to the navigation computer for station keeping. Now torpedo room, launch my drone."

"Drone away."

On the one-hundred-foot view screen the commodore saw the small torpedo-shaped drone shoot out just aft of the deflector plow. The probe fired her booster engines and shot around the moon.

"Launch relay drone."

Soon the first pilotless information-gathering drone shot free of the *Lee,* only this one stopped at seven hundred miles above the moon and still in visual range of the battleship. There it fired its automated breaking jets and came to a complete stop. She waited there to receive the information the first Black Bird drone sent back. Then it would relay the telemetry to the *Garrison Lee.*

The bridge personnel waited silently for what the drone would tell them they were facing.

"First images coming in," the intelligence officer called from her station.

Freemantle and the rest of the bridge leaned forward as far as their safety harnesses would allow and watched the screen closely.

"Oh, Lord," said one of the younger radar officers.

"Stow that, sailor," Freemantle said, though he too was stunned at the first image.

There were at least a thousand smaller attack saucers sitting in formation, six rows deep. The computer was rapidly counting and printing their type on the large screen. The message wasn't good. Sitting on the outer rim of protecting attack craft were at least ten of the processing ships. They were at minimum the same size as the two that struck Mumbai and Beijing. Then in the exact center was the power-producing and transfer ship that would feed the invasion force the resupply of energy they would need to take on the lacking defenses of Earth's military power.

An attack saucer broke formation and shot toward the probe. The little missile stayed in place and kept broadcasting as long as it could, and that was only a few seconds as the bridge crew saw a bright flash of light and the telemetry being sent to the relay went dark. But before it did they all saw the fleet of enemy warships start their advance.

"Number One, I would like to address the crew at this time, please," Freemantle said as he straightened up as best he could.

"Aye, sir, one MC is active."

"All hands, man battle stations," Freemantle said calmly. "All sixteen-inch gun turrets, charge your particle canisters and energize your Argon systems. Ladies and gentlemen, the battle we trained for these past four years is now upon us. We must destroy as much of this fleet as possible to give the boys time to destroy their only power ship. Assault element, man your attack ships. Good luck, Admiral Everett."

Throughout the HMS *Garrison Lee,* men and women tensed for the first outer space battle in history, and as most of them thought, the shortest and possibly the only battle.

The *Lee* turned to starboard, exposing all of her sixteen-inch laser cannon toward the curvature of the moon, waiting to discharge a full broadside into the first saucers that showed themselves.

Not since the end of World War II was a battleship more prepared for offensive action with naval gunfire.

Carl Everett looked Jack over as he sat up and winced at his broken ribs. He tried desperately to clear his eyes as the announcement was made about the testing of the power plant. He was finally able to focus on the face in front of him. As he tried to speak he felt sick as he started to float up into the air. Everett reached out and pulled him back down.

"I thought that letting you float away would be faster than explaining to you where you were at." Carl smirked and then realized the last thing his friend had seen on the surface was more than likely his command being blown to pieces, and the death of Will Mendenhall. "I'm sorry about your command, Jack." He looked over at Tram, who was sitting next to the now-spacesuited general. "And about Will."

Jack Collins was still dazed, but not quite enough not to feel the pang of guilt over how he had failed. And now there was no telling what was happening below on the surface.

"Camp . . ." He swallowed and tried again, "Camp Alamo?" Tram handed him a Mylar bag of Dr. Pepper and he took it as his eyes searched Everett's face.

"No word. Hell, we just got this big bitch back under control, thanks to the master chief." Carl had heard the coolant pumps engage just a moment before.

Collins took a drink of the sharp-tasting liquid, coughed, and then drank again. He handed the empty bag back to Tram. He reached out and squeezed the boy's shoulder. "The rest of the staff?"

Tram lowered his head and then started to clean the old M-14 rifle once again. The gift he had received from Jack in South America had never been out of his sight. Luckily when the Black Hawk went down he had it strapped to his back.

"Sebastian and the others are dead, Jack."

Collins leaned back as he held firm to one of the many canvas straps that hung from the bulkhead.

Suddenly the feel of movement was pushed throughout the ship as the *Lee* started to control her roll.

"We're headed for one hell of a gunfight in just a few minutes, buddy. I have to go. You and Tram take the number two lift to deck six, and then take the tram to the forward spaces nearest the escape pods. That's the safest place on board, right by the plow. Thicker steel."

Jack started to say something in protest, but Carl shook his head. "Not this time, pal, it's my turn. You and your men have done enough." He looked at the Vietnamese lieutenant. "Tram, you take command of the staff of General Collins, and if things go bad get him off the ship. That's an order, you understand?"

Even Tram hesitated, making Everett shake his head. He then turned to an SAS military security man.

"Sergeant, you take these two men to the escape pod. You'll know real fast if this attack goes south, so get them the hell out. The general's flag is being transferred."

The SAS sergeant came to attention and nodded.

"Sorry, Jack, but the fight's in the navy's corner now." He peeled his feet off the floor, pushed off, and floated through the open hatch to the shuttle bay without the slightest hesitation. Collins knew he couldn't say good-bye like he wanted to in front of the men around him.

The two assault teams of Delta and SEALs moved off with a nod of thanks to Jack for giving them a shot at their jobs. The last man by was the young SEAL who had recently shaved his beard. He smiled. "Thank you, General."

Jack watched the young SEAL sail through the hatch, knowing every man on that detail knew they wouldn't have the time to get back to the shuttles before the detonations of the warheads turned them to nothing more than light particles.

Throughout the *Garrison Lee* every person onboard felt

the ion-drive engines come to life just as the announcement from the commodore sounded through the loudspeakers.

And General Jack Collins never felt so helpless in his life.

CHATO'S CRAWL, ARIZONA

The two men in black Windbreakers waited inside the Cactus Bar and Grill. One was shooting pool on the filthy and beer-stained table that had seen far better days; the other walked up to the old Rockolla jukebox and not too gently shoved the long-haired old man away. The old man walked to a crooked and slanting table and slowly sat, placing his head on the tabletop. He looked like he had fallen asleep, which is the way the alternating watchers, the men in black, had seen him do most of the long and boring days in the time they had spent here.

The bartender was his usual self as he stood behind the bar and just watched the men. He had been kept busy in the kitchen serving these men sandwiches and cheeseburgers at least five or six times a day. He knew the bulk of the eight men kept low in the Texaco station across the way but never enquired personally. He wiped his bar and tried to ignore the two men until they ordered something, usually just water to his great dissatisfaction.

The small bell above the double doors chimed and the leader of these men came in and walked straight to the bar. He was soon followed by the redhaired man in the now dirty blue suit. The skinny one sat at the bar as the leader called the other two black-clad men over to where he pulled out a barstool, looked it over, and then decided to forego the seating as it looked like it would collapse under his weight. The two men came forward. The one playing pool placed the old, crooked pool cue on the bar and gave the heavyset bartender a dirty look until he moved down to what used to be a waitress station that hadn't seen a waitress in six years.

"This little safari is at an end. We've been ordered to pull out and head our separate ways," the larger of the three said.

"Our target seems to be a lot smarter than our man Vickers here thought he was." He glanced at Hiram, who just stared at the stained bar top with his hands hidden out of sight. "For all we know the asset is holed up at the Motel 6 in Apache Junction, drinking Coronas and lying by the pool."

"He will be here, eventually," Vickers said, not bothering to look up.

"Maybe he will and maybe he won't; that's no longer a concern of ours, or of Mr. Peachtree's." The man glanced at his two partners and slightly nodded his head. "We've been ordered to clean up our mess here and leave." The man suddenly pulled out a silenced nine-millimeter Glock and started to clean up.

He never saw the maniacal smile of the redhead's face as he just sat there. The other two slowly went for their hidden weapons, not feeling any need to hurry on this occasion—after all, there had been nothing more threatening to them since they arrived than a small, yellow scorpion walking slowly across the cracked and slat-missing hardwood floor. That was their mistake.

The other major mistake was for them and their new employer Daniel Peachtree to have not enquired as to what Vickers had been doing in the hours leading up to him being found in Las Vegas. They would never know he had found the Cactus Bar and Grill, along with the entire town of Chato's Crawl, deserted and abandon. Life could never have returned to the small place after the events of 2006. The town had been gutted of life and no one who lived there before could ever get the images of the slaughter out of their minds, so every one of the surviving townies had packed up and headed to where there were people—a lot of people where they would feel somewhat safe. Vickers had taken precautions against this eventual turn in fortune. He had stocked the bar in preparation for him to go it alone in securing the asset. He would have waited forever if that's what it took because he knew his life depended on a deal to trade the asset for his freedom. He never trusted Peachtree or Camden—Hiram knew how this particular game was played because he had written the rules long ago.

The shotgun blast caught the largest of the three men in the chest, taking his gun hand off before the double-ought buckshot tore into his body, flinging him back into the second and third man. Hiram easily raised his hand and fired three more very loud shots into his face and head as the old man sprang from his chair where the men in black had thought him drunk and passed out. The bartender with the sawed-off shotgun still smoking ejected the spent casing and easily walked up and fired again, this time catching the last man in line as he attempted to rise off the floor. The shot caught the man in the head, turning the air into a bloody mist of brain and bone.

The old man jumped on the second man's chest as he too tried to rise. With his legs pinning the man to the ground the codger, who wasn't so old and never drank a day in his life, pulled out his weapon of choice, an eight-inch switchblade. He smiled and slowly cut the man in black's throat from ear to ear. Then he stood with the dripping knife as the frightened man grabbed at his torn neck. The gun was kicked away from his grasping fingers and it slid away.

The bartender ejected the second shell from his sawed-off shotgun and then fired a round into the struggling man's upturned face. It was all over in five short seconds. Vickers placed his own nine millimeter on the bar top and then turned to face his number one team of assassins: a man and his quiet older brother who had set up the brownstone in Georgetown the night he had to eliminate the sister of Jack Collins. They were also the murderous siblings who had placed the two bodies on the turnpike later that night.

"So transparent and predictable," Vickers said.

The bartender and his brother stood next to Hiram. The older, silent one wiped the blood from his switchblade on the bar rag that was tossed to him by his brother.

"This thing is nearly over one way or the other. Either the president's plan will work, or it won't. Either way we take the asset."

"We wait?" The old man bent over and started removing money and identification from the slain agents.

"Yes, we wait. The asset will be coming home very soon." Vickers took some stale peanuts from the wooden bowl in front of him. He tossed away a few that had drops of blood on them and then lazily threw the remainder into his mouth and chewed. "You'll find the rest packing their bags over at the station." He looked at his personal employees. "I assume you won't have any trouble taking care of them?"

The burly man behind the bar took up his shotgun and started replacing the spent shells and smiled.

"Good, now go show them how real bad guys operate."

WALTER REED NATIONAL MILITARY MEDICAL CENTER
BETHESDA, MARYLAND

The president, as tired as he was, waited with General Caulfield inside his room as he spoke by phone to the prime ministers of two allied countries. The conversations were short and to the point. Caulfield knew he wouldn't last that much longer as he took in the beaten and worried countenance of the chief executive.

"Where is Dr. Compton?" the president asked quickly, fearing something had happened to his friend. The first lady looked up from the paperwork she had been trying to keep busy with since the attorney general and the chief justice had left the previous hour after the launch of the *Lee*.

"Calm down, he's right out in the hallway. He's about as bad off as you; you both have to stop for a while. Everything else is out of your control for the time being. You've hamstrung Camden, so he can't order lunch without congressional approval. Your military knows who is in charge and what's happening up there"—she looked toward the ceiling—"is out of your hands at the moment." The first lady stood, felt the president's forehead, and became worried as his fever had risen by seven degrees in the past hour. "You and Niles are both going to fall over and then you are back to square one with that son of a bitch."

The president looked at General Caulfield. "I think the wrong person has been in charge the whole time." He smirked as his wife kissed him on the forehead.

Niles closed his good eye and sighed. He was well aware of what the ground element at Camp Alamo was facing. He didn't know which of his people were alive and who were lying dead on the snow and ice. His leg was propped up in his wheelchair as he spoke to Virginia Pollock and Lee Preston. The attorney had never seen a battered man who refused to rest like this Dr. Compton had. The man frightened him as he realized that if all government employees were as tenacious as this man was he would run as fast as he could to the nearest border and get out, because the pencil pushers and the slide-rule boys would inherit the Earth and men like him would soon be out of work.

"I'm authorizing you to pass Mr. Preston through security at the complex and retrieve Matchstick. He's done as much as he can do, and Gus wants to be at home." Niles looked up and slowly blinked his left eye underneath the glasses that were propped as best they could be on his bandaged head. "We owe the old man that dignity. Mr. Preston, thank you for your assistance thus far, but with Camden, you never know what kind of legal maneuvering he'll pull and I don't trust anyone when it comes to Matchstick and Gus. Get them out of the complex and secure them the best you can away from Nevada. Chato's Crawl should be the safest place. We should be getting our military contingent back soon, one way or the other, to secure him better. Virginia, see to it."

"Niles, you have to rest. I'll personally take the little guy and Gus home. I've already notified Denise Gilliam, Charlie, and Pete, that they will accompany us, because Matchstick will need friends around him as Gus . . . well, he's too tired to keep his eyes on Matchstick all the time. We should have enough old-timers providing security at the two houses; I don't anticipate any trouble from now on."

Niles looked up and bobbed his head. "Tell Matchstick . . . tell him . . ."

Virginia thought Niles had fallen asleep and became worried as she looked at his battered and bruised body.

"Thank you." Niles's head dropped to his chest once more as Virginia leaned over and kissed Compton's forehead. She wiped another tear away like she had been doing most of the day as a nurse took Niles away.

Virginia had come to the conclusion earlier in the day that she could no longer fulfill her duties at the Group. She had become far too attached to the people she worked with, especially far too close to Niles.

Virginia halfheartedly smiled at Lee Preston as he waited patiently for them to leave for Nevada. He smiled his charming smile and then said what was on his mind.

"If you plan on quitting, I would at least leave Dr. Compton a note telling him why you are going to do what it is you're doing. He deserves to know that you love the little bald guy. Lord knows he's about the toughest son of a bitch I've ever seen that wears a suit and tie for a living."

Virginia looked shocked as she blew her nose on a handkerchief. She made a distasteful face.

"Here," Preston said as he held out a pen and notepad. "No charge, but I want the pen back."

Virginia accepted the pen and paper, smiled a sad smile, and patted the attorney on the shoulder. She went into Compton's room to explain the whys of her leaving.

"What a fucking day," Preston said as he watched the door close behind Virginia.

CAMP ALAMO
ANTARCTICA

Sarah held Mendenhall as upright as she could. The vision of another two thousand Grays and their automatons broke the spirit of many of the men, women, and soldiers. And the sound from above was mind-shattering as even more of the saucers were making their way down from high altitude.

Henri took hold of Will's other side and Anya scooped up both Sarah's and Farbeaux's weapons. They struggled in the snow to get the seriously injured captain to safety.

"Over there," Henri said with a nod of his head. Fifty feet away was the burned-out remains of a German armored personnel carrier. It had been blasted by one of the robotic automatons and the steel monstrosity was just starting to rip the hatches from the carrier. "Set him down," Henri said to Sarah.

Will was laid not too gently into the soot-covered snow and Farbeaux looked at both women.

"I'm going to get that metal bastard to chase me. It won't last too long, but see that Bushmaster cannon lying on the upper deck? Get to that and blast that thing to hell."

Sarah shook her head. She yelled as she tried to be heard above the din of battle and the constant whoosh of laser weaponry flying past as the Grays came on in force, heading straight for Camp Alamo and the hidden entranceway.

"You'll never make it," she finally managed to say.

"You know me, any chance to get away, I'll take." Henri grabbed the Heckler & Koch automatic weapon and sprinted a few steps, then started firing at the robotic monster. It had succeeded in ripping open the top of the personnel carrier and had one of the dead armor soldiers in its clawlike hands. Sarah had to turn away from the horrid sight.

Suddenly the metal beast felt the heavy blows of the 7.65-millimeter rounds as they slammed into its chassis. The large red eye imbedded in the front of its head slowly turned toward the man who caused it not pain, but irritation as it had been programmed to kill and collect. The metal monstrosity let go of the dead soldier and then nimbly hopped from the armored vehicle. Henri added more fire, and then Sarah and Anya added their own. Hundreds of bullets met the strange alien steel. A survivor of either the 101st or 82nd added a light 40-millimeter mortar to the assault but the automaton shook off the blows and started forward. It raised both hands to waist level and curled the long sharp fingers inward as it started to take aim with its heavy caliber belt-fed kinetic weapon.

"Get down!" Henri shouted, but knew it would be too late as the evil red eye had the two women and Mendenhall locked in. Farbeaux raised the Heckler & Koch to his shoulder and that was when he noticed the slide was locked open. The weapon was empty.

Before they knew what was happening they were all knocked off their feet as two Tornado fighter-bombers bearing the insignia of a blue circle with a red Kangaroo inside of the Royal Australian Air Force and twenty Gazelle Attack helicopters with the blue circle and red kiwi of the New Zealand army screamed by. The earth erupted as four laser-guided smart bombs struck the metal giant, blowing it into a thousand pieces. That was followed up by fifty-caliber machine-gun fire from the Gazelles as they strafed what remained.

Sarah, Anya, and Farbeaux raised their heads long enough to feel the blast of jet engines and rotor wash as the sky quickly filled with aircraft of every sort. Henri wanted to shout but was quickly inundated with debris from the robot that lay shattered on the ground only a hundred feet from the two women and the unconscious Mendenhall.

The roar from the high clear sky above continued and they all chanced to look up just as a thousand parachutes broke into the clear through the low clouds that covered the battlefield. It was the white canopies of the 12th Australian and 3rd New Zealand Parachute Brigades. This time Henri did cheer and shout as he stood and shook his fist at the stunned Grays. Ground fire and Gazelle attack choppers were knocking them down as fast as they could charge down the ramps of the hovering saucers. And they too were being hit by a multitude of weaponry such as Sidewinder, Phoenix, and AMRAAM missiles. At that moment, the powerful assault from the sea was timed perfectly as forty Tomahawk Cruise missiles were directed at them from the faraway coast. Sixteen missile cruisers of both Australian and New Zealand navies had joined a force of cruisers from the U.S. Navy and five Royal Navy and Los Angeles–class subs. Explosions tore the battlefield apart as all three surviving saucers were soon a smoking ruin on the melting ice field.

The Anzacs and the U.S. and Royal navies had arrived in force.

20

An hour later Mendenhall was in the hands of New Zealand army medics. They rushed him inside Camp Alamo for immediate emergency surgery. Sarah watched him being taken away as Anya took a deep breath beside her.

"I understand it was you two who rallied the workers and remains of our army to our defense?"

Sarah and Anya, with Farbeaux sitting down in the snow getting tended to, looked up to see a heavyset man in an expensive winter coat with three others standing beside him. They all had weapons that looked as if they had been recently fired.

"Pardon me," the man with the bow tie and glasses said as he gave his smoking M-16 assault rifle to the burly and smiling man next to him. "Very rude of me. I am Lord Durnsford, of Her Majesty's MI6; I am the person responsible for this . . . this . . . mess." He gestured around the battlefield as SAS men and the rescuing Anzacs were busy dispatching Grays one at a time—there would be no prisoners taken, not after Mumbai and Beijing. "These men are Admirals Kinkaid, of the U.S. Navy, and Huffington of the

Royal Navy. And this is my good friend, Sir Darcy Bennett, in charge of the Overlord Project."

Sarah and Anya said nothing. Their faces were bloodied and looked as if they had nothing to say to the four men.

"I believe you two were on the Russian vessel which brought the alien power plant through safely?"

Sarah nodded her head and then looked at the sky. She only wanted one question answered. She looked directly at Durnsford.

"General . . ." She paused as the question caught in her throat; she tried again with encouragement from Anya. "General Collins?" she finally managed.

The silence from the four men who could not look them in the eyes told her everything she needed to know.

"The *Garrison Lee,* any word?" Anya asked as her hope remained even as Sarah's was dashed.

Lord Durnsford was just about to say there had been no word as of yet when the high sky lit up. The battle in deep orbit between the moon and the Earth had started. All heads turned up as small, dot-sized flashes were seen in the crisp blue sky. It was almost like an illusion they were all witnessing. The dark of space was being inundated with small sparkles of gunfire as high as the human eye could see. Many more faces turned upward, as the powerful weaponry was bright enough to cut through not only the darkness of space, but the atmospheric blue of the planet's air.

The battle for Earth had commenced.

BETWEEN THE EARTH AND THE MOON
(MOON GAP)

The HMS *Garrison Lee,* with her powerful ion-based engines, had covered the seventy thousand miles to what would be forever known as Moon Gap in Earth's history books in a matter of ten minutes. She was now facing the strength of the Gray invasion armada. If the *Lee* failed to stop this assault it was only the opening vanguard, as the rest of the Gray civilization would soon follow the initial assault element and inundate Earth until it was totally subdued.

The full 1,865-foot length of the *Garrison Lee* was side-on to the first of the small assault ships as they exited the orbit of the far side of the moon. They came on at fantastic speed as the battleship before them flew on, seemingly oblivious to what was coming her way. The enormous sixteen-inch guns of all six massive turrets were trained directly at the Grays, but the large-bore weaponry must not have been seen as a major threat, because instead of slowing, the first one hundred attack saucers sped up to meet the Earth's last defense.

Commodore Freemantle watched as the small dots illuminated against the glare of the distant sun came at them without hesitation. He smiled and winked at the nervous female yeoman at his side. She was rapidly recording everything she was to be witness to in the upcoming battle. It would be her job and her job alone to back up the ship's log if and when it was jettisoned after the battle. She nervously and bravely smiled back, but the commodore could see her fear, and it was no less than he was feeling.

"Weapons status?" he said calmly to his fire control officer on the next lowest tier.

"Mounts one through six are fully charged with particle shot."

"Close-in defensive weaponry, please." Freemantle studied the fast-approaching saucers just as the largest section of saucers—along with the processing ships and the power distribution vessel—made their first appearance as they rounded the moon.

"Five-inch rail guns are manned and ready, they have individual fire control at their command. Ten-thousand-watt laser mounts are operating on computer control, all systems report ready." The officer swallowed his fear and stated as clearly as he could, "Power plant operating at 100 percent efficiency."

"Very good. Defensive shield status?" Freemantle proudly watched his people calmly go about their duties—knowing they were in for the fight of their lives, they all had resigned themselves to a grisly, but honorable death.

"Water tanks at maximum, smoke generators at 100 percent."

"Thank you. It seems we're as prepared as we'll ever be."

Commodore Freemantle looked at every face that he could on his, the highest tier of the bridge, trying to burn the faces of each of these brave kids into his mind. All nationalities, Russian, British, American, Middle Eastern, Canadian, Australians, and Chinese, he was proud of each and every one of them and the nations that bore them. He thought for the briefest of moments that his swelling pride in the youth, the very best of the planet, was going to swell so that he couldn't give his next command.

"Attack element, arm your weaponry," he said, warning the two attack shuttles they were now on their own and would be the judge on when to launch. It was dangerous arming the newly redesigned AMRAAM missiles while still in the bay, but he wanted those young men to have every advantage he could give them, as he knew they would never return from their mission.

He cleared his throat as he watched the telescopically enhanced view screen. The first one hundred saucers were at thirty thousand kilometers and closing fast. Evidently the arrogant Grays thought they could plow right through their ship without even slowing. The smile on Freemantle's face grew and his anger was a match for that smile.

"For all the wars fought; for all the injustice quelled; for the men, women, and children of our world, we fight for what we call home. Ladies and gentlemen, we shall engage the enemy at Moon Gap. All guns to fire on my command."

The HMS *Garrison Lee,* with the giant, aluminum, one-hundred-foot blue-colored flag of the United Nations flying at her stern, flew proudly and defiantly as she sailed to the exact center of space between the Earth and the moon—a place that would be forever remembered as the coordinates where the battle for Earth would truly commence.

Ryan listened to the Marine colonel as she slowly explained the attitude jets to him. Jason knew the maneuvering thrusters well, as they were the same design as the LEM that he had set down, albeit roughly, on the moon's surface at Shackleton Crater. The Marine shook her head when Ryan accidentally tripped the inertial navigation system when he toggled the thrusters.

"Now look, Commander, you can't have heavy fingers on this thing or it will come back and bite you in the ass and everyone else back in the crew bay, you got that?"

"Boy, you turn the nicest color of pink when you're angry," was all he said as he reset the inertial navigation system.

"Knock it off. You're speaking to a United States Marine Corps officer, jerk!"

Jason only smiled as he corrected the order of firing the attitude jets without a single mistake the second time. The colonel shook her head in frustration. The crowded cockpit was lit like a Christmas tree and Ryan was afraid of hitting something that would send him and the attack crew hurtling into deep space.

"Okay sweet cheeks, I'll take it from here." Jenks maneuvered inside the shuttle and waited while she exited the second seat. The master chief watched as the colonel slid close by, knocking him into the bulkhead. He raised his eyebrows several times as he got a real good feel of her heavily clothed chest. He looked at Ryan and then back at the floating form of the Marine.

"Gladly. You two dicks deserve each other," she muttered.

"She acts like she has something against the navy." Jenks tossed his helmet to Ryan, who caught the floating cover and then held it while Jenks strapped in. He reached out and hit the monitor that showed the assault team as they stood against the interior wall of the cargo bay. Once near the power resupply vessel the bay doors would be blown free and the Delta and SEAL assault element would be strung together in a long line being pulled by the first two men with their limited-range jet packs.

"Well, Officer Meat, you think you can control this thing for the five thousand meters it will take to get there?"

"No, I don't, but what the hell." Jason grinned at Jenks, who narrowed his eyes at the commander.

"Typical jock. Just do as I say when I say and we'll at least crash into that big bastard."

"Check, crash, that I can do."

"From what Toad told me a few years back you tangled with these boys before, that right?"

"Yeah, I got my ass shot right out of the sky." Ryan pulled his helmet over his head.

Again Jenks narrowed his eyes as he wasn't used to anyone returning fire on him. He soon shook it off and then placed his helmet on as Ryan turned and looked at the gruff old man.

"If it makes you feel better, Master Chief, I shot one out of the sky before I ejected. Does that count for anything?"

"No, because you'll probably be running into the son of a bitch's brother, cousin, and daddy out there in the next fifteen minutes—if, that is, this big-ass battlewagon doesn't get shot right out of the sky with us inside her belly."

"Does this assault really have a chance in hell of working?" Jason asked, finally getting serious.

"Look, Commander Shit-for-Brains, I got this contract because I said I could build the system used to get us from point A to point B. I never really thought we would get this far. So, no, we'll probably get our asses shot off when we open those doors."

"Hey, I'm brimming with confidence now."

Jack and Tram floated along hand over hand on the traversing line between sections with the two SAS guards as best they could as the announcement was made that every hand should man their battle stations. Collins gave a sideways glance over at Tram and the two men stopped, holding on to the line just inside the thick girder system of the main deck. The large windows showed the nothingness of space and that made Jack far angrier that he could no longer do anything to help his friends.

"Look, I guess you're going to have to shoot me, but as an allied general I sincerely hope you won't." Collins allowed a far more mobile Tram to pull him down from his free-floating status until his feet met the deck and the Velcro took hold. He slowly removed his helmet, as did Tram.

The two SAS men inside their red-topped helmets looked at each another and then pulled themselves down to the deck and joined the men they were supposed to take to the evac stations near the extreme bow of the warship. Many other crewmen shot past on lines above their heads as everyone had a duty to perform.

"Look, you men want to be with your unit. If I'm not mistaken you're supposed to be standing by in case the Grays start to board the *Lee*, am I correct?" Jack wiped a line of sweat from his forehead.

The two British commandos didn't respond; they just looked at the American general inside his ill-fitting space-suit. The two men had heard the scuttlebutt about what this man had done during the assault on Camp Alamo while they launched into space. He had given his entire command to give this ship a fighting chance. Finally the SAS sergeant slowly removed his helmet, as did the other. He faced Collins and then held out his gloved hand.

Jack shook it.

"No, General, we were ordered to stay with you two and that's just what we'll do, but your orders will supersede any previous command we were given." The sergeant looked at his partner. "And in the heat of battle we, like you, must overcome, adapt, fight from wherever we are at—wherever *you* are at." The SAS men replaced their helmets and then waited as Collins and Tram did the same. "What are your orders, General?"

"Can you take us to the command bridge?" He gave the helmet a twist to secure it.

"That we can do, sir." The sergeant gestured for Jack and Tram to get on the six-man tram that was situated against the interior bulkhead. "Right this way, gentlemen."

For the first time in hours, Tram smiled as he adjusted the old M-14 rifle and the many magazines of 7.62 rounds.

"One hundred and fifty thousand meters and closing. Magnetometers are pegged in the red, the attack saucers are powering their weapons systems," came the call from the third tier.

"Hold, hold," Freemantle said into his 1MC communications. The order reverberated off the heavily reinforced hull plates throughout the *Lee*.

As they watched the view screen, the saucers maneuvered into a wide *V* formation as they came on. They were using this tactic so the rest of the fleet could get in behind the screen for protection. Freemantle knew the Grays were sacrificing the forward element to protect the power-distribution vessel and the processing ships.

"Main batteries one and three will concentrate long-range fire on the power-distribution ship. Obviously they don't think we have the power plant. They must assume we will use long-range missiles."

The commodore turned and saw four men enter the battle bridge. He was about to order the newcomers off when he saw one of them was General Collins. He nodded his head and gestured the men down to his station.

"I would have assumed you had enough of our Gray friends down on the surface, General." Freemantle kept his eyes on the one-hundred-foot monitor.

"You have my apologies for not knocking more of these bastards out of the sky for you, Commodore."

Freemantle finally turned and faced Collins. Jack could see that the man had changed in just the past ten hours.

"I think you and your command did an admirable job, my good man. Now let's see if the navy can accommodate

these buggers and give them the fight of their lives, after all."
He smiled for the first time since Collins had met him.
"We're not the Martians, are we?"

"Not at all, Commodore," he answered as Tram strapped
the injured Collins into an upright chair. "Permission to
watch you work, Commodore?"

"By all means, sir, by all means."

On the view screen the attack craft were nearing the
point of full impact from the Argon particle systems.

"Turrets two, four, five, and six, target the head of
the attacking formation and fire at will at targets of opportunity."

Inside the six upper and lower sixteen-inch gun turrets,
the fifty-six man crews closed their eyes and waited for the
order. The last to load were underside turrets five and six.
First the men placed the silk-lined particle bag of miniature
ball bearings, a thousand pounds' worth, into the thirty-inch
breach. Then a two-inch steel-rounded plate designed to fit
snugly against the non-rifled barrel followed the particle
sacks. The plate would be used as a simple push-plate for
the powerful Argon laser to slam into the particle bag. The
resulting collision would jettison the short duration laser
beam into the steel, spreading out and slamming it through
the twenty-inch-thick barrel of the cannon. Once it hit the
muzzle guides, redirected rifling would push the steel shot to
form a circle as it passed by the expensively made crystal
laser-enhancer developed by the British, tripling the power
of the 1.67-second-duration laser, thus producing a blast of
twenty million volts of power that would rejoin with the steel
particles once outside of the barrel and hurl the shot toward
the enemy. It had been tested many times at the cost of several nuclear reactors.

The men and women of the gunnery sections were sweating profusely inside their reinforced suits as they waited for
the orders that would send the *Lee* to war.

The attack saucers came on arrogantly and didn't break formation as they broke six hundred miles.

"Open fire!" Freemantle called, far more loudly than he intended.

On the upper deck, the first to fire was the number one gun turret, followed a split second later by number three mount. The two were separated by a higher and lower platform, just like the battleships of World War II. The blast of all six guns rocked the *Lee* and propelled her on her side by more than two thousand feet just as turrets two and four let loose. The maneuvering jets activated to keep the *Lee* straight and then push her back to her original station keeping. The underside guns let loose their salvos at the closer ships flying in their *V* formation.

The first to hit were the guns of two, four, five, and six turrets. The particle beam, which actually looked like a short duration blast instead of the long-lined laser systems of the enemy, tore into the first three saucers, blowing them to bits and slamming their remains back into the widening formation. It was as though the remaining ninety-six attackers didn't know what had hit them. They kept coming in their suicide alignment instead of breaking apart and scattering. The Earth ship had caught the Grays napping.

After the discharge of the large-bore sixteen-inch guns, a burst of over five hundred kilos of liquid nitrogen burst from the cannon. The steam curled to almost nothing as it hit the vacuum of space. The *Lee* was only momentarily inundated by the nitrogen particles as they rapidly dissipated, sliding by the speedy warship to its rear. The men inside the gun turrets quickly reloaded before the attackers broke formation, and before the enemy knew what was happening twenty more exploded.

The six particle beams of the upper six guns hit one of the processing ships trailing far behind the vanguard of attackers. The shot caught it on the right side and the large craft started spinning crazily until it slammed into six of the surrounding saucers, also knocking them into a fast-decaying orbit over the moon. The seven ships vanished almost immediately. Three particle beams hit the larger power distribution ship but all it did was punch a hole in its

forward section; the damage was short lived as the powerful saucer started to heal itself immediately. The scab was
clearly visible on the monitors on the *Lee*'s battle bridge. The
power-replenishment ship immediately took evasive action
and slowed, allowing the bulk of its protectors to front the
important vessel.

"Damn," Freemantle said angrily as he saw the large target fall behind a screen of over seven hundred of the smaller
attack ships. Still, it was satisfying seeing the main guns of
the *Lee* reload and start pummeling the attackers in front
and at a distance. Over a hundred of the attackers were
burning in space as the giant battleship continued on.

"Incoming!" one of the techs shouted. Freemantle reminded all to be calm.

Jack Collins and Tram, along with heir SAS escort, saw
the bright flashes of over a thousand incoming streaks of
laser light. They were also of short duration. The crewmen
hung on as the first tendrils of light slammed into the broadside of the *Lee*. The jolt to her was wild. The ship banked
hard right as fires erupted in the interior spaces. She rolled
as she brought her underside to bear against the enemy
fire. This was intentional, to give her main batteries time to
reload.

"Defensive measures, now," Freemantle said.

All along the length of the enormous ship, one hundred
and twenty thousand gallons of ionized water was released
into space, where it froze instantly into tiny crystal beads.
The lasers of the enemy hit these and the powerful light
weapons were fractured and defused before they hit the armored underside near turrets five and six. Three of the
smaller twenty-millimeter laser cannon were knocked free
of their mounts and thrown into the void of space with all
twenty men and women inside. Then before the water dissipated the *Lee* rolled back to zero bubble and fired another
powerful salvo from all sixteen-inch guns. The fire was devastating to the enemy formation as they finally got the hint
and started to disperse in a wide arc.

The *Lee* stayed upright this time as her smoke generators

were now assisting the water jets in weakening the Grays' laser weapons. The beams still contacted the Martian steel but her damage was light compared to what it would have been. The vanguard of enemy saucers was now closing to close range of the *Lee*.

"Close-range batteries, open fire!" the commodore shouted purposefully this time.

The twin-barreled rail guns opened up. With the alternating poles of current they hurled a solid steel projectile weighing three hundred pounds straight at the closest saucers. The impact was tremendous as the saucers crumpled from the inside out from the electrically charged kinetic weaponry. Then the twenty-millimeter 1,000-watt laser cannon opened up on the streaking and closest saucers, slicing them into pieces. The rest backed away as they realized the weapons of the Earth ship had been vastly underestimated.

Inside the two attack shuttles, the pilots and crews felt the impact of the enemy weaponry. The bay shook and sparks flew outside the cockpit windows. Admiral Everett looked at the young faces around him in the shuttle's crew bay. The men had their eyes closed for the most part as they waited for their section of decking to be blasted away. He just prayed that the *Lee* could get them close enough.

"We've just lost water tanks six, seven, and eight, smoke generators six and nine!"

Freemantle felt the large explosion amidships.

"Helm, hard over one hundred degrees, bring us bow on, all-ahead flank. Let's close the distance, gentlemen, before we lose anymore countermeasures. Turrets one, two, and five, continue fire, clear us a path straight for the heart of their rear formation. All rail guns and laser cannon take the enemy as they close. Attack shuttles, launch in approximately three minutes—all nonessential crew to their evac stations."

The *Garrison Lee* fired her aft and starboard maneuvering thrusters, bringing her into a head-on flight toward the largest enemy formation, and centered on the two-mile-wide power distribution saucer.

The 4,000-man crew knew this was the moment of truth for the *Garrison Lee* as she made her way through the densest part of the enemy formation. They were going to take a pounding.

The *Garrison Lee* shot forward with her six powerful blue-flamed ion engines firing full. The enormous warship rammed everything that got in her way as her powerful sixteen-inch guns continued to clear a path of destruction as she charged forward. The small mounts were blasting saucers as they came in to attack the exposed side of the battleship. Saucers were struck at close range by the powerful Argon-based particle cannons and disintegrated as their debris peppered the thick girder lines of the ship. Still she came on at full speed.

A saucer slammed into the lower section of deck fifteen, knocking out number five turret and her fifty-plus-man crew above and below the guns. The men and women passing particle bags were jettisoned as a massive hole burst outward as the destroyed saucer entered the girder protection and exploded deep inside. Fires were now raging out of control, licking against the lower bridge section. Freemantle ordered the lower reserve bridge abandoned as the flames became untenable. Damage control crews had to give up in frustration as they lost all pressure to the foam firefighting equipment. The Halon 1301 gaseous firefighting tanks exploded, taking out three hundred of the lower sections' precious damage control crew. The lower decks were now awash with flames as they curled into the now exposed lower bridge. Still the number six gun kept up her fire, her gun crew refusing to leave their station.

Jack grimaced as he heard the emergency calls coming in. His frustration was only equaled by Lieutenant Tram as he gripped his safety harness with his gloved hands as he watched the *Lee* coming apart around them. Large cracks formed in the five-foot-thick plastic composite glass of the bridge as Freemantle ordered her steel shutters closed. Jack felt claustrophobic as the outside battle raged on unseen with his real eyes. The view screen at the front of the battle bridge rocked and went askew but held on as the enemy fire increased in effectiveness. Water and smoke discharge was down to 30 percent effectiveness with the loss of more water tanks and kerosene dispensers. The *Lee* rocked as the mixing chambers of maneuvering jets eight, ten, and twenty exploded outward, luckily taking out five saucers as they attempted to get close to the speeding battleship.

Jack frowned as the large power-regeneration saucer looked no closer than it had been when the *Garrison Lee* started her run at full speed one minute earlier.

"Stern section has taken an indirect atomic strike. We've lost two of the engines!" The *Lee* seemed to whiplash as the enemy started to play dirty in their fear of the battleship.

"Close-in batteries, I need those damn saucers off my ass for two minutes, don't let them launch again. AMRAAM stations, fire everything you have."

All along the centerline of the *Lee,* missile tubes opened wide and fired three hundred specially designed AMRAAM missiles. The American-made long-distance, dry-fueled antiair missiles were specially equipped with fifteen-megaton warheads. They cleared the superstructure and sped to thirty miles' distance before their small warheads detonated. The resulting explosion rocked the *Lee* and the surrounding void of space. The pressure wave backfired into the girderlike superstructure and started three hundred different fires. But the real damage was done to the attackers. The AMRAAMs caught over a hundred saucers as they maneuvered toward the sides of the *Lee* to come into port and starboard attack profiles. They never stood a chance as the weapons melted their special skins and blew them inward, crushing and burning to death the Grays inside. The debris field was far and wide as the battleship barreled her way through. The giant plow at the far forward section slammed into damaged and burning saucers, knocking them clear.

"Good show, targeting, that's the way to hold off and draw the bangers in. You got quite a few of the buggers with that one," Freemantle said just as an enormous explosion threw him and the rest of the bridge crew forward, even snapping the safety harnesses of some.

At three hundred miles the processing saucers and the power-distribution vessel opened fire with their vastly superior laser cannon. The forward number one gun blew up as the first strike hit the Argon delivery system. The resulting cataclysm engulfed the battle bridge and the superstructure from frames twenty-one to forty. The HMS *Garrison Lee* was now a hurtling ball of flame as she approached the largest ships at the center of the armada.

Before anyone could realize it, six of the smaller attack saucers made a suicide run for the stern of the *Lee*. They slammed into her graceful and curved fantail where the United Nations flag stood out straight, and exploded into the thinly armored rear. A catastrophic explosion rocked the *Lee* from her stern section all the way to her forward areas. The remaining four engine bells blew outward as her power plant was struck. The ripple effect of so much energy traveled to the areas of least resistance, downward into the bowels of the great warship. The resulting explosion snapped the *Lee*'s hardened back in two as her bow sank fifty degrees. Her large deflector plow was now at a downward angle as the battleship continued to push forward in a blind desire to hit the power-replenishment vessel, which was now helpless to get out of the way. One of the five hundred crewmen ejected into the freezing void of space was Captain Lienanov, who died bravely with the men he had been assigned inside the power plant section.

Freemantle was assisted back down to the deck by Jack and Tram as they fought to get the commodore to his station. The ship was rocked again as turrets four and five exploded from the immense heat buildup after the cannons were refused the coolant they so needed to freeze the hot barrels. The resulting backlash of energy traveled through-out the ship and she shuddered under the stresses of coming apart. The great battleship heeled to port and then seemed to magically correct its trajectory, as if with a mind of its own it was intent to finish the task.

The estimation by Matchstick, that the *Garrison Lee* could only last fifteen minutes against the Grays, magnificently exceeded his prediction. The *Lee* had lasted twenty-five minutes and had destroyed well over seven hundred of the invincible armada.

Commodore Freemantle was seriously injured as Jack and Tram strapped him back down. The noise inside the bridge was nearly unbearable as the venting of O_2 started in earnest. Men, women, and debris were flying around as if a tornado had erupted inside the enclosed spaces. Freemantle hung onto Jack, his face shield misting over with escaping gas and blood.

"Maneuvering thrusters to full, ram the bloody bastard!" he said as loudly as he could into his 1MC mic.

In the vacuum of space it's impossible to feel the forward momentum of any hurtling object, but the surviving crew of that day would swear they felt the *Lee*, with her last remaining working thrusters, shoot forward. The power-replenishment saucer actually saw the *Lee* bearing down on it from six miles but could do nothing about it as the downward-angled deflector plow slammed into the strange metal skin. The resulting deceleration threw every surviving crewman forward and killed many of the remaining men and women. Jack Collins lost his handhold on both the commodore and Tram as he was tossed like a flying rocket into the now blank view screen. The *Garrison Lee* and her sharpened deflector plow were now lodged deep inside the two-mile-wide saucer. The giant battleship would never move again.

Everett saw that there was no use in checking the vital signs of the Marine colonel and her copilot. The large girder had pierced the windscreen of the number one shuttle, impaling both. They sat in their seats, never knowing what hit them after the destruction of the engine room spaces. Everett saw that the damage the attack shuttle sustained was beyond repair, and floated back to the men in the cargo bay. Two of the insertion team was wounded as the thick-tiled skin of the shuttle had been penetrated by flying metal. Their suits had vented and they had almost succumbed to the harsh environment before adhesive patches could be placed over the punctures in the outer skin.

"What a mess," the admiral said as he started getting the remainder of his men moving. "Sergeant, you and Haley get to the rescue stations and jettison, that's an order. Your suits are too damaged. I'll ingress with the assault team."

Carl looked around at the shaken men as he searched the wreck for the special weapons that had broken free of their restraining straps. He saw them floating toward the rear bulkhead and ordered them secured.

"Lieutenant, get on the comm link and find out how number two shuttle is. If we've lost her too, we're truly fucked."

"Aye, sir." The SEAL officer hastily unstrapped after the massive explosion only three hundred feet above their shuttle bay. "Tell Jenks we're dead in the water over here and two men short."

"Done. The rest of you get the special packages out of here before this entire bay breaks loose. We need cable, lots of it."

"Jenks reports they're shaken and stirred but not broken, Admiral."

"Good, the number one shuttle must have shielded them from the main blast. Inform the master chief there's been a change of plan. We need to hitch a ride."

The remaining twelve men looked at the admiral for the barest of seconds.

"Move, damn it, before we're vented out of the damn ship!"

Before Carl realized it, Jason Ryan was in the open hatch, gesturing for the men to step it up.

"Hurry, gentlemen, hurry, we have Grays docking with

this wreck. We're out of time. The rest of the *Lee*'s crew is evacuating. Move, move, move!"

Jason assisted each man with their loads of weapons and ordnance from the wrecked bay of the first shuttle. He waited on Everett and assisted the big man free, then turned to help the men find added cable for their ride on the remaining shuttle. Jenks had quickly explained Everett's makeshift plan, as they both thought along the same lines in a split second of consideration.

"The rest of you get to number two shuttle, now!" Carl said into his internal microphone. "Duct tape those packages to your suits; we can't afford to lose any of them."

The men were again shocked at the order. This was turning into a real high-tech endeavor. Another explosion rocked the stern of the *Lee* as three of the ion gas-mixing chambers burst and sent a high-heat energy wave outward, engulfing two saucers as they tried to dock with the flaming battleship. The men were knocked around and one of the Israeli weapons broke free of a SEAL's grip and headed straight at Ryan's faceplate. He batted at it and slammed to the deck in the zero gravity. He cussed and then easily tossed the two-hundred-pound yellow box back to the SEAL.

"Try and hang onto that damn thing, okay?" The SEAL took the package and started hand over hand for the undamaged bay thirty feet away.

Everett floated up to Ryan, tossing him a five-hundred-pound coiled cable. Ryan caught it, but the force of the blow almost sent him through the large hole that looked out onto the oxygen-fed burning superstructure.

The minute they gained the access port to the bay Everett started unreeling the thin cable. "Hook to your backpack harnesses. We're going space skiing."

Jenks was leaning out of the forward hatch of the number two shuttle with his gloved hands taking a tight grip of the frame.

"In case you boys didn't realize it, we have a shitload of ugly bad guys breathing down our necks. Now get hooked up and be sure you're clear of the main engine bell and the thrusters." He eyed Everett. "And don't think I'll forget you fucked up another one of my boats, Toad, you shithead!"

The master chief vanished before the middle finger of Carl's gloved hand shot up.

"And to think I almost forgot what a lovely man he was." Ryan hooked up the last Delta man to the lifeline. "Now for God's sake, take a firm hold on the running rail of the dorsal or we'll lose the bunch of you!" Jason slapped Everett on the top of his helmet. "Good luck, buddy." He shot off toward the cockpit just as the inducers kicked in for the main engine.

Everett floated to the top of the shuttle and then made sure his team was secure. He knew they had just cut their chances by half as the second shuttle would have to travel twice the distance with the same amount of fuel, and that wasn't enough.

Before he could think further the attitude jets started pushing attack shuttle number two toward the still-closed bay doors.

"Goddamn it, Jenks!" he screamed. He knew the master chief was just showing off. Ten feet before the crumpled doors smashed the shuttle's stern, the doors slowly creaked open and the shuttle was free.

Attack element Pershing entered a kill zone of saucers.

The commodore was dying and Jack could see that. He and Tram lifted him to his station once more as the fifth explosion of the number three armory went up.

"We have to cover the assault element," Freemantle said in a barely audible whisper. "We have to order the remaining rail gun and laser cannon crews to remain at their stations." He pushed his way along the rail toward the damage control station. He harshly shoved a dead technician away as he floated over the shorting-out computer boards. He looked closely at the computerized silhouette of the *Garrison Lee*. He quickly saw that they had little hope of covering the assault teams as three quarters of the giant battleship were awash with flames that blazed even in the vacuum of space. "General, order rail guns six and ten to cover the remaining shuttle." Freemantle's hopes quickly dimmed when the computer told him shuttle number one had been disabled. "We have to give those chaps all the help we can."

Jack pulled the commodore away and said into the command mic the orders the commodore had spoken. He felt a shattering vibration rend the ship as the two remaining rail guns opened up on the six saucers that were tracking the fast-departing shuttle. He prayed that Carl and Jason were onboard the surviving craft. Round after round of high-strength tungsten steel blasted the saucers before they knew they were being targeted.

"Gentlemen," Freemantle hissed through broken teeth. "Get my people clear now. The remaining gun crews will stay their post and cover the shuttle and the escape pods."

Collins looked around and saw that most of the bridge crew was dead or just gone, vented out through the large holes in the pressure hull. He quickly gestured for the survivors to get out. He looked at Tram and then helped the commodore back to his command station.

"Thank you, gentlemen. I'll be staying with my ship and crew. Tell them down below how they performed, will you?"

"Yes, sir." Jack and Tram looked away from the dying Englishman. He watched hundreds of six-man pods eject from their small tubes as the crew abandoned ship.

"That's my good chaps." Freemantle leaned forward, unable to stay upright any longer. "Now, it's time for you to leave the *Lee*. Good show, by the way." And then Freemantle died.

As the remainder of the bridge crew went to the escape pod underneath the battle bridge, Jack looked at Tram.

"I don't suppose it would do any good to tell you to get the hell out of here, would it?"

The Vietnamese lieutenant frowned as if he didn't understand, then tapped his helmet, pretending a short in his communications.

"That's what I thought, you're just like Ryan and Mendenhall." Jack shook his head inside his helmet. He quickly reached for the plastic laser rifle once owned by the dead SAS sergeant. "Well, let's go and see if we can get a few of those pale-skinned bastards."

Tram smiled, clearly understanding that order.

Collins looked out of the large hole in the bridge where the view screen used to be and saw the deflector plow dug deeply into the two-mile-wide saucer as smaller craft buzzed around it.

"Feel like taking a walk out there? Maybe we can find some targets inside. After all, we put the hole in the son of a bitch."

Tram removed the M-14 from his back, charged the weapon, and nodded his head.

"Jenks, we need a place where there's already a hole, got that?" Carl could swear he felt the speed of the shuttle as Ryan fired the main engine just as the two remaining rail guns took out the six saucers at their rear. The men inside the shuttle didn't realize how close they had come to being destroyed a few seconds out, but the men hanging on for dear life had a front-row seat and stared with wide eyes at the expanding destruction around them.

"I thought I would tell Ryan to pull into the drive-thru, Toad. Of course that's what we're doing, we're dropping you off at the front door of this fucking thing!"

"I swear I'm going to kill that mean bastard if we live through this!"

Inside Ryan was trying desperately to avoid the saucers that zipped in and out of the burning superstructure. He rammed some of the floating debris and thought for a moment he had holed the shuttle.

"Now *you* get on my shit list, all right?" Jenks grimaced at the loud bang as a large chunk of destroyed saucer bounced off the nose of the small shuttlecraft.

"Master Chief, I've got an idea. This big bastard doesn't have the shielding to defend against anything this small." Jason used the small joystick on the left-hand armrest to avoid another large chunk of steel from the *Lee*. He tried not to notice the hundreds of floating bodies from the *Lee* as he dodged them the best that he could, but still heard the occasional thump as one of the crew would bounce off the shuttle's tiled surface.

"Your point?" Jenks used his body to turn the shuttle as if his added weight would drive the ship farther to the left. "Damn it, do you have to hit every piece of crap in space?"

"We use our six AMRAAMs and punch a hole in her skin right here, and then get our asses over to the hole the *Lee* made in her and enter from there. If we stay out here much longer we're not going to be mistaken for floating debris."

"You're the fucking pilot, what in the hell are you asking me for?"

Ryan cursed and slammed his stick as far right as he could, praying the men attached to their roof stayed right there.

"Firing braking jets," Jenks called out as the shuttle approached the silvery skin of the enormous power replenishment ship. The forward thrusters fired, using up precious JP-5 fuel. Jenks shut them down even before the shuttle stopped. Still drifting forward and before they got too close, Ryan flipped up the cover for his weapons selection and hit the switch six times. Under the stubby wings of the shuttle, six large AMRAAMs slid off their rails and went straight for the saucer. The small weapons would do relatively light damage to the behemoth, but maybe it would be just enough to create the hole they needed.

The missiles struck at one time, creating a straight line of destruction and making Ryan fearful of not concentrating the powerful conventional warheads close enough together. The resulting detonation rocked the shuttle and pushed it away from the saucer. Jason saw a thirty-five-foot hole had been blasted into the material—but the hole started to repair itself. Ryan saw the material start to scab over a foot at a time.

"I'll be damned," Jenks said as he saw the first of the SEALs and Delta team start moving toward the hole. Everett was the last, using his little bit of fuel to propel himself after his team. He turned on his back and gave Ryan and Jenks a thumbs-up. For once Jenks didn't have anything to say as he saw his old student head into the damaged section of saucer, just as the material completely covered the hole. Jenks hit the forward OHMs engines and the shuttle quickly backed away. "Good luck, Toad."

As Jason backed out he didn't see the small saucer waiting for the shuttle.

CHATO'S CRAWL, ARIZONA

Gus, wrapped in a blanket, smiled at Matchstick as the small alien sat next to him. Denise Gilliam kept a close eye on the prospector as they neared the compound.

Pete Golding and Charlie Ellenshaw dozed in the seat facing the trio as the large Black Hawk circled the old house and the two-story Victorian before setting down. Pete awoke and looked at Corporal DeSilva, the lone security man onboard, as he looked out the wide window. The old Marine looked troubled as the helicopter slowly started to settle.

"What's the matter?" Pete asked as he nudged Charlie awake.

"Half of the compound security lighting is dark," DeSilva said as he continued to study the grounds.

"Partial blackout, you think?" Pete asked as Charlie leaned over and also looked at the ground far below.

DeSilva got on his helmet mike and called to the pilot. "Get ahold of gate security or the main house and find out what the deal is. I haven't worked with these retirees before, and I don't know what they're thinking."

The pilot nodded his head. He banked the Black Hawk into a wide turn and remained at altitude.

"Sienna One, to Crow's Nest, Sienna One, to Crow's Nest, what's the deal down there?"

"This is Crow's Nest, we have a power line down between here and Chato's Crawl. We're running on generators but expect to have the power up in fifteen, over."

"Look, Doc, I don't like this." The old corporal leaned closer to the window to study the two houses below. "Our gennies can run the two houses, the security lights, and the whole damn town if we have to."

Gus frowned as he listened to the men speak. Matchstick placed his long-fingered hand on Gus's and then smiled. He then looked at Denise.

"Look, fellas, I don't pretend to know your business, but we have to get Gus inside pretty quick. I was against this little foray from the beginning." Denise looked at Pete and raised her brow, asking him to overrule any security concerns. Gus was exhausted and just getting him home would do the man wonders as far as recovery went.

Pete shook his head as he raised his glasses and looked out over the semi-dark compound. He looked from that to Gus, who laid his balding head against the padded support of the Black Hawk.

"Ask the gate guard to show himself, DeSilva," Pete said.

The pilot relayed the request and as the helicopter banked once more the guard stepped from the darkened booth and waved. DeSilva sat back and cursed under his breath, then looked Gus, who wasn't looking that well. He had the cold chills and Matchstick was staring at the Marine like it was his fault.

"Look, I want our friends up front to stay with us until we can confirm what's going on." DeSilva nodded toward the pilot and the copilot of the Black Hawk.

"Whatever you think is best, Corporal," Pete said, relaxing somewhat.

"Okay, take us down," DeSilva said, not really happy with the compromise.

The burly gate guard lowered his waving hand and then turned to the man hidden well inside the gate. The man who had been a bartender a day ago was satisfied as the Black Hawk started to settle onto the pad. He turned away from the blowing sand as he eased the shotgun free of the shack. His brother, hiding near the bodies of the six-man security team they had killed earlier, smiled as the helicopter touched down.

Hiram Vickers watched from the darkened window of Gus's old shack as he slowly pushed the screen door open. The taking of the compound had been too easy as the fatal flaw was quickly found in the replacing of the normal military security team. That flaw was about to cost the strange group under Nellis Air Force Base their asset.

The tall redhead smiled as he thought of Daniel Peachtree and the now-disgraced President Giles Camden.

21

The armada of saucers had covered the distance between
Moon Gap and Earth in less than half an hour. The burning
Garrison Lee was still hanging onto the huge power-
replenishment ship and her superstructure was now covered
in space-suited Grays as they boarded looking for anyone
still alive.

Ryan saw how big the Earth was growing in the windscreen and hurried the shuttle toward the enormous deflector plow embedded deeply in the saucer, which had already
healed itself as much as the deflector plow would allow. The
battleship was now attached to the large saucer. Jenks again
hit the braking thrusters and was satisfied when the shuttle
started to slow. Then the fuel lines quickly ran dry as Ryan
saw the fast-approaching deflector plow growing larger in
the windscreen.

"Oh, shit."

The shuttle first slammed into the bow of the *Lee* and then
careened into the thick steel-reinforced plow. The shuttle
slammed to a stop.

"All hands, time to go." Jenks blasted open the twin bay

doors. As the men started to use their backpacks to get into the air, several laser shots blasted by their heads. The men slowed, as they didn't know where the fire was coming from.

"Damn it, they were waiting on us." Ryan wished he had a cannon mounted on the nose of the shuttle.

Suddenly a rail gun sprang to life, firing a single round in front of the fast-moving assault element. The tungsten round slammed into the opening of the damaged section and took out five Grays as they thought they had easy floating targets. The rail gun fell silent as a team of Grays hit the mount, blowing it into oblivion.

The assault element entered the saucer though the giant hole created by the *Lee*.

Jenks removed his helmet, forgoing the danger of a hull breach, and then popped a dead cigar stub into his mouth.

"Well, all we can do now is wait, flyboy."

Everett had lost one man as they floated through the strange interior of the large craft. The curved walls were luminescent in a soft green glow. The expanse of deck was empty, with the exception of debris that had blasted into the interior from Ryan's AMRAAMs. As they gained a foothold, they found the farther they got from the damaged area, the more gravity they were feeling. Soon they were able to place feet on the deck and move far more rapidly. They soon found the flooring to be slimy underneath their boots. The vessel seemed to pulsing with a life of its own.

Suddenly they were confronted by an unhelmeted Gray as the creature rounded the curvature of the corridor. The Gray reacted faster than the assault team as it raised its long staff of a weapon and fired point blank into one of the Delta team as he was caught totally unaware. The laser weapon tore a large hole into the kid and he was blown backward. Before the Gray could re-aim his clumsy weapon, Everett and three others opened fire with their seventy-five-watt laser rifles. The beams caught the Gray and neatly sliced its head and arms away as if he was cut with a butcher's saw. Everett checked on the downed Delta man, who clearly was dead. He quickly removed the large nuke from his back, cutting easily through the duct tape, and slung it over his oxygen tanks.

Everett knew then the assault team was bound to run into more Grays inside the vast ship, and the admiral also knew they would never make it as far in as they had planned.

"Attack team Alpha, we're placing charges right here. We'll get cut to pieces before we get to the target area."

"Attack team Alpha, this is Bravo, we understand, we are running into heavy Gray activity. Will progress further and see if resistance is lighter, over."

"Bravo, negative, say again, negative. Set your charges at current pos. I repeat, your current position. I believe the nukes will be enough to set off a chain reaction inside the ship. Look at the walls, the whole thing is one big massive power cell, over."

Ryan and Jenks heard the radio calls and exchanged looks.

"Carl will never have the time for his team to find another way out. And we're all out of heavy ordnance." Ryan felt helpless as he knew Everett would set off the charges regardless.

Jenks looked frustrated as he tried to think. He removed the cigar and threw it hard against the glass. "Goddamn it, I knew that asshole Toad would go and blow himself up!"

"Ryan, do you copy? Over," a call pierced their helmets. "Ryan, do you copy? Over." The call came in the clear.

"This is Ryan. Jack, is that you?"

"Listen up, we have control of the last functioning rail gun, but we have Grays crawling all over the place. Leave the section you're currently in and make your way back to the same location where the admiral and his men entered the saucer. We have the coordinates and will blast open the hole again. Get those men off that are near you, and Lieutenant Tram will bring your team over to the escape pods, over."

Jenks whistled. "Ballsy, but that may be the only way of getting two birds with one stone."

"Roger that, what about you?"

"Just follow orders, Jason. Now get a move on; I fire this thing in two mikes, over."

Jason saw the first of his assault team as they started to gather at the damaged section where the deflector plow was buried deep into the saucer. That was when he felt a strange vibration course through the shuttle.

"What in the hell is that?" he said to Jenks.

"Oh, shit," the master chief said as he looked closely at his radar screen. The familiar displacement of space and time started to show up on the sweep of radar. "We have a large buildup of power emissions coming from that ship. I think it's trying to power up to form a time-displacement wormhole. Goddamn it, can we catch a break here?"

Jason didn't hesitate further. He tried to fire his maneuvering thrusters, but they failed to fire.

"Forget it, mister, we're bone dry on JP-5 for the thrusters. All we have is main engine power. You're going to have to push us through the steel of the *Lee* to get us out." Jenks quickly replaced his helmet. "Bravo team, do you understand the plan? Over."

"Weapons set and operational—ten minutes to detonation. Team Bravo regressing to evac point, I hope someone's there to cover our asses," said the SEAL lieutenant.

Jason grimaced as he looked over at the master chief. "Sorry about this." He pushed the joystick on the left armrest to its stops, at the same time firing the starboard maneuverings jets. The shuttle started coming forward, farther into the damaged section of saucer. The large deflector plow scraped hard against the tiles of the shuttle as Ryan applied more forward pressure. They heard cables and electrical wiring snapping like piano wires as the shuttle cut through the stabilizing rigging for the plow. Jason applied more fire to the starboard OHMs burn. The shuttle started turning as they entered the interior of the giant saucer. The inside of the cockpit glowed green and blue as the walls of the ship illuminated the men's two faces. Then Jason felt the pressure holding back the shuttle ease as he broke through. He turned tight and then she was free.

"Go, go, go!" Jenks shouted. The small shuttle broke into the open with her main engine shooting a long flash of bright blue flame, her engines at full power. She sped along the centerline mass of the saucer, heading for the scabbed-over area where Carl and his men had vanished, hoping Collins was right about a rail gun being operational.

Tram was at the very bow of the *Garrison Lee*, waving the attack team forward. He saw Grays close behind and so he lowered himself behind the large deflector plow, then brought the very old gift he had received from Jack Collins four years before to his shoulder. The M-14 was settled into a conjoined seam of steel for a steady support, and the Vietnamese sniper took careful aim. The Grays were firing at the men trying desperately to escape through the hole. They started to scramble over the area the shuttle had just destroyed when the first of the Grays started shooting.

The SEAL lieutenant was shot in the back before Tram could cover him. The small man cursed his slowness but still drew a bead on the monstrous being bearing down on the retreating assault team. He fired. The 7.62 millimeter round caught the first Gray in the exact center of the helmeted head, dropping him immediately. The second powerful round took the next one in line and was just as deadly. The third took two shots to bring it down. The assault team now had the time to go hand over hand across the plow to reach Tram's position.

Tram raised the rifle and pointed back toward the very bow of the *Lee* and the escape pods waiting there.

"General, we have succeeded. I will now come to you," Tram said in broken English as he moved to follow Team Bravo to the superstructure of the burning *Lee*.

"Negative, Lieutenant, get the hell out of here. That's an order!" Jack said forcefully.

Tram looked amidships, where Collins was inside the number fifteen rail gun. He watched as the small turret turned toward the formerly damaged area where Alpha team had entered. Tram cursed and then followed the team to the escape pods. His battle was now over.

Everett watched as the last charge was set. He felt the hair inside his suit rise as power coursed through the ship around him. He had heard the master chief and his opinion earlier that the saucer was trying to open a wormhole. The giant saucer started to shake as the power increased.

"Last charge is set," he called. A rocking explosion sounded from close to a half mile away. Jack had done what he promised and opened the hole. The rail gun discharged once more, opening the hole wider and slowing the reatomizing of the material making up the alien saucer's hull.

"Okay, Alpha, your door is open!" Jack called as he saw the shuttle limp close in. The braking jets were still and silent as Ryan slammed the black nose into the void. "Your ride's here, Admiral, move it!"

"Jack, get the hell out of there, don't worry about us!"

Collins escaped the turret just before the Grays blew it to shreds. Fifteen of them fired continuously and didn't even notice when Jack slid out of the opening between the two electrically charged barrels. He thought for a moment that his bulky suit was going to get caught, and then with a deep intake of breath he pushed through. He floated freely for a brief moment until he was able to reach out and grab a floating cable that arrested his flight before he drifted away between the flaming wreck of the *Lee* and the power-distribution saucer. Steady explosions were starting to rock the broken battleship from stem to stern as her munitions and coolant tanks started to cook off as the flames reached the many storage lockers buried deep inside the ship. As Collins watched the bridge area finally let go as the *Lee*'s forward particle and Argon gas storage area exploded in a blue cloud of debris. The bridge separated itself from the superstructure and went hurtling into the large saucer. The steel slammed into the large alien craft, creating a large hole that quickly started to heal. Jack chanced a look at the hole he blasted through the saucer's hull and saw Ryan taking on Carl's assault team.

Suddenly the area of space around the saucer started to waver before Jack's eyes and he thought that he was finally succumbing to his head wound. Then his stomach started to turn over as his gloved hand tried to keep a hold on the drifting cable holding him in place. As he spun he saw the whiteness of Antarctica far below. He wondered if Sarah was safe, and that was all his mind could take in at the moment. A hand took hold of his suit and he thought he saw Carl's face.

"Damn it, Jack, you accidently shut down your oxygen mix."

Collins felt himself rolled over and then the cold, refreshing blast of air as it filled his helmet.

As Everett turned him over he saw that the shuttle was ready for them. He pushed and pulled Jack free of the wreckage of the *Lee* as she shuddered, and then there was silence as she started to wrench away from the fast moving saucer. Everett saw the shuttle as Ryan tried in vain to hold her in place, but the *Garrison Lee* finally broke in two directly amidships. The stern section whipped around and in its wake it slingshot the shuttle forward and away from the two men.

Carl reached out and grabbed the remains of the aluminum United Nations flag as her battered stern came around. That was when his eyes fell on the tunnel opening for the escape pods.

"Make a run for home, Ryan, we can't make it!" Carl said into his mike as Jack started to come around. His eyes tried to focus but all he could see was the deflector plow finally releasing its hold on the giant saucer and go hurtling into low orbit.

"No fucking way, we're coming to get you."

Jenks came on next and belayed the order. "We don't have the fuel, we're going to have to find a clear and very long runway as it is. We've lost lower hydraulics, and that means no landing gear."

"You heard the man, Jason, fire your main engine and get back to Camp Alamo. You can't miss it, use the ice for a runway. Now get to it!"

With one last look at his two friends Ryan realized he had to save the men crammed into the cargo hold. Angry, he throttled the shuttle forward.

"I take it the rescue didn't go well," Jack said as he finally came around. He grabbed for the dislodged stern section that held the battered flag.

"We only have to float here for a few seconds longer, buddy," Everett said as he held onto Jack tighter.

"How much longer?" Collins asked, knowing what Carl meant.

Before he could answer, a small rescue pod bumped into them. Inside they saw the serious face of Tram as he guided the escape pod closer. He threw open the Plexiglas cover and then gestured for the men.

Carl knew the limitations of the pod. It held six and Tram already had six plus himself inside. He pushed and pulled Jack along the flag and then shoved the weightless body toward the open hatch.

"Take him, Lieutenant; I'll catch the next one."

Collins tried to reach out and take hold of Everett's arm but it was too late. He felt hands on him as the men of the Bravo assault element pulled him inside the small pod.

Tram placed the escape vehicle into automatic and the small craft shot forward, hurtling toward the ice continent far below.

Everett watched his friends leave and was content.

The swirling pattern of the vortex started in earnest as the dimensional wormhole started to form. To his surprise it whipped up a debris storm and his eyes widened as he saw an empty escape pod come at him from out of nowhere. He let go of the flag and reached for all he was worth. He caught the open canopy of the dislodged and empty pod.

He held on as he tried to pull himself up and in. He finally managed to make it and immediately buttoned it up.

"Carl, damn you," Jack was heard saying.

"I'm not dead yet, buddy." He placed the pod into automatic to allow the computer to take him home.

"Get away from there, the wormhole is on you!"

To Everett it looked as if a kaleidoscope had opened up and the colors of the universe filled the black void of space. The sight was amazing. The saucer was creating something only found naturally in deep space as stars collapsed in on themselves. The swirling tornado of dust particles, debris from the battle, and dust from space filled his vision as the saucer started to make a run for its home fleet. The smaller saucers fell into formation with it and Carl's pod was pulled up at the same moment.

Every event of Everett's life soon flew past his vision. He knew this to be illusion as his body and mind were caught in the displacement of time as the escape pod shot up into the swirling tornado of light. The large saucer, the processing ships, and the smaller attack craft were three hundred miles ahead of the small pod and much farther into the tornado.

"I don't think so," Carl said as his smile grew wide.

The twenty-four Israeli-built nuclear charges detonated right on time, catching the large saucer before it exited the displacement into the deep-space home of the floating home fleet carrying the remains of the Gray civilization. The power replenishment ship blew outward with the power of an exploding sun, vaporizing the other ships and sending them to their doom in the wink of an eye.

"Oops," was all Everett had time to say as he glanced at the watch he had attached to his spacesuit's sleeve just above the thick glove. He saw the exact time that was recorded on the damaged and ancient watch found in Antarctica by the British five years before, and the blood-streaked crystal. The small pod was violently thrown backward as the wave of superheated gases slammed into Everett. The pod was immediately and violently thrown free of the displacement wormhole and sent tumbling through the tunnel until it exited somewhere over Antarctica—two hundred thousand years before the *Garrison Lee* ever took flight.

The great mystery that no man could avoid came to pass and Admiral Carl Everett vanished into a distant past.

Soon the dimensional wormhole dissipated and nothing was left but the floating wreckage of a once proud warship of human and Martian design.

CHATO'S CRAWL, ARIZONA

Matchstick held the hand of Gus, and Dr. Denise Gilliam had her arm wrapped around the old man's waist as they were led from the Black Hawk to the front gate. Gus wanted nothing more than to get inside his old, comfortable shack and rest with his best friend. Before they reached the gate, the copilot of the helicopter hurriedly caught up with Pete and Charlie. Matchstick stopped to see what the excitement was about. They failed to see the burly man with the cowboy hat at the open gate tense up.

"Dr. Golding, we have a flash message from Group," the young copilot said as the pilot also joined the three men. The Marine corporal was eyeing the big man at the gate suspiciously as he noticed the man's eyes never left the small form of Mahjtic.

Pete took the hastily transcribed note and read it. His smile was cautious as he looked up at an expectant Matchstick.

"The power-replenishment saucer and the processing ships no longer appear on long-range Earth-based imagery."

Matchstick momentarily let go of the hand of the old prospector and took an expectant step closer to Pete. His small blue jumpsuit was too large as the pant legs dragged on the ground.

"The *Garrison Lee* has been destroyed."

Charlie placed a hand on the small shoulder and lowered his head.

Pete seemed to take heart with the next paragraph written on the notepad.

"The *Lee*'s escape pods are parachuting into the sea and on land near Camp Alamo and rescue operations have commenced."

The small alien took hold of Gus's hand and smiled up at him.

"Well, you did it, you little shit," he said with his old smile that made Mahjtic feel good inside that he could please Gus. "Don't go braggin' 'bout it," the old prospector said to Golding. "He's gonna be a bear to live with now."

Charlie, Pete, Denise, and Matchstick, in his strange cottony voice, all laughed.

"Come on Gus, we can talk about this inside," Dr. Gilliam said.

Marine corporal DeSilva moved closer to Matchstick. He also looked at the guard shack closest to the fence and slowly started to reach for the old Colt .45 at his belt. The young pilot of the Black Hawk saw the movement and unsnapped his holster that lay across his chest and then nudged the copilot, trying to get his attention. The corporal saw something that gave him pause. The big man at the gate kept flicking his dark eyes toward the old shack and then back again. He also didn't particularly care for the way he looked back at the group and the uneasy smile that appeared. His old combat hackles began to rise.

The Marine corporal pulled the Colt from its holster, but before it cleared the leather a shot rang out and DeSilva fell into the copilot. The pilot was much faster, as he had his Beretta nine millimeter in his hand, and shot the big man who had fired into the Marine with a gun he had hidden at his side. The large round caught the man in the shoulder, knocking him off balance; and before anyone knew it, Charlie Ellenshaw was on the man, taking the giant down, beating him with his fists.

Gunfire from their rear struck Ellenshaw in the back of his shoulder blade and sent him flying off the wounded bear of a man. Charlie hit face-first, his glasses flying from his face. Gus pulled Matchstick and Denise to the ground just as flying bullets caught the pilot. Three rounds stitched his flight suit but the tough Air Force lieutenant managed to get off one round as he fell backward. The nine-millimeter bullet struck the man directly in the center of his forehead, freezing him like a statue.

Gus saw the fallen weapon of the man as he fell and it clattered next to him. He started to reach for it when Denise screamed for him not to.

"Stop shooting!" Hiram Vickers shouted as he sprang from the open doorway of the old shack. He was waving his hands as the giant's brother was screaming as if he had gone insane. "Stop, we need them alive!"

The crazed brother of the dead man wasn't listening. His M-4 opened fire on full automatic. Gus was struck in the head and chest, and he was thrown off of Matchstick and Denise Gilliam. Pete tried desperately to retrieve the falling gun that flew from the old man's hand and in a near state of panic allowed it to slip through his fingers. He turned just as the charging man that had lain like a snake in hiding emptied half of the magazine into Pete Golding, sending him flying backward. Then he turned the weapon toward Denise and a frightened and stunned Matchstick as she tried to protect him the best that she could. She threw her body once again onto the alien. She felt the bullets pass through her back.

Vickers took quick aim and fired his nine millimeter six times. The bullets finally dropped the crazed fool, first to one knee, and then with a blank look on the bearded face, he fell forward dead. Vickers looked at his weapon and then lowered it in stunned silence. He raised his eyes and looked at the complete disaster that had unfolded in the blink of an eye.

Vickers stood there with the smoking weapon in his hand and looked at the carnage before him. Denise Gilliam's body twitched, then he saw a small arm and hand reach out and try and touch the hand of the old prospector who lay not far from the two bodies. The fingers twitched and as the long digits came into contact with the old man's still hand, the hand then quit moving.

Vickers saw his life coming to an end as his last hope of getting a trade for his life was now gone.

He slowly made his way to the car that was hidden behind the old shack. He looked back once more at the eight bodies that lay there as the hot desert wind started to pick up. His red hair blew into his eyes as he saw the carnage not as a disturbing scene, but as a man would look at a broken dish he had dropped in his kitchen. He knew now he would have to run.

Hiram Vickers had one last hope, and that was to blackmail Camden and Peachtree. After all, he had been under orders to secure the asset known as Magic.

As the red taillights of his car vanished in the distant desert night, another Black Hawk came low over the desert scrub. The pilot took the large helicopter to two hundred feet as he looked on in shocked silence at the scene below. He switched on his powerful searchlight and scanned the area below. His heart sank when his mind took in the carnage.

Dr. Virginia Pollock, tired and weary from her flight from the east, saw the scene in slow-motion detail as the searchlight played over the fallen. Her head slowly slid against the glass and a loud moan escaped her lips.

THE WHITE HOUSE
WASHINGTON, D.C.

The president was wheeled into the Oval Office by the first lady. Four Secret Service agents flanked them as the commander-in-chief saw the man stand from the couch he had been sitting in. Before the door closed, General Maxwell Caulfield entered and was followed by the reaffirmed director of the FBI and the newly reinstalled director of the CIA, Harlan Easterbrook.

The president reached out a hand and touched his wife's

as he neared the window that looked out onto Pennsylvania Avenue. He swallowed and pulled back the lace curtain and took in the view. Gone were the thousands of protesters that had lined the avenue. Being packed up and crated were the many missile batteries that had not only covered the White House grounds, but the entire city. Gone also was the innocence of the nation, along with that of the entire world. Not one person living could ever have that sense of security again. It had been ten days since the battle for Earth and they had lost too many of their own and others. The entire planet was in mourning over the death and destruction.

Speaker of the House Giles Camden watched the president as he allowed the curtain to fall back into place. The small man adjusted his gold-rimmed glasses and sternly looked on as the broken and wounded man was turned in his wheelchair by the first lady to take his rightful place behind the Lincoln desk.

The other men in the room flanked the desk and looked at the former acting president.

"Your friend and ally, Mr. Peachtree, is nowhere to be found," the president started saying. "The FBI says he's somewhere in Panama, but they suspect he will try to eventually make his way to a nonextradition nation."

Camden remained standing and silent as he eyed his most hated enemy.

"He should know that there is no such thing as a safe haven any longer. The entire world is searching for Mr. Peachtree and his trained monkey, Hiram Vickers—who, by the way, has forwarded to this office a very cryptic message. It said that he has information on not only who ordered the hit on our asset in Arizona, but also an unsolved double murder in Georgetown last year."

"I don't understand, Mr. President. Who is this Hiram Vickers?"

The first lady scowled at the question and wanted to jump over her husband and strangle the man. But the president patted her hand that was gripping the wheelchair so tight it turned her knuckles white with rage.

"Well, I'm sure we'll know everything in a few days. In the meantime, Mr. Speaker, I have had conversations with members of your party and the rest of the House. It seems you have been relegated to minor status—in other words, they want you out. The loss of two hundred and fifty thousand American lives in Antarctica, at sea, and in space has been charged to your account."

"I only did what I thought—"

The president's hand came down hard on the reports of death and destruction that lined his work area, and his face grew grave as he slowly stood on his shattered legs and leaned on the desk.

"Peachtree and Vickers will be caught, Mr. Speaker, and we will get to the bottom of this, and your resignation will be the last thing you are thinking about. The FBI and the IRS have uncovered some very interesting paper trails from your office that wind through many foreign bank accounts, and those countries you thought would assist in hiding that paper trail have suddenly become very cooperative. It's not the same world any longer, Mr. Speaker."

Camden looked closely at the man behind the desk as he tiredly slid down into the wheelchair. His eyes then went to the men around him and even the Secret Service agents who only days before had guarded his life. The hate there was enough to send chills down the most coldhearted man ever to hold public office. He reached down and retrieved his briefcase, nodded at the president, and then left the Oval Office.

"Mr. President, that's enough for today," Max Caulfield said as he took in his exhausted features.

"No, I have one last task to perform. Mr. Easterbrook, do you have that address?"

"Yes, sir, right here." The silver-haired man reached out and gave the first lady the note.

"Do we have enough to put that son of a bitch Camden away for life?"

The director of the FBI smiled. He just nodded his head.

"Then the testimony of the two traitors, Hiram Vickers and Daniel Peachtree, will not be needed?"

"Not at all, sir," the director said as he and the others started to leave.

The president waited until he and the first lady were alone before he picked up his secure phone. Before he made the connection he looked up at his wife. She only nodded and smiled, giving her tacit approval of what he was about to do.

"We owe him at least this much." She patted him on the shoulder and then reached down and pecked him on the cheek.

The president watched the first lady leave the office and then he turned to the phone and made the call. It was answered.

"The Juarez Hotel, Panama City, room 817," the president said calmly into the phone and then hung up. He then made another connection. It was also answered on the first ring. "After this I cannot protect you. Your status will be as before in the eyes of American law enforcement."

"I understand," the voice said from the other end.

"But before I say anything, in my eyes and the eyes of many others you have shown your true quality. I won't ever forget that."

The phone was silent.

"1262 Norman Drive, Beverly Hills. He's there now."

The phone went dead and the president slowly hung up.

"All family business," he said to himself. The Oval Office door opened and the Secret Service man allowed the president's two daughters to come in running. They threw their arms around him and hugged him. His eyes went to the window as he returned their hugs. "All family business."

BEVERLY HILLS, CALIFORNIA

Daniel Peachtree was staying at the richly appointed home of an old college friend, one who'd invested the millions of dollars he and Camden had made during the technology buy-up of the past four years. He casually walked out to the pool that was a part of the thirty-five-million-dollar home and told the houseman that he wanted a drink. He had been doing a lot of drinking since Vickers's small fiasco in the desert. He shook his head, slowly sat down, and leaned back in the expensive chaise longue. He closed his eyes until he heard the tinkle of ice inside a glass. He smiled and looked up as his drink was handed to him.

He took a sip and then noticed the houseman had not moved away but continued to block his sunlight. He glanced up and became confused, as he didn't recognize the man standing over him. The gray suit and white shirt bounced the sun off of him and Peachtree became concerned.

"Who in the hell are you?" he asked as he placed the drink on the glass table next to the lounge chair.

"I, Mr. Peachtree, am no one but a messenger."

Peachtree swallowed at the blond-haired man standing over him. "What message?"

The man didn't smile, he didn't even blink as the large knife was plunged deeply into the former CIA's director of Operation's chest. The blade was twisted and the breath exploded from Peachtree's lungs. Blood flowed from his open mouth.

"Colonel Jack Collins sends his regards."

Henri Farbeaux pulled the knife free and then slowly and mercilessly sliced the American traitor's throat.

With that, Colonel Henri Farbeaux once again assumed his most-wanted status in the world. He disappeared into the backdrop of a tired and war-weary society.

PANAMA CITY, PANAMA

Hiram Vickers was whistling as he turned the old-fashioned lock to his room. He had just left two messages, one at Camden's Georgetown residence, and one at Peachtree's. There had been no answer at either home but that didn't dampen his mood, as he knew the men had been forced into a corner with the simple threat of exposure. He slowly pushed open the door and flicked on the table lamp by the frame. He closed the door and then tossed his room key in the ashtray there. As he turned he saw the man sitting in the room's only chair.

Jack Collins.

He tried to say something but the words froze in his throat. Collins tilted his head as he looked at the man who had so ruthlessly murdered his little sister. The man was an enigma to a man like Jack. The way he arrogantly pranced through the world affecting the lives of others with no regard to who the men or women really were, and how his decisions affected not only them, but the families of those unfortunates.

Jack Collins was still bandaged from his forehead to his arms from the ordeal in Antarctica and outer space. His eyes were blackened and his nose broken. This made his appearance that much more menacing, even though Vickers easily recognized the man from his apartment in Georgetown and the many nightmares since.

"I—"

Collins shook his head and Vickers stopped before he started. Jack nodded for Vickers to move to the couch and sit. He did.

Collins slowly stood, feeling every one of his injuries from the previous week. He stood before Hiram Vickers.

"I didn't know what I was going to say before today. What you did to Lynn, and then the taking of so many innocents in Chato's Crawl . . ." Jack stopped, unable to continue for a moment. "What turns a man into an animal?"

The redheaded man swallowed and looked away from the piercing blue eyes.

Jack Collins made his way to the door, opened it, and stepped out into the warm day. He took a breath and spotted a small housekeeper making her way down the second-story balcony. Jack placed his sunglasses on and then smiled as he approached the old woman.

"*Llamar a la policía y el cuerpo de bomberos, por favor,*" he said with a smile. "*Vámonos!*" he added and slapped her ample behind.

The housekeeper left her cart and started hurriedly walking away. She turned and with one last look back at the bruised man who had sent her off to call the police and fire departments, decided that she should run.

Jack Collins slowly walked away and down the nearest set of stairs. He was almost to the rented car when a whoosh was heard from above. The large window of the room Hiram Vickers had rented blew outward. Flames licked the hallway as the screaming sounded in the nearly empty hotel.

Jack opened the passenger door of the rental car. Jason Ryan was behind the wheel and he placed the car into gear. The two Event Group officers moved away from the cheap hotel as fire alarms and the distant sound of sirens pierced the beautiful day in Panama City.

EPILOGUE

It's never good-bye, just farewell.

The conference room was silent as the department heads filed out. Niles Compton, looking like a smaller version of Senator Garrison Lee, sat with his head down as the six remaining men and women waited for the director to speak. The bandage covering Compton's face was still in place, and a new black eye patch covered his right eye. The rest of the occupants were in no better shape than Niles.

Virginia Pollock wasn't injured, but the dark circles under her eyes attested to the mental shape she was in since the night she came upon the slaughter at Chato's Crawl. She had cried endlessly since that night. Alice Hamilton took her hand as her sobs escaped when she looked up and saw all of the empty seats around them.

"Did Anya Korvesky make it back safely to Tel Aviv?" Niles asked without looking up.

"Yes, I put her on the plane myself. She's . . . she's . . . well, she's not taking the loss of Mr. Everett all that well," Jason Ryan said from his new appointed place beside Jack Collins.

Niles nodded his head and then let out a breath.

Charlie Ellenshaw, with his eyes downcast, just stared at the polished table. He slowly shook his head, wincing slightly at the bullet wound to his back. He had been released from the hospital the day before and had been silent ever since. Gone were the silly comments and the quizzical looks. Now he was broken, saddened beyond measure. He swallowed and looked at the chair Pete Golding used to occupy. He slid his own chair back and slowly stood. He started to say something, but instead just turned and paced to the far wall and leaned his gray and disheveled hair against it. They saw his shoulders heaving as he cried for his lost friend.

"The president is speaking at the memorial in Arlington for . . ."

Niles removed the glasses that were only assisting one eye and stopped speaking. Alice wiped a tear away. She knew the director was blaming himself for the loss of Gus, Pete, Denise Gilliam, and Matchstick.

Jack Collins reached out and took the hand of Sarah McIntire, then he stood. He walked over to the far wall, brought over a tray of glasses and a large bottle of Kentucky bourbon, and placed it on the table. He then walked to the still crying Ellenshaw and guided him back to the table. He winked at Jason Ryan, who stood and poured out the whiskey. He even poured one for his friend Will Mendenhall, who was in New Zealand recovering from his extensive wounds, and one for a fugitive who was again on the run: Colonel Henri Farbeaux. He passed around the glasses and then waited for Jack.

"I once heard this in War College. I always knew what it meant, but never once did I think the words could ring so true."

The men and women around the table stood with the exception of Niles Compton, who replaced his glasses and watched the recently demoted U.S. Army colonel raise his glass. The others followed suit.

"It was a quote from Robert E. Lee after the Battle of Gettysburg."

Virginia couldn't hold it in as the images of Gus, Pete, Denise, Carl, and Matchstick filled her memory. She placed a hand over her eyes and openly wept.

"We gather around our nightly dinner table and we see an occasional empty chair, but we are never, ever, prepared to see them all empty." Jack looked from face to face, pausing at Virginia Pollock as she finally looked up with her glass in hand. "I want to say to each and every one of you, these chairs will never be empty, not as long as we remember those men and women who occupied them." He raised his glass higher. "To absent friends."

The others echoed the sentiment as the conference room door opened and an Air Force messenger in his blue jump suit entered carrying a message. He placed it before Compton and then quickly left.

Niles placed his glass on the table and retrieved the message. He read it and then handed it over to Alice Hamilton. She also perused it and then sat down as the others did also.

"It seems our contact inside the Vatican archives, code-named Goliath, has uncovered a rare find indeed. Our lieutenant has discovered an ancient map of an area inside the borders of the modern state of Georgia, the former Soviet Republic, depicting the possible resting place of an ancient artifact of legend."

Niles smiled for the first time in weeks.

"Georgia—the old Soviet State that was once known to the Greeks as Colchis."

Sarah looked at Alice with a question written on her face. Alice, instead of answering, turned to Charles Hindershot Ellenshaw III to respond for her. Charlie cleared his throat as he placed his empty glass on the table.

"Colchis is the supposed resting place of a relic you may be familiar with. In the *Argonautica*, Appollonius Rhodius's third-century BC epic poem about Jason and his Argonauts, Colchis was the home of the legendary Golden Fleece."

"The Vatican hiding this map is at the very least intriguing," Niles said. "Jack, would you get in touch with Goliath and request more information?"

Jack Collins looked from face to face of his remaining friends, took Sarah's hand in his own, and nodded his head.

The group started talking about the impossibilities, the possibilities, and the way in which to discover the truth.

The closed doors of the conference room were no different than they were last year, or the year before that, and the year before that.

The thick oaken doors hid the secret Department 5656, also known as the Event Group, and it was now back to doing its job.

Read on for an excerpt from the next book
by David L. Golemon

THE MOUNTAIN

Coming soon in hardcover from Thomas Dunne Books

1

The eight members of the Senate Oversight Committee were stunned to silence. The same could not be said for the press seated inside the crowded room. Even military officers were visibly shocked at the comment uttered only moments before by the United States Army officer seated before the panel. As the room was silenced, several of the higher ranking military men; mostly Army officers, glared at the man seated at the table with his JAG attorneys and then angrily left the chamber. The U.S. Army lawyers were all still shaking their heads at his statement as the men implicated in the cover-up stormed out. After all, it wasn't every day that one of the official wunderkinds of the U.S. military so readily committed career suicide right in front of the entire nation.

Senator James Kellum, head of the Joint Arms Services Committee, hammered the gavel several times to get the observers and guests to quiet down.

"Ladies and gentlemen, I will clear this chamber if there is one more outburst like that. This is not a soap opera with good guys and bad guys, this is an investigation into the charges of misconduct by supreme command authority in a combat area. People's lives and careers are on the line here and I will not let these proceedings devolve into anarchy."

The C-SPAN cameras seemed to be locked on the tired and scarred face of the young army major sitting beside his JAG council at the table. The man didn't seem to hear the commotion that his last statement had unleashed. The major pursed his lips and then shook his head as he must have been feeling his career slipping right out from underneath the polished chair he was sitting in.

He looked up and then calmly poured himself a glass of water from the decanter in front of him. He sipped from the glass and waited for the senator to regain control. On the television screens of millions of viewers nationwide the C-SPAN cameras had zeroed in first on the green beret that sat upon the table's top and then the view easily moved onto the rows of ribbons on the left breast of the green uniform jacket. The first ribbon on the top row was the one the cameras sharp eye was focusing on. The ribbon wasn't much, but those few who knew the powder blue ribbon with five stars represented the Congressional Medal of Honor. The camera's lens lingered and then slowly moved to the heavily tanned face of the army major who wore it. Although seemingly unfazed by the words he had spoken a moment before, the few men and women who knew him also knew the major was dying moment by moment as he sat before the senate. The chamber finally became still as the last of the high ranking officers left the room.

Major Jack Collins calmly waited for the hearing to continue.

"Major Collins, to clarify your last, rather harsh statement," the senator from Missouri broke in before the head of the committee could continue his line of questioning which drew the ire of the representative from New York, "that the decision to alter the highly detailed plans of the assault were ordered from CENTCOM?" he asked as again the raised voices of questions sprang from the onlookers inside the chamber. "Can you explain why someone would override a battle plan that had already been approved by the commander of Central Command?"

The young major thought before he answered. He knew that the question was a loaded one that had been specially prepared by the only man on the committee that Major Collins trusted, The Senator from Missouri who had asked the question now so it could not be shunted aside by the Oversight Committee Chair, Senator Charles Fennel of New York. Collins, without glancing at his fidgeting JAG representatives, leaned forward as did half of the nation toward their television screens as he prepared to end not only his career but possibly many others in and out of uniform.

"The answer to your question, Senator, is not an easy one. It took me seven months to get to the truth after my assignment in Iraq was completed. By then the people responsible thought it would have been put to bed, or as they hoped, forgotten."

"From my understanding the investigation into the debacle had been completed eight months before, soon after the events had taken place. Which was a little faster than I thought it should have taken, but the results of that investigation did not sit well with you, am I correct in saying that Major?" "the senator from Missouri asked.

"You are correct. When you're speaking about the lives of twenty-one men—men who I trained, worked and lived with, no sir, the investigation in my eyes fell far short of the truth."

The head of the armed services committee, James Kellum, was staring at his colleague from Missouri as did the C-SPAN cameras. Everyone in the country could see that the senior man from New York was as angry as anyone had ever seen him.

"I'll ask you directly, Major, were numbers of Apache Longbow gunships and Blackhawk helicopters allowed for in the planning of Operation *Morning Glory* adequate for the mission to succeed?"

"In my original operational plan there were more than enough evac and support ships to cover all aspects of the mission in Afghanistan. Every soldier on that raid should have been lifted out safely from the area after the operation was complete."

"Yet almost two full squads of Special Forces personnel, including twelve Army Rangers were," the senator from Missouri looked down at his notes momentarily for emphasis to his question, "in your words, Major Collins, 'left on the deck' because of inadequate evac response. Is this more or less correct?"

"The plan called for all personnel to be evacuated at the same time. The Taliban insurgents have a bad habit of waiting for the initial first wave to lift off and then strike at those troops left uncovered in the LZ, or landing zone. That was why the extra Apache Longbows were allotted for, the added firepower to assist those left on the ground until the second wave of evacuation Blackhawks lifted off the last of the rear guard. The second attack group of gunships never arrived. The Apaches that were there had RTB because of fuel concerns. My men were left out there with no air cover whatsoever with over three thousand Taliban insurgents in the mountains surrounding them."

"How many of the twenty seven American boys made it off of that mountain, Major?" the senator asked as the chamber became silent.

"None."

"Major, what happened to those men?" the senator continued.

"Six were taken alive into the mountains, we found their bodies three weeks after my return to Afghanistan."

"The rest?"

"The description of their condition the next morning is not something I will go into here. Suffice it to say these men were massacred."

"During your personal investigation what was it you uncovered in regard to the missing element of air cover on April 6, 2005?"

"That three Apache and six Blackhawks had been reassigned in my absence for escort duty by CENTCOM, not in Afghanistan but in Florida through MacDill Air Force Base."

Again the gavel silenced most of the shocked and angry people watching inside the chamber.

"The decision was not made in theater, but at MacDill? Is that unusual, Major Collins?"

"Highly. Someone at CENTCOM changed the orders on the logistics of Operation *Morning Glory* to provide security in another area of responsibility."

"And what area of responsibility is more important than the lives of twenty-seven American soldiers?"

Collins stayed silent as the head of the services committee's face grew red and he began to fume as he awaited the guillotine blade to fall. Thinking now that this committee should never have been formed and wouldn't have if that bastard from Missouri hadn't taken it to the press. He slammed the gavel down again as he angrily silenced the room. The major looked from the table top to the man glaring at him from the center of the podium.

"The commanding general at MacDill changed the orders to provide security for a fact-finding inquiry from Washington on the conduct of operations in the Kabul area. This committee was escorted by the six Blackhawks and my three missing Apache Longbows. The area commander in Kabul ordered the helicopters to leave the investigative committee at a secure location and proceed on mission for dust off of my men. The order was overridden from Kabul after the senate and committee complained about staying over in a small village. Because of their comfort concerns twenty-seven men won't be coming home."

It had been the former CENTCOM commander who had angrily left the chamber a few moments before when he realized Collins was not going to play the game. The threats to Collins and his career had not had the desired effect on the obstinate major.

"Major Collins, according to your investigation, what civilian personnel were involved in the fact finding mission to Afghanistan that month?"

Collins looked straight at the head of the senate oversight

committee. "Senator James Kellum and several civilian contractors from various corporations."

The gavel slammed on the table again as the room erupted. The senator from New York shot to his feet as the wooden gavel fought for order. "I pray you have proof of that statement, especially after the commanding general of CENTCOM cleared my committee of all of these rumors?"

Collins smiled and then reached down and retrieved his briefcase and then placed it on the table before him. The room hushed as Collins removed a plastic-covered sheet of paper. "Yes, Senator Kellum, I do have proof." Jack held up the plastic-covered paper and placed it on the desk before him. His JAG lawyers frowned as they all knew Collins had just officially ended his military career. "The order was issued by the commander of CNETCOM and countersigned by yourself, Senator."

That was it. The statement was out and entered into the official record. The first soldier to turn on a four star general and the civilian senator who controlled the purse strings of the military. As the words and career of Jack Collins faded, the eruption inside the senate hearing chamber exploded into a cacophony of shouts and gasps. The Major easily slid the plastic-protected memo over to the front of the table where a senate aid removed it for the committee as the room continued to erupt and Senator Kellum kept slamming down his gavel.

EVENT GROUP COMPLEX, NELLIS
AIR FORCE BASE, NEVADA

Almost a full mile beneath the sands of the abandoned WWII target range was an ancient underground sea that had vanished over six million years before. All that remained behind was the largest cave system inside the continental United States. While dwarfing the Carlsbad system of caves in New Mexico, the Nellis system is not a park or recreational site. The cave system was never placed in any registry of geological wonders as its sister in neighboring New Mexico's desert, but had been kept secret since its discovery in 1922. The reasons for this silence was rumored to have been built in 1943–1945 by the same men and women who had designed the new Pentagon building in Washington. Their final architectural drawings would never see the light of day in any public or federal planning office in the nation, though.

The cave system was home to the darkest organization in American governmental history. Department 5656 was officially a part of the U.S. National Archives and was darker than most aspects of the National Security Administration. The department, unofficially named the Event Group, was assigned the task of discovering the truth behind world history. To investigate how and why we got to where we were. To avoid mistakes of history so they can never be repeated. The head of this Group now sat inside of his office on the seventh level of the complex that was situated above seventy-five more levels of archives, specimen vaults, engineering and science laboratories.

The small balding man looked over at the former head of the agency, who was sitting across from his large desk. The tall man had a black eye patch over his right eye and had his cane propped against the director's large desk. The bald man shook his head sadly as he watched the developments on C-SPAN. He looked over at the six foot six silver-haired man across from him who had stayed on long after his official retirement four years before to assist in the daunting task of assisting the new director in navigating his way through the ends and outs of keeping the facility, their duty, and their personnel secret above all government agencies.

"So, I wonder who assisted Major Collins in obtaining that top secret memo?" He smiled at his former boss and the man that had recruited him fifteen years before. "I suspect it had to have been someone who knows where to find such things inside the Washington trash heap."

Former United Sates senator Garrison Lee of Maine smiled and shook his head in the negative.

"Nah, my days on the Hill and absconding with the secrets of others have long been over."

"How about the old OSS days, you still know how to get things others don't."

"The Office of Strategic Services would have resented that statement, we were as honest as the day was long, Director Compton."

"Uh-huh, just like its little bastard offspring the CIA?"

Again Garrison Lee laughed as the double doors to the office opened and a lady with silver hair and gold-rimmed glasses hanging from a chain entered. Alice Hamilton, assistant to the director of the Event Group, came toward the desk and placed a file on the top.

"There you go, the Major's orders have been cut and the President has signed off on them."

Garrison Lee reached out and picked up the flimsy set of papers. "You don't know how many favors I had to give up to get that signature. The President is not real happy with our Major Collins."

"I wonder why," Alice said, never afraid to speak her mind, especially after serving with the Group almost as long as Lee himself. In fact, speaking her mind was just why she was retained by the newest director of Department 5656, Doctor Niles Compton.

"Well, the president's and the army's sad demeanor toward one of its own means that we get the man we wanted all along." Lee stood and with the assistance of his cane walked toward the far wall to pour himself a cup of coffee. "Did you put in the correct date of Major Collins's arrival in Nevada?"

"Yes, as you requested, he has the needed time off. The two weeks off to think about what a mess his career's in should make the Major at least listen to your pitch to join our underground ship of fools," Alice Hamilton said as she headed for the double doors, but she stopped before opening them and turned to both men. "But you better be careful just what it is you wish for gentlemen, because this Major Collins is unlike any soldier you have ever met. I mean, what other officer would throw it all away out of principle and dedication to his fallen men? I would think that would make him dangerous to bureaucrats like yourselves."

Alice smiled, batted her eyelashes as was her irritating trait, and then left the large office. She hoped that they understood that they were about to deal with a career officer who was shockingly, to the army's sadness, a man of deep convictions on the right and wrong of things. It was what they were looking for, and she knew the two men in the office were just like Major Jack Collins, therefore they were comfortable with their choice.

"That damn woman is as irritating now as when she worked for me," Garrison Lee said as he sat back down into his chair facing the director. "But she's right as always about one thing," Lee finished as he sipped his coffee.

"What is that?" Compton asked, really not wanting to know.

Lee smiled and then placed the cup on the desk top. "Men like Major Jack Collins have a very low tolerance for people like us."

"You really mean people like me, don't you?" Compton asked.

"Not at all. But one thing I do know, if we hadn't interfered, Colonel Collins would have had this shit pile land right back on the president's desk as being ultimately responsible for the fiasco in Afghanistan. I'm just glad my old friend from Missouri changed his avenue of attack and left the president out of it."

"Your point?" Niles asked, getting a little nervous.

"Just the same as Alice's point I guess. If the man was willing to bring down the President of the United States, do you think he would hesitate to do the right thing in this agency if we let him or his men down?"

"Well, you took a lot of years of research to find out just what kind of man he is, now you know. With this new insight into the Major's character, do you still want him to lead the security department?" Niles asked with a smirk.

"Absolutely."

EVENT GROUP COMPLEX, NELLIS
AIR FORCE BASE, NEVADA—JULY, 2006

The Event Group complex was relatively quiet at 3:40 a.m. on Sunday. Director Niles Compton moved through the deserted serving line inside the vast dining hall. The on-duty chef was wiping his hands on a white towel as he came from the kitchen after hearing the director was in the dining area. He, along with the entire mess crew, knew that Doctor Compton often toured the facility at the oddest hours, but this stop-in was unprecedented as the director usually just called and had coffee or a meal delivered to his office on level seven. For Compton to be in the serving line at this hour woke the sleepy-eyed mess personnel like no alarm ever could. As he approached the serving line, the director was pouring a cup of coffee and was perusing the pastry selection.

The chef looked over the interior of the cafeteria and saw only one other person at far end of the room sitting alone. It was the new head of Group security, Major Collins. He was sitting and staring at a cup of coffee. The man had not moved since coming in an hour before. The entire complex was in a mood because of the extreme loses the Group and the 101st Airborne sustained in the desert event last week. It was well known that the new major was not taking the death of so many lightly and it was now rumored that Collins was going to turn down the offer of permanently staying with the Group because of those deaths. The man looked as if he had had enough of fatalities in any form.

"Doctor Compton, can I get you some breakfast, or maybe a late dinner?" the tall, very thin chef asked. The military rank displayed on his chef's whites were that of a United States Navy chief petty officer.

Compton stifled a yawn and then turned to face the navy cook. "No thank you, Chief, just trying to stay awake for the most part," Niles Compton said as he nodded at the taller man.

With one last look toward the major, the chef moved back off to his kitchen and Niles Compton steeled himself for what was to come. He took his cup and saucer and then turned and saw with relief that Garrison Lee had come in early as promised to go over the situation with Jack Collins. Lee was fresh off a heart attack brought on by the events in the Arizona desert. It had been extremely hard to keep him isolated long enough to get the heart condition under control for the simple fact that Garrison wanted to be in on the extensive debrief of the small green alien, the Matchstick Man, the lone surviving extraterrestrial crewman from Chato's Crawl, Arizona. Lee had undoubtedly used that excuse to get out of the house he shared with Alice Hamilton in Las Vegas. The main objective was to conclude Major Jack Collins's introduction to a federal agency in which he had already taken life, and ended it. It was rumored that Collins was about to officially turn down the opportunity to remain with the Group and fall into an uneasy retirement from the U.S. Army.

Niles waited for Lee to get himself a cup of coffee and then they both moved through the deserted cafeteria to confront Jack Collins about his upcoming decision. As they approached they saw that Jack was perusing the personnel files of the Event Group personnel that were killed in action the month before. His face was stone as he read the names to himself. He was so absorbed in his task that he failed to notice that Niles and Lee had joined him.

"I was wondering when you were going to corner me, but I suspected with the senator's health problems I would have had the time to formally commit my answer to paper."

Niles realized that Jack had not even looked up as they had approached, probably because he already suspected they would attempt to corner him. Niles was slowly learning that Collins was not your ordinary military officer. Jack was a thorough, analytical thinker, and that was what Lee and himself were after.

"We figured the ambush technique was best for the situation," Lee said as he placed his cup and saucer down without waiting to be asked. "I suppose you wouldn't mind the company of an old fart and super nerd long enough to bend your ear a while?" Lee finished as he sat, placing his cane against the table as he gestured for Niles to do the same. "Besides, with my retirement, Alice has me doing some very strange things around the house, like fixing things, or cutting this, or trimming that. I would rather be here bothering you than turn into Mr. Fixit at home."

"I take it Alice doesn't know you left home?" Jack inquired.

Lee pointed to the double doors of the cafeteria and Jack saw Lee's assistant, Alice, standing there with her left brow raised and shaking her head.

"Don't be foolish, it would be easier escaping a Russian Gulag than escaping her scrutiny . . . she drove me here, which means I have very little time to conduct business, so I will get started."

"I've pretty much decided what I'm going to do," Collins said as he pushed the cold cup of coffee away.

Niles stirred sugar into his own cup and then looked at Collins. He removed his glasses, a move that Jack had learned meant Niles was about to get serious, which meant he was removing those glasses on a constant basis.

"Last month when Alice and Lieutenant McIntire gave you the grand tour of the vault levels, we never got a chance to ask what you thought of our finds and artifacts," Niles said as he placed his glasses on the tabletop and slowly raised his coffee to his lips.

"The tour was cut quite short as you well know when you called the event in the desert."

"Well, the Senator and I would like to finish up that tour before you make your final decision on your appointment to this Group." Niles placed his cup down and looked at Collins, who still hadn't committed to anything. The deaths in the desert had really affected him.

"Major, you have to understand what we do here far better than we have been able to explain thus far," Lee said as he joined Compton in trying to persuade the major to give them a chance to show him why it was they needed his expertise so badly. If the fight in Arizona didn't explain it, they knew exactly what would. They were about to pull out the ace they had up their sleeves.

Jack glanced up, and he saw that Alice was still at the double doors watching them. He knew then that Alice was also a part of this plot, not just Compton and Lee.

"I'm afraid young McIntire doesn't know the full story. There are only three people in the world that have all the puzzle pieces, Major, and that is what we wish to finish up tonight. The right tour, the right artifact that will tie this whole thing together for you," Lee said as he too looked back at Alice and then slowly stood with the aid of his cane. "Mind joining us Major Collins?"

Jack stood along with Compton and started a journey into the past that the major would never would have dreamed about.

"Okay, where to?"

"The largest, most secure depository in the United States. Level sixty-one, vault one," Niles said as he led the way out of the cafeteria.

Lee placed a hand on Alice's shoulder and then turned to face Niles and Jack. "Its story time, Major Collins, and you are about to get wowed."

Collins raised his eyebrows but followed them out of the door, only pausing long enough to receive that knowing smile and wink from Alice Hamilton.

"Wowed is just about right," she said as she fell into line heading for the elevators.

The tube elevator ride was on air-cushioned propellant and traveled close to fifty mph. The four stepped off and went to the security arch where one of Jack's people accepted ID's and proceeded to send them through the eye-scan check, clearing them all for entrance into the vault level. Jack followed the three inside the enormous hallway that had the dream-like facade of several hundred bank vaults. The most secured location outside of Fort Knox and the NSA building. Each vault contained an artifact from the history of the world, and Jack had not returned to the vault level since his mission to Arizona, simply because he never wanted the wonders of the vault levels to sway his decision about staying or leaving the Group. The magnificent finds had the ability to cloud the mind and could make the process far more difficult in coming to a conclusion on his destiny.

Lee and Alice stopped at a familiar spot. It was the first vault Jack had seen at the Group. It had been pointed out to him by Lee the first day of his arrival. He knew by the size of the reinforced steel door and by its size what artifact lay beyond—the Ark. The last time he saw it he'd never had time to explain to Lee and Compton that he was far from being a believer in the fantastical story of Noah and his Ark. Collins found it hard to believe in anything other than his own ability and keeping men under his command as safe as he could.

"I suppose you need no explanation of what's behind this door?" Lee said as Niles Compton scanned his ID into the reader and then stepped back as a smaller access door opened beside the larger, impenetrable stainless steel door.

"I know what you claim it to be, but I've yet to be convinced, and to tell you the truth, gentleman," he nodded at Alice, "and lady, I am skeptical in the least, and unbelieving at the most."

"That's exactly how you should feel, Jack," Niles said as he stepped aside to allow the three to proceed him into the giant vault area.

Collins saw it in person for the first time and he had to admit the monitors inside Niles's office did the artifact no justice. No matter what this object truly was, Jack knew it to be impressive. The Ark was a broken wreck but discerning its age could be summed up in just one word—ancient. It was the oldest thing Collins had ever laid eyes on. He didn't need too many impressive degrees to see that. The ship, *if that was what it really was*, was only a quarter of its former tonnage. The object ended in a jagged and twisted wreck. The beams and what remained of her wooden decking had long turned to petrified stone. You could see the grain in the wood and know what it was immediately. The bow of the vessel soared into the heights of the giant vault. Spotlights illuminated the scaffolding placed around the artifact where many a teacher, professor, and student had crawled over her exterior searching for clues as to her real identity.

It had been explained to Collins that the Ark had been officially carbon dated to over thirteen thousand years old. That was still a bone of contention inside the Group because the theology department espoused the accepted theory that the Noah civilization was only five thousand years old. The Event Group and its personnel never argued between departments, but everyone knew it was an accepted fact that Virginia Pollock and her Nuclear Sciences Division was never, ever, wrong in their time and age calculations, and if you knew Virginia Pollock you better not begin to question the science. She was a firm and adamant believer in dating material and had never been proven wrong on any established date.

Jack followed Niles, Lee, and Alice up the staircase of the closest scaffolding. Their footsteps made loud clanging sounds as they moved across the steel. Collins saw amazement in everyone's eyes. They must have already taken in the sight of the artifact many, many times before this morning, but clearly the viewing never failed to put everyone in awe. Collins didn't feel that way. It wasn't because he was a cold military analyst, or that he didn't have a great imagination. It was because he knew he did, it was the given fact that Jack knew something described as divine providence in believing this vessel was ordered contracted under the direct supervision of God was just about ridiculous in his thoughts. A romantic would always love to believe that God had mercy on man and saved them with the Ark of wood, but Jack was a realist and knew that God had long abandoned mankind, including men from antiquity.

"Fairy tales, right?" Lee asked, penetrating Jack's inner thoughts. Lee placed his cane on the railing overlooking the ancient vessel.

The wooden construction on the centerline main deck looked as precise as many a painting proclaimed. Collins could see the hairline fractures where the Ark had either been dismantled or damaged. The reverse engineering reconstructing the Ark must have been a massive undertaking. There was a house-like structure on the upper deck and about eighty-five feet of the pitched roof and frame remained intact and looked as if this is where the supposed family of Noah would have lived high above their animal pens. Collins moved his eyes from the sight below to the single piercing eye of Lee.

"Excuse me?" Jack said as he failed to get the point even though he had been thinking about the same word only moments before.

"Just fairy tales. Stories that make for good Sunday school lesson plans. Good versus evil, the fight of man against nature, the determination of the human soul. Yes, many a good lesson is derived from such a story, wouldn't you say?" Lee said as he moved to the major's side and then gestured with his free hand as the other stabilized his weak frame against the railing. "But a fairy tale nonetheless," he said when Collins remained silent. He patted Jack on the back and then held out his hand for Alice to continue.

"The Ark, if that's what it is, and you will have to decide for yourself if that's the case, is not the only artifact we have here at the Group that substantiates the data we have collected." Before Jack knew it, took out a large aluminum box which she opened the lid and held out to Lee. Garrison Lee, reached inside and gently, as if he were handling crystal, removed a leather-bound book. It was though Lee were touching divinity itself. "The real treasure here, Jack," he said as he felt the warmth of the leather beneath his fingers, "is not that petrified jumble of wooden beams, but this."

Collins looked at what Lee was holding and was satisfied that he was looking at a journal, surely not as old as the object below in the vault, but old, within a hundred or two hundred years would be his estimate.

"Major, you are a student of your family lineage, correct?" Niles asked as he placed his hands behind his back, which he did every time he went into teaching mode.

"Yes, my mother and sister have concluded we started somewhere in Ireland, came to the colonies in 1678, and that's where we started, nothing before that though. On my father's side of things they arrived even earlier."

"Military men, I must admit I never felt the calling, Major," Niles said almost apologizing for that fact. "Special people I have come to admire." Niles turned and nodded at the book Lee held in his aged hand. "How many in your family have given the ultimate sacrifice, Major?"

"Three, at least as far as my mother and sister's limited history tells of both my father's and my mom's side."

"Yes, your file says Civil War, cause of death unknown. The Spanish American war, I believe you lost your great uncle in Santiago, Cuba. And then finally your father in 1972, somewhere in South East Asia."

Jack remained silent, as he never spoke about his father to anyone. That area of his life was off limits to anyone and everyone. He just continued to eye Niles Compton as he spoke.

"This journal is from 1864 through 1865. It covers the event that brought the artifact before you back to these shores. It was written by a man much like you, Jack. A person such as yourself will be able to determine its value, its very validity. You'll know after you study this what to think about that down there." He waved at the Ark below them.

"I have learned in life, gentlemen, that the same people who wrote stories about things like this," he also gestured toward the ravaged vessel, "also wrote in journals, and they both usually have the same failing, if it was written by men, be it the bible, the Koran, or anything else, its fallible. Men love to embellish. Stories told about things like this," he nodded at the journal and then the Ark, "or that, are sometimes made more readable, more exciting if they just add this, or add that. No, I'm not a big believer in journals or the writings of ancient scribes who told tales of the power of God or the foresight of a single man to construct that."

Alice smiled and it was almost as loud as a shout. Jack looked at her, and she stepped up to him and patted him on the shoulder.

"I told them they would have to allow you to read the journal to make you a believer."

Lee held out the leather-bound journal.

"What do you say, Major, a little light reading and then we'll meet again and discuss your future with Department 5656, fair enough?" Niles asked as Lee continued to hold the journal out for Jack to take, or leave it and the group behind.

Collins nodded and took the offered book, and before he could change his mind the trio left the major and exited the largest vault ever constructed.

Collins watched them go and then slowly paced toward the viewing stand that served students when they were being taught in one of the varying tasks that the faculty had arranged for them. He sat and then looked at the Ark below him and then at the leather journal. He read the words in the lower-right-hand corner that used to be gold inlaid but were now just a discolored indentation.

"John Henry Thomas, Colonel, United States Army, August 1864 – April 1865."

Jack ran his fingers across the broken and cracked leather where the gold lettering used to be, and then again looked away and wondered why Lee, Alice, and Niles believed this would have any bearing on his decision. He took a deep breath and momentarily thought of the men and women he had lost just this past month in the desert. He closed his eyes, so desperately tired of writing letters to his dead soldiers' parents, wives, or husbands. Collins was sorely tempted to leave the journal on the seat beside him and deliver his resignation to Compton. Instead, he held onto the old book and decided that he would give the Group this one shot to sway his choice—to stay, or retire into a bleak future without the career he had chosen.

He opened the one hundred fifty-year–old journal and started to read.